THE MESSAGE

THE MESSAGE

a Novel

Jaime Espiritu

www.americanfiction.com

iUniverse, Inc.

New York Lincoln Shanghai

THE MESSAGE
a Novel

iUniverse books may be ordered through booksellers or by contacting:

iUniverse
2021 Pine Lake Road, Suite 100
Lincoln, NE 68512
www.iuniverse.com
1-800-Authors (1-800-288-4677)

ISBN-13: 978-0-595-34715-5 (pbk)
ISBN-13: 978-0-595-79458-4 (ebk)
ISBN-10: 0-595-34715-0 (pbk)
ISBN-10: 0-595-79458-0 (ebk)

Printed in the United States of America

ACKNOWLEDGEMENT

To my wife Nancy, a friend, a partner, whose hardwork and loyal support moved this novel from the first draft to the second…and finally to print, my many thanks and deep gratitude.

Author's Notes:

- The events during and after the attack at the Pentagon are of course fictitious. But the participants in the gathering of government officials such as those from the newly formed Homeland Security are not. In [October] 2002 when the event in the story took place, the Department of Homeland Security had not yet come to being. What existed then was the interim Office of Homeland Security which is accurately referred to in the novel.

- Since the time of the story (Oct–Dec, 2002), the FBI had undergone a major reorganization. The CID (Criminal Investigations Division) and the ISD (Investigative Services Division), for instance, no longer exist as they did then.

- *On May of 2002, the U.S. Attorney General issued a revised investigative guidelines to assist the Bureau's counterterrorism efforts. To support the Bureau's change in mission and to meet newly articulated strategic priorities, the Director (Robert S. Mueller III) called for a reengineering of FBI structure and operations that will closely focus the Bureau on prevention of terrorist attacks, on countering foreign intelligence operations against the U.S., and on addressing cyber-based attacks and other high technology crimes.

*Quote from www.fbi.gov/libref/factsfigure/shorthistory.htm

Contents

▼

PROLOGUE

▼

~ 1 ~

Sister Caterina, RGS, hurried back into her workroom after picking up the mail in the rectory front office. The post stamp on the envelope showed May 20, 1975—seven days ago—inside a red circle formed by the letters *P h i l i p p i n e s.*

It had been over three weeks since the last one, six months since the first. In that half-year period, she felt as if she'd known Mother Teofila most of her twenty-one years in the Church. Not including the six years between her postulancy, which she spent here in Rome and partly in Florence from the age of eighteen, and her final profession to sisterhood.

In the first letter which came soon after they spoke on the phone briefly about the Sister's year-long mission, the Filipino nun wrote how happy she was to have spoken to the Sister, and that she looked forward to working with her in their apostolate soon.

The island of Mindoro is a fascinating place to be, she wrote. There are great challenges that will put one's faith and endurance to a test. It is a place like many others in the Philippines where, by the grace of our Lord, your calling leads you directly to your flock. You see how little you've come with to give. It's never enough, but then you see how far it goes, how fast it multiplies, and you realize it's not the measure of giving that matters. It's the act of giving itself, regardless of how generous or how little.

Sister Caterina tore the envelope open and dove into the letter. Writing in her beautifully disciplined handwriting, Mother Teofila wrote first about the weather. Rain, rain and more rain, she wrote. For the past nine days now. It's good for the forests, the coconut trees, the fish in the shallow waters and the rice fields. But it's not good if you live in a house with a leaky roof, or if you have to travel to your ministry in a rural area through muddy roads.

And when it finally stops, the sun boils in the sky with a vengeance and bakes the earth. Then you need an umbrella, this time not against getting wet but against burning in the heat. But in the evening, the air cools and everything smells so fresh and fragrant from the tropical blossoms.

That's just part of what makes the island, the whole country, what it is along with the culture which was the result of more than three hundred fifty years of foreign rules, Spanish and American. I have never been to the countries you said you've traveled—in Africa and eastern Europe. I've only been out of the Philippines twice, once during a short visit to Hong Kong and again to Bangkok, and those are places closer to home in many ways. So I couldn't begin to imagine how if I were you—having lived in a great city like Rome all my life, coming to live here for the first time—I would find it.

I once knew a Belgian missionary who came here for the first time. I worked with her for a while and we got to know each other very well. She had since left to retire in Belgium, about two years ago, after living here for thirty years. That gives me some idea.

Mother Teofila then wrote about the work ahead of them.

Sister Caterina's living space as well as that of her aide, the young and newly professed Sister Natala, and their office in the convent would be ready for them when they arrived in the first week of June.

Father Benedicto himself, the Vicar Forane of the Good Shepherd Vicariate of the Apostolic Vicariate of Calapan, Oriental Mindoro, had put together a committee to officially welcome the Sisters from Rome and to take them to a reception banquet in Victoria, the parish where their mission operations would be based. Speaking of the mission, there is much to be discussed not only between them, the Sisters and Mother Teofila, but with other people, among them the Vicar, the parochial school Director, Principal and some community leaders. It's best, wrote the Mother, that they wait till the Sisters get settled first after they've arrived and had a little time to adjust to the climate and the culture. There's no need to rush. They'll have plenty of time to get down to work once they got started.

Later in the day, Sister Natala, a modest but intelligent young woman of twenty-three years came to her office. Like Sister Caterina, everyday as their departure date drew nearer, she awaited any news from Mindoro; any word about the mission. Her face lit up as soon as Sister Caterina showed her the letter. She sat in a corner of the office and read it anxiously.

Nine days later, the Sisters left the routine of daily life in their parish in Rome, in the school, the church, the rectory, the Residence of the Sisters of the Good Shepherd. They took a jet plane to the Far East via Frankfurt and Bangkok and, after being airborne for over sixteen hours altogether, they landed in the sizzling summer of Manila.

The following day, after yet another two-hour journey by bus from Manila south to the city of Batangas and a ferry-boat ride from there to Calapan City, the capital of the province of Oriental Mindoro, Sister Caterina finally met Mother Teofila. From the moment they laid eyes on each other, it looked as if they'd met many times before and now, after a long separation, were brought together again. The two nuns put their arms around each other for a moment then held each other at arm's length with happy smiles on their faces. The welcoming committee let them have their moment for a while before they gathered them in a bus and took them to the reception banquet in the church hall in Victoria.

It was the beginning of a close friendship that was to develop over many months. Months of building a school and shelters for the underprivileged in the surrounding rural areas, ministering to them daily, bringing them sustenance, both material and spiritual. As Mother Teofila had written in her letter, Sister Caterina found out how true it was that she did not have enough to give. She wished, after several months, that she could give more of her time if nothing else, but even that quickly ran out.

A whole year passed. When it was time for her to leave, she felt grievously that she had barely accomplished her part of the mission. But her time was up. The young Sister Natala would stay to carry on with the work in the mission as part of her continuing formation in her sisterhood.

In her daily prayers, Sister Caterina thanked God for having allowed her the privilege to serve 'this flock'. She gave thanks for the time she shared her life with these poor and innocent ones, and most important of all for having come to know and work with Mother Teofila.

In the short year she was with her, there were many things she learned from the Mother, not just about their apostolic life, but about herself—her own weaknesses and how to correct them, her own virtues and how to enhance them.

Yet, even more than that, Mother Teofila taught her what she had always believed she understood of the virtue of kindness and humility. This came to light when the two of them went to a Barangay (a council district similar to a barrio or a village) near the foot of the 8,400-foot Mt. Halcon. There, they met a fifty-seven year old man, a former Japanese Army officer who after the war lost himself in the jungles and became what was known as a straggler.

There were several Japanese stragglers found in the island years after the war. Many of the Filipinos wanted them executed but the peacetime authorities, with the urging of the Church, prevailed to have them rehabilitated and returned to their homeland. Captain Hiroshi Yamada was found in 1960, fifteen years after the war. When he was brought into the parish church in Calapan where then Sister Teofila first met him, he was full of shame and, he told her, he should have killed himself. He was a well-educated man, had traveled to Europe and America before the war and spoke several languages.

He could not be persuaded to return to Japan. Through the support of the Church in the parish and the personal guidance of Sister Teofila, he remained in the country, converted to Christianity from Shintoism and devoted his life to making up for the suffering the war had brought to the islands.

Earlier, he was constantly threatened with death by some men who were survivors of the victims of Japanese war atrocities. Sister Teofila learned of these men and spoke words to them that Sister Caterina would remember for a long time.

"Be kind to your enemy," Sister Teofila said to the men in Tagalog. "Do not be cruel to him, even as he might have been to you. For what good is a victory if it turns you into your enemy?"

Working as a member of the laity with the apostolates of the diocese for years, the missionaries, the nuns and the priests of various religious orders, Hiro—as he later became known to everyone—won the acceptance of the community. Soon, no one seemed to even remember who or what he was before. He was looked upon with reverence, especially among the *Mangyans*, the indigenous tribe of Mindoro to whom he demonstrated acts of kindness, humility and the respect most Filipinos would not afford them. He found peace in himself and brought it to everyone he touched.

On their way back to the mission office from the Barangay, Mother Teofila summed up what she saw as the working of the grace of God in the life of Hiroshi Yamada as well as the people he served.

"You can see," she said, in her eyes an outpouring of that forgiving look that reached out into Sister Caterina's soul. "In kindness, there is no greater wisdom. In humility, no greater peace."

~ 2 ~

It had been eleven years since an Italian-American who immigrated to America at five returned to Italy, in Rome, twenty-two years later. Not to stay but to visit.

He went back to America with a bride he met in Florence. The bride was Sister Caterina's younger sister Cecilia.

The siblings hadn't seen each other since then until four years ago when Sister Caterina went to a world congregation of the Sisters of the Religious of the Good Shepherd in Washington, D.C. Cecilia was having a time of her life then as a happy wife and mother of two—a five-year old girl and a two-year old boy.

It was a sad day when Sister Caterina left Mindoro. She wished she could have stayed longer. Another year or two, perhaps more. She promised Mother Teofila and everyone in the mission she would work out something in Rome to return as soon as possible.

She flew out of the country with great reluctance, a heart sad but filled with the satisfaction of having given of herself all she could. It was an enriching one year of her life and she looked forward to adding to it.

In the meantime, she had this four-week sabbatical ahead of her that she would spend in America to see her sister Cecilia in the Washington, D.C. suburb of Bethesda, Maryland. She couldn't wait to share Mindoro with her. Mother Teofila, Hiro, the Mangyans, the local people, the places they live in. But more than all that, she wanted Cecilia to be the first to hear of the words of Mother Teofila. The message that had etched itself in her mind, in her soul, from the day the Mother spoke it to her.

The siblings were never before happier to see each other again. Caterina stayed with Cecilia and her family, in a room next to the children's, for two weeks. The rest of the month she kept busy with Church activities in the Capital area.

Cecilia's children were darlings. The girl was now a pretty nine-year old, the boy a handsome six-year old first-grader. At first, the boy was afraid to come near the woman who suddenly started living with them in the next room and came out into the house dressed in that strange garb with a hood over her head. Cecilia took care of this by explaining to him what nuns are and why they dress and live like they do.

The girl knew better and quickly got acquainted with her aunt. It was with her that Sister Caterina, one day, unexpectedly found herself sharing the words of Mother Teofila.

Several days before, the niece got into a fight with a girl, a schoolmate her age who lived three houses down the block. The quarrel was over a book the neighbor claimed the niece had borrowed sometime ago and wanted to have back. The niece insisted she had returned it, the other insisted she hadn't. It went back and forth resulting with the neighbor avoiding the niece and refusing to even talk to her. The niece did the same and from being friends and neighbors, they became enemies.

In the morning of this day, a Saturday, the niece was sharing a moment with the aunt on the front porch. The girl told Sister Caterina that she saw the neighbor at school carrying the book that broke up their friendship but the neighbor would not acknowledge it and continued to refuse to talk.

"I hate her," said the niece. "I don't care if she never spoke to me again. It's not my fault. She made a mistake and she doesn't want to admit it. I'll never speak to her again either. Ever!"

Sister Caterina took out an English copy of the Holy Bible she always kept handy. She placed it on her lap with the back cover up and laid a hand over it.

"It's not good to let hate come between you," she said to her niece.

"But she won't admit she was wrong!"

"There's nothing you can do if she wants to be that way, sweetheart," said Sister Caterina gently. "The important thing is—you know you're right. You know the truth. You've won the argument. You have a victory."

"I hate her! I hate her! I hope something bad happens to her." The girl was nearly crying with anger. Sister Caterina put an arm over her shoulder and comforted her.

"Now, you really didn't mean that, sweetheart," she said. "You wouldn't want someone wishing something bad to happen to you, or to someone you love. It's cruel. Whatever anybody has done to you to make you feel bad, you don't want to do to her or to anybody else."

"But why not?"

"Because then you would be no different than her." Here, Sister Caterina lifted the back cover of the Holy Bible and showed her the words of Mother Teofila which she had handwritten on the inside of it. "This was said to me by a very nice Mother nun in the Philippines not long ago," she said. "I wrote it here so I won't ever forget."

> Be kind to your enemy. Do not be cruel to him,
>   even as he might have been to you.
> For what good is a victory if it turns you into your enemy?
> In kindness, there is no greater wisdom,
> In humility, no greater peace.

They sat motionless for a while as they both read it in silence. Then the girl inched closer to Sister Caterina, leaning on her slightly. The angry look had vanished. In its place, an expression of calm and regret as she turned her face up to her aunt. "I'm sorry, Sister," she murmured. "So sorry."

"You're forgiven," said the nun. "Now, the next thing to do is patch things up between the two of you and be friends again."

"But how?"

"One of you will have to break the ice. And since you're the one who's here, you're it. Don't worry. I'll help you. It'll work out."

They walked to the neighbor's house a few minutes later and knocked on the door. The niece, holding behind her red and white roses held together by a rubber band, hid behind the aunt as they waited for someone to open the door. Sister Caterina had to work her up to this a little.

A girl, not the soon-to-be-friend-again, opened the door. She was bigger and older than the other girls probably by at least four years, and even prettier. Once she saw the nun standing outside, she backed up wide-eyed and called out to her mother inside. A woman came to the door quickly and showed surprise at seeing the nun. But she managed to bring on a smile and didn't back off in mortal fear as did her daughter.

Sister Caterina introduced herself and explained what her visit was about. No, it's not a charity solicitation. No, she's not going around the neighborhood recruiting young girls for the convent life. She came to help the two young girls become friends again.

The mother said that her daughter wanted the same and that she had tried to talk to the nun's niece but the latter wouldn't speak a word to her. It turned out the niece was the one who was being stubborn and not telling part of the truth about the continuing break in their friendship.

When they finally got the two face to face, Sister Caterina prodded her niece to step up to her neighbor and offer the flowers for their reconciliation. The two women watched happily as the two children made up. The daughter accepted the flowers and thanked her friend. They shook hands and gave each other a hug and they were off together to the niece's house to get back to their Saturday morning routine of watching the 'toons on TV.

Her last week at Cecilia's house, Sister Caterina saw the mother a few more times and they became well acquainted. She learned that the woman, Minnah (Arabic for kindness, politeness), was herself in a situation in life, one that may not be as simple to 'patch up' as that between neighbors with a gift of roses on a Saturday morning. Both she and her husband were Lebanese. She was a Christian and he a Muslim. They were moving back to Lebanon the following year for business reasons back home, she said.

During one of their talks when Minnah visited the Sister, she said that her husband was not as open about his religious beliefs in Islam as she was trying to be with hers in Christianity. He was very strong-minded about it with her and the children, the two girls. But Minnah was no pushover herself, as Sister Caterina saw in the way she talked about her husband. She stood up to him, she said, when he required everyone in the family to read and study the Koran and no other religious book—meaning, the Holy Bible. She claimed he stole the only copy she had of it and wouldn't give it back. He denied it. They had a constant battle. She went as far as threatening separation to soften him up.

And she did.

The next time she visited the Sister, she reported that he had backed off some and was allowing the family to read both the holy books. But he still refused to admit he took and hid her copy of the Holy Bible. She began to have doubts about what really happened to it. Maybe she simply lost it and he really didn't have anything to do with its disappearance.

Anyway, now that she had him in good measures, she told the Sister, she didn't really mean her threat of separation. She knew he had some soft spots in him and she knew how to get to them. Sister Caterina couldn't help feeling amused at knowing this, and glad, rather than seriously concerned about the future of this family. She decided she would save Minnah the trouble of getting a new copy of the Holy Bible and went into her room for a minute to get her copy to give her.

"Please take this," she said, putting it on Minnah's lap.

"No, I can not," Minnah refused. "I will get my own."

"Please," the Sister insisted. "I want you to have it. My gift to you and your family."

She took the book and held it to her breast in both hands. "Thank you, Sister," she said, her eyes brimming with gratitude.

They were sitting out in the front porch and it was around the time in the afternoon school busses started dropping kids off from school. Just then, Minnah saw her eldest daughter get off the bus. The girl headed their way upon seeing her mother waving at her to come over.

Minnah asked how was school. "Fine," the daughter responded politely, still feeling her way in the presence of the nun.

"Look," Minnah said, showing her the book. "We have a new bible. Sister Caterina just gave it to us as a gift."

The girl's face lit up. "Oh, that's wonderful," she said, taking the book from her mother, looking at it happily and holding it close to her like her mother did. "This is really wonderful especially coming from a…"

Minnah caught on quickly during this one awkward moment and intervened.

"By the way, you haven't been properly introduced," she said, looking at one and then the other. "This is Sister Caterina," she said, turning first to her daughter and holding out a hand to the nun. And then going the other way, she said: "Sister, this is the one who ran away from you the other day, my eldest daughter—Kamilah."

~ 3 ~

The four weeks seemed to have come and gone in only half the time, just like the year in Mindoro. Now it was another day to fly away, to say goodbye again to people she loved.

"Will you come back soon?" asked the niece, her whole family standing behind her at the passenger departure concourse of Dulles International in Virginia.

"Of course, I will, sweetheart. I promise," Sister Caterina said, already thinking of her return trip to Mindoro, hopefully not too long from now.

"Say goodbye now to Sister Cathy," Cecilia said to her family. "We don't want her to miss her airplane."

Everyone said goodbye to the Sister and gave her a hug. When it was her turn, the niece said: "*rivadarci,* Sister Cathy."

The nun bent down to the girl affectionately for the hug and said in her natural Italian: "*Arrivederci.*"

PART I

▼

THE PENTAGON— OPERATION NORTH 27

CHAPTER 1

▼

October 2002.

Office of Civil Defense Logistics, Treasury Department. Sounded so…tactical, militaristic, protective. One wondered where else in the country can you hear something like that, find an office-name like that, except in Washington, or inside the Capital Beltway. Geographically it was in Virginia, on the ninth floor of a glass high-rise among several at Skyline Center near Bailey's Crossroads on Route 7 just inside Fairfax County from Arlington County on the north and Alexandria City on the south.

Coming out of the elevator, you saw it as the doors slid open, spelled in sharp white letters on a marble panel above a glass wall with a pair of double glass doors. And one wondered what went on beyond those doors, past the reception counters, behind yet another pair of doors, these ones of solid metal finish. To Robert Grundell, 42, who had been in and out of those doors the last ten of his fifteen-year career with the federal government as a program analyst, nothing much.

If it were talking about his career with OCDL, not a hell of a lot. Not as far as promotion, recognition and respect were concerned. Ask anybody in the office, including those assholes in management who had kept him down at the bottom of the career advancement ladder. Even those they had favored for promotion over him. They know what's going on in this office, but none of them would talk about it. They simply want to make the impression that…that's just the way things are around here. And there's simply nothing he can do about it, except maybe get himself another job someplace else.

Now, talking about the job, what he did and how much of it he did, it was a different story. There was a lot going on, a lot he did over the years, most often more than he was called upon in the duties and responsibilities listed in his position description.

There was handling highly critical-sensitive data created within the office and coming in from other federal agencies, top-secret documents both civilian and military, to providing security to these information and conducting background checks on anybody requesting access to any of the information; designing a computer system for the storage and processing of the data and managing the operation and maintenance of the system to keeping track of the IT people working on it. He did so much, and he did his job so well that when he thought about it, maybe that's why, ironically, he never got the recognition he thought he deserved.

Because everything worked so well—the project didn't go over budget and it was finished on time as the contractors had quoted, everybody thought everything he did was easy to do and, therefore, anybody else could have done it just as well, and perhaps even better.

For his sake then, it might have been better if he had deliberately botched up a couple of things here and there to show management how not so easy things really are if he didn't know what the hell he was doing or if they had picked some second-rate program analyst to do the job. Make them see the difference, what kind of service they get and realize how tough things could get without the right man on the job. Then maybe they would have appreciated him more.

This was a few years ago and nothing had changed. At this point, he had resolved that the only thing to stop the aggravation is to get away from it, get another job. Fine. They win. Who gives a shit anymore. The first job he sees out there that fits his resume, he's out of here. But this resolve amounted to no more than a quiet wish, a mute idea. Unless he got extremely lucky, spotted a job-posting in another agency that matched his credentials and beat all the other applicants to it, he knew he wasn't going anywhere.

So, what's left to do besides wallowing in the aggravation? Maybe get even. Give them back some of the aggravation. Play the same game they play on him. Fuck it. Why not? Sabotage their career, do things to make them look bad but make sure to leave no traces. The worst thing could happen is they find out he was doing it. So, then what—make his life miserable? They couldn't do better than the way they've been doing it for years now.

They could fire him. But that could take ages if he contested which he'll of course do. Also, that's really a two-way street. He could file grievances against them too. Write them up and get the EEO on their backs like the minorities did all the time. And did he have plenty to write and substantiate as well.

He—and his lawyer—could have personnel dig up all the hiring and promotion that had taken place in the office, say, the last five years and see how each one was done, if the jobs were posted in a timely manner for all applicants to get a shot at the opening, how a promotion was justified, examine the performance and accomplishments of the successful candidates at the time and match them against those who weren't selected then scrutinize them in detail. Open up every can of worms there is.

Fuck it, maybe that's what he'll do if they got to that. Why not? Could be fun.

Today, this was just what he was thinking, looking through the tinted glass window in his office at the 4:00 o'clock traffic on Route 7 and the shopping plaza across, nine stories below. Earlier, he had received data from OSERS of the Interior Department headquarters in D.C. about the completion of the last of the three projects they had out in the Midwest. There will be an opening celebration with a dedication ceremony at each one of them. Most of the members of the senate Subcommittee on Water and Power, about a half a dozen U.S. senators, will take a ceremonial train ride to North Dakota and Montana from Washington, D.C., and Treasury had designated OCDL to manage security and safe passage for the senators, round trip, throughout the scheduled activities.

Now, what he could do is play with this assignment. Like maybe put the senators on a train to Juneau, Alaska instead. Or detour them down to Vegas for a night. That would be a sure bet to make his boss, Milton Pheasant, head of Interstate Logistics Division, red in the face, and Pheasant's boss, the Treasury Undersecretary for the Office of Civil Defense Logistics, shit in his pants when he had to answer to the senators and maybe even Congress. Then maybe one of them, or both, could get fired before any of them could find out what he did and fire him.

It was time to go home but even this wasn't a welcome relief from his life at work. He had nobody to go home to, not since four years ago when he and his ex first separated and it became permanent through the divorce a year later, after a barren five-year marriage. He went out to the singles scenes in the Virginia suburbs, dated some the past couple of years but none of that came to anything life enhancing.

It was mid-October and there was a good hour and a half of daylight left. He felt it was too early to go home and decided to go over to the Palm Grove, a short walk across the Skyline Plaza, as he did occasionally, for a drink. There he sat at a tiny table for two in a high bar stool facing the TV hung below the ceiling. A baseball game was on. It sounded like a recap or re-run of the latest game of the World Series.

Across the room, sitting at the far end of the bar, two men watched him turn away from the TV a minute later to get his order of beer from the server. One was taller, heavier and older than the other by a whole generation. Late forty, early fifty at least. They were dark-complexioned, Middle-Eastern, both bearded. The younger one said something to the other, nodding at the subject of their attention and took a sip of the drink in his hand. Then he put a grin of familiarity on his face as he left the other man at the bar and began to approach Robert.

"Bobby!" he greeted as he stood beside Robert at the little table. "What a pleasant surprise."

"Ahmed, my man," Robert said, genuinely happy to run into his nextdoor neighbor at the garden apartment building in South Arlington where he had moved to since the separation. "Have a seat, my man. Have a seat."

"So, how was it today?" asked Ahmed Khalifa, a native resident of Hyderabad, Pakistan to the age of twenty-seven when he succeeded in getting a tourist visa to Canada three years ago for a visit made necessary by a very sick close relative. It turned out to be a very long visit which had stalled his return to Pakistan indefinitely. "Long day? Busy day? Happy day?"

"Shitty day, as usual. But now I feel better 'cause I'm out of there."

"Ow, c'mon, it couldn't be that bad. Don't forget how lucky you are to have a job nowadays. And a government job at that. A career job."

"Yes, and some career it turned out to be too," Robert said after downing a third of the beer in the mug. "And how was your day, hotshot?"

Ahmed laughed. More than three years after he finally escaped a life of nothing but material hardship to look forward to, he hadn't exhausted the pleasure of seeing these north Americans take the ease and comfort and security of their social, economic and political life for granted.

He'd like to, if he could, take this Bobby to Karachi or Calcutta one day, leave him there for a month, maybe even only a week in a one-room apartment without heating, air-conditioning, television and with no car and nothing to do but forage in the public market everyday with just a pocketful of rupees to find something to eat and at the same time see some of the lowest of all the lowest of human conditions possible on the face of the earth. Then we'll see how much he appreciates his 'shitty government job' and the quality of life it affords him. He'd probably go back to work and, first thing in the morning, see his boss whom he said he hates and kiss his hand and feet, maybe even offer to get him coffee and donut.

In the seven months since he moved in the one-bedroom across the courtyard from Robert, it had been like they knew each other from twenty years back in some old hometown. They went out to singles bars weekends occasionally, watched a ballgame on TV in one or the other's living room over beer and pizza and got to know each other pretty well. However, there was no telling how much one really let the other into his closet.

Robert had a thought at first about whether or not the Pakistani was an illegal alien. What he'd heard from the man, so far, began with his two years in Toronto, Canada where he first landed with a six-month visitor's visa he later managed to convert, with some relatives vouching for him, to a student visa which allowed him to work parttime at certain times of the year. Then, after completing a curriculum at a tech school in Toronto, on to Detroit where he got a job offer from MidEast Continental, Ltd. which petitioned the INS for his working visa. The company traded in Middle East oil, owned part of several refineries in Canada and the U.S. and operated a chain of gasoline stations in Detroit, Philadelphia, Baltimore and the Capital area.

After six months in a desk job in Detroit, he was picked for the job in the Northern Virginia suburb of Washington, D.C. to help run the gas station operation here as an assistant to one of the area managers. Sounds legit enough, thought Robert.

Anyway, what the hell did he care? The man appeared civilized enough, was educated, friendly and made good company. And so he didn't mind at all when Ahmed took the liberty of calling him Bobby after hearing an uncle visiting from Ohio a few months ago call him that while the three of them were watching an Orioles game. Only thing was, Ahmed liked to cook that curry stuff which sometimes stinks up the whole place. But even that, Robert—Bobby—didn't mind as much now since Ahmed had invited him over for dinner a couple times and he actually liked the dish.

Ahmed didn't care much either who he came to know in Robert Grundell as long as Robert didn't start acting like some of those snotty Canadians he met at school and at work. Prejudiced, ignorant, narrow-minded. All that considering the country was practically made up of new immigrants from all over the world as well as first generation Canadians, many of those very same snotty ones he encountered whose parents surely must have gone through the same shit they were dishing out on him. That's why he didn't have a second thought about coming to the U.S. the first chance he got.

Here, he didn't think he'd run into as much of that ugly stuff, thinking as he'd heard from many people both sides of the border that this is an older more established society of immigrants and that people here are long past that, more liberal and intelligent. Not only that. There are all kinds of laws—civil rights laws, human rights laws, equal opportunity laws that are enforced and work equally even for those in the lowest rank in society, and even for immigrants.

Of course there are some people, Americans, who still wallow in their old prejudices. Racial, cultural, religious. And he had run into a few of them in Detroit and here in the Washington Capital area. But so far, those he'd known who were the opposite had made him feel better about himself, and life in America. This included Robert although as a rule, after what he'd experienced and seen happen with others of his kind—dark-skinned, south Asian or Middle-Eastern, Muslim, he was always cautious, tentative, distrustful especially about throwing his allegiance to any persuasion and giving up any part of his own.

He could almost say he considered Bobby not just a neighbor with whom he knocked down a six-pack in front of the TV once in a while, but a friend. But he can't say he gave a shit either if he never saw him again. The reason was, everything in this country, this culture, felt so temporary, so fast-paced and quick-changing that it didn't make sense to feel any attachment to anything, or anybody. You just can't nail anything down.

"I had a nice day today, thanks for asking," he replied to Bobby who had turned his face back up at the game on TV. "A good friend of my boss dropped by this afternoon but he, my boss, had to leave early—some family errand he had to do for his wife—and I ended up taking his place. Boss for a half a day. So I took care of the man. We had a late lunch at the Olive Garden across the street and came here for a drink."

"Who's he?" asked Bobby.

"He's one of the major stockholders of the company. He's sitting right there at the bar. Mr. Abu Kamal Ramshallah."

"Moving up in the world, aren't we?" said Bobby after glancing at the man in what looked like a million-dollar suit and tie. "Swimming with the big fish, power-lunching with the elite, huh?"

"No big deal, man. He's just another small fish in a big tank. The big ones are in Michigan. Besides, I just happened to know him personally myself back when I was in Detroit. Actually, he recommended me for the job here."

A big uproar in the game suddenly interrupted them and for a moment they watched three Yankees touch home base.

"I hate those damn Yankees," Bobby said after almost emptying the beer mug. "Why can't anybody else be as good as they are? Or better."

"They *are* better than everybody else and there's nothing anybody can do about it. That's the way the game is played, man. You got to be better than everybody else."

"No, no. In this game, you got to have the best hitters and pitchers there are. And you know how you do that?"

"Yes, yes, I know," Ahmed said. "You buy them, steal them from anybody you can get them from."

"Exactly. And that's what I hate about this whole business of the big league ballgames. Every time I think about a twenty-five-year old player being lured to play a team for seven million bucks a year for six years, and a signing bonus of two million to start with, I feel like…like I could throw up."

"I agree."

"It's disgusting. Here I am, forty-two years old, working in this piddly-shit government job for fifteen years now and probably for the next fifteen, for an annual salary this guy under thirty years old right here on the mound," Bobby said, now pointing up at the TV set, "earns in two innings."

"You should've gone into sports. Did you ever play the game?"

"Baseball? Yeah, in high school. First base. I was a lead hitter too."

"Pretty good."

"I should've stayed with it."

"Why didn't you?"

"That's not the thing to do at the time. Nobody thought it's any way to make a buck. No. Gotta finish high school, go to college and get a good job."

"That's the sure way. And there's nothing wrong with that. If you think about it, things could've been worse. You could've dropped out of high school and now might have been delivering pizza or shoveling dirt in a construction site or doing some blue-collar job like that to make a buck."

That brought Bobby's eyeballs to level with Ahmed's from the TV set.

"You know, that's one advantage you guys just come from a Third World country have over us homegrown folks," he said, sizing up the Pakistani man. "You know the difference, and you remember it."

"We've seen worse than you ever did, not just on TV, but in person."

"I know. I have an idea, but—that doesn't change the situation I'm in where I am now. Heck, I understand a twenty-something guy getting paid seven million a year if somebody thinks he's worth it for what he does and is willing to pay him that kind of money. But I don't get it when a guy does good in his job, me to be exact, makes everybody else look good especially his freakin' bosses, and gets his career fucked up instead."

"What can you do? Anything?" asked Ahmed.

"What the hell can I do? Yes, there's lots of things I can do—"

"You know, for what you told me about your job," Ahmed interrupted, "it sounds like you do very responsible and important things for your office handling top security data for the government."

"Darn right I do."

"Some people would pay you a lot for doing that kind of work, someplace else, for somebody else."

"Yeah, I thought about that. Getting another job."

"I don't mean that, exactly. Tell me," Ahmed said, pausing a moment to eye Bobby as if to scrutinize how the man fit in his clothes. "How pissed are you at your boss, your job, the whole situation where you are?"

"What do you mean pissed? I've told you lots of times and I'll tell you again, I am pissed. Irritated, angry, frustrated. How else can I tell you how that feels?"

"Pissed enough to make something out of it?"

"Make something—what?"

"Like I said, a lot of money."

"Where? How? What kind of money?"

Ahmed turned to look at his companion at the bar and raised a hand slightly in his direction to give a signal.

"Listen, man, I got to get back to Kamal over there," he said to Bobby, "I told him I'd just be a moment to say hello to my neighbor. Let's talk about this some more later, if you want." He picked up his drink and started to move.

"How much money are you talking about?" Robert asked quickly.

"I'll call you tonight and we'll talk some more, okay? Bobby?" Ahmed said, giving Bobby a light jab on the shoulder as he stepped away towards the bar. "Take it easy."

"Alright. Talk to you later."

*   *   *   *

The E320 Mercedes eased out of the Skyline Center parking lot and headed west on Route 7 to Tysons Corner.

"Back to the hotel, Ghulan," Abu Kamal Ramshallah told the driver, shifting to a more comfortable position in his end of the back seat facing Ahmed Khalifa from whom he awaited hopefully some good news.

"Yes, sir," Ghulan Wahid, the driver, replied obediently even after chauffeuring his passenger most of the day, hanging out at parking lots patiently for stretches in between destinations.

"So, how did you do?" asked Abu Kamal.

"Very well, I would say," replied Ahmed in a measured voice to the man who saved him from having to go back to Canada or, possibly, back to Pakistan.

Now, Abu Kamal, in a tone of voice to someone who owed him plenty: "And what is—very well?"

"It means that for a first attempt, I got a bite. The man is angry, as I told you I thought he is. And he is. I think we can get to him. But, still, I have to be a little careful."

After what Ahmed Khalifa told him the first time about this nextdoor neighbor of his who worked for the federal government with a Treasury and Pentagon top secret clearance, Abu Kamal Ramshallah—a Syrian, but also part Saudi, Egyptian, something else, and senior board member of MidEast Continental, Ltd., wouldn't rest till he heard more about what kind of a man this Bobby was. It sounded like a lot of potential, this civilian government employee and what he did at work—maintaining an information system that passed top security data between civilian and military agencies involving the whole intelligence circuit of the United States, local and state to federal government level.

Goddamn! This guy could be a gold mine of information.

His bosses in Detroit were ecstatic when he mentioned this to them last month. And soon after that, they said they got the go ahead from Cairo to work on the guy, with instructions to be as 'generous' as they needed to be.

So the next time they got together, he told Ahmed see what kind of an American Bobby is: a southerner? a redneck? a northerner? a westerner? Listen what comes out of his mouth when he talks about things like God and country. Is he a radical or a moderate what—Democrat or Republican? Is he the patriotic type or the type who doesn't give a shit who he works for like if Toyota bought the whole country, as long as he eats well and drives a nice car?

Next, figure out how stupid or how smart he is. Is he a thinker? An intellectual? When you're in his apartment, look at the bookshelves and see what he's got in there and talk about books. Find out his ideology, his beliefs. Is he a Jew? A Christian? And which type is he of either—a Conservative? Reform? Catholic? Protestant?

Ahmed told him everything he already knew: definitely not a redneck; man's from Cleveland, Ohio, born and raised; married five years, divorced, no children.

"He told me he voted Democrat the last presidential election but he said never again," Ahmed related. "He's a Presbyterian of some kind but does not do anything about it. Does not go to service, nothing. A thinker? As far as his work is concerned, yes. He sounds like a very capable worker. I don't think he's an intellectual. Not that kind of thinker, anyway. He's not a politician so he's not a radical, I know this from his attitude particularly about his office. 'Parasites, phoneys, high-salaried assholes, that's what most of them are,' he says about the people in his office especially those in management.

"He's on his own, an individual whose only concern is his own. That's why I said I think we can get to him. It's not like we'd have to worry about a whole bunch of other people. Now, stupid? He's the kind of man who would hate to be made to feel stupid, by his own doing or by someone else's. I think he feels stupid about his situation at work but doesn't want to admit it to himself because he can't do anything about it right now. This is how I see us doing business with him."

Abu Kamal sat back, looking pleased. With a small grin under the beard on one side of his mouth, he said: "So, somebody offers him a half a million dollars for some classified government information which he can spill out to a diskette from the database in less than two minutes, he certainly wouldn't want to feel stupid by turning it down, after all these years of getting treated like a piece of shit by the office, huh?"

Ahmed didn't say a word and just let that sink in between them, bobbing his head ever so thoughtfully with that same grin the other man had on his face.

"Very good," Abu Kamal said next, more like thinking it. "Very good. Work on that angle. Dangle a carrot"

"That's where I'm at right now," Ahmed said and proceeded to tell what kind of bite he got from Bobby before he withdrew quickly lest the man start getting leery. You don't dangle a bait, let your quarry take big bites at once and risk making it look too good to be true. Although with this one, Ahmed expressed with confidence, he was almost sure they faced very little risk. They could offer to buy some classified information from this very disgruntled, itching-to-get-even employee for a certain amount of money and he'd accept with no qualms at all.

"I'll start him with a small offer," Ahmed continued.

"Good. I'll tell you what the deal is," said Abu Kamal. "If he accepts, pay him. And once you're sure he's in the bag, so to speak, I want to meet him."

CHAPTER 2

▼

Job. Love. Health. Family. Personal interests.

Chris Phillips, at 35, sitting in his ten-by-twelve office in this government job he'd had for seven years now, ran that through his head. He did this every now and then when something or somebody stimulated him to do so. It was a self-evaluation of his life, to check where he was headed, how far along he was, and if he was headed in the right direction.

At the moment, the stimulus was a man who just went past his door and sat in the office next to him—Homer Pinckney: 53, 27 years government service, divorced, three kids, single, dateless, depressed most of the time, ran up the health office in the fourth floor at least twice a month thinking he was having a stroke or a heart attack.

The guy was a specimen of midlife deterioration. A case like that, when he saw it, Chris Phillips wished there was some way he or somebody could intervene. But, hell, for every Homer here, there's dozens, hundreds of other Homers out there, everywhere. Who knows? Besides, he had his own life to worry about, steer in the right direction, not where Homer is now. He's working on it. And he's pretty much on track, he thought.

Now, the job? He believed he could do better in another agency if he's willing to fight for it, be a top bullshitter, a sleazy politician, an asshole like the few they had in the office now. But it's just not worth it, turning into somebody he didn't want to be. Besides, it's tight in government now with all the downsizing and job freezes all around, not just here in the Capital area but all over the country.

He could live with what he had now, salarywise, workwise, as a program analyst with the Office of Socio-Economic Reserve and Security of the Department of the Interior in the agency's headquarters in Washington, 19th St. NW and Virginia Avenue. And he earned his GS-13 paycheck as a socio-economic program specialist handling vital government data for OSERS, keeping them current by monitoring the country's human resource and natural energy reserves, keeping the information secure and sharing it with other authorized agencies.

It was a lot of work, but challenging. And he liked it. Kept him busy. The only sore spot here, at work, was a little bit about some of the people. The usual government deadwoods, the make-work paper-shufflers, the bullshitter politicians riding on the backs of those who produce real work, the vintage assholes. But at this point in his work career—including three years in private industry before government, he didn't mind.

Experience had upped his tolerance enough to accept the fact that assholes are everywhere and there's no getting rid of them. Things could've been worse. Things had been worse as he'd seen in his other jobs, in private industry and the two prior government jobs where he lasted exactly a year each: first with the Military Personnel Command of the Department of the Army where it took the entire top brass of the Command to move a piece of paper from one desk to another all day long, sometimes all week long if nobody's around, and the Air Force Information Service Center in the Pentagon where the whole place crawled with high-paid bureaucrats, civilian and military, who knew and did no more than be loud, look good and kiss ass.

Here at Interior, he felt better putting in his forty hours a week, for seven years now. Not only that there were less of what he saw in his other government jobs but because there were some, enough, of those like him, and Homer Pinckney who was actually a productive worker, to balance against the assholes and the politicians.

Next—love. Relationship. Involvement. Entanglement. Or whatever people like to call it these days.

Currently, it's Julie going on two full years now. Julie Santorelli, 36, divorced, math teacher at St. James College in Falls Church, Virginia. That's her maiden name which she never gave up when she got married and was glad she didn't after it was over three years later.

Julie is 100% Italian. Well, Italian-American. Her family saga goes: grandparents with three small kids—two boys and a girl—left Rome for America two years after WW II. The two boys survived, the girl died of dysentery. Father, the oldest child, went back for a visit twenty years later and met mother in Florence, brought her to America; two years later had a baby girl—her.

Like the job, there were precedents to Julie. But none of them made the distance this relationship had so far gone. Not much more than whole weekends together, the dinner-and-movie routine or an out-of-town holiday vacation drive on occasions, but nowhere near talking live-in full time as they were now exploring seriously.

She told him she loved him, a lot. He told her he cared about her, deeply. She never pressed the issue of making him say the three big words to her. She figured if it's there it's just there and if it's not, she wouldn't want to hear about it anyway. This was one thing Chris *liked* about Julie: she's level-headed. Not just *liked* but *loved* about her, among other things.

They got along well, shared interests in different kinds of book, music, history. They fought over stuff in the guise of a mild disagreement. They were good friends. One paid attention to what the other was saying or might be ranting about. They kidded each other and laughed together. And they had good sex which they did at least twice a week at present.

He thought he's doing pretty good in that arena. Love, or whatever you want to call it.

And Health? Heck, for somebody in his mid-thirties, likewise, he knew he's in top shape. A lot better than many he'd seen his age: potbellied, balding if not graying, couch potato, high-cholesterol, kidney problem, emphysematic from smoking, beer-guzzler, you name it. He's none of that. In fact, he's the opposite of all of that.

He drank beer only with meals and he loved it, especially with steak or kabob. He didn't smoke, never did since he quit inhaling those Salem menthols twelve years ago when he started running instead. Running at first two miles every day till he built up to five a few months later. Now he ran three, four miles consistently—rain or shine all year round, every other day. And this was another thing Julie loved about him besides all the others they enjoyed doing together.

On his running day, she'd go out with him to the park and she'd walk while he ran. He'd finish first and join her walking the next fifteen, twenty minutes, the two of them side by side around the park talking, kidding around, having fun.

Next he thought about his family.

For a start, his mother and stepfather in Pittsburgh, his retired unmarried father in Manassas, Virginia and his only sibling, a brother five years his senior, in Falls Church, Virginia. But then he glanced at the time on the corner of the computer monitor screen—11:25 AM—and that broke his concentration, bringing him back to...lunchtime in a few minutes. Also, the weekly updates he was to give his boss and several inhouse and outside-agency analysts on a new database they were building. That was supposed to be at a meeting earlier at 10:30 this morning which was postponed till 2:30 this afternoon because Stan Ranceid (pronounced the same without the e), one of the analysts, a co-worker most people in the office avoided having anything to do with, couldn't make it and asked to move it later. There's one really irritating, rancid co-worker.

There wasn't much else to do after all the preparations he'd made for the meeting so he got on the internet and read the news. The system was annoyingly slow and while waiting for the news to download, that's when he saw Homer Pinckney and got into his life-overview exercise.

Now he turned to the news on the screen and read about an unidentified man, a runner or a walker, found dead on a street in a neighborhood in Arlington. Except for what appeared to be some house keys, he didn't carry one piece of information that might help identify him. The police put out a telephone number to call for anyone who might happen to have any lead on the identity of the man.

He sat motionless for a minute thinking about what he just read.

And about Julie.

She went out from her townhouse-condo in Fairfax City after work for a forty-minute walk a couple of times during the week. He remembered asking her if she carried any ID with her when she goes out and she said no. He made a lot of noise to her about it, telling her how irresponsibly dumb that is but she didn't pay much attention to it.

He carried an ID whenever he went out running. Whenever he went out anywhere. He used to carry his driver's license with him running but he thought of something better. He typed his name, address, SSN, license plate number, home and work phone numbers on one side of a piece of paper within two square inch. On the other side, he put 'Emergency Contact:' and under that the name and phone numbers of his brother who lived in Falls Church, Virginia. He made several copies and wrapped each one in double layers of transparent waterproof tape. Now he carried one copy in his wallet, one in his running shorts or pants when he went out and one he left in his car for reserve.

He ran yesterday, Monday, so he would go out again tomorrow, with Julie. She came during the week, usually Wednesday, after work. So now he clicked on the Microsoft Word and brought up the file ChrisID.doc. He replaced all the information in it with that of Julie, as much of it as he knew and saved the file as JulieID.doc. Then he called her cell phone.

"Hey, kiddo. Where are you?"

"On my way to my room from my 10:30 class," she said. "Next is lunch in half an hour. Brown bag today. Tuna salad and peach yogurt. How's life in government today?"

"I'm doing okay. Not much politics today and no assholes in sight. You coming over tomorrow, correct?"

"Unless otherwise noted."

"Don't forget to bring your walking gears. Running day tomorrow."

"I know."

"Listen, I need some personal data from you. SSN, license plate number, and your mom's home and work phone numbers."

"What are you up to?"

"I'll tell you later. Tomorrow. Just let me have them."

"Whatever it is, better be good. Better than good," she said, entering her workroom and dropping papers and books from the last class on the desk. Without further inquiry, she gave him the information.

He typed the data, printed three copies of the document and made the two-inch square ID's out of it exactly the way he did his own. Tomorrow, no matter what she says, how paranoid and silly she thinks he is, he's going to make her carry one with her, leave one in her car and another in her purse. That's that. Now lunch.

On the way to the cafeteria downstairs, he detoured to the men's room but as he turned a corner, he found himself walking behind Stan Ranceid and Willie Gonzales, one of a rare few who didn't mind being within an arm's length of Stan. He thought he spoke too soon when he told Julie on the phone there were no assholes in sight.

He slowed down behind them and when he saw them go into the men's room, he turned around and went to the one downstairs near the cafeteria.

$$* \quad * \quad * \quad *$$

The days were getting shorter. And colder. But Chris liked that part of it. The autumn chill. He liked this season of the year better than all the others for running. He'd rather be cold on the outside and building up sweat on the inside than gasping for air on a hot and humid summer day. So he told Julie when she called before coming over, "Bring your sweatsuit and let's be out before it gets dark."

She got to his two-bedroom townhouse in Fairlington, a sober World War Two community in Arlington, a little after 5:30 carrying a tote bag containing a change of clothes for next day's work and her walking gear—sweatsuit and walking shoes and socks. Wednesdays had started to become routine—out to their run-walk venue, usually the nearby Fort Ward Park in Alexandria or the Episcopalian seminary campus across Braddock Road from the park, the Mt. Vernon trail at Old Town by the river and a couple of other places nearby; home-cooked dinner at his place, a little TV afterwards if there's a show anyone's interested in, or book-reading.

They nibbled on energy food, part of the routine, before going out. She on high-fiber crackers she pasted on one side with babaganoush, a spread made of eggplant and mayonnaise she learned to eat when she dated a Jewish guy briefly. He on pitted California prunes he simply loved to chew on. Then they went to Fort Ward, a four-minute drive from his place in Fairlington which he usually covered on foot, running from his front door when he went out by himself. During the three-minute stretch at a picnic table nearby, he told her how he was going to do the three-mile run.

Once around the park on its 5-MPH road was six-tenths of a mile. When he first discovered the place several years ago, he ran the regular five laps around it and walked a sixth to wind down. Then some months later, it got monotonous and he would do just one or two laps inside the park then take off across Braddock to the sidewalks alongside the seminary grounds, do a mile out there then come back in to finish the run.

If she went the same way, what he would do was flip-flop every two or three minutes to stay with her and keep her company especially when it starts getting dark. She usually started out first, walking, then he would catch up with her after giving her a two-minute lead in the park. Today, he told her, he would do two laps inside then take off to the seminary.

"If we get separated, be back here at the car in forty minutes," he said, looking at his digital watch while she stepped backwards away from him checking her watch too.

"Worry wart," she kidded, hopping in place in her Nikes, sniffing the crisp early autumn air.

"Give or take three minutes, ok?"

"Yes, sir." And she was off.

He did some more stretches for one minute before switching his watch to the timer and starting it as he began the run, going the opposite direction at first for a half a minute then turning around to catch up with her. There weren't many people left in the early evening hour using the park. Some walkers and joggers, old ladies walking their dogs. None of the picnic benches were occupied. Not many cars either, parked or moving at the speeds of a little above the five-mile-an-hour limit. It was a good time to be out in the park.

He liked running here more than any other place in the area except perhaps by the river which she also liked even more. In two or three weeks, the leaves would start turning into blazing colors and later drift in the autumn wind to cover the ground. He wished this time of the year would last much much longer than it did.

Coming to a bend by the sunken amphitheater to the right where he had watched some local performers—country bands, folk dancers and singers in the summer, she came into view some two hundred yards away. It was here that he pulled out the face towel he had in his jacket pocket and spilled the two-inch square ID's, four of them, he had brought with him and forgotten to give her. He picked them up fast and sped up to catch up with her.

"Hey, you unidentified walking woman," he said, hopping by her side. "I got something for you."

She turned to him questioningly, keeping her pace, and said: "You talking to me?"

"Yes you, Ms. UWW."

"I'm sorry, but I don't know you. Please go away or I'll call the cops."

"How?" he asked. "You don't carry a cell phone." This was another thing he had nagged her about a couple times.

"I can scream."

"Here," he finally said, holding out the ID's to her, three of hers and one of his. "Carry one with you whenever you go out, especially when by yourself. Put it in a place near the door where you won't miss it going out of the house for a walk. Keep one in your purse and one in your car, ok? The other one there is mine."

She took them from him, saying with just a trace of skeptic disbelief in her smile: "My guardian angel. What'll I do without you? So, does this mean I can drop dead now, disappear, and nobody'll have to worry about it 'cause now I can be identified and be disposed of properly?"

"I wish you'd quit fooling around like that about this and be more serious, really," he said and told her about the news item on the unknown dead man he saw on the Internet yesterday. "So, carry that from now on and no more arguing about it."

"Yes, sir."

"See you in a few minutes." He gave her a wink and sped up.

"Have a good run," she called after him, elated at seeing how concerned he was about her well-being even as she thought it, indeed, a little paranoid. But she didn't mind. In fact, she was touched, seeing it as a genuine sign of his caring, the value he placed in the part she played in his life.

When they first met at a friend's house-party nearly two years ago, she didn't think there was anything there between them. In fact, the first conversation they had ended up in an argument. But the more they argued, the more interesting it got as they opened up to each other and learned what one is made up of. He learned she was into astronomy, the planets and the stars, the galaxies of the universe, space exploration, Star Trek which she said fired her imagination when she first saw a few episodes. Small wonder, he thought later that evening at the party, when she told him she is a math teacher.

His, she learned in their subsequent encounter at the party, wasn't too far from that realm either: statistics, computers, IT in government socio-economic applications. The only thing that gave a bad taste in her mouth in that is the thought of him being a bureaucrat. Here they had another mild argument with him defending, explaining to her, his position in government saying he resists being branded a bureaucrat since he is one of the guys, the good guys, who does work to minimize and eventually get rid of red-tapes and bureaucracy in government.

The other side of that about him, she felt, is actually quite good: a career job, not a super-great income but steady, as long as people pay taxes to support the government, good benefits, pension plan, lots of vacation leave. The man is solid, in his early thirties, not like her 40-year old ex whom she had to support half the time they were married while he was 'in between jobs'.

After they got the personal bios out of the way, the matter of chemistry came next. They didn't know what they had there going into the second date. They were both aware they adapted to each other's presence and had become friendly. In the third date, they looked forward to it and enjoyed each other's company throughout. First came the kidding around, the jokes. They had more than a few laughs and enjoyed the whole evening. Then at the moment of parting—the short good night hug, the kiss that one felt the other didn't want to end and which then turned sexual and became an overture to a passionate relationship in the months that followed.

What's good about this one boy-meets-girl story, each of them agreed, is that they started out as friends, even as antagonists at the first encounter, and they turned that around and managed to see through each other later on. And now, they could turn this whole relationship around upside down inside out and it would still land safe on its feet. The worst could happen is they break-up, become just friends again, then jump-start the relationship which they shouldn't have any trouble doing. And that had happened before.

Twice before. The last time when she was at his place in the middle of the week and the phone rang, she picked it up and it turned out to be one of his ex-girlfriends, she figured out after she handed him the phone, sat nearby and listened, pretending not to pay attention as he spoke to the mouthpiece in a low voice.

"So, is that the one immediately before me?" she asked without malice, just curious, when he hung up. "Or two before me?"

"Honey, what does it matter? It's over between us a long time ago."

"Then why did she call? Rita, is that her name?"

"Yes. She called to ask if I still had the book she had me read one time and I said yes I still do. She said she'd like to have it back."

"Sounds good," she quipped, perking up a bit. She meant to simply tease him at first but now she started getting agitated. "So when will it happen? The rendez-vous. After work at Starbuck? Lunchtime at that good old favorite café in Georgetown?"

"Julie, please stop this," he begged while she picked up her things in the living room and started to leave. "I'll just put the damn book in the mail."

"Well, since you still have her address," she said on her way out the door, "why waste the stamp? Just drop it off at her door. And maybe go in for a quick visit?"

That rift lasted ten days. They were back together two weekends later after a few phone calls, both ways, as if nothing had happened.

She watched him as he got farther away in his blue cotton-polyester jogging suit, now thinking as she did occasionally for nearly two years now about how sure she was, the first time she talked to him, that she wouldn't have anything to do with him, a man obviously lacking in social skills and any knowledge in making the acquaintances of women. How wrong she was after uncovering the man behind the first impression he projected to her. First, the good humor which she now knew he uses to start a rapport as he did with her. Then, once he got the two of you opening up to each other, all the finer things she wanted—any woman would want—to see in a man: kind-hearted, good-natured, innocent as a child in the sophistication of women, sweetly innocent but not helpless where it mattered to be a man.

CHAPTER 3

▼

One thing Robert Grundell looked forward to coming to work every morning was breakfast at his desk especially when he decided on his way down to the cafeteria after taking his coat off and turning the computer on, that he's okay with bacon and egg and hash brown today. He tried to limit this to twice a week to keep his cholesterol in check. The rest of the time it was donut and pastry, one of each.

One thing he didn't relish upon settling down in his office to begin the day's work was going over the emails and finding one or two from Herod Hardin, his second-level boss, the Branch chief of Plans and Security Database, reminding the staff to 'be on time turning in your weekly work status report', or one addressed to him personally, saying something like 'Call me as soon as you get in.' or 'Meeting at 9:30 with DOT people, don't forget. Bring your stuff'.

Of his ten years in the office, the last five had been with Herod Hardin as the Branch chief. And all those five years, no one including him had gotten over how any mother on earth in this day and age could name her son Herod. It sounded like a joke when the man first came to the Branch to replace the one there before who retired. Not only that—the last name following the first came to his ear in a beat that compounded a sense of ridiculousness.

Herod Hardin. King Herod, someone said when, not long after he came, the man indeed turned out to be the despot that everyone in the Branch had hoped he wouldn't prove to be. Herod hardon, Robert Grundell said next among his peers in the office, to which none disagreed.

There were nine emails, only one from Herod, King Herod, which he read last. Most of the rest were what he considered junk messages from the LAN

Administrator's office, the OCDL Director's office, Personnel office, making agency-wide announcements about office policies that don't amount to anything more than make-work for those high-grade bureaucrats who had nothing else to do but send those emails to everybody. He deleted every one of them after reading only the first few words, except one that created an instantaneous burning effect behind his ears. The one sent out Division-wide by Milton Pheasant, the Division chief, about Leon Justice, one of King Herod's do-nothing senior-grade minions, announcing Leon's grade promotion and re-assignment to a management-level position.

Leon! That friggin' faggot, he thought. The guy came on board three or four years after he did and all these years he'd been with the agency, they didn't know where to fit him in. He'd been moving around between the Branches in the Division. One got the impression that nobody wanted him around. Meanwhile he kept getting promoted. For what?

With the burning-ear sensation came a sinking feeling in his stomach, churning out everything he had in it—bacon, egg, potato, coffee. His fingers literally froze on the keyboard, his breathing slowed as a wave of anger and disgust built up inside him at the realization once again that it's not enough that you do your job well in this fucking place; in fact, it's not even necessary that you do your job well, to get ahead. All you need to do is have friends, make friends, kiss ass, lick ass, suck ass, laugh at unfunny jokes, kowtow to assholes, and be an asshole yourself.

It took him about three minutes to start breathing normally again after that and proceed with what he was doing.

The email from Herod read 'Anything new from OSERS about the Senators' itinerary out west? You need timeline data by the minute from them if we want to know exactly what kind of security to come up with from beginning to end. Let me know if there's any problem. Give them a push if you need to.'

Like he needed to be told how to do his job he'd been at for ten years. The dumbshit. Get a life. Get a hardon!

Reluctantly, he hit a Program Function Key to toggle to the mainframe and look at the file he had received from OSERS two days ago. He didn't do anything about it after he read it for there was nothing for OCDL to do yet going by the data in the file. In one part, it contained pages of historical background from the initial conception of two water and power projects in North Dakota to its economic, environmental and national-security impacts, congressional funding and presidential approval. In another part was a description of the projects detailing the geographic location, topography, existing and proposed road accesses and the man-made structures above and below ground. There were pictures and site survey drawings too that came with the file.

The same materials were in the file for the third project farther west at the foothills of the Rockies in Montana. The last page gave a summary of the activities of the opening celebrations at each of the three projects sometime in the middle of December, week before Christmas. But there was no program of activities by which OCDL could map out security plans for the dignitaries attending the projects' inauguration. He expected Interior was still working on that and would get it out to him later.

He looked at the calendar beside the computer monitor. Two months, he thought, to mid-December. There's no cause for anybody to wet his pants over this. What's the big deal finding escorts for a bunch of senators on a train ride out to those back countries?

Alright, maybe he ought to call Interior's OSERS people for some details of activities of the coming event, see if they got anything he could start with to put a plan together, get an idea at least how many federal plainclothes dicks would be needed for those Capitol Hill bigwigs, then maybe call in a couple of them dicks, the headmen, for an advanced debriefing.

But first, the next item in the morning routine after the emails: check the TSL bin, the phone voicemail and the priority return calls to make, if any. Actually, checking the Top-Secret-Log bin took a higher priority than anything else in the morning routine. But because it's such a pain in the butt going through the procedure doing that, he was always tempted to go over the emails first.

First he had to get the day's password to access the bin file. He among only a few other people in the office got a new one everyday. And that was done by calling a number at Fort Meade in Maryland, some NSA prick over there with an attitude.

"Hello, my name is Robert Grundell, Office of Civil Defense Logistics, Treasury Department," he would start out every fucking morning like the prick at the other end hadn't heard him say the same thing a million times. "Calling for my TSL password today, please."

From that, he was taken through the following telephone queries:
Social Security number, please?
Date of Birth?
Mother's maiden name?
And your password yesterday or the last one you were authorized?

There were times when, because he only used it one day, he never committed it to memory long enough to remember it the next morning, let alone over a weekend. And they were strongly advised not to write it down anywhere so when this happened, he had hell to pay going to King Herod and King Herod's boss, Milton Pheasant, to substantiate to the NSA prick who he really was, where he worked, who he worked for, what he did and what business he had trying to access the Top-Secret-Log file that contained today's collection of the government's security data gathered and submitted daily by all the federal intelligence agencies, civilian and military, as well as the local law enforcement of the Capital area.

After the third time he went through that the past couple of years, he decided—the hell with it, he's going to write the damn thing on a tiny piece of paper and stick it in his wallet everyday. It's so damn ridiculous. Who's going to frisk him thinking that's what he'd done?

When he finally got to access the bin, he completely forgot the rest of the morning routine the next hour and a half. A matrix of security entries he kept an eye on everyday had an entry from the FBI with the label ATTN blinking at him in bold red font. The text box read:

> *OCDL alert. Item-Israeli Defense Minister ETA Reagan National 1130am Oct 24.*
> *Item-suspected attack, imminent.*
> *Item-require airport security sweep and two-layer stakeout 12 hrs prior.*

First things first, on a red alert. Finish going over the TSL bin, see if there were any more red-blinker and if there were, decide order of priority. Then take immediate action going by the book in a vault under his desk. Everything needed to be done when he got a red-blinker was done by the book.

A couple of years ago, during a U.S. visit of the foreign minister of Japan, some people in the front office—management—King Herod among them, didn't know this about the duties and responsibilities written in Robert Grundell's position description and in the book. They thought they were the first in line of command to take action on a red-blinker and that he should notify them first upon his discovery of the red alert before doing anything else. He did what he knew he had to do upon seeing the red alert: contact the Deployment Division, relay the situation details, the timeline and request security; then respond to the source of the entry in the TSL bin, that one the CIA, to tell them OCDL has done its job.

To cut red tape and bureaucratic tie-up, the book instructed the staff on the job to do just what he did—respond to the red alert quickly, follow procedures to the last critical step required of the Plans and Security Database Branch, then report the status to management. They didn't like that and they pounced on him like a pack of baboons but drew back later after he dropped the book on them and let them read up on it some.

Dumb assholes. They sit everyday doing nothing but collect their fat government paychecks every couple of weeks while workers like him do their jobs, keep an eye on the systems and their knowledge up to date, then when hell breaks loose they want to jump on center stage, get in all the action and look like big stars without knowing the procedures. Assholes.

He finished scanning the rest of the TSL bin, didn't run into another red-blinker and went into action to secure next week's arrival of the defense minister at the airport from the enemies of Israel who, according to the specifics in the alert entry, were suspected sleepers assigned in the Capital area by an Al Qaeda terrorist cell working the Mid-Atlantic region.

It sounded pretty grim but he had seen this a few times before over the years and nothing happened. It's either the bad guys were tipped off that their cover had been blown and so didn't show up or the red-blinker was a dud. Some government spook tricked into staging the alert as a joke or the spook himself started it so he and his fellow spooks would have something to do.

But...who knows what goes on with government intelligence work? There had been instances when neither the White House nor Congress knew what the CIA and the FBI were up to both at home and abroad until the media happened to stumble upon it. All in a day's work, as far as he's concerned. He does his part in it as far as his job takes him and beyond that, in all honesty, those Middle Eastern people could blow each other's head off any day for all he cares. Nothing he did at work, big or small, obscured the magnitude of how pissed he was at the way he had been trashed in the office and what he'd do to either get the hell out or get satisfaction at getting even.

After following the last in the procedures which was reporting the status of the alert to its FBI source and to the OCDL management, he went back to the rest of the morning routine. Next was checking the voicemail.

It seemed today was fast turning into one of those piss-me-good days when he listened to a message from Herod Hardin talking about the promotion of Leon Justice to Project Management Coordinator for the Branches in the Division. He'd be coordinating the work between the Branches so that he, Robert Grundell, the same as the other program analysts throughout the Division, would have to submit weekly activity reports to him starting the end of this week. Leon would be setting up a meeting with them early next week.

He gasped for air momentarily. There's no end to the bullshit that goes on in this fucking place, he thought

The next message was from Ahmed Khalifa. The call was made late the day before just after he left. The man apologized for not having gotten in touch with him as he said he would two nights ago and suggested they get together tonight for dinner if he's free. There was no other message so he hung up. But as soon as he pulled away, the intercom line rang. He picked up the phone again with a grunt halfway between indifference and relief after reading who it was on the caller-id window.

"What's up, Max?" he said to Max Poysen, a co-worker three away from him across the aisle and a more senior program analyst by eight years over his ten in OCDL. The fifty-six year old man recently became eligible for regular retirement a couple of months ago when he made thirty years of service. Max was one of a very few people in the office with whom he could have a no-holds-barred rapport once in a while.

"Got the email about Leon Justice, the dumb prick?" Max asked.

"Yes. Two of 'em. One from your Uncle Miltie, one from King Herod. I just about threw up a minute ago."

"Yeah, me too. And, hey, I don't have a relative working here."

They laughed briefly then fell into a grim hush.

"I don't know how much more I can take of it here, Max," Robert said first. "You're in a better shape. You're almost out of here, out of this whole federal government bureaucracy and bullshit politics."

"Almost is not quite the same as out of here. Meantime, I have to put up with bowing to that prick twenty years my junior and doesn't know shit of what we do here and how we do it. That promotion puts him in a position to order us around, in case you don't realize it. And you know he will do it too if for nothing else but to show us some muscle."

That brought back the burning-ear sensation to Robert. He didn't think about it but Max was right. He drew one loud deep breath of revulsion in response to Max over the telephone.

"I don't want to talk or even think about this now for one second," he pined. "If that's all you're calling me about, you might want to talk to somebody else about it."

Max Poysen understood as they hung up. Poor miserable Bob Grundell. He could feel what he was going through. He'd seen it himself, what those assholes in management had done to the man's career, keeping him holed up in a corner for years with no advancement. What he didn't understand is the man is about the best analyst there is around, good thinker, effective, puts out good work, dependable. He knew. He'd worked with Bob on several projects in the past. The man is an asset to the agency.

Maybe he didn't have the type of personality they admire, the way he presents himself, the way he looks at you, talks to you or doesn't laugh at your jokes. But that's no reason to dump a guy and forget everything else he is. The only thing he could think of behind this was they considered Bob a threat being so much more productive and accountable than they were and allowing him to get up there in higher position would certainly expose their incompetence and make them look bad.

Lunchtime, Robert Grundell decided he needed a walk and bought two hot-dogs, a regular and an eight-inch half-smoked with everything on it, at a stand across the street. He ate them at a concrete bench beside a tree out at the Skyline Plaza. After finishing the big one and washing it down with the caffeine-free coke, he took out the cell phone and dialed Ahmed Khalifa's work number.

*   *   *   *

He got off two hours early to have time to shop at Saheed's South Asian Imports in Clarendon, a short drive from work in the Ballston area of Arlington, and pick up some stuff he needed for Bobby's favorite tandoori chicken, in addition to the curry vegetable dish he himself liked. He had it all planned when Bobby called at noon, as Kamal had thought out mostly and discussed with him the day before: get him into your apartment, make him feel comfortable, at home; dinner, drinks, whatever, but make sure nobody else is with you.

For what you want to get him to talk about and hopefully you would and how far you go into it, Abu Kamal had said, we don't want to take the chance that his place is bugged. Get an extra six-pack, let him load up, and stretch the evening as long as you can till you get him to do business with us. Then drop the envelope under his nose. Let him smell it.

Bobby sounded very cheerful, even eager, he could tell in the sound of his voice over the telephone, when he told him come over for the chicken dinner at six-thirty, don't worry about anything, just bring yourself. It was now half past five. He'd been working in the kitchen over an hour and was just about done. He bought the marinated chicken pre-cooked in a clay oven at the store and all he had to do was restore the herb seasoning and warm it up before serving. He took a little time doing the curry dish but even that was no big production: peel the veggies, cut up to bite-size pieces, open a can of the pre-mixed Bhuna, a medium-hot dry type of curry mix with peppers and onions, Bobby's favorite, throw in a pot with the veggies and stir to desired blend.

He kept an eye through the kitchen window at the entrance to the apartment building across the courtyard. At ten past six, he saw Bobby come up the walk through the courtyard and up the entrance. Even from this distance of his second floor apartment, he could see how laborious Bobby's step was getting home from his government job. There is one unhappy man who needs a way out of where he is bad, the thought ran in Ahmed Khalifa's mind as much a cold, calculating observation as a feeling of sympathy.

Seeing the man so distraught made him hope and wish Bobby would do business with him regardless of who he'd be doing it for, as much to screw those making his life miserable as to at least make it pay. Turning away from the window just now to turn the gas oven on and start warming up the chicken, he had the strongest urge to just blurt out to Bobby what this whole evening was all about when he comes in.

"Take the money man, it's in the envelope. All...twenty thousand of it. Then tell me anything you can to fuck every one of them up, defeat their usefulness in their jobs and to whoever and whatever they're protecting in the country. Make them all pay and look bad."

Fifteen minutes later, he led him to a seat in the living room and brought him a beer and a glass.

"You look terrible, Bobby," he joked, not thinking Bobby would take it seriously. "Drink up. We'll have a feast tonight."

"So, it shows, huh?" Bobby said, picking up the bottle and pouring it in the glass. "Well, I can't help it. I had another terrible day today."

"Forget about it for now. You can tell me later," Ahmed said from the kitchen, checking the oven. "Just relax, man. You're on your own time now. Don't let them get to you all the way home."

You're so right about that my man, Bobby thought, and drank nearly half of the beer in the glass. No sense using up your own time getting worked up over the job. The beer tasted so good he felt he could down a six-pack before he said another word. And as Kamal coached him, Ahmed made sure that Bobby did, before and after dinner. In the course of that time, a man employed by the U.S. federal government in a position entrusted with a mine of classified top-secret national security data, feeling unappreciated, trampled and discarded by government bureaucracy and cronyism, sold out to America's enemies.

It was a breeze leading him on to the night's prime objective, Ahmed told Abu Kamal later. He didn't have to walk the narrow path of feeding him a cue a step at a time. During his second serving of the tandoori chicken, Bobby came right out and asked about a deal Ahmed talked about before for his services which he said his government office does not seem to put much value in, much less— appreciate.

Still, Ahmed remained cautious. "Well, Bobby," he said in between spoonfuls of the vegetable curry, "my company for one, as well as its subsidiaries, which as you know is in oil and energy business, they're constantly looking to expand their market and so they're always doing research, gathering data. All kinds of data, not just trade and marketing information but...stuff like business competition, demographics, and even—as a matter of fact, even more important, security data. Stuff like you do at work."

"Oh, yeah?" queried Bobby, busy on a leg of chicken.

"Yes. Like I told you before, they'd pay big bucks to get an idea of how to protect their interests, learn how to do it better, perhaps the way the U.S. government does it. Model their facility and security design for their water, power and communication resources after those of the government."

"Oh, hell, I can get you all that easy. I got a database full of that sort of thing. Nothin' to it."

"Maybe to you it's nothing," said Ahmed, throwing a quick glance at Bobby across the table. "You work with it day in and day out."

"Darn right I do. And I'm getting tired of it."

From there on, Ahmed started to fan Bobby's confidence and enthusiasm, at the same time raising his antenna to make sure he didn't miss any signal or misunderstand anything. It wasn't easy reading Bobby at first. But after they loosened up near the end of the first six-pack of beer, he had a good idea how to pace himself toward making Bobby an offer, and dropping the envelope in front of him.

He knew what he had here was a very disgruntled employee of the U.S. government who hated the people he worked for, but he had no idea what Bobby's position would be to the idea of selling classified data. Would he be doing it for the money or out of spite, or both? He tossed this out fast, thinking what do I care what he might do it for? The more important question was if Bobby might view it as a betrayal of his country. A criminal act that could get him in serious trouble. Did Bobby think it's anything to worry about? Or did he give a shit at all?

This is where Kamal's idea to study the man, check out the books he read, the TV shows he watched, and to listen carefully to the way he talked and what he liked to talk about paid off. He believed he knew the man enough, after cultivating a neighborly rapport with him for months, to broach the idea of making money, a lot more money than he made in government wages, with what he knew and did. Given the way he felt about his government job and the things he had said about the government, the parasites, the ass-kissers he'd seen in the civil service, Ahmed had no doubt about where any sense of patriotism, if Bobby had any at all, placed in his personal life at this point.

The signal he'd been hoping would turn up came when Bobby, going into his fifth bottle of beer, said: "Now, what exactly is the deal working for somebody else for a lot more money doing what I do now for Uncle Sam?"

In that, Ahmed heard the answer to one of his questions: Bobby didn't give a shit; not at all. And the key to it which was more than the money part in it was the most reassuring: '*working for somebody else*'.

Thus, now feeling more certain where he stood, he went down to business. "Alright, Bobby," he began with a nonchalance he could believe himself, "let me get straight about this. I told my company about what you do and how you could really, really help them with the great amount of information, data you work with, which could be very valuable to them."

Bobby took a deep breath without doing or saying anything, his eyes fixed on the glass of beer in his hand. They were now sitting in the living room, Ahmed in the armchair adjacent to Bobby in the near end of the sofa. Something was dawning on him, Ahmed could tell.

"Bobby, you alright?"

"I'm fine...fine," Bobby uttered, still focused on the glass of beer. "Go on. Give me the rest of it."

"They asked if you could get me some sample data I could show them..."

"That guy you were with the other day," Bobby interrupted without looking at Ahmed, "Who's he again? Your boss?"

"No. He's a friend of my boss. One of the big stockholders and member of the board of the company."

"Ah, yes, I remember. The money man. So, they want samples."

"If it's possible. If you can." Ahmed got up from the table and went to get a manila envelope around a half inch thick sitting on a shelf of a bookcase across the room. "They said they'd appreciate it a lot. This is just a token of that appreciation, they said to tell you." And he dropped the envelope on the coffee table in front of Bobby. Then he went to the dining room to clear up the table some more and get Bobby another beer.

Neither one said a word for a long time. Ahmed to give Bobby time to weigh things over and Bobby...he had considered the possibility that the Pakistani man could be telling him something, wanting to break something to him earlier in the evening and even going back to their previous meeting. Even if he was right, he didn't think it would be coming along this fast between them. He wasn't totally caught unaware but the envelope was a big surprise.

Ahmed excused himself to go to the bathroom after giving him the beer. When he came back out three minutes later, he found Bobby standing by the living room window looking at the trees in the courtyard outside. Just standing there looking out. In that time, a torrent of ideas, thoughts and emotions, past and present, had come and gone through his whole being.

It was a series of imagery he had experienced before when he felt its full impact on his personal life but which now he resolved to have little effect on him. His failed marriage and his aspirations in life then, his effort to recover and start over, his work career up to this very day, coming home from this government job feeling unhappy, looking terribly unhappy the whole world can see. Yes, now he resolved not to wallow in his unhappiness. He just wouldn't give a shit anymore. Not anymore.

He turned around just as Ahmed sat back in the armchair still keeping quiet.

"What kind of samples?" he asked suddenly after taking a drink of the beer in his hand.

A smile of relief broke on Ahmed's face. "It's all in the envelope," he said. "Go over it now if you want. Or do it in your place later. We can talk about it later, if you have any questions. I'd prefer later. Right now, I'm feeling so good I just want us to loosen up some more and forget about everything."

"You trying to get me stoned to get me to do business with you guys?"

Ahmed broke out laughing, raising his glass at Bobby. He got leery for a moment until Bobby said: "Hey, you don't have to do that. 'Sides, I'm already drunk!"

Now the two of them broke out laughing and the Pakistani man knew he had the American government worker in the payroll.

It was a good thing Ahmed preferred not to get into the business of the envelope right then and there. Because now, sitting in the living room of his own apartment at ten o'clock, even as the six bottles of Coors were now working to numb his face and fingertips, he realized how he would have flinched in front of Ahmed the way he just did—with a sudden loss of breath—at seeing the stack of the hundred dollar bills, at least a half inch thick in a paper binder, the envelope contained.

He wasn't really drunk, just whoozy from the amount of alcohol in his blood. And he wasn't tired. If anything, after such a good meal which he enjoyed so much—thanks to a neighbor's good cooking—he felt relaxed, comfortable, and awake enough to once again as he did earlier, weigh the situation he faced. He took the money out of its binder and spread it on the coffee table like a double deck of cards, guessing how much there was of it which he'd find out later to be exactly twenty-thousand dollars.

It didn't take him long, two or three minutes, to consider the choices he had and decide which one to favor. All he needed to do was consider the ten years he had spent at OCDL and remind himself of King Herod and his parasite minions, Leon Justice among them and what Max Poysen said about the latest development at the office today.

Fuck it, he thought once again. I don't give a shit. I don't give a shit anymore.

He then went over the five-page document that came with the money in the envelope. Like Ahmed said, it's all in there, what that stack of money was supposed to pay for. He was bobbing his head as he read through the materials, looking amused with an easy smile as if reading the questions in a school quiz to which he already knew all the answers.

CHAPTER 4

▼

It was a welcome event when the Alternative Work Schedule was implemented at Interior's OSERS three years ago. About time, everybody agreed, considering many other offices not only in Interior Department but other big agencies in Washington, D.C. and throughout the country had been doing it for years.

As soon as it was official, Chris Phillips signed up for it, opting for the AWS where every (two-week) pay period, you work nine hours a day for eight days, eight hours for one day and get one day off. And you're free to choose which day you want to schedule as your 'AWS off day'.

This pay period, he chose today—the second Friday—to be off. Unfortunately, he had some unfinished task from the day before—a report on current administration energy reserve statistics due the front office today, another one of those two-day research jobs they tossed at him now and then either because no one else could do it as fast or they can't find anyone else who'd take it. There were a few deadwoods in the office that management deemed pointless to bother with. But he didn't mind since he knew he only needed a couple more hours to finish it up. Besides, he could take comp time for it anytime he wants the next pay period.

He came in the usual time of seven-thirty, made a quick cup of tea and got to work right away. He planned to be out of there before ten and start his weekend by heading back home, maybe stop at McDonald's on the way for a hotcakes special breakfast, and putting on his sweatsuit and Nikes and driving down the riverside in Old town Alexandria for a nice early run.

By nine-thirty, he shot an email to his boss containing the report as a Word document attachment. That's that, he thought, then went over today's email, the last thing he intended to do before turning off the computer and getting out. There were five of them, mostly agency-wide public announcements, except one from the Office of Civil Defense Logistics, Treasury Department, sent by Robert Grundell. Ah, yes, OCDL, the Treasury spook dispatchers.

He knew immediately what it was about. Big Thunder, the upcoming inauguration out west of those water and power projects to be attended by the chairman of the Senate Committee on Energy and Natural Resources, and half the members of its Subcommittee on Water and power. And OCDL needs the events program so they can deal with security and safety of the projects, the senators and everybody else. He had heard from somebody in the front office the other day that the President might even be there for a sneak-peak appearance since he was scheduled to be out in that part of the country around that time, middle of December.

The file was ready in a secure folder, finally completed after weeks of planning and revisions by the Hill people and their office. He can now send it to Grundell who had called earlier in the week too about it, but not yet. He just needed to encrypt the texts—it's a classified sensitive file, same as the first part he had sent earlier in the week—and he didn't want to spend any more time here today. He wanted to get out of here now and go running by the river. It'll have to be Monday. What would anybody want to do with it over the weekend anyway?

He replied to Robert Grundell's email, saying—Monday, then logged off the computer and shut it down. But there was to be another delay, a few minutes longer, when the phone rang as he was getting up.

"Hey, kid," his father said from the kitchen of his condo in Manassas, Virginia, stirring powdered cream into a cup of decaf. "Remember me?"

"Hey, pops," said the son, suddenly thinking of something that caused him to move his eyes to the calendar on the wall—the date, which was yesterday, the man was supposed to be back from a two-week vacation in Europe. "You back?" he asked. "Or still out there?"

"I'm back," said Samuel Phillips, feeling bubbly, full of enthusiasm about the life he had lived for fifty-eight years including the past fourteen days he spent touring in Italy and Greece with a friend whom he planned to introduce to Chris tonight over dinner, if the kid is not busy with other plans, that is. "Just got back two nights ago."

"So, how was it? Any problem with the flying? Airports? Terrorists? Weirdos?"

"Nuh! Nothing. Everything went fine."

"Had a good vacation?"

"Great. Had a lot of fun. Tell you about it later. What are you doing today?"

"Nothing monumental I know of. It's my AWS off day. I just came in to finish up something due today. I'm on my way home now. I'm going running."

"Wanna come over for dinner later? You and….whatzername…?"

"Julie." Chris knew his dad remembered Julie but the man was always trying to make it seem like Chris had so many girlfriends he can't keep up with them. Chris thought it's the other way around the last six, eight years now since his mother, now remarried in Pittsburgh, divorced him for what she claimed as his infidelity.

"Yes. Bring her along. We wanna show you some stuff from over there."

"Alright, I'll tell her. What're you making for dinner?"

"I'm not. She is."

"Susan? I thought she didn't know much about cooking…"

"Nora."

"Who's Nora?"

"Nora, the one I went to Europe with."

"Weren't you with Susan?"

"No, kiddo, I haven't seen Susan in a couple months."

Chris buttoned up momentarily, puzzling over the women business of his unmarried father. He thought back to the last time he saw him with Susan, Susan something, 49, a blonde knockout, nice figure, young-looking for her age, three grownup kids one of whom, the eldest—a bright 27-year-old upcoming woman lawyer, he fancied at one time going out with if he hadn't been involved with someone else. Must have been early summer, right after July 4th, when the two drove to Rehoboth Beach. They insisted on him and Julie joining them later during the weekend which they did. It turned out to be an enjoyable weekend and they all had fun. He was convinced then his dad was ready to turn his back on the swingin' singles scene and get down to serious business. That was the last he knew about them

He liked Susan although he didn't know her close enough to see her personality. She was attractive, fun to be with and obviously was ready to go the distance with his father. But today, all of a sudden, he tells him what…it's all over with her? Now it's this…Nora?

Where in the world did he come up with this one so fast?

"Hey, kid," he heard his father say on the phone, "what's wrong?"

"Da-ad…" he said with all the moaning he could put in it so that his father knew right away what it was all about.

"Listen, I got to get going," Samuel Phillips said to his son now for the fast exit to avoid any further inquiry. "I still got some unpacking to do. See you around seven tonight, okay kiddo?"

"Don't run out now. Tell me first what happened with Susan. I want to know."

"What do you want to know?"

"What happened? Between you! I thought the last I saw you two together everything was looking good."

"Well, looking good isn't exactly the same as good good. We had a sort of a…falling out."

"What sort of a falling out? Who did what?"

"It's a long story and I don't want to get into it now, okay?" said Samuel, only now realizing how his son actually took interest in his personal life.

"Dad, if it's you who did something, how could you?" Chris was at a loss to nail him for anything for he didn't know what kind of a relationship the two had going. All he had was his personal impression of Susan and the hope that, after what—eight or nine months of them seeing each other, things would work out and the old man would finally settle down. "She is such a nice woman I really thought the two of you would do well for each other," he added.

"Son, there are others things you just don't see," Samuel explained. "We really didn't get along that well. We're two different types of people, that's all I can tell you, okay?"

Every time this thing came up between them, Chris always ended up just clamming up, facing the fact that it's really none of his business if his father bedded down every single middle-aged woman he could lay his hands on till he found the one he would want to be monogamous with. The most he could do was hope that would happen soon not with the next woman, or the next, or the next, but the one he's with now.

Nora? God, he thought as he hung up the phone, I hope this one not only turns out to be the right one, but knows how to bag him.

It was a few minutes past ten when he pulled in to MacDonald's at Bradlee shopping plaza across the street from his neighborhood. He loved these AWS off days. You've put in your time, you're done, he thought. Your time is yours. You're free from all that government bureaucracy and none of those bureaucrats and all their power politics can touch you. It's a sure three-day weekend every couple of weeks, four-day if Monday happened to be a holiday.

The way he usually spent the time off was simply by relaxing, doing what pleased him the most during his free time, not making any plans and pressuring himself with turning the day into a big production and a great success. It was simply a free day which he could very well spend sleeping all day if he wanted to, or doing the things he enjoyed doing, by himself or with Julie if she's with him. One of these, to start the day, was breakfast at the big arches and reading the paper. Next, without even thinking about it, was running, then whatever else he might have lined up for the day out of fancy or necessity: car oil change, mall shopping or foodstore shopping, cooking or going back to that award-winning novel he hadn't picked up in a couple of days.

It was a bright and pleasant autumn day, not too cold, just chilly enough to make a three- or four-mile run by the Potomac the centerpiece of the day. At the moment, however, while enjoying the hotcakes special—pancakes, scrambled eggs and sausage with plain black tea—his outlook for the day got dampened somewhat by what he read on the front section of the Post: Campaign Finance Reforms, Capitol Hill interns, corporate earnings reports, the new Redskins QB, war on terrorism.

He could never understand why the founding fathers, with all their wisdom that provided for the right of every citizen to exist in this country as free-thinking individuals, didn't think of putting in the Constitution something to assure that every candidate for public office enjoy equal exposure, equal time and equal expenditure, regardless of party affiliation or personal wealth. What's the problem with passing legislation setting a maximum campaign expenditure, with matching government allocation if necessary, to meet a reasonable estimate of a campaign expense from beginning to end? The way it is now, a candidate with lots of money, no matter where it comes from—personal wealth, party coffers, lobbyists, the Chinese, the Indonesians, white-collar criminals—practically buys his or her term in public office. The candidate with the most amount of money to blow in the campaign wins, plain and simple.

And now, that congressman who had a personal relationship with that vanished Capitol Hill intern half his age was back in the news: the sleazeball had the gall to start campaigning for another term in Congress. The nerve!

And here's what really got to him everytime he sees it on the front page, the front page of one of the most powerful, if not the most powerful, daily newspapers in the nation: a friggin' football quarterback (or a star basketball or baseball player) making the headline. This is the role model, the public image of what's desirable and ideal that's being hammered in the minds not just of the young but that of the matured in society, by those who decide what's news and what's not. Ballplayers whose views in life go no farther than the turf they play on. Mindless!

And it doesn't get any appetizing when, next, he parallels the acts committed by the terrorists with those of corporate executives and their accountants, those white-collar criminals. One destroys human lives and even a whole way of life if they could, literally, physically, any way they could think of; the other does the same thing, without the use of terror but with lies, thievery and deception. The end results, perhaps outside of the actual bloodletting and blowing up of human bodies to pieces, are not much different.

He turned to finish up breakfast before his stomach turned completely while reading the paper. Frankly, he thought to himself, he didn't know why he continued to read it. He used to buy it most days of the week and Sundays. For a time now, he did only once during the week, if that, and Sunday. Lately, though, he wouldn't even buy it anymore and read it only when he found it laying around at MacDonalds' or at a table in their office cafeteria or when Homer Pinkney next to him in the office was done with his copy. If not, he just read the news on the internet or got it on cable TV at home.

When he got home, he hurried through the short walk from the parking to his ground-floor apartment door, thinking he should've gone to work with the running bag like he sometimes did when he ran at lunch time, so he wouldn't have to go home and change. When he felt the cool air out, he wished he could've just gone out to the riverside or even the park right away. He didn't want to miss another minute of it any longer.

But coming back out a few minutes later all set to go running, he came across Daisy Campbell, 33, single and looking, a neighbor two buildings down the pathway from him, struggling with a piece of furniture—a mahogany nightstand she was moving in from her car. It was going on three years now when he dated her. Lasted about five months, give or take a half.

He had high hopes with her at the beginning, wanting eagerly to get out of the singles and bar scenes already which he got into not long after college with friends, many of whom were now married. But two months into the relationship, he realized she wasn't his type. And she knew it too. He was too serious for her and she was too independent, too fun-seeking and unpredictable for him. The rest of the time they dated turned into a friendship of convenience, for sex and companionship. They liked each other in the way that kept them together and accepted the fact that they could only stay in their situation until someone else came into the picture for either one, or both.

Someone did for him first so they ended their 'situation' with no one bearing grudges and became just friendly neighbors. He went and got into another relationship and she went on a dating binge. They were both in and out of relationships and occasionally, during a breaktime, they would get back together and resume their old situation temporarily. This went on for a few months until Julie Santorelli came along. And that, he assumed after he hit it good with Julie a couple of months later, was the end of the breaktime flings with Daisy.

With him it was. It had been. But not with Daisy. She continued to impress upon him to this day as they crossed paths coming and going, that she was open to it. He was glad they didn't live nextdoor to each other. But once in a while, like right now, it didn't matter.

"What—are you trying to induce a hernia or something?" he said as he saw her coming and hurried to take the furniture from her. They had always been on good speaking terms which included a friendly rapport.

"Not actually," she replied. "I'm wearing this heavy duty supporter that beefs up your groin muscles, the kind basketball players wear."

He cracked up as he hoisted the thing over his shoulder. "I hope you don't have anything else to bring in like an L-shaped sofa."

"Actually I do but I have it on layaway. I'll let you know when I'm bringing it in."

"Well, make sure you catch Pablo Sandejas nextdoor," he joked. Pablo was the gentle three-hundred pound Nicaraguan groundskeeper of their section of the community who lived in Daisy's building.

In her apartment, she directed him to place the furniture in a corner of the bedroom near the head of the bed, the same bed where they had made love countless times even a few weeks after Julie came into the picture but before he and Julie became exclusive. Before he could head back out the door, she quickly got them into a small talk.

"I see you must be on your AWS off day today," she said.

"Yup. And I'm going out running and enjoy it."

"I'm off too, on annual leave just today. Hang on a minute. Lemme get you something to drink."

"No, thanks. I just had breakfast and I got to go while the weather is good." He turned towards the door but as he stepped away from her, she took one of his hands and pulled him back hard so that he wound up turning around. She kept on pulling him hard towards her until they ended up falling onto the bed with him on top.

"C'mon, Chris, you got all day," she said, wrapping him in one arm and drawing his head towards her with the other hand. "What's your hurry?"

"Daisy, we can't do this anymore. We just can't"

"Why not?"

"Because…" Before he could say another word, she pulled his head down and sealed his mouth with hers. He struggled momentarily but not as much as he could have. He knew what she was trying to do—get him to relax and start a fire in his groin, rekindle the old passion, the physical drive that kept them together in the past even after they had known how they felt about each other.

"Alright, alright…" he gasped after forcing his face away from hers. "This is all…nice fun and games—"

"Then don't fight it," she interrupted, lifting one of her legs from under him and wrapping it around one of his. This she did to press his bottom half harder against hers after she felt him get hard. "Let's just have fun and enjoy."

"I can't."

"Yes, you can," she insisted.

"I shouldn't!"

"Just lose yourself to it. It's not that bad."

"Daisy, please don't do this."

She heard what he said and she knew he meant it, but she also heard how he said it not with a firm voice but a weakened self-control and will to resist. Thus, she pulled him back to her and was justified when he collapsed completely over her, wrapped his arms tightly around her and lost himself to his old sexual desire for her.

It was half past eleven when he pulled into a parking space at Oronoco Park in Old Town Alexandria. He could still feel her sensuality subduing his thoughts of loyalty to Julie while they made love. No. While they had sex. And this is the only redeeming thought he had of it. He didn't make love to her or with her. He just had sex with her. He simply gave in to the lust, the sexual drive of a healthy, physically fit 35-year-old man who found himself trapped in the arms of another woman.

Long into the first mile of the run, his shoes pounding incessantly on the pavement, he struggled to absolve himself of any wrongdoing. Could he have gotten out of the situation he was being forced into? Could he have resisted her more strongly? Was he a victim or a willing accomplice?

One side of him said yes he could have escaped the situation he found himself in and the fact that he didn't summon enough will to do so made him a willing accomplice. The other side said no, things happened so quickly that he had no chance to resist her assault on his manliness. He had become powerless and it would have been unnatural to overturn the forces that had engulfed him.

In the second mile right by the Washington Sailing Marina on Daingerfield Island, he set all that guilt-and-blame question aside and considered what next. He's definitely not going to let her corner him again and if she tried, he'd have to be firm about his rebuff in no uncertain terms, if it hurts her feelings and even angered her. And if she kept trying, of course there's the alternative to move.

Past the Marina, the trail came to an open area only yards away from the river bank with a long clear view of Washington, D.C. several miles upriver on the other side of the Potomac. Looking across the river at the city that to him for years represented, more than anything else, respect and power not just in America but throughout the world and now, recently—the last ten, fifteen years—sleaze-ball politicians, lying politicians, sex-addicted politicians, incompetent bureaucrats, he fell back to examining himself and his own actions the same way he scrutinized the politicians and his own womanizing father.

People's weakness with women, money and power—is it possible that all men are subject to the same degree of vulnerability, and that those who are not, only appear that way? And they do because they're better liars and hypocrites, and more importantly—they hadn't been caught in their cheating and thieving acts?

So, where did he place in that? And if he did at all, how could he then look across the river and feel the aversion he just did for the collective image of those Washington politicians, talk to his father on the phone and try to nail him on his casual relationship with women, without feeling the heat himself especially with what just happened between him and Daisy Campbell, let alone his own casual relationships with women in the past?

He felt caught in his own act and wanted to just run away from his thoughts, leave them behind at every stride he made. And he did, pulling for that side of him that said he was more a victim than an accomplice, and resolved to forget what happened this day and certainly not to let it happen again.

Before he knew it, he was running by the National airport, three miles from where he started, and turned around as soon as he became aware of it. He did another mile and a half which brought him back to the Marina where he slowed down to a fast walk for a minute while he took his pulse. A hundred and forty five beats. Not bad for someone starting to push forty, he thought, without dropping dead.

He walked the rest of the way back to the car not thinking, not feeling, just focusing his consciousness on his physical well-being as his body gradually recovered from the stress of running. The best part of being out here after the run. Just losing himself to his environment through a span of time when all other human activities and involvement, all his cares in the world were on hold. But this span of time didn't last as long as he wanted it to when his cell phone rang a couple of minutes later.

"Hey, where are you?" Julie's voice came clearly to his ear out in the open outdoors between the G.W. Parkway and the Potomac river.

"I was just getting ready to call you," he said, still puffing from the run.

"What's the heavy breathing? Let's see, you just got done running or having sex with an ex-girlfriend?" she joked.

He took a moment to catch his breath, stunned, before replying: "Both."

"Which one is better?"

His mind and body froze for a moment. He had no idea how he was able to say the last word he said to her without even thinking about it. Whether he said it to go along with her joke or because he feared by some unknown reason she knew the truth and he decided better to confess and await his fate, he couldn't be sure.

"I don't know yet," he managed to say in between puffs. "I'm still winding down from the run. I'll tell you when my pulse gets back to normal. Meantime, about tonight. If you don't happen to have a better offer, dinner at my dad's in Manassas."

"What's the occasion?"

"He wants us to salivate over his two-weeks in Europe with his latest partner. They got back a couple nights ago."

"Ow, this should be interesting," she chirped. "Is this latest going to be there?"

"She's cooking the dinner. That's all I know. I haven't met her, didn't even know she existed till he told me. Pick you up at around six?"

"That'll be fine."

"So, how's your day?"

"Busy. Got a tough one coming up before the next class," she said, her voice slowing down some while picking her words.

"A tough one what?" he asked.

"This girl I've been sort of counseling on my own, she and I have gotten to be confidants. The last time we had a talk, she opened up quite a bit, asked to see me again today. She should be here in a few minutes."

"What's her story? Acne? Boyfriend problem?"

"A little bit beyond that. She's Catholic and had an abortion three years ago. Now it's starting to get to her. Oops, she's here," Julie said turning towards her partly open office door where someone stood and knocked lightly. "Tell you about it later. See you around six."

CHAPTER 5

▼

Everybody got the email early Monday morning regarding the 11:00 A.M. all-hands meeting of the Division. It was a short notice for which the sender, Milton Pheasant, the Division chief, apologized but expressed hope that most people would make it.

What it was all about primarily was the presentation of Leon Justice in his new position in the Division. Around seventy people went, roughly two-thirds of the Interstate Logistics Division, spread out in the ground floor conference room thick from the middle to the back, sparse towards the front where most of the management people gathered.

Robert Grundell sat near the entrance door twelve back of fourteen rows. He'd rather be delivering pizza for a living, or making it himself, all sweaty in a pizza joint than hold a government job where he'd be sitting in a meeting like this one. He was going to dodge it as he'd done so many times with other admin meetings but it was too late. A lot of people had already seen him come in including the front office.

It was supposed to be a one-hour meeting but it went over because they waited fifteen minutes till they felt there were enough people. The meeting was one of those gatherings that many thought was not necessary and was a total waste of taxpayers' money, if you consider the average hourly rate of this type of white-collar professional government workers, senior to mid-level managers, senior analysts and mid-level bureaucrats. Salaries ranging from fifty to over a hundred thousand a year.

Robert was one of the last ones to show up. As he sat down, he did a quick take of the spread in the room.

There were several groups he could've color-coded and labeled in different ways. The group sitting in the first two rows, say Red—Management, big fat paycheck for not doing much, lots of government fat there. The next three rows—Orange, the minions of those up front, the ass-kissers, the Politicians, people whose main goal on the job is to be PC, right or wrong. Leon Justice sat among them.

The next two rows were nearly empty except for the front office admin assistants (secretaries and several temps). The rest of the spread was made up of several other groups, from Robert's vantage point. Say the Blue group—the Mid-level workers in journeyman positions, the employees who did the real work, the people who really mattered in government service or should, but unfortunately not all of them did.

For this reason, Robert broke this group into two subgroups—the Light Blue group which is made up of some minorities who got in government service mostly through an unwritten quota system or affirmative action, as well as several mainstream male and female workers. All of them did mediocre work or no work at all. Many had to be coaxed into doing their assignments by their project leader if they could get away from their various social activities in the office, that is, or be counted on being in their workstations once in a while to earn their paycheck.

The Deep Blue group—the real productive workers among whom Robert counted himself, those whose interest on the job is to face the challenge of their assignments, to get them done right and get them done on time. These are the kind of people who, should those managers and politicians sitting up front, in the exercise of one of their managerial and political blunders, happen to piss off thoroughly enough to make them quit, or for some idiotic reason suppress so that they cannot function in their positions, the office will simply cease to function the way it is meant to. And if somehow this sort of thing happened throughout the entire federal government service, the United States executive branch of the government will cease to function the way it is meant to and will collapse.

Finally, there's the Yellow group—the oldtimers with twenty to thirty some years of service, in their late fifties and early sixties just waiting for the right time to retire and couldn't care less what went on with work and with everybody in the office. They didn't sit in one bunch. They were scattered throughout, front to back, but mostly in the middle and near the back of the room.

Max Poysen, sitting behind and to the right of Robert was one of them. Next to Max directly behind Robert was Eddie Mahone, fifty-four years old with twenty-eight years service. Recently, Eddie had become known for being vocal with just about anything in the office. Many thought it was because the man didn't give a shit since he could go anytime while the OCDL was authorized by the Office of Personnel Management, the government's HR arm, to offer early-outs and some incentive to retire such as a twenty-five-thousand dollar farewell cash payoff. And the offer had been authorized successively for the last three years now.

"The fuck are we doin' here?" Eddie Mahone, leaning inconspicuously forward, whispered to Robert when Herod Hardin got up front to introduce the topics of the meeting and speak about one of them—some of the changes taking place in the Division, prior to turning it over a few minutes later to his boss, Milton Pheasant.

"You tell me," Robert, leaning back a bit, mumbled through the corner of his mouth to Eddie.

Max Poysen turned to one then the other, speaking only with his eyes, the lid halfway down in an expression of total disinterest, saying 'Get me outa here. I'm ready to throw up.'

And he nearly did when Milton Pheasant, after rambling for twenty minutes about—among other stuff that only he had a say and interest on—the Division's new fiscal-year budget and how sound it is with a surplus of so many hundreds of thousands of dollars for training money and equipment upgrades, started talking about Leon Justice, lauding the man's personal background and professional career in industry and government, prior to getting him up in front and turning it over to him.

"Thank you, Milton," Leon Justice, in his new position as the Division's sole Project Management Coordinator said. Robert Grundell along with several other Deep Blue group members and most of the Yellow group rolled their eyes, slouched in their seats and paid attention only out of civil politeness. "That sounded a lot better than the way I wrote it in my resume," Leon added.

That drew a thin applause from several people mostly in the first three rows. Everyone else in the back kept their heads low, their eyes angled up at the speaker in an expression of helplessness and boredom.

He went on to talk about the changes in the organizational chart which was handed out to everybody as they came in. In it, he focused on his position and how it relates to the workers in the Division—Branch chiefs, project leaders and staff members. He will be gathering data to track the work activities in the Division for a monthly presentation to the Division Chief and the Deputy Director for the Office of Civil Defense Logistics. To do this, the weekly activity reports would have to be at his desk by COB Thursday.

Contacts with OCDL customers outside Treasury, particularly with military and intelligence agencies, will have to be cleared through his office. There will be a semi-monthly meeting between his office, the Branch chiefs and staff members selected from each Branch particularly those working on considered high-profile, high-priority projects.

When he was done, Milton Pheasant got back up and opened the meeting for questions and answers. This lasted another fifteen minutes with some people asking about the training schedules this year, the IT people about any planned hardware and software upgrades and others about hiring and promotion.

By this time, Robert Grundell was bursting with impatience to get the hell out of there. And when, a couple of minutes later, the meeting was adjourned and he swiftly got up and was the first to stride out the door, Eddie Mahone with Max Poysen alongside was right behind him.

"We're in a real jam here now, you guys know that?" Eddie was saying.

"Yes," replied Max Poysen. "More than I thought we would be. That goddam prick Leon telling us all that shit—report to him, no outside contact unless he okays it, meet twice a month. That's the same as telling us he's going to keep an eye on us from now on. What for?"

"Yes," agreed Eddie. "What the fuck for? You know what we can do? Why can't we protest this?"

Robert Grundell slowed down in his hurry to get away from the crowd and turned his head halfway at Eddie. "Protest what?" he asked.

"Protest that dumbshit's appointment or promotion—whatever or however the hell he got to that position," Eddie Mahone replied, all steamed up.

"How do you do that?" asked Max Poysen.

"Somebody could write it up then pass it around through the entire Division for signatures," Eddie suggested after thinking about it a moment.

"That might not be a bad idea," said Max. "Shit, I'm gonna write it up. I'll start today, right now, as soon as I get back in my office. Strike while the iron is hot."

"I'll spread the word," Eddie added. "Get some solid support to back it up early. We'll send a copy to the Inspector General, one to EEO, and of course one to the Office of Special Counsel. That one could go to the White House and the committee of Congress that oversees our agency. Fuckit, we'll take it all the way to the top."

Robert Grundell nodded his agreement without saying a word and resumed his hurry to get away even from the two and get back to his office. He felt totally rattled even more than they were as they sounded but he simply didn't want to discuss it with anybody. He had been pissed enough long before that meeting, much much longer before so that it just made no sense to talk about it anymore. Especially now that he had decided to do something about it on his own, that's the more reason he didn't want to talk to anybody about it.

That would be a good thing, though, what Eddie Mahone thought about for the Division to do. And he's sure they could get a majority, a big majority of the Division to sign that protest letter. Put in why they don't want Leon Justice in that position and, better yet, why they don't want that position to exist at all, prove that it's not necessary and on the contrary would only be counter-productive, a waste of taxpayers' money, so abolish it.

Everybody knew how Leon Justice got to be known as the 'pompous ass' throughout the Division and even among many of its customers in OCDL. For years since the guy came on board, he got passed around to every Branch in the Division. Nobody wanted to work with him. The word was that the guy was one arrogant, demeaning son of a bitch to work with. And he played tricks on you. When he didn't know the answer or what to do about something, he'd ask you the question in a real bossy, superior way like he was quizzing you, making it look like he knew the answer and he was just testing you if you're any good by giving him the answer.

Son of a bitch is one contemptible scumbug. But being in the front office clique with Herod Hardin who was in with the upper management echelon that went all the way up to the deputy director in the power tree of the agency, none of that got in the way of his getting ahead in his service career. Personal reputations, personal differences with co-workers, personality clashes, none of that was rated in the performance appraisal and goes in one's personnel records. Only what one's friends in high places chose to put in them.

In his office, Robert Grundell gave himself time to recover from the boredom and the disgust and the ire he brought back with him from the meeting. After he'd been sitting for fifteen minutes, feeling, listening to the signs of his body functions—his breathing, heartbeat, a ringing in his ear, the arthritic pain in his neck and right elbow—closing and opening his eyes intermittently, he turned to the computer and clicked the left button of the mouse. The monitor screen that had blacked out while he was away came back to life, displaying his email inbox window.

After going over several messages before it, he read the one from the Office of Socio-Economic Reserve and Security, Interior Department, sent by Chris Phillips. Nice fellow, he thought. Nice doing business with you. He clicked the attached file named BigThunder and saved it in the C drive. It was an encrypted data file so he inputted it to DXD, the inhouse government-designed digital complex decoder authorized for use only by selected agencies, Treasury and Interior among them. He saved a decoded copy of the file in the C drive and another he dumped to a CD-RW disc he brought from home.

He imagined the data transfer from the C drive to the disc while he was doing it. The entire file containing all the critical-sensitive classified information OCDL needed to determine the type of security to provide in the December inauguration events of those big water and power projects out in the Midwest. Amazing, these information technology machines, hardware and software. It took no time at all to dump the whole thing, a little more than two megabytes of data, to the disc.

Same as he did earlier in the morning with the other file he received last week from OSERS, the one containing the documentation of the projects, even a bigger one—four megabytes, which he dumped to another disc. He had planned to make these two discs his first drop to Ahmed but changed his mind just now.

He was thinking, the anger and the feeling of helplessness against those people seated in the front rows at the meeting still lingering mightily inside—even if Eddie Mahone and the whole Division succeeded in throwing Leon Justice out and abolishing that make-work position they created for him, it could take a whole year or longer to get to that, if they ever did. Meantime the asshole would be taking a big fat paycheck every payday worth easily over a hundred thousand a year.

He sat with his eyes closed for a few seconds. When he opened them, they moved to his briefcase leaning against the computer tower under the desk. In it was the manila envelope containing the twenty-thousand dollars he hadn't found time to deposit. He planned to today at a branch of his bank near the office.

No, he now thought about the drop to Ahmed and his people, not these discs. Not yet. These will be for later. Another drop, for a bigger price. A much bigger price. He must learn the value of his commodity and of his position to them. He won't be cheap.

He turned back to the computer and browsed a file directory of the Deployment Division. Many of the folders were classified Top Secret but with his TS clearance, he was able to access every one of them like any ordinary folder. He expanded the ones he thought would be of any interest to him to see what files they contained and browsed as many files as he could, speed-reading them till his eyes tired.

An hour later, he had over a half a dozen floppies loaded with files he judged would be good-commodity drops. One of them which he intended to use for the first drop contained the security deployment data which originally covered the arrival of the Israeli Defense Minister from the airport through the entire route of the entourage which was to end at the river entrance of the Pentagon. This had been revised since his request for a new deployment based on the TSL alert. The Defense Minister now would be picked up by a helicopter from the airport and received at the chopper pad on the Washington Boulevard side of the Pentagon. In the diskette also was a file containing the site and security data of several nuclear plants in Virginia and North Carolina.

See how Ahmed's people like these ones, for samples, he thought. And there's plenty more. But—they got to pay for it, at least as much as they're paying that son of a bitch Leon in the office. Heck, no. A lot more.

He looked at the briefcase again under the desk. Checked the time. Shoot, it's close to one o'clock. How time flies when you're either pissed or excited. He logged off the computer, put the floppy in the briefcase and went out with it to his car down in the garage to head to the bank.

It was a short drive, less than ten minutes, down Columbia Pike to the corner of Glebe Road in Arlington passing by several fast food joints which made him think of lunch. Maybe he'll pick up a mushroom steak at The Broiler on the same side of the street near the bank after making the deposit. Good. He liked that steak sandwich. He'd been going there, The Broiler, whenever he got tired of KFC or MacDonald, ever since he discovered it a couple years ago.

Something else kept coming back to him as he neared the bank. Who goes to a bank with this much cash nowadays other than those armored trucks with armed guards carrying sacks of green bills? Another thing—the IRS, come tax time. How in hell is he going to declare where he got this money? At the parking lot of the bank, he sat for a while and thought hard about this.

Hold on there a minute! You can't do this, he thought in a flash all of a sudden, deciding right then and there not to make the deposit. Shit! Why didn't he think about this before? Every time money changes hands, Uncle Sam gets a percentage of it, how much depends on your tax bracket, unless it's tax-exempt money such as charity or capital gain under some amount from a home-sale, stuff like that.

This led him to do something else instead of going in the bank. He needed to call Ahmed right now, talk to him about payment arrangements. Several ideas raced through his mind. Maybe he'd need to talk to his people directly about this.

Get him on the phone quick. Maybe he can come out now, meet him for lunch at a park nearby. At Fort Ward Park. Yes. Ahmed worked in the Ballston area of Arlington, not far from where he's sitting now. They could both be there in less than fifteen minutes and he could make the drop too. That's right. Get that done at the same time. And lunch—forget that mushroom steak for now. Takes time ordering to carry it out. Just drive up MacDonald's a couple blocks down. But call the guy first.

CHAPTER 6

▼

He was having a very relaxed day. The weather was nice, unseasonably warm for October so he went out after lunch for a walk to Ballston Commons to do a little window shopping shortly before one o'clock. Then the cell phone rang. It was Bobby. From then on, everything in his day changed and it hadn't stopped yet, even now which is what—six forty-five in the evening, on his way to Westfields Marriott in Chantilly twenty eight miles away.

He agreed to meet him at the park. Bobby offered to get him a burger. "No, thanks," he said, "I already ate. Go ahead get your Big Mac and fries, I'll meet you there in fifteen minutes, give or take."

The guy was just now catching on to the…the trick of the trade, he thought. It's a good thing he didn't go ahead and deposit the money in his account.

"I guess you're just going to have to find a way to handle this," he told Bobby at the park, watching him work on his burger and fries across the picnic table under a pine tree.

"Heck, I never gave this any thought at all. You read about it all the time, especially here in Washington but you never really pay attention," Bobby said. "So how do people do it? Launder money?"

"I don't know. Open a Swiss bank account? Get it out of the country?"

Bobby stopped eating for a moment and gawked at him. "You're not serious," he said.

Both of them admitted never having thought that possession of money in large amounts could be a problem, as much of a problem as working and busting your guts for it and getting it in your name.

But spending it isn't, Ahmed told Bobby. Not if you don't make a show of it. Bobby took that one in and appeared to be working on some ideas in his head. Put it in a hole in the ground? Keep it under your pillow, use it a little at a time? In any case, Bobby asked if Ahmed could talk to his people and work out some kind of payment arrangement.

Perhaps partial payments like regular paychecks by electronic transfer or even hardcopy check for what could appear as legitimate services, that sort of arrangement. Make it look like he worked for them parttime, moonlighting as a consultant at what—two hundred bucks an hour? Something like that. Beats what Leon Justice would be making plus what a couple of his high-grade cohorts in the front office made. Why not?

He told Bobby not to worry, he'll ask his people. But when, he didn't know. On any given day, he had no idea how to get a hold of Kamal if he didn't answer the phone or return his call. It could be he's out of town, either in Detroit or New York. Well, today, it would turn out different starting with Bobby, after finishing his lunch at the picnic table, asking him to get in Bobby's car for a minute where Bobby handed him an envelope that looked like the same one that contained the twenty thousand dollars but this time had in it a floppy diskette.

They were both short of time, had to get back to work, so they split not more than a minute after Bobby made the drop. Also, knowing what just took place between them, they began to have the sense that it wasn't wise to stay in the same place too long. He got out of Bobby's car scanning the immediate vicinity of the park through the corner of his eye, the envelope tucked out of sight inside his coat and feeling it somehow weighing ten times more than it did.

And it might as well had because three days later, owing to the floppy diskette he carried in that envelope, many people will die.

As soon as he got back to work, Ahmed browsed the drop using the IBM laptop in his fifth-floor office, a cozy twelve by twelve room with a large window looking down on Fairfax Drive in Ballston, Arlington. Looks just like what Abu Kamal and his friends wanted from Bobby, he thought as he went over the file on the nuclear power plants. He was curious about the other file detailing the arrival of the Israeli Defense Minister at Reagan National. It appeared the route from the airport to the Pentagon had been changed drastically, and so was the planned security, as was explained with some lengthy footnotes on the pages.

He wondered what Bobby's idea was for making it part of the drop.

Oh, yes, he suddenly remembered. These were supposed to be samples only. But they're very good samples from what Abu Kamal told him they wanted to see from Bobby. He put the diskette back in the envelope and started reaching for the phone to try his luck with Kamal just as it rang. Weird, he thought when he picked up the phone and heard Kamal's voice, beginning to imagine that maybe the two of them communicated telepathically without being aware of it. The man asked about the drop and Ahmed was happy to say that he was just about to call him to let him know he had it and ask how he wanted to get it. Being in nearby Foggy-Bottom in D.C., he said he'll send Ghulan, the driver, to pick it up right outside the front entrance of the office building.

He went down the lobby fifteen minutes later and waited no more than five before he saw the Mercedes pull up by the curb. The window rolled down as he approached and he dropped the envelope into the empty passenger seat, waved at Ghulan while the window started rolling back up and the car was off on the road again.

Three hours later, Abu Kamal called again, his voice tense, agitated. It had an ominous tone in it as he said come to the Westfields Marriott in Chantilly around seven o'clock.

He was now on Route 66 approximately fifteen miles away according to directions given to him when he called the hotel earlier. He felt a bit uneasy as he got nearer with every mile that went by. Ever since he heard that tone in Abu Kamal's voice, he had been trying to figure out what might be going on. He was sure it had something to do with Bobby's sample drop.

He remembered hearing that tone of voice one other time, when he was working in Detroit in the company headquarters where Kamal had an office suite. There was a foul-up on an oil shipment Kamal had helped broker from Oman and a quick meeting was held. Ahmed was there. When the man responsible for the foul-up was pinned down, that's when he heard that same tone of voice from Kamal as he spoke next. But it sounded many times as ominous because you also saw the foreboding expression that went with it on the man's face.

Shit, I wouldn't want to cross this man, he thought then.

Up till then, Ahmed's impression of him was that of a good benefactor mostly because Kamal had put his signature in the INS petition form for Ahmed Khalifa's H-1B visa which got approved and allowed Ahmed to stay and work in the country. That impression grew stronger when Kamal recommended him for the plum job opening here in Virginia.

In all that time and to this day, a period of a little over a year, he had also built up an understanding in himself, and he's sure Kamal was aware of this too, that he owed Kamal more than he could repay him for. Thinking just for a moment about perhaps being back in Hyderabad had he not lucked out by knowing the man particularly that time when his temporary visas in the U.S. and Canada were about to expire gave him a painful jolt. Everytime.

He owed the man. So when the man told him to do something, to come and go somewhere, they both knew that Kamal only had to say it, any day, any time of day.

This was as much as Ahmed had known Kamal personally. He had known his goodness, and now on his way to obey the order for him to be at this Westfields Marriott hotel, that tone of voice still echoing in his head from Detroit to Arlington, he felt apprehensive and worried at the thought of possibly seeing the opposite side of him.

What could happen should he have a falling out with him, Allah forbid? He'd lose his job, the working visa, and he'd end up hiding from the INS as an illegal alien. Or, get out on his own, back to Canada maybe or someplace else, but definitely not back home. Not yet. Not while he's just getting his foot in the door, the door to material and economic freedom here in America. He's not especially thrilled at the idea of living here permanently, making a life for himself and his own family if he got to that. The three years he had been in north America, he had seen and felt things, many things that made him understand those who become disenchanted with life here, some even to the point of hating America and working against her.

Barring material and economic hardships, he would still prefer home, living in his own culture, with his own people and with their own spiritual life—Islam. He is a Muslim first before anything else, as is anyone who is.

He had fulfilled one of the Five Pillars (duties) of Islam which is a pilgrimage to Mecca at least once in a believer's lifetime. This he had done with his early life's savings the year he turned twenty-one. The other four—profession of the Faith, Prayer, Almsgiving and Fasting during the month of Ramadan, he struggled to make a part of his life. He admitted to his personal weakness in keeping the faith at times but continued to make the effort to improve upon it. He prayed and gave to the poor and the mosque and fasted during Ramadan.

He is a peaceful man. A moderate man who does not believe in violence and extremism, fanaticism and the use of terror to defend his belief and preserve his self-respect. And so, deep down inside and in the back of his mind, he had this mire he imagined he had stepped into. And he couldn't pull himself out of it since it became apparent what it was all about, after Kamal told him the kind of government information he and his associates were interested in, even before they knew about Robert Grundell.

He didn't want to believe it and tried not to think about it after that. He didn't want to be a part of it but he knew he was now, and no longer in a small way as when he first realized it a few months ago.

Something must be afoot and awaiting him in Chantilly. So now he cleared his mind of all thoughts, braced himself for what might be and drove the few remaining miles to the hotel dutifully.

Abu Kamal Ramshallah had been on the phone most of the afternoon since he browsed the diskette in his laptop in the Columbia Plaza apartment in Foggy Bottom where Omar Husain was staying. He did good calling Ahmed Khalifa while he was visiting Omar, a dedicated guardian of the Faith, a devoted believer of the Prophet Mohammed and servant of Allah. He was also a highly trusted intelligence officer in the U.S. operations of the Organization, one of the most active and well-financed radical Muslim groups operating worldwide, known as the *Global Islamic Defense Organization*.

Kamal was very pleased with the sample drop from Bobby especially when Omar came to read it with him, the two of them sitting side by side in front of the computer, going over the detailed description of the North Anna and the Surry nuclear power plants near Norfolk, Virginia, and the ones in North Carolina—the Brunswick plant by the Cape Fear river near Southport, and the well-protected 900 megawatt Harris plant near Raleigh.

They were particularly interested in the security that protected the plants. With the information contained in the diskette on the subject, they couldn't have asked for more. This isn't just a sample drop from Bobby, whoever this Bobby is, Omar told Kamal. This is as good as it gets, compared to what his spies had been feeding him, stuff anybody could get from the internet.

With this much detailed security information, we can find ways to penetrate these facilities, Omar had started thinking immediately and later told Kamal, blow them up to smithereens. No security, no matter how thickly layered, is foolproof if somebody knows how it's designed.

They went ahead and looked at the other file in the diskette. That's when their balloon deflated and came down to earth.

"Did you ask Bobby for this?" Omar looked grim, surprising Kamal at this sudden change.

"No, I didn't," Kamal replied positively. "I didn't even talk to him. In fact, I haven't even met him. Everything I said was through Ahmed."

"You know what this means?"

"If what that page on the screen says is real, yes, I understand."

"They changed the entourage of the son of a bitch. Now he's being picked up at the airport by helicopter and transported directly to the Pentagon. So, now we got to re-do our plan to kill the devil. We have less than three days to come up with a new plan based on this. But—"

"But what?"

"Let's slow down and think for a minute." Omar got up and walked to the window of the ninth-floor apartment, taking in the view that covered the Memorial Bridge over the Potomac river and across to Virginia—Arlington Cemetery, the Pentagon and beyond.

"They knew about our plan," he said after a half a minute, partly to himself. "They knew."

"They must have found out from some source," Kamal said. "They must have a source."

"Of course," added Omar, still looking out the window, thinking. "That's one thing—the who and the how of it. Another is—" he turned around slowly to face Kamal, gazing at him from under a pair of thick, dark eyebrows. "Why did Bobby pick this one to send you?"

They held their eyes steady at each other as if to pick each other's brains, Kamal moving his head slightly sideways, figuring, concentrating, either getting ready to spill a flood of ideas or waiting for Omar to do it first.

It was Omar who spoke first and with another question: "And did he know you, we, had anything to do with it?"

Kamal caught on to his mind-thrust and from there on they took turns at looking into all the possibilities at hand.

Kamal: If he did know we had anything to do with it, then he's not working for us; he's working against us and that diskette is a false lead; if we change our plan to kill the bastard based on that new entourage, we could be walking into a trap.

Omar: Why, they'd probably have a double in that helicopter when we attack it while he's being slipped away somewhere else. Further, they know who we are and even right at this moment, we're sitting ducks. But they won't do anything. Not yet. They're going to wait and see what kind of move we make from here on in. On second thought, giving it the benefit of a doubt, what if Bobby's on the level? Then what he gave us in that diskette is real. One way or the other, we got to make changes to our plan.

Kamal: Meaning, it's a pure coincidence that he picked this one to send us?

Omar: And a very fortunate one for us. Therefore, we have an ace up our sleeve and he's worth every dollar we pay him. But we don't know this. And we better find out starting right now.

This was where Kamal made the second call to Ahmed Khalifa, shortly before Ahmed's quitting time at work at five o'clock.

The possibility that they didn't have Bobby loomed larger than the opposite which urged Kamal to separate himself from Omar immediately. However, they needed to spend more time together to make some fast decisions, but not where they were. With the chance they're taking, they didn't consider the place in Foggy Bottom safe any longer so they agreed to meet later in the evening in Kamal's hotel office suite way over in Chantilly where he usually based his activities when he came to the Capital area.

Before they split, they made some hurried phone calls, local and long distance—New York, Detroit, Philadelphia, Baltimore—to people who needed to be told of the changes in plan which they didn't have yet; some of them—those within traveling distance to Chantilly and whom they got a hold of in Philadelphia, Baltimore and Washington, they directed to the hotel immediately.

In Chantilly, Kamal spent more time on the phone chasing after some of the people they weren't able to contact. Omar did the same with those he knew personally. There were several in Detroit and New York, the people they were answerable to and to whom they spoke dutifully, and respectfully.

It was now a few minutes past seven. Kamal's ear had started to feel sticky with perspiration from holding the phone hard against it for the past fifteen minutes while he listened to one of his superiors in Detroit. The conversation had consisted mostly of questions coming to him to which he gave quick, short and precise answers.

Yes, sir, the files are definitely authentic. Written in U.S. government bureaucratic language. No doubt about it.

Yes, sir, we will contact the man tonight. Our man Ahmed Khalifa is on his way here now to do that.

We will get back with you as soon as we come to a decision. Yes, sir.

While Kamal was saying that, he turned towards the door of the spacious office, saw Ahmed being ushered in by one of the men he and Omar had been gathering for the past hour in the outside room and motioned him to one of the seats in front of the desk.

Ahmed sat quietly for the next five minutes while Kamal finished up with Detroit, took two more calls apparently from people of lesser authority for he cut them short, and dialed a number to say: "He's here," and after a short pause, "Right. Tell Hassan to take all the calls from now."

After he hung up and set the phone down, his back to Ahmed, he took a few long seconds to turn around, quite obviously thinking and thinking hard among other things what appearance to put out when he turned around. The past few hours, it seemed like he had been puzzling over an enigma where there was absolutely no clue whatsoever. The possibilities he and Omar had explored earlier didn't stop at Bobby. It extended to Ahmed Khalifa as well.

Going back to what if they didn't have Bobby, and on top of that, things had gone further the other way where they, their enemies, got Ahmed too: Is Ahmed turned? Could he be? Is he or is he not? What should I assume, so I know what expression to put on my face to him? How to talk to him?

Quickly, just before he faced and walked up to Ahmed holding out a hand with a half-smile, he decided he was going to let Ahmed think that he's buying what Bobby put in the diskette. Because this approach worked with whether or not Ahmed was now working for the U.S. government and all the enemies of Islam.

"Thank you for coming," he said, leading Ahmed down a short side corridor to a glass-walled room. He spoke softly, but behind the calm in it together with the traces of perspiration on his face, Ahmed heard a slight tension. "Please," he said, as they entered the room half the size of the one they came from, motioning Ahmed to an armchair by the window.

In the corner of the room on the other side of the window was a table loaded with a hotwater and coffee maker, trays of cookies, pastries and fruit. Underneath the table was a refrigerator that hummed softly. Kamal said to help himself to anything in there, excused himself for a quick second and went out, closing the door behind him.

Ahmed who had been all eyes and ears since he arrived, got up to help himself to a cup of tea even as he saw Kamal through the glass wall just going through the outside room heading to the door. While he filled a cup with hotwater, he saw a man come in through the door. Light-complexioned, early forties. Egyptian or Syrian like Kamal. Middle Eastern people vary so much in appearance. Some are so light skinned and looked like southern or western Europeans. Others so dark it's hard to tell them from Africans. The man could even be Lebanese for his light skin and fair, more western European feature, he thought as Omar got closer.

Kamal stepped up to the man quickly and the two of them put their heads together and talked in a low voice with Kamal doing most of the talking, and fast.

Then they started moving towards him in the room, making small steps while hurrying up to finish their conversation practically in whispers.

Had he somehow gotten wind of what they were talking about since a couple of hours ago, he wouldn't want to be sitting in this room right now. Because earlier when they first touched on the possibility that he might be turned, Omar got overly incensed, almost foregoing any doubt and coming close to a decision to 'take care' of him immediately. But Kamal quickly talked him out of it, saying Ahmed does not know anything, unless he's really a mole way back in Detroit, or even Toronto where he came from. After weighing things over, Omar agreed, giving him the benefit of a doubt the same as they did with Bobby.

"But we'll see," he said in a low voice a few feet from the door. "After I talk to him. And Bobby too."

They hushed just before Kamal grabbed the door handle and turned it.

"Ah-h, good," Kamal said as he swung the door open and saw Ahmed with a cup of tea. "I could use some of that myself. Have something to eat too, please."

"Yes, I will, thank you," replied Ahmed, getting up to meet them halfway.

"Ahmed Khalifa, meet another one of the company's major stockholders," Kamal said, stepping aside between the two men for the introduction. "Rahim Akbar. From Baltimore."

"Ahmed," Rahim Akbar (Omar Husain) greeted. "*Salaam aleikum.*"

Ahmed said the same and they shook hands. They sat down across from each other while Kamal went straight to the corner table to make himself a hot tea. "Rahim," he said. "Hot or cold drink?"

"Light coffee, no sugar, please."

Kamal made small talk while he busied himself at the table.

How's work today?

Good, thanks.

Busy?

Yes, always.

Then without warning, Ahmed started talking casually about the diskette. Omar, using one of his many aliases, surreptitiously began homing in on everything he said and did. Every word, every movement, every gesture.

"It was an excellent drop, Ahmed," Kamal said, stirring a teaspoon of Coffeemate in Rahim's coffee. "We're all very pleased with it. We find the files extremely vital to our business and we sure can use every bit of information it contained."

"Good. Good," said Ahmed, working hard to boost his self-confidence. "I'm very happy to hear that."

Rahim watched him secretly, every moving part of him. The eye, the head, the hands and feet, even the reactive movements between his mouth, nose and cheeks when he drank the hot tea. He would read the thought running in Ahmed's head behind the expression on his face if he could.

Omar Husain, Chief Intelligence Officer and Commander of major U.S. operations of the Organization, was very thorough, very precise and careful with his work and expected no less of those under his command. Abu Kamal Ramshallah who held the position of Intelligence Liaison in the Organization respected his character and abilities both as a Muslim individual who lived by his *Shahadah*, a devoted follower of Muhammad and a defender Soldier of Islam.

Kamal took the seat against the wall between the other two, going around the marble-topped cocktail table after handing Rahim his coffee.

"Yes, yes," he said as he settled down, blowing on his tea. "Your friend Bobby did very well for us." He took a sip then lowered the cup on the table, adding: "What we want to talk to you about now, perhaps Rahim could explain better-"

"I will try to make it simple," Rahim began, sitting back after taking two small sips of the coffee and leaving it on the table too. "It's a common practice of the company to analyze—authenticate, you understand, all the data it receives. So, what we want to do now simply is to perhaps talk to Bobby, if that can be arranged."

"Of course," Ahmed said, leaning forward with the cup of tea in his hands and a compliant smile on his face. "I could call him right now if you want."

Rahim couldn't decide if the reaction was too eagerly contrived or too innocently real. Should we believe what this Pakistani says? Do we trust him, or shoot him? The way Abu Kamal described him, talked about the route his life had taken since leaving Pakistan sounded like he would be one to be trusted, as Kamal had since Detroit. Indeed, he might even be welcomed into the Organization. If he's not an enemy which leads us to see that Bobby's only using him, no, we don't want to shoot him.

Also, we don't want to talk to Bobby just yet. Find out about this one first so then we'll know how to talk to Bobby next. Bobby gets the idea his cover is blown because of Ahmed, knowing who we are, where we are, he and his people could just decide to cut the plan short, whatever the plan is, and come and round us all up.

"There's no big hurry," he said, sitting back, relaxed. "We don't want to rush you."

"No, it's not a problem," Ahmed countered. "In fact, right now is as good a time as any to catch him. He's probably just come home from a fast-food or a Chinese carry-out eating dinner in front of the TV. I know how the man lives."

He laughed and the others joined him with a snicker, Omar saying: "Do you?"

"Yes, 'cause I do the same thing and once in a while I'd join him."

That drew more snickers in the room.

"I can imagine what good neighbors you two must have become," Omar said.

"Oh, yes, yes," Ahmed said, now getting more comfortable. "I've gone out with him weekends to singles bars, dances, looking for women, or just having fun."

"Sounds nice," said Kamal. "Of course what's there to do for two single men on a Saturday night in a town like this teeming with single lonely women?"

"Any luck?" Omar asked.

Ahmed fidgeted in his seat a moment, embarrassed. "Depends what you call luck," he replied, now feeling a social connection with the two. "We met some ladies a few weeks ago and double dated. It was nice, but I don't know about these American girls, women. You can't be too serious with them."

"Yes, that we all know," Kamal said and as if all three of them agreed altogether, they turned to their cups and took a sip.

"However, it might be different if she's of the Faith," Omar suggested, gesturing with an open hand extended on an upright forearm as if to give a blessing.

"I have yet to meet one here," Ahmed replied. "An American Muslim woman. And one who had at least made the *Haj*."

Omar perked up, suddenly homing in on Ahmed's whole personality, not just parts of the person that might give telltale signs of what he might be lying about or concealing.

"Interesting," he said. "And have you?"

"Yes, when I was twenty-one years old," Ahmed replied. "My home village in Hyderabad, actually it was only a dirt road about four hundred feet long with about two thousand people living in shanties on both sides of it, I grew up with a group of boys who formed an alliance based on the ambition to make the pilgrimage to Mecca no later than the age of twenty-one."

The men's face grew with fascination. "Marvelous!" Kamal said. "What happened?"

"I only know of three others besides myself, out of fifteen boys, who made it. I used up all my savings and came home totally broke but very happy that I was able to say my *salat* in the holy land many many times."

Here, Omar regarded Ahmed with admiration and was close to forgetting any doubt about his loyalty to their cause—their faith, culture, beliefs and way of life. Everything that every true Muslim throughout the world had been fighting for and shielding against the decadence and tyranny of the Christians and the Jews here in America, back home in the Middle East and all over the world.

He'll never forget when he himself fulfilled that one Pillar of Faith, the one he, like many other Muslims, considered the grandest of all—the *Haj*. He was only thirteen when he made the pilgrimage with his parents—his dear beloved parents who were now dead, killed by the hated Israelis in that massive attack of their homes in southern Lebanon twenty years ago. Yes, the Israelis—the Jews, and those crusading Christians forever oppressing our people, turning us against one another. We must continue the struggle against them, stamp them out of existence, weed out the brothers whose minds and hearts they had poisoned.

And what of this young Pakistani who looked so innocent, sounded so naïve? Is he as pure-minded and dedicated to the ways of Islam as he just now appeared to us? Or has he sold his soul for the material comfort of life in America?

He turned to Kamal briefly and glanced Kamal's look of confidence, a little smile on a corner of his mouth as he drank his tea. It was at this moment that Kamal indeed felt inclined to trust Ahmed but without totally letting his guard down. There will be other times to look deeper into the truth that lay hidden in the young man's heart. Now, he wanted to hear about this supposedly angry American government worker who would sell his country to get even. Or maybe just to put on a good front to us? So they can get to us and catch us?

Kamal sounded very much convinced with what Ahmed had told him about the American, how the man does not give a damn about his government, the people he works with in that agency, whatever it's called, because they don't give a damn about him either. Well, first he'd want to hear it from Ahmed, then he'd want to listen to the man himself, picture his appearance from his words, maybe hear a sound of that anger and uncaring for his country.

"So, tell me," Omar said next, "how long have you two known each other?"

"Bobby?" Ahmed asked, caught unaware by the sudden switch of subject.

"Yes."

"Since I moved across the courtyard from him. Seven, eight months now."

"What's his full name again? Kamal mentioned it one time but it's been awhile."

"Robert Grundell. He works for the Office of Civil Defense Logistics of the Treasury Department."

"Ah, yes. Now I recall. How well would you say you know him?"

Ahmed took a few seconds to give an answer, thinking about some of the things he had told Kamal about Bobby.

"I know him only as much as he has told me about himself and what he does at work, and on his free time. That part of his life right now I know quite well," Ahmed said with a smile. "Like I just told you. Fast-food dinners during the week, weekend nights out."

"Yes, yes," said Omar, also with a smile. He turned to Kamal briefly before looking down, thinking, then continued: "Do you trust him?"

Ahmed knew this was what the two of them were after. He knew they were coming to this, and he was prepared to give them an answer.

"Yes, I do," he replied peremptorily. "I have no doubt about his motivation."

Kamal looked at his watch and said: "Let's see, would you say he's about done with dinner?"

"If he's home, it doesn't matter what he's doing. He'll talk to me, anytime," Ahmed replied, adding that Bobby had said at the park that he would like to talk with them too about something, if possible. He told them what when Kamal asked.

They said fine, by all means, and asked him to make the call. Kamal brought the phone at the end-table near him to the coffee table in front of everybody and pushed the speakerphone. Ahmed dialed and they heard Bobby's phone ring three times before it was picked up.

"Bobby!" Ahmed greeted.

"Ahmed, mah man! What's up?"

Omar and Kamal were quickly impressed at the cheerful sound of camaraderie between the two. Kamal was especially curious to hear Bobby's voice after all these time of hearing only *about* him. Omar tuned in on the man's tone of voice, how genuine or phoney it sounded, to perhaps catch any give away that might cue him in also on whether Ahmed or the both of them were just taking them for a ride. One question he had in mind: Does Bobby know ahead of time that Ahmed would be with them? Hence, is this possibly a rehearsed phone call?

"How was your day?" asked Ahmed.

"What part of it? You don't want to hear about the same friggin' thing all the time so I won't tell you about work."

Ahmed laughed merrily, at the same time talking to the men in front of him with his eyes by looking at each one back and forth quickly with a you-hear-that? or see-what-I-told-you? message on them. He would do this everytime something came up to substantiate what he had said about Bobby.

The men looked amused and sat quietly to listen.

"I'll tell you something nice for a change," Bobby said next with a tingle in his voice. "I got a call from Paula. She wants us to go out again. How d'yuh like that?"

"She must be desperate. It's only Monday. They usually wait till late in the week to see if they get a better offer," Ahmed said and laughed.

Bobby cracked up. He replied: "If you weren't my friend especially after that great Tandoori chicken dinner you made us last week, I'd feel insulted by that. She told me she had other guys calling her, but me I didn't even call her. She called me!"

"So what do you want me to say? You're hot, man. Whoop-tee-doo!"

"Actually, I want you to say you'll be okay Saturday. Paula says her friend too, the one you went out with-"

"Rosie," Ahmed threw in.

"Yeah. They would like to double up with us again. She said they really had fun with us that weekend."

Ahmed shot a timid glance at the men in front of him. "That's nice to know. Tell 'em yes, sure, I'm free Saturday."

"Great!" Bobby said, his voice filled with enthusiasm that couldn't sound more real to Omar and Kamal.

"Well, I'm glad I called."

"I was gonna call you shortly, tell you about it but you beat me to it. So, anyways, lemme ask how your day was? And did you talk to your people about what we talked about in the park today?"

"I had a good day, thanks. Busy, a little bit of work to catch up with. I earned my dollar today."

"That's more'n I can say about many of the people I work with. Fuckin' parasites!"

"You're not going to get into that again, mah man," warned Ahmed, but he was actually thinking let him get fired up some so these two in front of him would hear for themselves. Thus, he added as an opening for Bobby: "So what if all they do is collect their big fat paychecks for doing nothing. It's not your money. What do you care?"

"That's right, what the hell do I care?" Bobby, getting fired up now. "What do I care if they sit on their big fat asses all day and let the whole fuckin' country go down the sewer. Wanna know what I'm gonna do if that happens?"

"What?"

"Shit, I'll just pack up and move to another country. The fuck do I care?"

Ahmed raised his eyes at the men sitting quietly in the room, his eyes telling them 'Wanna hear more?', 'That's our man talking and that's what he sounds for real.' Kamal shook his head sideways for a moment then smiled and reversed it to up and down. Omar sat motionless, waiting to hear more, thinking, analyzing, no telling by the look on his face what he's coming up with from what he'd heard so far.

Ahmed decided to get some more poison out of Bobby.

"How about if you blow the whistle on them. Fuck 'em up like they fuck you up."

"Yes, I've thought about that a lot. We had a Division meeting today where they made an official announcement of the promotion of this one asshole to a new higher position. Fucking asshole got up and talked about what his job is about—keeping track of everybody's work, everybody turn in a work report to him every week, that kind o' shit. This guy has never done anything for years in the office but bullshit and kiss ass. Would you believe that? So some guys in the office are talking about protesting his promotion, saying we don't need this asshole around and his position is not necessary and is a total waste of taxpayer money; sorta blow the whistle on management waste and bureaucracy."

"So, are they going to do it?"

"Oh, yes. One of 'em said he's going to start the write-up today. I know him well. I'm going to help him do it. Another guy started going around spreading the word and collecting signature pledges this afternoon."

"Good. Good for you guys. I hope you win the protest. That'll be one parasite less. Anyway, to answer your other question—yes, I mentioned to my people that you would like to talk to them about what you told me." Ahmed turned up to Kamal and nodded, signaling get ready to join in.

"That's good. Thanks. When do I get to talk to them?"

"As a matter of fact, right now," Ahmed said, getting up and moving the base unit of the telephone to the middle of the table closer to everybody. "Let me introduce you to them first, tell you who they are. Then they can speak for themselves."

This went:

'Bobby, this here is Mr. Abu Kamal Ramshallah, senior board member of the company. Mr. Ramshallah, Robert Grundell, also known as Bobby.'

'Hello, Mr. Grundell.'

'Bobby's fine with me.'

'And you may call me Kamal. Pleasure to meet you, Bobby.'

'Pleasure to meet you, Kamal.'

'And this here is Mr. Rahim Akbar, a major stockholder of the company.'

'Hello, Bobby. How do you do? And you may call me Rahim.'

'I'm fine, thanks, Rahim. And you?'

'Very well, thank you.'

At this point, Ahmed said: "Gentlemen, if you'll excuse me a moment, my tea is cold. Care for a refill?" he asked the others who said they're fine.

"Bobby, Kamal here speaking."

"Yes, I can tell."

"Before we talk about anything else, first let us thank you for…the drop today."

"I read up on what was described in the envelope Ahmed gave me last week and just went by that. Is that alright with you?"

Kamal turned to Rahim who had edged closer to the telephone.

"Yes, Bobby, you did very well," Rahim said. "And I'm sure there is not a single reason to doubt the authenticity of the data in the files."

"Not at all," Bobby said, not defensive, not trying to convince, just stating a fact naturally. "Those files are kept current constantly. I know. It's my job to do that on some of them. Others I keep an eye on 'cause I have the 'need to know'. That's in my P.O. Position Description."

Rahim turned to Kamal, nodding slightly, a look on his face saying we're almost there, almost safe to count on what this guy, and Ahmed too, is saying, and therefore what the diskette contained. Which means re-drawing the plan, and we have three days to come up with a new one. To kill that Israeli bastard.

"We believe you, Bobby, and we want to thank you again for your help." Now he nodded at Kamal to express his full concurrence. Over at the corner table where Ahmed stood mixing a new cup of tea, he heard and saw everything and was finally relieved to see the men pleased at what they're hearing directly from Bobby.

"So, Bobby, what is it you want to talk to us about?" Kamal asked. "Anything we can help you with? Anything at all."

Here, Bobby discussed the predicament he told them he suddenly realized he faced minutes before he almost deposited the money in his bank account. He left it open to them to decide the best payment arrangement. The two men sounded to Bobby to take the matter lightly, even chuckled a little at this what they obviously considered a very minor concern.

In the end, they decided the best thing to do was to put Bobby on the payroll as a consultant. His designation, for accounting purposes, would be the good old job title government agencies use for many of their catch-all make-work positions—Research Analyst. Only difference is they'd be hiring him at an hourly rate about four times that for a federal government GS-14 do-nothing job held by a career bureaucrat with twenty-five years service.

Comes to a little under two hundred thousand a year. It'll come in a regular bi-monthly paycheck at Ahmed's office which he could just pick up there or Ahmed could bring home with him, hand over to Bobby or slip under his door if Bobby's not in.

The last thing they talked about was the location for future drops, personal contact and communication. Everybody agreed to the use of cell phones only when it's totally unavoidable. Public phone is preferred. They swapped phone numbers and at this point Rahim moved to end the phone call, suggesting that from now on, they avoid contact of any kind unless it's absolutely necessary.

After Ahmed left, Omar walked over to the corner table to make another cup of coffee, head down, thinking as if counting the number of steps to get there. Kamal sat back waiting to hear a word, anything from the Chief Intelligence Officer about his take of the situation. What's the bottom line? Do we go by what's in that diskette?

Two minutes went by in silence with nothing but the tinkling of the teaspoon in Omar's coffee at first, then his footsteps as he walked back to his seat, sipping the coffee standing up. When he finally raised his head, he nodded at Kamal and Kamal knew the bottom line then when Omar bent down to the telephone on the coffee table and pressed the intercom line to Hassan Bahaji who'd been sitting in the ante-room waiting for something to happen.

"Has everybody arrived?" Omar asked after Hassan got on.

"Everyone but two, boss," replied Hassan Bahaji, veteran of the fourth Arab-Israeli war in '73 from Damascus and now a high-ranking combat officer of the Organization. He was to lead the attack at Reagan National but shortly would learn of the final decision of the change of plan from that. "The ones from Philadelphia," he added. "They're on their way now. We'll bring them up on what's going on when they get here."

"Good," said Omar. "Is everything ready in there? The screen? The pictures?"

"Yes, sir. But which plan are we working with now?"

"The one for Operation North 27."

"That's the one I got in the machine now," said Hassan. "Everything's ready. We're just waiting for you."

"We're on our way."

As soon as he hung up, Hassan strode to the door of the meeting room behind him at the table, opened it a couple of inches and called on someone to come out.

"Take over," he said to the man. "Don't let anybody through no matter what. And don't take any calls, just messages, no matter who."

"Yes, sir," the man said. Hassan then stepped aside to let the man take his seat at the table while he stood by the door and waited.

Operation North 27, he was thinking. It's a totally different game plan. And could be many times as critical. This could take all night. He looked at a wall clock across the room which showed 8:05. All of a sudden he felt famished and remembered that he hadn't had dinner. When he got Commander Omar's high-priority call to his Baltimore apartment earlier at four o'clock, all he did was grab a soda from the refrigerator before jumping in the Toyota Corolla and doing Foggy-Bottom, D.C. in about forty-five minutes.

At Foggy-Bottom, due to some new development from intelligence, he and Omar quickly worked out a rough of the alternate plan they called Operation North 27. Very rough. No details. All times were approximate, nothing under a two-minute projected accuracy in all stages of the assault because of lack of detail information. Omar said he had the information they needed but had yet to do some authenticating, analysis work before they could apply them. And there was no contingency plan at all. Everything was up in the air. Then they had to round up everybody to this hotel in Chantilly, Virginia, in Abu Kamal Ramshallah's office suite, way out here a few miles from Dulles International airport. There were some brothers coming from Baltimore and Philadelphia. Others from central New Jersey and as far as New York City and southern Connecticut.

Only took the whole afternoon and early evening to do it.

A few seconds after he had been standing outside the door of the meeting room, Omar Husain came from the other room with Abu Kamal Ramshallah. He too glanced at the wall clock as they hurried. When they came near, the man at the table stood next to Hassan and the two of them bowed dutifully. Then Hassan turned to open the door.

Stepping into the meeting room, a sudden clamor of chairs sliding back filled the room as fifteen men who had been sitting around a long conference table, some for as long as an hour now, stood up to greet them. Those within arm's reach of Omar Husain put out a hand which he shook, recognizing several of them, close associates in the Organization. The rest acknowledged their entry by bowing quietly.

They walked around the table to the opposite side of the room where a six-foot square rolldown screen hung on the wall. Omar stood on one side of it,

Kamal on the other. When everyone was seated back and the quiet resumed, Omar nodded at Hassan who was now behind the digital projector on the other side of the room and an aerial site photograph of the Pentagon appeared on the screen. It covered an area one-mile all around the five-sided building of the United States Defense headquarters which is bounded in a triangular area on the east by the Jefferson Davis Highway 110, on the south by Virginia's I-395 and on the west, running north-south, by Washington Boulevard Highway 27.

CHAPTER 7

▼

It was a cold night. At half past eleven, the wind was blowing at thirty miles an hour with a chill factor in the low twenties when the rugged V8 Ford Expedition SUV, headed south on its final test run on Route 27, dropped them off the Columbia Pike exit at the perimeter of the Arlington National Cemetery.

It was dark too, and overcast. But they were actually glad about this because they needed all the cover there were in addition to the natural growth in the area—the grass, the bushes, the trees. Especially come daybreak.

They test drove the route at least ten times the past two days, the SUV carrying the two teams of three men each, up and down Route 27 coming from Route 110 at the Memorial Drive entrance to the Columbia Pike exit, a stone's throw from the southwest corner of the Pentagon. As part of the plan, one of the teams which was the command and control team led by Hassan Bahaji would take a camouflaged position directly across Route 27 from the west side of the Pentagon with a straight shot of the helicopter pad less than 300 meters away, a distance well within the effective range of the heat-seeking Stinger-RMP the team carried.

The other team led by Kashim Najoub, a 52-year old Egyptian and fellow veteran of Hassan Bahaji in the '73 Arab-Israeli war, using the SUV, would be coming south on Route 27 on the go-ahead word from Hassan anytime between the arrival of the targets and the time Hassan either decided to run and save as many of them as possible or to stay and fight to their death. Either case, Hassan told his team when the SUV dropped them off the night before, hopefully they would have accomplished their mission by the time he had to make that decision.

These two teams were meant to supplement the attack, one after the other, following that of the first one which would be coming from the south in a

220-horsepower Toyota Highlander SUV. Parked on a sideroad just off the Army-Navy Drive and the entrance to North 27, the five men in it led by Ahman Shahid, a 24-year old Palestinian suicide warrior, would get the word from Hassan Bahaji to move at a precise time so that they would be at the shoulder of the road with a flat tire, at a spot which would give them a clear shot with their RPG-7Vs of the target helicopter as it descended on this side of the Pentagon.

It was now 11:05 A.M. The wind had calmed down, moving at a pleasant cool-breeze temperature. The sun was up almost directly over the heads of Hassan Bahaji and his two soldiers, each of them hidden under the camouflage of thick evergreen shrubs they had brought with them at night and matted into four-by-six-foot covers they could lift slowly to survey their surrounding.

Traffic on Washington Boulevard (Route 27) was light. Hassan expected and hoped it would pick up in the next twenty-five minutes, the start of the lunchtime period. There would be people—mostly government workers from the Pentagon and Washington across the river—going out to lunch, doing errands. Once the shooting started, the enemies would eventually locate them and it would help to have some people cover. It could give them time to either change their position or run to escape.

Hassan had positioned himself five yards away from his men behind a pair of pear trees surrounded by an underbrush through which he peered with his field glasses at the Pentagon, the entire length of its west side. He zoomed at the heavily guarded entrance on the north end and the activities at the south end where he could see the buses turning into and out of the busy Metro station at the south side of the building.

He was now counting minutes, glad the long chilling hours of the night and early this morning were behind them. He kept his eyes trained between the Pentagon and the sky to the south of it, keeping alert for a sudden early sighting of their target. Occasionally, he glanced to his right at the two he could see through a small side opening they had made under the thick evergreen and brushwood camouflage. One of them, Nassar Madani, a 22-year old fellow Palestinian, born and raised in Nablus, West Bank, waited patiently for any signal from his team leader whom he admired deeply and would follow to their death.

Yes. He would do anything Hassan Bahaji told him to do if it meant killing as many of these American infidels and their Jewish soldiers as they could. Here, right here at the fortress of their armed forces or in Israel or back in the West Bank where he and his generation grew up eaten by deep hatred for these oppressors, or anywhere in the world.

For almost six hours now, he remained crouched on his stomach under the thick covers, the man-portable Stinger resting on his shoulder, ready to raise on his elbows and fire at the airborne enemies at Hassan's command.

The brother to his right, Jamil Sabayat, another soldier of Islam his age, likewise was ready to give his life for the destruction of the enemies at their leader's command. He hid dutifully under the brush covers on hands and knees beside a stack of high-explosive RMP missiles he and brother Nassar had trained for weeks before this day to load in the tube, target and fire.

There is much to be said about the thinking capability of the enemies to kill and destroy, they agreed during those weeks of training. This weapon, you get a fix on the target in the air, fire and you can forget about it and just re-load for the next shot. It will seek and find the target.

Less than a mile away on Lynn Street a block off the Army-Navy Drive, Ahman Shahid in the driver's seat, along with the four other suicide warriors with him in the tinted Toyota Highlander, awaited the call from Hassan Bahaji. They knew it could come any moment now so they hardly said a word to each other unless it was absolutely necessary.

Shahid kept vigil on the southern sky through his field glasses, his breathing short and tense while the four, one in the front passenger seat and the other three in the back seats held their weapons of war close beside them—M249 SAW machine guns, M-16s and AK-47s, several of which already mounted with 40mm UBGLs (Under Barrel Grenade Launchers) to supplement the Soviet-era RPG-7Vs.

Two miles north, at a parking space by the Iwo Jima Memorial park in the Ford Expedition SUV, Kashim Najoub and the two men he led sat quietly with the same weapons of war. The last call he got from his friend Hassan was ten minutes ago just to hear the man say everything is on schedule as is, hang on and get ready for his next call.

Two minutes later, he and Ahman Shahid in the south would get on the conference call with Hassan Bahaji on the radio after Hassan, at 11:40 A.M., finally spotted five helicopters approaching from the southeast.

Anne Durham, a 50-year old Department of the Army procurement specialist, sat in a window office on the fourth floor with a serene view of the Arlington National cemetery across Washington Boulevard. For fifteen years, she worked with her back to the window, facing the door from the E-ring corridor outside, until yesterday when she finally had her desk turned perpendicular to the west wall of the building so that with a slight turn of her head to the right, she had the full view through the window.

She could knock her head on the wall for not having thought of this years ago. Now, in addition to enjoying the view outside, she didn't have the direct glare and reflection from the window to hurt her eyes and muddle the image on her PC monitor while she worked.

The view outside, as she turned her head up and a little to the right just now while she was contemplating lunch after seeing 11:42 A.M. on her computer monitor, included a dark-colored SUV that had pulled over the shoulder of the road for what looked like a flat tire. Within a minute of this, her life would suddenly come to a violent end that none of her co-workers, along with the tens of thousands of other people in the building, could have imagined and thought possible.

First, after observing a man come out of the SUV to work on the right front wheel, she heard the muffled sound of the helicopters high above the building approaching the landing pad she could see below at least a hundred yards away and almost in a straight line of sight between her and the SUV. Then the helicopters, five of them, came to view—a Bell 412 transport craft rear-flanked above by two Army Kiowa combat gunships and forward-flanked below by two USMC twin-engine Supercobra. They hovered beautifully for a few moments at Anne Durham's fourth-floor eye-level altitude to get into position before the 412 began to descend. Then she saw a puff of smoke materialize on the side of the SUV, proliferating into a straight line from the tail of a rocket-propelled missile hurtling directly towards the helicopters. Another one followed within a couple of seconds.

The first one hit one of the Supercobras, the one nearer her, right below the double-bladed rotor where it connected to the top of the craft, severing it clean from the helicopter as the rocket-propelled grenade exploded. The second one missed completely and headed straight to Anne Durham's window.

The Kiowa Warrior at the rear flank staggered in mid-air momentarily, its two crews shocked at the suddenness of the attack as they watched the now rotorless Supercobra crash forty feet down and explode as it hit the ground. The other two escort helicopters were equally shaken. But the pilot of the Supercobra quickly became alert to what was happening and didn't lose a moment to maneuver in front of the 412 to cover it from another pair of RPGs he saw coming.

He knew they could evade these non-heat-seeking missiles if there's time and there was, but only in fractions of seconds now. The pilot of the 412 acted as fast as he could to maneuver the ship straight up and away over the roof of the Pentagon upon catching the signal from the Supercobra to abort the landing.

The transport craft carrying the Israeli Defense Minister and his entourage of six, four U.S. Army security personnel and the pilot, eluded the missiles, but the Supercobra didn't.

The missiles found their mark. One went directly into the cockpit and the other on the tail rotor, killing the two crews instantly and fragmenting the Supercobra into flaming chunks of metal that plunged violently on the helipad below.

The first Kiowa had at this time turned to target the SUV with its Hellfire missiles. The first one left its pylon even as the remains of the second Supercobra were crashing down on the first one on the ground. The SUV had started to run just as the missile hit on its rear end and set it aflame. The Kiowa gunner crew observed two bodies on fire fall out of the vehicle as it picked up speed on Route 27 north. The pilot homed in on the SUV while the gunner reset for the next shot.

While this was happening, the second Kiowa turned to follow the 412 up just as the pilot saw a trail of smoke from a Stinger missile fired from across the road just inside the perimeter of the Arlington National cemetery across the road. Unlike the Supercobra, this time the pilot didn't have time to provide cover to the 412 which had climbed up and over the top of the building to escape the attack. But he knew too that this time it was a different ballgame. The Stinger will chase its target unless, thought the Kiowa pilot, he can lure it away to make himself the target. And this was exactly what he tried to do, but to no avail.

As he climbed above the building to attract the missile, it went past over the top as if it had its own mind and it did, for it had been programmed so that nothing else mattered but the target it was aimed to destroy. The most he could do as a split-second move to help the 412 was shoot at the missile with his .50 caliber machine gun as it went by. But this actually made a difference in saving several of the lives in the Bell 412 transport including that of the Defense Minister.

The missile caught its target alright but was partially deflected by the spray of the .50 caliber rounds so that it hit at the rear of the passenger section, sparing five of the twelve people in the craft. What remained of the helicopter with the survivors in it fell and went partially through the roof in flames.

Now what's left to do, the harried look on the face of both the Kiowa pilot and his gunner said, was blow the hell out of the Stinger-shooting position somewhere out there inside the Arlington National cemetery without being blown out first by another RMP missile. So the Kiowa went south out of visual range of the enemy position, right above the median of Washington Boulevard.

On the ground around the Pentagon, they saw MP humvees mobilizing along with several DPS patrol cars and the Virginia State Troopers. They could hear the noise picking up down there from every direction. Traffic which did pick up in the last twenty minutes had slowed down as motorists became aware of what was going on, seeing the downed helicopters burning on the ground and on the Pentagon, the columns of black smoke filling the air, sirens screaming from near and far.

Suddenly, it dawned on the crew's mind in their mounting disbelief—the country is under attack, right here at the Pentagon, the headquarters of the government's Defense Department! In a blink of an eye and with anger quickly building up inside, they recalled that this was the very same side of the Pentagon where Flight 77 smashed back in September 11, 2001. Incredible! How could we have let this happen again!

No time for any of that at present. Right now the only thing that matters is to get those motherfuckers in the bushes inside the National Memorial Cemetery who didn't even give a shit about committing the sacrilege of hiding on one of America's most hallowed grounds to kill us.

"Steady!" said the gunner to the pilot as he locked on the target position with the Hellfires and released the two missiles simultaneously.

The missiles were on target, blew up a hole the size of a house foundation on the ground where Hassan Bahaji and his two warriors were, moments *before*. They watched the explosion from twenty yards away behind a clump of trees where they had scampered to unseen right after they had shot at the 412. Hassan prayed to Allah when he saw the smoke on the roof of the Pentagon then that they had done what they had come for and had quickly summoned his friend Kashim Najoub on the radio.

Kashim was now weaving through the southbound traffic in the Ford Expedition SUV and got a full view of what was going on.

The first Kiowa which had engaged the partly disabled Toyota Highlander SUV in a shooting match was now strapped from shooting back as the SUV moved close to the northbound traffic, hiding behind other vehicles. Seeing this, Kashim ordered his team to shoot at the Kiowa as they neared the scene. Unaware of another enemy attacker in the Ford Expedition, the Kiowa crew was surprised to see two RPGs streaking towards them at close range. Their effort to dodge the missiles was a few seconds short. It looked like the Kiowa disintegrated into hundreds of little scrap metal pieces when it blew up.

At that same moment, Hassan Bahaji had opted to take out the second Kiowa shooting at them from right above the middle of the road in the south. Nassar

Madani and Jamil Sabayat who had the second Stinger missile ready to shoot quickly acquired the target on the scope, and shot. The two men in the Kiowa, believing they had destroyed the enemy, were stunned when they saw the Stinger-RMP missile coming and made a run for it. But they knew it was too late.

At the Columbia Pike on-ramp to Route 27 where Ahman Shahid and his team launched the attack in the Toyota Highlander, Army Sergeant Tom Davis, hands gripped tight on the 40 mm Mark-19 Automatic GL atop the humvee coming from the Pentagon south parking lot, saw the Kiowa get hit and explode practically right above him. He had to duck to avoid pieces of metal crashing down in his direction.

"Move it!" he shouted to Corporal Jenni Wapner down at the wheel. "Let's go, Wap! The black SUV with the busted tail! Go! Go!"

"Yeah! Yeah! I see it!" Wapner shouted back, burning rubber while getting around traffic, avoiding big chunks of the Kiowa debris and the bodies on the road to make the open high-speed left lane.

Ahman Shahid and the two men left of his team in the Toyota Highlander saw the humvee bearing down on them. The two men opened fire indiscriminately, one with an M249 SAW machine gun, the other with an M-16 which slowed down the humvee. Sergeant Davis gave them back some from his MK-19, putting a hole the size of a cantaloupe in the upper torso of one of them. But the humvee was immobilized after a few rounds from the M249 blew its front-end wheels and busted its motor.

Corporal Wapner and Sergeant Davis then watched in horror for one instant as the remaining attackers in the SUV turned to the motorists around them and kept firing in random. It became clear that they intended to kill anybody in sight. It wasn't much different from what a suicide bomber did except in this situation, the killer must be killed by someone else to stop the carnage. And they did—the Army MPs that arrived in two other humvees, one coming from behind Wapner and Davis, another coming southbound against traffic on the road shoulder—but not after the attackers used up all their rounds and turned the northbound stretch of Washington Boulevard this side of the Pentagon into a bloody scene of battle-field devastation.

Ahman Shahid had stopped the SUV and got out on the road with the last man he had of his team. The two of them then, back to back, sprayed rounds first at the motorists around them then the humvees when they saw them coming from both directions.

"Die Americans and Jews! Die!" he yelled nearly as loud and violent as the AK-47 in his hands pouring rounds all over.

"Die! Die! Die!" the 24-year old Palestinian kept yelling to the last moment of his life when both the humvees returned fire with .50 caliber machine guns that ripped him and his companion to pieces.

On the other side of the road, the shooting had intensified with the arrival of several Defense Protective Service patrol cars from the Pentagon's north parking lot and the Virginia State Troopers from Highway 110. Four cars gave chase to Kashim Najoub and his team in the Ford Expedition. After they downed one of the Kiowas, Najoub had maneuvered to the Columbia Pike exit road to pick up Hassan and his team according to plan which didn't count on the four government cars on their tail. Thus, they went past the pick up point while Hassan and his team engaged the pursuer from their position behind the trees in the cemetery, shooting 40 mm M203 grenades from their M-16s.

Two of the pursuing cars took lethal fire, skidded in the ditch burning. The other two, a State Trooper and a DPS car took position against the median concrete barrier of Route 27 and got into a shooting battle with Hassan's team less than a hundred yards away.

Hassan Bahaji who had been in radio contact with Kashim Najoub throughout the assault talked on the radio while working an M-16.

"Leave us!" he screamed at his friend Kashim over the radio. "Save yourself! Go! Go!" he insisted as he saw the Ford Expedition stop on the side of the exit road and wait.

Now it started backing up. The rear door swung fully open on its hinges and the next moment an RPG came shooting straight out towards one of the government cars in the middle of the road. The missile went through the windshield of the State Trooper patrol car and blew its top off.

Seeing a moment of opportunity for Hassan and his team to flee, Kashim Najoub screamed back at Hassan on the radio.

"Come on! Come on! You can make it!" he urged while continuing to back up and close the distance between them.

Nassar Madani, one of Hassan's men, humped over a large tree branch let go of his AK-47 trigger for a moment and turned to his leader. "Sir, please go now," he pleaded. "Don't worry about us."

"I go we all go!"

"Go now, please, Commander. We'll cover you."

"You've done your duties. And you've done them well."

"It's still our duty to protect you, so please go now."

"Come on!" Kashim Najoub's voice again came through the radio.

"There's more coming." Jamil Sabayat, the other man of the team, cried suddenly as he saw two humvees jump the median from the other side of Washington Boulevard.

"*Salaam Aleikum*," Hassan Bahaji finally said to each one of the men who immediately resumed firing at the government forces.

"*Salaam Aleikum!*" they responded over the sound of their weapons.

He sprinted through the tall overgrowth at the perimeter of the cemetery, leaped out at the first clearing he came upon to the side of the road and ran to meet the SUV that was still backing up.

The first burst of 40 mm rounds from one of the humvees came and tore at the rear fender of the SUV. Kashim Najoub quickly shifted gear to drive and stepped on the gas as soon as he saw Hassan grab a hold of the open door. But before Hassan could haul himself into the passenger seat, a round struck his right thigh, sending a tremendous wave of pain through the rest of him as it tore through his muscles.

"Hang on!" Kashim Najoub cried as he floored the gas to get out of range of enemy fire. "Hang on, my friend!"

CHAPTER 8

▼

It was another one of those media frenzies in Washington. The lead was: Israeli delegation ambushed at Pentagon. Dozens of casualty. Civilian and military. Nobody knew exactly how many, or how it all happened.

Hordes of them—camera crew, reporters, anchorpersons—descended south of the Potomac and took pictures and videos they transmitted 'right on the spot' to their headquarters with quick, sketchy reports before they had all the facts. Those who were quick to get a special flashpass ventured beyond the yellow cordon and roamed the battle scenes where they took pictures of rescue crews still bagging bodies.

By 1:15 in the afternoon, every network and cable television had nothing else on but banner lines like 'Surprise Attack at Pentagon', 'War in Washington', 'Pentagon Attacked', 'Terrorists Invade Pentagon'.

It's 9/11 all over again, sans New York.

The report started coming in to the Office of Homeland Security shortly before the shooting ended which was when Nassar Madani and Jamil Sabayat used up the remaining Stinger-RMP missiles they had, three of them, by randomly targeting windows at different floors on the west side of the Pentagon, killing twenty-one more Americans. Infidels. Enemies of Islam. Oppressors of Muslims throughout the world. Then they emerged from behind the trees, their weapons blazing and faced their deaths at the hands of a gathering of federal, state and local armed forces.

Once he had a better picture of the situation after that part of the report came in, the OHS Director mobilized the office immediately. First, even before the

President, he reached the Secretary of Defense whom he knew was in his E-ring office in the Pentagon at the time. He reached the Secretary while the Secretary was out, minutes after the end of the shooting, surveying the devastation in the building and, looking out through the shattered walls, the bloody scene out on Washington Boulevard.

We're picking up bodies here inside the building, he told the OHS Director mournfully, and out in the street. Lots of bodies, he said. The Israeli Defense Minister survived but is critically injured and right this minute is in an ambulance on his way to the GW Hospital.

The Director expressed relief that the Secretary was safe and invited him to the White House as soon as he could make it any time at all today. He said he'll talk to the President next about gathering the advisers for an emergency Homeland Security Council meeting; he'll send out word to all the members to head to the White House situation room now.

Of the heads of intelligence agencies, only the FBI Director was available for the emergency meeting. Most of the others were out of town. So was the President who was at present in as far a place in the mainland from the nation's capital as he can be—San Diego. Thus, the Vice President, who was always up for grabs when the President is away especially at a time like this, pitched in along with the seconds in command of the absent agency heads, and several high Pentagon military and civilian officials.

The Secretary of Defense sent the head of Intelligence Operations of the Defense Intelligence Oversight, and appropriate aides, with a message that he'll join the meeting as soon as he can leave the Pentagon. The Deputy Assistant to the President for National Security Affairs and the Deputy National Security Advisor for Combating Terrorism were there, the CIA Deputy Director, the Deputy Director of the National Security Agency, the OHS Director, the Vice President and, lastly, the Chairman of the Senate Intelligence Committee who contacted the OHS Director and was promptly invited to the meeting which was to last for the next eight hours.

The meeting, presided jointly at first by the OHS Director and the Vice President, began promptly as soon as the last of the eleven men who were to be in the Council originally was seated. After the round of introduction for the non-regulars in the HSC meetings, the OHS Director opened by stating the sole purpose of the gathering, the single item in the agenda.

"We were attacked," he said, the expression on his face speaking of the embarrassment and the helplessness at having to say it. "And for the security and protection of the homeland, I declare that we *are* under attack."

He then turned everyone's attention to the 36-inch video screen on the wall behind the President's chair, turned the machine on and the President appeared on the screen.

"Mr. President," greeted the OHS Director, "we have everyone here as best we can put together at this time."

"The Secretary of Defense?" asked the President immediately.

"No, sir. He's still in the Pentagon."

"Is he alright?"

"Yes, sir. He's fine. He'll join us shortly, as soon as he's done over there."

"And the Vice President?"

"He's here," said the OHS Director and turned to the Vice President.

The Vice President then took over the direction of the meeting through most of its duration with the approval of the President who was to be air-borne in a secret military aircraft headed back to Washington, D.C. a half hour later.

"Mr. President," said the Vice President, scanning the few pages of the report handed to him first and the OHS Director only minutes earlier by one of the Defense people. "first thing—the Israeli Defense Minister is alive but in critical condition at the GW Hospital. At least twenty casualties inside the Pentagon, military and civilian staff. Many more injured. Outside, on the street…"

The President was on the screen for twenty minutes and got a full briefing on the situation from everyone in the room, then hurried on his way to a nearby Naval Air station. The next few hours were spent on assessing the loss in lives, the homeland vulnerability to such an attack, the required—and lack of—intelligence for countermeasures before it happens and, most importantly, the very real possibility of enemy penetration (espionage) of the American Intelligence Community being the source of this latest major catastrophe. Here, the FBI stepped in, addressing the Vice President and the OHS Director alternately.

"Gentlemen, when we re-routed the Israelis' entourage, all the information were communicated to all parties concerned through routine secure channels. There was no deviation of any kind from FBI and all inter-agency transmission procedures."

NSA pitched in quickly: "When we received the data, we ran it through our standard encryption analyzer, decoded them and catalogued them in the Top-Secret-Log bin. All standard procedure."

"There has to have been a leak," suggested the FBI.

"Who has access to the TSL bin?" asked the OHS Director.

"We have a list of selected IC-member agencies and their staff with read or update access," said the CIA. "The list is classified information."

"It has to be either a leak or an intercept during transmission," suggested the Senate committee chairman.

"Gentlemen," the Vice President interrupted with some urgency. "That's all fine and good to know everyone's doing things according to procedure. But the last thing we want to do at the moment is look for somebody to blame. The way things look right now, it appears we have some loose ends to tie up. Leaks, communication intercepts, acts of treason and outright betrayal of the country to our enemies—any of these could've brought this day upon us. This is not September 11 over again. This is a well-planned armed attack on our government, a blatant attack right at our military headquarters, for godssakes. And if it can be done at the Pentagon, couldn't it have been done here at the White House or the Capitol if they had a reason to? Or if they choose to? Think about that."

"Mr. Vice President, sir," the OHS Director said, "I believe our top priority here is intelligence countermeasures. We must be one up on them at all times. And to do that, we need more human resources, more surveillance capability, more use of state-of-the-art information technology."

The Vice President supported that strongly, and so did everyone.

Later in the afternoon as more data kept pouring in from the Pentagon, Defense finally brought up the question they'd been itching to toss in. "What we'd really like to know," said one of the Generals from the Defense Intelligence Oversight, "is how in the world did these people get a hold of all those Stinger-RMPs? Where did they get them?"

Robert Grundell went down the building cafeteria at 12:30 PM in a hurry for he was hungry. He was on his way a half hour ago but got held up when Eddie Mahone showed up at his office with the original of the protest letter bearing the signatures of over two-thirds of the Division staff.

"We have enough here," Eddie announced enthusiastically, taking the only other chair in the office, uninvited. "But I have a few more pledges I haven't seen. I'll do them today, while they're preparing their first weekly activity report to that asshole. Everybody I've talked to is so fuckin' pissed about it."

"So am I," said Robert, looking over the four-page protest letter. He flipped to the third and fourth pages which had the names of everybody in the Division, typewritten alphabetically with the underlined space after it for the signature.

The third page was almost completely signed up and about half of the fourth was. Robert found his name in the third page and promptly put his signature after it.

"I'll make you a copy later today," Eddie said, watching Robert now reading the top page of the letter.

Robert had thought earlier about what day this was—Thursday, which was the first day everyone in the Division was supposed to turn in their weekly activity report to Leon Justice, as Eddie mentioned. He hated the thought of it, felt a strong reluctance to do it, resented it. All those feelings had built up inside of him earlier that now it gave him a great sense of relief and satisfaction reading the protest letter, which said in part:

We, the employees of the

> *Interstate Logistics Division*
> *Office of Civil Defense Logistics*
> *Department of the Treasury*

write this letter in protest of the creation and staffing of the position titled Project Management Coordinator with duties and responsibilities written in the following Position Description:

> *'The incumbent performs the duties of the ILD liaison between the Division's branch offices and between ILD and other offices within OCDL, outside OCDL within the Treasury Department, and outside agencies. The person coordinates the work between the branches in the Division, between the Division and outside offices within Treasury Department or in external agencies, by establishing methods of communication, arranging meetings and conferences, tracking and documenting the progress of work on each project with data from the weekly activity report collected from the office staff as well as information gathered from outside agencies.*
>
> *'On projects that require the processing of classified data, the incumbent is the POC (Point Of Contact) in ILD/OCDL where outside agencies are involved. The person oversees the staff and data interface between offices working on the project and ensures that required security standard of procedures are followed at every instance.*
>
> *'The incumbent reports to the ILD/OCDL Division Chief and once a month makes a presentation of the Assessment of Work of the Division to the Division Chief and the Undersecretary of the Treasury [for OCDL].'*

Upon careful review of the above Position Description, a majority of us in the Division has come to the conclusion that the position simply duplicates the duties and responsibilities which are now—and have been for many years—effectively and sufficiently performed in existing positions in the Division. To delegate them to someone else would amount to introducing a 'middleman' that would interfere with the speedy communication now in place between staff within ILD and its customers within the Department and in outside agencies, would create unnecessary additional bureaucratic routing of information (red-tape) and cause delays in the normal work-pace in a project particularly in terms of problem prevention, recognition and resolution.

We not only think but know this personnel action is counter-productive and view it as a make-work effort for unneeded staff and, further, an unmitigated waste of taxpayer money at the annual (GS-14) maximum rate of $101,742.

Therefore, we the hardworking majority of employees of the Interstate Logistics Division of the Office of Civil Defense Logistics, Treasury Department, affix our signature freely to this letter and demand that the newly created and staffed position titled Project Management Coordinator be unfunded and abolished immediately.

We look forward to a quick administrative and personnel response within a period of thirty days, beyond which…

Robert Grundell turned his head sideways at Eddie Mahone with an approving look through the corner of his eyes. "Well done," he said. "I just wish we could've put Herod Hardin, Milton Pheasant and the rest of their minions on this same chopping block."

Eddie laughed. "Damn, wouldn't that be something. Herding a whole wagon-load of assholes to the gallows."

"I got just one question, though," said Robert. "What if management just trashed this letter and we never hear anything from anybody?"

"Which management? ILD? OCDL?"

"Yes."

"They better know what they got coming if they did that," Eddie said, ticked off. "See who else it's addressed to? With a preamble specific to each." He took out cover sheets to go with copies of the letter. "Our IG, EEO, OPM and lastly, the top federal whistleblowing investigator throughout the service—the Office of Special Counsel. That's the White House and Congress at its tail."

He came out of his office, after Eddie Mahone left to gather the rest of the signatures, feeling good though hungry and went straight down to the cafeteria. Coming out of one of the check-out lines carrying a tray of a roasted chicken leg, carrots, mashed potato and a can of soda, he stopped by a stand to pick up the napkins and utensils. There, he became aware of something peculiar going on in the cafeteria. Almost everywhere he turned, people gawked in awe while looking up at the TV sets on wall shelves around the room. He walked past two rows of tables and sat down at an empty table for two facing a TV set with a good view at an angle to his left and another to his right.

MSNBC, in one of the TV sets, had a camera covering parts of the collapsed walls of the Pentagon from inside one of the third-floor Army office areas hit by the Stingers.

"This is all so hard to imagine," said the reporter in a shaky voice, holding the microphone while leading the camera through the ruins of several office rooms, "how the terrorists were able to carry out such a devastating attack right here at America's national defense headquarters. So far, twenty-seven people had been found dead, killed, in here throughout this office area of the Pentagon. Dozens more are seriously injured."

The camera then panned through the large jagged wall opening to the view of Washington Boulevard which was now sealed from the Memorial Bridge and as far south as the intersection with I-395 and the Army-Navy Drive. The only traffic that remained were the Arlington Fire Department fire trucks, the Virginia State Troopers and the DPS patrol cars, and the ambulances coming and going. The camera zoomed in on the activities down on the street where rescue crews, military and medical teams, local police and firemen were looking inside disabled cars riddled with bullets, pulling out dead bodies, helping motorists who survived board ambulances on foot and on stretchers.

It was like a carnival scene with all the red and blue strobe lights on top of vehicles turning, sirens wailing as the dead and the wounded were driven away in ambulances. The camera panned closer to the exposed girder beam supporting the edge of the third floor and zoomed in on the wreckage at the helipad below. The ruins of the two Supercobras lay in separate large pieces still smoking. Those of the Kiowa, the one that took two RPG hits, were scattered in smaller chunks of metal, smoldering a short distance away near the road.

"What an incredible sight of devastation, right here at the Pentagon," the reporter kept saying over and over again, unable to control the impulse at what he was seeing. "The whole place is turned into a battlefield between here and across the road just inside the Arlington National Cemetery over there where some of the terrorists had taken up a position, and up and down Route 27 where others launched the attack, from the Memorial Bridge in the north and I-395 in the south."

Robert sat petrified in his chair in the cafeteria, unable to eat the chicken lunch on his tray as he couldn't move anything except his eyes, and then his head as he turned slowly to look at the other TV set up on the wall to his right. In it, CNN had on a bird's eye shot of the Pentagon from a news helicopter focusing on the still burning roof of the building where the Defense Minister's helicopter was shot, fell and went partially through. Part of the Bell 412 transport helicopter—its rotor and tail, could be seen sticking out on the roof, sending up a wide cloud of black smoke in the clear early afternoon autumn sky.

"Preliminary reports have it that the Defense Minister survived and is now in *a* hospital in critical condition," a reporter in the helicopter announced. "Several other passengers in the helicopter survived the attack. We have no exact numbers but the word is most members of the Defense Minister's entourage, along with some of their American military escorts, were killed when the helicopter was hit by a Stinger missile."

It was a long time, so it seemed to Robert, before he recovered from the shock and disbelief at what he saw. In that time, a flurry of uncertain thoughts and sudden awareness jolted him as if from a long state of unconsciousness. There was the sudden awakening to the fact that what he just saw was no longer just a possibility he had imagined when he met with Ahmed in the park and later talked to his people, Abu Kamal Ramshallah and Rahim Akbar.

It was all real now. As real as the wallet in his pants backpocket bulging with twenty-dollar bills from the stack in the envelope Ahmed gave him which he decided he'd just spend one day at a time. Like yesterday when, on the spur of the moment, he drove to Circuit City after work for the latest audio-visual system available out there—a 200-watt stereo receiver, CD/DVD player and a 34-inch TV set. And this weekend—the latest, most powerful Pentium computer.

Then there was the possibility—as real as the live TV coverage which now showed dead bodies being stuffed into zippered body bags—of the cause of all these carnage being traced back to Treasury, to OCDL and its staff. How long or how soon before anybody, any idea or anything led the investigation to the office—the question suddenly turned up front in his mind and he quickly filled with apprehension.

Yes, he got scared when he first thought about it, imagining some plainclothes government agents simply grabbing him from behind and hauling him away with no questions asked. As casually as he could, he made several moves like picking up the fork to begin eating while slightly shifting in his seat to a more comfortable position but at the same time so he could look around the cafeteria without turning his head too much. But other thoughts played in his mind while he fought with this feeling of apprehension. And with them, logic.

If anybody ever got to the bottom of this, meaning OCDL, a whole bunch of people would get dragged out in the firing line first before he did, not just in the Interstate Logistics Division but the other Divisions in OCDL. And why not other offices within Treasury that did business with OCDL, as well as outside offices which were mostly those of intelligence agencies themselves like the FBI, the CIA, the military intels and others?

In ILD, it'll be Milton Pheasant, the Division chief and his high-grade front office staff all the way to the Branch Chiefs and, yes, including Leon Justice who'd get in the line-up first. And what a thrill it would be to see the investigation end there. What a thrill it would be for everyone in the Division whose signature is on that letter to see every goddamn one of them hang.

The thought of that was so alluring that some ideas started popping up in his head. Yes, why not? he thought to himself as he began to entertain one of these ideas. There could be a great big golden opportunity opening up in all these to really get even with those assholes in every sense of the word.

He thought about the idea some more. He expanded it, looked into some details which opened the way to its possibilities, how to carry it through...no problem.

Shit, why not?

CHAPTER 9

▼

Just keep an eye on them a little longer, their Section Chief at the FBI's CID headquarters had told them several times and they heard him loud and clear even now as they focused their powerful field glasses through the second-floor window on what's going on down there, the gas station across the street. They could bust the place right now, agent John Jacobs was thinking as he watched Elmo Cooney, one of the pump attendants, go in to the glass-partitioned office room behind the front store of the filling station after he got done with a full-service customer outside. In the room, he sat down at a corner table behind the one with a man who had come in earlier with a magazine and a brown bag which he was now digging into for his lunch.

"There, there," Jacobs, known to his peers in the service as JayJay, said a few moments later to his partner, agent Richard Bartley positioned a few yards away on his elbows behind a small worktable, peering through the dusty blinds behind the window in the darkened room with his glasses. "See what that dope is doing?"

"Yeah, what else is new?" Bartley said quietly, watching Cooney, a tall skinny African-American, twenty thirty years old, snort a half a teaspoon of the white stuff right behind the man eating his lunch. The man turned halfway and said something to Cooney, apparently to refuse an offer for a hit 'cause he's busy eating right now. "We've seen this before, with the other guy too, that one in the cashier's booth."

"And we've got pictures of both of 'em doing it and doing business out on the street and right there at the pumps. Selling the stuff! The fuck more do they want at headquarters? What are we waiting for?" Jacobs had been impatient for weeks now especially when he saw an easy bust like this at hand.

Bartley, the senior, older, bigger and apparently more mature of the two FBI field agents reminded his partner of their orders, saying that unless they hear otherwise, they're staying put even if the place started to look like a controlled-substance supermarket. All they do, as they'd been doing for a month now, is keep track of who comes and goes, take pictures, plate numbers and keep feeding them in to the computer at headquarters for their boss and the brains with him there to look at.

"Mind telling me what else they expect us to see here?" asked Jacobs, taking his eyes off the glasses to look at the other man.

"Or hope to see," added Bartley, now focusing on the man having lunch at the table in front of the one now sitting back in his chair with eyes and brain floating high up on the ceiling.

"Something you know I don't?" Jacobs sounded irritated. "Something they tell you you don't tell me?"

"Nothing," said Bartley assuringly. "Your guess is as good as mine. Or as far off. And my guess is, knowing some of those guys at headquarters, they're fishing, foraging for some intels that might connect things."

"Things? What things? Fishing, foraging for what information? Why don't they just tell us? If it's something to do with South American drug, Asian drug or the Middle East drug traffic, or even the terrorist connections over there?"

"Why? Because there's enough guys they've told, guys they work with not in the same way they work with us, guys doing things different from what we do, guys who have the need to know."

"And we don't?

"Yes. Correct."

"We're the ones out here day after day on the lookout and we don't? That supposed to make sense?"

"Yes. To them it does."

"Sounds like a lot of bureaucracy to me," Jacobs moaned, turning helplessly back to his glasses.

"Look at it this way, JayJay—we all have a job to do. What you and I do goes only so far. For us to do, to know more'n what we're supposed to could create problems. It's the same with them at headquarters. They do only what they're supposed to do. This is the same with everybody."

"Yeah, yeah," Jacobs groaned, loathing what he was looking at across the street. "The same old rank-and-file follow-the-leader routine." God, how he'd love to throw those guys up against the wall, cuff them and haul them away in the backseat. "I want to go down there right now and get a real good smell of the joint," he said partly to himself.

But Bartley heard him clear and said: "That's an idea. See the guy eating lunch?"

"Yeah, whatabout him? We've seen him there before. I've never seen him do anything but eat lunch and read or watch TV."

"Maybe we should know more about him. Remember what they told us and all the agents at headquarters after 9/11? Come to think of it, they did tell us something."

Bartley may have meant to say that without sarcasm but when they both thought about what began to happen at the Bureau after the attack on America, they knew better than to take it lightly. Day after day for weeks, months, after September 11, 2001, they were flooded with special memos, bulletins, directives for just about everything they did, not only in the performance of their government-paid duties and responsibilities as employees of the Department of Justice but in the way they conducted their personal lives at home and everywhere. Consider yourselves on duty twenty-four hours a day, the word came from the higher ups and everyone down to their immediate supervisors.

We are fighting a war, they were told, not the ones you just read about out in Nicaragua or Southeast Asia and are not directly involved in. It is here at home and you are in it. You and your family. All of us, fighting for our beliefs, our freedom and our way of life.

On the more specific matters in their line of work, they were reminded as in the past not to sacrifice justice in the conduct of their investigations particularly in profiling potential suspects—except under the present circumstances faced by the nation but only where there is sufficient probable cause or strong underlying intelligence need related to national security and homeland defense. With that came the order for more cooperation and data networking with the INS, DEA/ATF, the Coast Guard and other domestic intel agencies, followed by the big increase in deployment of agents for drug operations and money laundering investigations nationwide.

There wasn't much time to prepare for so much activity and educate every field agent thoroughly on what he was sent out there for, undercover in some ethnic community, or working in a multi-national company, or hiding in some abandoned building or a 20-foot square rented office space across the street from a known drug market that could have a connection with some big money-laundering operation or even a terrorist network.

They were both quiet for a minute. Jacobs, especially, who lowered his glasses down his nose while he got his mind going. What he remembered specifically now was, after that one last big Division meeting they had at the Bureau, their immediate supervisor and dispatcher briefing them more thoroughly on the investigation of some obscure terrorist suspect they knew existed, one who had been the brains behind many terrorist activities around the world and in the United States. They were told to keep quiet about it the way the Bureau had been keeping it hushed all these years because it was simply too embarrassing to admit that outside of his existence, they knew practically nothing about him.

Nobody even knew what his real name was because he used and changed aliases frequently. The Bureau had several on record but nobody thought they're any good unless the man chose to use them over again: Yussuf Zadran, Mullah Bassyir, Rahim Akbar, Muhammed Moussa. And nobody knew exactly what he looked like because he disguised himself physically, culturally, spoke several languages fluently including American English in which he could speak with different accents. Thus he could assume different types of personality. He was a creature who easily adapted to the physical and cultural environment he ventured into. A chameleon, they were told. A very cultured and intelligent, careful and elusive one. For a matter of reference, the Bureau decided to give him a name of their own choosing—Saladin.

After he learned about this, agent Jacobs as did many of the field agents he knew simply put it on the backburner, thinking what could a small-fry agent like he was, let alone the hundreds of other lesser and no-brainer agents in the Bureau, do to contribute to an investigation of that nature? He didn't even know who or what to look for. Or how.

And this was what he told Bartley unenthusiastically, when he said: "Yeah, I remember."

To which Bartley replied purposefully and without making it sound like a lecture: "So how do we look for something, somebody we don't know much about? This is how, just what we're doing. There's something out there, somebody we're looking at right now. That's something, isn't it? Well, let's start with this, what we have. Do the best we can."

"You're right," Jacobs agreed thoughtfully, focusing his glasses back on the lunch-eater.

"What do you think he looks like?" Bartley asked. He was thinking—the people in the office analyzing what they'd been turning in from here for the past month would have said something by now if they had anything on the guy showing in the computer. But all they got were pictures of the guy. No name, no data of any kind. They didn't know diddly about him whatsoever.

Well, they knew that he's friends, acquainted, with the drug addicts working in the gas station. They knew that the druggies in there knew him. Question was, what is he to them? And why is he there only at lunchtime? Where does he come from? And where does he go when he leaves?

Jacobs zoomed in and got a closeup of the man—dark-skinned, not African-dark, Indian-dark, Pakistani, some kind of Arab, late twenty, early thirty. The man was eating leisurely and reading what looked like a copy of the Reader's Digest.

"South Asian, Arab," he mumbled to Bartley, "definitely Middle Eastern, can't tell which type. Hell, they all look alike to me. Let's go down there right now and check him out if you want. Somethin' to do."

"No, we don't want us seen together. You go. Pick up the paper too, and get me a caffeine-free coke. The regular one, not diet."

"Yes, sir," Jacobs sounded a little cheerful now as he stood up from leaning forward on the back of a chair he was using to look out the window. "Anything else? Want me to pick up your underwear at the chinese laundry nextdoor too?"

"Listen," Bartley said as he turned to his younger partner momentarily, "try not to attract any special attention from anybody down there. Make it so, as far as they're concerned, you're just a guy probably working nextdoor or across the street, maybe even in this building, and you happened to be on that side of the street when you decided to get the paper, a soda, a candy bar. Take your time…"

"I know, I know. I'll see how I can maybe find a way to get a close look at the guy."

"That'd be good. With some luck, he might come out for something too while you're in there. Talk to him, get anything you can out of him."

Rocko Diggs got busy in the booth for a minute when several cars rolled up to the pumps. Two of them used credit cards, one came up the window to pay cash first and he took care of him. As soon as he shut the cash register, he turned to look through the glass wall of the back office, at Elmo Cooney, and laughed to himself.

Crazy mothuh, he thought. One o' these days, we all gonna get busted including him just for sittin' there eatin' his lunch. The one he was referring to was Ahmed Khalifa who came down once in a while from his office nearby to eat his lunch here. He liked to watch the 27-inch TV in the room while he's eating.

It's nice he don't mind a thing, Rocko mused, even if he could get us thrown out of our jobs by his office which owns the station among a chain of others, but it's not all good either 'cause cops could suddenly walk in and catch us in the act. Like this guy walking in now, dressed casual, not too dumpy-looking and not too straight either. Average. The type could be an undercover. Shit, I hope he isn't, with fuckin' Cooney in there gettin' his high.

"Help you?" he asked through the pass-thru gap below the front glass wall of the booth.

"Still got the paper?" the man asked nice and friendly, looking around like he wanted to buy the whole place or maybe turn it upside down for drugs.

"Yeah, it's right here right outside my door. There's a couple left."

"I only want one," said the man being funny. Maybe he ain't no cop.

"He'p yourself."

The man looked at the newspaper rack and waved okay at Rocko but stayed where he was in front of the soda displays looking for a brand. He was there two, three minutes looking up and down the three tall soda display coolers for something apparently not in there. John Jacobs knew they didn't have the caffeine-free regular coke Bartley wanted the first time he looked and spent the next couple minutes stealing glances at Ahmed Khalifa in the office room.

The man didn't look any different up close. Definitely Middle Eastern or South Asian. When he finally moved to get the newspaper by Rocko's booth door and got hit by the smell of curry from inside the room, he became certain the man was either Indian or Pakistani. Who else eats that shit for lunch, godssakes?

He was in no hurry to get what he came for but didn't appear intent on checking up the place to either rob it or conduct a secret investigation. He was just a little slow reading the newspaper headline, bending over to pick up a copy and scan the front page to see that the President was in Ottawa, Canada the day before and addressed the parliament over there, told them how to run their government, the Redskins broke a loosing streak of four.

He was fishing for loose change in his pants pocket when the curry eater inside the room called out to the man in the booth, speaking with a distinct South Asian accent.

"Hey, Rock-o! What's wrong with the TV?"

"Nothin'!"

"It's not on!"

"Well if it isn't, then turn it on, man! What's the matter, somebody broke both your hands? I see you eatin' that stinkin' stuff again so they can't both be broke!"

John Jacobs was caught in the middle of this and he and Rocko exchanged amused looks.

"Where's the remote?" asked Ahmed Khalifa.

"It's in there somewhere, cryinout loud," Rocko called out but then held himself as he saw the thing sitting in front of him in the booth. He took it and got up slowly, shaking his head, smiling silly at Jacobs like sayin' hey, I'm not perfect, what's he expect?

Jacobs didn't find any change in his pockets so he gave Rocko a five for the paper and a candy bar when Rocko came back. While Rocko rang up the purchases in the cash register, Jacobs had his eye on Ahmed in the office room just as Ahmed, less than half a minute after he turned the TV on, dropped his hands on the edge of the table, spilling food particles from his fork, looking stunned as he became transfixed at whatever he was viewing on the television.

"Thank you, sir," Rocko said as he slid the change out to Jacobs then turned to look at Ahmed too when he saw the weird look on Jacob's face while looking at Ahmed.

"What the hell is going on there?" he mumbled to himself as he now saw Ahmed get up, staring at the television with utter disbelief on his face. Behind him, Elmo Cooney had sat back up and opened his zombie eyes. He too gawked at the television with surprise on his face.

Rocko rushed back into the office room, Jacobs right behind him pocketing his three-dollar-and-some change.

"Unconfirmed reports had the number of fatalities inside the Pentagon alone at twenty-eight," the CNN reporter said as the camera zoomed in on the west side of the Pentagon, focusing on the parts of the wall where the missiles had hit and demolished large sections of it. "Most of these are civilian and military personnel on duty at the time on the third and fourth-floor levels of the building which were hit, we were just told, by a number of Stinger missiles, the type that are shoulder-fired, the same type that hit the helicopter carrying the Israeli Defense Minister as it was maneuvering to land on this side of the Pentagon. Many in the helicopter were killed as it crashed and burned on the roof of the Pentagon but the Defense Minister was not one of them. The Secretary of Defense was in his office at the time of the attack but is unharmed and we were told that he is in constant communication with the President who is right now on his way back to Washington in a secret military transport flight. And down here on the ground along this quarter-mile stretch of Washington Boulevard by the Arlington National cemetery on the other side, there's blood everywhere…"

Across the street behind the blinds at his second floor window, agent Richard Bartley was puzzling over what was going on. Whatever it was, all he could think of was Jacobs must have gotten real lucky. He's in there with everybody looking at something on TV that's apparently of common interest to all of them. And he talked briefly to the Middle-Eastern guy.

Something strange happening to that guy, though. He looked like he was ready to puke, horrified at what he was watching on TV. He had totally forgotten about his lunch. But then Bartley zoomed in on Jacobs and noticed that Jacobs too looked quite taken aback. They stood close enough to each other in the room so that he was able to focus on all of them at the same time.

The Middle-Eastern man appeared to be unusually agitated. He was definitely affected by what everybody was looking at more than the rest. He saw that Jacobs who divided his attention between the television and the man noticed this too. This went on for three minutes before the man packed his lunch back in the bag and hurried out the front door of the store to the building a block away on the same side of the street.

Bartley followed the man with his glasses only as far as outside the store before focusing back on Jacobs because the man went out of range halfway down the block due to physical obstructions. But Jacobs had that covered. As he watched the man go out, he noticed the magazine the man had left on the table. He picked it up and looked at the address label quickly, held it up in front of him long enough for Bartley to zoom in on it and photograph it, he hoped, then rushed out the store to go after the man.

The way it all looked to Rocko and Elmo, Jacobs was being nice enough to try to catch the man and give him back his magazine but he wasn't fast enough to see where he went so he came back in to leave it with them. Jacobs actually had no intention of catching up with the man. He just wanted to see where he went, which building, and he did. On top of that, he had his name and home address.

They sure lucked out, the two undercover agents thought. Later, they would find out how much they actually did, more than they could have imagined.

Hassan Bahaji didn't expect to still be alive. Now, two hours after they began the attack, he had mixed feelings about being alive. On the one hand, he longed for what would have been one glorious and triumphant last day of his life, as it had been to his team, if he had stayed with them to the end. He would have journeyed with them to Allah in heaven, believing they had accomplished their mission on their last day on earth.

On the other hand, now knowing from the radio in his car that they did not, the Jew they came to destroy was not one among those killed in the helicopter, the lucky bastard, he thanked his warrior friend Kashim for rescuing him that he may live even just another day to do his duties in life in the name of Islam.

It had been almost just a fast ride—over the speed limits on the streets of Arlington, Virginia, getting away from the noise and frantic activities at the Pentagon and giving their pursuers, what's left of them, a slip. Kashim Najoub had planned it well, studied the roads, the traffic lights and signs along all the possible alternate routes for just such an escape although none of them, he and Kashim and the two men with him in the Ford Expedition SUV thought it possible.

But how surprisingly easy it looked when Kashim bolted at top speed for a mile on Columbia Pike west, quickly losing the humvees and a couple of state troopers at his tail. Once he did, he simply turned south into a minor street in the neighborhood where he and one of his soldiers had left the two cars the night before, his late-model Ford Taurus and Hassan Bahaji's Toyota Corolla. The four men split in the two cars, abandoning the Ford Expedition, then got on the road again at normal speed. They drove to Glebe Road two blocks out of the neighborhood, turned south a few miles down on Route 1 through Old Town Alexandria to get to the Beltway, away from the turmoil they created which had now begun to shake the political and military establishment in Washington, D.C. and send shock waves throughout the nation.

They crossed the Wilson Bridge into Maryland and headed north on the Baltimore-Washington Parkway I-295 on their way to Baltimore where their Commander, Omar Husain, awaited word from anybody Allah might have spared in the battle to bring him a message.

Hassan Bahaji, keeping a hand pressed against his right thigh above the bullet wound to help stem the bleeding, rode in the passenger seat of his car with one of the men at the wheel—Samir Osmani, a 30-year old Soldier of Islam, born in Syria, raised in Maryland. The man was one of hundreds of children from the Middle East sent to America years ago by the Organization with legal immigrants they supported. They are now American citizens in their twenties and thirties living in various parts of the country, the very same people among other groups of Muslim activists all over the world whom many in the American intelligence community and the media had, since 9/11, routinely referred to as the sleepers.

It was a flesh wound inflicted by the bullet that entered the back of Hassan's right thigh and exited clear through the front without severing any arteries, touching the bone or doing anything more serious than ripping through the tissues. Samir, who he learned quickly had trained in paramedics in addition to his college degree in Medical Technology, knew precisely what to do with a first-aid kit Kashim carried in the SUV during their escape. But now, glancing at the wound occasionally while keeping their speed under 70 miles an hour on I-295, Samir saw that the dressing he applied from the first-aid kit was not large enough as it was now saturated with blood. He decided they needed to get more materials and told Hassan.

"There's a town coming up," Samir said, speaking in a natural eastern American English with a slight southern Maryland-Virginia accent. "Laurel. We can go to a drugstore and get something thicker'n that. Get the blood to clot more and stop the bleeding completely. And you must be getting hungry too, sir."

"And you?" asked Hassan back, feeling deeply appreciative and now almost totally trusting of this *American* man who—from his appearance, mannerism and speech—could have been any natural-born American who knew and valued nothing more than his own materialistic western culture and beliefs, an arch-enemy of Islam.

"I sure am too. I could have a bite of something. I bet they could too." Samir glanced up at the rearview mirror to indicate the two men in the Ford Taurus following them at a cautious distance of five car lengths.

He got off the BW Parkway on Route 198 west towards Laurel and found a shopping center where he bought large sterilized dressings of thick pads and wide gauze and bandage at a drugstore. On his way to the store, he walked to the Ford Taurus which followed them and parked a section away from them in the parking lot, talked briefly to his leader, Kashim Najoub at the wheel and the man with him, to ask them to wait for them at a table in a pizza restaurant nearby.

Several minutes later, he tore at Hassan's trouser some more, as he had done earlier, so he could add the thicker dressings on the wound and around it, making sure the blood that had already clotted and partially stopped the bleeding did not get disturbed. That was all he saw needed to be done at the moment. The man was not in danger of going into shock for the amount of blood he had lost. All he needed now is some nourishment, and rest. And so did he, and all the rest of them, for it had been a long sleepless day and night the past twenty four hours for everyone.

Realizing it wouldn't do for Hassan to walk to the restaurant in his condition, they agreed the only choice they had was for him to stay and wait for Samir to bring him food. But Hassan Bahaji had another pressing matter on his mind.

"I must contact Commander Omar as soon as possible," he said, adding that he must get to a pay phone. Everyone had strict instructions not to use cell phones at this time unless there's no other way to communicate.

"But you can't get out of the car, sir."

"I know, I know." Hassan was at this moment deep in thought, his right hand laying firmly on his right thigh near the bandage, his left supporting his weight laterally on the seat on the other side. "I want to make a quick report that we're on our way back to Baltimore."

"Couldn't I do that?" Samir asked.

Hassan fell quiet for a few moments while he wrestled with the last weak remnants of his distrust of the American sleeper. Only he knew the telephone number of Commander Omar and his location.

He did not know this man and the one with his close friend Kashim Najoub, not like the two younger ones whom the Organization had selected for his team through Omar Husain's recommendation, the two who had made their ultimate sacrifice for Islam and are now with Allah. But they can't all be wrong, now he was thinking, he and Kashim and above all Commander Omar who had spent years between here in America and the various homelands of these Soldiers of Islam in the Middle East, indoctrinating each and every one of them on the keeping of the Faith, the defense of their Muslim traditions and belief in the teaching of Mohammed and the Koran against the Judeo-Christian acts of desecration that had been going on for centuries throughout the world.

"Yes," Hassan said, turning to Samir Osmani with a discerning but trustful look. "Why didn't I think of that?"

He then gave Samir Osmani their Commander's telephone number—a suite in the Courtyard by Marriott Hotel at the BWI airport, and the message saying the four of them are now halfway to BWI from D.C., they need to know their next order from the Commander before he leaves on his long journey to Mindanao in the southern Philippines later in the afternoon and if the Commander would not consider it careless for them to proceed to and meet with him at the hotel or another place at his discretion.

Hassan Bahaji knew he had done the right thing when the 30-year old Muslim American, defender of Islam, looked at him obediently with a deep resolve in his eyes, a mirror of determination and courage, before he left the car and headed to a public telephone outside the pizza restaurant.

When Omar Husain picked up the phone in his hotel suite and heard the first few words from one who survived the battle at the Pentagon, he almost fell to his knees with a heartful of gratitude to Allah. All the television coverage he'd been following the past hour and a half had mentioned only casualties in reporting about the 'terrorists', nothing on whether any escaped or were captured. Now, after learning that four out of eleven of his warriors lived to tell about the battle where the enemy suffered dozens of casualties and the humiliation of being attacked, penetrated right at the doorstep of the center of their military power, he felt a surge of triumph, victory beyond anyone's expectations.

Let that Jew devil, the Israeli Defense Minister, live a day longer for now, a week, a month, a year. The Soldiers of Islam will come again, and again, and hunt him down, and his leaders and followers alike and destroy them wherever they may be. Just like they destroyed his family, his life, his country.

"Samir Osmani!" he said happily after the caller identified himself. "Yes, brother Samir, I remember you well. Allah be praised you live."

"Allah be praised, Commander," the young Muslim replied.

"And are you well?"

"Yes, thank you, sir. Not a scratch. And so is our team leader Kashim Najoub and brother Sabah Ahmaddi. But our mission Commander, Hassan Bahaji, is wounded."

"Thank God he lives too. How bad?"

"Not seriously, sir. He'll live to fight another day. I took care of the bleeding but I'd like to get him to a clinic soon to clean up and close his wounds before they get infected," Samir Osmani said.

He then proceeded to deliver the message from Hassan Bahaji for which Omar Husain made quick but careful decisions. One of these was an instruction for them not to come to him at the hotel but to meet him in one hour at a 'place where the orchids bloom', saying that Hassan and Kashim would know exactly where that is. It was a comfortable little Chinese restaurant in nearby Glen Burnie where they had dined not long ago the last time Omar Husain was in Baltimore.

Before they hung up, Omar Husain took a moment, although anxious about taking any more time on the line, to inquire about the others. Samir Osmani reported that they were all good and unharmed. And for those who died in battle, he paused for a moment of silence, not to express sorrow but relief in the thought that they were now with Allah, then uttered a brief prayer for their souls.

It was the other man's turn to speak but he didn't. And he had his own moment of silence pass, a moment which spoke of their solidarity no word could have spoken any better. That solidarity forged between him and the young Muslim and many others like him throughout the world in their maturing years while they prepared to be called upon to their ultimate service to Allah one such day as today, or another day soon.

Omar Husain—senior Commander of missions operations worldwide, teacher, trainer and ideologist in Islamic culture and traditions, also known in the Muslim world here in America and abroad by such names as Sulaiman Zatari, Yussuf Zadran, Abu Saeed Muhammed, Rahim Akbar, Sultan Salahudin, among others, and by any Anglo-American name when in his guise as such—sat quietly by the telephone after he hung up. He recalled many of those young men, their names, faces and personalities. Among them—Hassan Madani, Jamil Sabayat, Hamad Salim, Sabah Ahmaddi, Samir Osmani, and many others. Lebanese, Palestinians, Indonesians, Saudis, Egyptians, Filipinos, Syrians, Malaysians. Yes, those young men who grew up here in America, western Europe, Southeast Asia, from between the ages of two and five, and became his pupils in Islamic fundamentalism in their teens and twenties the past fifteen years.

He was a part of their lives, in their hearts and minds, and they became a part of him so that proud as it made him to see or hear of any one of them give their lives willingly, joyfully, defending Islam in the name of Allah, he grieved deeply in his heart as if he grieved his family over again when they died. But hearing from one of them such as brother Samir especially—one he knew well among the many he had taught to be a loyal and strong defender of the faith—back from a call to duty, alive and well, made up for much of that grieving. Thus, he pulled himself out of his stupor, picked up the phone again to make the call that Abu Kamal Ramshallah in another suite away at the farthest end of the hotel awaited anxiously from him.

Immediately after listening to what Omar spoke about, Kamal was in a public phone booth in the hotel relaying what he just learned to Mahmud Mahran, his boss and financier in Detroit, who in turn a few short minutes later was relaying the same information in a deeply coded Arabic lingo to his superiors in the Organization at its home base in Cairo, Egypt.

PART II

▼

HAWAII—OPERATION PUNCHBOWL

CHAPTER 10

▼

This one looks like a possibility, thought Jerome Bolden, a lead analyst in the Data Security Section of the FBI Investigative Services Division. He was looking at the screen output of a query he executed in the TRIDEX—Transaction Identification and Data Extractor—a network application system that reported on, among other things, accesses to classified government data files. Date and time of access, duration, userid, agency code, I-O activity.

It was two-thirty in the afternoon, the worst time of day for trying to stay awake especially if you're working on a high-priority task and you're not quite sure where the hell you're going with what you're doing. What's needed here, he had been thinking the past couple days, is a simple stat program to gather a profile of accesses. Profile for each accessor by frequency of access, by duration, by day of the week or time of day. That kind of thing which is what he was trying to do here and taking him an awful long time. To top that off, with more and more users getting on the system, the network had slowed down to a crawl. Now the response time was almost two seconds each command, up from under one only yesterday. So irritating.

The day after the attack six days ago, a directive had come down from the front office and launched a massive activity to investigate a suspected leak of classified data that—according to the White House, Homeland Security and Fort Meade—allowed the terrorists to execute their plan with such lethal high precision as they did and even allowed some of them to get away with it. Look into every nook and cranny of data traffic throughout government service, they were told. Networking between agencies, any kind of interface even in non-classified data.

Work with the other intel offices—NSA, CIA, and all the branches of the military. And the local governments too. Get all the leads you can from everybody. The situation here is either the enemy has penetrated our IT systems or somebody's selling us out to the enemy. We got to find out what or who, fast.

So, these past few days, Jerome Bolden had been busy doing just that, working with his contacts at State, the CIA, among other agencies, but more closely with his counterpart at NSA in Fort Meade, Maryland. Their hands were full over at NSA, he was told, even before the attack, so he was given all the lead they thought he could use on his own which was almost saying—here take these and work with them. Like getting an assignment from them which he didn't mind. He needed all the help he can get.

The query he executed read a network database NSA shared with all the Defense agencies and recently with the FBI. It was a virtual clearinghouse of access logs for use by the intelligence community and select agencies involved with homeland security. It took around thirty seconds for the query report to spring up across the screen. He almost gave up on it but when it came up and he started looking at it, he understood why it took so long.

The query command was set to read the log files of the State, the Navy and the Treasury departments. That plus the input he entered requesting selected data going back to a week before the attack up to current date took a good amount of processing, now he realized. Indeed, this appears to have great possibilities—possibilities for some hard analysis, he thought again as he scrolled through pages and pages of the data. There were over 35,000 report lines the query returned as shown in the upper right-hand corner of the screen.

It'll take hours, maybe even days to go over this one report even just to see what files are accessed the most in each agency, let alone establish a pattern, a profile for a single accessor.

He stopped for a minute, thinking hard.

Scrap this one. The thing to do is run them one at a time. Each agency. That would be more manageable.

He had a second thought. The stat program, which would actually be just another query, perhaps a little lengthier, but it'll make his work a lot easier, more targeted and faster. He wished he was a programmer, not just an end-user, and knew how to code this query language they use in the system.

It shouldn't take any time at all for one of their IT specialists down the hall to code the query, catalog and can it and log his userid as an authorized user. He picked up the phone and began to dial a number but held himself halfway through. He had in mind this guy, one of the top computer programmer/analysts in the office, but working with him was like making yourself a footstool for him to kick around or rest his stinking feet on. Arrogant, bossy. Pain in the ass. What's with these IT people? They all have this attitude of self-importance about them. Maybe they got the smarts to know what they know, but it also makes them ignorant about everything else which isn't so smart.

After thinking a few more seconds, he dialed another number.

"Hey, Mr. Hunglow, howzit going?" he said as soon as Ray Huai-lo picked up and said hello. Ray was a contractor staff and a U.S. citizen of Chinese extraction whose parents brought him over from Kwangtung Province via Hong Kong in 1955, when he was two. In the seven years his company had him assigned to their contract with the FBI to maintain the agency's system software, he had become just about the most dependable analyst, troubleshooter, help-desk man and all around consultant in the office.

"Jerry, listen, man. I got no time to bullshit right now," he said to Jerome Bolden who never hesitated to shoot the breeze with him whenever Jerome felt like it, it seemed. The two of them had this kind of rapport where they took turns irritating each other when one felt like it. They went out to lunch at least once a week. "I got a half a dozen irate end-users around me right now and every one of them's ready to kill me."

"Tell them to hold off till you write this one itty-bitty query I need you to do for me right away." Jerome spoke quickly upon sensing that his buddy might actually be busy with something.

"Can it wait? And if so, how long?"

"Any chance getting it done before COB today?"

"Depends what it is you need."

"It's nothing complex," Jerome said assuringly. "I know you can do it quicker than I get back from a trip to the washroom after I tell you what it is."

"Well, what application?"

"TRIDEX."

"Geez, Jerry," Ray groaned, "I thought I taught you how to code that a long time ago, man? Any dumbshit can…"

"That was a long time ago, Ray. And I'm no ordinary dumbshit. Listen, seriously, I never have a need to code the damn thing so I never use it. I forgot everything."

"Alright, tell you what—how about you email me the requirement. Tell me exactly what you want and from which database."

"Sounds good to me."

"I'll give you a call when it's ready or send you an email and tell you the name of the query to execute."

It was ten past four when he ran the query in the production computer. He started with the Navy database, requesting a report of accesses two weeks back to current date. Within minutes, he got the online report back, saved it to his work library and did a thorough analysis of the data. He sorted the report and pared it down into a select group by userids—the twenty-five percent with the most number of accesses not just to Navy classified files but to those of any agency government-wide, and wrote a summary of his analysis. Next, he did the State Department database. That took a few minutes longer doing the same thing. It was a larger database.

So far, he had a file of dozens of userids from each agency, showing the office they belonged to within the agency, the files they accessed and the rest of the access-log data. There were some showing up in both reports. These were people, he assumed, who had data interface between the two agencies. What they do with the classified data once they had them, who the hell knows. That's what FBI analysts like Jerome Bolden are supposed to find out, identify these people, scrutinize and profile them if need be and catch them in the act—in cyberspace or in person—if any of them were doing something with those data other than what they're authorized to do.

Once again he brought up the input screen of the query program that Ray Huai-lo wrote and tested for him in a little more than an hour and keyed in his request, this time for a report on the Treasury database. Just before he submitted it for execution, he glanced at the time on his watch and thought, shit, can't do this now. He had less than ten minutes to get down the garage for his 4:30 car pool.

Tomorrow, he said to himself, then hurried to close up shop which usually consisted of shutting down the computer, a trip to the washroom to wash the coffee-maker and mug, gathering stuff into the briefcase. He had three minutes left when he ran out to the elevator.

Had Jerome Bolden not run out of time and executed his query, it would have returned a report of over ten thousand lines showing log data of accesses by Treasury people to classified files within Treasury, NSA, State, FBI and several other agencies. And when he sorted the report by userid and pared it down to the top twenty-five percent, he would have seen all the accesses to the TSL bin by OCDL staff, among them those of Robert Grundell. But not tomorrow. At least not exactly the way he would have seen them today.

As Bolden was hurrying out to join his car pool, Robert Grundell just decided to spend another half hour, maybe even an hour, at work to finish up what he was doing.

After watching the flash news on television in the cafeteria on the day of the attack, his apprehensions grew to a level of paranoia that three days later, he got together with Max Poysen to ask a favor. Max was one of the analysts who handled the maintenance of the application and some of the system software of the Branch. Somebody comes on board, needs a userid, password, auth-id to specific application functions, he goes to Max. Somebody goofs and loses his password after three unsuccessful attempts accessing the system using a wrong password, he goes to Max. Somebody leaves, Max takes care of the archiving and cleanup.

Robert Grundell needed something else from Max.

"I need to be able to update the records the system creates in the access-log database everytime somebody accesses a file, any file," he said to Max.

"You need read/write access to it," Max said flat out. "What for? That's the most boring, uninteresting data you could look at in the whole world. Who ever uses that file for anything, I don't know. Not even the systems programmers downstairs."

"Can you give me read/write access to it?"

"Sure. Nothing to it. I'll do it right now."

For two days now, he had been browsing the log file, eyeballing the access records containing his userid. There were lots of them with accesses to many classified files. He also kept an eye on accesses by several people in the Division particularly his boss, Herod Hardin, and Leon Justice.

So, today, the past couple of hours now, to finally ease his apprehensions for one reason and to fuck up the hated assholes for another in the event of an investigation, he got busy changing the userid of his access records in the file to mostly that of Leon Justice, some to Herod Hardin. He deleted many of the records of his accesses to the TSL bin outside of the routine during the regular time in the morning. The ones he left he changed the userid to that of Leon Justice.

Since the day of the attack, he had been thinking of any possible way an investigation could eventually implicate him. The first thing he did was clean up his computer of any copy he had of any classified files. He dumped some of them to diskettes which he took home. The rest he deleted. Even his email folders he cleaned up of any message with reference to any top secret, critical sensitive, classified information. Then he thought about the access-log database which he just now took care of.

Unlike the past few days, he went home relaxed, feeling confident that he had covered all the angles, and glad that he did what might just possibly amount to Leon Justice's doom should things come down to the wire at OCDL.

Pulling into a space at the parking lot outside the apartment building, he saw Ahmed Khalifa just walking up the front door of the building across the courtyard. He hurried to catch up with him, getting out of the car quickly and hopping up the few steps to the pathway leading to the building entrances on each side.

It was dusk but there was still enough light for the two men, sitting patiently in another car three spaces away, to distinguish Robert Grundell's features, approximate height, weight and age as he went by looking glad to see Ahmed just before the latter entered the building. One of the men immediately took out a pen and scribbled some notes on a pad in the pool of the map light below the dashboard.

They watched the two talk for less than a minute before Robert Grundell turned to enter the building across the courtyard. From the looks of it, Ahmed didn't want to prolong the conversation beyond a quick handshake and a neighborly greeting. One of the men in the car, FBI special agent Richard Bartley, didn't think it was because Ahmed needed to run up to his apartment quick to take a dump because when he went by them shortly before Robert did, he was in no big hurry. On the contrary, he was walking rather sluggishly and appeared to be deep in thought.

The day after they learned his name and address at the gas station, they found out everything else they thought they needed to know about the Pakistani. His H-1B visa, its petitioner and the sponsoring company—MidEast Continental, Ltd., his employer with main headquarters in Detroit and owner of the gas station, the time he lived in Canada and Detroit before coming to the Capital area for the job he now held in Ballston, Arlington.

With MidEast Continental, an energy trading and shipping company more than eighty percent owned by Arab capitalists, coming into the picture, their section chief at CID and his bosses got curious. A case file was opened for the company, and changes happened quickly. The stakeout at the gas station was finally turned over to the Arlington County police although one new field agent was still assigned to it together with a couple of dicks of the local jurisdiction. Bartley and Jacobs were turned loose full time on Ahmed Khalifa.

They were told to find out more about the man, where else outside of work and home he spent his time and who he came in contact with. Anybody.

As soon as Robert Grundell had entered the three-story garden apartment building, John Jacobs got out of the car quickly and walked away from the building. He stood some twenty yards away at the median between the street and the parking lot with a view of the front and side of the building, and waited. Within seconds, a window on the second floor adjacent to the entrance and stair lit up. Another, a smaller one probably the washroom, did too after a few moments. Jacobs then went up to the entrance door and was delighted to find out the door was not latched when he tried it and it swung open.

The units were numbered consecutively, clockwise from the left as he entered the lobby and staircase, starting with 101. There were eight units each floor. He guessed that the one he was interested in up in the second floor would be 201 and found that he was right when he checked. On his way out, he scanned the mailboxes and noted the name R. Grundell on box 201.

"We got one," he said to Bartley back in the car as he began a white-page search for 'R. Grundell, Arlington, VA' on the internet.

"Good," Bartley replied. "Now we're getting somewhere, maybe."

This was their fifth day on this new assignment and the closest they got to seeing Ahmed make contact with anybody on a personal level was two days ago when they followed him to the Sheraton Premier Hotel at Tysons Corner, where they lost him. Lost him for three hours while he apparently met with somebody he had to see, somebody important to him. He took most of the afternoon off work. He was in there, in one of the hotel rooms while they waited for him to come back out to his car in the parking lot.

"Name is Robert Grundell, 312 Highland St, Apt. 201," Jacobs said, now turning off the computer. "Got his phone number too. Shall we give him a junk call? One of those charity fundraising call? See what he sounds like?"

"Sure. Go ahead."

Jacobs got on his government cell phone and dialed the number. The line was busy.

"I think we're done here for the day," Bartley said, sitting up at the wheel and aiming to get the car started. "Let's get outa here. Try him again in a few minutes."

"You're right," agreed Jacobs. "It's been a long day. I could use a beer right now."

"Hang on. We'll get one."

When Ahmed called Bobby after they got in their apartments as he said he would downstairs at the door, the first thing he said was for them not to stay too long on the line. Bobby said he understands although the thought of their lines being bugged couldn't be farther from his mind.

Bobby had been anxious to get word from anybody the days following the attack. He waited a few days before even thinking of calling Ahmed but the day he decided he'd call him, he didn't.

He thought maybe Ahmed or one of his people would call instead, or Ahmed and he would run into each other at home, somewhere. If not, he thought of just buzzing his apartment one evening. He would have done just that if he hadn't seen Ahmed coming home tonight. In spite of his reluctance to make contact with anybody so soon after the attack, Bobby still didn't think there was any possibility of anybody getting wind of the deal he had going with them.

"What's going on?" Bobby asked up front. A few long seconds went by before Ahmed spoke.

"Bobby, I understand how curious you are at the moment," Ahmed said gingerly. It sounded strange to Bobby hearing him talk that way. Ahmed then went so far as to tell him what time it was now—ten after six—and suggesting they meet at the Sheraton National a mile down Columbia Pike. The bar at the top in…thirty, forty minutes, he said, and Bobby agreed.

Bobby was there first, taking a table for two by the window with an excellent panorama of that part of Northern Virginia that ends at the Potomac river, including a view of the Pentagon. He hesitated a moment before taking a seat, thinking if he should take another table, but then decided he didn't care. There are other things to look at through the window.

Five minutes later, he saw Ahmed appear at the door to the restaurant cocktail lounge. The place was half full so Ahmed spotted him quickly and headed his way.

They ordered the same drink—vodka tonic, which they sipped gradually while they made small talk. Work, social life. The girls, Rosie and Paula, from last weekend's double date which turned out to be another happy event. When Bobby said that he got a solo date with Paula Saturday, Ahmed confessed the same thing with Rosie. That's where their conversation stalled.

In the silence that followed, Ahmed sized Bobby up through the corner of his eye, trying to figure out the best way to talk to him about a number of things he needed to, among them, of course—what Bobby's take was about the attack, his part in it. Another was Ahmed's meeting with Abu Kamal two days ago at the

Sheraton Premier hotel at Tysons Corner where he came out with a bonus pay for himself, and another one for Bobby. He broke the silence first.

"Bobby," he said, turning from his view of the Pentagon where the scars of the attack were visible from his seat, to the man across the table briefly and down to his half-full glass. "How do you feel?"

Bobby waited a moment, second-guessing the meaning of the question, before answering: "I'm fine. I'm doing just fine."

"Good." Ahmed sat straight and turned his eyes back up at Bobby. "Good," he repeated.

"And you?" Bobby asked back.

"I'm...alright."

It was clear Ahmed was burdened with some thoughts. Bobby was quick to catch on to it so he started over with the same question he asked on the phone: "What's going on?"

"Kamal asked to see me two days ago," said Ahmed, pulling out a standard business envelope from his coat pocket and laying it on the table under a napkin. "He asked about you, how you're doing. I told him I haven't talked to you but I said I would. He gave me this for you."

He slid the envelope over to Bobby halfway across the table with as little noticeable movement as possible.

"What's this?" asked Bobby, eyeing the napkin with the envelope.

"He said they didn't want to take the chance you might be feeling short-changed," Ahmed said, taking a sip of the vodka tonic and putting the glass back down empty. "They wished you well and said they hope to continue to work with you for a long time."

Bobby took a few moments to take all that in. He felt touched, but reluctantly so. This is getting a little too close to *them*. And too quick. But thinking about the forty hours a week he spent in that government job unappreciated, putting up with the assholes, the politics, week after week all year round, overcame his reluctance and he reached for the envelope. He casually slid it out of sight in his coat pocket.

"Thank you," he said, now thinking how right they are. Nobody's going to be short-changing anybody around here anymore. Anybody wants something out of Bobby Grundell, he pays for it, buys it, for a price.

"Tell them it's good doing business with them," he added, "and I will continue to do business with them."

Ahmed decided now it's time they leveled with each other inside out.

"I want to tell you something, Bobby," he started out.

"Go ahead," Bobby prompted softly. They spoke in low voices and showed no animated movement or expression on their faces. He noticed Ahmed's empty glass and signaled their server for another round.

"You never asked me this but I know it's on your mind, you've wondered about it."

"Right so far, but let me hear how right you are."

"I'm not one of them," Ahmed said practically without moving his lips. "Not initially. And I'd still like to consider myself not one of them, even if Kamal and Omar thinks I am now which I hope they don't. I just work for the company, and that's the honest truth about my being with these people."

"Right you are," Bobby said. "I've wondered about that."

"I just work for wages, a salary, for a living. To pay the bills just like you. It could've been with another company. But I'm obligated to Abu Kamal and Mid-East Continental. I'm only on a working visa through their sponsorship, I told you that before. They dump me I'm out in the street on my own with no place to go. Either I go hiding or get out of the country."

"I understand. You don't have any problem about that with me. Why should you?"

"Thank you."

"Hey, none of my business. I don't work for the INS. And you're not an illegal alien. You're in the clear so you got nothing to worry about."

It was comforting to hear that, especially thinking of the time he waited for several months to hear about the status of his visa application, not knowing what to do in case it fell through. He remembered how sickening it was to go through the uncertainty of it all.

"Anything else you want to tell me?" asked Bobby.

"How about you take your turn for now," replied Ahmed. "Start with how you feel now especially about—" he nodded out the window in the direction of the Pentagon. "-after what happened."

Bobby took his time opening up. He finished his drink just as the server came with the next round.

"I feel the same as before it happened," he said coldly. "As a matter of fact, I feel the same about everything before it happened. That's the honest truth, mah man." He paused a moment to take a sip of the fresh drink, continued: "Now, should I ask you no such question so you won't tell me no lies?"

Ahmed picked up his drink, a wave of uneasiness weaving its way through him as he took a sip of the vodka tonic.

"You may ask but I can't give you a straight answer right now," he replied, wishing he could give as straightforward an answer as Bobby gave him, but he needed some time to sort out what he was feeling now before he could talk about them.

In the meantime, he did what Kamal had asked, something he was reluctant to do, which was to deliver a verbal message to Bobby. Another diskette, Kamal had said to him at the hotel for Bobby, by this weekend or early next week, would be greatly appreciated. Something for the Veteran's Day holiday which is coming soon in a couple of weeks.

Also, to satisfy Kamal's now growing concern with security, Ahmed worked out a code language with Bobby to be used during their telephone contacts. Particularly, Kamal had said, when Bobby is ready to make a drop.

'All set?' Ahmed would ask Bobby when Ahmed calls for the drop and Bobby would simply respond with a 'no' or a 'yes' for an answer. Bobby would say 'I'm all set' when he calls to indicate he has the goods and is ready to make the drop. For now, the drop site would be the same venue as the last—Fort Ward Park in Alexandria.

They sat facing each other without saying a word after Ahmed gave that to Bobby almost word for word. Bobby now sitting there not giving the world anything about what he was thinking with a calm, unaffected look on his face. Ahmed, just the opposite, as he appeared to restrain an inner agitation after he delivered the message and pulled away from the table to the back of his chair. He had a look in his eye that contemplated a multitude of thoughts he did not have the words for.

Later, when he was in bed going over those thoughts, one by one, he put them in words he derived from the depths of his spiritual beliefs, his lifelong presumptions about his faith in those beliefs, his personal convictions as a follower of Islam.

He was a Muslim first before anything else, a voice re-affirmed in himself once more in the silence of the night. And he did despise the Jews and the Christians for how they had been treating the brothers here in America, the Middle East, South Asia and all over the world. But he can not support righting one wrong with another. All those suicide bombings and acts of terrorism.

Not all Jews and Christians are enemies of the Faith. Not all Jews and Christians are evildoers. There are good ones as well as bad ones, and it's the same with the Muslims. Therefore, he can not condone these indiscriminate killings, the taking of lives without regard to one's guilt or innocence; these acts of destruction, by one or the other, driven by blind rage and hatred.

Hence, he had found it increasingly difficult—much more than before the attack—to face Abu Kamal Ramshallah when he asked to meet at the hotel two days ago. He thought of making excuses, ways to delay the continuity of his association with them till perhaps he gathered enough guts to sever his ties with them and just disappear. But the unlikelihood of this only made him see realistically what perilous circumstance he was in.

He found Kamal in unusually high spirits when he walked in to the hotel suite. Lively and forthcoming. He was happy. Happy that, he saw quickly, many he presumed were enemies of Islam, people whose belief differed with theirs, were destroyed.

There were two other men in the room, younger men closer to Ahmed's age—thirty and up. They looked equally pleased. Both were naturalized U.S. citizens and raised in America, he learned later.

One was Mustapha Khan, a tall, dark Egyptian-American. He was a powerfully built man whose feature was defined by a hooked nose and deep-set eyes that focused at you intently. He looked like a foreigner on a tourist visa. Ahmed was used to seeing people who looked like that, in Pakistan, Egypt where he had traveled once for several weeks and even here in North America. If he saw him again out in the street somewhere, Ahmed wouldn't know it was him.

The other, a Syrian-American, was the opposite. Light complexioned, handsome, well-educated. Everything about Samir Osmani, from his external appearance, mannerisms and speech was mainstream white America. He *is* an American, but not the stars-and-stripes, mom's-apple-pie type; not inside with what he held in his heart and mind as a Muslim, Ahmed would realize later.

Food and drink were ordered in the suite. They were celebrating. It was clear that the three men had a kind of fellowship he did not yet share but into which they were drawing him, especially Kamal.

He tried to blend in, loosen up, but in the three hours he was with them, he couldn't get comfortable especially with the two younger men. They took turns speaking to him and when they did, it was only to scrutinize him, one part of him at a time, not to show their confidence in his presence and to open up. Kamal made up for the distance which appeared to be building up between him and all of them, repeatedly complimenting him on the good work he had done with the company including the time he was in Detroit.

The deal with Bobby came up ultimately and it was then that he understood why he was summoned to the hotel and realized the value they placed on the deal more than he or Bobby thought.

"A little something extra for you," Kamal said while Mustapha and Samir were away at a distance in the room, handing him the first of the envelopes, "for the good work you're doing for the company."

He took the envelope with some hesitation, surprised. The two men looked through the corner of their eyes not at the envelope but at Ahmed's expression.

"And this for our friend Bobby," added Kamal, giving him the second envelope.

After Ahmed left, the two younger men took no time letting Kamal know what they thought.

"I don't trust him," said Mustapha Khan.

"I think he's a risk," added Samir Osmani.

"He's harmless," countered Kamal. "He would do anything I tell him, no questions asked. And what made you think that of him?"

Mustapha, speaking in earnest: "He wasn't among us. He didn't appear to be one of us, like he didn't want to come any closer."

"You didn't look too friendly towards him either," replied Kamal.

"We didn't want to open up before he did. We don't know him," Samir said.

"I've told you everything I know about him since he first came to us in Detroit," said Kamal. "His time was running out in Canada and he had no place else to go. No money, no help from anyone. And he'd rather be eating crumbs under my table before he even thinks of going back to Pakistan, he told me, in so many words. He hangs by the thread of that work visa we got for him with our petition."

"That's not the point, Abu Kamal," Samir said, now looking more thoughtfully serious. "Sure you got him on a short leash, but what matters is what's inside the man. You don't have that, you don't have a leash on him. He's fair game. He could turn given a better offer by someone else."

"Our Commander Omar himself who raised you two, taught you, took care of you and shielded you against the infidels, against these damn Jews and American warmongers, he trusted him, and this Bobby Grundell!" Kamal suddenly exploded causing the two to inch back some. "Don't you think he has the intelligence to know what's inside these men enough to trust them as much as he did?"

He snorted and bristled as he drew a deep breath, drilled a fierce look at each of them before turning to the window with the view of the commercial spread of Tysons Corner along Leesburg Pike. Mustapha, the more impulsive one, moved towards him to continue the argument but Samir held him with a hand on his shoulder.

Everyone held his place in silence. It was Kamal who spoke again two minutes later. He turned back to them and asked: "So you don't think he is one to be trusted. Then what would you have us do?"

He was looking at one and then the other as he spoke and ended up addressing Samir last. So it was Samir who responded.

"Learn more about him," he said. "Not what he had done where he was before, but what he does now where he is and where he goes."

Kamal listened to that grudgingly, expecting to hear more but Samir wasn't going to say anything else and was just waiting for his reaction.

"You mean keep an eye on him," he said. "Put him under surveillance."

"Yes," Samir said.

"I'd be glad to do it, if you'd let me, Abu Kamal," Mustapha said.

"You would, uh?"

"Yes. I think brother Samir is right. This we need to do, or we could face some very grave consequences if there is even a single possibility that this man may turn against us."

Kamal turned back to the window, this time head down between his shoulders. It took another two minutes before he turned around and said: "We have a very good deal in place, a direct contact with a prized access to sources of classified federal government data. And he's cheap, and easy to deal with."

"I understand the value of the information we're dealing with here, sir," said Mustapha. "The more reason we should exercise extra caution. Let me do it, Abu Kamal."

"Very well. But be careful you don't ruin a good thing we have going here. And I hope you don't prove us wrong about it."

CHAPTER 11

▼

Most of the people who signed the letter protesting the creation and funding of Leon Justice's position were members of the American Federation of Government Employees. One of them, Elga Bailey, a 42-year old paralegal specialist, was a union steward. As such, she had agreed to take the letter, through the chief steward, to the union president who after studying it took no time to deliver the copy to the Treasury Department EEO, the copy to the Inspector General's office, and the copy to Milton Pheasant, Chief of the Interstate Logistics Division, the office which officially employed Leon Justice. The rest of the copies, Elga herself sent to the other addressees. Any response to the letter or correspondence to the Division staff would be addressed to the EEO and AFGE who had concurred to arbitrate.

It was now four days since the letter went out, eleven since Milton Pheasant made the announcement of Leon filling the position and officially introduced the man to the Division staff. Today, Thursday, was the second time everybody was required to turn in the weekly work activity report to him. And once again, everybody was pissed; many like Eddie Mahone, Max Poysen and Robert Grundell could hardly contain their resentment.

And then as if to deliberately aggravate them further, Leon Justice, late in the afternoon after going over many of the work activity reports, called a select number of people to come in to his office. It wasn't anything critical, he said. He just wanted to talk about the current high-visibility assignments some people are working on right now. He asked them to be in his office in half an hour.

Eddie Mahone and Robert Grundell met in the hallway on their way to the meeting two minutes before the time. They were moving slowly, clearly not overly eager to get to where they were going.

"I want to strangle that son of a bitch," Eddie said.

"You're gonna have to get in line, after me," replied Robert.

"He starts bossing us around, I'm just gonna give him the finger and walk out."

"Anybody heard anything about the letter?" asked Robert.

"I called Elga this morning. She said she doesn't have anything yet. She'll let everybody know as soon as something breaks."

"Think the asshole knows about it by now?"

"That's an interesting thought. I hope so," said Eddie. "And if he does, let's see what he says about it."

While people stepped into Leon Justice's office, all seven of them and not one turning any kind of a face to him with more than a civil nod after being motioned to a seat, Milton Pheasant, his boss the Division Chief alone in his office, pulled out his copy of the protest letter for about the fourth time and went over it again. He read it two days ago and had been putting off breaking the news to the rest of management. Including Leon.

Months ago, he didn't think it was a good idea to go ahead with funding the position just so the Division wouldn't have to 'fess up having a surplus and possibly cutting down its allocation when he submitted his budget request this fiscal year. But his buddy Herod Hardin said we got 'our man Leon' who really had nothing to do and it would be nice if we could finally find a slot for him where he might actually look good.

That was another thing. He had heard word around the branches of the Division about Leon Justice and not many of them were too complimentary. So, now look what he's got on his hands. The AFGE, the EEO, and God knows who else might jump in on this thing. In most parts, he agreed with what the letter contained. That job is a make-work position. What he should've done, now he was thinking, was move quick, before the budget deadline came around, and distribute the surplus through all the items in the Division budget. Simple.

He picked up the phone and dialed Herod Hardin's number on the intercom.

"Yeah, Milt. What's up?" asked Hardin.

"Got a minute? My office, please."

Next, he called Leon Justice who said he's having a staff meeting and asked if he could come after. The Division Chief said it's fine, tomorrow morning will be just as good.

He put down the phone and sat back in the leather executive chair, holding on to the letter on an outstretched arm as if ready to crumple it in a second and toss it in the trash can. Then the phone rang. His admin assistant outside said she had a man from the Treasury's Inspector General Office on hold on line one.

A man spoke, identified himself by name and position and just as Herod Hardin appeared at the door, the man on the line said:

"Sir, I have here a copy of a letter, delivered to us through the AFGE and the EEO, regarding a staffing matter brought up by the employees in your Division. Would you happen to be aware of this letter?"

"Yes," he answered promptly, motioning Hardin to a seat at one end of the desk.

"Sir, we've routed it through our reviewers and have come to the disposition that this is a matter that merits an inquiry by the Inspector General's Office. Therefore, we would like to discuss the matter with you when you are ready."

As Robert Grundell thought walking into Leon's office, his mind would be made up many more times than before to do everything he planned to do, by the time he walked back out. Eddie Mahone, he noticed, was visibly red in the face with exasperation halfway through the meeting which didn't have to last all of the one whole hour that it did. Max Poysen looked the same.

Nobody said anything unless Leon Justice asked one a question to which the person gave a curt, direct answer. There were long silences, awkward moments, when Leon paused and waited for somebody to pitch in something. Anything.

Nobody did. Not once.

The only time somebody spoke to him voluntarily was over the phone, when it rang once. He excused himself while he picked it up and spoke in a low, subservient voice to the caller. Probably his wife, or his boss, thought Robert.

From beginning to end, it appeared everybody was just waiting to walk back out again as quietly as they walked in. In between, Leon carried on—as the seven senior program analysts he gathered in his office expected he would—with what amounted to pulling rank, making them aware who he was to them, to the entire Division; making clear what his duties were which behooved many of them, he emphasized, especially those working on 'high-priority', 'high-visibility' tasks to be answerable to him directly, not just to their respective branch chiefs.

From the way he sounded, everyone had the impression that he hadn't known or heard about the letter from anybody. They hated every minute of it, sitting there in front of him, waiting to be spoken to, answer his questions, under his control and waiting to be dismissed—at his pleasure.

This guy is a total asshole and has no place in this office or anywhere in the entire Department of the Treasury, said Eddie Mahone's eyes when he turned to Max Poysen at one time, and then to Robert Grundell.

No doubt about that, said Max's eyes back. Robert thought the same.

Robert hurried back to his office as soon as he got out of there, eager to logon the computer and get busy. But it was past his quitting time. Fucking Leon ate up the rest of his afternoon for nothing.

The next day, he took care of legitimate work, duties and responsibilities for which the U.S. government paid him a salary, timing his activity so that he was free the last two hours in the afternoon. In that time, he cruised through the classified files throughout most of the major federal agencies, looking for logistics security data connected with Veteran's Day events throughout the country, including Hawaii and Alaska.

It was a tedious process, much like surfing the internet for references to some obscure artifacts belonging to an obscure period in history. He was interrupted at one time by a phone call from Eddie Mahone.

"Got a call from Elga," Eddie announced. "The IG has reviewed the letter and they're setting up a meeting to discuss it with Milton Pheasant and company, next week sometime."

Good, he said to Eddie. Looks like things are starting to *happen*.

It better, said Eddie, 'cause the next time that dickhead calls us in to his office to pull that kind of show, I'm not showing up. He wants to see me, he'll have to come to my office, sit and wait till I got time to pay attention to him.

Shortly before he quit for the day, Robert Grundell noticed something else that had started to *happen* and happen, on the computer monitor, more frequently. A userid he first saw the day before while browsing the OCDL access-log database had shown up again today several more times. xxxxJKB.

He would have known what government agency it belonged to but the first four characters which was the standard agency system ID was encrypted. So he called Max Poysen.

"Can you break it?" he asked Max after telling him about it.

"Authorized staff can, like…me." Max replied.

"What's the big deal?"

"Confidentiality, secrecy, security, all that. That's what we're all about here, otherwise we wouldn't be doing the work we're doing."

"Max, I need a lecture I'll sign up for some classes and go back to school."

"Alright, alright, Bob, what else do you need?"

"Well, what do you do to break it?"

"Simple. Just get authorization to use TRIDEX," answered Max. "I can put in a request for you to the NSA guy…"

"That same guy I have to call everyday to access the TSL bin?"

"Yeah, that guy."

"Never mind. Guy's a prick," Robert said irritably and Max agreed.

So he just asked Max to look at the access-log database and search for xxxxJKB.

"You want to know who this guy is?" Max said, looking at the access-log records on the screen with the userid, several of them dated yesterday and today. "Hold on."

After about thirty seconds, he told Robert: "Name is Jerome K. Bolden. He's with the ISD, FBI."

"What's ISD?"

"Investigative Services Division," replied Max.

"Hey, Max," said Robert.

"Yeah?"

"What are we to do without you, man? Thanks."

CHAPTER 12

▼

"**I manage** a chain of gas stations here in Virginia," Ahmed had told Rosie Fletcher at the club during their double date with Bobby and Rosie's friend Paula last Saturday. And that was about all she remembered of everything he told her. There was so much going on at the club with the music and dancing and drinking that it was hard to carry on a conversation and stick with it longer than two minutes.

"We still have so much to talk about yet," Ahmed said when they dropped her off her apartment on Armistead Street in Alexandria.

"Most definitely," she replied.

So at the end of the evening, they agreed to pick up where they left off, the following Saturday. Tonight.

He didn't expect to feel any different seeing her again for the third time. But when he picked her up at seven, he felt a kind of excitement he never felt before.

The thought of him and her alone together the whole evening through dinner, and then movie later as they planned earlier, now struck him as such a pristine idea. He didn't—couldn't—even begin to imagine the possibilities that lay beyond the evening.

With this excitement, however, came rising in his consciousness, the back of his neck as real a pain as it had been, the other aspects of his life in America, starting with the clutch Abu Kamal and the Organization had on him. How truly peaceful and orderly, and happy, his life would have been here in America had such complications not been a part of it, he thought while he escorted Rosie Fletcher to her seat in a Thai restaurant in the Shirlington Village of Arlington.

He shoved all that aside the best he could and tried to enjoy the evening. What will happen will happen. Beyond doing your level best, he said to himself, there's nothing else you can do to prevent it, so live and enjoy life now while you can no matter how it turns out later.

"So, you're a manager," Rosie blurted out, rehashing what she could from last weekend while they worked on their drinks waiting for their dinner. "Big time, eh?"

Ahmed was still getting used to her openness. She held back little in the way of being sociable. Only thing was, she didn't seem to remember much of what she'd said or heard. So Ahmed practically had to start over with everything from their first encounter.

"Actually—an assistant manager," he recanted slightly, "although most days, which is almost everyday, I act as the manager since the boss is hardly ever in. He's always out somewhere making the rounds of the stations all over the area."

"Which suits you just fine," she threw in, her head going from side to side in a jolly way, "'cause you like being the boss. The man in charge."

"You might say that," he admitted, smiling coyly at her.

"So what do you actually do at work? Just point and tell everybody else what to do?"

Ahmed laughed. "Sometimes, yes," he said. "But there are other things I have to do myself."

"Like what?"

"Well, like, um…keeping track of stock inventories everyday. Things we sell at the service stations. Including gas, of course. A little bit of accounting and payroll. Personnel staffing. We have a lot of turnover and we have to constantly recruit new employees."

"Busy man, you are. So you like your job?"

"Yes. Very much."

"Lovely," she said. "That's just lovely."

He liked the way she said the word in that very British way, coming from her mother, she had told him, who is half Brit and half Indian, an outcome of a World War II romance between a young English diplomat and a lovely maiden from Jaipur City, in the state of Rajasthan. She was born in India, grew up in England and married an American she met in New York where her parents had taken up residence while her father worked in the British Consulate there later.

She herself, Rosie, was born and raised in Pittsburgh, Pennsylvania, a half American, a quarter Brit and a quarter Indian.

Their conversation progressed during dinner through most of what they had touched on the week before, and some even the time before when they first met. It had been Ahmed's impression early since last week that she, born in the early seventies, had been one of those over-indulged although well-mannered children of the upper middle-class American suburban society. Watching her with her carefree behavior, body language and a playful air about her, he became more certain of this as the evening wore on.

Another impression he had of which he was even more certain now was that she honestly enjoyed his company, and liked him. Just about every other time she raised her drink to her lips, she extended it to touch his glass as if to make a toast for their lovely evening together. And when she spoke, she touched the back of his hand for his attention even when their mouths were full. Thus, he did not completely dismiss the idea that he may successfully invite her to his apartment for a cup of tea after the movie.

From a distance of three tables away such as where special agent Richard Bartley and John Jacobs sat, one might think that the couple was thoroughly intimate, that they weren't only on their third time out but thirty times over many months. Jacobs sat facing Bartley who sat against the wall. To his left three tables away sat Rosie facing his side where he had his ultra-sensitive listening earpiece tuned in to every word she and Ahmed spoke between them..

"So, what's going on over there?" asked Bartley, the words coming out of small gaps in his mouth as he chewed on a piece of the spring roll on his plate. "Anything about crashing a jumbo jet on the White House any time soon?"

"No such luck so far," said Jacobs, pouring himself a refill of the jasmine tea from the kettle, listening to the couple. "She's working him up fast and he's slow catching on. She definitely wants it. This guy could get laid tonight if he knew how."

"I go home to Pittsburgh at least twice a year," Jacobs heard her say now along with the clatter of her fork on her plate. "Christmas and Thanksgiving. And how often do you visit India?"

Ahmed raised his head from his plate chewing on a lump of boiled potato. "Not often. In fact, not at all."

"Oh, so sorry. But don't you miss home?"

"Rosie, I'm not from India," he said, hurrying to clear his mouth so he could straighten her out once and for all about his person. "I'm not an Indian. I wish I were, now that I know you. Even partly, like you."

"Oh, thank you. Sorry, but I thought—"

"I'm from Pakistan. And, yes, I do miss home occasionally. But only that part of it worth missing. However, I've started growing roots here in America, and this makes home seem more and more distant."

"America grows on you very quickly, don't you think so?"

"I can't deny that."

"My mother had said the same thing many times, since she moved here from London after marrying my father, she told me. So say, what's it like living in Pa-a-kista-an?" Her part British accent never ceased to fascinate him. Once in a while it would sound to him like she would abandon her American accent and go British completely for a spell.

"Wretched. Quite wretched," he said, mimicking her accent some.

"Ow, c'mon. You're joking, of course."

"Well, there's good and there's bad in every place, I grant you that. But in Pakistan, it seems the only good it has is good only for itself, and even that in the end isn't good at all."

"You're talking about it being one of the nuclear powers of the world, I presume," she said which surprised him momentarily.

"Exactly. On top of that add all the political and religious extremism, fanaticism that go on in there, not to mention the territorial conflict with its big neighbor."

Hearing that, Jacobs said to Bartley: "I got news for you and the bosses at the office—this guy doesn't sound like a suicide hijacker or any kind of a terrorist at all."

"So what does he sound like?" asked Bartley, now working the phad thai noodle on his plate slowly. They took their time with everything starting with choosing the table they wanted to be at, once they saw the couple seated. It was their plan to finish after them so once seated, they ordered drinks first—tea for both, then the spring roll appetizer before deciding minutes later on the entree.

"I don't know," answered Jacobs. "I can tell you what he's not—a killer, a nut, a fanatic, a date-rapist. One thing I know he is—a dumb guy when it comes to women. What did they say at headquarters about how long he's been here from Pakistan?"

"A little over three years. First two in Canada."

"No wonder. He hasn't been weaned from the culture in the old country," Jacobs said.

"I love going to the movies," Rosie's voice came loud into his electronic earpiece. It's an amazing piece of device. Didn't use a bug to listen from. Worked just like a hearing aid except it was smaller and less noticeable; fit inside the ear snugly. And it had a few added features that made it perhaps twenty times more powerful by using a sonar homing technology which allowed the listener to adjust the breadth and distance of coverage so that only the sound you're interested in could be selectively collected and funneled into the eardrum.

Jacobs hadn't seen much use of it, unlike his older partner, so Bartley let him do all the listening tonight. Should this Ahmed Khalifa turn out to be hot, headquarters had told them, the next step which should make this assignment less stressful for them would be to stick a bug in the guy's car. And if he got even hotter, wire his apartment and tap his home phone.

What got them really hopping over at headquarters as a result of work on Ahmed Khalifa was the company he worked for. Just the day before, the report file on MidEast Continental came in from the Detroit field office. There's definitely 'a lot of ground to cover' in that report file, said the head of CID in agreement with their section chief.

Contraband shipping in arms and drugs, money-laundering, hostile foreign connections and who knows what the hell else, with an Arab-held company like this? Energy trading and shipping. Sure, it could be totally legit—its stock closed at $21^{5/8}$ yesterday—but that's what makes it more viable to be involved, and be above suspicion, in illegitimate activities.

So it's profiling, stereotyping, whatever. But what's the alternative to fighting terrorism? Who else is there for the role of suspect after what we've seen beginning with 9/11, and now 10/24 just a week ago?

Two names figured prominently in the report file on the company, for now simply by the frequency of their occurrence in the papers. Mahmud Mahran, the CEO, and Abu Kamal Ramshallah, a vice-president who appeared to function as a PR man, liaison, primary contact man. He traveled a lot, all over the country but mostly the east coast. Here in the DC-Baltimore area, Philadelphia and New York.

So, yesterday, headquarters added an order to agents Bartley and Jacobs to make sure they take notes if and when Khalifa made mention of either one of those names. And with that, they reiterated being thorough about who he made contact with anywhere, particularly people from Detroit and especially those two.

So far, they'd only reported on Khalifa's personal contact with his neighbor Robert Grundell. And so far Grundell looked straight, according to CID—42, fifteen years civil service, the last ten with Treasury, divorced, no kids, single, born and raised Cleveland, Ohio, no police record, no drugs. Clean. Heck, this town's populated with Feds, like us, Jacobs told Bartley. That whole apartment complex they live in is probably full of them. It's possible nine of ten of Khalifa's neighbors could all be Feds. You or I could've been living there, he said.

After tonight, they would have another one to report in Rosie Fletcher. But were it not against orders, they could very well skip her unless Khalifa was using her—or was planning to—for something devious and evil other than just for sex after the dinner-movie routine which Jacobs doubted would happen.

"You may be right," Bartley was now saying to Jacobs about what he thinks of Khalifa. "The guy seems harmless, but—you can't go by looks. For all you know, he changes to a dozen different personalities under different settings. We could be looking at whatzis name? This guy the Bureau doesn't want anybody talking about much?"

"Saladin."

"Yeah, him.'

"Could be," said Jacobs, shrugging. "You can't be too sure about any one of these guys nowadays. Even those who grew up here."

Across the aisle against the opposite wall, someone else had a similar thought about Ahmed Khalifa. Someone who grew up here and had the appearance of 'one of these guys': dark complexioned, deep-set, piercing eyes, South Asian-Middle Eastern countenance. But his thought about not being too sure about Ahmed Khalifa was of a different sort—not on the question of Ahmed's capacity for violence, murder and terrorism but more on the matter of his religious faith and practices, fundamentalism, adherence to cultural tradition, all of which right now Mustapha Khan, who had been keeping the couple in sight through the corner of his eye from four tables away across the aisle, doubted very much in the way Ahmed Khalifa was living his life in America.

This Pakistani, he was thinking more strongly after observing Ahmed's behavior with that airhead of an American girl he's with, is not one of us. He is not to be trusted. He is a brother lost to the West, to this mundane and materialistic American culture that values nothing, believes in nothing but the dollar and all the lust and greed and instant gratification it can afford them.

"Sabah," he said across the table to his companion, Sabah Ahmaddi, a 23-year old sleeper and one of the survivors of Operation North 27. "I don't care to see anything else about them for now. I've seen enough tonight. Let's get out of here."

"I'll catch our server when he comes by," said Sabah, hurrying up to polish off his bowl of vegetarian noodle soup.

"What time is the show?" Jacobs heard Rosie say as if she was sitting next to him and Bartley.

"Nine-thirty," replied Ahmed, glancing at his wristwatch.

"Do we have time?" Rosie asked, enjoying the last of her combination seafood dinner.

"Plenty. Give you an idea, we could drive home—to your place, or mine— have sex, jump in the shower together, dry up, come back here, over there across the street to that ice cream parlor, have some ice cream and still make it to the movie and get good seats."

Bartley was seriously alarmed when he saw Jacobs jerk his head straight up at him, a face looking at first horrified, then surprised, exhilarated and amused, followed by a laugh which he contained in the hand he cupped over his mouth.

"Ahmed, dear God almighty!" Rosie gasped, not believing how Ahmed just spoke to her. "Where did all that come from?"

A big jovial smile broke on Ahmed's face, his head bobbing back and forth mischievously. "I just wanted to impress upon you that I'm not as conservative as you obviously thought I was all along. If I wanted to, I could be as American as any apple pie there is you can find although I may not lookit."

"Now, re-a-al-ly?"

"But of course I was only kidding."

"Why, I didn't think you were."

Jacobs held his hand out to Bartley to hush him up for a moment. He wanted to hear clearly where this would lead up to. This guy Ahmed may actually be a sleazeball swinger, not at all the puritan Muslim he sounded earlier. As American as any apple pie...! Geez!

"Well, I'm sorry if you took me there seriously for a moment," Ahmed said. "But you certainly may—if you wish."

Rosie broke out laughing, amused at this totally absurd line she never heard before from any guy she'd ever dated in her entire life.

"Now, that—" she started saying, catching her breath, "that is just absolutely marvelous. Very clever, and funny!"

Ahmed didn't say anything but simply joined her laughing.

"But wouldn't that be cutting it a little too close?" she continued. "Sex and ice cream dessert? Oh, and the shower."

"Not actually," he replied. "The movie theater is just across the street from here."

"Oh, I see. Well, I'll tell you what. Why don't we do one thing at a time. Let's have the ice cream now, and we'll see about the others after the movie. But no promises."

"Goddamn!" Jacobs almost said aloud instead of murmuring to himself.

"The hell is going on?" asked Bartley.

"This guy is a pro!" said Jacobs excitedly. "I couldn't have been more wrong about him. He just played her into his hands, and she practically told him she'll go to bed with him after the movie."

"How did he—" Bartley started to say just as two men led by a tall dark one, coming up the aisle on the way out, fumbling with his wallet, not looking ahead, got too close to Jacobs and bumped him on the shoulder, almost knocking Jacobs out of his seat.

"Pardon me, sir," Mustapha Khan apologized earnestly, hanging on to the back of Jacob's chair and helping him right himself on it "My fault. Totally my fault."

"It's alright," said Jacobs, looking up at the man as he pulled himself back in the chair. For a moment, he thought he was looking at Ahmed who finally got wind they had been spying on him and decided to confront them. But—no, this one was a lot taller and built heavier, not at all the light frame of Ahmed. "No harm done. I should have been sitting closer to the table rather than halfway across the aisle."

"Not at all," replied Mustapha, looking across the table at Bartley with a dreadful smile, and then back at Jacobs. These assholes look like plainclothes local cops, he thought. They look gay too, especially that one against the wall with the high shiny forehead and a girlish curl at a corner of his mouth. "I should've been looking where I'm going. I'm sorry, and have a good evening, gentlemen."

"You too," said Jacobs and, once the two men were out of sight, commented to Bartley: "What's with this place tonight? It's crawling with them kind of guys."

A few minutes later, the two special agents watched their quarry go by along the aisle, out of the restaurant and across the street to the ice cream parlor.

Jacobs told Bartley, practically word for word, exactly how Khalifa played Rosie into his hands. And as they watched the couple across the street, he said: "I should've learned to use that kind of line a long time ago. It works."

"You don't know what she'll decide after the movie," said Bartley. "I don't know about you but I'm calling it a day when we get out of here.."

"Shucks, I sure would like to see him drop her off at her door later," said Jacobs. "Find out which way he goes—back to his car or into her apartment."

Had they stayed with them to the end, Jacobs would have found out how wrong he was about which way Khalifa goes after the movie. First off, they wouldn't have seen him drop her off at her door.

At eleven fifteen, going south on Shirley Highway in Arlington, Ahmed said to Rosie: "I live nearby here. Ten minutes, depending on how lucky you get with the traffic lights, and traffic."

"I don't imagine there'd be a lot of traffic this time of night," said Rosie.

"Well then let's find out how right you are."

"And how lucky you get, with the lights."

"Yes, that too," said Ahmed, his head suddenly filling with excitement, numbing his normal senses. He couldn't believe everything he pulled now seemed to be working.

Thus, he got off at the next exit, Route 7 West. She didn't say anything, knowing clearly then that they weren't headed to her place but his. They rode in silence for the next few minutes, then shortly before they reached his apartment complex on Highland Street, Rosie asked: "You wouldn't happen to keep an extra toothbrush, would yuh? Ever since I was small, I got into this habit of brushing my teeth as soon as I get out of bed in the morning."

It would have been a perfect right turn to Highland Street as he had done hundreds of times before, but having lost most of his composure after hearing what Rosie said, he drove the right wheel halfway up the curb, pulled back left a little too far and nearly went on a head-on collision with a car coming out before he got back on his lane and headed straight to the apartment parking lot.

CHAPTER 13

▼

For three days, Jerome Bolden debated with himself whether or not to make the stakeout request to CID. Is it too soon to do this? Is he being too hyped up by what he'd seen since last week? Maybe that's normal with some of those people at Treasury—surfing the gov net for classified government files the way he sees them do, much the same as he's doing gathering data. Some kind of data for their agency use.

Gathering data? What kind of data? And for what use?

Any kind of activity you deem suspicious, now he recalled everybody being told in the emergency meeting by their chief of the Investigative Services Division hours after the 10/24 attack at the Pentagon, initiate action to investigate. Use your judgment. The price is too high to pay for a near-miss or any slip-up no matter how unlikely you think your hunch may be.

It was one thing to assume someone is an authorized user with at least a TS clearance and not a hacker. It was another to question what he or she is doing and why. He rated their IT security analysts highly so it was his hunch that what he might be looking for, if there is anybody out there doing bad things, would not be a hacker but an insider.

After some intense monitoring of the daily activities of users at several agencies, a pattern began to emerge with selected ones. He took notice of several at Navy's Personnel Command (Bupers), State Department's Near East Affairs office of the Undersecretary for Political Affairs, Commerce Department's Bureau of Industry and Security, and Treasury's Office of Civil Defense Logistics. He got particularly curious at first about two userids each in State, Commerce and Treasury.

The next day, after more hours of tracking accesses, he decided to drop the two in Commerce and one in State. He kept monitoring the remaining one in State and the two in Treasury. He picked up on several others here and began keeping an eye on their activities too. One of them caught his interest the most— xxxxLTJ, which TRIDEX identified as Leon T. Justice.

Most of them were with ILD/OCDL—Interstate Logistics Division of the Office of Civil Defense Logistics, the Treasury office that mapped out security for significant domestic public events such as those at major infrastructure sites: water and power plants, transportation and communication stations; directed planning and deployment during such times and at such places in cooperation with other federal intelligence and security services.

Heck, thought Bolden, we might as well be checking up on the Bureau itself.

The government was right about consolidating a lot of those agency offices that did mostly the same things, into a central agency. But, still, there were a few like this OCDL that remained intact under Treasury, much the same as many parts of the Bureau remaining under Justice because of mission activities that had become highly specialized under the Department.

Looking at the query reports he had pulled out the past few days, he felt disturbed by the idea of putting somebody—one who could very well be a Fed just like him—under investigation. Somebody with duties and responsibilities similar to his, enjoying the same trust by the government, becoming a subject of an FBI stakeout.

If we can't trust us, he thought with a sinking feeling in his guts, who can we?

He started feeling a shortness of breath, a heartsickness, and thoughts of desperation ran in his mind: Goddammit, what are we to do? What am *I* to do?

Shit, you're one of the good guys looking for the bad guys out there. Doesn't matter who they are, who they work for and where they are—the guy two doors down the hall or two thousand miles from you. You got your orders. Do it!

At that point, early morning yesterday, he made the request for a stakeout at OCDL. Two special agents were fielded immediately in a matter of hours: agent Nancy Schneider, 30, an IT specialist ex-Navy lieutenant now four years with the Bureau, and Frank DiPaolo, 35, small-arms specialist, ex-Army staff sergeant, now five years with the Bureau. Good professional people. Arranged through the Treasury Undersecretary and its IG and installed through the 'backdoor', they were Treasury staff called in to OCDL's D.C. headquarters from one of its regional offices for interim assignments.

Their orders were to target their investigation on a number of personnel. They were to refer to each subject by code, never by the person's name. Leon Justice was code JS001 (Justice-Subject one), Robert Grundell—code GS008, Pacifico Inocentes, a hardworking Filipino-American systems analyst in the Deployment Division who was among others who showed up in the top twenty-five percent in Jerome Bolden's query report extracts—code IS004.

*   *   *   *

Damn, I was right! thought Robert Grundell as he browsed the access-log database. The spooks are out in federal cyberspace checking up on what people are doing, what they're looking at.

Can't blame them after what happened recently. They're sniffing for anything they can get their hands on. Any lead, clue, pattern that could possibly point someplace, at a group of people or an individual, a corporation, a government agency, to cut a profile, a cross section. Anything to give them the smallest reason to focus their attention on a subject.

He didn't worry himself about it, thinking he was now clean, thanks to Max Poysen. He's one step ahead of them and he'd just have to stay that way. Clean and one step—or two, ahead of them.

It was a few minutes before noon. He and Ahmed Khalifa had been playing cat-and-mouse on the phone for an hour now. First Ahmed called when Robert wasn't in and left a message. Then Robert returned the call twenty minutes later while Ahmed was out. He called again fifteen minutes later and left a second message when the answering machine picked up again.

A few minutes later, his phone rang but it wasn't Ahmed. It was Eddie Mahone bringing bad news which made Robert more eager to hear from Ahmed. Milton Pheasant met with the IG and the president of the AFGE Local yesterday. Elga Bailey was there too. She 's now officially representing the Division staff. Good for her, said Eddie Mahone. Good for us.

The bad news is, from Elga's report which she'll email to the Division later in the day, management is keeping Leon Justice in his position, saying that there's nothing they can do about it now because the position is funded, the FY budget has been approved and money allocated for the position is already money spent even if the incumbent, Leon Justice, has not actually received it all in his annual GS-14 salary of $91,308.

"Fuck!" said Robert Grundell.

"There's more," Eddie Mahone hurried to say, and not too enthusiastically. "Milton Pheasant did agree to review the position to determine what to do about it—next year."

"And who's to say they're even going to talk about it next year?" said Robert. "Meantime, we're stuck with that asshole Leon for a whole year, at least. Or permanently."

"That's not a sure thing yet. That's just what Pheasant is saying—that they can't do anything about it now. The IG for one doesn't agree and suggests a review of the need for the position. Meaning, let the Division staff's unanimous voice—the voice of the people, so to speak—be heard, before anybody makes any decision."

"And what about the union?" asked Robert. "What did they have to say?"

"The union said something even better—take it up to the Undersecretary of the Treasury for OCDL. After all, the Undersecretary is the office that approved the budget with the funding for the position."

"Good move."

"I agree," said Eddie Mahone. "So, the battle is on. We haven't lost. And there's a good chance we'll prevail over these assholes especially when the Office of Special Counsel gets in on the action. Elga says she'll follow up on the copy of the letter we sent them."

Robert Grundell sat thinking hard after they hung up, thinking what it would have been like if he had happened to be one among those, like Leon, who belonged in the office power circle, protected, promoted and recognized even for the smallest piece of work he ever accomplished in the Division. He found he couldn't even begin to imagine this. His loathing and hatred of them were simply too powerful to consider being one of them even for one moment, going out to lunch with them, skipping some Friday afternoon to play golf with them, pulling for each other, making each other look good at the expense of others.

Motherfuckers!

The phone rang.

"Hey, government worker," Ahmed said and his voice couldn't have sounded sweeter to Bobby's ear at the moment. "Guess what?"

"Ahmed, mah man," Bobby said happily. "What?"

"I got laid last weekend."

"You're lying."

"Hey, do I look like a Washington politician? A government worker?"

"Watch it, mah man. Watch it! Tell me, did you really?" Bobby asked nicely.

"Yes!"

"I take it you're talking about that sixty-eight-year old nextdoor neighbor of yours."

The two of them cracked up at the same time. Ahmed waited impatiently, while Bobby enjoyed a good laugh, before boasting: "Rosie, mah man. Sweet, delicious Rosie."

"I don't believe you," said Bobby.

"Believe it, man. I'll tell you all about it later. But first I got to ask you something."

"Yeah, what?"

Ahmed took a short pause then asked: "All set?"

"Yes," replied Bobby, feeling the diskette sealed inside a 4-inch square opaque envelope in his coat pocket. He then looked at his wristwatch and said, "I got five minutes to twelve. See you there at 12:30, give or take. Is that alright with you?"

"Yes," replied Ahmed, looking at the time too on the PC monitor in his office. That should be enough time to pick up a burger on the way to the park, he thought.

Two days ago, he had just returned home in the morning from dropping Rosie off her place, feeling happy and as uncaring as he never felt before about anything that ever burdened him in his life. Then Abu Kamal Ramshallah called to summon him to a hotel in Baltimore.

It was a repeat of the meeting he had with them in the hotel in Chantilly, Virginia. Them being Abu Kamal and Rahim Akbar. When asked if he had settled on a routine with Bobby regarding the drop: their method of communicating, the venue, the preferred time and day, he said he had and told them when the next one will happen. Bobby had found what they asked for and would be ready to deliver in a couple of days within the time of day they worked out.

"Between 11:30 in the morning," he told them, "and 1:30 in the afternoon." The peak time block for lunchbreak in government offices, he said further, which makes a convenient time for both of them for a drop.

He explained also that Bobby didn't want to hang on to the data once he had them downloaded in a diskette. He wanted to make the drop immediately and be rid of it. It's getting somewhat thorny, he said, quoting Bobby, handling classified data since 10/24. Kamal then gave him a number to call immediately after the drop so they could send a pick-up right away.

"Very good. Very good," praised Rahim Akbar, "you can't be too careful nowadays. Take every precaution you can. You've both done very well. And, please, give our many thanks to Bobby once again."

"I will," said Ahmed, turning to face Rahim Akbar directly only for the second time since Chantilly. And for the first time, he confronted the question he had had in himself about the man who appeared to him the first time they met as someone in a position secondary to that of Kamal but later, especially now, seemed to be in command, someone Kamal obviously deferred to. He remembered how Kamal had introduced the man to him as one of the company's major stockholders. It sounded like a thin cover for something else, now he thought, and wondered who he really was to Kamal, the company and everyone else involved in MidEast Continental here and the Middle East.

He held his eyes steady on the man for a few moments, curious to see finally how they took to each other. Rahim Akbar did have that air of authority and power about him. Ahmed sensed it, felt it in the look in his eyes, the mirror of intelligence in them which he now saw the man played down while talking to him. There was distance between them though they were at arms reach.

He is definitely not the man, now Ahmed thought, he would have you believe he is. Unless perhaps you were someone he had known for a long long time. Someone close, someone he trusted. Rahim Akbar did not trust him, this he now knew.

There was something out of the ordinary about the man, one sensed especially in the presence of those who knew him well. He was also a handsome and attractive man, quite young-looking for a forty-year old globetrotting Islamic fundamentalist, teacher, educator of young Muslim minds, and supporter of worldwide reprisal and terrorism against America and the Judeo-Christian world. The man his American enemies, for lack of knowledge about his identity, had named Saladin.

"And when you do thank him for us," Kamal followed after Rahim Akbar, taking out a business envelope from his coat pocket, "give him this as well. His second paycheck including the pay statement, complete with all the deductions—social security, federal and state taxes—and company benefits. Tell him he's on the payroll and has nothing to worry about."

"I'm sure he'll appreciate this very much," Ahmed said.

He then left a minute later under the watchful eye of the men in the hotel suite, including Mustapha Khan who listened and watched from behind a curtain in a separate room.

"That man will eventually betray us, I tell you, Commander," he said to Omar Husain as soon as he came out. "He goes out with this…this American whore, watches those mind-rotting American TV shows and movies, consumes anything he wants of this western culture. He is totally absorbed outside of the Muslim way of life and…and everything we believe in and are fighting for."

Kamal raised a hand between the two men for calm. "We have no evidence he will betray us—"

"So we just wait till he had us all routed, bound hand and foot in prison?" Mustapha cut in vigorously.

"We can't just go by loose assumptions. Everything we do we take a chance in doing. We take some risks. We have to or we'll never get anything accomplished."

Omar Husain kept silent in all this with eyes cast down at his feet. He heard little of the words spoken before him by the two men while he recalled the image of Ahmed looking directly at him a few minutes ago: eyes seeking entry into his soul, trying to penetrate his mind, prying into his identity, asking what manner of a man this Rahim Akbar is.

Mustapha is right, he thought. That Pakistani is a risk that can not be taken lightly. He is like a pawn, there for the taking by any bidder, or one of his choosing. At the moment, he chooses to be on our side because it is to his personal benefit, not because he is of the Faith and a devoted follower of our lord prophet Mohammed. He is not a true defender of Islam.

So, what to do about him? For now, use him to our advantage, and carefully. Keep him in sight, he told the men before him.

Mustapha Khan was instructed to continue to spy on Ahmed Khalifa. Hide under his bed at night if you find it necessary, he was told. Listen to his dreams if you can, to know what's in his heart and mind. Go to the park on the day of the drop, precede him there, and the American Bobby. Watch every move, every gesture and listen well to every word you may be fortunate the wind carries to your ear.

In addition, should everything go well with the drop, he was told to go ahead and make the pick-up by calling either Kamal or Ahmed directly.

*   *   *   *

It was twenty after eleven when he arrived at Fort Ward Park. He drove in just a little above the 5-MPH speed limit on the one-way road that looped sixth-tenths of a mile counter-clockwise around the park. He kept his head low while he surveyed the surrounding, the few cars in the parking lots, the walkers and joggers, not many of them.

He drove the whole loop and came back to where he started to park in the lot behind the two-story Civil War museum facing the entry gate from Braddock Road. He was confident neither of them, Ahmed or Bobby, was in the park yet. He knew the car Ahmed drove—a four-year old silver metallic Toyota Corolla— and had its license plate number written down. He didn't know Bobby at all and couldn't wait to see the man in person. He was curious to see what an angry, dis-gruntled federal government worker looked like, a man who didn't give a shit about his country, his government, his people.

A woman walked by on the park road carrying a plastic poop-bag in one hand, in the other a leash with a fox terrier straining ahead of her. A minute later, a car driven by an elderly man came in slowly through the gate. Definitely not one of the men he expected to see.

He glanced at his wristwatch, snuggled comfortably in the driver's seat of the late-model Honda Accord and waited patiently.

A few miles away, at a little after twelve noon, Ahmed Khalifa got out of his car at one of the pumps at the gas station in Ballston and told Elmo Cooney to 'fill 'er up, man; be right back', then went to a burger joint across the street for a takeout. The more he thought about it—without all the monkeys on his back, namely Abu Kamal, that Rahim Akbar, the company, and the INS—he couldn't have asked for a better life on earth right now. What with Rosie, this nice job, good pay and all the perks—company car, free gas, bonus once or twice a year.

But, shit, the price he might have to pay for all that later. The only thing he could think of right now is to save up as much as he could so if he decided to skip the whole situation, even get out of the country, he could be on the run for a long time and not be stranded hungry, penniless, hiding out in the cold somewhere.

Across the street, not far above the burger joint, special agent John Jacobs hur-ried up the stairs to the second floor stakeout room where he and his partner Richard Bartley had spent many long hours for weeks before. He walked in to see the two Arlington county detectives and the one federal agent who replaced them lounging about by the window.

"Anything new happening down there?" he asked no one in particular.

"You ever watch grass grow?" said one of the detectives.

"Out of a crack in a street sidewalk?" said the other.

"That's about what we see happening down there," added the federal agent. "So, what's with this Khalifa guy? We just saw him pull up the gas pump and cross the street."

"We're on him, twelve, sixteen hours every day now," Jacobs said. "More stuff came in from Detroit about the company he works for and owns that gas station. Guy's getting hot on the headquarter's list."

And things seemed to be happening fast at headquarters. Even Ahmed Khal-ifa's nextdoor neighbor, Robert Grundell, was now on the list. They just learned that ISD had installed a stakeout where he worked at Treasury.

The federal agent asked, "Where's your partner? Whatzisname—"

"Bartley? He's down there in the car keeping an eye on him. I just thought I'd stop in see how you guys are doing."

"We're here," the three of them echoed each other.

Then after a couple more minutes of bantering, one of the detectives added, echoing what Jacobs had said many times during his time at the window: "Man, I wish they'd let us bust this place now. We've seen more drug activity here now than I have in fifteen years in service."

"I know how you feel, buddy," Jacobs sympathized. "I know how you feel."

He patted the man on the back, shook each one's hand and headed back out the door.

"Stay alive, man," said the federal agent.

"You guys do the same."

He got back in the car parked three parking meters away from the gas station with Bartley at the wheel waiting for Ahmed to come out of the burger joint. They followed him a discreet two cars back when he finally got on the road heading west on Fairfax Drive. He turned left to Glebe Road and from there, a few miles later, got on I-395 South.

The two special agents following him started getting curious where he was headed. With the carry-out burger Khalifa had in the car, Jacobs guessed he had an outdoors lunch date with somebody, probably Rosie.

In his Honda Accord over an hour now, Mustapha Khan finally decided to stretch a leg and got out for a leak in the men's room a few yards away from the car. He wasn't there two minutes before he was back in the car, worried that he'd miss somebody after waiting all that time. The time read 12:28 P on his wristwatch.

Indeed, he would have missed Ahmed Khalifa if he had delayed going to the men's room a little longer because now, three minutes later, the car he had been waiting to see just turned off Braddock Road outside and slowly went through the gate onto the park road. Mustapha, sitting low, watched intently as the Toyota Corolla went by. Yes, sir. That's him alright. Our man Ahmed Khalifa.

He waited till the car was far enough he couldn't distinguish the driver's feature before he moved. But turning onto the road, he had to wait for another car that came in to pass. It was an old-model American junk, a Chevrolet Cavalier or something with two men in it—driver and a front-seat passenger.

He followed close behind the Chevrolet which was moving at just under 10 MPH for a couple hundred yards, keeping an eye on the Toyota Corolla ahead of them. Now the road curved left at a bend. He felt a little impatient about the Chevrolet keeping the same distance from the Toyota. He wished it would turn off the road and park on one of the plentiful parking lots along the side, or speed up some.

Past the bend, he saw the Toyota pull into a space near the end of a parking lot close to a bench under a tree on one side and a picnic table in the grass area a short distance in front of it. He slowed down and expected the Chevrolet ahead of him to keep going past the Toyota and get lost. But it didn't. Instead, it did what he wanted to do himself—pull into the space at the other end of the parking lot where it would have been ideal for him to watch everything that was now happening and about to happen.

Shit. Those dumb pricks, he thought. Probably a coupla gays out to get their fix in the park in the middle of the day. Watching them pass no more than five yards in front of him back at the parking lot near the gate, they did look gay. But, hey—wait!

It happened like a lightning flash, a spark in his memory illuminating the night at the Thai restaurant, when he had a similar thought about some guys he saw...yes! A man he bumped partially off his chair, and the man sitting across the table against the wall.

It can't be! Not the same guys. He sat for a moment feeling weird about the whole thing. Then an *idea* dawned on him, turning weird slowly into alarm and then into a numbing sense of danger. With it came a kind of fear, fear of the unknown, of someone else being in control; and then a loathing and hatred of the enemy.

He was now only two car lengths behind them and didn't know what to do at first, whether to pull into a space he just passed by backing up or to keep going. He stopped for a moment in the middle of the road to eye the two men without turning his head, just his eyeballs. But all he could see were the back of their heads. After he read and memorized the license plate number, he decided to pull ahead, get a closer look.

As he crept past the Chevrolet, he turned his head right partially for one quick look at the man in the driver's seat just as agent Richard Bartley glanced at Ahmed Khalifa far to his left getting out of the Toyota with his carry-out burger. Great Allah in heaven, Mustapha exclaimed in his mind. The shiny forehead, that girlish curl at the corner of his mouth. And the one next to him. The same man he bumped accidentally in the restaurant.

Now nearly petrified with a sense of real danger, he sped up some but without looking in a hurry to get to some distance from there. He didn't turn his head and only had a partial view of Ahmed Khalifa walking towards the picnic bench with the lunchbag, as he drove past the Toyota.

He came to another bend on the loop where the road was bordered by a long row of parking spaces. Looking at the rearview mirror, he saw that he was now at a right angle with the parking lot occupied at one end by the Toyota and the Chevrolet at the other. He pulled into a space that afforded him the whole view of both cars, turned the engine off and took time to finally calm his nerves down and think straight.

He remembered his first thoughts about the men in the Chevrolet when he first saw them in the restaurant: plainclothes local cops. But now he had a more troublesome thought about them of which he had grown certain just the past thirty seconds—federal agents.

So, what's this Pakistani infidel doing? And Bobby?

And those agents—who are they with: Ahmed or Bobby? Wait till Bobby shows up. Keep a sharp eye on everybody. See how things go.

But even while he was pulling in to the parking space, he already missed seeing something: the passenger in the Chevrolet getting out of the car carrying a newspaper, moving quickly away from the car to make sure Ahmed didn't notice where he came from even by going the opposite direction first and then coming back and walking leisurely past the Toyota to the bench under the tree beside it.

The Acura Legend went through the gate at about 10 MPH over the speed limit in the park, catching the eye of the groundskeeper in his green coveralls standing beside his pickup truck at the edge of the service parking lot near the gate. Bobby saw the man and immediately slowed down to a crawl, acknowledging the man's look with a friendly smile. He could have waited till traffic on the road outside was all clear, like the man's look was telling him, for a slow turn into the park instead of rushing in to beat the oncoming traffic.

From there he drove in at the speed limit past the first bend of the loop to the parking lot where he saw the Toyota Corolla, and Ahmed at the picnic table having lunch. Agent Jacobs, sitting on the bench facing the road and holding up the sports section of the Post in front of him, watched Robert Grundell through the corner of his eye park two spaces from the Toyota. He was right about Ahmed having a lunch date with somebody and wasn't at all disappointed, in fact, was glad to see it was with Robert Grundell instead of Rosie. He can't wait to hear in his earpiece what goes as the man walked to the picnic bench carrying a Macdonald's bag and a medium soda to join Ahmed Khalifa on the same side of the bench.

From his vantage point, Mustapha Khan realized what a disadvantage he faced keeping track of what's happening from a distance and only through his rearview mirror. So as soon as he saw Bobby come, he turned the car around and sat low behind the wheel. The first thing he noticed was the man sitting on the bench behind a newspaper a few yards from the Toyota. Then he almost laughed to himself when he looked at the Chevrolet and saw only one man inside. This left no doubt about his suspicions.

No matter how this turned out now, he thought—whether Ahmed Khalifa was dealing with one or the other or neither, he must tell the Commander and Abu Kamal that they must sever *all* ties with the Pakistani as soon as possible. And they must not have any contact with Bobby from now on whatsoever.

He watched them eat lunch for half an hour, talking, laughing and enjoying each other's company. But that was all he could do—watch from a distance. He couldn't hear them, unlike agent Jacobs who was much closer to the two and could hear almost every word they spoke to each other through his hi-tech earpiece. Except at one point when they seemed to have lowered their voices to say a few words to each other, words which they sounded like they were trying to avoid saying to each other.

Actually, that was during a short break in Ahmed's narrative of his date with Rosie when Bobby surreptitiously slid the diskette envelope on the table seat over to Ahmed. "It's all yours," Bobby mumbled faintly while chewing on his french fries. In exchange, Ahmed did the same with the pay envelope which he folded in half and slid over to Bobby. "Payday," Ahmed said softly. "Everything's fine now."

All that came to the agent's earpiece as fragments of unintelligible mumbling. And nobody saw the exchange, not even agent Bartley in the Chevrolet who had been keeping an eye on them through his field glasses. He couldn't because the subjects were sitting on the other side of the picnic table from him.

A few minutes later, even as their quarry gathered their litter on the table and headed back to their cars, agent Jacobs was reluctant to give in to the idea that the two neighbors met just for an honest-to-goodness lunch at the park and not for some criminal activity. He did find some of the details of Khalifa's date with Rosie, particularly those in the bedroom where Khalifa said she wouldn't quit deep into the late hours, quite entertaining, and authentic.

"She just wanted to keep going," he told Bartley, from Khalifa's testimony to Bobby, later in the car as they drove a few car lengths behind Robert Grundell, past the Honda Accord with Mustapha Khan crouched low in it in the driver's seat. "Deep into the night. Even when he was barely awake. She was insatiable."

"That sounds like one of those fish tales from an angler with a terrific imagination," said Bartley disinterestedly. Jacobs laughed.

"Hey, I'm only telling you what I heard."

"Now, talking about that—so, what else did you hear?"

"That's about it," replied Jacobs. "Mostly about their dates. Sex, women, sports. Nothing about what we hoped we'd get. Unless something else went on there I missed out on. See anything?"

Bartley shook his head sideways. "Nothing I could lay a hand on," he said, "I can't be sure, though. They were sitting behind the table from me. I couldn't see below their waists."

"Something must've gone in there for them to come out here. I don't imagine they come out here just to eat lunch."

"Could be," said Bartley, glancing up the rearview mirror, taking in a Honda Accord four car-lengths behind but paying no attention to it. "Maybe this is a thing they do sometimes. When the weather's nice. Like today."

"Could be," said Jacobs. "What're we up to now?"

"I was counting on something breaking back there," replied Bartley, weighing stuff in his head. He could tell Jacobs was getting weary of this assignment, keeping track of the Pakistani. He was starting to feel the same although he thought this was still better than working the second-floor stakeout room watching dope in that gas station across the street. One thing he planned they'd do today which should free them up some from this assignment was plant the bug on Khalifa's car. After they heard about the stakeout at Treasury the day before, they got the go ahead from the office to do it.

Things are starting to heat up, they were told by their Section Chief. But nobody knew where all this was leading up to. The Bureau's working closely with NSA and the other national security agencies. We got to move as much as we can with what we got, the Chief said. Yeah, put the homing device on the underside of the guy's car. Then if nothing breaks, wire his apartment, tap his phone, do the whole shbang later on.

"What's the time?" Bartley asked. Now they're heading out of the park the same way they came in—Braddock Road to North Van Dorn to the Route 7 entrance to I-395 North.

"Geez, it's a quarter after one. What do you want to do for lunch?"

"Let's do his car at the parking lot as soon as he goes back to work," Bartley said. "Then lunchtime."

"Sounds good to me."

At Van Dorn and Route 7, they watched Robert Grundell head straight west on Route 7 to go back to work in his office at Treasury's Office of Civil Defense Logistics in the Skyline Center. They went down I-395 North following Ahmed Khalifa at a discreet distance. Behind them, even at a more discreet distance, was the Honda Accord.

They tailed Khalifa till they saw him park in one of the spaces assigned to his office on one side of the building on Fairfax Drive. Then they drove behind the building and parked at a meter within sight of the parking lot. The Honda Accord, ever so careful not to be observed by the occupants of the Chevrolet, had managed to get itself caught at the red light across the street from the building with a clear view of the parking lot and the Chevrolet.

Mustapha Khan watched Ahmed Khalifa get out of the car and disappear into the building, then the two men come out of the Chevrolet and one of them, the smaller one, feed the meter. At the turn of the green light, he drove across the street alongside the parking lot and parked at a meter a half a block away from the Chevrolet.

While he fished for change in his pockets, he watched the two men talk for a few seconds, walk through the parking lot and enter a restaurant across the street. He fed the meter with the last of the quarters he had in his hand, patted the 38 caliber blue Smith & Wesson he carried in his right rib-cage holster under his jacket and headed toward the restaurant.

It was half past one and they were both starving so Bartley thought it a good idea to get a table first, look at the menu and get their orders in, then go back out to the parking lot to plug the homing bug on Khalifa's Toyota Corolla. Also, it's good practice to give a guy time to remember something he might have forgotten in the car, come back out and get it, before you mess with the car and possibly get caught redhanded.

The restaurant was still half-full even as it was near the end of the lunchtime peak hours. They got a table one off the aisle, midway between the entrance and the rear where a 'Restrooms' sign hung from the ceiling. They sat looking at the menu for six, seven minutes. Then the server came from seating another customer who came in right after them across the aisle near the entrance, and took their orders.

"And a caffeine-free Coke for me, please," Bartley threw in lastly before the server finished up jutting down their orders. Then to Jacobs, once they were alone: "I better get this thing done right now. I'll be back a few minutes."

He got up and headed out the front door. On the way there, he bent down to pick up an insert page that had fallen out from the menu, unnoticed, of the lone customer—a tall, dark and well-dressed man—who was just seated. Bartley handed it to the man who barely turned his face up at him, thanked him briefly and took it.

Sitting with his back to the aisle, Mustapha Khan only had to turn his head slightly to the right to see which direction Bartley went from the restaurant—back where they came from across the street and through the parking lot. Probably forgot something in the car. Then a couple of minutes later, turning his head slightly this time to the left, he saw Jacobs get up and go into the men's restroom.

Without marking time other than to take a drink of the icewater on his table, he got up and followed Jacobs in the restroom. In there, he saw Jacobs at the near-end unit of a bank of urinals behind a row of toilet stalls on the left. Another man, two units away from Jacobs was just zipping up. Mustapha stood one away from Jacobs and pretended to unzip himself, actually just waiting for the other man to get out.

Once sure no one else was around, he sized Jacobs up through the corner of his eye just for two seconds: poor man must be at least eight, ten inches shorter than him who was six-foot-four. Let's see now, he thought, do I just blow his head off? No, that won't do. If he had one of those silencers, yes. He's got to get himself one soon, no question about it. He decided against using his gun altogether.

While Jacobs was zipping up, Mustapha stepped over, grabbed him by the back of the neck with the left hand, twisted his right wrist behind him with the right hand and smashed his face and head against the wall as violently as he can over and over again. Jacobs' facial skin broke in a dozen different places and while his consciousness ebbed from the brutality of the sudden attack, the glossy tile oozed with gobs of blood from around his eyes, forehead, cheekbone, nose and mouth.

Mustapha moved very quickly, dragging his victim into the handicap toilet stall and closing the door. In there, he looked at Jacobs' wallet and confirmed his suspicion once and for all.

Just look at that shiny badge the little twit has. Fucking undercover FBI agent.

He regarded Jacobs, sprawled on the floor beside the toilet bowl, completely out, in some kind of triumphant satisfaction for a moment. Then, hearing people coming in, he hurriedly slipped the wallet into his coat pocket and went back into the restaurant.

The next thing to do was make the call for the pick up of the drop.

But first, get out of the place before the other agent comes back and he had to, maybe, shoot the son of a bitch to get away from him and the whole U.S. armed services. He stopped briefly at his table to take another drink of the icewater and drop a five on the table before going out the door.

In a phone booth across the street from his car, he talked to Abu Kamal who said that Ahmed Khalifa had the drop and was waiting for him to pick it up. He then called Ahmed who said drive up the front door of the office building, they agreed, in fifteen minutes; he'll be waiting inside, just roll down the passenger-side window and he'll toss it in. He got in the car and sat for fifteen minutes, looking straight at the front of the restaurant where he had come out five minutes ago a block away and across the street from the front of the office building.

In that time, he saw an ambulance pull up the restaurant, two paramedics hurry in with a stretcher and come out a minute later with a man on it under a blanket. Cars swarmed around the restaurant, local police with strobe lights turning, some just plain dark-colored ones.

He drove slowly when it was time to go and got to the front of the building just as the ambulance started to leave, sirens whining. He looked across the street where the door of the restaurant was wide open and saw people standing inside, talking. One of them was the other FBI agent taking notes while talking to the server right by the table where Mustapha was sitting.

Then he heard a rap on the passenger-side window. It was Ahmed leaning out on the curb. He rolled down the window just low enough for Ahmed to drop the four-inch square brown envelope containing the diskette, waved at him and drove off.

CHAPTER 14

▼

"The world is at war. Our world," Sabah Ahmaddi thought, gazing at the blue Pacific Ocean from the balcony of the twenty-fourth floor suite in the Rainbow Tower of the Hilton Hawaiian Village hotel, "against their world; against them, the enemies of Islam, the killers of our mothers and fathers, our women and children and babies.

"We must fight with all our might to subdue that world that seeks to destroy ours. One's life is too little to sacrifice for this cause. It is a great honor to be chosen for such a sacrifice not only that it is one's precious duty to defend our families, our honor and self-respect—our world, against their world."

It was near the end of day, moments before the first of the evening prayers began. The cloudless eastern Hawaiian sky was just beginning to fade into one vast expanse of a quiet night firmament. The 23-year old Lebanese, born American, nurtured and molded in the ideals of Islamic fundamentalism throughout his young life, turned further eastward as far as he can see in the weakening light of day. In his mind, the voice of Omar Husain, his teacher and mentor, echoing from the past four days of the intense planning and preparation he went through for his ultimate sacrifice for the Faith.

It soothed him even now just listening to the voice in his mind. Intelligent, all-knowing and wise, but kind and understanding; soft and assuring but strong and firm.

"No sacrifice is too little or too much," the voice sounded. "To give for the sake of what lends meaning to our lives, is to live life. To defend our faith, our own belief in what is good for us and what is not good for us—this is what we live for. We must therefore defeat the forces that seek to impose its self-righteous ways upon us. The infidels who never cease to muddle our vision, our mind and spirit with their own values, self-importance and materialism. This we must do, even at the small sacrifice of giving our own physical life."

He lowered his eyes from the far horizon to the near view of Waikiki Beach below, the endless stream of pleasure-seekers coming and going in every direction, the rich, the mindless, the hollow in spirit. His mind, primed with the ideals of absolute submission to the will of Allah from his early youth in the Madrassas back in Pakistan, rebelled at the sight of this. So he lifted his eyes, gazed beyond the horizon, up to the peace and tranquility of heaven above and slowly closed them. Risen from his physical existence to a sheer spiritual consciousness, he went down on his knees, bent to touch his head on the floor and began his evening prayer.

This, God willing, will be the last of his early evening prayer. He shall not see this hour again when it comes the day after.

The man came out of the elevator from the garage level and walked up to one of the straight-backed, neatly dressed men behind the long desk in the hotel lobby. He wore a brightly-colored Hawaiian short-sleeve shirt, tennis shorts and a pair of walking Nikes. His light-red hair looked as though it had just been blow-dried and he pressed it against his scalp occasionally to keep it flat on the sides. He did the same with his bushy eyebrows as if to keep them from flying off his face. He had a slight tan which showed around his eyes when he removed his sunglasses and asked if he had any messages, giving the man behind the counter his name and room number.

"Yes, sir, Mr. Tyler," said the hotel clerk, looking at a message envelope he took from a shelf behind him. "John Tyler?"

"That's me," said the man, a hotel guest in one of the premium suites on the 26th floor of the Rainbow Tower the past five days now. Looks like one of those single swingers either from L.A. or New York, another rich mainland *haole*, thought the hotel clerk who was half native Hawaiian.

"Here you go, sir," he said dutifully. "Came in just over an hour ago."

"Thank you very much," John Tyler said, swapping a five-dollar bill for the envelope and, before heading back to the elevators: "*Mahalo.*"

"You're very welcome, sir," replied the Hawaiian, smiling appreciatively.

The man calling himself John Tyler took one of the elevator cars with several other people and pressed button 26. Five days ago, he boarded a plane at Baltimore-Washington International where he began to assume his present identity from that of Omar Husain.

He was in a hurry to get back to his suite and became terribly impatient as each of the five other passengers in the elevator got off one at a time before the 26th floor. Eager to read the message in the envelope, he was hoping he'd do so while riding the elevator so he could take action immediately if he needed to as soon as he got in. After having accomplished the bigger and more difficult tasks he had worked hard on since arriving in Honolulu, he was anxious to make sure he took care of any loose ends and didn't overlook anything.

Kelly Rodman, 31, known before—sometime ago like fourteen years—as Khalid Rahman when he was under the tutelage of Omar Husain, now proprietor of Kelly's Automotive Service and Body Shop in the town of Waipahu just west of Pearl Harbor, had made it all possible by presenting him with the fruit of two days' round-the-clock labor: the mobile newscast van, newly-painted ivory-white, all equipped with a satellite dish, cable hookups and a fifteen-foot mast antenna. A sign on both sides read HTV WorldNews, Honolulu.

When he first got word of the assignment a few days before Commander Omar arrived, he felt the same kind of excitement he did when he first saw the early television videos of the World Trade Center Towers collapsing, then the Pentagon burning with a gaping hole on one side of it, and again only weeks ago. It took some footwork first finding the van with help from two other sleepers like him in Hawaii, rigging it with all the works on the outside, making it look like what it's meant to look like. Then the paint job, and the signs, with an added precaution not to make the vehicle look fresh out of a body shop by putting some scratches on it, some dirt; re-doing parts of the paint to make it look off-color and old.

Seeing John Tyler so pleased with the result was almost enough reward for their dedicated hardwork in the name of Allah and the great Prophet Mohammed. They would do anything, give anything—their lives, willingly, to see that their beloved teacher, revered leader and great bearer of the Faith succeed in his mission, their mission, and what must be the mission of all Islam—to bring America to its knees.

It was dusk when John Tyler entered the suite and proceeded directly to the lanai at the beachfront end of the living area facing the southeast. The message in the envelope was from Abu Kamal in Virginia, relaying in coded texts an inquiry from Cairo, via Detroit, regarding the status of the mission in Hawaii. He also confirmed all the arrangements for his return trip to the mainland under the name Charles Robiski, with a roundtrip ticket departing at 10:30 AM tomorrow morning to L.A.; a separate flight from there to New York, a hotel reservation in

Manhattan, and the company car to use for his return to Baltimore the following day.

He vacillated for a couple of seconds between responding to it now, by email or telephone, or waiting till after his evening prayer. After a quick glance at the now deepening silhouettes over the eastern sky, he took a beach towel from the bathroom, spread it on the hardwood floor of the lanai and sat on it on bent knees facing Mecca. He then closed his eyes, shed all his thoughts of the world and, touching his head on the floor, began the fourth of his *salaah* for the day.

Originally called Armistice Day to commemorate the end of World War I and in 1954 renamed to honor all men and women who have served in the armed forces, Veterans Day is one of the most hallowed remembrance federal holidays. To express defiance of America and inflict harm to her pride and self-respect—so goes the thinking in the hierarchy of the Organization, Omar Husain was told, those who seek to do so would do well to commit such acts on this day.

At a quarter past nine in the morning of the day, Sabah Ahmaddi strolled through the sands of the Ala Moana Beach Park from the Hilton Hawaiian Village hotel. He had just concluded the last meeting with Commander Omar in the hotel the past half hour for the final rundown on today's activities: the launching of Operation Punchbowl.

What does one think about on the last day of his life? Experiences of joy and sadness? Triumph and failure? Peace and hatred? As he watched his shoes make footprints in the sand, he thought that none of that mattered now. Nor do they ever, really, at any time in one's entire life. Such life experiences are fleeting no matter how long one may think they last or let them linger in memory. Life itself is fleeting, so temporary that once risen from the cradle, one simply goes into the daily activity of meeting the demands of his physical existence, pursuing pleasure while, in the process, forgetting—intentionally or not—that all of that comes to an end sooner or later, one way or another.

For the unbeliever, that is all what life is and ever will be. Not for the children of Allah, the followers of the Great Prophet Mohammed, the believers in Islam. A life spent in the pursuit and defense of one's faith, as Commander Omar said to him one last time in the hotel, is a life well-lived no matter how short it may need be: ten years, fifteen years, twenty-three years. The ultimate purpose of life is its surrender to Allah—Islam!

At fifteen minutes to ten, sitting on a bench by the Beach Park Drive, his back to the ocean, he watched the van come into the park from the Ala Moana Boulevard, turn into the parking lot directly across the drive and take a space facing him. He got up and walked straight to the passenger side. Kelly Rodman, in the driver's seat keeping the engine running, unlocked the door.

They said little to each other as they rode out of the park and headed west on Ala Moana Boulevard. Traffic wasn't as heavy as on a workday but there were plenty enough cars, buses full of tourists, and locals off work in their RVs and SUVs to make it seem like a regular day.

In less than three minutes, they were making a right turn to Ward Avenue going north toward the foot of the Puowaina Crater, better known as The Punchbowl, site of the National Memorial Cemetery of the Pacific. In about an hour, dozens of local and foreign dignitaries, civilian and military—active and retired, and veterans from the Second World War to the Gulf War, including Afghanistan, would be gathered in the park for a memorial ceremony. Most of them had in fact at this moment arrived, and so had hundreds of spectators along with the early morning tourists.

Security was beefed up starting from the base of the dead volcano at Prospect Street all the way up to the crater with local and Federal Park Service police, and MPs. Just like it was described in the file contained in Bobby's diskette which also told Omar Husain, among other things, how to get past them, place the van as close to the dignitaries as possible, the size, content and color of the press passes needed to do this. Kelly Rodman and his team of sleepers had done an excellent job with that as well, gathering data which was practically offered to them by both the press and the Park Service, and then producing the passes, all in a matter of days.

Traffic came to a crawl during the ascent to the crater at the intersection of the popular scenic Tantalus Drive. At one instance, though, a Park Police walked up to Kelly Rodman at the wheel and upon seeing his press pass directed traffic to let the van through even past some of the official participants in the ceremony still arriving.

They reached the park which overlooks the city of Honolulu from five hundred feet above the sea and is site of the 115-acre memorial cemetery developed from what was known among the native Hawaiians as the Pu'owaina Crater, or the 'Hill of Sacrifice'. Approaching the ceremony grounds from the far end on the perimeter drive, the van slowed down to ten miles an hour. After it got another hundred yards closer, it pulled to the side of the road and stopped.

There were people everywhere. On the rows of grave markers, the walkways, the Link Drive that circled the park grounds. A big crowd had already gathered at the foot of the memorial shrine at the other end. There was a platform built at the bottom steps of the shrine ringed with flagpoles displaying the colors of various countries. Across the drive from it extending to the grass area were rows of seats for as many as five to six hundred people. Around this were wide open standing-room spaces that could accommodate hundreds more.

Below the platform and to its right was a group of seats already more than half occupied by ceremony guests, old veterans in military uniforms accompanied by some family members. Up on the platform, some workmen hurried with the last-minute check-up of the equipment, the microphone on the lectern and the sound system and made sure the seating arrangements for the dignitaries in the back half of the platform were in order.

Kelly Rodman looked at the time on his watch. Commander Omar should be along in about fifteen, twenty minutes to pick him up, as planned, after he and Sabah Ahmaddi had everything set up in the van. He surveyed the area around the platform and the shrine up the steps where more people had gathered. Mostly tourists, he imagined, admiring the Statue of Columbia, reading the patriotic inscriptions carved in stone up there and taking in the panorama of the solemn majesty of the whole scenery around the crater.

Everything looked as they were told to expect. Commander Omar had some reliable sources in Washington, D.C.

Sabah Ahmaddi fought with some emotion that started welling up in him about the place, the thought of what it represents not just to Americans but to other people, other countries. He can not, must not allow himself to feel or think of any such thing now. He must concentrate, as he had from every waking moment since arriving in the islands, on his final mission in life *today*. Nothing more, nothing less.

He snapped out of his musing suddenly when they heard the wails of sirens heralding the arrival of a motorcade from behind them. A string of black and white stretch limos, stars and stripes fluttering on their hoods behind escorts of local police motorcycles, went by. A second group followed, this one consisting of five black limos preceded by military escorts, each one with the stars and stripes mounted on its right fender; on the left the flag of the countries each represented: Japan, China, Korea, Vietnam and the Philippines.

The two men watched the activities around the ceremony grounds for a while, waiting for the appropriate time to move and play a part in the scene around the platform—that of a TV news crew doing a satellite broadcast of the event. They could see two other news crews—real ones, already in position. One was already shooting the scene, the other setting up some equipment beside a truck parked near the platform at a space near the one Kelly Rodman would be pulling into shortly.

At ten minutes before eleven, the van pulled up slowly towards the platform. Halfway there, two fully armed Army MPs waved them down and approached on each side of the van. They were ready to pull out their fake credentials and press passes when they were asked for them.

The soldiers took them and examined both sides of the passes, held the picture side for a few seconds and looked each of them squarely in the face.

"HTV," said the one by Kelly Rodman's side.

"That's us," he replied. "Still waiting for our producer to show up. He's running late."

"Well, better get in there now," said the MP, handing back the pass. "The program's about to begin. Get yourself set up, right next to that other media truck on the side."

"Yes, I know. Thanks."

He drove past several other security guards who simply waved them through into the area reserved for the media. The space was just to the side of the park drive that cut right through the front of the platform where the dignitaries from the limos were now being seated. The appearance of some of the more recognizeable ones drew the attention of the audience now filling up the seats fast. Among them one of the U.S. senators of the island state, the Governor, the President of the Philippines and the U.S. Secretary of State.

The color guards soon appeared, marching to the sound of the drums front and back of them, and stationed themselves in front of the Statue of Columbia at the top of the shrine. Then the emcee, a Navy Commander in dress blue, approached the lectern and announced the commencing of the Veterans Day ceremony.

Coming up the last curve of the access road to the crater, Omar Husain had to pull out his press pass for the third time. This time, there was a stretch of about forty-five seconds of uncertainty while the two Army MPs stood at each side of the car, one scrutinizing the pass, the other eyeballing the inside of the rented Ford Taurus while taking notes in a palm-size logbook, his M-16 hanging on his shoulder. The soldier noticed how slightly edgy the media man in the car was, obviously for being a little late, he thought. At one point, the soldier bent down to look straight at Omar Husain's face. Finally, the one holding the pass stepped back and Omar Husain wasn't sure if he was going to be asked to pull over or be let through.

"You're going to have to hurry up a little, Mr. Tyler," said the MP, actually just moving out of his way. The tightening in his chest let go slowly. "Things just started happening up there."

"Yes, I hear it," he said with a tone of urgency. "I got a camera crew come early, though. I told them to roll it if I don't get here on time."

"Good thinking," said the soldier, handing him back the pass. "Go ahead, sir. Right down the press area."

"Thank you."

He drove slowly to the designated parking area, observing the event now taking place up ahead. The emcee was winding down with the introductory remarks. Just as he pulled in to a space a short distance back of the van and facing the platform, the emcee introduced a young Filipino female entertainer to sing the national anthem.

Sabah Ahmaddi was standing at an angle to the front of the platform this side of it, the camera going on his shoulder while Kelly Rodman stood partially in front, microphone in hand. They had the appearance of airing the event but at the moment were just keeping still like everyone else in the entire place while the singing of the anthem was in progress.

Omar Husain remained in the car. He had a clear view of the dignitaries standing at the front row of the seats near the back of the platform. He noticed in particular the President of the Philippines where he had recently traveled to boost the morale of many of the suffering brothers, as well as deliver some badly needed funds for the fight against the Christians and the government, out there south of the country in Muslim Mindanao. The same as what's going on here in America and everywhere else in the world.

Next to the leader was the U.S. State Secretary whom no one expected to be in the event till the eleventh hour when, according to news, his plane coming back from a trip in South Korea was delayed, allowing him time for the appearance here during the layover in the islands. Couldn't have happened at a better time, thought Omar Husain. Too bad he wasn't with his boss or some of those devils at Capitol Hill, members of Congress who keep pumping billions into Israel to keep up its military strength and continue the slaughter of the brothers in Palestine.

Well, he thought as the singing neared the end, what's about to happen here does not come close to a smidgen of the kind of killing and oppression of our people in the Middle East and all over the world; the kind of destruction of our culture and human dignity, the denial of our freedom and human rights in our own countries by the Jews and the Christians.

The singing ended, followed by a long enthusiastic applause.

The Navy Commander was now back to the lectern to start the next activity in the ceremony which was the presentation of several groups of Pacific war veterans, starting with that from World War II. Everything is right to the minute, thought Omar Husain after looking at his watch as he now approached the van.

Kelly Rodman opened the rear door and Omar Husain hopped inside. In there, he lifted the green plastic cover around a three-foot high cardboard container that took up about a third of the area of the van inside. He opened a toolbox, took out a screw driver and a pair of pliers, all he needed to wire the detonator terminals and hook it to a circuit-loop line that went through the panel behind the front seat. The loop had a switch, now in the off position with a safety latch, fixed just above and to the right of the driver's seat back.

He put his arm through the square opening in the panel and made sure the switch was off and safety latched. Then he hooked up the line to the detonator, completing the power loop that would send electrical charges to detonate the two tons of high-power explosives in the container when the switch was turned on.

From here on, every minute was critical. First, the disguise: the blonde wig came off first, then the bushy eyebrows, next the tan with the help of a squeeze of the skin lotion and some warm water Kelly Rodman left him in a thermos. Now the new look: short dark brown hair, the mustache and wire-rim glasses, and a plain light-blue short-sleeve shirt.

He looked through the panel opening to see what was going on outside. The last of the old veterans had just gone up and assembled at the center of the stage and now the color guards were coming down the steps of the shrine onto the platform for the veterans' salute. Below, Sabah Ahmaddi looked busy with the camera and Kelly Rodman with the microphone whereas they were just waiting to see him come out of the van and walk back to his car.

And he did, five minutes later when he felt the ceremony had progressed enough for everyone, including security, to settle down. Kelly Rodman followed him into the car without appearing in any hurry and got in the driver's seat. This is the sticky part, Omar Husain thought as they drove out of the park at ten miles an hour without attracting attention.

There were still some cars coming into the park but theirs was the only one going the other way. They passed the same guards they did before on the park drive and to their relief none of them took any interest in them. The last of them, the pair of MPs stationed near the top of the access road, were the only ones who seemed to have looked their way as they approached.

One of them, the one with the logbook and 'Cpl. Wembley' showing on his front name panel, came a couple of steps closer for a quick look at Kelly Rodman and simply waved them out. For some reason, though, Omar Husain noticed through the right side rearview mirror, the soldier kept his eyes at the rear-end of the car even as they descended on the access road and disappeared.

About the same time Corporal Wembley got curious enough to pull out his logbook from his side pants pocket, Sabah Ahmaddi dropped the camera on the passenger seat in the van and got in behind the wheel. He had seen Commander Omar's Ford Taurus leave the crater at least three minutes ago. It's time, he thought. He started the engine.

Corporal Wembley leafed through his logbook and found the license plate number he had written down of the car that just left. He remembered specifically that there was only the driver in it. And now the driver was not the same man and there was a passenger as well. Also, he wondered briefly why they left so soon during the ceremony.

While he had this thought going, he glanced at the ceremony in progress at the bottom of the shrine, noticing oddly a van moving straight to the front of the platform stage and stopping there. It sat there for just about three seconds, right in between the stage with all the dignitaries on it and the hundreds of spectators on this side. This was the last image he retained in his memory of these hallowed grounds, the serenity of the environment, the sense of tranquility evoked by the face of the Statue of Columbia at the shrine, all of which, from the next second, together with most of the people attending the ceremony would be obliterated.

In that second, Sabah Ahmaddi looked up in the sky through the windshield as if already rising from his earthly being into immortality as he had been told over and over again in the past and believed would happen. Then he turned the switch on, and his earthly being together with the van seemed to just disintegrate into millions of pieces along with the entire surrounding: all the people around, the chairs they were sitting on, the platform and everyone on it, the steps to the shrine, the shrine itself—its walls, the Statue of Columbia and what's behind these. Trees nearby were uprooted, some splintered and fell. There were body parts everywhere.

The shock wave from the horrific explosion reached throughout the entire plateau of the crater, scattering debris in every direction. The explosion itself was seen and heard throughout downtown Honolulu and for miles away. People spoke of it later as if the dead volcano suddenly came to life and blew up.

Corporal Wembley stirred slowly on the ground as he was examined by an Army medic who was being careful not to move him too much at once. He opened his eyes straight to the clear blue Hawaiian sky and thought for a moment perhaps he was in the hereafter, until the face of the medic came into view and spoke.

"Corporal, can you hear me?" the medic asked. "Can you talk?"

"Yes," he replied normally, now coming to gradually and remembering everything clearly. A large piece of debris had shot straight to the side of his head, knocking him out completely and putting a big gash on his right cheek.

"Can you move?" the medic asked next.

"Yes, I'm alright. I'm alright. Let me up," Corporal Wembley said rapidly as if he were in a hurry to go somewhere or do something.

The park was now filling up fast with military ambulances and personnel transports as well as commercial emergency vehicles. The city of Honolulu was placed on a state of emergency and the entire island of Oahu on red alert.

There were debris everywhere. Local and federal rescue workers poured in and were now looking for survivors, rushing the few they find out to a hospital or flying them out in helicopters. Many moved about carefully, carrying stretchers and body bags, assessing the damage, identifying bodies, tagging them or parts of them, removing those already positively ID'ed.

The medic and another worker helped Corporal Wembley up. The first thing he did was feel his pants side pocket where he kept his logbook. He felt his other pockets when he didn't find it there, at the same time looking around on the ground. Finally he spotted it a few yards away.

"Get the police," he called out to the men around him as he went to pick up the logbook. "Somebody get the cops quick!"

"What is it?" asked the medic.

"I got a positive lead," he said as he walked back, leafing through the logbook. "We can find the bastards who did this."

The police came a few minutes later and inputted the license plate number he gave them in the computer. It was a rented car picked up at the airport several days ago by a John Tyler. A police APB was issued for the car and three hours later it was found abandoned at a McDonald's parking lot off the Kamehameha Highway in Mililani Town several miles west of Pearl Harbor. Everything moved fast from there on, until the search for John Tyler himself was launched.

The massive investigation turned the guest registry file in the computer of every hotel in Honolulu inside out, eventually leading to the Rainbow Tower of the Hilton Hawaiian Village hotel. Squads of local and federal forces put the entire hotel complex under siege, searched every square inch of John Tyler's suite and found absolutely nothing, not a piece of paper to connect to the Punchbowl suicide bombing. It was the same with the car which turned up nothing in the way of finding John Tyler at this time, other than a collection of some sets of fingerprints.

The search continued nonstop into the next day with police and FBI agents conducting investigations, questioning anybody who might have been in contact with John Tyler in any way at all. At the airport, the car rental, the hotel, the restaurants he might have gone to and, of course, the Punchbowl starting with Corporal Wembley and any other survivors who were able to talk. Corporal Wembley was taken by the FBI to sit with an artist who drew a composite from the Corporal's descriptions of the man he saw briefly in the car.

But it was all for nothing because the man they were looking for ceased to exist moments before the bombing. And by noon, it was the more futile with the 10:30 AM departure of a flight from the Honolulu International Airport carrying Charles Robiski direct to Los Angeles.

CHAPTER 15

▼

It was almost noontime when she finally got done with another one of those quick after-class tutoring and got back to her room. She loved teaching and didn't mind putting in extra time to help someone who might be having a problem. And not just classroom problems. Any problem, academic or personal. Maybe, she thought occasionally, she could branch out into counseling come burnout time in teaching.

She'd been at it six years now and her enthusiasm hadn't peaked yet, still in the upswing and she didn't see it leveling off another five, maybe ten years down the work-career path. By that time who knows what lay ahead. Another thing, she hadn't completely given up on the idea of *starting over.*

Heck, that was only a three-year marriage she got detoured into. She still had time. Not a whole lot, but at thirty-six, she's still in the running. Lots of women go through worse—ten-, fifteen-year marriage into their fortys, fiftys, and in the end…nothing. No family, no money, no home. Some not even a job and nothing but lots of therapy bills.

Uh-h…no. Not Julie Santorelli. No burnout in her agenda. Not with work, relationship, family or anything in her pursuits in life. By what anyone can see happening out there, she had just barely started. She had some pretty good things going. She liked what she was doing for a living. And it's a pretty stable living. She's in good shape healthwise, moneywise. Very important, especially that last one. And on top of all that, she had this government worker, very stable guy, with whom she connected, finally, in the way she had always thought a woman should connect with a man.

It had been a promising relationship all along, so far, for almost two years now. They've had some ups and downs. The usual stuff—lack of communication, some non-lethal bad judgments from both sides, friction coming from personal idiosyncracies as what happens with other couples. But they always got over the hump. The only thing that really bothered her was the thought of his past flings. And there were a good few of them.

Every now and then, while at his place, she'd pick up the phone when it rang and it would be one of them. She'd hand him the phone and watch him ease out of earshot maybe in the bathroom and she'd be getting hot behind the ears while waiting for him to come back out.

"One of those, huh?" she'd say while he replaced the phone on the rack a couple of minutes later.

"That was Donna," he'd say, convincingly innocent and clean. "I've told you about her before. She's like my sister, or I should say, I'm like her brother. We've been friends for years now. We never had sex. Never even kissed."

"So, how many other sisters do you have waiting in line out there?"

He would laugh and run up to her and hug her and kiss her all over and she would believe him, let it go at that and her trust would be restored. Lately, she decided that anything you get into involves a risk. A guy is either trustworthy or not. No two ways about it. Whether or not you believe him is your choice. Same as whether you stay or not. If he meant to do something behind your back, no point telling him or compelling him not to. The point of the matter is the intent to do it. If he had it in him, that's all you need to know and it's your choice whether to hang around or not.

Altogether, she's convinced she has a good thing going here and feels comfortable—daring, enough to look forward to what's ahead, way ahead. Like a house, a baby. And hopefully before she hits forty.

How wrong could she be, after the first one? She couldn't be any dumber now than she was before, if at all. She knew that one had a high probability of not going far even before she married the guy. There were a few loose ends she couldn't quite tie up, but she took a chance anyway. She was thirty-one and was too daring and much in a hurry to think things through more clearly.

She didn't think they came any better until a few months in the marriage when the guy started slacking off, not responding physically, emotionally. Then he changed jobs a couple of times. It turned out that had been the pattern of his work career. The guy was forty years old and all he had for a nest egg was a few hundred dollars in the checking account. But what got her was he didn't care. He didn't care if he, they, lived from one end of the dollar to the other. Not that she intended to live off of him.

It took her three years to get out of it. Part of it was, alright, being still a little young to know better, which is not far from saying too dumb to know better and, it follows, lack of life experience. Fine. But now, she knows better. She thinks.

How she wished times were back when values were simple, people were more honorable, trustworthy and conscientious. Like even when her parents married, thirty-nine years ago. Or even her uncle Steve and aunt Ida, thirty-five years ago. Theirs were marriages in the sixties when things were turning inside out, traditions were being upended full swing, old ways were on the chopping block of the libbers and all those non-conformists. New values, new role models were introduced in the psyche.

You'd think that Joe Santorelli (her Dad) and his younger brother Steve would have succumbed to the liberalism of that age and possibly ruined their marriages, but they didn't. They hung in there and to this day you couldn't see either one without the only woman he vowed to love and respect for as long as he lived.

Tradition, values—these are what made them hang in there, she often thought to herself during and after her short married life. Credit the upbringing their parents afforded them coming from the old country. What else could it be, in most parts? Love? Yes, it had to have been in there too. The right kind of it, if not all of it at the time but over the years. Now, out there, nobody even knows what the word means anymore. Many, especially the young, the mindless, mistake a lot of other things for it—sex, money, power, stardom. All the time.

Friendship? A caring and trustworthy one, yes. In fact, this was basically what she had going with Chris Phillips more than anything else. One of respect, fairness and comradeship.

She had made a quick stop at the school cafeteria for the chicken salad and the Diet Coke, picked up a copy of the Post at the teacher's lounge and now was having a quiet time at her desk in her work room having lunch.

She turned away from the chicken salad for a moment to look at a couple of family pictures she had on the base file cabinet behind her. The one on the left taken in 1976: Mom and Dad standing next to each other; in front of them her aunt, Sister Caterina—older sister of her mother, visiting from her native Rome, Italy—sitting in a chair, dressed in the full habit of the Religious of the Good Shepherd, flanked by nine-year-old Julie standing close on her right and six-year-old brother Charles on her left. The other picture with everyone standing in two rows seven years later: Mom and Dad, sixteen-year-old Julie and thirteen-year-old brother Charles on the left half of the shot; Uncle Steve and Aunt Ida, cousins Jake and Brigit, thirteen and ten at the time, on the right half.

She loved that picture in particular, taken twenty years ago at her aunt and uncle's wedding anniversary, each half of it like a carbon copy of the other, except her family is three years older than her uncle's. But what was seen in the picture, the closeness, togetherness, was what it was actually like in their lives. Even today.

She became particularly close to her aunt and uncle from the time she was barely two years old. Uncle was only a year back from his last tour of duty in Vietnam when he got married. They were anxious to start a family and took every opportunity to see what it was like to have one by babysitting her. Naturally, her parents were only too happy to share their experience with them.

For a time, it was as if she had two sets of parents. Then their first child, Jacob, came a year later. But she remained just as close with them. In fact, it grew even more as the years went by and the rest of the children arrived. Later, when she got older, starting from her early teens, she returned her uncle's favor by babysitting his children.

They were one whole family, it seemed. And they still were even as the nests— her parents' in Chevy Chase, Maryland and her uncle's in Vienna, Virginia—had been empty for several years now. All four of the children went through college and were now in pursuit of their separate work careers.

Her brother Charles went to New York City three years ago in pursuit of large sums of money, he told everyone in the family, as a Certified Financial Adviser for an investment company, and planned to quit working at age forty. Cousin Jake, now thirty-three and, unlike Charles, appeared to be more the conservative type, was a lawyer, engaged to be married soon, and had taken a job in the federal government with the Office of General Counsel of the Commerce Department in D.C. His sister, Brigit, now thirty with a master in Computer Science, was a co-founder of a dot-com company in Herndon, Virginia that went belly-up twice, reorganized and stayed with the business and was now finally starting to turn up a profit.

She turned back to the chicken salad and the paper feeling thankful for having come from…yes, she could say, a good, happy family background. The only sore event in it had been, so far, her failed marriage.

She hoped that would be the last in both families. With her thoughts of Chris Phillips and the optimism she had for the future, she resumed eating and reading the paper.

What an awful thing to happen, she was thinking as she read the front-page article on the suicide bombing at The Punchbowl in Hawaii. It had been on the front page since it happened two days ago. There was nothing else on the TV newscasts, round the clock, but the horrifying event.

How could anybody think of doing such a thing? the thought went on in her mind. On such a day, and at such a place? She turned the page, read on and came to the list of victims who had now been positively identified and whose next of kins had shortly been notified. She moved her eyes quickly down the published list of two hundred fifteen names so far, chilled by the thought of this, another horrible act of terrorism against America.

Then her eyes caught a name and froze. Everything seemed to have suddenly stopped. Not just her chewing, but her breathing, her heartbeat, the world around her, and time.

It can't be. It's got to be somebody else, another Vietnam veteran. No, it can't be! she cried aloud in her mind. But as she remembered how Aunt Ida was having a bout with a flu last week and Uncle Steve and both her parents were so disappointed that the poor wife couldn't take the trip with her husband to Hawaii for the Veterans Day celebration, she closed her eyes and tried to black out everything. But when she opened them again, she knew she wasn't dreaming or hallucinating. She blinked at the name and looked at it again, hoping it wouldn't read the same this time, the last name spelled differently perhaps. But it wasn't—Steve Santorelli

She grabbed the phone and with hands shaking, heart pounding, dialed her aunt in Vienna. She hung up as soon as she heard a busy signal and dialed her parents' number in Chevy Chase next but then remembered that they had driven to New York City four days ago and would just be on their way back today.

Now she thought furiously where she might have her cousins' numbers. The cell phone! Why hasn't she heard anything from anybody? she thought while she dug the phone out of her handbag. She found Brigit's work number and called. She was told that Brigit had not been at work all morning. She was about to call Jake at work in D.C. next when her desk phone rang. It was Jake calling from Vienna. She was ready to jump on him, the moment it was her turn to speak, for not having let her know sooner but changed her mind when she heard his voice.

"Mom just got word late last night from the government," he explained in a very subdued voice. "She got a hold of Brigit first. I came right over as soon as I got her call."

They were up most of the night, he said, looking after their mother who was still sick with the flu while they tried to get information from anybody in the government—the military, the Veterans Administration, the Defense Department at the Pentagon and in Honolulu.

They didn't, couldn't, say much else to each other during the next three minutes as she began sobbing and tears rose in her eyes and rolled down her face. She glimpsed the family picture just for one moment and that, with cousin Jake at the other end of the line, set off an image of a bigger picture in her mind: first her Uncle Steve and Aunt Ida looking after her when she was little, bringing her gifts as if she was theirs; the coming of their own children, and Charles, her brother, too; then the growing up years; she taking care of little cousins Jake and Brigit. Everyone was always there for each other so that now, for anyone to be suddenly taken away was just too severe, too difficult and hurtful to accept.

Elsie Caravella, a co-teacher and a longtime friend at the school, walked right in through the partly open door just as Julie was fumbling in her handbag for tissues. She tiptoed over to her side at the desk and seeing she was on the phone, simply laid a comforting hand on her shoulder, trying to guess what was going on.

She watched Julie's free hand move slowly on the newspaper page and lay a finger listlessly at the name, and she understood.

Chris Phillips hated going to meetings. He hated meetings and thought very little of people who spent a lot of time going to meetings, especially those who attached an air of self-importance to it as you see them get up and go, saying to those around:

"I don't have time now. I got a meeting at ten." Or simply: "I got one at ten."

Like that's what they come to work for. To go to meetings. You wonder—when do they ever do any actual work? He can see it with somebody, a businessman, some vice president of sales or marketing for instance, who had to go out all the time to make a pitch to potential buyers, drum up business.

But that's in private industry where you work your butt off to bring in business or you don't eat. This is government service. You live off of taxpayers' money for which it's only fair for them—the people, the taxpayers—to expect some honest-to-goodness government service out of you instead of just looking important, wasting time bullshitting in meetings.

He'd been in plenty enough of those meetings these past few years in the service that he knew a lot of them were absolutely unnecessary and a total waste of time. A lot of times, there'd be nothing in it that couldn't have been handled by a couple of phone calls or emails between two or three people. Many of them amounted to not much more than pure bullshit sessions between bureaucrats who either had nothing to do in their positions and were always happy to take an opportunity to get out of the office or were simply too lazy to do any real work and just wanted to go to a party all the time. That's what most of those meetings were, as a matter of fact—parties. Social events. And even those that may be thought necessary, they usually turn out to be the result of some disoriented high-grade newcomer, didn't know shit about his assignments, being so dreadfully unprepared or unqualified to do the job and needed to be educated on it.

Then why not hire somebody else better qualified?

Coming out of that eleven o'clock *one* today which lasted an hour and a half, that was exactly what he thought about several of the people in the conference room. Towards the last half hour of it, he realized everything that had taken place so far had been just that—to educate these two GS-14 newcomers of what they should have prepared themselves for before day one on their high-salaried positions in government, as well as a couple of old-time slackers in the office who needed to be hand-held with everything they did, all the time.

Over eighty percent of the work in the office was surveys, statistics, demographics and research. The rest was documentation, IT and automation. Those high-paid newcomers had never done surveys and statistics of any kind. All they'd ever done was research. Shit, anybody with two good legs and who knows how to read could do that.

Of the fourteen mid-level and senior bureaucrats in the room, each pulling between eighty to a hundred-twenty thousand a year, only four should have been there—the two newcomers and the two, of whom one was Chris Phillips, who supplied them with most of the knowledge they lacked. The two slackers should have been fired years ago and the rest stayed in their cubby holes playing games on their computer.

It was now twelve forty-five in the afternoon as he headed down to the fitness center in the basement rec room of the Interior Department Headquarters building. He hadn't had lunch yet but he wasn't all that hungry, his appetite shut coming out of that meeting. But he ate a Hershey bar for some fuel to use up in the thirty-minute workout he did at least twice a week at work. He did this for the upper-body exercise and running every other day for the lower which he would do this evening, with Julie for their Wednesday after-work routine.

The workout consisted basically of Tae Kwon Do routines: ten minutes of floor and upright stretches with a little bit of those yoga twists Julie taught him from her yoga classes, ten minutes of the *poomse's* or Forms—these were punch-kick-stance routines of different combinations, and ten minutes of letting it all out on the kicking pads and the punching bag.

He had done some of this occasionally on weekends with Julie in her condo community gym. He held a second-degree blue belt by the time he quit going to that martial arts school in South Arlington over a year ago. Julie held a second-degree brown belt, the next higher rank color, from another school, in Fairfax, long before he even got into it.

They did *poomse's* together and once in a while did light contact sparring, with pads. When he attacked, he would always hold back the blow a split second before it landed so that it wouldn't deliver a full impact. She would get mad at him and tell him to quit doing that and just hit her good, if he could. He did one time with a roundhouse kick to the rib cage that sent her to the wall. But she bounced back up quick, unfazed, and decked him with a poke punch to the nose and a follow-up front snap kick to the chest.

"I thought this was supposed to be light contact," he said, coming up slowly on his hands and knees.

"Yes. But nobody said how light. Or what's light," she replied.

He went through the workout routines and the half-hour was over too soon. When he got out of the shower room, he had a sudden hunger attack and remembered that he hadn't had lunch. He stopped by the cafeteria and took out two slices of pepperoni mushroom pizza at the pasta counter. While he ate at his desk, he remembered something else—he was supposed to stop at the foodstore after work to pick up some ingredients for the spaghetti dinner with Julie tonight after the run.

He checked the time. He knew she had a one-thirty class and she couldn't talk until after that so he finished lunch, went back to work and waited till a quarter of three before calling her. He tried her desk phone first and hung up after four rings. Then he dialed her cell phone.

"I can't make it tonight, Chris," she said, after he asked what kind of pasta sauce she'd like for the spaghetti.

"What's going on?" he asked, feeling a little uneasy fast. She usually said honey or sweetie, not Chris. See you later, sweetie. Bye, honey. "Something I did? Forgot to do?"

"No, no. I'm on my way to Vienna right now," she said in a fragile voice he didn't remember ever hearing from her. "My uncle..." a pause. "He was killed in the Punchbowl bombing. His family just learned late yesterday."

It sunk in quickly when he thought about how close she was to Steve Santorelli and his family. He himself liked the man the first time they met and learned to like him more after that when he and Julie started seeing each other regularly.

He liked to talk about his ten years in the Army both as an enlisted and an officer, culminating with two tours in Vietnam in the late sixties. Wounded twice in separate engagements with the enemy, he said. Once in Da Nang in '66 along the Han river, with a non-lethal bullet hit on the right hip and again in his second tour in '68 during the Tet Offensive in Hue with a grenade shrapnel, this one he said—just below the left collarbone—he was lucky to survive. It was a big chunk of metal that cut nearly clear to his back and would have pierced his heart and killed him had it entered a couple inches lower.

He also liked to talk about Italy. Rome, Florence, his father and mother's hometowns respectively, and the many trips he had made there over the years. He had just turned sixty-two a few months ago and was going to retire later in the year. Thirty-one years of service, the last twenty with the Army Materiel Command in Alexandria, he told Chris and Julie the last time they were over for dinner at his house in Vienna

It made Chris Phillips sick now that he thought about it. The man looked forward to it and, especially with his son Jake getting married soon, perhaps being a grandfather not long after.

Chris Phillips had always felt, since 9/11, that everytime a terrorist attack happened, it's always someplace else involving somebody else. Now, it suddenly occurred to him that he wasn't that far removed from it.

Later, he would know that he was even closer to it than he ever imagined he was.

*   *   *   *

It was a clear mid-November day. The trees swayed gently in the autumn breeze, their boughs turning bare as the colors drifted quietly to the ground. This would have been a perfect time to run, Chris thought, as he drove down Memorial Drive towards the gate of the Arlington National Cemetery. Up ahead was a car driven by Charles, Julie's brother, with their parents Joseph and Cecilia Santorelli, and some relatives on Joseph's side in the passenger seats. And ahead of them was the car with the family of the deceased following the hearse.

He remembered the times when he ran here once or twice a week, at least ten years ago. He'd park by the Iwo Jima Memorial nearby and do two miles by the river, along the way enjoying the scenery running just outside the cemetery and through the Memorial Drive with the view of the Lincoln Memorial across the Potomac river and the Memorial Gate to the cemetery at the other end.

He still did it occasionally and all those times he'd been here, he never thought what it would be like to come here one day and, in a way, be a part of the place. A participant in what it was meant for, which today, beginning with this morning hour, was a full-honors military burial ceremony for Vietnam veteran Steven Santorelli, former Captain, U.S. Army.

It was half past ten. The wide sidewalks on each side of the road were starting to fill up with tourists, the rush hour traffic had come and gone so that a head-lights-on funeral motorcade with police escorts easily drew attention. Chris Phillips thought of the pictures and news film clips he'd seen of the Kennedy funeral ceremony where crowds of people in grief stood on each side of this same road.

Looking at Julie Santorelli next to him in the passenger seat, he saw the same grief a thousandfold. It was a grief that came with a sense of helplessness at the loss of someone dear, a grief of deep sorrow and loneliness. Being so close to her, today he saw this place not as another tourist stop in the Capital area but truly a shrine, a memorial to those who have earned a resting place here among the many other honored men and women of America.

She wore a pair of sunglasses but he could still see that her eyes were now swollen from crying since they left the funeral home. One of the two women in the backseat, close Santorelli relatives of her father's generation, placed a hand on her shoulder when she sobbed and patted her gently till she calmed down.

At the transfer point inside the Memorial Gate, the flag-draped casket was received officially at the cemetery and transferred to the waiting horsedrawn caisson. From there, the funeral ceremony began, starting with the formation of the funeral procession. This was headed by a band which—at the family's request—consisted only of four drums, followed by two escort squads of soldiers of the 3rd U.S. Infantry, the official Army Honor Guard also known as The Old Guard; the color guards bearing the Stars and Stripes and then the chaplain accompanied by the ceremony's Officer-In-Charge. Behind these was the caisson flanked by three Old Guard pallbearers on each side, and the mourners trailing.

He had seen rituals, ceremonies for various events—birth, marriage, gradua-tion, private funeral, religious holiday memorials, but Chris Phillips had never felt the kind of solemnity he did now while holding Julie's hand and walking behind the caisson with the rest of her relatives. It felt as if there was nothing else going on in the world except what the steady beat of the drums and the sound of the horses' hooves brought to one's awareness of the moment—the loss of a friend, a brother, a husband, a father, an uncle, a fellow 'Nam vet.

During the few minutes that took the procession to the gravesite, he glanced occasionally at the mourners behind them. There were lines of other people who were touched by every part of Steven Santorelli's life—neighbors, co-workers, fel-low ex-soldiers and war veterans. They walked quietly in this cool November morning to bid farewell to someone they knew well, would miss and remember in one way or another.

Each group of mourners or perhaps each mourner had a different sense of loss which came as a result of that heinous Punchbowl bombing. Of course the greatest of this was in the next of kin of the victim. With Julie Santorelli, her sense of loss didn't just bring sadness and grief. It also brought anger and an urge to find an answer to—why this? Why the innocent? The harmless bystander who couldn't care less what fanatic beliefs you pursue in life? What religion? What Ideology? What grievances you harbor against the world?

At the gravesite, after the service, Captain Steven Santorelli was afforded the traditional three-gun salute and the playing of the Taps. Then the presentation of the flag to Brigida Santorelli followed.

Julie watched and listened intently to every part of the ceremony, the step-by-step procedure executed by the Officer-In-Charge and the pallbearers from transferring the casket from the caisson to the grave, to the precision-handling of the flag until it was handed by the chaplain to Steve Santorelli's widow.

She watched her Aunt Ida take the neatly folded American flag in her hands and shed her tears over it, her children next to her looking utterly helpless in wanting to lift her from her sorrow. And she too, Julie, shed some more tears. And with those tears, her anger grew stronger.

CHAPTER 16

▼

While agent John Jacobs recuperated for a whole week from a massive facial and head injury, his partner, agent Richard Bartley, now with a sense of being personally confronted by forces he felt far more lethal than he imagined, began to think more carefully of what happened, what they might have overlooked on their assignment. Instead of grappling with some wild guesses, he thought of backtracking to the day they started working on Ahmed Khalifa. But as soon as he did this, he realized there wasn't much point to it. Because what's there to backtrack to? Not a hell of a lot happened since they got the assignment other than the contacts with Robert Grundell the neighbor, that Saturday-night date and the day at the park that led to the assault on JayJay at the restaurant washroom.

Then he thought of something else—the day they followed Khalifa to the Sheraton Premier Hotel and lost him for a few hours. Another day when nothing happened. But...maybe not.

Since then, they'd learned about the company he worked for, and some of the people in it, with that report the Bureau got from Detroit. Now that they had some names associated with Ahmed Khalifa's existence besides his neighbor Robert Grundell and his girlfriend Rosie Fletcher, why not backtrack to the hotel? It's a long shot but anything at this point is better than nothing.

That, it turned out, wasn't as long a shot as he thought.

The Sheraton Premier guest register computer file showed that Abu Kamal Ramshallah, a vice-president of the company, had stayed in a suite in the hotel up to three days after Ahmed Khalifa went there. As soon as he knew this, Richard Bartley ordered the suite, which happened to be unoccupied at the time, a restricted area.

Print experts were brought in and went through every square inch of every room in the suite. Accessing the IAFIS (integrated automated fingerprint identification system) in Clarksburg, West Virginia using RFMRS (remote fingerprint match reporting software), they found out that some of the prints they lifted in the suite matched those lifted in the restaurant where agent Jacobs was assaulted. Learning this raised some hair on the back of agent Bartley's neck. Nothing spookier than a fear of the unknown.

What in the hell is going on here? he thought, trying to calm himself down and analyze the situation. So what he had was: it's a sure thing Ahmed Khalifa was in that hotel suite with this Abu Kamal Ramshallah who was probably one of his bosses in the company, along with agent Jacobs' attacker, whoever the devil that person is. Skip what they were doing there for now. So, three sets of fingerprints tie these three people together. Except for Ahmed Khalifa, two of them were unknown but it's only a matter of procedure—open or covert—getting the whole spread on Abu Kamal.

But who in the world is this other guy with them in the hotel, the same devil who stalked the agents in the restaurant and beat up on JayJay in the washroom? He must've known they had Ahmed Khalifa under surveillance and been on their tail all along. Back at the park. Maybe even before then, days before. But why the assault?

Simple—the devil wanted to know why we're following Ahmed Khalifa around, possibly by finding out who we are. Explains agent Jacobs' stolen wallet too. If the attacker's intent is to make it appear a robbery assault, it's now nullified.

We got some real work to do here, now agent Richard Bartley thought. One thing needed to be done now more than anything else is find out what these people are up to and who they are, starting with the unknown attacker.

This time, with what he had on Abu Kamal, in addition to Ahmed Khalifa, Bartley didn't have to take any long shot or be like shooting in the dark. He could pick and choose how he wanted to go about it

He could have the Bureau officially contact MidEast Continental and request a visit with one of their officers, Abu Kamal Ramshallah, question the man about that day at the Sheraton Premier Hotel, make him identify everyone he was with in the suite and bring them all in. Simple, but a dumb thing to do.

Why? Because this is where the question of what they were at the hotel for that day, what these Middle Eastern bozos are up to, comes into play. You bust them now, you catch one bad guy and that's all you get. The rest comes clean unless you dig up something on them which you know they are going to make sure doesn't happen.

Alright, then bring in Ahmed Khalifa on probable cause based on evidence of complicity in the commission of a crime against a federal law officer. Same thing. Only, even dumber. Whatever they're up to, the real reason for the assault on agent Jacobs including his wallet being stolen, the whole operation—whatever it may be—they're going to fold up, hide, put away until things settle down.

So, Bartley chose instead to be patient, and clever. He had one of the Bureau's Arab-language experts, a woman, call Abu Kamal's office in the company's Detroit headquarters, impersonating an oil trader's representative needing to discuss business with the man. She was told the man was out of town but was promptly given the hotel and suite in Baltimore, Maryland, where he was staying.

Abu Kamal was immediately put under surveillance the day after the assault on agent Jacobs at the restaurant. That same day, he drove a man calling himself John Tyler to Baltimore-Washington International from the Courtyard by Marriott Hotel.

✳   ✳   ✳   ✳

Abu Kamal Ramshallah liked staying at that Westfields Marriott in Chantilly, Virginia whenever he came to Washington, D.C. mostly for its proximity to Dulles International. And it was nice and quiet, away from the congestion of the big Capital city. But it was far out there, thirty miles away from places he needed to go to, people he had to work with, plan things with.

So, occasionally he used the ninth-floor Columbia Plaza office apartment here in Foggy Bottom. It's convenient, near the subway and the GWU campus where, too, he could always call upon several of the sleepers attending the university for help of any kind in the event of an emergency. As a matter of fact, he had two of them downstairs now on duty through most of the day—and night, as needed, equipped with beepers and cell phones and on the lookout for trouble.

Since the day Mustapha Khan discovered those government tails on Ahmed Khalifa, everyone agreed to exercise added precautions and increase security. No one can be too safe especially at a time like this. Mustapha had argued once again that Ahmed Khalifa as well as Bobby should now be viewed as high security risks, a danger to all of them and the Organization, and that perhaps something must be done about them soon. This time, Abu Kamal couldn't argue much about it but cautioned him, as well as Commander Omar, about doing anything rash.

He imagined the entire American intelligence community and its forces, civilian and military, now like a mad dog, some kind of a tortured beast, snarling, rearing to unleash its anger and ferocity at the tormentor it can not find, or see. Thus, it was wise to take precautions and consider alternatives now should they be needed later.

A week after Operation Punchbowl, he couldn't get enough of the media coverage of the event. Just like with Operation North 27 a few weeks ago which, in fact, was still very much in the news everyday and was now commonly referred to as the Second Pentagon Attack, or Pentagon II. Both were on all the cable news networks every hour of the day. Every single development about the events were out quickly. Among the latest:

'Three of the high-ranking officials who were among the victims at the Punchbowl bombing are now counted as survivors of the attack. The President of the Philippines who suffered life threatening injuries and had been in a coma for three days had regained consciousness yesterday but remained in critical condition.

'The Secretary of State had just been taken out of the intensive care unit at the Tripler Army Medical Center in Honolulu after exhaustive hours of surgery. Likewise, the Governor of Hawaii just emerged from a third operation since entering the hospital and is now out of the intensive care unit.

'Another high-ranking American guest at the Veterans Day event, unfortunately, did not survive his injuries. U.S Senator Ignacio Lorenzo of Hawaii, the first U.S. Senator of Filipino-American descent, expired from massive internal injuries yesterday morning.'

A front-page item in the copy of the Washington Post he was reading said: 'So far, no evidence had been found to establish a link between the Punchbowl bombing in Hawaii and Pentagon II.'

Funny how irreverent the American media is. They make it sound like a movie sequel. Rocky II, The Godfather II. Even as many of their countrymen, women and children are dying, their sacred grounds desecrated and spilled with the blood of their heroes and veterans, they had the gall to be so casual about such tragedies in their lives. It just shows how disrespectful and wanton these infidels are and how much more they could be to others the way they have been all these years. Arrogant bastards.

But what a wholesome, satisfying feeling it gave him. It was the same with Omar Husain and the leadership of the Organization in Cairo and Riyadh when word got to him through his boss in Detroit. They were no less exuberant.

Were it only possible, he wished they could all gather for a celebration. Everyone, from the headquarters in Cairo, the offices in Detroit and New York, London, Paris, Madrid Hamburg, Kuala Lumpur and Manila; the operatives in Baltimore, Los Angeles, Miami, Chicago, and especially their heroes in Honolulu.

But of course that was not possible. Even this small gathering he was setting up here in Foggy Bottom with several men the next two days, he felt a little uneasy about. The crazed and bleeding beast is on high alert, its senses honed a hundred times to pick up on the slightest scent of its tormentor and strike with no warning whatsoever.

They must exercise great caution at every turn each of them took. Most especially their brilliant young Commander Omar who was due in the apartment this evening along with a fresh stock of several of their select Soldiers of Islam from New York and Baltimore.

In their telephone conversation two days ago, Omar Husain—just back in Baltimore from New York, had asked what is 'next in the agenda'. Thanksgiving is coming, he mentioned, which ushers in the Christmas holiday season. This would truly be a good time to send these Christian and Jewish oppressors of our people a message they will long remember and which perhaps would eventually make them realize what they have been doing to us. Give them a good taste of their own medicine, he said. The same type they've been shoving down our throats in the lands they occupy of our beloved Palestine, in the land of my father, Lebanon, the stolen Golan Heights, the West Bank and the Gaza Strip.

For a moment there, the Commander got emotional, his voice echoing the sound of a war-cry in an open battlefield. How he understood the man only so well.

Twelve years ago, when he was Omar Husain's age, he had the same strong feeling of revulsion against Israel and the enemies of Islam that he finally decided to join the Organization. The hatred he felt of the Jews—which had been building up since way back in the Six-Day war in '67 when his entire family and two generations of all their relatives lost their land, all their possessions—finally reached a peak where he could no longer live with himself without doing something about it, without doing something to get back at the enemy of his people, of his family, of his country.

He knew that emotion now boiling in Omar Husain only so well that after they talked on the phone, he got in touch with Ahmed Khalifa and Bobby immediately to order another drop either for Thanksgiving or Christmas. We will hit them where it hurts them the most, as often as we can and when they least expect it, he could still hear the Commander's voice saying as he spoke to Bobby from a phone booth in the lobby of the St. Regis hotel, a designated historical landmark of the city, two blocks from the White House.

Somehow, he felt how ludicrous it was that here he was, within sight of the house where America's president lives, plotting the next attack against the country. Three of his men—Kashim Najoub, Hassan Bahaji and Hamad Salim, surviving warriors of past operations, sitting in the hotel restaurant having lunch among some of the most influential power brokers in Washington, D.C.—defense contractors, government bureaucrats and civil servants, lobbyists, many of them Jews no doubt with their hands out asking for an additional billion for arms buildup against the Arab countries surrounding Israel.

Damn Jewish puppets. They can't see that they are just being used by this Christian American empire to carry out its economic colonization of our part of the world. Puppets, being used in another Crusade, just like the Christians did for more than two hundred years between the 11th and 13th century, this time not just for religious purposes but for our oil. And the hell with our Faith and culture and our whole way of life.

Thinking about this, he got fired up himself just like when it first began in him decades ago. Too bad Omar Husain didn't think they could come up with a plan that would be successful in attacking those nuclear power plants in Virginia and North Carolina. The most recent reports Omar got from the research he ordered to supplement the data in Bobby's sample drop a few weeks ago did not recommend targeting any of the plants. Too protected, the reports said, especially now that the federal government had beefed up security in all the country's nuclear and other infra-structure facilities.

However, don't be too disappointed, Bobby said over the phone, telling him to look in page three of today's paper which he did immediately after they hung up. Bobby said that he had a couple of diskettes ready and that he could make the drop anytime.

On page three of the Post was an article about several federal water and power projects in the west, named The Big Thunder, nearing completion. There were pictures showing the one near Lake Sakakawea just north of Bismarck, North Dakota. It was to be inaugurated in December, before Christmas, the celebration to be attended by the chairman of the Senate Committee on Energy and Natural Resources, and half the members of its Subcommittee on Water and power. The senators were to take a train ride from Washington, D.C. to North Dakota, an act symbolizing the westward push of the industrial age in the nineteenth century.

Some of these Washington politicians like to be dramatic once in a while, thought Abu Kamal, at the same time picturing the event. First, say a half a dozen U.S. Senators chugging along in a train halfway across the country. They'll be well guarded of course. We'll see what's in Bobby's drop about that.

Then the inauguration program. Who else will be there? Probably many of the big fish in state and federal bureaucracy in addition to the senators. Maybe even some cabinet members. And the project itself—what's to do about it? Bobby said the drop will have everything they'll need to know about the event. The timeline, the participants, and most important—security, including that for the senators' itinerary.

This sounded just like what he would have asked for had he read the paper before he talked to Bobby. He called Omar Husain in Baltimore to tell him about it and the Commander agreed after he read the article in the paper. He was so enthusiastic that he unexpectedly called back the next day and said that he would like to meet Bobby himself by taking part in the drop. Ahmed Khalifa was nowhere to be found. It was learned from Bobby when they set up the drop that Ahmed took a weekend drive to Virginia Beach with his girlfriend.

The drop was set up for tomorrow between twelve-thirty and one in the afternoon in a different area of the park. Bobby said it made no difference to him who picks up the drop.

∗　　∗　　∗　　∗

With the tightening of the cyber security in the office and throughout the federal government, Robert A. Grundell decided it was now still too risky covering up his track in the access-log database by manually switching his userid to that of Leon T. Justice. So he wrote a four-line utility to automate the switch as soon as he logs on the computer:

```
If &&userid = OCDLRAG and &&termid = ILD41 and &&time = 1000 thru 1200
    userid = OCDLLTJ, termid = ILD70      endif
If &&userid = OCDLRAG and &&time = 1500 thru 1700
    userid = &&enter      endif
```

and had Max Poysen add it to the online system monitor software.

Now, when he logged on to the network at his terminal between ten in the morning and twelve noon, his userid (xxxxRAG) and terminal id number (ILD41) were replaced with Leon's (xxxxLTJ, ILD70). Between three and five in the afternoon, he can log on at any terminal in the Division and he could switch his userid to anyone's by entering it on the keyboard at a prompt line on the screen.

When he asked Max Poysen to do it—load the utility program with the system monitor software, Max looked at it for a second, turned to him with a funny smile on his face and said: "I don't give a shit. Do your thing, man. I'm with you. Fuck 'em."

"I knew you'd say that," Robert replied, giving Max a light jab on the arm.

The move to oust Leon Justice and abolish his high-paid do-nothing job, to the growing pain of the majority in the Division, hadn't made much progress with management. Meaning—the Division chief, Milton Pheasant and the head of OCDL, the Treasury Undersecretary.

Robert Grundell, for one, along with Max Poysen and Eddie Mahone who penned the original of the letter had started to sense the momentum of the protest slowing down. It had been a month since the letter went out, two weeks since anything was said or done about it by any of the recipients of the letter. The Inspector General's office earlier had expressed interest in supporting it but now seemed stymied while waiting for any response from the Undersecretary's office. And who knows how long it'll take before anybody in that high office, let alone the Undersecretary himself, decided to take up the issue. For all anybody knew in the Division, they could all be in cahoots to keep these freeloaders in place.

There could be as many assholes and parasites up there, Eddie Mahone told Robert Grundell, doing nothing but collecting big fat government paychecks every couple of weeks, same as down here in the Division and everywhere else in the agency and throughout the whole friggin' federal government service.

The Office of Personnel Management which is the agency that sets the standards of hiring and firing responded to the letter saying it had no authority to rule on the issue or intercede for anyone in that regard. OPM had no business interfering with how an agency used its allocated budget.

The last hope was the Office of Special Counsel. And the latest from Elga Bailey who was pursuing the issue through the union, AFGE, where she served as a steward, was that she had talked to an official the union president knew personally there. The official had agreed to start an investigation as soon as they had examined all the facts. A word directly to the Undersecretary, Elga said she suggested to the official too, could make a lot of difference.

In the meantime, Robert Grundell had resigned to the idea that Leon Justice along with all the rest of Herod Hardin and Milton Pheasant's cronies were here to stay and that there's really nothing anybody can do about it. Nothing that can be held up against the accepted politics and cronyism in the office, that is. Maybe not, he thought, but as far as he's concerned, the point here now is to do something the same as what they're doing. Something they can't get back at you for. Something to fuck 'em up and at the same time either give you the personal satisfaction of being able to get back at them or to make some personal gain out of it, or both.

So far, besides a new home entertainment center in his living room, not to mention his rapidly growing bank account balance, one other personal gain he had coming was the year-model Lexus GS430 luxury sedan he had ordered from an Alexandria dealer a couple of days ago. And for his personal satisfaction, for now he continued to imagine Jerome K. Bolden of the FBI's Investigative Services Division keeping track of Leon's activities over the government network, especially after the Punchbowl bombing, and one day the asshole being yanked out of his office for questioning, along with Herod and his other parasite minions.

Since Max Poysen loaded the utility program, he had logged on as Leon T. Justice dozens of times, other times as Herod L. Hardin and a couple of others in the Division, friends of theirs, at one of the open workstations, cruising the government networks, accessing top secret, critical-sensitive and all kinds of classified files and databases; downloading and decrypting files which were possible future drops. One of these was for the drop he had offered Abu Kamal Ramshallah, the inaugural programs for The Big Thunder projects. One file, in particular, was the security design for the event at the project in North Dakota which was the first one scheduled for inauguration.

The event made a spread in the paper and Abu Kamal and his associate liked it so much after they read the article that they immediately set up a drop for three days later. Day after tomorrow, in the afternoon.

*   *   *   *

Electronic eavesdropping, sleuthing, snooping. Call it whatever you want, but that's what it all boils down to, agent Frank DiPaolo said to agent Nancy Schneider one lunchtime at Friday's Restaurant, corner of Beauregard and Route 7 not far from their 'office' in the Treasury Department's Office of Civil Defense Logistics at Bailey's Crossroad. And he likes it, he added. It's exciting, clever and very interesting.

In his five years with the Bureau, he'd been to many computer classes—a load of those OJT's: some computer programming, systems analysis and user requirements, networks and communications. A little bit of everything. A big switch from his Army MOS—small arms specialty. He wished he had gotten into computers sooner and now aimed to get more into it.

"Never too late for anything," agent Schneider, who had been in the IT field for years since her Navy days, told him. "As long as you have the enthusiasm. Tell you what—you teach me how to shoot, I'll teach you how to snoop."

"Deal," he said, enthusiastically.

A few days after they got set up in their workstation, his concern earlier at working with an ex-Navy officer, and a woman at that, five years younger than him, quickly dissipated. Now he was actually glad he was teamed up with agent Nancy Schneider who turned out to be a real pro at what she was trained for and did both in the Navy and the Bureau.

Assigned as the lead analyst in the stakeout at OCDL, she did practically everything for them to 'fit in' with the career staff, from talking to others about the kind of work they'd be doing—security, disaster recovery—and, likewise, learning who did what, to picking up fast on the day-to-day conduct of business between the shop and its customers both inhouse (Treasury) and with outside agencies.

With the necessary help from a contractor staff, a system software engineer, it took her one day to get familiar with the technical lay-of-the-land—the global network and communication system, the mainframe system, the local area network, the major applications running in the systems, and the authorized end-users or customers accessing the systems. Each day, she took time for him to catch up by sitting down with him for a half hour here, an hour there, soaking his head with the seemingly magical workings of state-of-the-art high-technology.

By the middle of the first week, they were both doing what they were fielded out there to do—snoop. Case the joint. Find out how grim the situation might actually be, from what it looked like with the access-log profile Jerome Bolden had cut of some of the authorized accessors of the networks.

With the software tools they were provided by the software engineer, they were able to do more than Jerome Bolden was doing remotely in his office in the Bureau headquarters. They not only could monitor authorized accesses to classified files but know what the accessor was doing with the files—reading, updating or downloading. One of the tools journaled the entire session they were monitoring, saving every keyboard entry and the resulting internal processing in the computer, and they could re-play the whole session later.

In their second week, they had gathered enough data to support Jerome Bolden's findings in his top twenty-five percent TRIDEX query report, and more. Several more people were added to their target staff. Martin R. Hawkins (HS003), Ralph D. Robson (RS004) and Herod L. Hardin (HS002) showed up among the top accessors of classified files and the TSL bin along with Leon T. Justice (JS001), Pacifico M. Inocentes (IS010), Robert A. Grundell (GS012) and several other people in the Interstate Logistics and the Deployment Divisions.

Leon T. Justice whom they now referred to as JS001 appeared to be the busiest cruising the government networks and accessing classified files, along with HS002, HS003 and RS004. Agent Schneider wished they had two or three more terminals they could log on to simultaneously everyday so they could monitor every one of them at the same time and capture a copy of their sessions for later viewing. They would just have to work hard at it. Keep themselves glued to the computer every minute of the day and journal as many of the top target sessions as they could.

Near the end of the week, Frank DiPaolo thought they had enough to make their case against the target staff stick. They must begin talking to these people, find out what they're up to without scaring them away, though.

Schneider agreed, reported to headquarters and got an okay—not to start an investigation of each individual, but to simply 'feel' them out by talking to them. Find a way to do some work with them so they could observe them more closely, in person, but without making them suspicious.

"We'll do," Nancy Schneider told Jerome Bolden and his boss, and to her partner Frank DiPaolo: "Leave that to me. Here's what we'll do—"

That same day, they worked out a plan to pay each one a working visit by arranging it with their respective branch chiefs. Their requirement, they stated to the branch chiefs, was to know the impact of a cyber attack on the work of selected analysts, particularly the senior staff who handled classified data, so they could find ways to recover from it, but more important, to determine counter-measures now.

They started with GS012, Robert Grundell, at eight-thirty in the morning the next day. They decided they'd start with someone at the middle of the twenty-five in the list, work their way up through the top half, the high-risk half, for the next couple of days. After they'd done this, they'll report back to headquarters and get a decision on the next move which agent Frank DiPaolo hoped would result in some real open activity. Like search and seizure (of evidence), apprehension and arrest.

Robert Grundell was about to go to one of the open workstations a short hallway walk away from his office to logon either as Hawkins, Robson or Justice—he was going to decide at the workstation, when he got the phone call from this

Frank DiPaolo, one of the people brought in from the Phoenix, Arizona regional office to work on some interim assignment, so they said. When he first met them the day they were shown around by the admin staff, he had a funny feeling they didn't come from Phoenix, nor were they Treasury people.

The call was to tell him they were coming in a couple of minutes for the visit which was announced in the email sent out Division-wide by Milton Pheasant yesterday explaining what it was all about. Backup operations, disaster recovery, security, crime prevention and countermeasures.

"That's what we're here for," Frank DiPaolo said a few minutes later after he and Nancy Schneider were seated in front of Robert Grundell.

"Sounds like a lot of work," Robert commented. "So, what do you have to do—go all over the place and check how business is conducted?"

"Exactly," replied Nancy Schneider. She had been busy secretly eyeballing the twelve-foot square office—workstation, the preferred term nowadays in management—through her peripheral vision when she was not in direct eye-contact with Robert. "Look for areas vulnerable to, let's say, outside disruption."

"Hackers, viruses and worms, cyber attacks," added Robert.

"Yes. Security holes, logical as well as physical, and figure out what best to do to plug them."

"And to do this, we need to talk to you guys," said Frank DiPaolo, real casual and friendly. "Ask a few questions about the work you do. How you do them. Who you do them with. Data exchange, that sort of thing."

From there, the two agents took turns every few minutes talking to Robert. While one talked, the other did the eyeballing of the place, and of Robert—his behavior, the way he said things, his eye and body movement. Basic stuff they were trained to do when they joined the FBI.

It took them forty minutes to get through with all the questions they had prepared and jot down a page of notes each. Robert Grundell looked natural throughout. There was no sign of discomfort or hedging with any of the questions he was asked to which he gave quick, straight answers, including the one about the procedure for accessing the Top-Secret-Log Bin where he had to get a new password from a guy in Fort Meade every morning.

They shook hands with Robert Grundell and thanked him as they got up to leave and move on to the next worker. They didn't speak a word to each other about what they saw or thought. They just moved on from one worker to another, using their time frugally and discreetly to get as many of them done as they could through the day. Several of them weren't available, out of the office, on leave or something, so they lined them up for another day and moved up the ones they had scheduled for later and who were available. One of them was Leon Justice. Another was Martin Hawkins.

Shortly before noon, they'd done five of them—JS001, HS003, IS010, PS011 and GS012—and were back in their workstation comparing notes. They ran into a problem with Leon Justice (JS001) and Martin Hawkins (HS003) over the same question—How often do you log on the system daily, on average?

"Three times, tops, on average," was Leon's response. This raised a red flag with the agents instantly. In their monitoring records the past whole week, the userid OCDLLTJ showed up more than twice that often. It was the same with Hawkins who said three to four times on average when his userid showed up at least twice as often in the agents' monitors.

They had no problem with the others, including Robert Grundell whose records showed exactly what he told them. Four to five times, at least, depending on how busy his day was, Robert said. Almost all of his duties at work are done on the computer, he said. The global network and the mainframe, mostly. The rest on the local area network and the telephone.

"The man certainly appears to earn his paycheck," agent Frank DiPaolo told his partner on their way to that Peruvian roast-chicken short-order place they discovered a few days ago, a quick five-minute walk from the office on Route 7. "He's too busy to be doing anything else on the networks."

"I was just thinking that," agreed Nancy Schneider. "We could pretty much leave him alone. The same with IS010 and PS011. I don't think we have any problem with them."

"This assignment sure is getting more and more interesting each day," said agent DiPaolo. "I can't wait to get to the bottom of this."

"If there really is something going on in that office," said agent Schneider thoughtfully, "it could be pretty serious. Really serious."

"What do you think?"

"I think there *is* something going on there. Something back of my mind tells me."

"What if you're right. What then?"

"Depends on what it is. Let's finish up with the rest of the top twelve today and tomorrow. If we run into more problems, we'll see what headquarters decides. I'll suggest we start gathering physical evidence to supplement our Q & A notes and our monitor journals. Then bust the high probables, without setting the alarm on the rest, on grounds of national security risks."

*   *   *   *

They're here! thought Robert Grundell minutes after they had left, trying not to panic and scare himself stiff. Phoenix regional office my foot.

He went about doing his morning routine normally including that to access the TSL bin and check for entries addressed to OCDL. The question that loomed big in his head now was—how foolproof had his actions against the assholes been? When he was doing it manually and, now, that utility program he had Max Poysen load in the system monitor software recently?

Could there be a way his userid and terminal ID were still captured somewhere in the system when he logged on using somebody else's userid? When he was doing the switch manually in the access-log database, wouldn't his userid show as the one that updated the log record? That's the way it works when updating mainframe application files. The system captures the userid, date and time to the hundredth of a second.

Shit!

He struggled to think rationally, now saying to himself: "Maybe not. In the mainframe, yes. But this is client-server file...network architecture...think, think fast! Shit, yes, it's the same thing...maybe even worse. It's the same as in the internet where personal data can be captured, then bought and sold or used to ruin people's lives!"

His heart raced as fast as his hand did to pick up the phone. "Max, how yuh doing, man?"

"You know what day it is, don't you?" Max Poysen said to remind him that it was Thursday, the day they openly submit to the authority of master Leon Justice by turning in their weekly work activity report to him.

"Damn that sonofabitch, you're right," Robert grumbled, then sighed as he now wrestled with anger and anxiety inside.

"Hey, did you get a visit from those folks from Phoenix?" Max asked.

"Yes, they were just here an hour ago."

"They left here ten minutes ago. Wanna know what I think?"

"Tell me." Robert was dying to ask Max what he called for but thought this might have a bearing on it by chance.

"I think Herod did it again. These two guys from Phoenix who are probably his relatives ran out of work over there, didn't have any place to go since nobody else wants them so Herod got them in here on another make-work assignment."

I hope like hell you're right, Max, Robert thought for he was still really not a hundred percent sure about his suspicions. At the same time, he hoped Max was wrong but that he, Robert, would turn out to be safe from them.

"Listen, Max, tell me about that access-log database."

"Yes? Whatabout it?"

"When you update a record, does it show who updated it?"

"Yes. The userid is trapped with the other audit-trail data. It's placed at the very end of the record."

Robert Grundell froze. He felt like he was being sucked in a whirlpool that's increasingly turning violent and there was no escaping from it. Like grabbing the last straw to stay afloat, he asked: "It's archived like any other online files, right?"

"Yes."

"How often?"

"I don't know," replied Max, causing Robert to stomp hard on a pile of print-outs under his right foot. "It gets pretty big fast," Max continued. "Imagine everytime anybody in the Treasury Department with access authorization logs on the system gets an access-log record created in the database. I say it would have to be rolled out to an archive backup, um...at least once a week to free up space. Maybe even twice a week."

Robert drew a deep breath at hearing that. Some relief. At least now, he knew, there was less chance of being caught—unless somebody dug into the archived database—hoping Max was right about what he said. And Max was more often right than wrong when it came to stuff like this. System maintenance. That's what Uncle Sam was paying him for.

But Robert would not rest with perhaps half the chance, or even less, of one day getting shackled in chains and hauled in a high-security federal prison. He would do all he could to see that that's what happened to Leon Justice and his friends first, before it happened to him.

At two-thirty in the afternoon, he dialed Leon's number from the telephone at one of the open workstations, hoping the man would be out of his office. But he wasn't. As soon as the phone was picked up, Robert hung up.

He did this at between ten- to fifteen-minute intervals. At ten after three, the phone kept ringing. On the tenth ring, he hung up and went over to Leon's office. In his hand was the two-page weekly work activity report he had prepared earlier, as usual, full of resentment and nagging anger much the same as everybody else felt in the Division.

It was less than a minute's walk from the workstation but he wished he could fly to get there and get the weekly report off his hands before he changed his mind and tore it to pieces. He stood at the doorway momentarily to scan first the immediate areas outside quickly, then the inside of the office. No one was around. It was nearing the start of the early quitting time and most people were at their desks clearing up stuff.

It was easily twice the size of his crammed 12 x 12 workstation, with lots of room for all the fancier office furniture Leon had in it. A dark hardwood executive desk eight feet long with an ergonomically engineered swivel chair, a computer workstation to the left side with lots of shelves and drawers and a large surface for the keyboard. Behind, under the window stool were full-length base cabinets and more drawers. To the right were full-height bookshelves covering half the length of the wall. Across on the opposite wall hung artwork in expensive wood frames. In the middle was a conference/reference table with four chairs around it. Robert felt he was in some CEO's office suite.

"What in the hell does this guy need this fancy office for, with what little he does in the office and for something the U.S. government does not need?" he thought disgustedly. A wave of revulsion coursed through his insides at the sight of such a senseless waste of taxpayer money. It's not fair, he thought, this parasite riding high on the backs of those who produce real work, those who were the true bread and butter of the federal government service.

He had one other reason for going into Leon's office besides dropping the work report in the inbox on top of the expensive desk. The one reason why he also didn't want Leon to be in the office when he went in there and why he now moved very quickly to pull out the top drawer behind the desk. Reaching into the back of the drawer, he slipped two of the diskettes he carried in his pocket and buried them deep at the bottom of a pile of papers.

Next he pulled out the bottom drawer which was half-filled with vertically stacked folders and slipped two more diskettes at the bottom rear. He wondered what the guy kept in those folders, got curious enough to pry some of them open and found most of them empty. He needed to get out of there now twice as fast as he went in or he might throw up. So he moved quickly, slam-dunking the work activity report in the inbox as he hurried out

Going by Herod Hardin's office, another habitat that was even more posh than Leon's, he glanced the two 'Phoenix' people as they were getting up from their seats, one of them, the man, shaking hands with Herod. It looked like they were going around seeing as many people as they could through the day. He didn't think they were Herod's relatives.

He headed back to his workstation feeling more secure than earlier in the day, and satisfied, with what he was doing and was yet to do including the drop tomorrow afternoon at the park. Abu Kamal Ramshallah had hinted at another cash bonus coming with the drop, in addition to the regular legit consultant-fee paycheck every couple of weeks. Good. With the bonus from the previous drop which he had hardly touched and this next one, he should have more than enough cash for the Lexus GS430. With some luck, the dealer in Alexandria could deliver the model package loaded with all the top-of-the-line options he ordered, early during the day Saturday. Then he might just get lucky with Paula while hauling her ass in the spanking brand new luxury sedan with that fresh new-car smell during their date in the evening.

Damn Ahmed, he sure got way ahead of him in this dating game. Now he's out there in Virginia Beach lounging around with Rosie Fletcher getting laid left and right.

About a dozen steps to his workstation, he saw Ralph Robson, a model paper-shuffler and free-loading bureaucrat, office politician, known for having no qualms about taking credit for the hard work and accomplishment of others, coming up the hallway. He was another member of Herod's squad of ass-kissing deadwoods, an arrogant, sarcastic bastard he couldn't bear to look at, hear, smell or sense within a mile.

As they passed each other two steps from his room doorway, he turned his head sideways to proceed into his workstation just as Ralph afforded him a frugal nod which he acknowledged with an equally dismissive wave of a hand. With his piss-off scale up a couple of notches just by getting near Ralph Robson, he pulled over a disk tray from beside the computer monitor on his desk, selected a half a dozen diskettes from it and started making labels for each with the word processor. The same kind he put on the ones now in Leon's drawers.

Several of them read:

> 'To: Abu Kamal Ramshallah
> Subj.: Big Thunder 1, North Dakota'
> Disk 1: Inauguration Pgm and Security'

> 'To: Abu Kamal Ramshallah
> Subj.: Big Thunder 3, Montana'
> Disk 1: Inauguration Pgm and Security'

> 'To: Rahim Akbar
> Subj.: POTUS Inauguration Day, D.C.'
> Disk 1: Inauguration Pgm and Security'

He looked at the time—3:45PM. He had a little time left to go back to one of the open workstations and log on as Ralph D. Robson. Maybe do some more downloading, park it in a mainframe sequential-file format with RDROB as one of the file-name qualifiers. Make a copy of it too in Robson's mainframe work file. Do several of them. Fuck him up good. The maggot! Then wait till the guy left for the day—in another fifteen minutes—and slip a couple of the labeled diskettes in one of his drawers.

And tomorrow morning, before he goes for the drop at the park, he could do Leon T. Justice some more. Martin R. Hawkins and Herod L. Hardin too. Fuck 'em all up good.

CHAPTER 17

▼

The day after the Punchbowl bombing, the trace on John Tyler from the suite in the Rainbow Tower of the Hilton Hawaiian Village hotel, the abandoned car and the airport led back to Baltimore-Washington International. And from there to the Courtyard by Marriott hotel near the airport. It was as simple as a connect-the-dot exercise. The same with the Bureau's web of investigative assignments. Just linking one with another, see if they connect—a field agent's assignment with another.

When agent Richard Bartley learned of the origin of John Tyler's itinerary to Honolulu, he didn't need a crystal ball to pick the hotel to check near the airport, especially knowing of someone else staying in that same hotel who was seen dropping somebody off at the airport five days before the Punchbowl. Two days after that bombing in Hawaii, late at night, prints were lifted from Abu Kamal Ramshallah's car in the Courtyard by Marriott hotel parking garage near the BWI. The following day, shock gripped most of the Divisions in the FBI Headquarters in Washington, D.C.

One set of fingerprints from the car matched every one of the sets previously recorded in the IAFIS database of the fingerprints of Saladin. Then within a couple of hours of this finding, the report reached the Bureau headquarters that prints lifted in John Tyler's rented car in Honolulu also matched those of Saladin.

A beehive of activity erupted at headquarters, the suddenness of it catching Richard Bartley unprepared for a non-stop twenty-four-hour duty including an all-night meeting with dozens of analysts from CID, ISD and several from CJIS, Clarksburg. Everyone was literally patting him on the back. No federal intel service had come this close on the trail of Saladin. Not since the existence of the faceless, nameless, unseen mastermind of several acts of worldwide terrorism was first established back in 1989 after an assassination attempt on a group of Israeli diplomatic officials in Greece (25 people killed including three Israelis), and the bombing the following year in front of the U.S. embassy in Paris (15 dead including four Americans). No trace of him had been found in any of the succeeding terrorist acts anywhere in the world since, not in the U.S. Embassy bombings in Africa, the USS Cole, the 9/11 suicide hijackings or the recent 10/ 24 attack at the Pentagon.

But now, thanks to agent Bartley's patience and thoroughness, at least it was established that Saladin is around, and here in America. This was no small break in the investigation of the unknown man and hopefully it would be the beginning of a continuing process to capture or kill him.

With his now known connection to MidEast Continental which was now under intensive but hush scrutiny by the SEC, the Attorney General and the IRS, it could be a matter of picking on one lead after another, starting with this Abu Kamal Ramshallah, followed by the rest of their people in Detroit and elsewhere, to finally identify and bag Saladin.

But it was too late, much too late for the hundreds of people who were killed in the horror of the Veterans Day Punchbowl bombing which came five days after John Tyler flew from the mainland to Honolulu. Five days which was all Saladin needed, coming from Baltimore, to plan and execute the attack. For he was a decisive man, quick thinking, intelligent, and very elusive.

And how elusive this time became a test on the capability of American intelligence and its power to capture him especially when it was determined that he was responsible for that latest attack on America. The all-out manhunt, classified top secret and kept from the press—perhaps the most far-reaching and intensive on record of such an event in the country, was launched nationwide and later worldwide hours after it was confirmed that John Tyler was Saladin.

*   *   *   *

Samir Osmani drove dutifully on the Baltimore-Washington Parkway towards Washington, D.C. as if mindful only of the road. But he heard every word of what Mustapha Khan, in the front passenger seat of the rented Buick Regal, had been telling Commander Omar in the back seat. Glancing at the rearview mirror, he watched the Commander respond with short, thoughtful comments.

Since early morning at breakfast in the hotel lounge, Mustapha had been trying to talk Omar Husain into a number of things, mostly about the Commander's safety. He had already succeeded in doing so with two things.

One, not to go back to the same hotel, the Courtyard by Marriott at BWI, when he arrived in Baltimore from New York. The Commander had seen the reasoning behind it and agreed to check in at the Comfort Inn Baltimore West, a not-so-fancy lodging on Security Boulevard just off the Baltimore beltway I-695 where Mustapha had booked three modest single rooms for each of them.

It was wise, he suggested to Commander Omar, to lay low for sometime and avoid exposure at airports and fancy hotels. Comfort Inn West was a smaller hotel, only three stories and ten miles away from the airport.

Two, that the four other men—the two sleepers who traveled with the Commander from New York and the two others who joined them when they arrived in Baltimore several days ago travel separately from the three of them to Washington, D.C. The four sleepers were even advised to split up and travel only in pairs, and stay at different hotels in Virginia, Maryland or the District, which was done. Two of them checked in at the Springfield Hilton in Fairfax and the other two in the Hilton Alexandria Mark Center, just a few miles apart off I-95 in northern Virginia.

Now Mustapha was trying to convince the Commander to change the location of the meeting from Foggy Bottom to someplace else.

"You make it sound like things are so difficult now," Omar Husain said as Samir Osmani drove them out of Baltimore a little while ago. "And you're going to keep that up till I agree, aren't you?"

"Commander," Mustapha pleaded. "All we have to do is put ourselves in the position of the FBI. Those two agents I discovered, in particular."

"Let's do that, then. Go on."

"Alright. Now, they followed that Pakistani Ahmed Khalifa instead of Bobby. Let's forget what Bobby had to do with those agents for now. The more important thing is how much do they know about Ahmed Khalifa, where he works, what company. I don't know how long they'd been on his tail but I'd bet anything they now have a case file on MidEast Continental. I wouldn't be surprised if they now have a list of all the officers, board members and employees of the company."

"Go on," said Omar Husain, deliberating.

"That leads them, easily, to Abu Kamal Ramshallah," Mustapha continued, his voice now pitching his argument a little harder. "And that's where it gets scary. You've made several contacts with him since the drop at the park, before you left for Hawaii." He paused for effect, allowing the Commander to chew on that a moment.

Samir Osmani, the driver, threw a quick glance at each of them then turned his eyes back on the road. They were now going by Fort George Meade on the BW Parkway, about halfway to Washington.

Omar Husain in the back seat behind the driver now turned his head up to Mustapha Khan and said slowly: "So, now you think we could be walking into a trap. They've now had Abu Kamal under surveillance for sometime, the Foggy Bottom apartment bugged, his phone tapped, their fishnet in place there and they're just waiting for more fish to swim in before they haul it in. And the worst part of this is they've established a connection between Abu Kamal and us, although they don't know who we are. But that's elementary. Once they got us all in the fishnet—"

"You're a little ahead of me," said Mustapha, now realizing how the man was just holding back. "But that…that's about the size of it, Commander."

They were once again silent in the car for two minutes. The next one to speak was Samir Osmani, the 30-year old sleeper, native Marylander and one of the survivors of Operation North 27 now better known throughout the world as Pentagon II.

"Commander," he said without taking his eyes off the road, "I think we should not go to Foggy Bottom. And I think we need to stop somewhere out here and work this out before we drive into Washington."

Another stretch of silence before Omar Husain said just as they entered the city of Greenbelt, going right by the Goddard Space Flight Center: "Alright, get off at the next exit."

They were right, he thought. Perhaps he had been taking the cunning and vicious reach of the American intelligence, especially now in light of the recent attacks, too lightly. They wouldn't pass up the slightest possibility of catching the least significant of those responsible for them, let alone their leaders.

A single piece of evidence, one seemingly insignificant lead, with the advanced investigative technology now in their hands, could tie things up together and point them to any one of the operatives of the Organization.

Mustapha was right. The FBI could now have a case file filling up on the company, MidEast Continental. It would have been as simple as following Ahmed Khalifa and finding out where he works. That leads them to Abu Kamal, and once they're on to him, it's a matter of time before they're on to the rest of them, watching, hiding and waiting for the most opportune time to spring the net.

He must give this much credit to the abilities of the enemy or he could, quite possibly, suddenly be staring a costly surprise in the face.

A half a mile down the road, Samir Osmani got on the exit lane to Route 193 West, drove another half a mile and went into Greenbelt Park where Omar Husain told him to pull into a space at a parking lot near a public phone booth.

It was almost two o'clock in the afternoon. There were few people in the park. Mostly older women walking their little dogs, and some younger ones walking and jogging. They were about to get out of the car when Omar, for the first time, held himself, took time to look discreetly through the window before opening the door and stepping out. The others did the same, giving each other a sense of wariness over something undefined.

They started walking on the park road slowly, heads bent slightly, working things out. Samir Osmani fell behind the other two so they wouldn't take up half the road.

"Tell me something," Omar Husain said to Mustapha, "Have you considered how Ahmed Khalifa happened to pick up those FBI tails?"

"No idea," Mustapha replied after a few seconds, shaking his head slightly. "We've been working on the assumption Bobby put them on him. That Bobby's working with the undercovers."

"I don't think so," said Omar. "I never thought so since before Operation North 27, and especially after."

"I agree," said Samir Osmani behind them. "I think he's a genuinely disgruntled government worker wanting to get back at the people he works with, and even the entire government he works for. He did exactly what we're seeing him do. Selling out the country."

"We got what we paid him for," said Omar. "They're real. Those drops contained all the data, the logistics we needed to get the jobs done. Like Ahmed Khalifa said, the guy doesn't give a shit. Because nobody at work gives a shit about him."

"Commander, I have no answer to how that Pakistani picked up those FBI agents," Mustapha said. "The only thing I know now is that he is a risk to all of us. And so is Bobby. And I think we all agree, as we have in the past, what must be done to eliminate such risks."

"I want that drop tomorrow," Omar said. "We will go ahead as we set it up, at Fort Ward Park. After that, I want nothing more to do with Bobby. A man who can sell out his own people, his own country over his personal gripes is not to be trusted in any way."

"Exactly," agreed Mustapha. "He can turn against us in a blink and not give a shit either. We can take care of this business with no problem, Commander, I assure you."

"We'll get back to that later," Omar said. "Right now, let's figure out where we're at. We don't want to go to Foggy Bottom, I agree with you both. So, we're saying Abu Kamal is under surveillance. Therefore, we must get him out of there, and everybody else with him, and meet someplace else."

"We need to call him right now," said Samir Osmani, "and the four brothers who went ahead of us. Hopefully, they haven't gone there yet."

"I told them to meet us there at seven tonight," Omar Husain said and stopped walking, a calm in his eyes concealing a buzz of intelligence crunching in his head. Unknown to the other two, he had been busy analyzing, planning, visualizing in minute details as fast as he could, based on the fishnet theory, what to do to outsmart and outrun the enemy. "Alright, here's what we'll do—"

*   *   *   *

Working on the premise that government intelligence, in a worst-case scenario, had the Foggy Bottom apartment staked out top and bottom—right on the ninth-floor corridor and downstairs at the main entrance lobby, the only way for any of the men to get out of there undetected was through the garage, preferably by taking the stairs rather than the elevator. Even the garage would be staked out but there are more ways of evasion they could resort to down there than by coming straight out the entrance lobby.

Now, the streets around the apartment complex could be staked out as well. Two ways to get past this—either an all-out shooting battle, punch a hole in the fishnet so the men could swim out, or trick them. Lead them out—those undercovers sitting in their cars on the streets around the complex—23rd Street, Virginia Avenue and E Street, and possibly even as far as G Street. Get them to move, go someplace else. The latter would seem to be a better choice. And it was, especially when Omar Husain learned during the call they made to Abu Kamal from the public phone at the park that, indeed, Abu Kamal had considered the possibility of the fishnet theory and for that reason had posted GWU sleepers downstairs. One nearby to cover the lobby, another outside to keep an eye around the area of Virginia Avenue and G Street where Ghulan Wahid, the driver, had parked the rented Ford Taurus. A third one was posted in the garage near the entrance to the elevator.

That would have to be done first, to prove the fishnet theory. For all they knew, they could be wrong about the whole thing—no stakeout upstairs or downstairs, and they could just walk out of there as if they were simply going to a dinner party. But they would have to prove that and to do so, a decoy would have to be used. A bait. The rest of the plan to get out of Foggy Bottom then depended on the outcome of this.

Kashim Najoub, an Egyptian, at 52 was a year younger than Abu Kamal Ramshallah who is a Syrian. But outside of these differences, they were cast from the same mold. One fit in the other's clothing almost perfectly, vertically and horizontally. And with the cold-weather outerwear, what slight difference in height or weight there were between them were lost. The difference in physiognomy was quite distinguishable up close, but from a distance of twenty feet and beyond, it was easily obscured by an upturned winter-coat collar.

At a few minutes before five o'clock in the evening, with a dark sky casting an early night shadow over Washington, Kashim Najoub and Ghulan Wahid came out of the ninth-floor apartment not as unwarily as when they arrived the day before. Two men in suits in a lounge area at the end of the corridor took notice and were immediately astir. One of them got on the phone in a hurry. Kashim and Ghulan took the elevator to the lobby and walked out through the open plaza of the office-apartment Columbia Plaza complex to 23rd Street. They were carrying on a normal conversation, unhurried. But the calm in their voices didn't coincide with the grimness of the words they spoke to each other.

"They're there," Kashim Najoub, Abu Kamal's double, muttered to Ghulan Wahid as they walked on the plaza towards the street, "the lounge at the end of the hallway on the ninth floor."

"Yes, I saw them too," replied Ghulan softly. "And in the lobby too, by the mailbox room. I could've spotted them from a mile away. The suit and tie, and the head and body always turning stiff at the same time in that macho pose. Not too undercover. Dumb dicks."

"Good for us."

On 23rd Street, they turned north and crossed the diagonal Virginia Avenue. They surveyed the surrounding—the cars parked on both sides of the street, the people moving on the sidewalk and standing at the bus stop—just by rolling their eyeballs and not moving their heads even slightly. They turned left and a short distance from the corner got into the Ford Taurus.

"I see our GWU brothers two cars up," Ghulan said, locking the doors and starting the engine.

"They know what to do? And where to pick us up for sure?" asked Kashim, now surveying the area a bit more openly from inside the car.

"Yes. They know that restaurant inside out. They eat there all the time."

A Malibu sedan parked on 23rd Street close to the corner of Virginia Avenue started maneuvering to pull out of the tight street parking space. Agent Richard Bartley hated driving in the District. That's why he was glad at least to be driving this newly issued Bureau car—plenty of horsepower, good handling and smells good.

While he was busy keeping an eye on the Ford Taurus visible at a distance and hurrying to get out on the road, his front-seat passenger spoke rapidly on the radio to his counterpart in a second car, a Buick Century, down in the garage of the office-apartment complex. During the few seconds the car passengers spoke over the air, the Century's driver had started the engine and pulled out of the parking space which commanded a good view of the garage entrance to the apartment elevators. It sped out of the garage up the exit driveway that was the dead-end of 24th Street at a diagonal intersection with Virginia Avenue outside.

Ghulan, in the meantime, had nosed the Taurus out slowly on Virginia Avenue to make sure he cleared the car in front, at the same time looking at the side rearview mirror. He had to hold for a few seconds while some asshole wouldn't let him out and sped through. Another one came close behind and did the same.

Motherfuckers! Driving in this town is insane. No wonder some hotheads get into road-rage mode so quickly.

The next car that came was the Malibu sedan from its left turn from 23rd Street, coming up slow, allowing Ghulan plenty of time, and space, to pull out and get on the road. The Taurus turned north at the first intersection which was 24th Street, coming into plain sight of the Buick Century, with the Malibu now trailing right behind it. The Century then shot straight across Virginia Avenue illegally, drove past the intersection of G Street and got behind the Malibu.

Now Ghulan, driving the Taurus, drove a couple of blocks to Washington Circle and turned left on Pennsylvania Avenue towards Georgetown. The caravan of cars behind him and Kashim Najoub now consisted of the two FBI tails and the Ford Escort carrying the two young GWU sleepers at the end.

The evening rush hour was at its peak, as usual, especially around this area near Georgetown. Thus, the caravan got separated at one time on Pennsylvania Avenue as the road merged with and became M Street. At that point, neither the Taurus nor the Escort could tell if the Taurus had picked up a tail. Not until the Taurus reached and turned north on Wisconsin Avenue. Here, as had been planned, it turned off the main road into a small neighborhood street, traveled two blocks and circled around the blocks a couple of times as if looking for an address. The two cars behind it, though keeping a discreet distance back, stayed the course—stop and go, even when Ghulan stopped at a corner for an extra time to pick up a newspaper from a newsbox, sat for a half a minute and started moving again.

Coming back out on Wisconsin Avenue from the neighborhood road, Kashim Najoub, in the passenger seat of the Taurus, looked at the Escort which had parked on a standby at the corner. He motioned to the driver with his head, eyes rolling backwards to indicate the cars coming up behind them. The two young men in the Escort, undergraduate students at the George Washington University, understood, nodding back at Kashim.

Everything Commander Omar had theorized about the fix they were all in now had been right so far. Allah be praised for such a brilliant, able-minded leader, Kashim Najoub thought. He got on the cell phone quickly and talked to Abu Kamal in the apartment to tell him in rapid Arabic to get out of there now. The whole place is under surveillance including the ninth floor but it's possible the ground is clear for now since they picked up the tails right behind them. But there could be more of them down there. There is a real possibility, he said, they might have to shoot their way out of there in a hurry and, if they could, without attracting anymore Feds or local cops.

Within minutes, the three men remaining in the apartment—Abu Kamal, Hassan Bahaji who still limped from the leg wound in Operation North 27, and Hamad Salim, a 32-year old seasoned fighter of the Organization's Soldiers of Islam, had picked the place clean of everything that might leave a trace of their activities—papers, receipts, maps, and got ready to leave.

Hamad Salim inched the door open enough to get a one-eye view of the lounge at the end of the corridor about thirty yards away. They were there alright, as Kashim Najoub had told them on the phone. Two suits, one of them holding a cell phone to his ear, probably getting an update from the ground team tailing who they thought was Abu Kamal Ramshallah, their main quarry. The other standing near a window just outside the lounge facing the apartment doors.

There's no way they could have missed Ghulan Wahid and Kashim Najoub when the two men left the apartment earlier, but these two suits stayed. That could only mean they had instructions to hold the fort up here when they called the ground team to inform them that their quarry was on the way down.

After a quick discussion about it, they decided the only choice they had was to simply walk out of there as if they had no concern about anything. Two things could happen—first, the Feds decide there's plenty enough fish in the net and the suits come up to them openly to arrest them; second, they don't and continue to keep them under surveillance.

Being captured was not an option, thus the three men agreed on a plan of action before they walked out the apartment door. Abu Kamal went first, followed by Hassan Bahaji. Hamad Salim came out last, taking an extra moment to close the door behind him and glance at the government agents down the hall.

As soon as all three of them were in sight and moving towards the elevators, the agents hurried towards them openly. Abu Kamal and Hassan Bahaji did not heed the call for them to stop and continued walking towards the exit door to the stair a few yards from the elevators. Hamad Salim slowed down and turned partly towards the advancing agents, his right arm hidden on the side of his body from them. When they were within five yards, his right hand emerged from his side pointing a powerful 10 mm Glock-20 with the silencer tube he had attached to it before leaving the apartment.

The agents dropped face first one after another a few feet from him as he pumped three rounds into each of them in rapid succession. The pistol produced a noise no louder than that of a beer can popping open. Puff! six times. And the two government agents fell dead.

Down the ten flights of stairs they descended with the wounded Hassan Bahaji dragging his right leg a bit but without holding up the rest. They hurried down to the fire exit in the rear of the garage level and out to E Street where a third GWU sleeper was standing by in a Toyota Highlander SUV. Kashim Najoub was right. The sighting of Abu Kamal Ramshallah leaving the building had cleared the area of the government stakeout. They could've walked, taken their time and hailed a taxi on the sidewalk.

However, they won't be foolish enough to go back up the lobby to see if this was completely true and find out that there were two more FBI agents hanging out there who were at the moment trying to contact their dead colleagues upstairs.

On Wisconsin Avenue, at Tenleytown, the Taurus turned right to 39th Street a couple of blocks before Tenley Circle and pulled into a metered street parking in front of a kabob restaurant. In the back alley, the Escort sat in the shadows of the buildings around it right by the backdoor of the restaurant.

Up front, Ghulan Wahid and Kashim Najoub got out of the car, fed the meter and walked into the restaurant, all under the watchful eye of the four FBI agents in two cars a short block front and back of the Taurus. Within two minutes after their quarry disappeared behind the door of the restaurant, a call came telling them of the fatal hit on two of their colleagues back in the apartment.

With that news came the order to open-pursue and arrest or, if resisted, launch the assault and shoot to kill.

They jumped out of the cars all at once, burst through the restaurant door, weapons drawn, and swept through all corners of the restaurant. But there were only the few terrified customers sitting at the tables, a couple of servers and the cashier to be found inside. At this same moment, the screen door of the back exit was still swinging close while the Escort with the four men in it sped through the alley, drove around the block and headed west on Van Ness Street to Nebraska Avenue. A few minutes later, they entered Canal Road, traveled less than a mile and crossed the Potomac River on Chain Bridge Road to Virginia.

CHAPTER 18

▼

At 9:55 AM, Robert Grundell had done what he expected would be the most of what he had going for the rest of this Friday morning. The routine with the TSL bin—checking for red alerts, if any, and working with the Deployment Division. Nothing. Priority phone calls on current projects. Nothing. There were a couple of emails he had to respond to regarding one assignment, an application software development he as the end-user in the Branch had been working on with the developers.

He decided he'd take it easy and get himself a second cup of coffee from the dispenser out in the hallway. On his way, he glanced Ralph Robson in his office talking to the two Phoenix people. Seeing them again this time left him no doubt about who they weren't saying they were and what they were doing.

On his way back, he passed by Leon Justice's door and saw the man sitting in his executive chair facing the window, feet up on top of the base cabinets while talking on the phone. It was such a revolting sight—a freeloading parasite burrowed in a government bureaucracy, living a life of ease and luxury—that he spilled a few drops of the coffee he was carrying, in his hurry to get past the door.

He couldn't move fast enough logging on the computer as soon as he got back in his workstation. It was a little past ten o'clock already. Anybody whose business it was to check the access-log database and see who was logged on the system and looking, downloading or updating any file, here or at the FBI, NSA or any place else in the government network would see Leon's userid instead of his. Between now and twelve o'clock.

He was on the system for over an hour and a half, cruising the network, accessing classified files, downloading some of them, doing what he did the day before logged on as Ralph Robson. When he was satisfied, he looked at the time and decided—lunchtime. He logged off and got ready to leave first by making sure he had the diskettes for the drop at the park. He had an hour to eat and get there. He decided he'd go to Bradlee Shopping center for lunch, the usual Northern Virginia neighborhood mart—foodstore, fastfoods, drugstores, bakery—two blocks from the park and less than ten minutes' drive from the office.

He felt good as he put his tweed sportscoat on and took the elevator down to the garage, looking forward to that cash bonus envelope from the drop and driving that brand new Lexus. The dealer had called early evening yesterday to tell him they got it, as he ordered, and would be ready for him to pick up Saturday morning.

*   *   *   *

Julie Santorelli felt as if she had a ton of unspent energy waiting to be burned from every strand of her body tissues when she got out of Chris' car at Fort Ward Park. The loss of her uncle had turned the past seven days of her life into an undefined emotional and physical stupor. It's because it all happened so quickly, so unexpectedly. Like a deafening thunderclap that suddenly exploded all around her. But then how else do these things come into one's life?

Today you're here, tomorrow who knows?

The day Chris Phillips told her he was switching his AWS off day to today, Friday, because he just felt like a short week this week, she thought it's probably a good idea for her to do the same thing. She worked it out with her school admin and got the day off too.

There was a chill in the air that forebode of the coming cold in the days ahead a week before Thanksgiving. The trees had now turned a blazing kaleidoscope of colors. It was a pleasant autumn day, ideal for being out there, brisk-walking, running, or just being a part of the outdoors. On a park bench, sitting in your car eating lunch or reading as they saw people doing when they got there at ten minutes before noontime.

Chris loved this kind of weather for running, another good reason why he wanted to have his AWS day off a week sooner. Days like this, he felt he could run twice as long as the three to four miles he had been doing the last few years.

He got out of the car, raised his face to the sky and filled his lungs with the cool air. Julie on the other side did the same, then the two of them went to a bench nearby and did the routine stretches for a couple of minutes.

"Any thoughts about lunch?" he asked while he had the back of the heel of his right foot over the backrest of the bench stretching his calf muscles. He turned to Julie after a couple of seconds when she hadn't answered and asked: "Big Mac? Popeye's? KFC?"

Everytime he carried on like that, she always assumed he was kidding—knowing he knew what she thought about fastfoods—but she knew he wasn't, really. Because he ate fastfood for lunch nine out of ten times on his days off. But what else is there to eat for lunch in America, he would ask?

She had thought about that a few times in the past and realized—he had a good point.

"I'll think about it while we're exercising," she said faintly with her back turned to him doing a backstretch. Then she kept a silence which Chris had noticed about her since she arrived at his place a couple of hours ago. The same kind of silence, a quietude he had noticed about her as a matter of fact since her uncle's funeral.

He finished his stretches first and stood a few feet from her for a while, looking at her close. Then it dawned on him that she was still grieving as much since the funeral. When she straightened up and turned to face him, he closed the gap between them and took her in his arms.

This was one part of her he hadn't seen before. He had seen her get angry, irritated, pissed off and even quarrelsome, but never when she was in deep emotional distress, suffering some real hurt.

He spent many hours with her the day after the funeral and ended up spending the night at her place. He learned a bit more than she had told him before about her family background, how truly close her family were with her uncle's. They weren't just relatives. They were one big family.

He felt good about being with her at such a time in her life, understanding and sharing her grief. He comforted her, sympathized with her and listened kindly to everything she said. Even when grief sounded to be overtaken by anger in her as she talked about how such a tragic event had come to touch her family along with hundreds of other innocent people.

"There's no excuse for such brutal acts," she said softly in a measured voice while they sat close to each other in her living room couch. "Whoever they are, whatever they believe in. No belief of any kind based on anything—religious, political, social, ideological, justifies doing any such act. I don't care who they are—Muslims, Christians, Jews, pagans, atheists."

"I agree," he said. "But these people are trained, brought up, to respect no other belief but their own. The only thing that matters to them is their kind of life, not ours. Not anyone else's. They're fanatics."

"They're animals," she muttered angrily. "Not even real animals are capable of doing this sort of thing. And to their own kind. Their own species."

It lasted only a few short moments, the two of them standing there in each other's arms this beautiful cool day amidst the blazing colors of autumn in the park. One knew exactly what went on inside the other. It was all in the silent words in their eyes when they pulled apart and looked briefly at each other.

Chris decided grief, and anger, had used up enough of her for today and she could use a break from them by allowing herself to indulge in what this charming day could do for her. He gave her an inviting, friendly smile, drew a deep breath and said: "How about I spring for lunch and you decide dinner."

A smile broke on her face. She said: "Not fair. Dinner's more expensive than lunch. Bigger production too."

"Alright, you do lunch. I'll do dinner," he said.

"How about you shop and we both cook? Anything you want for lunch after your run. All the fastfood you want. Knock yourself out."

"Deal."

They checked their watches before they started out. Chris said he felt so energetic and that, because it was such a gorgeous day too, he'd probably run an extra mile. Do one and a half inside the park, then take off to the side of the seminary grounds up to the football field inside there and do a mile and a half around there too, then head back. They figured forty-five minutes, give or take five, to finish their exercise and be back at the car in that time.

As usual, Chris was the stickler for details and made sure Julie was carrying her ID before they took off. It turned out she wasn't. She forgot, she said, earning her a long eye of reprimand from him. He went back to the car and got her a duplicate of his ID.

They started out at the same time, both running the same pace for about a minute before Julie dropped to her regular walking pace and Chris took off at his usual eight-and-a-half-to-nine-minute-mile pace. It was five minutes past noon.

Julie flushed everything out of her while she exercised. And it did her well. She felt emotionally and mentally unburdened the next thirty-five minutes. She was all physical. All skin and bones, body tissues and working organs; a healthy heart pumping rich, oxygenated blood throughout her system. She gulped a lungful of the cool air every two or three strides most of the time.

It was fifteen minutes to one when she finished her usual four laps around the park. She decided she'd wait for Chris at a bench by a broad thicket of evergreen bushes a short distance from the car. It was off the park road up near one of the Civil War Fort bastions with the big guns behind the parapets high above the surrounding deep trenches. From there, she watched people—runners, walkers, dog-walkers, and cars traveling at five miles an hour go by.

Chris must have gotten carried away again and didn't look at the time, she thought, as he did once in a while on a good running day like today. He also liked to finish up his run a few minutes away from the car so he could enjoy a leisurely walk while recovering from the stress. Thus she stretched on the bench and relaxed, turning away from the road for a moment to look at the bastion.

It was the sound of footsteps she heard at first coming from behind and some distance beyond the bushes near the edge of the trenches. Dry leaves crushing. And then there were more of them, footsteps, and she was certain there were more than one person making the sound.

She looked for a place to see through the dense bushes by switching her position on the bench until she found a small gap between the tangle of twigs. Peering through the small opening, she saw a man in tweed sportscoat standing with his right side to her facing two other men. The one farthest from her was noticeably taller than the others by at least six inches. He was also noticeably Middle-Eastern—stark, deep-set eyes and darker complexioned. The other one was closer to the man he was facing in build and height, as well as general appearance—light complexioned, reddish hair, more caucasian American. A handsome man, she thought. He wore a gold earring on his left ear. Something semi-circular, slightly smaller in diameter than a quarter. When he moved his head while speaking to the man in front of him, it caught the noon-hour sun and reflected its full image to Julie behind the bushes. It was the shape of a crescent moon with a star suspended in the middle of it.

She kept her place on the bench where she found the small gap through the bushes and relaxed for a few moments, waiting for Chris to show up on the park road. Then, peering through the gap again a minute later, she saw the taller man take out a long-nozzled handgun from his coat and shoot the man in front of him three times. The only report she heard was a faint succession of short pops like those made by small firecrackers exploded at a good distance. The man in the tweed sportscoat didn't have an instant to even move a limb before he was shot and simply collapsed backwards.

She came close to sounding out her shock with an instinctive shriek but managed to hold herself. Then as she watched the gunman point his gun again at the fallen man and shoot a fourth time, she let out a short gasp but it was loud enough to attract the attention of the handsome man with the crescent-moon earring.

For a moment, it looked like he was looking directly at her although she knew he couldn't possibly see her face or any part of her in whole through the dense thicket. Engulfed in fear, she jumped from the bench and tripped on a trash can near it. She fell momentarily, got up and bolted to the park road toward the park gate where she expected Chris to come back in.

Hearing the noise of the trash can following Julie's gasp, Omar Husain pulled out his own handgun and hurried around the thicket to the bench. By the time he focused on the direction Julie went, she was near the park road, running hard towards a group of people coming the opposite direction. All he recognized of the person who had occupied the bench and certainly witnessed the killing of Robert Grundell was a white woman in a warm-up suit and athletic shoes, around five feet six inches, 125 pounds thereabouts, straight light-red hair tied behind her head. The way she moved so briskly, especially when she turned her head partially to look back as she ran hard, she must be between her late twenties and early thirties.

The incident nagged at Omar Husain like no other that had happened to him in any of the operations he had been a part of in the past. He had no doubt that she saw his face and would recognize him if she saw him again. But there's no point working this out now, he thought. She's gone, whoever the hell she is, and there's nothing he can do right now unless…

He was about to turn and hurry back to help Mustapha Khan hide the body as they had planned when he glanced at the seat of the bench. He saw a white card of some kind, around two-inch square laying there, and picked it up. It was actually a piece of paper wrapped in transparent tape. One side of it read 'PERSONAL ID:' on top. Below it was the name, address, social security number, home telephone number, and the car license plate number of Chris Phillips. The other side read 'EMERGENCY CONTACT:' on top and below it was his work address and telephone number, and the name and telephone number of his brother James and their father Sam.

Allah be praised! he murmured to himself as he pocketed the ID card and hurried back behind the bushes. He found Mustapha standing by a large oak tree, Bobby's body slumped against it in a sitting position away from a narrow line of view of the park road curving some fifty yards in front of them. To their right, however, which was the 45-degree trench wall topped by the parapet that enclosed the bastion, they were completely visible. Anybody standing inside the bastion behind the waist-high parapet would be looking straight down at them. Thus, they hurried to move the body and hide it as they had planned: each man holding it up under-arm on each side and walking it as fast as they could towards the trapdoor entrance of the bastion's filling room, an underground storage where armed shells and other firing implements for the big guns of the fort were kept during the Civil War.

There was never a big crowd in the park especially on a weekday. It was used mostly by joggers and walkers, and weekend picnickers. Around the bastions and the surrounding trenches below it, there was seldom anybody to be seen so that they were able to walk the body to the trapdoor, open it and drop Bobby in without anybody seeing them.

That done, they covered their tracks, the traces of blood, between the trapdoor and the murder scene with the combination of the wood chips, fine gravel and dried leaves that were in abundance on the ground. Afterwards, Mustapha led their way back to the Honda Accord across the park grounds on the other side of the fortification with Omar Husain scoping the surrounding as far as he could see—the sparse traffic on the park road, the restroom building, the parking lots and the museum building near the gate. Most of the people in the park were either on the park road or at the picnic tables and benches. He focused closely on some who sat in their cars. He didn't see any woman resembling the one he was looking for.

When they got in the car, he read the license plate number written in Chris Phillips' ID and memorized it. He thought about telling Mustapha to drive around once and look for it but changed his mind and decided to just leave immediately. He knew *her* name, where she lived. He knew everything he needed to know about her, as a mater of fact, to find her and do what's necessary. Every moment they remained in the park was a risk they didn't have to take. She could have had the police coming right this minute. He got what they came for from Bobby, the three diskettes now in his coat pocket containing classified government national security data which he and Abu Kamal and several of his lead Soldiers of Islam would analyze as soon as they got back in the hotel.

He had argued with Mustapha Khan about the fate of Bobby, believing the poor man was really nothing more than what he had become—a broken-down civil servant who had lost all sense of self-worth and self-respect along with whatever values he once upheld as an American. He felt sorry for the man, apparently a good hardworking employee who earned his paycheck but went unrecognized, unrewarded for his good work because of office politics and personal bias, that kind of management shit that went on in government bureaucracies.

So he had come to a point where he didn't give a shit about anything, and even far beyond that where he could sell the country to its enemies and not give a damn. And that's where Omar's argument to spare him came apart.

To a man who had come to such a state of uncaring, the only thing that mattered in life is himself and his satisfaction. Now it was not just between him and his employer, the U.S. government, America and its people. Now it's between him and the whole fucking world. The man was now a risk to anyone he dealt with. He held no values, no respect and no loyalty towards anything or anyone.

Why face a risk they didn't have to? Besides, why should one more dead American matter? After all, the only good American is a dead American.

*   *   *   *

Julie literally fell into Chris' arms as soon as she saw him walking on the park road by the museum. She was panting and quivering as if she just came in from a freezing cold.

"What's going on?" he asked, becoming seriously alarmed as she turned up an ashen face at him.

She caught her breath a moment, looked frantically around and pulled him in the direction of the museum entrance. "In there, quick," she told him.

Seeing how desperate she was, he followed her without a word into the museum. Inside, she pulled him farther aside into a corner past the vestibule, away from some people viewing the Civil War displays, and told him in harried whispers what she saw.

"We must call the police immediately," Chris said after listening to her.

"I know, but we got to get out of here first," Julie said rapidly. "And we must not be seen together. They could be looking for me right now. They see me with you, we're both in trouble."

"Alright," he said calmly after thinking a moment, amazed at the courage and clear thinking she showed. "You stay here. I'll get the car and pick you up at the entrance from the parking lot in the back. Give me two minutes." He went out the back entrance and started what must be a four-minute running pace through the parking lot, back out to the park road and to the car a good quarter of a mile away.

Left alone, Julie scanned the inside of the small museum quickly. Like the park outside, there weren't many people in it. A family of four—young parents and two boys, were viewing a bullet-holed Confederate officer's uniform and its accessories in a tall glass case. Hat, gloves, boots, and the weapons of war that went with it—saber, pistol, knife. She quickly moved across the display room past several waist-high glass showcases to the rear entrance and stood to the side of the door with a view of the parking lot outside.

She suddenly realized that the killers could come in the back entrance as well as the front so she stepped away from the doorway to a window next to it and checked out the parking lot. There were only a few cars scattered out there but she saw no one.

Now the front entrance door swung open. She turned, hiding behind the wall that separated the display area from the back doorway. She stood there breathless as she watched two people come in. First a man she couldn't immediately distinguish from one of the two she saw through the bushes. The man held the door open until the other visitor entered, a woman.

Chris had the car key ready long before he reached the car. The bench where Julie had sat and witnessed the killing through the thickets behind it was visible from the park road as he approached the car. He tried his best not to look that way even as he reached the car, taking no chance that the killers might still be around, until he was in the car, got the doors locked and the engine started. And even then, he only glanced at the rearview mirror quickly and got a partial glimpse of the thickets.

He backed out of the parking space quickly but smoothly, now taking the opportunity to look at the bench and the bushes behind it in full view as he turned to look at the side rearview mirror. For one moment, he wondered what the killers did with the body. He stepped on the gas wanting to eat the one-third mile on the park road to the museum in the blink of an eye but checked himself, remembering the five-mile-an-hour speed limit in the park. But after he looked front and back and saw no traffic at all, he pressed on the gas pedal harder, pushing the speedometer up to twenty-five, until the road curved left and he had to crawl back down to five when a Honda Accord just pulled out of the parking space along the side and got on the road at the speed limit.

From there, his right foot tap-danced between the gas and the brake pedal in his impatience to get to Julie in the museum, tail-gating the late-model Honda Accord ahead of him. At one instance, he nearly rear-ended the car when it had to slow down even more coming to a speed bump. He noticed the driver looking up at his rearview mirror several times, apparently starting to get pissed off. His front-seat passenger even turned around to stare at him for a few seconds.

"What the fuck does this asshole want from us?" Mustapha Khan, the driver, mumbled.

"I don't know," Omar Husain said, thinking FBI undercover, the same as the day Mustapha ran into them. But they wouldn't be so stupid, coming out to them like this on the road. The car didn't look like a federal government car. A Toyota Camry, '97, '98 model. But that's no giveaway with undercover agents. They could be driving anything between a luxury brand or any old clunker. And he couldn't see the license plate number because it was too close. But that's no clue either even if he could read it. He told Mustapha: "Just keep going. Speed up a little and let's just get out of here quick."

They finally came to the gate where they sat and waited for traffic to clear up to make a right turn on Braddock. Omar Husain was expecting the Camry to sit close behind them but looking on the side rearview mirror, he saw it turn left in a hurry instead. On a last second thought, he turned around to read the license plate number but Mustapha had already started to make the right turn. As they got on the road, Omar Husain looked back to see the Camry going into the parking lot behind the museum.

Chris Phillips drove out of the park and headed home. The first thing he did as soon as he got Julie safely in the car was take out his cell phone and give it to her.

"Call 911 or Alexandria police, now," he told her. "It's on," he added when Julie started fingering the keypad uncertainly.

She was sitting low in the car, her head below the window sill facing him. She got as far as pressing 91 on the keypad then stopped and looked up at him.

"No," she said, thinking to herself.

"Why not?" he asked.

"Let's go to the shopping center. Turn left at the light coming up. I want to use a public phone."

Chris read her mind, nodding without taking his eyes off the road. "Anonymous call?"

"Yes," she answered promptly. "We don't want to get involved in this. They'd have your phone number on their case file and it'll become a permanent piece of data in it. You want that?"

Chris didn't have to think a moment about that one. "No. You're right. Thanks," he said as he made the left turn at the light to the parking lot behind Bradlee shopping center.

"We could end up becoming suspects in this," she said further. "You know how the police think. It's part of their job."

"I'm with you, honey," he said, pulling into a space..

They got out of the car and went to a phone booth nearby. She made the call to report the murder in the park while he stood behind her keeping an eye on the people around.

C H A P T E R   19

▼

Agent John Jacobs got up from the living room couch when he finally saw his partner—or former partner, temporarily—Richard Bartley, pull up to the curb in front of the house. It was an old house in this quiet middle-class Falls Church community called Fairmont. At least sixty years old, he was told when he bought it four years ago from the children of some old lady who lived most of her life in it. Two stories with an attic and a basement, twenty-foot long front yard and a big backyard, about three times longer, with big trees. Gave him something to do this time of the year raking sacks of leaves. Especially now that he was sidelined from the service on injury leave for a few weeks.

It had been over two weeks now since he was mauled by that big bad animal in the restaurant washroom. Totally surprised him. He was just peeing there at the urinal. He did notice him standing there for just a couple seconds. Well-dressed, dark but not African dark, and tall, at least six or eight inches more than his five eight. Didn't even seem to pay attention to him.

Then all of a sudden, just as he was tucking himself in, he was seeing stars; his head being used like a wrecking ball to demolish the washroom wall, he thought then, before he passed out. Sonofabitch. He swore if they ever found out who he was...

He watched Bartley get out of the car and walk up the door. Good man, he thought. He was glad to have been teamed up with him. No personality conflict at all between them, unlike a previous partner. A real pain in the butt, hard to get along with. Arrogant, bossy and too political. He threatened to quit the service unless he was reassigned with someone else.

"Hey, JayJay, how yuh doing?" Bartley greeted as Jacobs swung the door open.

"Good, good. C'mon in, pardner."

"You look much better," said Bartley, peering at Jacobs' face as he stepped in.

"Yeah, yeah. The buzzing in the ear finally went away," Jacobs said, motioning the other to the armchair next to the couch. "I still got to get the teeth fixed."

Also, the last of the fifty some stitches he had to have to put his face back together after the assault were finally gone. The swelling around the eyes had settled down although some dark patches remained on the right cheek. And he had to get one upper front tooth recapped. Another, a lower incisor, was completely broken and had to have a crown. He had dental appointments for the next two months.

"Want somethin' to eat?" asked Jacobs as he cleared the mess on the coffee table. "I got chicken and beer. I just gotta nuke it a coupla minutes. The chicken."

It was one-thirty in the afternoon. Bartley had just come from the Washington Field Office to pick up the latest follow-up on Ahmed Khalifa in Virginia Beach from the Norfolk Division. They had no one left, for the moment, to recover from the Columbia Plaza disaster except the original subject, Khalifa, from whom this whole thing began. Everybody got away without a trace for them to pick up on. Two fatalities, and they had nothing to show for it.

The ninth-floor apartment at the Columbia Plaza complex was literally turned inside out. No lead turned up on Abu Kamal Ramshallah who was now on the Bureau's MWL (most wanted list).

They were back to square A, so to speak.

"No, thanks," replied Bartley, sitting back in the armchair, relaxing. "I just had lunch. I can use the latter."

Jacobs went into the kitchen and came back with two cans of Milwaukee Best. For about a minute and a half, they just sat sipping the beer in silence. It was clear what ran in their minds. One sensed the other racing, or more like groping, for an answer to how the whole operation could've turned out the way it did. And not just the fiasco at the Columbia Plaza but going back to Jacobs' getting banged up on that washroom wall. Damn, everybody was so sure, including the heavyweight analysts at headquarters, that Saladin was as good as in the bag, finally. Then suddenly the whole setup got blown

The way it looked, they were simply outsmarted by the bad guys. They, the bad guys, knew something or found out something. And they analyzed it, tested it and proved they were right about it and that's what put them one step ahead of the game. That's how they gave the agents the slip, cutting down two of them in the process.

Whoever engineered it must be one hell of a good analyst. A brain, Bartley had thought over and over again. He wasn't even there. He just thought it all out, and who else could it be but the very same man the Bureau had been trying to catch for years now. Who else could it be but Saladin himself?

"Tell me something," Jacobs started out after the beer was more than half down. "The monster who did this to me?"

"Yes?" said Bartley.

"Ahmed Khalifa must know him well. They were all in that Sheraton Premier hotel at Tysons Corner the day we lost him. They could very well be good friends. Maybe even relatives."

"Could be. We don't know who he is. All we got is his fingerprints. He has no record in the IAFIS. He's a no-show anywhere, local and federal."

"Yes, we all know that," Jacobs said eagerly. "Now, given what just happened at Columbia Plaza, our investigation is literally hanging by a single thread with only one subject left—Khalifa. Every minute he's out there in Virginia Beach banging his girlfriend, he could give us the slip too. Then what? So, what I'm saying is, bring him in now. Let's not take any more chances the same thing might happen over again."

"That's just what I came to tell you, JayJay," Bartley said. "We're bringing him in soon. He can't give us the slip. We got his ass bugged real good. He farts, we hear it. Norfolk's on his tail all the time while he's down there. We got him 24/7. We'll give him a couple more days after he comes home tomorrow. See if he gets us anywhere."

"And what about Robert Grundell?"

"We've taken him off the probables. We got nothing on him other than he lives across the courtyard from Khalifa. Lots of other people live in the neighborhood."

"Of course we got nothing on him now because we haven't worked on him. I wouldn't count him out yet," Jacobs said, collapsing the now empty beer can in his hand. "That day in the park, something must have taken place there we didn't see. The fact that he's a Fed—I know, I know, there are other Feds in the neighborhood but he's the one we see with Khalifa. I think it's the more reason we ought to put more weight on that. I think he should have been put under surveillance too. I think he should be now, same as Khalifa."

"Wouldn't hurt," agreed Bartley. "Like we were told after 9/11, especially after what happened this past couple of weeks—the Punchbowl, and now Columbia Plaza: No lead is too small or insignificant to risk a slip-up."

"No question about that."

"But you want to know what the word is, though, from our guys now working in Grundell's office at Treasury, Bailey's Crossroads?"

"You mean that guy, whatzisname? Small arms expert. And that Navy girl—"

"Frank. Frank DiPaolo, and Nancy Schneider."

"Yes. Tell me," said Jacobs interestedly.

"Well, they're the ones who said Robert Grundell is clean. Out of a couple dozen people. So far, they got four, five people they've ID'ed prime suspects in the office on possible unauthorized handling of classified government data. They're getting ready to make a low-keyed bust and toss the suspects' workstations inside out. Some people at the Bureau think this could blow into something big."

They sat in silence for the next minute as if conscious they had run out of things to say to each other but didn't want to move on to other things. Jacobs got up from the couch after a while, thinking.

"This Abu Kamal Ramshallah, Khalifa's boss, whatever," he said, looking out the wide glass window of the living room to Bartley's car out on the street. "We know he's in business with Saladin on the Punchbowl bombing. No doubt about that. He drove him to the airport five days before. And he stayed at the Columbia Plaza apartment when he was here in Washington. Do you see a possible link between him and what could be going on at Treasury, Bailey's Crossroads?"

"Yes, our analysts have thought about that. I have."

"Removing Grundell from the picture, you see how that breaks the link?"

"That's one way to look at it," said Bartley. "If that's the setup you're working with."

"Assuming it is, if you were Grundell, wouldn't you perhaps take extra precautions to make sure you come out clean in the event of an investigation?"

"I would be wise to do so, yes. Save my ass."

Jacobs took an extra long pause before saying: "I wouldn't count him out yet."

*   *   *   *

Everybody's hunches just kept turning out right on the money, thought Abu Kamal Ramshallah, vodka tonic in hand, as he sat in the seventh-floor room that was booked for him—under an assumed name—by one of the sleepers at the Hilton Alexandria Mark Center on Seminary Road. Everybody's, including his which prompted him to post the GWU sleepers at the apartment. And it's a good thing they did, or he might now be sitting someplace else much less pleasant than this luxury room.

Every time he had stayed at the Columbia Plaza apartment since the company rented it a year ago, he had it in the back of his mind that something like this might happen. He had always had some sense of insecurity being in that place. One good thing about what happened was that he wouldn't have to worry about that again.

However, he must now face what could be the biggest change in his life since he left Syria twenty-two years ago and came to America. He was now a wanted man, a fugitive from the American justice, if there is such a thing. He can't go back to his office or his home in Detroit; he can't have anything to do with the company anymore. In fact, the company will disavow any complicity with his unlawful activities. It had been under probe by the SEC and the Justice Department as it was, and the last he knew from his boss, Mahmud Mahran, was it would do everything it could to prevent discovery of its association with the Global Islamic Defense Organization. *The* Organization.

The life he had lived here in America for the past two decades was no more. But he knew that all along. So did everybody, especially one such as Omar Husain. No one's personal welfare and security, no one's life came before the Organization and its mission throughout the world, especially here in America, the seat of all evil that sought to defame and ultimately destroy their faith and way of life.

The life we live here in America is not life, Omar Husain had declared an hour ago before he left for his own room in the Sheraton Suites Hotel in Old Town Alexandria. It is a dead life, he said, for it is the kind of life that values nothing and respects no one. So you live it outside of yourself, outside of your heart and soul. It is nothing but a facade so that for you to lose it as I did many years ago, said Omar, amounts to nothing more than losing a few material conveniences.

The past forty-eight hours since they escaped from Washington had been nothing less than a test of endurance and their will to continue to fight America, in defense of their Islamic faith and in the name of Allah. It had involved careful maneuvering to escape detection once they entered northern Virginia, deciding which hotel to check in and get out of sight safely as quickly as possible, and re-working a new timetable and agenda for the gathering that had been originally planned at the Columbia Plaza apartment.

Then there was the gathering itself in his room, first of the operations commanders—Kashim Najoub, Hassan Bahaji, Omar Husain and himself. The drop Omar Husain had brought in from the park—three diskettes, were duplicated immediately upon his arrival and studied separately by two pairs of men. Omar

Husain and Hassan Bahaji at one laptop, Kashim Najoub and Abu Kamal at another.

It was just like the other drops—except that this one came stained with the blood of a disillusioned U.S. government worker. All the logistics data they needed for their purposes were there: the timeline of activities—to the minute, the guests' entourage, itinerary, arrival and public appearances, transportation and communication and, most important of all, the security design for the entire duration of the event.

They worked late into the night, planning the next assault on America, the U.S. government and its leaders, each one introducing ideas for everyone to analyze, reinforce or rebuff, or work into a new one, another possibility. There was no word to describe the determination and singleness of purpose in each of them as they pooled their mental and physical energies to come to a common resolve. What they labored on, clearly, was what they lived for. Nothing more, nothing less. With a legion of men like these and one like Omar Husain at its head, he imagined the end of this oppressive American culture and way of life.

It was a few minutes past eight in the evening when Omar Husain left Abu Kamal's room. He looked forward to returning to his own hotel room, finally, and to a good rest after what had been a draining but productive and satisfying two days. He was almost done for the day but there was just one more thing to take care of.

Instead of heading straight on Seminary Road out to his hotel room in Old Town, he turned north towards Arlington. He got off Route 7 east, drove a couple of blocks and turned left at the light into the community of Fairlington. He knew exactly what street he was going to and what block. He had no trouble at all finding the address in the map just as he didn't have any locating the townhouse unit in one of the one-and-a-half-story World War II brick colonials.

It was on a softly lit tree-lined street, very settled-looking and quiet. He parked under the shadows of a tree, at a space past the end unit of the building. The units faced a landscaped courtyard across from an identical building and were entered through a front stoop with a gable-roofed canopy.

He sat in the car for two minutes to get accustomed to the surroundings. Across the street, he saw a figure move and disappear behind one of the buildings. On his side of the street, another was approaching on the sidewalk towards the building across the courtyard. This one got into a car in the off-street parking lot on the other side of the four-foot wide median from him and drove away. There was no traffic at all on the street except for one car that came by just as he was getting out of the car. He waited till it was gone and quiet again, then closed the car door and walked on the shadowy sidewalk to the walkway leading to the unit with the address on Chris Phillips' ID.

It was the second unit from the end. Two steps up from the walkway to the front door under the canopy supported by a pair of Tuscan columns. Old but elegant. Omar Husain made out the number on the door in the dimly lit front stoop, confirming the address. There was no light visible from anywhere inside the house, on the ground floor and the upper level. From all appearances, it looked like there was no one in the house.

Still, Omar Husain crossed his right forearm across his waist under his coat, wrapping his hand around the grip of the 38 caliber with the silencer before knocking on the door three times. He waited ten seconds and knocked again four times. Another ten seconds, then he stepped back out to the walkway and looked up the upper level windows. No light turning on, no sound of any kind. He turned and walked back to the car. A woman came by past him on the walkway and exchanged 'good evenings' and a quick glance with him. He slowed down to half-step and turned to watch where she was going. She went past the second unit, kept going till she turned to the fourth.

Perhaps it's best that she wasn't home now, he thought, for he was suddenly feeling exhausted, the thought of a cold drink and stretching out in bed so alluring. This can wait another day. He'll come back tomorrow night. There shouldn't be much of a problem, if any at all. He was almost sure she lived alone. One of those young career professional women, great social life, always busy trying to get way ahead of everybody, to have it all. Naturally, she shouldn't be expected to be home so early on a Saturday night.

✳   ✳   ✳   ✳

Coming home from the park Friday, Chris Phillips packed a bag for two days' change including a set of running gear and drove behind Julie to her place in Fairfax City. They had completely forgotten the deal they made about lunch and dinner. She just wanted to get away from the park as far as she could after she reported the crime she witnessed behind the bushes.

It didn't take the Alexandria police more than a couple of minutes to become convinced her call was for real. They pressured her for more details in addition to the description of the people she saw. Her identity, of course, and where or how she may be reached. She declined and begged them to please hurry to the scene of the murder and even suggested they seal the entire park and check everybody before they let anybody out. She hung up after that and she and Chris got back in the car fast and drove away.

She suggested they leave his place which was just a close walk to the park and go to her place. "Stay with me, please," she told Chris as he was packing after a quick shower, the gruesome image of the real-life killing burrowing into her consciousness. "I don't want to be alone."

When they got to her place, she went directly to the bathroom and showered. She spent a long time in the room before she came out in jeans and sweater and snuggled with Chris in the living room couch. They both realized she was still in denial when she said she was having a hard time convincing herself that what she saw wasn't a TV show but a live act of one human being killing another. Neither of them had ever seen anything like it and he was just as disturbed even only hearing it directly from her.

But more than that, the possibility of her now facing real danger loomed large in their minds. They sat in silence for a few minutes, at last finding the time to really feel the impact of the experience. Then without moving a limb, her face pressed against his chest, she said to him: "What are you thinking about? I can hear your brain cells cranking out waves of electrical discharge."

"That's my stomach waiting to get some lunch," he replied.

"I know you're thinking when you're thinking about something."

"Alright," he said a couple of seconds later. "Tell me, if you saw him again, the one who came out after you, do you think you'd recognize him?"

Julie took a few moments to answer while she recalled the scene she saw through the bushes, that time lasting perhaps three or four seconds when she thought the man was looking directly at her. It was so clear in her mind, the look on the man's face—alert, suspicious but without losing its composure. It was a determined look on a handsome, masculine face.

"God, yes," she said slowly. "I was looking straight at him some fifteen yards away, maybe less. And it was clear daylight. There wasn't even a shadow on his face."

"If you were able to see him as clearly as you did through the bushes, don't you think he might have been able to see you too?"

"Not at that distance," she said positively. "It was a pretty dense bush. He'd have to come as close as I was to it and I'd have to be as far back from it as he was for him to see me as I saw him. In other words, we'd simply have to switch places."

Chris thought a moment and said: "Makes sense."

She clasped her hands around his forearms to draw away from him, sat up straight and looked deep in his eyes. "Do you think they might come after me?"

"I'm sorry, honey, I didn't mean to frighten you—"

"Do you?"

"Julie, you're a witness. A sole witness to a murder, the only person who could possibly identify them. I'm sure they would if they could. So, they decide to come after you. How? Where do they start? They don't know where you live. They don't know you, what you look like."

"The man saw me running away. I saw him come out from behind the bushes."

"How far were you when you saw him?"

She turned her head side to side approximating the distance when she glanced back after she bolted from the bench. "I don't know…I was just running as fast as I could. Twenty, thirty yards."

"You looked back and saw him?"

"Yes, but I didn't make a full turn," she explained. "I just glanced him and looked forward again as soon as I made out his figure standing there."

"So, he didn't see your face."

"No, he couldn't have. Not at that distance. All he saw was my back."

He took her hands in his with all reassurance he could put in them, inching closer to her on the couch. "I think you made a clean getaway," he said. "All he saw was your back. A woman in a warm-up suit with a ponytail."

"What do you think we should do now? Anything?" she asked.

"Yes. Let's not take any chances. Ditch the warm-up suit. Hang it way in the back of the walk-in closet. And the hair—"

"What about the hair?" she asked pensively.

"Lose the ponytail. Spread it, just let it hang or do something to make it look different."

"No problem at all."

"Good. Now, how about some lunch?"

"My treat, remember?" she said, now feeling relieved, cheered up. "Just give me a sec to do the hair."

CHAPTER 20

▼

When he was a young teen in Hyderabad, Ahmed Khalifa never imagined living a long weekend like he just did. Four days of nonstop leisure with not a care in the world. Waking up every morning and looking forward to another whole day of pleasure-seeking in an American resort city. Plenty of money, a car, and an American girl. Good food, entertainment, and lots of sex.

No wonder, he reflected every once in a while when something would trigger a quick recall of the life he had known in Pakistan, millions of people all over the world would do anything—throw in a life-savings, sell their house, their land, prostitute themselves, rob, steal, borrow, to buy, fake, or make possible for themselves an opportunity to come to America. Even on a tourist visa, on a fake passport, a bogus green card, in a container ship, a slave ship, a dinghy or the trunk of a car.

What a life. The only way to live on this planet. Coming back home after dropping off one happy and exhilarated Rosie Fletcher at her place at about the same time Chris Phillips, likewise, was leaving Julie Santorelli to head home, he couldn't imagine ever going back to the life he left behind three years ago.

He resolved to himself that he would do anything, from now on, to maintain the lifestyle he now had or even a near likeness of it should things take a slight downturn. He would explore every avenue to remain in America, work his way out of his dependence on his employer, and especially Abu Kamal and his associates. He would still keep his basic values and cultural traditions as long as they did not get in the way, that is, of allowing him to pursue his lifestyle. But he will not support the destruction of this way of life and no longer contribute to the effort of those opposed to it. No matter who they are, what their beliefs are—Islamic, Jewish, Christian or anything.

Coming out of Rosie's apartment complex on Armistead in Alexandria, he turned right on Beauregard towards Seminary Road to pick up I-95 and head north to Arlington. Each turn he made showed as a bleep—transmitted by the homing bug under his car—on the monitor screen inside a van carrying a load of electronic equipment operated by three men: a computer specialist, a satellite relay expert and one known among the others as the topo man. The topographist, ground surveillance expert, the earpiece of the stakeout operation. The van was parked inconspicuously at a space in the big parking lot on the other side of a landscaped rotunda across from Ahmed Khalifa's apartment building.

All those men and machines, posted on-site three hours earlier, were to support the work of the two Bureau undercover agents now assigned on Khalifa—Richard Bartley and his interim partner Eddie Green, a 32-year old African American, newly transferred from New York to Washington. Green was a good agent, mature, no attitude, very professional, not like some Bartley had seen acting like rookie local dicks. Bartley had no problem with him at all. They got along and worked well together. With them were two other agents Bartley had requested the field office for temporary duty the next couple of days to provide additional muscle in the stakeout operation.

At the moment, Bartley was in front of the monitor in the van watching the electronic bleep turn from Seminary Road east to I-95 north. Green sat low in the driver's seat of a Bureau car parked in the dark several spaces away from the walkway to the courtyard leading to Ahmed Khalifa's apartment building entrance and the one across from it. The two temp agents—Doug Jones, 36, a 290-pound former D.C. detective and Hector Gomez, 37, an ex-Marine lieutenant, ex-Virginia State Trooper and now a three-year Bureau UC, sat in another car on the other side of the walkway a few spaces from the entrance to the parking lot.

They now had more than probable cause to bring in Khalifa by virtue of Khalifa's contacts and association with Abu Kamal Ramshallah who was now as sought after by the government as Saladin himself. The order from the Assistant Director In Charge of WFO was tight: don't lose this guy for any reason whatsoever; he is the only subject left who could lead us to identifying, finding and capturing Saladin; this is a matter of national security at a level that doesn't go much higher.

Their Section chief and case supervisor wanted to bring him in tonight as soon as he got home but Bartley convinced him to give them another day or two. It was too soon to cut the only connection there is to the ones we're really after, he said. Since Columbia Plaza, it stood to reason the guy would have contacts either direction and they, the undercover agents, might pick up some real hot leads that could make things move a lot faster.

"Almost here," said Lou Heywood, the topo man who had the apartment bugged so Khalifa couldn't scratch an itch without them hearing it. "We'll soon see—hear—some action." He and Bartley kept their eyes on the monitor, watching the bleep now approaching the exit from I-95 to Columbia Pike west.

"I can't wait to find out who this man is in there right now," said Bartley, taking a sip of the decaf from the mug he held in both hands. He was thinking Robert Grundell, the neighbor across the courtyard, but what would he be doing in there by himself? He turned to Heywood and asked: "How do we know for sure it's a man?"

"I heard him clear his throat twice," said Heywood. "Once in the kitchen, another time in the living room."

Bartley nearly laughed, thinking how in the world did the surveillance expert even knew what room the man was in. But he wasn't about to ask him and question their confidence in the man's skills and qualification in what he did for a living for the FBI.

When they turned on the audio monitors, everything was quiet in the apartment. Nothing was heard but the low hum of the refrigerator in the kitchen. Then, ten minutes later, Heywood heard footsteps coming from the bedroom moving into the kitchen. Whoever it was opened the fridge, popped open either a can of beer or soda, cleared his throat before taking a sip, then went to the living room where he cleared his throat again before taking another sip. The strange thing about it was, when Bartley asked Eddie Green in the car to go to the courtyard walkway to take a peek at the second-floor apartment from behind a broad pear tree across the courtyard near the building across, all the lights were out. It appeared nobody was inside.

Learning this, Bartley even then thought of questioning Heywood—but he didn't—if he perhaps might have bugged the wrong apartment unit. The expert couldn't have possibly made such a gross mistake.

The bleep was now moving west on Columbia Pike. Three minutes later, Eddie Green and the temps, after getting an alert call from Bartley, sat up just enough to see the Toyota Corolla drive into the parking lot and pull into an open space near the walkway to the courtyard, three away from Green.

It was a few minutes before ten at night. A quiet night, chilly with a gentle autumn breeze just enough to make Ahmed Khalifa move a little faster getting out of the car and walking up the courtyard walkway to the apartment entrance. Eddie Green was out of the car, back behind and in the shadow of the pear tree as soon as Khalifa disappeared behind the entrance door of the apartment building. Bartley sat tight next to Heywood in the van, the volume of the speakers in their earpieces turned up a couple of notches.

"He's in," Heywood said softly though he didn't have to. Bartley heard everything as it was happening—Khalifa inserting the key outside, unlocking the door and swinging it open, stepping inside then closing it and locking the deadbolt again.

Eddie Green, peeking from behind the tree, saw the light in the living room come on. He didn't hear the key-chain dropping on the coffee table, Khalifa sliding the living-room closet door open and hanging his coat. The men in the van did loud and clear with agent Bartley thinking what an amazing leap technology had taken in the last few years with these electronic eavesdropping gadgets now at their fingertips.

Next they heard what would answer Bartley's question earlier without a doubt, and reveal more than what any of them had anticipated. One word was spoken and it was, indeed, by a man.

"Hello," the voice of Mustapha Khan reached their earpieces as if the word was spoken directly to them.

Ahmed Khalifa was stepping towards the sliding glass door to the balcony to open the blinds when he heard and pivoted around scared shitless.

"How did you…?" he started to ask the instant he recognized the man. Those were the last words he spoke which the men in the van heard.

As soon as the sound came to his earpiece—two pops in quick succession as Mustapha pumped two rounds of the 38 caliber through the silencer and into Ahmed Khalifa—Lou Heywood knew exactly what happened. He'd heard that kind of suppressed report enough times in the past to leave no doubt about what kind of a situation they now had at hand, even before they heard Khalifa's body crashing on the floor.

Bartley immediately told Heywood to keep an eye out at the courtyard through the view window of the van and get handy with the floodlights at his call. Then he alerted the men outside and burst out of the rear door. He posted Hector Gomez at the rear exit of the building, Doug Jones at one end of it, himself at the opposite end at the edge of the parking lot behind a car and kept Eddie Green behind the tree.

They waited in the dark, guns drawn by their side. Heywood peeked through the view window in the van, one hand cupped over his earpiece waiting to hear from Bartley, the other on the power switch and swivel arm to the three-hundred-watt floodlight mounted on top of the van.

Two minutes later, the entrance door swung open. A man in a long winter coat, at least six-foot-four, emerged from the doorway. Bartley felt a little spooked at first seeing the figure loom above them in the dark. He sensed a menace emanating from it even at a distance. Unless they were wrong, this man had just committed murder and no matter what his reason was, he must face the law for it. But more than that, it was the loss of Ahmed Khalifa that now concerned him the most.

Mustapha Khan stood a moment at the top of the flight of four steps above the courtyard and sniffed the air. He did a quick take of the surrounding, at one instant looking directly at the tree covering Eddie Green on his left and then the other tree and the shrubs underneath it at the end of the building to his right behind which Doug Jones crouched low.

Once he saw the man step down in the courtyard and start walking towards him in the parking lot, Bartley gave the word to Heywood over the microphone. Instantly, the dark in the courtyard and part of the parking lot vanished as a wide column of white light shot from the top of the van and illuminated the area. It was as if night had suddenly turned to broad daylight.

Mustapha Khan froze at his last step on the walkway, shielding his face from the bright light. Meanwhile, the agents emerged from their cover and converged towards him, pointing their guns at him on an extended arm and flashing their shiny service badges in the other hand.

Bartley ordered the man to put his hands behind his head and squat, but the man had quickly recovered from the initial shock and summoned enough calm to speak.

"What's going on?" he said to no one in particular as he turned from one man to another, each one keeping his gun pointed at him. Now he was thinking he should've known better than to come here tonight to get rid of the Pakistani. He could've done it someplace else safer. He knew all along the Feds were on Khalifa's tail. He protested: "You're making a mistake!"

"Sir, I say again put your hands behind your head and sit on your heels. Now!" Bartley commanded this time but again the man showed no indication that he cared to do as he was told. Instead, he began to look agitated as he backed away from Bartley, shuffling left and right looking as if aiming to bolt.

Windows in apartment units on both sides of the courtyard lit up and people looked out to see what was going on with the bright light and the loud voices.

Doug Jones who had advanced within two arms' length behind the man decided this is where he comes in. He pocketed his badge, put away his gun and grabbed the man's elbows with his powerful hands, pulling them together behind the waist so that Eddie Green didn't have any trouble at all cuffing him.

While Bartley recited the Miranda in front of him, Mustapha Khan took a moment to have a close look at the FBI agent. And look who we have here, he thought, if not that same one at the two restaurants, once in Shirlington and again in Ballston. Now he wished he could've taken care of this one too the same way he did that little twit partner of his.

They led him back up to the apartment where they found Ahmed Khalifa sprawled on the living room floor soaking in his own blood from two shots. One through the forehead and the other through the heart.

*   *   *   *

The same minute Ahmed Khalifa met his death, Omar Husain was pulling into a parking space on the same side of the street in Fairlington as the night before. Only this time, he was back two spaces along the curb which was better for viewing Chris Phillips' townhouse unit.

As soon as he turned the engine off, he looked through the passenger-side windshield and saw that there was light in the downstairs windows of the townhouse. He scanned the surrounding briefly and sat for a minute when a group of noisy young people came by on the sidewalk. While he waited, he looked through the windshield again and saw the upper-level windows light up.

He got out of the car once the coast was clear and headed towards the walkway to the townhouse, hands jammed deep in the coat pockets, shoulders drawn up to the ears. He glanced up at the windows still lit up above as he approached the stoop. Still upstairs, he thought. He took the two steps up to the front door, right hand around the grip of the 38 caliber in his waist, and pushed the door-chime button three times with the left-hand thumb.

He leaned closer to the door to listen carefully for any sound coming from inside. It was a quiet neighborhood and it was easy to tell approximately where a sound even inside a house was coming from. Not hearing anything twenty seconds later, he pushed the door-chime button again five times this time just as Chris Phillips was coming out of the bathroom upstairs.

On his way to the stair, he glanced through the bedroom door at the duffel bag he had dropped on the bed to unpack when he came up a couple of minutes ago. Who could it be this time of the night Sunday? Probably that old lady two doors down having a home maintenance problem again, needs a quick help like he'd given her several times the past couple of years. Plumbing or electrical problem, a creepy bug in the kitchen or the laundry room in the basement.

No, not her, he saw, peering through the peep hole before turning the outside light on. And it didn't look like a home invader either, or a mugger, when he turned the light on. It was a man, a neat-looking white man—light-brown knee-length winter coat wearing a tie. And something else which caught his eye from its reflection of the light outside when it came on. The earring on the left ear—a crescent moon with a star in the center.

What? Men wear earrings nowadays. Athletes, professionals, businessmen. Some even on both ears. He unlocked the deadbolt and opened the door halfway.

Omar Husain looked directly at Chris Phillips, blinked once but without showing any sign of the surprise he felt. A bit of a complication here now, he thought. But, what the hell. Too bad somebody else might have to get involved in this, thinking the man he was looking at was either the husband or the boyfriend or some relative of the woman. He just hoped there wasn't anyone else in the house besides him and this woman named Chris Phillips.

"Hi, may I help you?" the man asked, nice and friendly.

"Good evening," he said, giving him an innocent smile. "I'm looking for Chris Phillips. Is *she* home?"

Chris perked up momentarily. The man spoke with no accent and by every indication in his speech manner, he had to be a born speaker of American English. It must have been a slip in his use of the personal pronoun. He'd heard some people do that once in a while.

"I am Chris Phillips," he said flatly.

"I'm terribly sorry," Omar Husain said, putting on a lost look. Thinking quickly now, he moved the right hand from the gun in his waist to the left shirt pocket and took out a piece of paper which he pretended to decipher under the light. "This is a mistake. They must have put the wrong address on this."

"Maybe," Chris said. "Although I don't know of anybody else around with the same name as mine."

"Maybe it's the wrong name and the wrong address altogether," Omar Husain added. He decided at this point to figure this out more and leave. "I'm sorry again, sir. Sorry to bother you this late at night."

"No problem. Good night," Chris said and closed the door.

As baffled as he first was at seeing a man instead of a woman, he knew there was a simple explanation to the whole thing. So what could it be—among a few possibilities? Start with the ID he found on the bench in the park. After all, that's what started it all. Thinking about this, he took it out of his wallet as he was walking in the off-street parking lot of the townhouse building. He read the license plate number in it under a light pole and looked for it in the parking lot. He found it attached to a gray Toyota Camry, model '97 or later. He looked briefly inside but couldn't see too well and, since it was dark and he had no reason to look anyway, just went back into his car to continue with his figuring.

So, he started thinking in the car, one possibility is maybe this guy Chris Phillips was at that bench in the park earlier and lost the ID there. That means the young woman he saw running away knows nothing about the ID at all and she doesn't know Chris Phillips. Which also means he's lost her since she left no trace of herself and he knows nothing about her at all. This placed him in a rather discomforting position because she could identify him and he couldn't her. This was of course counting on her having reported the killing she witnessed to the police and that they found the body and they were now looking for him.

The other possibilities all fell under the assumption that the woman and Chris Phillips know each other. He couldn't quite bring them to bear with great confidence, but they are definitely worth exploring. He had to connect the woman with this man or he had nothing on her.

First, the man who opened the door, say, is lying. His name is not Chris Phillips. He is somebody else. Who? The woman's husband or boyfriend. Whatever. The woman he saw in the park is Chris Phillips. Christine. Christina. And she did unknowingly drop her ID on the bench.

This means then that they've discovered that she lost it—where, she's not sure—but the worst-case scenario for them is just what happened. She lost it on the bench when she panicked and ran after witnessing the killing, and the killers found it.

Now he, the man she saw at the killing scene, shows up at their doorstep looking for her, as they've been imagining. A nightmare come true. So what could they be doing right now after he left? he asked himself. But a more important question he asked himself was—what should *he* be doing right now?

Two things. Either get the hell out of there right this moment, fast, before the place swarmed with cops, or go back and do what he had come to do. This last he didn't favor at all. They're not about to open the door again for anybody unless it's a cop.

He started the car without delaying any further and got on the road to the hotel in Old Town Alexandria. One last possibility he thought of while driving—the man at the door is not lying. He is Chris Phillips. The woman for some reason was carrying his ID with her while they were in the park. Maybe she didn't have one and he gave her his to carry with her. And why was she sitting on the bench by herself? Could be she's waiting for him to come back from the men's room. Maybe he was a runner and she was waiting for him to finish running.

There's only one way to figure out which of the possibilities is right, he thought as he neared the hotel. Keep track of the man. Hopefully, if they know each other or are related in any way, it wouldn't be too long before she showed up with him somewhere.

PART III

▼

SALADIN

CHAPTER 21

▼

Exactly three weeks after they came to *work* in the Office of Civil Defense Logistics, undercover agents Nancy Schneider and Frank DiPaolo now had very little doubt about the outcome of their investigation into the activities of several workers in the office. They agreed to head out to headquarters to turn in a complete report to their case supervisor and recommend an immediate action: interdict any activities in the office by the suspects and bring them in quietly now for questioning.

The supervisor and the other analysts assisting in the case, including Jerome Bolden, cautioned them to slow down some. Did they have physical evidence yet? Concrete proof to support their accusation? Is there any outside entity—such as that which may be considered an enemy of the United States—with whom the agents can tie the suspects and their activities?

Between the data they had accumulated in their monitor of the suspects' work activities and those gathered in their interviews of each of them, agent Schneider told them, they are clearly not telling the truth. They are hiding something. They are doing something they don't want anybody to know. Many of the classified files they had been accessing—browsing and downloading, based on what they told us in the interviews, she said, they have no business looking at. But because they have TSC (top-secret clearance), they are able to.

The headquarters analysts insisted they needed more concrete evidence. Material evidence. Record of accesses to secret government data alone constitutes no ground for accusation of any wrongdoing, especially with a user authorized to access the data. Any wrongdoing such as illegal use of the data would need solid evidence as to how it was used and by whom especially an outside entity with insufficient clearance.

"There's only one other way to find out what they're really up to," agent Frank DiPaolo said. "Toss their workstations and see what material evidence we come up with. Something's bound to turn up if they're hiding anything. It's got to be in there somewhere."

After going over the reports thoroughly into the late hours Friday night, headquarters gave them the go ahead to 'toss' the place. They asked for a backup, another agent to assist them and got Elmer Banks, a 38-year-old expert security undercover, eight-years in the service now after spending as much time with the Interior Department's National Park Service.

They brought him into the office today, Monday, as a 'contractor consultant' to assist them with their front work and got him a visitor building pass good for three days. The plan was to work overtime tonight and do the job late after the regular hours. Agent Banks was to be their lookout, make sure the coast was clear before they came out in the night. He'd keep an eye on the two entrances to the office—the one from the reception and the other from the rear which was actually an exit near the elevator banks and the stairs. They realized late in the day this might pose a problem because the doors were far apart and can not be seen at the same time. A security guard could come in one door, unseen and unheard by Elmer Banks who might be at the other. They didn't know what time and interval the security guards made their rounds

He would just have to be on his toes patrolling the distance between the doors while agent Schneider and DiPaolo were doing the job, they all agreed. With their radio earpieces, however, agent Banks didn't think they should have any problem.

The office started emptying noticeably at four o'clock. By five, the whole place looked deserted and was almost completely quiet except for a few late starters who had to leave later than the early birds. Agent DiPaolo went to the watercooler once to check what the situation looked like, going by the office of Leon Justice on his way back. The door was closed and no light shone underneath.

At six-thirty, the entire office was completely empty except for the three of them in their workstation. To make absolutely sure, they went around separately and checked every room—all the workstations, the coffee room, supply room, copy room, all the front offices, even the washrooms.

Their prime suspects were Leon Justice, Martin Hawkins, Ralph Robson and Herod Hardin. Agent Schneider started with Ralph Robson's workstation which was near the carousel of common workstations where she could sneak into quick should she need to get out fast and look legitimately busy working. Robson's workstation was also close to the rear door so agent Banks was posted there from the start.

Agent DiPaolo went into Leon Justice's office. Unlike the open workstations of the other workers, the office had a door which Leon locked. But Frank DiPaolo didn't have any trouble at all. One of the basic trainings UCs had to have at the FBI academy in Quantico was exactly for this kind of operation—tossing a place, starting with gaining access into the place. This it took him less than a minute to accomplish with the tools he had brought with him.

They did the job according to procedure: leave the place the way you found it, and remove, destroy or take back out everything you brought in, including fingerprints. They used surgical gloves to take care of that.

Agent Schneider timed herself and saw in her watch, after she tidied up and got out of Ralph Robson's workstation, that she took exactly seventy-two minutes to finish the job. She flipped through every book and folder on the worktops, looked into the boxes of diskettes and CDs next to the computer. She went through more files in three-ring folders on the shelves of the built-ins on the wall, the drawers in the base cabinets and under the worktops. It was here, laying at the bottom of the top drawer in the back, behind more files, that she found two diskettes labeled:

> *To: Rahim Akbar*
> *Subj: Harris Nuclear Plant, Raleigh, NC*
> *Disk File 1: Plant Security Data*

> *To: Rahim Akbar*
> *Subj: Harris Nuclear Plant, Raleigh, NC*
> *Disk File 2: Utility Site Plans, Surveys and Topography*

After turning practically every piece of material that moved in Leon Justice's office, agent DiPaolo came up with a similar find back and at the bottom of the top drawer behind the classy executive desk. Two diskettes labeled:

> *To: Abu Kamal Ramshallah*
> *Subj: North Anna Nuclear Plant, Norfolk, VA*
> *Disk File 1: Plant Security Data*

> *To: Abu Kamal Ramshallah*
> *Subj: North Anna Nuclear Plant, Norfolk, VA*
> *Disk File 2: Utility Site Plans, Surveys and Topography*

"Son of a bitch," agent DiPaolo muttered to himself in alarm. "What the hell is this guy up to?"

Nancy Schneider was so eager to see what was in the diskettes. She was about to head back out to their workstation and make a quick copy in the desktop PC when she got a rap in her earpiece from Elmer Banks.

"Break! Break!" Banks whispered through his micro-mouthpiece, the warning they used to mean 'take cover, somebody's coming'. A guard had started to open the door from the reception just as he was walking away from it to return to the rear exit. He thus rapped the others quickly so they could hurry back to their workstations and look busy working.

Nancy Schneider ran out of Ralph Robson's workstation into the carousel of common workstations near it and quickly logged onto the computer in one of the workstations.

Frank DiPaolo had no choice but to turn the light out in Leon Justice's office and lock himself in there in the dark, the office being just two doors along the hallway from the entrance way. He heard the guard's footsteps coming near, stray across the hallway for a few moments then continue on. The guard stopped outside Leon's door and tried the doorknob a couple of times. Then he moved on down the hall.

Nancy Schneider made as much noise as she could with some papers she had with her, the keyboard and the chair when she heard the guard coming in her direction. When he finally got to her, she took time looking away from a file she had brought up on the monitor to pay attention to him.

"That must be some mighty interesting piece o' work you're doing to keep you here all by yourself into the night," the guard, a husky middle-aged man, probably a retired policeman, Schneider thought when she glanced at him, commented with a slight southern Virginia accent.

"Yes," she replied with a snap. "I'm nuts about it. Just love this job. And how are things with you this evening?"

"Oh-h, everything's doin' good," he replied in a monotone, and moving on to the adjacent hallway added: "doin' good. You take care now. Don't work too hard."

"Have a good evening," she replied.

He moved on down the hallway to the agents' workstation where Elmer Banks, hearing him coming, opened a file folder before him on the worktop and got busy on the laptop.

"Good evening," he said when the guard poked his head in the open doorway.

"Evenin'," the guard replied. "Boy, I hope they pay you enough to be working on that thing this late hour."

"Hey, you gotta do what you gotta do, man," FBI undercover agent Elmer Banks said, "when you gotta do it."

"I hear yuh," said the guard. "Same thing here. I know exactly what you mean. You have a good evening now."

"You too."

As soon she got the okay from Elmer Banks, Nancy Schneider went back into Ralph Robson's office to tidy up things in there, make sure everything was back to the way she found it, then hurried into their workstation to make a copy of the diskettes. Then she brought the first one up on one of the laptops with Microsoft Word.

After browsing it a couple of minutes with Elmer Banks, they agreed it was time to make a bust in the place starting with this guy Robson. And when they saw more of the same with the diskettes Frank DiPaolo brought in a few minutes later from Leon Justice's office, they all agreed the Bureau must be notified immediately, right this minute, to plan a bust for no later than the next day.

They took close-up digital pictures of the label side of the diskettes then Schneider went back to Ralph Robson's workstation, DiPaolo to Leon Justice's to return them where they found them. DiPaolo then went on to do Martin Hawkins' workstation while Schneider, instead of doing Herod Hardin's office which they planned for her to do next, got on the phone with headquarters.

It was now a few minutes after eight. Most of the analysts, including Jerome Bolden and their case supervisor had to be roused from their home life in the Maryland and Virginia suburbs. She had spent better than thirty minutes on the phone by the time she succeeded in making the arrangements for the analysts to meet them at headquarters at ten.

A little after nine, Frank DiPaolo came back from Martin Hawkins' workstation looking all puffed up. He was carrying two more diskettes labeled:

> 'To: *Abu Kamal Ramshallah*
> Subj.: *Big Thunder 3, Montana*
> Disk 1: *Inauguration Pgm and Security*'

> 'To: *Rahim Akbar*
> Subj.: *POTUS Inauguration Day, D.C.*
> Disk 1: *Inauguration Pgm and Security*'

They browsed each diskette and after only a few minutes, agent Schneider, momentarily shaken by what they read especially about the POTUS (President of the United States), decided to make a copy immediately, took the digital shot of the label and got agent DiPaolo to return them to Hawkins' desk drawer. It was a stunning discovery. They couldn't begin to gauge its impact to national security. All the files they found addressed to those two names on the label. Obviously Middle-Eastern.

Anyone care to guess what they're up to? Nancy Schneider imagined asking the analysts at HQ after they've browsed the diskettes, reminding them of the people they had monitored in the office and in whose workstations they found the floppies.

It was going on nine-thirty and clearly, there was no time for them to do Herod Hardin's office. They picked up in a hurry, turned the lights out and in five minutes were on their way to the WFO headquarters.

Four people had left a total of seven voicemail messages in Robert Grundell's office phone yesterday. Today, by nine o'clock in the morning, three of them had left four more messages. Two of them, recorded fifteen minutes apart, were from Herod Hardin wanting to get some update on one of the major public events coming up soon in North Dakota—the Big Thunder projects. They were the third and fourth call he'd made to Grundell since Monday, yesterday, when he called once in the morning and again in the afternoon.

"Let me know how things are coming," he said. "Gotta get all that logistics data over to Deployment now, if you haven't already, so they can wrap up security plans. The inauguration is coming up soon. Call me as soon as you can."

In one of the messages the day before, he said two more senators—the majority leader and a ranking member of the Committee on Energy and Natural Resources—had decided to participate in the event. Eight members of the U.S. senate would be traveling to North Dakota and would need good security.

Chris Phillips of the Interior Department's Office of Social and Economic Reserve and Security had left two messages yesterday, another one today at eight thirty. He needed verification that Grundell received the file on the Big Thunder events he sent a few days ago containing revisions to the previous copy.

The other two messages today were from Eddie Mahone regarding some good news about the protest letter to abolish Leon Justice's do-nothing position, and from Max Poysen about the same thing. These same two had each called Grundell once the day before too. The Office of Special Counsel, Eddie Mahone said in his message, had taken up the protest letter, categorized it a whistleblower case of waste and fraud and had scheduled a meeting with the Undersecretary of the Treasury for the Office of Civil Defense Logistics.

The other caller yesterday was Paula Lambert. "I have just been wondering what it is—if it is—about me that made you just...just stand me up cold last Saturday," she said in the message, trying not to sound too peeved, holding on to her dignity. "I'm not looking for any explanation, long or short. Just the decency of a call would do, even only to say something like sorry I screwed up. On second thought, just in case you do have a real reason why you couldn't make it, can't even call—maybe you're in an accident and couldn't communicate right away, had a seizure or something like that, God forbid, I'd still like to know what the hell happened. Just out of curiosity. Not that it's going to destroy me if I never saw you again."

At ten o'clock, impatient to hear from Robert Grundell, Herod Hardin called Lou Atkins, chief of the Deployment Division's Security Audit and Evaluation Branch, with whom Robert Grundell was supposed to be working on the Big Thunder security plans.

"Haven't heard from him, Herod," Atkins said when Hardin asked about Robert Grundell. "Not since early last week. He was supposed to update us on the job."

"I know, I know. We'll get back with you as soon as I find out what's going on."

He checked his inbox sitting on a low cabinet outside his office and looked at everything in it, sure to find the leave slip Grundell must have filled out and turned in before he went on leave. That's it—the guy must be on vacation, or sick leave, he thought. But he was wrong. He looked at all the papers on his desk too, thinking he might have already picked it up. Nothing there either.

There was nothing else to do but go out there in Robert Grundell's office area and find out if anybody knew his whereabouts. He went around the whole Plans and Security Database Branch and asked every one of his subordinates. Nobody had seen Robert Grundell today or yesterday. Several people remembered seeing him the week before. A couple of people said the last time they saw him was Friday around noon when he apparently went out for lunch. Nobody had seen him since.

He went back to his office and asked the admin assistant outside, a late middle-aged African American woman named Petronia who had been in the same civil service position in the same office for eighteen years, to call Grundell at home and if he's not there, any number that's in his personnel record. She called the home number and left a message on the answering machine to return her call immediately. There was only one other number in the personnel record, a younger brother in Richmond, Virginia. Petronia talked to the wife who was at home taking care of the children while her husband was at work. She knew nothing about Robert's whereabouts, hadn't heard from him for a while, maybe a year, she said. She'd ask her husband and tell him to call if he knew anything.

At around ten thirty, Herod Hardin made the decision to declare Robert Grundell missing and reported it to the DC Police Department which in turn notified the entire Capital area police jurisdictions in Maryland and Virginia.

Word spread quickly within the Branch and throughout the Division. Being a federal employee and especially one with a Top Secret Clearance, the Department of Justice was notified as well which then turned it over to the Federal Bureau of Investigation. An FBI missing-person investigator was assigned to the case immediately.

It took no more than a couple of hours before Henry Tucker, the FBI investigator, was talking to agent Richard Bartley. When he noticed that Robert Grundell's home address was one odd number away on the same street from that of Ahmed Khalifa who was murdered the night before, he did a quick footwork to find out about the case, the agent assigned to it and locate the man.

"Between these two cases, it's like I can smell something from a mile away," Tucker said to Bartley on their way to Grundell's apartment later in the afternoon. Now Bartley was really feeling spooked but at the same time anxious to get into this Grundell case. JayJay was absolutely right when he said they shouldn't count Robert Grundell out yet and that he should have been and should now be put under surveillance.

Khalifa's killer, Mustapha Khan, who was as cold-blooded a murderer as any he had ever seen, gave the interrogators the run-around from the beginning, first by denying the killing, taking everybody around him for a fool. When the prints came from the lab, along with all the physical evidence, including ballistics, and put him in the scene of the crime at the time it was committed, he invoked the Fifth and clammed up. But in spite of this, Bartley was ecstatic. The man's prints matched those found in the restaurant where his partner John Jacobs was assaulted. They finally caught the sonofabitch. He couldn't wait to tell JayJay.

To this moment, however, Bartley was still unable to make a connection between Ahmed Khalifa and Robert Grundell outside of their being nextdoor neighbors and friends. Thinking back to that day they tailed them in the park, the only other thing they had in common was Mustapha Khan, this same man who had followed, watched everybody in the park and later banged Jacobs' face on the washroom wall.

Now Bartley wondered as they neared Robert Grundell and Ahmed Khalifa's apartment complex in Arlington, if being dead, killed by the same man, might be another thing they now had in common. He fidgeted in the driver's seat as he thought about what they might find in Grundell's apartment.

They drove into the parking lot of the apartment complex and parked a few spaces from the same one where the surveillance van was only two nights ago. They saw two Arlington Police cars next to each other as they stepped up the walkway to the courtyard.

"Looks like the locals beat us to it," said Tucker.

"I hope they know what they're doing and don't mess things up." Bartley increased his stride as they neared the front door of the apartment building.

An officer posted just inside the door let them in after they flashed their badges. Upstairs in the second floor, they found three law men, another officer and two plainclothes detectives. One of them was a good deal larger than the other. At least nine inches taller and maybe seventy pounds heavier than the other's five-foot-seven 150-pound build. The smaller one was busy taking notes while the bigger one was quizzing a gray-haired skinny man who would turn out to be the apartment manager.

After they got past the introductions and clarified the order of business between the local and federal authorities, the Arlington detectives brought the Feds up to speed. From what they got from the apartment manager so far, there hadn't been anything out of the ordinary happening in the place involving Robert Grundell. Either at his apartment, in the building or any other building in the complex.

There was never any trouble with the guy. He's always on time with the rent. He's quiet; there was never any complaints from the neighbors.

And the last time you saw him?

Geez, I don't know, sir. The only time I see most of them, the tenants, I mean, ordinarily is when they drop off the check at the office on a weekend. Many of them just slip it through the slot in the door in the morning on their way to work.

Not much from all that, the Feds agreed with each other in a low voice after a few minutes. Agent Henry Tucker then asked to go over the place which he and agent Richard Bartley did for some twenty minutes.

From the look of things—the kitchen, the bathroom, the bedroom, nobody had lived in the apartment for days now. Maybe as long as a week, Tucker told Bartley, coming from years of experience with missing-persons investigations on dozens of cases in the Bureau.

The only food particles he found in the kitchen—on the floor, the countertop, the dish tray and the refrigerator were all dried up; had no moisture content whatsoever that might indicate consumption within twenty-four to forty-eight hours. The bed certainly hadn't been slept in for days. The bathroom—not a drop of water sitting on the sink and the tub, and the toilet likewise hadn't been flushed for days.

Something that caught their attention in the small bedroom Grundell used as an office workroom—the brochure of a Toyota Lexus, model GS430 luxury sedan. Inside it was a receipt for a five-thousand-dollar down on an order price of forty-nine thousand dollars for a premium-package copy of the model. A hand-written note at the bottom line said 'No loan. To be paid in full'.

"If I didn't know any better, I'd say this guy is on vacation," Tucker said as they were coming out of the bedroom.

"Not according to his boss," said Bartley. "No leave slip, no notice of absence of any kind."

"Maybe the boss went on vacation himself and just got back and it's sitting at the bottom of his inbox he hadn't dug into yet."

"Maybe. Let's hope so." Bartley couldn't have meant and wished that more honestly. It was a relief that Robert Grundell wasn't found dead in his apartment. But if he was missing because somebody had killed him, he'd still be quite dead someplace else.

Then as if simply by thinking his thoughts out loud, things started to unravel before him and Henry Tucker. Stepping back into the living room, they saw Zak Porter, the note-taker and the smaller of the two Arlington detectives listening intently on his cell phone which they heard ring earlier.

"When?" he asked to whoever it was at the other end. He listened for a short while and then another question: "Has it been secured?" A short pause. "Alright, good. We'll be there in…twenty minutes," he hung up, pocketed the cell phone and turned to Joe Riley, the larger one.

"What's that all about?" Joe Riley asked.

Zak Porter took a moment to collect himself. He appeared visibly excited particularly to the two FBI agents.

"We got something real big come up, Joe," he said, an expression of delightful discovery opening up on his face. "Remember that bulletin from Alexandria about a woman who called regarding the shooting she said she saw at the park which they later decided was a prank call?"

"Yeah? what about it?"

"It isn't. Well, I'm saying it could be that it isn't. Guess what was just found at a parking lot in the park?"

"Zak, I'm gonna wet my pants in a second here now."

"Okay, okay. This guy's car. It's been sitting there for a few days now and the groundskeeper finally noticed it and reported it to Alexandria police."

"You mean this guy? The guy who lives in this apartment and who's missing?"

"Yes. This Robert Grundell."

These two guys work real well together, thought Henry Tucker as he and Richard Bartley now moved closer into the living room. Now he was thinking, as he said earlier to Bartley, he could smell something about this whole thing from a mile away. He finally decided to get some attention from the two locals.

"Somebody want to tell us what's going on?" he said.

It was Joe Riley who cued them in, being the lead man in the police investigation, apparently. He started with the call received by the Alexandria police early afternoon four days ago from a woman reporting a killing at Fort Ward Park she said she witnessed first-hand. Two men together and a third man. One of the two men shot the third man three times.

People went out there, at the place in the park where she described seeing the crime happen. Behind some bushes. Nothing was found. No body, no cartridge, no blood. They decided it was a prank.

Now Zak just got a call from one of their buddies in Alexandria PD. He knew they're assigned to this Grundell missing-person case.

"They're back out there now combing the place," Zak Porter told everybody in the room. "We got to get over there quick."

That woman's call wasn't a prank, Henry Tucker was thinking. This guy is out there somewhere in that park dead. He looked at Bartley and he could almost read the same thing on his mind.

Before they left, Joe Riley had the officer that was in the apartment tape the door off-limits and ordered the manager to make sure nobody entered the unit.

Coming out of the building into the courtyard right behind the two local detectives, Henry Tucker said to Richard Bartley: "You know about what's going on in Robert Grundell's office, I assume?"

"Office of Civil Defense Logistics. OCDL, Treasury, Bailey's Crossroads," Bartley said. "I know about the two agents, Nancy Schneider and Frank DiPaolo, we got *working* there right now looking into unauthorized access and use of classified federal data. Why? Anything?"

"I was told when I got this assignment they found some serious stuff going on in that office. In fact, they got a plan to bust some of the workers either today or tomorrow."

Bartley stopped walking just as they were stepping down to the parking lot and looked straight at Tucker. "What kind of stuff?" he asked.

"They found floppy diskettes loaded with classified data. Outside labels were addressed to some Middle-Eastern names. One of them I remember is Abu Kamal Ram...something."

"Ramshallah!" Bartley barked, giving Tucker a slight jolt.

"Yes. That's it. What's going on? Know the guy?"

"No. Just the name," Bartley said, now hardly able to contain his excitement, eyes widening like a madman. "I haven't met the man or seen him. I just know about him."

He had finally found the link between Robert Grundell and Ahmed Khalifa outside of their being good neighbors and buddies—Abu Kamal Ramshallah, the very same man who was their sole lead to Saladin! He hit pay dirt at last. Damn! Why didn't he look into this angle before? It was there all the time. They even had Nancy Schneider and Frank DiPaolo right in that office and he could've just asked them to see if that name popped up anywhere not just in that office but anywhere inside the whole building.

Now he remembered that Toyota Lexus brochure back in the apartment and the receipt inside it. An order for a forty-nine-thousand-dollar luxury car. How does a mid-level bureaucrat taking in something like sixty grand a year blow forty-nine grand on a car? No loan. Paid in full. He must have another source of money besides his government pay unless he won the multi-state lotto recently.

He wondered how much a floppy diskette full of classified federal government data is worth to some people who might fancy an attack against America similar to the Punchbowl bombing. Maybe even Pentagon II. Then, looking stunned senseless, he grabbed Henry Tucker on one arm while fumbling for something in his coat pocket with the other hand. Thinking of Abu Kamal and Ahmed Khalifa that day in the Sheraton Premier Hotel, he suddenly remembered that there were others with them, from the prints that were lifted in the hotel suite. One set of prints matched that they found in the restaurant washroom where John Jacobs was assaulted. That of Mustapha Khan.

Now it all tied up even more. Mustapha Khan, Abu Kamal Ramshallah, Ahmed Khalifa and now, possibly, Robert Grundell, were all in on this. And who else? Those other workers in Robert Grundell's office that agents Schneider and DiPaolo were getting ready to bust!

But why the killing of Khalifa? And now perhaps Robert Grundell.

One thing at a time.

First, now that they've lost the only subject they thought could be a lead to Abu Kamal and Saladin, it wasn't a total loss because now they had another in Mustapha Khan. And more—the workers in Robert Grundell's office, including Robert Grundell although the chance of him being alive now looked pretty slim.

"Henry, you go with these local dicks," he said. He let go of Tucker's arm and started dialing on the cell phone he had pulled out of his coat. "Call me on this phone later, let me know what happens. I need to get back to the office to make sure nothing happens to Mustapha Khan. He's the only first-hand case subject we got left—alive. We got to keep him that way. Then I got to butt heads with the analysts handling the operation with Schneider and DiPaolo at OCDL. I'd like to talk to the two of them too." He walked quickly to the car with the cell phone pressed to his ear.

"Wait a minute," Tucker said right behind him. "Anything I need to know? Do? What the hell is going on? Who is this Abu something?"

"I'll cue you in later. Haven't got time right now. Call me or Eddie Green—I gave you his number—as soon as you find out if Robert Grundell is dead. If he is, we'll have to get back into his apartment—hey, Eddie!"

"What's up, Richard?" Eddie Green's voice sounded out loud through the cell phone just as Bartley opened the car door and got in. Henry Tucker stood nearby and all he could do was just that—stand there holding out his hands, palms up and with a lost look on his face. And he stayed that way till he saw Richard Bartley drive out of the parking lot, after which he got in his own car and followed the local detectives to the park.

"Where are you?" Bartley asked Green on the phone.

"At WFO."

"I'm on my way over."

"I thought you're on temporary detail with Tucker on that missing-person case."

"Yeah, well, I still am but something more important, hugely more important came up. I got to get together with the analysts working on Schneider and DiPaolo's stakeout at OCDL. You'd probably want to join us. I'd like you to."

"I was just getting ready to pay Mustapha another visit in the Alexandria Detention Center. See if he gets us anywhere today," Green said.

"No, wait for me. I'll go with you after we talk to the analysts."

"What've you got?"

"Our guys at OCDL are getting ready to bust some of Robert Grundell's co-workers who are trading on classified government data with some Middle-Eastern people. One of them is our man Abu Kamal Ramshallah who gave us a slip at Columbia Plaza and left two of our men dead. He's also our link to Saladin. One more thing—Robert Grundell is dead."

CHAPTER 22

▼

It had been another busy and tiring day, Omar Husain thought after the meeting at the hotel, but a very productive one. And a lucky one too, for him, he thought just now as he saw Chris Phillips get into his Toyota Camry at the townhouse parking lot and get on the road. It was a few minutes before five in the evening and he had been sitting in the car across the street for just over fifteen minutes when he saw Chris pull into the parking lot, get out of the car and hurry into the townhouse. Five minutes later, he was out again carrying a gym bag and was back on the road going somewhere. And that's what he wanted to find out, where the man was headed, as he now tailed the Toyota Camry on the residential road out of Fairlington community to Route 7.

Things were starting to fall in place pretty clearly with the plan for the next operation. Operation Capitol West. That's what they had decided to call it after going over the details in the diskettes.

There were still several major items which they didn't get into during the all-day meeting. But they had plenty of time between now and the second weekend of December which was the date he and the other commanders—Hassan Bahaji and Kashim Najoub, along with Abu Kamal Ramshallah, agreed would be the target date for the launching of the operation. A couple of the younger men he had selected to join the operations planning got so involved with their own ideas at one point he decided to call a break so he could pull them aside and talk to them.

They suggested launching three separate operations at the same time in the first day of the two-day inauguration of the project. One in the train before it got to North Dakota, to take care of the senators right away. One at the inauguration site during the opening celebrations, the speeches by the local and state officials. Get them all at the same time. And one at the water and power project itself.

It certainly sounds so grand and exciting, he told them but expressed doubt they would have enough time to gather all the resources they would need for such operations. He didn't want to discourage any of these devoted Soldiers of Islam, especially these ones who respected him highly, many of whom he helped mold in their youths and early manhood. From the madrassas in Pakistan to the Islamic schools in the Middle and Far East, and even here in the hidden enclaves of the Muslim faith in North America. He left their ideas open as options to whatever plan of operation they arrived at by the end of the coming week.

At the moment, he put all that aside and focused on the road, the Toyota Camry that had just made a right turn to Route 7 while he now had to wait for traffic to clear before he could do the same. He stepped hard on the gas as soon as he was able to make the turn and barely saw the Camry go down the entrance ramp to I-95 South. He followed the car discreetly on the highway, staying between two to three car-lengths behind it on the same lane or on its right.

Going to Julie in Fairfax City from home, once in a while Chris Phillips preferred taking the Beltway, looping around part of the way and getting off again on Route 236 west and heading straight to the city from there. Other times as now, he decided it's just as fast getting there all the way on the surface road which was a shorter and more direct distance, but for the lights. Besides, he needed to stop by a Seven-Eleven to pick up a quart of 2% milk for Julie and a six-pack of Sprite. So, instead of going all the way out to the Beltway, he planned to get off I-95, a couple of miles down at the exit to Duke Street west, the same road as Route 236 but a different name at this end of it. Except that he didn't decide on this till the last three seconds he had the chance to exit which he did but only by driving as if he would score a 1.0 on a breathalyzer.

Unlike the Toyota Camry which was only two car-lengths ahead when it suddenly jerked to the right and cut fast to the Duke Street exit, Omar Husain didn't have a chance at all to make the exit. He had no choice but to keep going, picking up speed as soon as he lost the Camry, thinking fast what to do next.

Make the next exit which was Edsall Road west, get off there then cut back north on any road that intersected 236 and head west. Try to catch up with the Camry. He got off on the exit, drove a few minutes on Edsall till he came to Backlick Road and turned north on it. After about a mile, he decided to pull over to the side of the road and check the map. By the time he saw any chance of catching up with the Camry, he gave in to the thought of the comfort and rest in his hotel room after a tiring day.

The Camry could have made a turn on any road shortly after it got on Route 236. It could be anywhere, any road in the area or off the road by now, parked somewhere. He decided to let this one go and head back to the hotel in Old Town. He'll give it a try again tomorrow, the day after, and the next, till he found out who that woman was and what this Chris Phillips had to do with her.

Everytime he went to Seven-Eleven, he always picked up more stuff than he meant to even when he's in a hurry. He got the 2% milk and the Sprite. In addition, he picked up a box of Klondike ice cream bars, a bottle of spring water and a 32-ounce bottle of Lemon-lime Gatorade. So now, seeing how it was starting to get dark, he hurried out of the store into the car and got back on 236, three miles from Julie's place in Fairfax Square, Fairfax City.

He should've remembered to pack the gym bag when he went to work this morning so he wouldn't have had to come home first, he was thinking as he got out of the car at Julie's condo parking lot a few minutes later. It was running day and it was supposed to be at her place today, including dinner afterwards.

She was sitting in the living room all dressed up for the outdoors in her warm-up suit and walking shoes, ready to go when he walked in.

"Hi, hi, hi, sorry I'm a little late," he said to her, walking straight to the kitchen to unload the Seven-Eleven stuff on the counter and then to the bathroom to change.

"Lemme guess," she said after him. "You forgot to pack the bag in the morning—"

"Got up late, got ready in a hurry and forgot about it."

Five minutes later, he came back out in a light-blue warm-up and sat next to her in the couch to tie his shoes. "Where are we going?" he asked.

"The park," she said, referring to the one behind her subdivision community, a small but scenic retreat from the city's traffic and commerce. Sometimes they went to the high school across Route 236 and used the quarter-mile track there.

"Ready?" he asked as he got up, rotating his head and flexing his shoulders. "I'm all tensed up. I need to loosen up."

"Yes, you look like you need a good workout," she said, getting up too. She stood a few feet facing him, did a couple of knee-bend sit-ups then assumed a tae-kwon-do stance. "Let's see what you do with this," she said and before he saw it coming, he was staring at her right fist a half an inch from his face. He turned to his right and there was her left foot coming from a roundhouse kick which she held an inch away before it made contact with his nose.

"That's not fair," he complained. "You're supposed to bow before your opponent first and challenge him."

"It could've been worse," she replied. "I could've come from behind."

"It's getting dark fast out there," he said, changing the topic. "We might not be able to do the park now."

"And whose fault is that? Who was late coming?"

"Alright, alright. Let's see what it's like outside. If it looks like we're going to get caught in the dark before we finish, we'll go to the high school track across the street. It's well lighted and better for running and walking."

They headed out the door and just as she was locking it outside, he remembered the Gatorade and the spring water and went back in to get them from the kitchen counter.

"Anything else?" she asked, eyeing him from the corner of her eyes when he was coming back through the doorway.

"Well, let's see—"

"Sweetheart, if we don't get out of here now, we're never going to get anywhere before it's pitch dark out there."

"Alright, alright, just one more thing I remember," he said, looking at her meekly.

"What now?"

"Got your ID?"

"Oh-h, Christopher…"

"Honey, would you just make sure you got it with you, please?"

She searched all her pockets but found no ID. "I don't have it," she said. "It must be in my other warm-up suit."

"What about the one I gave you at Fort Ward park?"

"I'll go get it," she said grudgingly and hurried back into the bedroom feeling totally impatient but way down, deep inside, grateful for his concern for her safety and well-being.

"I got it, right here. See?" She came back out holding her ID out close enough for him to read before putting it away in her zippered pocket.

"Where's the one of mine I gave you?" he asked again.

"I can't find it. It's not in the other warm-up suit. I must have lost it."

"It's alright," he said. "I got another one with me. Let's go."

CHAPTER 23

▼

The night they met with their analysts at WFO after tossing the workstations of several of the top suspects at OCDL, Nancy Schneider and Frank DiPaolo didn't have any problem convincing the office not to wait any longer to do the bust. Immediately, they urged. The analysts agreed, but asked for one more day until the two agents had finished tossing the workstation of all the other suspects. The two agreed, when they thought about it more.

If they busted only some, the others could—and surely they would—take flight. The agents could end up losing the bigger, more important catch. They had no way of knowing beforehand.

The following day then, they went through three more workstations late after close of business. One of them was Herod Hardin's where they found two more diskettes addressed to Abu Kamal Ramshallah.

That was last night, after which they headed back to headquarters, worked till midnight with the analysts and got the go-ahead to do the bust the next day. Early on during the night session, news of an event that potentially brought the operation up five or six levels in criticality broke with the arrival of agent Richard Bartley.

New developments had come up in the disappearance of Robert Grundell, missing since late the week before. Agent Bartley and Henry Tucker—the agent working with the Arlington locals in the investigation—thought the missing OCDL analyst was dead somewhere in a park in Alexandria. They searched for the body all over the park through the afternoon. It got dark late in the day and the search was called off till the next day.

Meantime, hearing of one of the names on the label of some of the floppy diskettes found in the office, Bartley declared that the operation may no longer be considered just an investigation in unauthorized use of classified government data. The Bureau may have to re-classify it as a top-level national security operation. The name Abu Kamal Ramshallah on the label of some of the diskettes had been positively identified as an associate of Saladin, the main figure in the recent Punchbowl suicide bombing under the assumed name of John Tyler.

When he saw the content of the diskettes, he went so far as to urge that the Director be brought in on it, who should then consult with the NIPC, the Homeland Security and the President. To clear up some of the cobwebs in the now dual investigation—that of the operation in OCDL and now the search for one of the most wanted men in the history of the FBI—the case files on Saladin were pulled out and the CID chief and his lead analyst made sure that everyone became familiar with the case.

There was no doubt about it, Bartley said later after the planning for the next day's operation got back on track. This is the biggest break we've had since we learned about the existence of this man years ago, and a dozen suicide bombings and other attacks later against Americans and the Jews here at home and abroad. Make sure nothing blows this investigation with some piddly legal technicalities, he said. Once we have the suspects in custody, we have to do all we can to hold them, squeeze them dry of anything we can get out of them. Same as what's now being done with the killer of Ahmed Khalifa, Robert Grundell's nextdoor neighbor. They haven't gotten much of anything out of the man so far, but some of the discoveries in Mustapha Khan's apartment in Annandale, Virginia brought more grimness to the investigation.

Materials linking this Abu Kamal Ramshallah with the Pentagon II attack, the Punchbowl suicide bombing and the more recent Columbia Plaza event were found. Another name on the label of the diskettes found in OCDL were on some of the papers found in the apartment—Rahim Akbar, along with Commander Omar Husain, Kashim Najoub, Samir Osmani, and several others. Any one of them could be Saladin himself. What concerned the analysts more, on top of everything else, was that the papers bore the letterhead *Global Islamic Defense Organization*. Everyone, the whole world in fact, knew about GIDO and how often the organization had been investigated for money laundering and implicated in many terrorist attacks in the West, the Middle East and as far as the Far East, in Malaysia, the Philippines, Indonesia and Singapore.

Richard Bartley wanted to get to the bottom of the Robert Grundell case thinking that it, the killing of Ahmed Khalifa and this whole operation that had now snowballed beyond anyone's expectations were all linked together. He wanted to go with agents Schneider and DiPaolo in the morning to talk to Robert Grundell's boss, Herod Hardin. When he learned that the man was one of the top suspects they were getting ready to bust the next day, Bartley asked to talk to the man first in the morning.

The bust was to start in the early afternoon, one-thirty, the end of the lunchbreak when most of the workers were expected to be back in their workstations. There was no search warrant, court order or permission of any kind needed from any government authority. The Department of the Treasury's Office of Civil Defense Logistics being an office under the Executive Branch of the U.S. government, the only red tape involved to carry out the 'search for evidence of suspected activities against the homeland and the United States government' was the White House approval which the Bureau's Director obtained with a phone call.

Every piece of information, material, equipment, discovery, invention, writing; every piece of paper, software, hardware, CD, floppy diskette an employee used at work belonged to the office. And the boss, the President of the United States of America, through his agents and representatives, had the right to access them, read them and allow or prohibit their use. He had the power and authority to investigate and seize them and the persons using them especially where it involved activities that threatened national security.

Agent Bartley went with Schneider and DiPaolo in the morning and they took him to Herod Hardin in the man's office. There Bartley questioned Robert Grundell's boss just short of an hour, took some information about the missing federal employee and then left to join agent Tucker in the search taking place in Fort Ward park in Alexandria where Grundell's car, abandoned for days now, had been found.

Shortly after one o'clock in the afternoon, as soon as the Treasury Secretary and the Undersecretary for OCDL were officially notified, a dozen agents with Jerome Bolden of the Bureau's Investigative Services Division, one of the case analysts who approved the bust, arrived in the office. Agents Nancy Schneider and Frank DiPaolo cleared them quickly at the entrance lobby security and took them into a large conference room first on the same floor where agent Elmer Banks waited. There, Schneider and DiPaolo gave them one final briefing on the conduct of the operation.

At exactly one-thirty, an agent was posted at each of the two entrances to the office. Then agents Schneider, DiPaolo and Banks took the rest with them and stationed a pair at the doorway of the workstation of each of the suspects. They lucked out big time. All the top ones, suspects they had hoped would be in—

starting with Leon Justice—were in their workstations either on the phone, finishing a brownbag, cruising the internet or the government network.

Once everyone was in place, Schneider and DiPaolo went around to each workstation to properly identify themselves to its occupant, displaying their credentials while stating their business and the authority under which they were performing their duty. Then agent Schneider, leading the operation, gave her first official order to the suspect worker which was to cease all activities at once and remain in his workstation (under guard) while the FBI agents conducted their business.

They caught each of them off-guard. Leon Justice started to protest and attempted to pick up the telephone but was quickly restrained by one of the agents. Ralph Robson took a step towards the doorway but the agent who stood guard there stared him down and he simply went back down in his chair looking pale with disbelief.

One of the agents then began the search, knowing exactly what to look for and where to find it while the other stood guard at the doorway, one hand positioned near his weapon, a pistol holstered under his coat. The procedure was to do a ten-minute search before making the 'discovery'. Then the suspect was declared under arrest, cuffed and read his rights. If the suspect protested, he was advised of the appropriate event and place where he may do so, with counsel.

At the headquarters meeting with the analysts the night before, the agents were directed to conduct the operation from beginning to end quietly, without attracting a lot of attention and, most important of all, without allowing the leak of a single word to the media.

The delicate part was getting the suspects out of the office one by one, in cuffs, escorted by the agents front and back. Several of them had the agents cover their hands and forearms with a sweater or a coat but those who didn't have anything to hide the cuffs and were too dazed to even think about it just walked between their escorts in plain sight of the other workers who happened to be around at the time.

One of them was Max Poysen, just coming through the main entrance door when Leon Justice was being led out, in handcuffs, by two large men in suits and with those thin wires curling out of their collars to their ears. Another was Eddie Mahone who was talking to another worker in the hallway near the entrance.

"What the hell is going on?" Max Poysen asked the two men in the hallway as he approached them.

"Beats the hell out of me," said Eddie Mahone, all at once surprised, puzzled and covertly delighted at seeing Leon Justice being hauled away like a criminal.

"I have never seen anything like that around here in my twenty three years here," said Felix Andrioli, a forty-something career bureaucrat, one of the oldtimers in OCDL.

The three of them searched each other's face for an answer but found nothing but a lost look, a bewildered expression and apprehension. Max Poysen was the first to offer a speculation, moving closer to the other men as he spoke.

"You think maybe that has something to do with Robert's disappearance?" he murmured to the others.

"I don't know," said Felix in a low voice. "But now that you mention it, maybe."

"Let's go ask Herod. He should—" Eddie Mahone started to say but held the rest of it when they saw Herod Hardin himself being escorted out the door in handcuffs by two men, both as large as the ones they saw before, also in suits and with those thin wires curling up behind their ears.

*   *   *   *

Samir Osmani was more than happy to take the Commander's order early today. It didn't matter what it took to find out how this U.S. government worker Chris Phillips would live his life today, at work, at home or someplace else. He would find out for Commander Omar. He was prepared to track the man all day but as it turned out, coming upon the idea after following Chris Phillips for a while on his way to work, all he had to do was give the man a call at work at half past nine o'clock in the morning.

"O-S-E-R-S, Department of the Interior, good morning?" Chris Phillips greeted in an official-sounding voice as per the standard of office telephone conduct.

The man means business, thought Samir Osmani. Very prompt, opening up to you not with just a plain hello but a greeting in the form of a question saying 'How may I help you?' without saying it. And it's a good thing Commander Omar told him where the man worked: Office of Social and Economic Reserves and Security—O.S.E.R.S., or he wouldn't have known what the hell it stood for. Not that it mattered an iota to him.

"Mr. Chris Phillips?" he asked while sitting in his car at a parking space across the street from the Interior Department headquarters building on Virginia Avenue.

"Speaking. Who am I talking to, please?"

"Sir, this is Jeff Carter from the Office of Civil Defense Logistics, Treasury Department," Samir Osmani lied, finding it easy to sound like one of them—a Washington career bureaucrat just like the one he was talking to now. After all, he grew up in America and in fact was an American, spoke American English, lived like any born-American, acted and appeared on the outside like an American. Except that he did not think like real Americans, did not share their ideology, religious beliefs or cultural traditions. He did not look forward to American things like July Fourth, the Super Bowl game, Halloween; things like the big year-end holidays, for instance, beginning with tomorrow's Thanksgiving Day. He was a Muslim, one who would uphold and defend his faith in Islam to death. "I have some materials I need to deliver to you personally for your signature. Would you be available sometime today?"

"What is it? Never mind, it's alright," the man said, and Samir Osmani was glad he changed his mind for he didn't have a ready answer. "When are you coming?"

"If it's alright with you, sir, around three-thirty, four o'clock this afternoon would be good for me, but if it's not for you—"

"Afraid not," Chris Phillips answered. "I'm leaving for the day in a couple of hours. Going home to get out of this work clothes, get into my grubbies and get some shopping done for turkey day tomorrow."

"Ah, I can understand that," said Samir Osmani agreeably. "Good idea. In fact, I need to do the same thing. Start out early, beat the rush at the store. I'll see if I can make it before you leave. If not, would it be alright Friday?"

"Yes, I'll be in all day."

There you are, thought Samir Osmani, after he hung up. Simple. Now he can relax, call the Commander and ask what he'd like to do.

"Good work, brother Samir," Commander Omar said on the phone, very pleased.

He asked his former pupil in Islamic fundamentalism from twelve years ago in Lebanon to pick him up at the Hilton Alexandria Mark Center hotel where he was continuing work with the other leaders on the planning of the next operation. No later than ten-thirty, he said. The plan was for them to wait for Chris Phillips to come home, keep track of him when he goes out again, hoping this time he would lead them to the woman. This was of course working on the theory that they knew each other—boyfriend-girlfriend-lover, whatever their relationship was.

At a quarter of eleven, Omar Husain was once again sitting in a car across the street a safe distance from the townhouse building, except this time he was a passenger and brother Samir sat in the driver's seat.

"There he is," he said ten minutes later as they watched the gray Toyota Camry pull into the off-street parking lot, Chris Phillips come out of the car and walk to his townhouse unit. He cautioned Samir Osmani to make sure he stayed alert and did not lose him, telling the young man what happened the day before.

"No, sir. We won't lose him," Samir Osmani assured, left hand firmly on the steering wheel, right hand on the gear shift ready to put the Ford Mustang Cobra in motion at a moment's notice. "Unless that Camry can fly."

Chris Phillips had just glanced at the dashboard clock which read 11:07 AM when his cell phone rang. He knew who it was, going by the time. He and Julie whose school was closing early before noon to give everybody time to prepare for Thanksgiving Day traveling, shopping, cooking, made a shopping date at Fair City Mall near her neighborhood.

"Hi, sweetie, it's me," Julie Santorelli said from her cell phone.

"Hi to you too, sweetie. Where are you?"

"Just got on Route 50 out of Falls Church," she said. "I should be at the mall by…11:30, give or take five minutes. And where are you?" she asked back.

"Now on 95 near Duke Street. I'm going on the Beltway. It's faster this time of day. I should be there about the same time."

"Don't forget—right in front of Shopper's Food Warehouse," she reminded him of their exact rendezvous point.

"I won't. See you there, honey. Bye." He put the phone back in his coat pocket and stepped on the gas a bit more, checking the traffic around him. It was perhaps a little heavier than normal for this time of day, apparently because of the holiday. People were taking off work early like they had done.

He sped up by five, seven miles an hour more when he pushed on the gas pedal. So did the Mustang Cobra three car-lengths behind him. It kept its distance no less than that, sometimes more. It even changed lanes so it didn't appear to be keeping anybody company on the road through the four miles on the Beltway, the exit to Route 236 west and the three miles on it to the shopping center.

At the parking lot in front of the foodstore, Omar Husain watched the Toyota Camry cruise on the entrance drive, turn right into a lane and then stop after a few cars in front of a blue Toyota Corolla. A woman in the driver's seat had her left arm out waving at Chris Phillips who then pulled right into the parking space next to her.

He had Samir Osmani go past them to the next parking section and pull into a space with a clear view of the two from five spaces away looking at the rear of the Corolla. He watched Julie get out of the car, turn and close the door. She had a winter coat on that went down just below her hips over her work clothes—a three-button shirt blouse and a knee-length skirt. Omar Husain matched her figure with the image he retained of the woman in a warm-up suit with a ponytail at Fort Ward park.

It was hard to tell with her inside that winter coat, but she looked like the same height, and weight, approximately. The hair of course would be different—no ponytail—since she apparently wasn't out for leisure or recreational activity but professional. It was just loose down to past her ears, curling in just before it touched her shoulders. Definitely not the same look as he saw of her at the park, if she was the same woman. But he could imagine—looking at her now walking with Chris Phillips toward the foodstore—how easy it would be to turn her back into the woman in the park simply by tying her hair behind her head, putting her back in that warm-up suit and the athletic shoes she had on. With the way she moved, the youthful energy she displayed walking—firm stride, brisk arm and head movement, she had to be the same age as the woman in the park.

She had to be the woman in the park!

Strange as he felt about it just now while watching her, he didn't see her as a threat to his safety or his life. He saw her more as a woman, a fairly attractive woman who would have turned his head at a social gathering, a chance encounter at a public place, and he would have definitely found a way to make her acquaintance. For a few moments, without questioning it in himself, he was saddened that he gained this insight about her while back in the obscure recesses of his mind lurked an awareness that he might have to destroy her.

They sat in the parking lot and waited for them to come back out of the store. Omar Husain would not dare follow them in. Chris would recognize him, and so would the woman, assuming she was the same one he was after. There was no reason to get closer to her than where he was now. Besides, all he wanted to do, for now, was find out where she lived. The rest of what he might decide to do later would just be a matter of when and how.

There was a steady flow of customers, holiday food shoppers, in and out of the store. These Americans, Omar Husain observed mentally, they love this Thanksgiving Day holiday. The women cook all day while the men and boys sit in front of the TV watching football, the men filling themselves with beer and junk food. Then, later on, the guests arrive, relatives and friends with no relatives of their own, lonely people anchoring themselves with their friends' families. Dinner is served and everybody stuffs their faces with turkey and everything else that traditionally comes with the meal—dressings and gravy, cranberry sauce, potato salad, pumpkin pie, apple pie, all kinds of dessert.

They consume to excess, fatten themselves up and then suffer from high cholesterol, heart disease, high blood pressure, alcoholism and depression. No wonder the health maintenance industry in this country—health insurance, doctors and hospitals and other service providers—makes up one of the most powerful drivers of the economy and lobby in government politics. Here is an entire population, in the hundreds of millions, engaged constantly in avaricious consumerism, pursuing a culture, a lifestyle that eats itself up from the inside, and then spends billions trying to make itself better.

What a despicable culture, thought Omar Husain now as he watched more people come and go to the store and the parking lot. Selfish, arrogant, destructive, and very stupid.

Twenty-five minutes after they saw Chris and Julie go into the store, the couple came back out to the parking lot carrying several plastic bags of groceries. They loaded these in the trunk of the Toyota Corolla then got into their cars and drove out of the parking lot, the Camry behind the Corolla.

The Mustang Cobra moved inconspicuously out of the parking lot, following the Camry at a discreet distance as it turned west on Route 236 into Fairfax City. It was a short drive to Julie's place, a community of rental units, condo apartments and townhouses on a quiet neighborhood street off the main road. There were always ample parking especially at this time of day so that they had no problem finding spaces next to each other and right outside Julie's ground floor condo apartment.

Going into the development, Samir Osmani took the extra precaution of slowing down to fall farther behind them but without losing sight of the Camry. As soon as they saw them finish unloading the groceries and shut the trunk lid of the Corolla, he pulled up quickly and parked two spaces past them across the parking lot driveway with a clear view of the entrance doors and the inside of the lobby of the three-story apartment building.

They had no problem seeing, through the glass doors, Chris Phillips open the door of the apartment unit to the right of the stairwell which was set back clear of the foyer. Julie followed right behind him carrying the rest of the grocery bags in both hands.

"She's the one," Omar Husain said partly to himself after studying her figure some more, as she got out of the car, took the groceries out of the trunk and carried some of them into the apartment behind Chris.

"Anything you want me to do, Commander Omar?" Samir Osmani asked dutifully.

"You've done a good job, brother Samir," said Omar Husain, regarding the younger man approvingly. "Yes, there are things that must be done, but you have done enough for today. The rest is up to me. I'll let you know when I need to call upon you again. We need to get back to the hotel now."

"Yes, Commander."

While the Mustang Cobra was pulling out to the parking lot driveway, Julie was turning around after having made just two steps into the living room to head back out to the Toyota Corolla. She suddenly remembered that she didn't need to bring in the bags of groceries she was carrying because she was supposed to bring them to her aunt Ida in Vienna where she and Chris would be going shortly.

Thanksgiving for the two Santorelli families had been held alternately for years, since the children were little, between Chevy Chase, Maryland—Julie's parents, and Vienna, Virginia—her aunt and uncle's home. Though it was in Vienna last year, it would be there again tomorrow. It was the right thing to do, everyone in Julie's family had agreed. It was simply too unbearable to imagine Ida Santorelli and her two children going through this usually joyful family gathering for the first time without the head of the family.

Standing behind the car, she freed her right hand of the grocery bags to unlock the trunk by putting them down on the ground. One of the plastic bags tipped on one side and a large eggplant rolled out to the middle of the road right in front of the Mustang Cobra which came to a full stop as it got closer.

At that same moment, Chris had come out the entrance door and called out: "Julie, watch out!"

Samir Osmani quickly shifted the gear to park and got out of the Mustang Cobra to pick up the eggplant.

"I'm awfully sorry," Julie apologized as she turned from inside the trunk to take the eggplant from the man.

"Not at all," replied Samir Osmani good-naturedly. "That is one beautiful eggplant. I'm afraid it might be a little sore in some places."

Julie chuckled, amused. "It's alright," she said. "It'll be fine. Thank you very much."

Omar Husain saw and heard everything even as he crouched low in the passenger seat. He sat up and watched Chris come up to Julie at the back of the Corolla as Samir Osmani drove them out of the parking lot to the street.

Up close, he found her even more attractive than he had thought earlier. Once more, he fought with that sad feeling inside even as he found it more strange, impossible that he should feel this way. Especially now that he learned and heard her name even as it was spoken by the man whom she, in all likelihood, loved, and with whom she slept and shared most of her life. No! He must not allow himself to wallow in this kind of personal feeling. There can be no room for sadness at what might have been in his life here in America, nor for any kind of regret, mourning for whatever possibilities might have awaited him in the past and lost for the rest of his life.

She is a threat to his life, he now forced himself to think. And therefore a threat to everything he and his people believed in; a threat to their way of life, and to Islam.

Chris followed Julie back into the apartment, finally closing the door behind him. They went straight to the kitchen and unloaded the grocery bags into the refrigerator, the pantry and the cupboards.

"Anything else you need to remember you might be forgetting?" Chris asked when they had put everything away.

She shot a look at him through the corner of her eye for a few seconds, giving him that don't-rub-it-in look but actually thinking what else, indeed, she needed to remember before going to Vienna. Any dish? Container? Pots or pans? Any more foodstuff? Thanksgiving cards? Yes she had them in the car already. She and Chris just had to sign them.

"Nope," she said confidently. "I got everything in the car. I just need to change and we're ready to go."

She started for the bedroom but held herself when the security intercom on the wall buzzed. Being the one near it, he pushed the answer button and responded: "Who is it?"

"We're disciples of the Universal Christian Bible Church," a young female voice came through the speaker. "We have some materials we would like to share with you which we believe would help you understand the direction you are taking in life."

"That's very kind of you, but no thanks," Chris replied and released the button.

"Are you quite sure you want to pass that up?" Julie kidded.

"I have a crystal clear understanding of the direction I'm taking in my life. Yes, I'm quite sure, my dear," he said and before Julie could turn, added, "That's one advantage you have living in a security building like this. They can't just walk up to your door and get you behind it. Not like at my place. Anybody could walk up my door outside and knock. Like last Sunday night when I got home from here. Some guy came and rang the door chime. I'm glad at least I have a peep hole I can see who it is before I even say anything."

"Who was it?"

"Some guy looking for…" Chris stopped and looked at Julie thoughtfully, suddenly remembering something. Then his expression gradually turned serious with a grimness he tried to avert but not quite successfully.

"What's the matter?" Julie asked, puzzled. "Who was it?"

It must have been the power of the subconscious that finally connected Sunday night with yesterday evening when they were about to go out and Julie said she must have lost the…ID. Not hers but *his*. Now this man who had found it in the park where she must have lost it, the same man Julie saw at the killing site, came to his place looking for a woman named Chris Phillips, the woman he saw running away from him after witnessing the killing.

"Honey," Julie inched closer to him now as he simply stood there, his face becoming ashen every second. "Are you alright? Is it a heart attack? A stroke? Please don't scare me like this."

"In the bedroom," Chris said, leading Julie by the arm through the bedroom door after glancing over at the big picture windows of the living room that overlooked the parking lot.

Sitting on the edge of the bed with her, he raced to find a way to tell her without frightening her out of her skull. The best he could do was sound as gentle and assuring as he could, in a tone of voice that gave her a sense of protection. But— thanks to her great intelligence, she appeared to have partly figured it out by herself when he turned that grim look on his face and he couldn't tell her who it was that came to his door Sunday night.

"Something about what I saw at Fort Ward park?" she asked, looking inquisitive, tense, more than worried. He figured the moment that possibility dawned on her, she had prepared herself internally to deal with it instead of letting panic take over.

He nodded, holding both her hands in his and said: "It was a man looking for a woman named Chris Phillips. When I opened the door and he saw me, he asked if *she* was in."

He told her the rest of what happened, the man taking out what Chris now realized was a phony piece of paper to the light outside to check the name and address written on it, then apologizing for the apparent mistake before leaving.

She asked what he looked like and he gave her a physical description which matched that of the man she saw at the park and described to the police. She stood up beside the bed, thinking. She remained calm, not outwardly worried but with her logical mind working, looking deeply concerned.

"You notice anything else about him?" she asked. "Any particular feature? Beard, mustache?"

"No. He was clean shaven. Wearing a coat and tie under the winter coat."

"What else was he wearing?"

Now he recalled one particular feature: the crescent-moon-and-star earring. When he told her this, she fell silent for a moment then raised her head at him looking very serious.

"That's him," she said, not at all frightened but instead with a firm voice.

"We must tell this to the police immediately," he said. "Right now."

He went around to the other side of the bed where the phone was but before he did stepped over to the window to close the blinds, lift a slat and scan the parking lot outside briefly. Julie caught one of his hands as he was stepping away from the window and turned him around.

"Do you think he knows where I live now?"

"Honey, I don't know," he said now with some urgency in his voice. "It's possible someone could have been following me around since Sunday night. Someone could be sitting out there now in a car in the parking lot—" He caught himself before he scared the wits out of her, pulled her with him in a hurry, away from the window-side of the bed and picked up the cordless phone on the nightstand.

"I'll let you talk to the police. Alexandria police," he said. "You'd have to identify yourself and tell them everything including what we learned just now."

"And then what?"

Thinking quickly now, moving as fast as he could and with the urgency in his voice now more pronounced, Chris said: "The most important thing right now is your safety and protection. We take the worst case scenario which is they're out there in the parking lot or somewhere else planning to come here. That means we have to get out of here right now. And you can't come back here."

"Christopher," Julie said aloud to interrupt. She used his full name either when they were having a fight or in some crisis as now. "What are you saying? How am I going to live from now on?"

"Honey, please listen to me. We don't have a moment to lose. We need to get the police here right now. Right this very second if we could. Do you understand?"

He drilled a look on her that made her understand what he was saying—someone could be on his way right now to kill her—and caused her to simply bob her head in agreement.

He dialed 911 and after being juggled in the Alexandria Police Department a couple of times reached its Investigations Unit. Chris then handed her the phone and she started telling the man at the other end what it was all about. She was asked to hold for a few seconds and then another man came on the line.

"Detective Harold Duke, speaking," said the man.

His voice sounded familiar to her. She told him over again what it was all about, giving him the most vital information she needed to give him quickly, as Chris instructed her—her name, address and telephone number. He remembered the case as it turned out he was the same man who took her call the first time.

Detective Harold Duke, 41, an eight-year veteran with the department, weighing the situation the caller was in about halfway through what sounded like a rapid two-minute question and answer drill, stayed with Julie on the line while he got on another one to the Fairfax City PD. He talked to Criminal Investigations for three minutes with the telephone on the left side of his head while holding the other on the right with Julie at the other end. She heard just about everything he said on the other line, thus learning that an emergency dispatch for the units nearest her location was being sent out as they spoke on the phone.

Duke asked to speak with Chris to get a firsthand account of Chris' part in the situation. Since the call came in, the detective had begun to feel this was coming out to be another lucky day following the discovery of the missing Robert Grundell's car at Fort Ward park only yesterday. He needed to take a break from the search at the park to tend to some urgent paperwork at the office and had come in just before noontime. He had just walked in when he got the call.

With a crime-scene eyewitness, now they could have a positive ID of a suspect. A few things left to do, though, which should keep him busy from now on: find the victim's body, see if it was the same as the missing person, protect the eyewitnesses, keep them out of harm's way, and hunt the killer.

The detective verified with Chris what he got from Julie which Chris summarily confirmed. "Yes, I can identify the man if I see him again," Chris said on the phone.

"Alright then, sir," said Harold Duke, sounding all official police business. "I do think there is enough reason to believe the two of you are at some risk. Especially Ms. Santorelli since she had actually witnessed the man at the scene of the crime. Stay where you are. Keep out of sight of the outside. We've asked for an immediate security dispatch from the Fairfax City police. They should be there any minute."

He made no mention of the investigation of the missing-person case which was taking place in the same place as they spoke. His reason was it could turn out to be an entirely separate case. In fact, that's how it was right now on record. He had two separate case files. But at each turn in the investigation everyday, it had become more likely than not that the murder victim whose killing Julie Santorelli witnessed was the same man, a federal government worker reported missing by his office—Robert Grundell.

Less than three minutes after the phone call, they heard police sirens coming at a distance from Route 236. They got louder and louder when the police cars turned into the community road and sped towards the apartment parking lot.

Julie and Chris looked out the window through the blinds and saw two city police cars, strobe lights turning, pull up right in front of the apartment building entrance. The sirens died down and an officer came out of each car in a hurry. They did a quick take of the surroundings before stepping up to the entrance. Each driver then got out of the cars and spread out in the parking lot looking for anyone on foot or inside a car.

Chris was poking his head out the apartment door even as Julie was still buzzing the two officers in. They obviously knew well ahead of time, in detail, the circumstances that brought them here in an emergency dispatch. As soon as they stepped in the living room, they inquired politely how things were with them and then started asking routine questions—police procedure, thought Chris.

Has there been any sign of forced entry? Ground floor apartment units, especially, are naturally vulnerable to this. Have you observed anyone suspicious near the premises? Any suspicious phone calls?

One of them did most of the talking while the other kept busy writing on a notebook. He looked up once in a while to say something, mostly to confirm or supplement what the other was saying. Then they told Chris and Julie that a plainclothes detective who had just been assigned to this case should be along shortly. They, the uniforms, were dispatched solely to provide an emergency security coverage. But they will be here, the talker explained, to give them protection until the detective or detectives arrived, or even after, if they were ordered to stay.

Julie offered them refreshments while they waited. One accepted and asked for a glass of water. The other declined, thanked her, and sauntered to the window to look outside. Whoever might have been around thinking of doing harm to anyone here must have been scared away by the sound of the sirens, not to mention the presence of the uniforms out there now, he thought as he watched two fellow officers making themselves quite visible in the premises. There was no one to be seen in the parking lot.

Chris was quite impressed by the promptness of the police from both Alexandria and Fairfax City, considering they were separate jurisdictions. It had only been less than twenty minutes since he picked up the phone and here they were, secure with armed police protection. Then another minute later, the intercom buzzed again. Julie pressed the answer button on the box on the wall and asked who it was.

"This is Detective Earl Stone of the Fairfax Police Department, ma'am," said a man's voice, brisk but polite, just like the uniforms in the living room.

Julie buzzed him in, telling him the ground-floor apartment number, first door on the right. A thirtyish man in khaki pants and corduroy jacket with elbow patches walked in, nodding at the uniforms, one at the window and another near the door holding a notebook, as he surveyed the living room quickly even before turning his full attention to Julie and Chris.

After the introductions, Detective Stone excused himself and conferred with the officers for a few minutes. Julie took this opportunity to finally let Chris in on what she'd been tossing around in her head with a growing discomfort since Chris told her she can't stay in her apartment anymore. Seeing how the atmosphere in her home where she had been living for a few years had suddenly transformed into some kind of a crime-scene investigation, now she was able to comprehend the real situation she was in. And she now understood how quickly Chris saw into telling her that they got to get out of the apartment and that she can't come back here.

But now the question was: What is she going to do? Where is she going to live?

What? Hide?

"In a way, yes," Chris said helplessly, in whispers, when she asked. "You're not going to stay here by yourself. You'd have to have 24-hour police protection. I could stay with you everyday but that doesn't change the situation much, unless perhaps we arm ourselves to the kazoo and use a guard dog at night."

After they talked about it some more, they agreed she had three options: stay with relatives, move, or stay in a hotel. At this point, she was prepared to make a phone call to her mother in Chevy Chase, Maryland, when the detective's cell phone rang, interrupting them as well as the conversation the man was having with the officers.

He turned away from everyone while he listened on the phone momentarily. "Uhm, I got all that," everyone heard him say. He listened some more, then: "I see...understand...ok. I'll see to that right now. Thank you." He pushed the end button and slipped the phone back into its holder on his belt.

"Ms. Santorelli?" he said, turning to Chris and Julie. "That was Alexandria police. I was just told that a thorough investigation is now underway at Fort Ward park. Two things I need to talk to you about right now, both of you—they would like to know what your plans are today. And so would I, since we have been put in charge of protecting you at this time. They asked when you could come down the headquarters, some time at your convenience, but the sooner the better. They need to get more information about what you saw, particularly the persons involved."

"I understand," said Julie. "I would—" she glanced up at Chris, then continued, "we would be glad to go down there but probably not today. We were just getting ready to leave for my aunt's in Vienna to bring some holiday stuff over there when this...whole thing suddenly occurred to us."

"And tomorrow wouldn't be good either because of the holiday," said the detective. "Perhaps if we could arrange for you to meet with them where you are instead, sometime today, you think that might be possible?"

Again, Julie looked at Chris and saw him already nodding in agreement.

"Yes, that would be fine," she answered, turning back to the detective. "In the meantime, we need to get going to my relatives right now."

"Yes," said Chris. "And that brings us to—what do we do from here on? She can't come back and stay here."

"Yes, yes, I am well aware of your concerns, of course. Both of you, as a matter of fact," Detective Stone said, stroking his jaw with one hand, contemplating. "I don't imagine you've talked about what the possibilities are at this point? Any alternatives?"

Yes, they have, just a few moments ago, Chris told the detective. And he and Julie went ahead and told the man the three options they had considered. There was a fourth one Chris alluded to briefly, that of having police protection, which the detective took as an open possibility. But that wasn't just up to him, he said. He'd have to take that up with the Lieutenant at Criminal Investigations back at headquarters.

After discussing all the options, everyone agreed with having Julie stay with relatives. And Chris would have to be very careful when meeting with her, making sure he didn't lead anyone to her. For now, Fairfax City police would provide them security while they're in transit. Julie got on the phone with her parents in

Chevy Chase. She spoke first to her mother who, upon hearing of the circumstances her daughter suddenly found herself in today, handed the phone to her husband.

After talking to her daughter for several minutes, Joe Santorelli urged Julie to hurry up, pack up and get out of the apartment immediately with the police security; proceed to Vienna where her aunt Ida was expecting her and he will meet her there. Get out of there now, he repeated to her. And tell the police, he added before they hung up, be damn sure no one is following you.

CHAPTER 24

▼

On his way to Fort Ward park fresh from meeting Herod Hardin at OCDL, Agent Richard Bartley remembered some of the things the case analysts at head-quarters had said about the investigation on the possible criminal mishandling of classified data in that office. Something like it could blow into something really big.

They must know plenty more than they're letting the field agents in on. But being the analysts, the brain thrusts of the Bureau, it's their job to be a step ahead of the game, figure things out ahead of everybody including—and especially—the bad guys. He had to hand it especially to that guy at Investigative Services Division, Jerome Bolden. He worked his brains out doing all that electronic monitoring, analyzing all that access-log data government-wide to zero in on some top suspects.

And look what agents Schneider and DiPaolo had come up with at OCDL because of that. No less than the expose on the connection between one of the Bureau's most wanted men in the world—the nameless, faceless Saladin, and people employed by the U.S. federal government with top-secret clearance doing business with him and his associates who were, in all likelihood, all working for one of the world's most powerful and well-financed militant groups—the *Global Islamic Defense Organization*.

He'd seen a report from the Bureau's Detroit Field Office detailing some of GIDO's connections with MidEast Continental of Dearborn, Michigan, through one of the company's vice-presidents, Abu Kamal Ramshallah, the man who drove John Tyler (Saladin) to BWI five days before the Punchbowl suicide bomb-ing in Hawaii. Copies of documents of money transfers in discreet five- to six-figure amounts to several Muslim charity organizations which later funneled them to Abu Kamal and one Rahim Akbar—a name the Bureau's analysts now firmly believed as one of the aliases used by Saladin—had been dug up by the SEC and the Justice Department.

Talking to Herod Hardin—Branch Chief of Plans and Security Database of the Interstate Logistics Division of the Office of Civil Defense Logistics of the United States Department of the Treasury—it was hard to believe he could be talking to somebody who would, and may already have, betrayed his country and caused the deaths of hundreds of his fellow Americans. What could bring a citizen to commit such an act against his own country, his own people?

Anger? Hatred? Money? Ideology?

One would have to be an avowed enemy—born and raised—of what he was trying to defeat and destroy to come to such a resolve. And the others? Did they all share that same resolve? And how many more of them were there throughout the government? Throughout the country? Were these people sleepers? Sworn enemy of America, the Christians and the Jews?

Knowing what he knew about the man and what was about to happen to him in a matter of hours, agent Bartley kept his senses sharp for everything Herod Hardin, Robert Grundell's boss, said and did during their forty-minute meeting. Early fifties, Bartley guessed of the man who said at one point that twenty-five of those had been with the federal government. And he looked it too, Bartley thought, the way he appeared to be so holed up snugly in his government job—a typical paper-pushing, Washington career bureaucrat, if he ever saw one. Well honed in the art of government politics, appearances and Washington bureaucratic gibberish.

"When was the last time you spoke to Robert Grundell in person, Mr. Hardin?" he asked some twenty minutes into the meeting after he had analyzed the man.

"I'm not sure. I don't ordinarily work directly with the program analysts," Hardin answered. "But I remember calling him in here early last week, or it could have been late the week before, about a high-visibility assignment with a due date coming up fast."

"Anything in particular you noticed about his actions? Language and behavior? Anything odd at all about him?"

"Not that I could think of. He was just...himself—Robert Grundell."

"And how would you describe Robert Grundell as an employee? A staff member?"

"In what respect?"

"As a worker. Did he do well?"

"Are you asking about his job performance?" Hardin asked, now looking as if he had something he knew well enough to talk about.

"Yes, exactly."

"Yes, he did well. Got his assignments finished on time, pretty much. He had a good track record from what I heard from my predecessor in the Branch. I consider him one of the most dependable of the senior analysts in the office."

"And you've been with the Branch how long, Mr. Hardin?"

"Five years."

"Would you say Robert Grundell was happy with his job? I mean, to your knowledge, and you may not know this for sure unless you consult occasionally with your staff on a personal level—do you have any reason at all to think Robert Grundell might be angry about something?"

That made Herod Hardin pause a moment. He had long ago noticed Grundell, along with several other workers in the Branch, as not being too sociable, at times outright unfriendly towards him and the people he, Hardin, associated with closely. There was a polarization there that had been quite noticeable. One group avoiding another. He always took it as the usual detachment between management and employees but of late had sensed that it went beyond that, especially with the flack about Leon Justice's recent promotion, and that protest letter which had now gone as far as the Office of Special Counsel. It was more like open resentment, the kind he could almost read on some people's faces, including that of Grundell, like a sign hanging in front of them.

"I really can't tell you," he said to the FBI agent. "I know some people in the office had long been due a promotion, including Grundell, but he had never made it an issue with his job. I guess the reason is he knows, as everyone else does, about the hiring and promotion freeze that is still in effect in a lot of offices throughout the Treasury Department."

"What about this office?"

"If you mean the Office of Civil Defense Logistics, the freeze had been lifted two years ago for most job categories. Especially the hard-to-fill jobs as in the computer specialist job series, for example."

"Sir, do you still have a freeze on the hiring and promotion for the job such as the one Robert Grundell has in your branch?" asked the FBI man more specifically, now with some impatience rising inside.

"His job title, no. We're now open to hire personnel in his job category at a grade level we have approved budget for. There were openings we've filled this past year as a matter of fact but at grades lower than Robert Grundell's position."

And how about promotions? he wanted to ask next, but at this point, Richard Bartley looked at the time and decided talking to this man was like talking to a drone that had been programmed to talk in circles. He could ask the man two more questions and it would probably take another hour to get a straight answer from the bureaucrat.

He had one question, though, he would twist the man's arm till it broke if that's what it took to get a straight answer from him.

"What was Robert Grundell doing before he disappeared?"

"You mean—the work he was doing?" Herod Hardin asked back.

Richard Bartley was dying to say, "No, sir, I mean—was he, like, masturbating at the time?" He had a second thought about what to do to get a straight answer out of the pesky bureaucrat. He was thinking, instead of twisting his arm, just pick up a chair and smash it on him till either his head or the chair broke or he gave a straight answer, whichever came first.

"Yes, sir," he said, mirroring his impatience by lowering his eyelids halfway down.

"Well, as I indicated earlier (God, how he hated that word—*indicate*—Bartley thought as soon as it came out of the man's mouth; why can't these fucking people just say things in plain simple words? How does one *indicate* something—by blinking an eye? raising a hand? sticking out a middle finger? This bureaucrat must be a failed lawyer who couldn't make it in the real world out there and came scooting into a cozy management job in the federal government.), he was working on this high-visibility assignment which incidentally involves handling of classified data."

"I understand he has TSC," said Bartley.

"Yes. We normally don't discuss assignments like this with outsiders but in your case, I don't see any risk. Robert was working on the security plans for this upcoming event in North Dakota called the Big Thunder."

Hardin went on to describe what the assignment was all about and Bartley was glad he didn't have to smash a chair on the man's head after all to get something out of him.

"Anything else you might add? What work he was doing last week?"

"Yes, let me see," Hardin said, turning to a sheet of paper taped on the wall to his right. "He was on call last week. You see, we have this weekly on-call rotation when an analyst may be called for any emergency task twenty-four hours a day for a week. A computer application system blows up middle of the night and operations needs somebody with a TSC to access and fix some data files, that sort of thing."

"I understand. So that means the person on call carries a cell phone he can be reached at anytime during the week?"

"And a beeper," added Hardin.

Bartley asked for the number of both the cell phone and the beeper and, with no desire to prolong his stay another moment, thanked the man and left.

He had just entered Fort Ward park from Braddock Road and was now headed to the crime scene near the northwest bastion, going at just under ten miles an hour. He pulled into the parking lot where Robert Grundell's car, which had been trucked away by the Alexandria police yesterday, was found. The report that had come in about the car was inconsequential. There were no prints found on it other than Grundell's. Not a single material found in the car linked to anything outside of his being an employee at OCDL where he was *not* one among a half a dozen people who were about to be busted in a couple of hours. Thus far, Robert Grundell was just a missing person. Somebody who could have been a fatal robbery or a kidnapping victim. Or he might just be playing hokey for whatever reason—to see if he would be missed by anyone, anything.

Bartley got out of the car and looked around for a few moments, didn't see anyone he knew, then crossed the park road and walked up the gentle slope of the grounds towards a sculptured green hedge on the other side of a clump of trees. Beyond this was the bastion around which the search for the victim of the shooting, reported by an eyewitness, was resumed yesterday. It got dark fast late in the afternoon and the search parties which consisted of both the Alexandria and Arlington investigators, in addition to himself, agents Henry Tucker and Eddie Green had to call it off till today.

About an hour after they, the Feds, had joined the locals in the search yesterday, he didn't think they were going to find any body. From the looks of things around the reported crime scene, the killers had done a good job of cleaning up if, indeed, there had been a killing and a victim. There were footprints in the area where the woman who called said she saw the killing, but they could be from dozens of other people, park visitors, who had come since and obliterated the subject prints. And there wasn't a trace of blood.

This meant, thought Bartley as he climbed up the slope, the body may not be anywhere in the crime scene at all or anywhere in the park. The killers could have carefully moved it and taken it someplace else. In that case, they could pick the whole place apart all day and it'd be a waste of time.

"Bartley!" a voice called after him from the other end of the hedge on the right. It was Henry Tucker coming his way with Eddie Green and another man, one of the locals he met yesterday—detective Harold Duke, Alexandria PD. He waited for them and they all walked in the direction he was headed.

Hey, what's happening? Anything new?

Nothing.

Not around here.

No stiff anywhere.

That could very well be. The bad guys could've taken it with them and dumped it someplace else.

That's what it's beginning to look like, considering there was an eyewitness who saw one of the killers. Get out of the scene of the crime clean. No body, no evidence of any kind. Nothing.

They got past the clump of trees and were now within sight of the bastion high above the trenches surrounding it. To their left was the evergreen thickets that had hidden the eyewitness from the killers.

Harold Duke himself had just arrived and joined the two Feds when they saw Bartley. He'd been waiting for the right moment to break the news to them and decided to do so now that they're all here.

"I do have something new," he started out. "It may not necessarily help us decide to continue the search here, but it might."

He told them about the call he got at the office from the eyewitness who finally agreed to identify herself and come in. She and her boyfriend had both seen one of the killers, he said, because the boyfriend got a night visit from him last Sunday. He explained how this had happened, the killer locating the boy-friend and through him, possibly, the eyewitness.

"Spooked the hell out of both of them and now she's in hiding," Duke went on, now getting everyone's attention one hundred percent. "She agreed to meet today but she can't leave where she is now, so we're going to go to her instead. Two o'clock. Any of you guys want to come along? You're welcome."

All three raised their hands.

They kept walking till they came to a clearing that led to the entrance to the bastion. To the right were the steps to go up the walkway leading to the big guns behind the parapets surrounding the bastion. Near the steps just inside the assem-bly grounds of the bastion was a pair of trapdoors labeled 'Filling Room', under-ground storage where armed shells were kept. On the other side of the entrance was a similar pair of trapdoors labeled 'Magazine', another underground storage where gunpowder was stored. These were of course during the Civil War when dozens of forts were built around Washington, in Virginia and Maryland, to defend the capital city against the rebels.

Bartley turned from the others and went up the steps to the parapet. Henry Tucker was right behind him. The view behind the parapet wall covered the southeast approach to the fort. Beyond the trees, less than a mile straight out, was King Street, also known as Leesburg Pike at its west end, where the Yankees at one time anticipated an attack by a contingent of Robert E. Lee's forces coming from southern Virginia.

The two men stood next to each other for a couple of minutes, enjoying the scenery, the blazing colors of autumn throughout the park. It was cool, chilly, but not winter-cold yet. The air felt good to Richard Bartley as he watched a few joggers and walkers go by on the asphalt road that looped around the park six-tenths of a mile.

"So what the hell are we doing here if you think there's no stiff to be found here?" Tucker asked.

"I said it could've been taken someplace," replied Bartley, enjoying a good sniff of the cool autumn breeze. "That's the same as maybe. I didn't say it's not here for sure."

"We've had the groundskeeper take us just about everywhere in the park," said Tucker. "The amphitheater, that little ancient cemetery near the park gate, the children's playground, the restrooms, the rifle trenches and all around this bastion."

Bartley turned around to look at the inside of the bastion, the big guns, six of them, poking out through openings in the parapet wall that enclosed the fortification above, the assembly ground below and the trapdoor entry to the magazine and filling rooms near the entrance to the bastion.

"I just talked to Robert Grundell's boss in their office at the Skyline Center, Bailey's Crossroads not far from here," he told Tucker, one hand coming out with the cell phone from inside his coat.

"Anything there?"

"He told me Grundell was on call last week when he vanished. He was carrying the on-call cell phone and beeper."

"So?" asked Tucker disinterestedly.

Bartley didn't say anything. He was busy reading the numbers Herod Hardin gave him which he wrote on a piece of paper. He dialed the beeper number first, thinking the cell phone wouldn't be on since it's used only after the contact with the on-call person was made through the beeper.

He waited ten, twenty seconds, keeping the phone receiver pressed tight on his ear. Tucker kept quiet, looking at Bartley, waiting for something to happen. Then Bartley's eyebrows flipped as the ringing began. He pressed the speaker button so he, and Tucker as well, could hear the ringing and at the same time listen to the sounds around them.

The first few times they heard the beeping, it sounded very faint and distant. It was as if it was coming from beyond the entrance to the bastion, way out in the trees that lined the park road some thirty yards away. Then as they descended the steps to the ground and listened more closely, it was coming from the area around the magazine trapdoors across the entrance to the bastion.

But as they approached there, they heard it coming from the filling room trapdoors. They turned and bent down on top of the white-painted wooden trapdoors. This time there was no mistaking where the beeping was coming from. They had found Robert Grundell's body.

*   *   *   *

Shortly after they got on the road to Vienna, Fairfax City Detective Earl Stone, driving on the tail of the patrol car carrying two of the Fairfax City PD uniforms behind Chris in the Toyota Camry and Julie at the head in the Toyota Corolla, he got the call from Alexandria Detective Harold Duke telling him of the discovery of the victim's body in the park. From this, he learned that because the victim was a U.S. government employee who worked with top-secret data, the Feds were now getting involved in the investigation. Duke was finally able to turn the two case files he had—that of the missing federal employee and the killing at the park, into one. He re-confirmed to the Fairfax City detective the two o'clock meeting with Julie and Chris in Vienna, adding that he would have a couple of Feds for company, and got an assurance from Stone that they would be there, in safe hands.

As soon as the Fairfax City detective said that and hung up, he suddenly realized why he was where he was—driving behind the three cars supposedly as an incognito lookout escort for an eyewitness to a murder. Julie had just made the right turn from Fairfax City's Main Street to Route 123 (Chain Bridge Road) on the six-mile journey to her aunt Ida's house in Vienna. The two cars behind her did the same but without making it look like they were a convoy, one of them keeping a distance from the other on another lane. Earl Stone, now fully aware of his role in the transit, kept an eye on the vehicles all around, front and back of them on all the lanes of the road, keeping track of the ones that may appear to be keeping them company. When they first left Julie's apartment, he stayed way back of the others to see if anyone would tag along.

By the time they entered Vienna, a city of less than five square miles and a population of under fifteen thousand middle-to-upper-income Northern Virginians, none of the vehicles he saw three miles back on Route 123 was still around. The road had now changed its name to Maple Avenue, the main artery of the little city. Julie led them through it for a mile before turning right to Branch Road, drove a few blocks on this and then turned left to Echols Street. She pulled into the driveway of a brick split-level on the right. The police car pulled up in front of the next house, Detective Stone right in front just past Julie's car in the driveway and Chris parked a block away and across the street.

Ida Santorelli, a woman newly widowed at 59, saw her niece coming up the frontyard walk. She was at the door when Julie got there. They hugged briefly then Julie started to explain that she had company. Her aunt waved her down while telling her in the distinct Italian accent she never completely lost since her late husband took her away from her family in Rome thirty-five years ago, that she knew. She knew because Joe, Julie's father, had called, told her what was happening and that he was on his way here too, coming from Chevy Chase, Maryland.

Julie had to calm her down a little especially when the detective, followed by Chris, came up the door. The uniforms stayed in the car.

"I'm doing fine, Ida," Julie assured. "I'm fine."

"I worried about you when Joe called," her aunt said as they moved into the living room, the men following. "I thought maybe you were hurt or something."

"No, nothing like that."

They turned to the men and asked them to sit down. Chris got up a moment later, taking Julie's car keys to bring in the stuff from the trunk.

Ten minutes later, Julie's parents arrived. The family spoke for a while with Julie doing most of the talking at first. Then there were discussions about what they should do, where she should stay, her father weighing seriously how much her daughter was in danger. Here, he left the women and joined the two men in the living room. It was reassuring to hear from the detective that not only were there two police officers out there near the front of the house but that another detective, from Alexandria, with some federal government investigators were coming.

After Joe Santorelli had heard everything that happened, from the day Julie sat on that bench in the park where she dropped Chris' ID to the last couple of hours today, he was at a loss to say anything about how or why his daughter got involved in all these except that it was out of sheer dumb luck! Why couldn't she have been someplace else when that crime was committed? Maybe just on a bench in another place in the park instead of the one where she witnessed the shooting. Now he wondered what the story was behind the killing of this government worker. Who the killers were. What the stakes were. The only thing Detective Earl Stone was able to say about it was that the victim handled top-secret information in his work with the federal government.

An hour later, his view of the situation got a bit more foreboding when four more men came: Alexandria police Detective Harold Duke and three Feds—FBI agents Richard Bartley and Eddie Green, who brought with them Earl Franks, a graphic artist from the Bureau headquarters. From them, he learned a few more things about the victim and the latest development on the investigation. But he could tell, after having dealt with some of these government people as a Beltway defense contractor for most of his thirty years in private industry, that they were not telling it all.

He sensed something ominous about the way they were withholding what they didn't want to talk about. But they weren't short on giving their assurances that they would be available on a moment's notice anytime of day if they were needed.

"And we will be working with the local police," Agent Bartley added, nodding at the Alexandria and Fairfax City detectives, "throughout Northern Virginia and nearby Maryland jurisdictions, in this investigation. Every local law enforcement agency will know its case number so they will know the appropriate actions to take and to respond quickly when they get a call."

After they had been talking to him for a while, they asked to talk to Julie and Chris, for the record. Meaning, as part of the official investigation—the questioning of the eyewitness and others involved which now included Chris Phillips. Julie's parents and aunt then went out into the kitchen with Ida offering coffee to everyone. The Feds and the two detectives all accepted the offer, thanking her politely.

During the questioning which lasted just over an hour, Julie wondered how many more times after Chris, her parents, Detective Stone and now the FBI and the Alexandria detective, she would have to tell the same thing over again. Chris had the same thought while he sat listening to Julie most of the time before it was fully his turn for the questioning.

The interesting part about the whole thing came after the questioning when the artist, Earl Franks, took his turn with the two of them. Franks was one of several field men assigned to WFO in its IT Section office, from the CJIS Division, Clarksburg, West Virginia. A Graphic Imaging Specialist, he and his type was commonly referred to in the Bureau as the *gooey* man, from the thing they do that goes with the IT acronym GUI (Graphic User Interface).

A man whose power of observation obviously was above that of most ordinary people, he spoke very little during the questioning. He just sat, looked and listened. And the times he said something when he needed to, it was only to ask Julie and Chris for additional details about what they saw. He wrote down what they said, then shortly before he took his turn with the subjects, he powered up an IBM Notebook on a high chair Julie brought out from the dining room, clicked on a GUI icon on the desktop and started a base definition of two images of a man, a front and side view, from the notes he had written down.

He started getting more data first with Julie by asking her to describe what the man she saw at the park looked like. At different instances. When she first saw him from behind the bushes, in profile, when he heard her and turned her way, and then when she was running away from him and she turned briefly to glance at him.

Everything Julie said in answer to his question, he entered into the computer by clicking on an item in a subject index on the right side of the monitor, adjusting the image on the screen. Other times, he would use an electronic pen and adjust the image manually with it, the same process as drawing on a sheet of paper.

As he progressed, his questions became more specific and detailed, and the image of Omar Husain began to take shape on the screen.

Was the light coming more from behind him or his side?

How bright was it? Look outside, please. Like that? Brighter? Or less?

Now, the eyebrows. Was it a natural frown you said you saw, or a reactive expression?

Reactive. This was when he heard my gasp after the man was shot a third time and he turned towards me. Other than that, his expression was…quite normal. I mean, no likeness to any reactive expression at all. I might say it was a pleasant-looking face.

The likeness of a man, indeed one might say pleasant-looking, even handsome, a caucasian, youthful-looking middle-aged man in his late-thirties to early forties, began to emerge on the screen. Here, the detectives and the Feds all got up and bunched up behind Earl Franks.

"Amazing," Eddie Green murmured as he watched Franks make adjustments to the picture, the lighting, the flesh tone, the bone structure with data coming from the high-speed calculations the computer did at billions of instructions per second using input given the artist by Julie.

Earl Franks flipped back and forth between the frontview and the sideview images of the subject everytime he got a new data to input in the computer. Everyone kept their eyes glued at the monitor, fascinated, as the pictures developed to near completion in a matter of minutes.

Then it was Chris' turn.

Again, Franks started two images in the computer and began querying Chris for data. This time he created a night backdrop, working first with the frontview of the man that stood at Chris' front door Sunday night under the canopy light. He took Chris through the same process as he did Julie, developing the two images alternately as he introduced new input into the computer from Chris.

The people around him which now included Julie watched with great interest. Her aunt came out of the kitchen at one point to ask if anyone wanted more coffee. All the four men behind Franks raised a hand without even looking her way.

Finally, some fifteen minutes later, with the front view of Omar Husain on the screen, Franks clicked the Save button which stored the latest copies of all four images in the CD. He then clicked the 3D Mode Function button in the toolbar of the GUI application and started rotating the image on the screen slowly, full circle. Chris had stood up from his seat and joined everybody around Franks. After watching the three dimensional image for a few moments, he and Julie exchanged looks. While they did, Franks brought up the frontview image he developed from Julie's input beside the other on a split screen.

"No doubt about it," Detective Harold Duke said first. "They're the picture of one and the same man."

Everyone agreed as they were looking at the two pictures that were ninety-nine percent identical except for the lighting and the contrasting backgrounds.

Julie said something to Chris which made him nod quickly in agreement. "We forgot something else," he said. "But it doesn't make any difference at this point."

"What is it?" asked Earl Franks.

"The earring on the left ear," said Chris.

He described what it looked like and in no time at all, Franks had it added in all the four pictures and re-saved them on the CD. The one he had on the screen, the frontview from Julie, he saved on the harddrive before he got out of it. He then removed the CD from the computer and inserted another one he got out from the computer case.

"Is that the one the Chief asked to bring along?" asked Bartley.

"Yes," said Franks. "The one that came from Hawaii, taken from...what's his name? The Army MP who had a close look at John Tyler."

"Corporal Wembley," said Bartley.

Franks brought it up. The image of a man at a quarter turn to the right from the frontview appeared on the screen. Next, he split the screen and brought up the copy he saved in the harddrive on the right half of the screen. Now Bartley understood what they at headquarters—their Chief and the analysts working with him, were after; the possibilities he now realized they were constantly looking into.

The two pictures looked different at first but on closer look, everyone began to see the unmistakable similarities. John Tyler was blonde while the nameless one on the right had dark red hair. But he had the same greenish-blue eyes as the other. For an exact parallel viewing, Franks put the nameless one on the 3D Mode and turned him a quarter to the right at exactly the same angle as on John Tyler. Then he edited John Tyler on the left, highlighted the hair and changed its color to that of the other. He lightened the complexion which was probably a fake tan, to match the other. He trimmed the eyebrows which again didn't look natural, to match the other. The two pictures now looked almost exactly identical. Franks rotated both of them slowly at the same time clockwise, full circle, stopping at the same angle he started with.

After that, no one in the room needed to be convinced another second that the pictures they were now looking at were of one man. Richard Bartley was the first to see the parallel but the last to accept the single identity of the pictures. He didn't count entirely on the matching of the physical descriptions given by Julie from the park and by Corporal Wembley at the Punchbowl in Hawaii when the MP bent down at the driver's side of the car and got a close look at the driver, John Tyler. Those could have a big margin of coincidence although all the features were extremely similar in both pictures. But when Franks had the pictures viewed from the same angle and Bartley finally saw in full view the crescent-moon-and-star earring—the symbol of Islam—on both pictures, he knew whose pictures those were. He knew they were all looking at the image of Saladin.

At last, after more than two decades of chasing a nameless, faceless, unknown enemy, they now had at least a likeness of him. More than a likeness, really. An accurate physical facial appearance, a technologically proven physiognomy of the man. He could now disguise himself as he had over the years, change his name a dozen times, speak in tongues and assume different personalities, and they would know him.

CHAPTER 25

▼

Once the identity of Saladin was officially accepted, approved and documented, a wave of excitement spread rapidly through the Bureau, starting with the Investigations Divisions. But it was quickly suppressed and allowed only to reach the higher ups. First, the Director, then the heads of other federal intel and security offices—the CIA Directorate of Operations, NSA, ATF, the Attorney General, State, the Homeland Security and the President.

The decision to keep it quiet, for the time being, was forwarded by those out in the field gathering intelligence, risking their necks to catch the man. Letting Saladin know he had been identified could actually help him make it more difficult for anyone to track him down, let alone catch him. But copies of the pictures developed by Earl Franks, both from Virginia and Hawaii, along with that of Abu Kamal Ramshallah from Detroit, were immediately mass produced wallet-sized and distributed worldwide to every field agent.

It had now been determined that Saladin's activities had reached into the top-secret data repository of the federal government, possibly by bankrolling its way to some people on the inside, although this had yet to be fully substantiated. After what agents Schneider and DiPaolo had turned up at OCDL, everyone in the Bureau believed it was only a matter of time, and procedures, before everything came to light, in spite of the vigorous denials and claim of a frame-up by the accused Treasury employees.

Finding one of the aliases Saladin had used in the past, in the offices of the employees, was a pretty damning discovery by itself, not to mention the same name appearing in GIDO's stationery found in Mustapha Khan's apartment and, now, Saladin's involvement in the killing of Robert Grundell, an employee of OCDL.

And it didn't stop there, as agent Richard Bartley realized how everything was now coming together since he saw the face of Saladin take shape on Earl Franks' computer monitor. Less than twenty-four hours after Robert Grundell's body was found, agent Henry Tucker called him from ballistics. Bullets found in Grundell's body were fired from the same gun that killed Ahmed Khalifa. The gun found practically still smoking in the possession of Mustapha Khan when they arrested the man. The same man Julie Santorelli saw murder Grundell in the presence of Saladin; the same man who broke agent John Jacobs' face on the restaurant washroom wall.

During a phone call by Agent Bartley over the weekend, Jacobs, now feeling well enough and eager to return to duty, got so excited and suggested the two of them pay the man a visit, perhaps take part in the questioning too, among *other* things. Also, he added, he would at least like to recover his wallet and badge if there's any chance at all the devil coughing it up.

The Bureau would have to work hard to find out how Saladin and his operations, led by Abu Kamal Ramshallah apparently as the liaison man, the pitchman, got through to the government employees at Treasury and succeeded in making insider deals with any of them. They're going to have to make someone talk, starting with Mustapha Khan which was the hard part as they had already found out the past couple of days of questioning. Especially now that counsel, a federal public defender, had been appointed for the killer. And it's not going to be any easier with Herod Hardin, Leon Justice and the others now being held without bail, pending a court decision on national security concerns, in the federal detention center in Alexandria.

Like an easy picture puzzle, everything in the entire investigation appeared to have simply fallen into place one piece after another since the day Richard Bartley thought of going back to the Sheraton Premier hotel after learning about Abu Kamal Ramshallah and the MidEast Continental in Detroit. The picture was nearly complete—from Jerome Bolden's initial request for the stakeout at OCDL, the surveillance of Ahmed Khalifa and the link found between Khalifa's boss, Abu Kamal Ramshallah, to John Tyler of the Punchbowl bombing, to the killing of Robert Grundell in the park.

A few pieces were still left out to complete the puzzle, involving mostly the money trail. But the government had been burning the midnight oil on this since Columbia Plaza with a coordinated paper-chase operation on MidEast Continental in Dearborn, Michigan, and its offices in Cairo and Riyadh, by the SEC, Justice and the CIA. The latest was SEC had subpoenaed the company's books, tax records, oil shipping deals and other business ventures and money transfers in the last five years.

Armed IRS audits and Bureau agents from the Detroit Field Office were posted round the clock at the lobby and at every floor the oil shipping and trading company occupied of the office building in Dearborn. A raid had been authorized to haul out the company's computers and other business equipment, but because of the Thanksgiving holiday, it had to be postponed till the start of the weekend.

Due to extenuating circumstances and the risk of flight of subjects under investigation, the U.S. District Court in Detroit issued orders to detain several of the high officials of the company. Among these was Mahmud Mahran, the COO and employer of Abu Kamal Ramshallah who was now in the Bureau's MWL, along with Saladin.

During the initial interrogation, as in earlier ones when Abu Kamal's name first came up from the surveillance of Ahmed Khalifa, Mahran dodged questions concerning Abu Kamal, gave answers that clearly avoided admitting any personal knowledge of the man outside of business. He even hedged when asked for a picture of the man but realized he couldn't go that far without making it look like he was hiding the man. The Bureau could have obtained a search warrant to raid Abu Kamal's office and home immediately after Columbia Plaza but had decided against it and placed them under surveillance for a few days instead. But since the open investigation of MidEast Continental had begun, the DFO had scheduled to do the raids all at the same time. They didn't expect Abu Kamal to come home and report for work in Dearborn at all.

Several government investigators kept the interrogation going, tried to wear him down by making the specter of deportation more real. That or facing federal prosecution on charges of aiding and abetting terrorist activities against the United States, for a start. Then early afternoon Friday following Thanksgiving, stressed out after hours of exhausting debriefing with Justice officials and federal prosecutors, Mahmud Mahran entered into a bargain with the government.

The company's Executive Vice-president and Chief Operating Officer, a long-time green-card holder (twelve years, according to the INS) who never gave up his Egyptian citizenship to become a U.S. citizen, met one of the government's demands for his part of the bargain by turning in first a list of the Muslim charity organizations MidEast Continental supported, and then the names and addresses of the company's foreign offices including their officers and staff. A combined task force from the IRS, FBI and the SEC went to work overtime over the weekend first on the charity list.

It turned out MidEast Continental didn't just make large contributions to a number of those charitable organizations in the list. The company single-handedly financed a couple of them. Used them to transfer large amounts of money to smaller organizations which then distributed funds to individual recipients.

The company also doled out large sums to the other organizations, practically supporting their existence. When the government investigators, working as fast as they could, went digging up every piece of information they could in hardcopy or in computers at the charity offices, they found records of dozens of wire transfers within the United States and many more to foreign individual and business accounts. The amount of transfers ranged in the hundreds to the hundreds of thousands of dollars.

Most of the records with the larger amount of transfer, five to six figures, showed the recipients as John Tyler in Baltimore, New York City and Honolulu, Rahim Akbar in Washington, D.C. and Arlington, Virginia, Abu Kamal Ramshallah himself in Washington, D.C. and Fairfax, Virginia, Hassan Bahaji in Baltimore, Samir Osmani and Mustapha Khan, both in Fairfax, Virginia. The biggest transfers, records of which were uncovered in the computers of the two charities the company financed solely, went to various business accounts owned by the *Global Islamic Defense Organization* in the U.S. and abroad, some by the company's own foreign offices in Europe and the Middle East.

The raid in Dearborn was made early from the start of the weekend. All the computers, entire filing cabinets in management and staff offices at every floor were carted away into a federal warehouse building in Detroit. Much of the same financial data obtained from the charity offices were found in the company's computer files and hardcopy documents. Enough hard evidence—proving not only the company's support of GIDO but its active participation in the militant organization's operations harmful to the United States at home and abroad—were gathered that the U.S. District Court ordered the government to continue to hold the company officials indefinitely.

Having risen to the level of national security from an obscure undercover stakeout on a suspected drug market at a gas station in Arlington, Virginia a few weeks ago, the investigation now commanded one of the highest priorities in the manpower and material resources of the Bureau. This had also brought some notice to the people involved in it, starting with agent Richard Bartley and John Jacobs. Thus, when Bartley asked for round-the-clock protection for Julie Santorelli, all he needed to do was tell his Chief and the case analysts at the debriefing in the office following the visit to the witness and her family in Vienna, Virginia.

He wasn't planning on pushing hard for it, knowing how some people in the office differed in opinion with them out in the field. But when he learned that Ida Santorelli happened to be a survivor of one of the victims of the Punchbowl suicide bombing, he couldn't see the family on the brink of another tragedy which, ironically, could come from the hands of the same perpetrator. He must do what he can to protect them.

Everyone in the investigation, including the local police, agreed about the risk Julie, as well as Chris, faced. Saladin was intent on keeping his identity unknown. He would not tolerate having a witness around and face the risk of being identified, let alone captured. During the debriefing in the office, the question of whether to publish Saladin's picture or not was argued. Putting it out would ease the risk Julie Santorelli faced from Saladin who would then see no point in killing her since the whole world would know what he looked like. On the other hand, it would become even more difficult to catch him. He would be doubly careful about what he did, where he went, how he disguised himself. He could just vanish without a trace from then on but still carry on with his militant operations.

Let him think his identity is safe as it had been for years, it was agreed in the office by everyone, including Richard Bartley, somewhat reluctantly. But, ok, put the witness under twenty-four hours.

So, what it amounted to, if one chose to see it that way, thought Bartley, was the witness was now to be used as a decoy to lure Saladin. When he talked to her to tell her that he had succeeded in requesting the Bureau to put her under twenty-four hour protection, he hoped she and her family wouldn't see it that way.

After much discussion, everyone agreed that Julie would stay and keep her aunt Ida company at her house in Vienna, since the widow now lived alone. They considered the risk of having Julie in her house but the aunt waved that down bravely. It was Julie's parents who expressed great concern and worried deeply. This was where Bartley spoke strongly of the protection the FBI would give Julie, helping calm them down a bit.

CHAPTER 26

▼

It was the earliest the family gathering ever began for the holiday. Not long after the police and one of the FBI men, Earl Franks, had left, Brigit, Ida Santorelli's eldest of two children, had called from her office in nearby Herndon. After talking to her mother, she got on a long conversation with her cousin Julie.

Like the rest in the two families, she continued to feel the pain of the loss of her father. The suddenness of it still fresh in her mind, slow at giving in to time. To help herself cope, she buried herself in work. Twelve, fourteen hours a day in her office. What hurt the most was the pain, and now the loneliness she imagined her mother must be going through. And so she was happy to learn that Julie would be staying with her.

She and her brother Jake who lived in Rosslyn, Virginia and worked in Washington had been talking to her on the phone almost everyday. They took turns visiting since the funeral. Julie and her family too made time to help her along.

It was near quitting time, the regular quitting time which was five o'clock, when she called. She had just come from a successful shop demo of a product her company had been developing for the past two years. It had been a long day and she was beginning to feel it, making her look forward to being home for the holiday right after she got out of work. But the result of the demo re-invigorated her and she didn't feel tired at all.

She could've gone another three or four hours plugging away at work pushing the project into its next phase which would be the market development for the product and the research that would be involved in this. She wouldn't have had any trouble at all gathering the other guys, along with the company's leading high-tech brains, into one of the conference rooms while they were still cheering the first full-function demonstration of the ESCard. The other guys being the two other co-founders of VersaTek, now the president and the CEO, along with herself, the executive vice-president. But she had another part of her life she must attend to. It was the eve of the holiday everyone in the family looked forward to and hearing especially from Julie and learning of what was happening at home, she locked up immediately and simply wished the office a good holiday on her way out.

Everyone was there, the house where she grew up, when she arrived thirty minutes later including her brother Jake who had come home from work to his place in Rosslyn briefly and drove to Vienna immediately. Agents Richard Bartley and Eddie Green were still talking to Julie and Chris and Julie's father who had held up the FBI men getting more assurances regarding her daughter's safety and protection.

Soon the night came and it was decided unanimously that everyone, including Chris, would stay for dinner. The agents couldn't be persuaded to stay, saying it's vital they report back to the office without delay. The two men left, thanking everyone especially Ida Santorelli for her hospitality, particularly after learning about her husband in the Punchbowl bombing. Upon resolving not to divulge the identity of the man in the picture in Earl Franks' computer as that of John Tyler, the known perpetrator of the Punchbowl bombing and in a true sense the killer of Steve Santorelli and hundreds of other victims, Bartley had to pull Eddie Green aside at one point to let him know to keep quiet about it.

He realized later, thankfully, that it was the right thing to do as everyone else in the Bureau agreed during the debriefing which—after the picture of Saladin was officially accepted and approved, turned into hours of ops planning. It was long and intense. Decisions had to be made fast because there were actions needed to be taken without delay. The agents on the case starting with Richard Bartley, Eddie Green, John Jacobs (just back on duty earlier in the day), Nancy Schneider, Frank DiPaolo and Elmer Banks, didn't expect it to be anything less. All the top case analysts were there, Jerome Bolden and his lead analysts, the Bureau Chiefs—Unit, Section and Division level, and some inter-agency guys, one from NSA and a couple of spooks from the CIA's Directorate of Operations.

Procedures for the current investigation were reviewed and quickly revamped. New ones were worked out based on the reports brought in by the field agents from OCDL, the murder site at Fort Ward park, the Detroit Field Office and the interrogators of Mustapha Khan in Alexandria.

Several major decisions of varying significance, depending on who was involved in either of them, came out of the operations planning. Among them:

the raid on the MidEast Continental in Dearborn, Michigan, the new strategy for tracking Saladin and Abu Kamal Ramshallah; the investigation and prosecution of the OCDL employees which included links to GIDO and certainly the murder of Robert Grundell; the twenty-four hour protection for the murder witness.

As soon as it was over, Richard Bartley got on the phone to Vienna immediately and, with a sigh of relief, told Julie Santorelli that she would have the round-the-clock protection starting, as a matter of fact, tonight. He gave her the name of the agents who had been given the assignment and told her to expect them within the next two hours. He also gave her their mobile phone numbers she can call anytime.

Julie tried hard to get Chris to stay after dinner, spend the night with the family. The house was big enough—four bedrooms with a large guest room, a basement rec room that was habitable as a separate dwelling, like an apartment. Days before, they had planned that they would go back to Julie's apartment for the night, go out in the morning the next day for her walk and his run, relax and enjoy the holiday by themselves for a while before going back to Vienna for the Thanksgiving with the family.

All that changed since he made the phone call to the Alexandria police. First, it was his idea before they drove to Vienna that he split immediately and not be seen with her. Someone could have followed him to her apartment, but if it were so, it was too late and wouldn't make any difference if he stayed with her or not.

If, on the other hand, he hadn't led anyone to her so far, she wasn't in jeopardy although it would still be wise not to take a chance on this and 'hide' her somewhere which they decided to be Vienna. Meantime, he remained to be the known link to her, leaving him the one in jeopardy. The killers could decide to come right out to him as the man Sunday night could have done and force him to lead the way to her. Thus it may not be good for him as well to return home in Arlington.

The thing to do then at the time was hide Julie which, hopefully, they did successfully during the trip from her place to her aunt in Vienna. Now, that left him, the police and, later, the Feds, to decide what to do about his situation.

On their way out, agent Richard Bartley laid a hand on Chris' shoulder and said in a low voice they needed to talk. Walking slowly to the car outside, Bartley re-affirmed that they will get protection for Julie.

"But there's a loose end I worry about," he added.

"Which is?" Chris asked.

Bartley and Green exchanged looks quickly, making Chris feel left out of something. He waited for either one to say what.

It was Eddie Green who said, "You."

Chris weighed that a moment and said: "Yes, I kinda knew what you're getting at."

"Which is?" Green threw back at Chris.

"Well, you tell me. It's just a guess."

"Alright," Bartley cut in. "You ever consider them thinking we've figured out who it was that showed up at your doorstep Sunday night? Now they realize you're another person who can identify him so they decide to go all out on you by coming back full force the next time, muscling you to take them to Julie."

"You think they'll do that?" Chris asked.

"I'm saying that's what could happen, regardless of whether or not they think we know who they are," replied Bartley.

"They know where to find you at home and at work," Green said. "Unless you decide to hide too."

Chris mulled over that a moment. He jammed both hands deep in his coat pockets out of the cold weather and glanced behind him at the house where Julie and her entire living immediate family, except her brother Charles who was due to come the following morning from New York, were gathered together.

"Damn," he muttered between the two men in front of him. "I'd hate to do that too."

With Chris Phillips, Richard Bartley didn't feel he had to hold out on the dual identity of the man they were trying to protect them from and capture. He saw no reason why he can't ask Chris to be discreet about it to the Santorellis and let him in on it, for a reason he now decided to bring out to him.

"I have a suggestion I would like you to consider," he started out. "But first, I'd like to tell you something."

"Go ahead." Chris couldn't help the eager look on his face.

"The man you and Julie have just identified is the same man we have been after for years. The same man who has been responsible for a number of terrorist attacks in the U.S. and abroad the past several years, including the recent Punchbowl suicide bombing in Hawaii. And we suspect, Pentagon II."

Eddie Green added that the other picture and the one they identified were of one and the same man. "We can not," he said emphatically, "impress upon you enough how important this discovery is to us. To the Bureau and the entire U.S. government. This is a matter of grave national security concern."

"Good God," Chris gasped, dumbfounded. "Who is he? What's his name?"

"We don't know," said Bartley. "We've been trying to find out for years. He disguises himself, as you saw in the picture, and uses many different aliases."

"John Tyler?" Chris said, recalling the name he'd seen and heard dozens of times from the newspapers and TV newscasts.

"Yes. We know of other names he had used in the past. And we didn't even know what he looked like. But now, thanks to you and Julie, now at least we do."

Chris once again turned behind him to look at the house as if expecting to find the whole family bunched up outside listening to their conversation and learning that the same people that took away Steven Santorelli from them was once again threatening to do them harm.

"We thought it wise to keep it to ourselves while we're in there," Richard Bartley said. "We hope you do too."

When Chris turned back to the men, he was a mixture of sadness and rage, his eyes moist. "Goddammit! How could this happen?" he growled in a restrained voice. "What can we do? Tell me how I can help. And dammit, I'm not going to hide."

Bartley and Green had been hoping one way or another they would come to this, Chris opening up as he just did.

"Well, as I said, I have a suggestion," Bartley began. "You could help us, by working with us."

It was a daunting thought when it first dawned on him and he realized what the Feds had in mind. But now, aware of how far-reaching the investigation was beyond the killing of a federal employee, the threat to Julie's life, not to mention his, loomed larger than they thought before. He couldn't think of himself turning his back on an opportunity to protect her by helping the authorities capture John Tyler or whoever else might want to hurt her.

"I realize we have no right to ask you—" Bartley began to say but Chris interrupted.

"What do you want me to do?" he asked.

"For now, here's what we'll do, Chris. We need to get back to the office and report all these to our superiors and the analysts so we all can plan our next move. Some of the things we figured we needed to do on our way here we already did. As I said earlier, all the local police throughout the Capital area now have this case on their hot list. Especially Arlington and Alexandria. We've already talked to the Arlington dicks, I mean—detectives—who were involved earlier in the search for the body, since the victim was an Arlington resident. They know about you, where you live in the Fairlington community, about your Sunday night visitor. They know everything, what happened with you and Julie, except what we learned here tonight. I told them we, federal agents, possibly with you, will be talking to them before late tonight. Here's what they're waiting for us to confirm with them we will do, with their help, and with your participation, if you agree."

"I do," Chris said peremptorily. "I want to know what the plan is right now."

The three men spent another five minutes out in the cold of the autumn night at the curb in front of the house. In that time, the two FBI agents alternated telling Chris the operation they had worked out with the local police in Arlington county and Fairfax City, with the participation of the city of Alexandria and Fairfax county police departments as necessary. They will talk to the Arlington detectives, name of Joe Riley and Zak Porter, on their way to the office and they will have them call Chris on his cell phone.

They gave him their cards, telling him call any of them anytime he needed to and then left. In the short walk back to the house, Chris had a totally different idea of the situation he and Julie were in than before he went out. What he just learned from the Feds and what he had agreed to do with them and the police now put him in a different state of mind. The biggest thing that concerned him now was how much he could rely on the police, and the Feds. Perhaps it's a good thing they asked him to be a part of the plan. He wasn't worried about the risk. He was at risk as it was so why not do something about it to help protect Julie and himself. But he mustn't rely solely on them for his part. He must think of protecting himself, and Julie, on his own. At least be prepared to, should a time come when he needed to. This brought him to thinking about his big brother James in Falls Church. But he was already back in the living room amidst everyone and had to tune back in to what's going on with the family.

Julie's aunt and mother, working together with great enthusiasm in the kitchen, produced a spaghetti-meat-sauce dinner that the family helped itself to as though everyone couldn't get enough of it. During dinner, they appeared to have put aside what had brought them together so soon before the holiday. There were moments when someone would stop eating and pause for a few moments to reflect. When Ida Santorelli did this obviously for missing her husband, Julie, sitting at her right, laid a hand on her forearm and complimented her for the pasta dinner or simply let her hand rest lightly on her shoulder.

Later, during coffee and dessert, an entirely unfamiliar hush suddenly fell in the dining room, in the entire house as a matter of fact, when knocks were heard on the front door. It was Chris who stirred first from his seat, getting up quietly to head to the door. Julie's father, Joe Santorelli, followed together with her cousin Jake. Then Julie suddenly remembered something and, in a low voice, told the men to hold for a few moments.

She picked up the phone in the living room and called one of the mobile phone numbers Richard Bartley had given her. While she waited to be connected, the knocks on the door came again. A few seconds later, the phone at the other end rang three times before it was answered.

"Agent Doug Jones, speaking," said a man's voice.

When Julie identified herself, the FBI agent, standing at the front door of the house holding the phone to his ear, told her it was them right outside—he and another agent, Hector Gomez, who would be doing the duty rotation with him and had come along for the introduction.

It was half past eight when Chris got on the road to Falls Church. Julie had walked him out to the curb in front of the house and tried to the last moment to get him to stay. He assured her he'll be alright and that the Arlington police would be looking after him from now on, that they're just one quick call away. So were the Feds. He told her that much, but not his agreement with them in which, in plain language, he would be used as a decoy to lure the killers. A bait. And, as he promised the Feds, he did not tell her who it really was they were trying to catch other than the man who was after her.

As soon as he got in the car a block away, he talked to his brother on the phone to tell him he was coming over. Within a half hour, without asking if it was alright. That's the way it was, had always been with him and Jim.

Big brother Jim had always been there for him since they were kids as young as ten and five respectively. Jim Phillips practically shared the male parenting of his little brother with his father into Chris' late teens. He loved his kid brother, looked after him, helped him out of trouble at school and in the neighborhood when they were growing up. And even now, Chris could call for anything—time, money (within a reasonable amount), advice, or even just a sympathetic ear.

His relationship with their Dad, Sam Phillips, however, took a different turn, starting with Sam's falling out with their mother while Jim was in the middle of college. It got worse during the separation which Jim blamed on Sam for being unfaithful to his wife, fooling around too much.

When the family finally broke up, it hit Jim so hard that he didn't speak to his father for a whole year. What saved Sam from total alienation from his children was the one naturally decent thing about him, Jim believed, which was his sense of responsibility for his children, feeling obligated to help them any way he could, including paying for their education all the way through college. If only he had been as generous to their mother with his attention—instead of to other women—as he had been with his resources to his children, Jim and Chris often thought even to this day.

But, perhaps it's best to leave well enough alone as it was meant to be. Everyone was now going on with life fairly happily, including their mother in her second marriage in Pittsburgh. And Sam? The man's happy with his ways, so let him be as he wanted to be.

"What's going on?" Jim Phillips now asked his younger brother on the phone, in the study room of the single-family house in East Falls Church he shared with his wife Linda and their two children, an eight-year old girl and a five-year old boy. "You sound like you can't go, kid. Ate something bad?"

"I need to ask you for something," Chris said, starting the car. "If you don't have it, you might...you'd have to get it for me."

"Sounds pretty serious. What is it?"

"I'll tell you when I get there. I'll tell you everything, but I can't right now. I need to get off this phone. I got a very important call coming anytime now."

"Alright," Jim said, wondering what this was all about. "Can't wait to hear it."

As soon as he hung up, Chris drove out of Vienna and got back on I-66 East, feeling a bit anxious about what he wanted to see his brother for. The last time he had held a handgun, he was thinking, was some months ago when he was visiting and a couple of guys, fellow members of Jim's in the Capital Region Practical Shooting Association, were in the house. It was one of them, a close friend of Jim's since high school, who got Jim into guns years before.

They were all in Jim's study room and talking about guns, range shooting and competition events. They were passing a couple of models around. A revolver and a pistol Jim's friend owned. Chris had come to visit and spend some time with his niece and nephew which he did as often as he could but ended up joining the guys as well for a little while.

When it was his turn to hold the weapons, he simply turned them sideways in his hands without slipping a finger around the trigger. He made no attempt to fool with a single moving part. That was the extent of his coming into possession of a gun recently. He had an even more distant memory of when he fired one. As far as he can remember, it had been years, six or seven, when he went with Jim to a pistol shooting range in West Virginia. There, he fired a whole magazine with a seven-round pistol, hit one bullseye, missed the target completely a couple of times. Jim thought he did pretty well. He thought so too, for a novice. But that's as far as he would go messing with guns, he told his brother.

He was now on Washington Boulevard after having exited I-66, in East Falls Church a few blocks from the house. He wondered what his brother would think about the whole thing, what he would do, or advise him to do. As he pulled up the driveway, he had a last-minute thought about telling him everything. Maybe he should just give him some other reason why he needed—would like—to carry a gun. The last thing he would want was to see Jim getting involved, risking his own life and perhaps his family too, all because of him.

It was near nine o'clock when Jim let him in. They went straight to the kitchen where Linda was working, preparing stuff for the holiday dinner next day. Jim went to the refrigerator to take out two cans of beer and went out to the study room while Chris took a moment to give Linda a hug. She had just tucked the kids in bed and everything was quiet.

"You can go in, say good night if you like," she told Chris when he asked about the kids. "They just got in bed."

"It's alright." he said. "I'll just peek in before I leave after they're asleep. I'll probably stop by tomorrow anyway and see them."

"Stop by?" she asked, frowning. "Aren't you coming for dinner?"

He explained that he had promised Julie first, weeks ago. She grumbled at him some before letting him off with his brother.

Chris sat in the armchair next to a glass-covered bookcase on top of a four-foot high cabinet with locked doors. Jim took the swivel chair in front of the computer workstation at the opposite side of the room. It took Chris but a couple of sips of the beer before he came right out and told Jim he needed a handgun.

Why? No, he's not mad at somebody and planning to kill the person. It's just for protection.

"You never had to have it before," Jim said. "Why now? Somebody threatening you?"

"No. Not exactly," Chris replied, continuing to make up his mind how much to divulge to his brother.

"Who? Is it Dad in trouble again messing with another man's lady?"

That drew a laugh from both of them.

"No, it…it's just me," Chris said, and after hesitating a moment, added: "And Julie."

That caused his brother to perk up a bit.

"What about you and Julie?" Jim asked and waited for Chris to tell him more. When Chris appeared to take his time, he said: "You want me to give you a gun to carry, I'd need to know what for, how many bad guys you plan to knock out, maybe you need more than one gun so then I would know how much ammunition you need to have too—"

"Alright, alright, here's the story," Chris interrupted and, at this point, decided to tell his brother everything. Five minutes later, Jim was pacing the floor repeating to himself some of the words he heard from his brother as if he didn't hear them enough.

Murder witness. Body found in the park. FBI. Police detectives.

Terrorists. Islamic militants. The Punchbowl suicide bombing! Pentagon II!

"This is hard to believe," he was finally able to say to Chris.

"Well, you better believe it. It's as real as me sitting in this chair right now."

"The guy actually came to your door at night looking for Julie?"

"Yes. The same guy she saw at the murder scene at the park. The same guy who turned out to be the mastermind of the Punchbowl suicide bombing."

"Shit," Jim muttered to himself, now looking deeply concerned. He stepped over to the cabinet under the bookshelves next to Chris, saying: "You should've called me sooner."

"We didn't find out until today," Chris said, watching Jim select a key from several in a keychain and use it to unlock the cabinet.

Jim swung both doors of the cabinet open, reached over the top shelf inside and took out two leather cases which he carried to a study table at the far end of the room. Meantime, Chris' cell phone rang.

He answered the call, asked who was calling and listened. Jim sat at the study table looking at Chris, listening intently.

"Yes, he told me about you guys," Chris said on the phone after a few seconds then listened again.

Jim watched him get up from the armchair, nod as he continued to listen, take a couple of steps forward and back and then look at his watch.

"That's fine with me. I'll see you then," Chris said last before hanging up. He then pulled a chair and joined Jim at the study table.

"That was the Arlington detective I'd be working with," Chris told his brother. "One of them. I'll meet them at my place at ten. Tonight."

"Shit," Jim said again. "You're really way deep into this, aren't you?"

Chris didn't say a word this time and only gave his brother a long knowing look. Jim then turned their attention to the two leather cases between them on the table. He turned the small table lamp on then picked a key from the keychain to unlock the top cover of the leather cases.

Inside one case was a copy of Smith and Wesson pistol model SW40E. The other contained another S and W pistol, model SW99. The two were nearly identical models where it mattered. Both were .40 caliber pistols, fired 10 rounds, black finish, seven-and-a-quarter inch overall length.

"The best I got," Jim said "Pick one. Or take them both."

"I just want one."

"I want you to take them both," Jim said firmly. "Carry one with you, leave the other at home. In the bedroom under the mattress."

"Don't you need them?"

"I have others. Hold on," Jim said as he got up to go back to the cabinet. He came back with boxes of ammunition for the pistols. "Take these with you," he said. Then he took one of the guns out of the case, had Chris take the other and started going over its operation.

"I'm going to a practice shooting in Woodbridge with the guys, one o'clock Saturday afternoon," Jim said after he finished with the demo which Chris followed step by step. "I want you to come. Be here at noon."

"That's great," Chris said, trying every moving part of the SW99. "Yes. I'd like to go. I'll be here."

Jim had Chris practice filling up the magazine of each gun with the rounds from the boxes and load them. He carried the SW99 in his coat pocket while Jim put the other with the cases and boxes of ammunition in a gym bag. On his way out, he went in the children's bedroom to take a look at his sleeping niece and nephew, kissed each of them then went back in the kitchen to say good night to Linda.

At the door, Jim held him for a moment. "Listen, kid," he said, looking serious. "I want to know what's going on from now on. You call me, alright?"

"Sure, Jim. I will."

"In fact," Jim paused to look over his shoulder briefly at his wife in the kitchen. "Why don't I go with you now. I want to know what those cops are doing."

"I'll be fine, Jim," Chris assured his brother. "I'll call you later tonight, let you know what took place."

"I don't mind. Kids are in bed. And we'll be up late anyway."

"Jim, listen. I know all this looks creepy, and it is. And that's the more reason I don't want you getting involved. You got a family. I can't see me bringing any danger to your home, your wife and the kids. I can't, won't let that happen."

"It won't come to that. It'll be just you and me."

"I'll call as soon as we're done tonight. I'll let you know everything. I will, okay, Jim? And don't worry," Chris paused and laid a hand over where the SW99 was inside his coat. "I got this now. I know how to use it. I just need some practice."

Jim thought a moment then raised his head and patted Chris on the shoulder.

"Alright. But you take care," he said. "And be sure to call tonight."
"I will."

CHAPTER 27

▼

It was difficult concentrating on his fourth *salat* even as he watched the remaining light of day fade into a quiet night. Bowing on his knees, facing east in the tenth-floor hotel room that overlooked the Potomac river, he tried to shut the world out of his mind and focus on his thoughts of the lord prophet Muhammad, messenger of the almighty God, Allah.

But there were nagging concerns that would not leave him in peace even for a moment. He was almost resigned to the possibility that Mustapha Khan had fallen into the hands of the enemy as he had not returned since his last mission nearly a week ago.

And then only yesterday, Khalil Majid, a ranking financial officer of the company in Dearborn, Michigan, had called, in spite of the strict rule against it, to tell him about the government raid of the company headquarters and the arrest of the officers, practically shutting down operations. He himself, Khalil, narrowly avoided being hauled into federal detention with the Organization's lead man in the company, Mahmud Mahran, and the rest of the brothers at headquarters. He had just come back from a short trip to Canada and was on his way to work. Lucky he called first and learned what was going on.

Next, there was this woman, Julie. It was the thought of her that nagged at him more than all the other concerns, even more than the remaining work on the planning of Operation Capitol West. It had been five days now since he located her, five days when the thought of her had not once failed to come forward in his mind. What a curse this was, at a time like this? He had meant to deal with her sooner but more pressing matters had taken up his time these past few days. But he would, and when he did, he would be quick and decisive.

It could very well be that time was running out for him and many of the brothers here in America. He could feel the enemy—the government and its hordes of intelligence and armed forces—reaching out to snare him and the others. First Abu Kamal Ramshallah, then Mustapha Khan, and now the brothers in Dearborn, Michigan.

He didn't need such a minor incident as that involving a witness to identify him and further hasten the time when he must leave the country to escape the enemy. That must not happen before he had completed this one other act of war against satan. He had a duty to fulfill in sustaining the global Holy War against this Western culture, this decadent Zionist power that had taken so much dignity away from his culture, his people.

He closed his eyes and bowed lower until his forehead touched the floor, humbling himself in an act of submission to Him. Then he finally succeeded in cleansing his mind of all worldly thoughts, his heart of all emotions. And then he prayed in the silence of the early evening, sending words of supplication to Allah to humble the enemies of Islam and raise His children—the listeners to His words through the Messenger, the prophet Mohammed—above them; to give them, His faithful and dedicated children, the will, the courage, and the strength to defend the Faith and destroy those who would dishonor it.

In the month of Ramadan which had ended only two days ago, he said the same prayers five times a day while fasting. And the times he had the rare chance to visit a *masjid* (mosque), once in Zamboanga City during the trip to the Philippines, another time in Falls Church, Virginia two weeks ago, he repeated the same prayers more arduously during the hours he worshipped, pleading at the same time for the repose and eternal life of his departed parents, killed by the enemies of Islam, the Jews; for the souls of his ancestors in Lebanon, Syria and Palestine, long departed through the cruel hands of the Christians over the centuries.

He prayed for the divine power of the Almighty to prevail upon the enemies by filling their hearts and minds with kindness. And he prayed that the enemies, together with all the brothers throughout the world, would humble themselves to each other, and to God.

He spent hours in prayer with these thoughts during the month of Ramadan, even at moments when he suffered the anguish of knowing that there was little hope in his generation, and God knows through how many others, for a reconciliation with the enemy; that humility and kindness, tolerance and acceptance of each other's existence were but illusions, noble hopes that did not stand a chance against the overwhelming reality of hatred and fear in everyone's heart.

And even as he had been a part of it for most of his life, he refused to accept the idea that the destruction of one by the other was the only way to peace. And so, while he planned the next strike against the enemy as was the bidding of the Organization and its leaders in the homelands, he prayed daily that the reign of bloodshed and terror would soon end, that he will no longer seek to destroy the enemy in order to live his way of life freely, without fear, without hatred, without violence.

Night had fallen when he concluded his prayers and raised himself on his knees. The first thing that came to mind as soon as he opened his eyes was *Id-al-Fitr*, the three-day celebration of the breaking of the fast now on its second day in the month of Shawwal, the tenth lunar month of the Muslim world, following Ramadan, the ninth.

He and Abu Kamal had summoned many of the brothers in the Capital area, including some from Baltimore and Philadelphia, to the hotel for the traditional feast which was to begin in less than an hour. Arrangements had been made in advance to prepare for the celebration down in a second-floor banquet room.

But before that, he awaited the arrival of Khalil Majid from a perilous journey from Detroit. Much depended on the news he bore for him and the other leaders. Now that they can no longer expect the support of the company in Dearborn, they were on their own and must be quick to regroup and protect the resources they had left to carry out their operation. Also, they must inform the leaders of the Organization here in America—in New York and Los Angeles—and in the Middle East.

Ten minutes later, he had just poured himself a shot of straight vodka on ice and taken a quick sip when the knock came on the door. He saw two men through the peephole. A lean man in a heavy winter coat wearing glasses and carrying a small luggage. Behind him stood the other man who was at least two hundred pounds and six feet three inches tall. His whole head stuck up above that of the man in front of him. Omar Husain recognized Khalil Majid immediately, the one in front. They had known each other years before back in the homelands, Syria and Lebanon, and traveled together to different parts of the world on various missions.

"*Salaam aleikum*," Omar Husain greeted as he led them into the room, shaking hands with each one.

They returned his greeting. Khalil introduced the other man. "Commander, this is brother Masoud Faisal," he said, "head of security in the company. The two of us were in the government list of the company people they came to round up."

"How did you find out?" asked Omar Husain.

"One of my staff found out about it and told me when I called," replied Khalil, feeling relieved at being where he was now. "Then I called Masoud and we got together immediately to plan our escape. We traveled together from Detroit after we secured some—" He glanced at the luggage he had placed next to a table by the window. "—assets we keep in several places there. We owe this man a great deal for a safe trip to here."

Masoud Faisal bowed his head dutifully. "Not at all, gentlemen," he said. "Anything for the cause."

"You did very well, brother," said Omar Husain. "I'm glad you've arrived safely. I'm happy to meet you."

"Thank you, Commander. It's a great honor to meet you, sir," replied Masoud Faisal. And it was as he said, to finally come face to face and shake hands with the greatly respected teacher and leader of his people. Before now, he had only heard of the man through word of mouth, learned about his teaching and work through those who had trained under him in the homelands years before, and even here in America.

"I hope you not only had a safe but comfortable journey as well," Omar Husain said, once he had them seated, and offered them drinks. Khalil asked for soda while Masoud opted for the same as Omar was drinking—vodka with ice.

The men had checked in a hotel nearby in downtown Old Town, Alexandria, Khalil said. Everyone agreed that it was good for them to spread out. But Omar Husain, as the other leaders had expressed, was concerned about staying in hotels any longer. In light of the heightened national alert and the increasingly aggressive government investigations against them, it wouldn't be much of an effort for the Feds to sweep all the hotels clean of any suspicious activities and people. As a matter of fact, that's how Abu Kamal Ramshallah was identified and subsequently linked to Omar Husain and the Organization. And that's what led to the raid of the company in Dearborn, and what brought the two men here now.

"What are we to do then, Commander?" asked Masoud Faisal, looking alarmed.

"We've made arrangements with several brothers who live in private residences," replied Omar. "Single-family homes, townhouses and condominiums, here in Virginia and the Maryland suburbs. After tomorrow, the end of the *Id*, we all check out of hotels and move to the residences. Everyone has been assigned a place to go to. You will be staying with a brother, a student at the George Washington University in the District, who lives in a house in Springfield, Virginia, not far from here."

They talked socially for a few minutes with Omar Husain speaking about the feast they would be having downstairs in a little while. Then Khalil proceeded to report, in more detail, what happened in Dearborn, Michigan, over the weekend.

"It happened very quickly," Khalil said at the end. "The Feds had all the papers, evidence needed to obtain a subpoena and go after MidEast Continental. Of course the company lawyers are going to fight all the charges, declare what was done to the company officials, including the raid itself, illegal. One of the lawyers I know personally told me when I called him before we left. But now that the government had the company papers, and not only that—they also raided the charity organizations and got their records as well, the Feds have made their case even stronger. Altogether, it doesn't look good at all, Commander."

Omar Husain fell silent for a few moments while he, once more, weighed the major consequences of the loss of MidEast Continental upon their operations here in the mid-Atlantic area of the country, not to mention the other operations the company supported in other parts of America, and the Far East, Africa and Europe.

He must move quickly from here on. Finish the plans for Operation Capitol West and everything else he had left to do in America. But it was vital that they get in touch with the leadership of the Organization in Cairo and Riyadh right away. Perhaps they would have a change of order for him and the rest of the brothers here in America with this recent turn of events in Michigan.

Indeed, time was running shorter than he had thought before the men arrived. And not only that. Now that the money supply was cut off, they must do with what they had left, make some adjustments to conserve their resources. He had started to feel the pressure back of his mind when Khalil Majid, Allah be praised for this man, picked up the luggage by the table and brought it in front of him.

"Commander Omar," he said, "I had the presence of mind to think about what you just said. So I took a little time to stop by our bank in downtown Detroit before we left."

He laid the luggage on its side. It was about half the size of a regular long-distance travel suitcase. Whatever was in it looked like it fit just right. It was full but not bulging. Khalil unlocked the small padlock, unzipped the top and flung it open.

Stacks of hundred-dollar-bills seven inches high lined half of the inside from end to end; the other half with five-hundred-dollar bills arranged in the same manner. With a mixture of disbelief and joy, Omar Husain stared at the pile of cash on the floor, all of the five million dollars Khalil Majid had simply hand-carried all the way from the Detroit headquarters of the First Gulf Bank of Michigan, a financial institution operating mostly with MidEast Continental, Ltd. deposits and other Persian Gulf states investors.

Words would not suffice to express his gratitude to the man so he stepped around the luggage and clamped his hands on Khalil's shoulders.

"May Allah be generous with your reward for this noble act, brother Khalil," he said in a solemn voice. "I thank you, and so do all our people, here in America, in the homelands and all over the world." He turned to Masoud Faisal towering above the other man next to him and shook his hand, saying: "And you too, brother Masoud. You have indeed done a great deed for our people, our families, our children, our homelands."

CHAPTER 28

▼

Brigit Santorelli got to her office a little later than usual this Saturday. Weekend work at least twice a month had been pretty common the past year and a half now, since VersaTek came out of the red.

With the thirty-million-dollar contract to build an application software system for a U.S. Air Force satellite network and a twenty-million-dollar one to design and develop a land-and-space-based intelligence signal system called CTS (Communication Tracking and Surveillance Security System) for Defense and the National Recon Office, the small but now flourishing company of thirty-five hard-working hi-tech people buzzed with activity seven days a week. Two and a half years ago, the company lost bids for several plum contracts to the big players around the Beltway in Maryland and Virginia. Lockheed, TRW, EDS. A dozen employees had to be let go, the rest settled for a pay-cut or reduced work hours. Four-day, three-day week.

The company couldn't stay afloat and declared bankruptcy for the second time in five years. It reorganized and started over again with ten people. Brigit, together with the other two co-founders of the company met with several old college classmates at a gathering—real hi-tech brains but unhappy with where they were—and pulled them in with no promises other than stock options and freedom of creativity. At that time, the company was once again playing with fire as if it hadn't been burned enough to learn its lesson competing with the big contractors.

This time, with the brains—some of whom came from the big players—now working with the company, it won the Air Force contract. A few months later, the company was awarded the Defense/NRO contract too. One year after it filed for Chapter 11 protection, the company was back on its feet, recruiting aggressively for the right people to fill in top-paying positions.

The company started out as one of dozens of startup dot-coms in the Capital region eight years ago, right about the time when investor confidence on dot-coms had started taking a dive. But it had raised enough capital to stay in business pursuing a market with its line of software products, some already completed, others still under development. It did well for a couple of years, compared to some other startups around who never turned a profit from beginning to end, before it ran into trouble with market competition, losing bids on large contracts it poured money into.

VersaTek actually made money for its investors and paid its workers well for a time, venturing into some highly speculative new product developments. One of them was the ESCard—a smart card that was supposed to become the smartest of them all. Its development was off and on since it actually started a few years before it finally picked up full speed two years ago.

An electronic data processing device based on nano technology, the ESCard was designed to function as a mini-palmtop computer. It looked like a credit card, a building pass card or it could be made to look like any card. It bent in half, and when it did, the top-half became a monitor screen, the bottom-half the keyboard.

It came with accessories, all loaded with what the company geeks declared as revolutionary microchips with new logic gates and circuit arrangements designed to conserve space. One of them was a data-entry electronic ring worn around the tip of the index finger and used to operate the tiny keyboard. Another was the card-owner's personal data strip (D-strip). It was a removable mini data-storage device, worked much like a removable flash drive. This came in multiples, depending on how much data storage the card-owner needed. It slid into a six-teenth-inch-wide strip notch across the keyboard-half of the card near the bottom edge. On the backside of the card behind the top-half was another strip notch where a processor strip (P-strip) could be inserted. At this time, VersaTek had a whole catalog of P-strips loaded with state-of-the-art application software. Banking, accounting, engineering math modules, socio-economic statistics. In addition to these, the card could be issued through a bank or other financial institutions as a credit, debit or ATM card.

A couple of other features of the product was what caused Brigit to be an hour later than usual getting to work, this time coming from her mother's house in Vienna where she had spent the past two nights. She had been thrilled to have Julie staying with her mother in the house. It was like going back to their childhood. They spent hours talking, doing things together, staying up late into the night.

They couldn't get enough of the old days back even when Julie babysat Brigit. So, this Saturday morning, talking to her cousin over breakfast about this revolutionary product she said her company had been developing for several years now and would soon start marketing, Brigit completely forgot about the time.

"We're all so excited about the project," she told Julie in the same breakfast nook at one end of the kitchen where they had spent many mornings years ago.

"So am I, from the way you describe what this card could do," said Julie. "Can it cook an egg?"

They laughed, trying hard to keep it low and not wake up Brigit's mother who was a late riser.

"No, but here's what else we're going to make it do," Brigit continued, sounding like a little girl getting ready to show a dear friend a birthday present. "ESCard V2, that's Version 2, will be able to access the internet, send and receive emails. And, get this—it will be a cell phone and a beeper at the same time."

"Oh, my God, Brigit!" Julie almost screamed at the top of her lungs. "How could all that be possible with such a small thing the size of a credit card?"

Nothing thrilled Brigit more than seeing big cousin Julie get excited, laugh and marvel over something she had said or done.

"Cousin Julie," she now said to her. "Size does not matter. It shouldn't. It never did and never does. Our outlook hinges on one thing—access. If you can get to it, no matter how small or how far it is, it's yours to do as you please. All you need is some creativity."

Julie couldn't admire her more. She knew all along that that little girl she babysat for a few years during her teen years had a good head on her shoulders. She had always seen it in Brigit—a mind of her own, curious, always probing, inquiring. She worked hard to find the answer to her questions. She didn't give up easily. And Julie loved her so much, just like the sister she never had and, in many ways, even more than her brother Charles.

It made her very happy to see Brigit so enthusiastic with what she did both in success and in failure. Therefore, it also made her feel sad when things went wrong with her life, her family. Now that she was with them, these past few days at least, there wasn't a moment of joy she felt as she did this morning, and especially during the past Thanksgiving family gathering, without the recent family tragedy clouding her thoughts. It seemed, with the loss of Steve Santorelli, the family, not just Brigit's but hers as well, was drastically altered. How telling it is to see something whole that works so well come apart when even a single part is taken away.

But life must go on. Everyone must accept change, or learn to, and move on. This brought her to the matter of what's ahead with the family, especially thinking about Brigit's personal life. She's still a young thirty, which didn't appear to concern Brigit whose sole preoccupation at this time was work, seeing her company make it big time.

She knew of several men Brigit had gone out with. But there wasn't one Brigit saw long enough for her to admit she *dated* him. This had concerned Julie occasionally about her cousin. But it didn't worry her. Brigit was enjoying the challenge of her work career right now. She had precious time left, not a whole lot, but Julie would rather see her spend that time doing something that made her happy than caught in a bad relationship, or even marriage, like what happened to her.

When Brigit finally glanced at the time on the clock up on the kitchen wall, she took a small packet case out of her purse, opened it and showed Julie the proto-type copy of the ESCard V2.

"We're actually ahead of our development schedule," she said cheerfully. "This is a model with all the features of V1 in it working, plus a couple still at testing stage for V2." She went ahead and started demonstrating the operation of the smart card.

She took out a P-strip from its niche in the packet case and inserted it in the strip notch in the back of the top-half. Once it was perfectly fitted in the notch, she bent the card in half. There was a click when the two halves were at 45-degree angle with each other, the operating system cold-booted and things began to happen. First, the background of the front of the top-half appeared to gradually change in shade. Then a swirl of colors began to emerge from the center until a menu appeared with a prompt for the userid and the password. The top-half of the card was now a monitor screen while, at the same time, the face of the bottom-half had displayed six rows of tiny keys clearly marked in the center by the character each one represented. It was now a keyboard.

"Incredible!" Julie marveled, wide-eyed. "It's a little laptop computer."

"No, dear cousin. It's a mini palmtop," corrected Brigit.

She wanted so much to give Julie a demonstration of some of the features of the machine especially its communicating capability which she said was still at experimental stage, but she didn't have time. Instead, she left her a copy of the manual with the packet case containing a set of P-strips and a couple of D-strips. She said she could actually make herself useful to VersaTek by testing the card.

Play with it using the P-strips in the packet, she told Julie and asked her to call her later at the office and tell her how hard or how easy it was to use. Let Julie be the first customer to give VersaTek some feedback. Then she took a last sip of her coffee and headed out to work in her executive office in Herndon. Julie walked her out to her car in front of the house, telling her she'll work on the manual as fast as she could and give her a call.

After she watched her cousin drive off, Julie's eyes fell on a gray four-door sedan parked across the street two houses away. In the driver's seat was FBI undercover agent Hector Gomez refilling a coffee mug from a steaming thermos bottle. This was Hector's second solo day on the job, having started three days ago with agent Doug Jones when they doubled up the first day just so they get organized, get oriented together on the routines. He took the first watch the next day.

Later in the evening that day, Julie had called to ask him into the house for refreshments. He told her procedure did not include open contact with the subject, for good reason. It's one thing to keep the agents undercover, unknown to the danger they're protecting her from. It's another to make the presence of the agents or their identities known which could either scare off the danger or put the agents themselves in jeopardy as well.

She ended up having a lengthier conversation with him on the phone. She learned some more things about the job he did for the FBI. She told him about the job she did, the places she went to at work—St. James College in Falls Church where she taught, and in her daily routine from sun-up to sundown which, he said, should help them give her better protection.

She also learned that the government had put her now vacant apartment under surveillance with 24-hour video cameras covering the building entrance, her apartment door and the parking lot in front. A man came to collect the tapes every night and replaced them with new ones.

Julie told the undercover agent how impressed she was at the attention the government had given her, the promptness of their action, making her feel like someone really important. Hector's response was brief and simple, making sure he didn't tell her any more than he should.

We do our best, ma'am.

It's all part of the job.

We get paid for it. They both laughed at this one.

But Julie couldn't help becoming curious about it. About the murder victim at the park which was how all these got started. She wondered who he was, what exactly he did for the government. Who were the people who wanted him dead and why?

A couple of times in the presence of the law enforcement people and especially after they left, she had a strong sense that something else, not just the killing of one man, was behind all the vigorous effort the federal people were putting into the investigation. Not that she and especially her family would have anything less than what she was getting in terms of her security. Could it be that the man was doing something crucial for the U.S. government but terribly bad for another government and that that, perhaps, was why the latter got rid of him? Or could it be something personal? It can't be. Otherwise the federal government wouldn't take such close interest in it.

The only thing she'd heard from both the FBI and the police, was that the victim worked with classified data in the federal government. When she thought about it more, it just seemed too obvious to her, as her father had expressed earlier, that they weren't being too open with what they were saying.

Julie spent the rest of the morning putting things in order in her bedroom which she hadn't been able to do since arriving a few days ago because of the holiday. Then she worked on the ESCard manual and test-used the smart card. All the features worked as Brigit had described. The damn little thing worked almost like its full-size laptop predecessor, or even its ancestor, the desktop PC. Except you had to use an electronic ring you wore around your index finger to use the keyboard. But it worked almost as fast as fingers on a full-size keyboard because it only had to pass over the keys without touching the surface of the card to make an entry.

She tested the communication feature last by installing the P-strip for the phone dialer and made the call to Brigit. To her complete astonishment, it did everything a cell phone did and she talked to Brigit for a few minutes. The super-mini speaker embedded in the card didn't deliver full volume sound but it was clear and intelligible. Incredible, Julie thought after they hung up. What's next? And where's all these taking us?

Then the house phone rang. It was Chris.

He asked how things were going. Her FBI protection, living in the house in Vienna, her aunt, how she thought her commute to work in Falls Church would be like. She said it's actually better since Vienna is almost half closer to Falls Church than Fairfax City. She added that she felt safe and not afraid.

She asked what the police were doing to protect him. They kept him company once in a while when he's home, he said. They too had installed video cameras to cover his front door, the walkway from the parking lot and the parking lot. He told her not to worry about him.

"I'll probably be over later in the afternoon. Closer to four," he said. Part of the plan this weekend was for him to come over for dinner. "I'm going to visit my brother, see the kids. They haven't seen uncle Chris in a while."

"That's nice of you," she said. "Keep in touch with the relations. Never know when they might come in handy." She had no real idea how right she was, notwithstanding her current situation.

Chris didn't tell her the other reason he was going to his brother, the pistols Jim lent him, the practice shooting in Woodbridge at one o'clock Saturday.

PART IV

▼

CAPITOL WEST AND BIG THUNDER

CHAPTER 29

▼

When Richard Bartley picked up John Jacobs from his house in Fairmont on the way to Fairfax City to look at the surveillance videos of Julie's apartment, Jacobs tried hard to convince him they had plenty of time to do that so in the meantime, why don't they head out to Alexandria for a little while and pay a visit to Mustapha Khan in the joint. It was nearing ten o'clock in the morning and the Washington/Northern Virginia rush hour traffic had pretty much cleared up. They were now on Route 50 heading west to the Fairfax City police department on Old Lee Highway.

"We won't be long, I swear," Jacobs said, not giving up easy. "We can just swing south on the Beltway right there—" he pointed up ahead at an interstate sign for the I-495 entrance. "Shouldn't take but fifteen, twenty minutes to get there."

"I know where it is and how to get there, JayJay," Bartley said, not at all listening to what his partner was asking. He knew what Jacobs really wanted to do. He wanted to kill the sonofabitch messed up his face and put him out of commission for a few weeks. Or maybe even just give Mustapha a taste of what he gave JayJay, let the sonofabitch know what it's like to crack some tiles on the washroom wall in the joint with his face.

"C'mon, Bartley," Jacobs pleaded as they neared the interchange. "Be a guy, huh?"

"I'd like to, JayJay, believe me," Bartley replied, staying on the left lane of Route 50. "But this Fairfax City dick's waiting for us. I told him we'll be there around ten this morning. He said there's something he'd like us to look at."

Late afternoon Monday, the day before, Fairfax City Detective Earl Stone had called saying they now have over forty-eight hours of digital surveillance videos from the apartment. They had looked at most of them and were almost done with the rest when they noticed something and figured it's time they get the Feds in on it. Could turn out to be something time or event critical.

"He's not going anywhere," Bartley added as they went past the entrance to the Capital Beltway, Jacobs shaking his head in disappointment. "You'll have plenty of time to see him, say hello. Maybe get your wallet back too."

Forget the fucking wallet and everything in it, thought Jacobs. He'd had the credit cards cancelled, the driver's license replaced, what else? The badge—he just had a new one made, shinier than the old one. All he wanted to do was have a look at the goddamn animal in the cage, poke him a little bit, maybe loosen a few front teeth with a baseball bat and shove it up his ass for good measure. Heck, it's early. Maybe they'll have time later in the day.

"You know, the office has got us locked in to priorities," Bartley continued. "And this is it. This is a national security concern, not to mention these two people we're trying to protect could wind up dead too. Everything else comes second. You can understand that."

"Yes, yes. I understand. So, what's this thing Fairfax found out and wants us to look at right away?" Jacobs asked.

"He didn't say exactly, this guy Detective Stone. He just said have a look for yourself and tell us what you think."

It turned out this wouldn't be the day Jacobs got to pay a visit to Mustapha Khan in the Alexandria detention center. They were at the Fairfax City police headquarters the rest of the morning and the early afternoon. And not only that. After watching hours and hours of surveillance videos on the computer in the police AV room, they had to run off to the Arlington PD and do the same thing over there—watch more videos, this time of the ones taken at Chris Phillips' townhouse.

Three hidden cameras were installed in the surveillance system at Julie's place. One outdoor to monitor the parking lot and the building entrance. One inside the entrance lobby and another in Julie's apartment. All three were motion-detector activated, programmed to pan, zoom and tilt, and transmit wireless to a video receiver hooked to a hidden laptop computer Lou Heywood of the Bureau—working with a Fairfax City PD audio-visual specialist and Detective Stone—had set up in the apartment using a surveillance software system called DVSR (Digital Video Surveillance Recorder).

Nothing was recorded inside the apartment. The camera in the lobby showed nothing out of the ordinary—just the residents coming and going, the mailman opening the mailboxes and delivering the mail. Detective Stone went over this quickly, fast-forwarding all the way to the end sometime after Bartley and Jacobs had pretty much seen the same people in the building over again.

Stone then brought up the video files recorded by the outdoor camera. These contained the first sixteen hours of the surveillance the past three days. Here, Stone let the video run at normal speed, fast-forwarding when nothing was happening. He would freeze a frame and zoom in when something of interest caught one's eye, pull back a few seconds and slow-replay till he was satisfied. By the time they were halfway through the video file, they'd seen most of the same people they did before, getting in or coming out of their cars.

Bartley hoped they wouldn't have to do this very long. So did Jacobs. They thought it was absolutely the most boring part of a surveillance job. Watching people in their most ordinary daily routines on a screen. Like watching grass grow. They felt very appreciative of Detective Stone for the enthusiasm he showed in taking them through the process.

There were two places on the video, two occasions, once at four o'clock in the afternoon, when a car drove into the parking lot and parked right across from Julie's apartment. A man came out of the car, walked to the building entrance and buzzed an apartment. He waited a good two minutes, buzzing at least three more times before getting back in the car and driving off. He showed up again at seven o'clock at night the same day. The same thing happened. He didn't show up again in the rest of the video.

There was another car that attracted Stone's attention. A late model Pontiac Grand Am. It would show up in the parking lot and pull into a space four or five away from Julie's apartment across the road. It would sit for two or three hours before it left. It showed up at varying times during the day and at night: six, seven o'clock in the morning and between five and seven in the evening.

The weird thing about it was nobody ever came out of the car. It appeared whoever was in it was waiting for somebody and must have a lot of patience. Stone kept hoping the car would park at a space nearer the mini-camera which was hidden above the entrance canopy so the driver would be visible but, so far, it hadn't.

Another car they got curious about was a Ford Mustang Cobra. It showed up only the day before, twice. Once at four o'clock in the afternoon and a second time at eight at night. This one had a man sitting in the passenger seat. But like the Grand Am, no one came out of the car as it sat there for two hours parked away from the building entrance but still close enough to have a good view of the people coming and going.

"So, what do you think?" Stone asked the two FBI agents as he finally got to the last of the video files.

"I think we got something going here," replied Bartley.

"I do too," seconded Jacobs.

"I'm curious to see what they've got in Arlington," Bartley said, still thinking about the Grand Am and the Mustang Cobra. "They said they too would have plenty for us to look at by now. They're expecting us there today as soon as we can make it."

Stone offered to get the sheets on the license plates of the two cars and of several others that looked suspicious. He also gave them a CD copy of the video file that contained most of the shots of the Grand Am and the Mustang Cobra. They thanked Stone who was only too glad to be working with the FBI. He told them he'd have the sheets on the cars to them as soon as he got them. Then they headed out to North Courthouse Road in Arlington after Bartley talked to Arlington police Detective Joe Riley on the phone. There, they spent several hours watching the surveillance videos from Chris Phillips' townhouse, with Detectives Joe Riley and Zak Porter.

When the Mustang Cobra finally showed up in one of the video files of the parking lot, Bartley asked Porter who was at the keyboard to freeze the screen and zoom in at a frame that displayed the license plate number of the car. There were two men in the car but they couldn't tell if they were the same people. And again, they just sat there, waiting. It was early evening Sunday and starting to get dark.

Bartley took out the copy of the Fairfax video and asked to load it in the other computer nearby. It was the same damn car showing in the other computer. Same license plate number, and probably the same two men in it.

Zak Porter fast-forwarded by half an hour. Now it showed Chris Phillips in his Toyota Camry pulling into a space two away from the car, getting out and walking past the Mustang Cobra without noticing the men in it. The viewers waited for something to happen, like the men going after Chris and doing something to him. They didn't, thank God. Chris kept walking towards his townhouse and went in. One of the men got out of the car as soon as Chris was out of sight. He was lean, young-looking in spite of the close-cropped beard he wore, dark complexioned and unmistakably Middle-Eastern.

He didn't follow Chris but went instead to the Toyota Camry, wrote down its license plate number on a piece of paper and went back in the car. They sat for another half hour and then left.

"Has Chris Phillips seen this?" Bartley asked the detectives.

"No, and we don't intend to show it to him," replied Zak Porter.

"We got the place staked out since then," Joe Riley said. "Two shifts. Four to midnight and six A.M. to three P.M."

"You're going to have to do better than that," Bartley said. "More like round the clock. They could have decided to take him out right then. Or whatever." The Arlington detectives fidgeted in their seats and stared at each other.

"I'm going to ask the Bureau for the same kind of protection for Phillips as we have for his girlfriend. Meantime, I'd like to ask you to give him that the next couple of days till we get some people to take over."

"Who's going to pay for all the overtime?" asked Zak Porter.

That drew a long look from the Feds. Joe Riley, the other Arlington detective, waited for an answer.

"I'll talk to the office. There won't be any problem. The Bureau will take care of that with your people. They'll work it out," Bartley replied.

They were about to turn back to the twenty-two-inch computer monitor when Bartley's cell phone rang. It was Fairfax City police Detective Earl Stone.

"I got the sheets on the cars," said Stone. "I can get them to you right now by fax or email."

Bartley put him on hold for a second to ask Zak Porter about getting an email on the computer. No problem, Zak said and gave him the email address. Three minutes later, they were browsing the data on the Mustang Cobra and the Grand Am. Afterwards, Bartley tensed. The other three men could almost hear his thoughts racing in his head. They waited for him to put them into words.

"We got to go after these guys," he said, referring to the names and addresses in the car registration information attached in the email from Stone. The Mustang Cobra which had a Maryland license plate was registered to a Samir Osmani with an address in Baltimore. The Grand Am was registered in Virginia to a Haji Madari of Dale City. He turned to John Jacobs sitting next to him and added: "We got to move fast."

While the FBI agents assembled a team to track their suspects, Omar Husain and his men, the past four days now, were busy looking for Julie. They stalked her apartment morning, noon and night but came up with nothing. She hadn't come home at all. She could've gone on vacation. Not likely, though. Not without her boyfriend. They'd seen him coming and going at his place in Arlington and he hadn't gone anywhere to see her.

There's only one way to find out. It's time to get inside the apartment and get some information. Addresses of relatives, workplace, school, gym, church. Or maybe put a gun to the boyfriend's head and get him to take them to her. Either that, or both. He didn't have anymore time to spare for this one little problem which could turn into a major one. The plan for Operation Capitol West was nearly complete and it was scheduled to begin the following week.

At eight o'clock at night, the Fairfax PD AV man came to the apartment to collect the surveillance CD from the laptop and replace it with a fresh one. A half hour later, Omar Husain and Haji Madari, a twenty-two-year old GWU sleeper he had recently activated, entered Julie's apartment and went through every room. They found all the information they came for and were out of there in twenty minutes.

About the time they were driving out of Julie's apartment parking lot, Samir Osmani, in the Mustang Cobra with Hamad Salim in the passenger seat, drove into the parking lot of Chris Phillips' townhouse building in Fairlington. The lot was full so he drove out again to park across the street from the walkway to the townhouse building. In the dark three spaces from the walkway in the parking lot sat police Detectives Joe Riley and Zak Porter in the unmarked police car.

Neither of them paid attention to the car that just went by and parked across the street. After four hours of watch, looking at cars and people in and out of the residential complex, everything becomes routine, boring, causing a slip in one's awareness at moments. But the detectives did notice the two men when they crossed the street and headed on the walkway towards Chris Phillips' townhouse unit.

They watched one of them stop at Chris Phillips' unit, go up the steps to the door and press the door-chime button. The other one continued on to the end of the building and disappeared in the dark.

"What do you think this is?" asked Zak Porter in the passenger seat, his eyes glued on the man at Chris Phillips' door.

"I don't know," replied Joe Riley, thinking fast, now realizing they hadn't given it much thought, in fact they hadn't thought about it at all—what to do on something like this happening—a possible suspect appearing at Chris Phillips' door.

Do they rush him before he could do anything? Before Chris opened the door? What if it turned out he was a friend or a relative?

But what if Chris opens the door and the man forces his way in at gunpoint?

Or simply shoots Chris?

Joe Riley told Zak Porter to call for backup immediately then started to get out of the car. His phone rang before he could open the door.

"Joe Riley," he said.

"Where are you, guys?" Chris whispered on his cell phone, his voice a bit shaky as he continued to back off the front door into the living room after peering through the peep hole.

"We're out here in the parking lot. We see him. Get away from the door and don't make any noise." Riley answered quickly.

"You better do something. I don't know this guy," Chris said nervously as he kept moving back in the living room to the wall at the foot of the stair to the second floor, out of sight of all the ground floor windows. He only had one light on—a free-standing shaded lamp by the TV at a short wing-wall that separated the living room from the dining room. With the blinds on the living room windows shut, the curtains over them drawn, which they were at the moment, no one outside could tell if there were any lights on inside, if anybody was home. He had come in an hour ago from a carry-out chicken fast-food at Bradlee Shopping Center and had just finished eating the dinner in front of the TV.

Now, as he stood quietly against the stairwall, he thought of reaching for the Smith and Wesson he had been carrying with him the past few days. But the .40 caliber pistol was in the coat he hung in the visitor's closet by the front door when he came in.

Without making a noise, he bounded up the stairs as fast as he could. He got the other pistol from the bedroom and started back down step by step, gun aimed straight ahead in the right hand, cell phone in the left as he now listened to Joe Riley say: "Get out the backdoor right now. We're moving in."

Chris reached the bottom of the stairs and headed straight to the backdoor of the house through the kitchen. The last door chime had come moments ago and now he could hear the man outside working the locks of the frontdoor. Whoever it is, he thought, is not going away; he means business this time and he's coming in no matter what. In the kitchen, he put on a jacket he had hanging on a nail and slipped the gun in its right outside pocket.

He got out of the house into the dark outdoor, taking the two steps down to get to the ground before closing the door behind him. It was then that he felt the cold muzzle of a gun press against the back of his head.

"Hands wide to your side," Samir Osmani ordered. "Walk towards the street, quietly."

The chill coursed through his body before he fully understood what he was told to do. And it was only when the gun pushed harder behind his head that he spread his hands to his sides. Then he started walking one slow step at a time.

"Move!" ordered the man behind him firmly. There was low light coming from their left but only some of it got past and over the six-foot high fence on that side. He could see from the chest up and hardly anything at all on the ground. But he knew practically every square-foot of the way out to the end of the building and the street sidewalk up ahead. The concrete splashblocks that caught the water from the downspouts on the side of the building, the stuff his neighbors kept just outside their unit—snow shovels, empty cans, firewood and every crack and pothole there was on the ground.

Inside the house, Hamad Salim had gained entry through the frontdoor. He had closed the door behind him and was now picking his way through the living room, pointing a 10 mm Glock 20 automatic pistol in the direction of every step he took. Outside, Detective Joe Riley approached the frontdoor as if he was walking a mine field. Zak Porter, likewise, tiptoed a few feet behind and off to his right in the dark. Both men led their way at every step with their service handguns.

Not finding anyone on the ground floor, the man in the house now moved stealthily up the stairs.

In the alley behind the building, Chris Phillips had calculated how many steps away he was to the pothole before he got there. It was one of several he knew well in the alley, this one in particular because it was the deepest and it paralleled a fence post on the left which marked its location. The man behind him poked him in the back with the barrel of the gun about every other step. Chris heard a genuine menace in Samir Osmani's voice everytime the man urged him to 'keep moving', 'hurry up'. The hard foreign accent made it sound more threatening.

As he neared the pothole, Chris widened his steps sideways to avoid accidentally stepping into it himself. Just as he was stepping over it, Samir Osmani poked him in the back, giving him reason to spread his hands wider to his sides. Then, exactly the same instant Samir Osmani stepped into the pothole and lost his balance, Chris swung his right arm backward, fast, hitting the man's wrist with a handknife chop. The gun flew from Samir's hand in an arch that extended way over the other side of the fence.

Surprised at suddenly finding himself unarmed and on the defensive, Samir Osmani rolled away from Chris far enough to get back on his feet. In the process, he felt for anything to pick up on the ground. A rock, a bottle, anything. He lucked out and found a two-foot-long pipe which he swung in a semi-circle at

Chris. It caught Chris partly on the left side of his forehead. Not a direct hit enough to knock him cold but good enough to open a cut and jog his brain a little.

The pipe kept coming at him, arching from different directions. He ducked and backed up, blood now starting to get in his eyes, until he found his back against the wall. The next time he saw the pipe coming, he hopped sideways and delivered a left-foot roundhouse kick to the right side of the attacker's face. Samir Osmani staggered backwards, dazed, but stayed on his feet. He suddenly had a change of mind about staying around and bolted.

Chris thought of going after him but after all the excitement, he felt totally drained and sank to his knees. Then he felt the gun in his coat pocket, took it out, aimed quickly at the escaping target and fired. Samir Osmani stumbled partly as the bullet struck his left shoulder. But he kept going and disappeared from Chris' view as he turned at the end of the townhouse building.

Hearing the gunshot, Hamad Salim hurried back down the stairs from the second floor. He was near the backdoor in the kitchen when Joe Riley, just stepping into the far end of the living room, pointed the gun at him and shouted the order to freeze.

Instead, Hamad Salim turned around, fast. Riley dropped on his left knee, crouching forward over his right when he saw the gun. He realized at that instant that one of them would fall and he sure as hell wasn't going to let it be him. He pumped two rounds into the upper torso of the man to make sure the arm didn't come around to aim the gun fully at him. But it did and the finger managed to squeeze the trigger once. Riley's third shot finally felled the man, tearing into the left half of the chest at the same time as the single 10 mm round from the man's Glock 20 tore just below Riley's left rib-cage.

Zak Porter burst through the frontdoor and poked the air in every direction with a gun in both hands. A moment later, Chris entered the backdoor into the kitchen. Huddled against the brick wall outside, gun aimed at the backdoor, he had waited for anyone to come out of the house when he heard the shots.

He called his name out to Zak Porter when he saw the detective looking in on his partner bleeding on the living room floor.

"Hang on Joe," Zak said to the wounded detective. Riley was in pain. He turned slowly side to side, a hand cupped over his bloody waist. "Help is coming."

Zak Porter was busy on the phone the next few minutes. After they called for the ambulance, he reported to his chief in the office. Then he talked to the Feds. FBI agent Richard Bartley said he'd be over right away. Next, the backups arrived which, as usual, didn't have anything to do but secure the area and protect evidence for the forensics. The other man on the floor lay still, quite dead as one of the uniformed backups found out when he checked.

As the entire event continued to unfold into the night, Chris simply rolled with the unreality of it all, as if he wasn't at all a part of it. Like he was just watching a movie or one of those regular police TV shows.

Pictures were taken throughout the entire scene which included practically every room in the house. Upstairs and downstairs, as well as outside where Chris was involved. The ambulance came and Detective Riley was moved carefully to a stretcher and carried out. The dead body was stuffed in a zippered body bag and moved out. One of the paramedics cleaned Chris' wound which turned out to be a nasty inch-and-a-half cut and was sewed later.

It all seemed so unreal but all along, Chris knew everything was happening right there in his living room. It wasn't till the phone rang and he heard his brother's voice when he finally accepted that he wasn't just watching; that it was all real and that he was not just a small part of it but the major subject of the whole event.

His brother inquired about his well-being in general. "How are things with you?" he asked.

"Jim," he said and let it hang a couple of seconds to set the mood. "I want you to know how grateful I am for letting me have the pistols, and taking me to that shooting practice last weekend."

CHAPTER 30

▼

Omar Husain made the right turn to N. West Street from Route 7 in West Falls Church and drove two blocks to St. James College on the right. It was half past ten in the morning, near the end of Julie Santorelli's first class of the day.

He pulled into a space in the parking lot at the end of a long five-story building, one of three in this main campus of the local school a block away from the Catholic parish church of the same name. Haji Madari, in the passenger seat of the Grand Am, scoped the surrounding immediately. There weren't many vacant spaces left in the parking lot, not like when they first came two days ago late in the afternoon to get familiar with the campus, see the routine activities outdoors and inside the buildings.

At Omar's direction, he had gone inside each of the buildings and located Room 1725L in the one across the grounds from where they were now parked. They were counting on Julie Santorelli now being in that room in front of her class, according to a copy of the class schedule they found in her apartment.

A few students went in and out of the buildings, walked on the grounds, to the parking lot or out to the street. Nothing that might pose an unexpected problem to what they had come for went on..

After sitting in the car for a couple of minutes, Omar Husain looked at the time on his watch. That signaled Haji Madari to start getting out of the car. But before he opened the door, Commander Omar picked up something from the tray under the dashboard and held it out to him.

"Oh, yes," said Haji, reaching for the shiny FBI badge and looking at it admiringly for a moment. "Thank you, Commander."

"That should make things go a lot smoother," said Omar Husain, smiling confidently.

When Mustapha Khan presented him with the badge several weeks ago, he had no idea what to do with it other than to marvel at it at the time. Satisfy everyone's curiosity as to what it was like to be in possession of such a thing. An object that symbolized power and authority, a right of passage, giving one permission to venture into places ordinary people were not allowed. They passed it around, some of the men mimicking an FBI agent by flashing it at each other.

Little did he know how useful it would be later, how much easier it would make taking care of this one little problem that had been nagging at him for sometime now. He watched Haji walk to the entry doors of the building. An ordinary college-age American male, or a faculty assistant, or maybe even a young government employee such as an FBI agent.

He sat in the car another two minutes after Haji entered the building. Hopefully, it wouldn't be one of those times when the class breezed through today's work in less than the seventy-five-minute period and the teacher dismissed them early. If everything worked out according to plan, Haji would have just the right amount of time—within the next three to five minutes—to look through the glass panel of the classroom door for a quick look at the teacher, hang out in the hallway a bit till the class came out and make his move.

Now Omar Husain pulled out of the parking space, drove slowly around the building and stood by the side of the campus road a few yards away from the rear entrance to the building. He looked at his watch again—10:42. At this same time, Haji reached the classroom door number 1725L on the left side of the hallway. Walking three feet away from the wall, he slowed down, actually lingered without looking especially curious, as soon as Julie Santorelli came to view at the front of the class. After a first glance and one quick good look, he went past the room to a shelf across the hallway, picked up a pamphlet to read and waited.

When the door swung open two minutes later and the class started pouring out, he turned and waited till the last of the students had come out, expecting the teacher to come out last. When she didn't awhile, he debated whether to continue waiting or enter the classroom. Then the door swung open again. Julie, dressed in a pantsuit, came out carrying a tote bag and turned his way. He immediately stepped to the middle of the hallway to meet her.

"Ms. Santorelli?" he asked as politely as he could.

"Yes?" she responded, stopping in mid-step and looking up at the dark-haired young man, twenty-something. Probably a senior at school, she thought. But she was totally mistaken when he identified himself—agent John Jacobs of the Federal Bureau of Investigations—at the same time pulling out the shiny FBI badge.

"I'm sorry to inconvenience you, ma'am, but I have orders to escort you out of these premises right now," he said in a hurry, giving her the impression of the urgency of the situation at hand.

"Why? What's going on?" she asked, suddenly alarmed.

"We have information about certain people who are here at school today to do you harm. We must get you out of here now. This way, please, quickly." Haji led her by an arm to the rear entrance a short distance to the end of the hallway.

"Where's the other man? What's his name...Gomez. Hector Gomez."

"He's out in the car waiting for us. Hurry, please."

Agent Hector Gomez wanted to stay a little longer at Burger King a couple of blocks away from St. James College on the same side of Route 7, finish the coffee while reading the paper. But he saw that it was time to get back to the school to check up on his charge. He took the coffee to the car and drove back.

As he pulled into a space in the parking lot, he saw Julie Santorelli come out of the rear entrance of the campus building with a man. They looked like they were in a hurry. She didn't appear to be under duress or acting against her will. A sedan pulled up as soon as they stepped onto the sidewalk. The man opened the rear door and they got in the backseat, the man right behind her.

Something didn't feel right about this, though. It wasn't quite eleven o'clock. Too early for lunch. She just finished her 9:30 class. He decided to get out of the car to intercept them on foot as the car turned towards him on its way out to the street. But there was no time as the car picked up speed. He put the car in reverse gear instead and was about to step hard on the gas pedal when a group of pedestrians strolled behind him.

He strained to get the license plate number as the car sped past but his view was obstructed by the car parked to his right. The only thing he could say to identify it was its make and color—a red Pontiac Grand Am sedan. It had turned left on West Street, left again to head east on Route 7 and was gone by the time he was able to pull out of the parking lot. At the intersection of Route 7, he looked east and west, cursed himself and made the decision to head west, hoping he was right. Perhaps it got caught at a traffic light, or hadn't made another turn anywhere so he'd still have a chance to catch up with it.

Meantime, he got the phone out and started dialing a number. While at it, he suddenly remembered hearing of the report on the incident in Arlington the night before. One of the local dicks taking out an intruder in Chris Phillips' house and getting shot himself in the encounter.

That's why he got a call early this morning from the office telling him to stay close to his charge. There apparently was an all out move by the bad guys to get to Julie Santorelli.

You're up shit creek, Gomez, he thought to himself. He should have listened, stayed right there outside her classroom door. Dammit!

He wove through the morning traffic on Route 7 towards the Beltway and Tysons Corner, switching lanes, cutting close in front of other motorists and paying no attention to their gestures. The Grand Am was nowhere to be seen. His call finally got through.

"Agent Richard Bartley," said the man at the other end. He was driving a Bureau car on I-95 south approaching the infamous Mixing Bowl of Northern Virginia with agent John Jacobs sitting in the passenger seat. Behind them were two armored personnel transport vans carrying the SWAT teams.

"Bartley, it's Gomez. I need assistance—"

"Hector, just the man I want to talk to," Bartley interrupted in a voice determined to be heard first. But Hector was feeling the heat behind his ears with the fix he was in and wouldn't be quieted down.

"Bartley, listen. I lost her. I think they got her. In a car. I'm in pursuit right now. Route 7 west near the Beltway."

"Shit, Hector, what happened!"

He related what took place in about three short sentences. He going for coffee while Julie was in class, and the rest.

"Tell me what kind of car it is," Bartley asked, his voice changed from urgent to steely calm. Like Hector, he started feeling shitty about what had happened. He meant to call Hector Gomez immediately, two and a half hours ago. As soon as Fairfax detective Earl Stone came to show him the video of the break-in at Julie Santorelli's apartment the night before. About an hour before the break-in at her boyfriend's townhouse in Arlington. The video showing two men, one of them Saladin, going through the apartment, obviously gathering information regarding Julie's possible whereabouts. Dammit. He should have called immediately, dispatched a couple of more men to protect her.

But a glimmer of hope came to light when Hector Gomez said: "It's a red Pontiac Grand Am. Four-door sedan, late model."

"Where are you now?"

"Just past the Beltway. I...don't see it anywhere. I've lost them."

"Alright, listen," Bartley said, drawing a great long breath as he drove under the multi-level skyways of the Mixing Bowl. "Get on the Beltway and head south on I-95 to Dale City. We're headed there right now with two SWAT teams. You shouldn't have any problem catching up. Rush-hour traffic's over."

He went on to explain what the operation was and why Hector shouldn't feel all was lost with Julie Santorelli. After they viewed the surveillance videos and saw the sheets on the red Grand Am and the Mustang Cobra, and especially after the following shootout in Arlington and the break-in at Julie's apartment, the analysts at headquarters had concurred with the agents out in the field to launch the operation to bust the house in Dale City where the Grand Am was garaged. A separate operation was at this very moment being launched in Baltimore at the address of the owner of the Mustang Cobra which showed up again last night in the video at Chris Phillips' place prior to the shooting.

Richard Bartley cautioned Hector Gomez that there was a good chance the Grand Am was on the Beltway and that they were all headed the same place—the house in Dale City. Hector said that they didn't see him, didn't know he existed. They hung up and Hector made an impossible u-turn on Route 7 to get back to the entrance to the Beltway.

Immediately after she settled in the back seat, a thought suddenly occurred to Julie Santorelli with all its numbing horror. First, she looked up in front of her at the driver and saw that it wasn't Hector Gomez. Or Doug Jones, Hector's alternate. Second, he only glanced quickly at her before she even saw his face, and drove out of the school in a hurry. And, next, the two men didn't say a word to each other. They simply nodded at each other, speaking with their eyes.

The air in the car got thick with suspicions quickly—they sensing that she knew right away they weren't who they said they were and she becoming aware of this in return. Coming to a red light, she gathered enough courage to escape. She sat up slowly while surreptitiously eyeing the controls of the car door on her side. There was a button for rolling down the window and another for locking and unlocking the door, the same as in her Toyota Corolla. She shifted in her seat so that her right foot, in her work-shoe with the half-inch hard-rubber heel, was free. As the car came to a stop, she delivered a vicious snap side-kick to the left ear of the man beside her.

The impact sent Haji Madari hard against the car door. Stunned at such an unexpected violence, from a seemingly defenseless woman, he had to take a moment to recover. This gave Julie time to push the unlock button and open the door. But Omar Husain immediately saw what was happening and turned around in time to grab a handful of Julie's hair and pull her back in the car. Haji

Madari then clamped a hand around her neck, twisted her right arm behind her and pushed her onto the floor of the car face down to keep her out of sight.

The light turned green and Omar Husain resumed driving, checking through his peripheral vision if anybody noticed what went on in the car briefly. Nobody did.

"That was good, lady," Haji said, keeping his hands tight on Julie although she wasn't struggling. He grimaced while he moved his jaw up and down to find out if it remained in the right place. "But not a very sporting thing to do to somebody who hadn't done anything to you."

"What do you want with me?" she asked no one in particular, her voice bouncing against the bottom edge of the backseat five inches away from her face.

Omar Husain heard it clearly and replied: "First, Ms. Santorelli, we'd like to talk to you. That's all. Talk."

"Who are you?"

They had reached Lee Highway on Route 7, in the heart of Falls Church, and Omar Husain was now waiting for through-traffic to clear to make a left turn. Their destination was a large single family house bought and financed by the Organization several years ago in Bellevue Forest in North Arlington off Military Road. It had been used by sleepers who came to the capital region to attend schools in the area, along with out-of-town guests from time to time. As a cover, the property deed and title were put in the name of a second-generation Egyptian-American family, a middle-aged couple who was one of the many strong supporters of GIDO in the country. They came and went normally as they needed to while Omar and his men were staying in the house.

"I believe you know who I am," Omar Husain said, making the left turn to Lee Highway. He spoke amicably, trying to establish an atmosphere of calm and, he hoped, some form of decorum between them later. "For a start, I would just like for us to have the opportunity to get properly acquainted. If that's possible."

"I don't see why not," replied Julie. "If that's what you want."

Omar Husain glanced back at Haji Madari and nodded a signal to release his hold on her. Julie pushed herself up from the floor of the car and sat in her corner of the backseat, eyeing Haji defiantly.

"It'll only be a few minutes to where we're going," Omar Husain said, keeping his eyes on the road. "If you don't mind waiting till we get there, for the proper introductions."

The soft talk worked with Julie. Listening to the man speak in that conciliatory voice, she became less fearful of them. It calmed her down and allowed her to think of many things, possibilities, she must now consider.

First of all, who else could they be other than the people the police and the FBI had been protecting her from? The people involved in the killing she witnessed in the park. And of course the matter of what they intended to do with her was right up there with that, along with when, how and where?

She was amazed at how she could now, in a situation she had never been before in her whole life, think methodically, analytically, without being paralyzed by fear and becoming totally helpless. So, now she started thinking as they turned to Lorcom Lane in a more affluent area of north Arlington, what she could do to help herself out of this predicament. One thing she must always do from here on no matter what, she thought, is make time. Do anything possible to delay whatever it was they intended to do to her—harm or kill her. Because whatever plan she might come up with to escape, or as a last resort to fight them, wouldn't be possible without time to prepare.

So far, she had learned something about them that gave her some encouragement. She could kick their faces, resist them physically, and they wouldn't just shoot her dead. That's something. Question was—how far could she go before they did shoot her dead? A more realistic one was, knowing that their sole purpose for capturing her was to prevent her from identifying them to the authorities for the killing in the park (what other reason could there be? they never knew she existed before then), how long did they intend to keep her alive?

Another thing that came to mind once again was, realizing what great interest the Feds had taken in the case, obviously it's not your routine homicide resulting from a robbery or a fatal assault out of personal grudges or vendetta. A drug-related mob hit, perhaps. Or something to do with government intelligence, espionage, terrorism, the victim being a federal worker.

Knowing this would give her an idea who these people might be, what kind of people they were: how ruthless, how intelligent or stupid. And, most important of all, she'd know how to talk to them, dig in to their values, probe them, and perhaps even challenge them.

The young man in the backseat with her, for instance, she could tell he wasn't American-born, if he was any type of an American at all. At least, with his slight foreign accent, Asian or Middle-Eastern, English was not his native tongue. The man at the wheel was much the same but with an accent different from the other. Not American. Definitely foreign. A bit of south Asian British, perhaps, and again Middle Eastern, the Mediterranean strain. Educated.

They turned north on Military Road. A couple of miles later, they drove into the sprawling, neatly landscaped frontyard of the large two-story brownstone surrounded by some tall trees, a few evergreens, hemlocks and red maples. Two men, these ones looking outright Middle Eastern—mustache and short beard, darker hair and complexion, came out of the house promptly. One of them held the door as the driver got out. The other stood on Julie's side of the car and waited.

"Good to see you back, Commander," Julie heard the one up front say. He was a large man, over six feet tall and had the weight and muscles to go with the frame. He had a thick Middle Eastern accent if she ever heard one. Now, in Arabic which only the men understood, he added: "How did things go?"

"As well as we had hoped for," Omar Husain said to the towering Masoud Faisal, recently of Detroit, whom he had now designated to replace the missing Mustapha Khan. He turned towards the rear door and motioned the other man, Yussuf Al Mukhtar, another GWU student sleeper he had recently activated, to open Julie's door.

She got out of the car, taking the hand offered by Yussuf, a younger but smaller one about the same age as the one she rode with in the backseat. She kept an eye on Haji Madari as he went around the back of the car carrying her tote bag which contained just about everything that told the world who she was and what she did in her daily life.

"I would have that please," she said when he came to stand beside her.

Omar Husain simply nodded at Haji Madari and the latter immediately turned the bag upside down on the concrete driveway, scattering everything she had in it—books, folders, test papers, purse, cell phone, lipstick, hair brushes and other cosmetics items. In Arabic, Omar told the young man what to do next which was promptly done—take the cell phone, open the purse and check what's in it; take any potential weapon or communicating device, put everything else back in the tote bag and give it back to her.

"Thank you very much," she said, grabbing her bag angrily and glaring at the young man. She turned the same angry look at the man who was obviously the leader of the gang, their 'commander', and she froze.

"I'm sorry to have to do that," Omar Husain said truthfully but unapologetically.

"It's you," Julie said, staring at the man. She inched back, the anger on her face turned into a look of cautious recognition of a familiar face.

It was the same face that emerged on the FBI's computer monitor, that day at home, after she and Chris described the man they saw in different places. The greenish-blue eyes with the discerning look that read your mind, the pleasant expression, handsome in a way you didn't associate with any wrongdoing or foul intent. It was a face she could've easily trusted under different circumstances.

Finally, it left her no doubt about Omar Husain's identity when she looked at his left ear and saw the golden crescent-moon-and-star earring shining in the daylight as it did on that day at the park.

"Please, allow me to introduce myself," now she heard the man saying to her. "I am Omar Husain. We will make your time with us as comfortable as possible, Ms. Julie Santorelli, with your cooperation, of course. My associates here will see to that."

Omar Husain led the way into the entrance vestibule and to a wide stairway that took them down to the basement floor. It was actually another living area of the house, complete with all the rooms and conveniences found in the upper living quarters. Living and dining rooms, full kitchen, a large master bedroom and a guest room each with a separate bath.

They deposited her in the master bedroom, all four men surrounding her every step of the way. Haji Madari and Yussuf Al Mukhtar left. Masoud Faisal, now Omar Husain's newly designated personal aide, stayed out in the living room while his Commander spoke briefly with Julie in the bedroom.

The pleasantries of the accommodations helped ward off any concern in her, physical or psychological. But the urge to demand to know what they intended to do with her had now become much stronger. So she faced Omar Husain and insisted to have an answer.

"I have to leave right now," he said instead, backing up to the door. "But I will be back and we will talk."

"I want to talk now!" she demanded. The anger she felt before was back but with it, now as she faced confinement in this room, in the basement level of this unknown house, was the apprehension at the thought that she might never see the life she'd known before, and worse. She was close to tears, wanted to beg, plead, but she held it all back. Her mind raced for anything she could tell him that might make him stop and listen. She thought of one. "You might want to consider there's no reason for you to silence me," she said as fast as she could.

It did stall him a moment and caused him to give her that discerning look.

"They know who you are, what you look like," she continued. "They don't need me as a witness—"

"You can tell me more about it later," he said calmly.

"I want to tell you now," she persisted, stepping up to him.

"Please, just make yourself at home for now," Omar Husain said as he stepped farther back out of the bedroom. "My associate, his name is Masoud, will be outside to attend to your needs." And he grabbed the doorknob and pulled the door shut.

Julie went after him and quickly found out that the door hardware was the type that locked from the outside. She was a prisoner.

Up on the ground floor, as soon as Omar Husain appeared before them, a group of men in the family room turned their attention to him, some of them rising from their seat around the table. Others scattered in the other rooms, some of them armed and just sitting near the doors to the outside, did the same.

"Gentlemen," he greeted, pausing a moment but not changing his direction to the stair to the second floor. "Please don't let me interrupt. I will join you in a minute."

Several of his veteran warriors—team commanders Kashim Najoub, Hassan Bahaji, among others from Philadelphia, Baltimore and New York, were present. So was a group of newly activated sleepers selected from the cells in the east and the mid-Atlantic regions, among them several of those GWU students such as Haji Madari and Yussuf Al Mukhtar.

Everyone responded dutifully before he continued on his way to the upper floor. He hurried through the spacious hallway of the big house, turned a corner to the bedroom wing and went into one of the rooms. In there were two men. One was Samir Osmani in bed for the bullet wound in his left shoulder from the night before. He had been in pain and was running a fever earlier but was now resting comfortably. Khalil Majid, the money man from Detroit, had given him a dose of painkillers and been keeping him company for most of the morning. He had just now stuck a thermometer in Samir's mouth.

"Commander," Khalil greeted, rising from a chair beside the bed.

"How is our man?" asked Omar.

"Getting better, I hope," said Khalil. "We'll see in a few moments."

"As they say in this country, you can't keep a good man down," commented Omar, sitting on the edge of the bed and laying a hand on Samir's arm.

Samir smiled and attempted to respond but managed only a short hum through his nose. Then the thermometer started beeping. Khalil pulled it out and read the scale.

"Hah! Much better," he said gladly. "Ninety-nine point four degrees. Down from over a hundred."

"Good," said Omar. "Get a good rest and get well soon. Don't worry about anything. I have good news to tell you. We have her."

"We do?" Samir said, inching up in bed.

"Yes, she's here. That's one thing we no longer have to worry about. So, now we can just concentrate on the work we have to accomplish. Very soon."

"I worried about you, Commander," Samir said. "We all did. This is indeed good news."

"You have made great sacrifices and have done very well, brother." Omar sounded genuinely comforting as he always did to all of his charges since many years back in the homelands. This was how Samir Osmani and all the rest of them remembered him and came to revere him, their teacher and Emir in whose presence they signed their *bayat* where they swore to obey his orders in the holy war against the enemies of Islam A sleeper, once activated and finally called to service in the Jihad under his command would follow his words to the letter. The Soldier of Islam sees his life as a humble flicker in the burning flame that illuminates the trueness of the one and only God of mankind—Allah.

"I wish to do more and I will," said the wounded young man in bed.

"I understand. Pray it is the will of Allah that you will continue to work with the rest of us to protect his honor and our faith in him," Omar said, bowing slightly and closing his eyes for a moment.

Abu Kamal Ramshallah who had taken up one of the rooms across the hall appeared at the door holding out a telephone in one hand. He was in a hurry. Omar Husain gave Samir one last reassuring pat on the hand before he rose to meet the man in the middle of the room.

Abu Kamal, one of the FBI's most wanted men, next to Omar, couldn't have spoken the bad news better than the grimness on his face did. He handed the telephone to Omar, only saying: "Dale City."

Omar took it and listened intently as the man at the other end spoke.

The government has invaded the house, he was told by the man, one of the sleepers who lived in the Dale City residence. He was on his way home in the car when he saw the vans, the soldiers with 'FBI' letters on their backs surrounding the house and in it arresting two of the brothers who were home at the time.

And where are you now?

Nearby Woodbridge, at the shopping mall—Potomac Mills.

Omar Husain paced the entire length of the spacious bedroom floor thinking fast even as he listened to the man. How did they find out about the house in Dale City? And did they also know about the other houses? Including this one? How about the one near Fort Hunt in Alexandria where he was staying? The one in Reston and Springfield? And the ones in Bethesda and Baltimore?

The man had asked what to do and was waiting for his order. Omar tried to maintain calm and had come to stand at the bedroom window overlooking the u-shaped driveway where the Grand Am, along with a couple of other cars, was parked. Then it suddenly occurred to him as his eyes fell on the license plate of the car.

The automobile was registered in the name of Haji Madari whose address was at the Dale City house. And how many times had they driven to Julie Santorelli's apartment, parked near the building and waited for her to come home? Finally, last night, when he decided to enter the apartment, they had parked right in front of the main entrance where the police or the FBI could have those hidden surveillance cameras both outside the building to cover the parking lot and inside the apartment in case of a break-in.

That means, possibly, they not only have the car license plates which include the other car—Samir's Mustang Cobra now sitting on the exit side of the driveway since last night—but his face on their surveillance video. Perhaps that's what Julie meant when she told him that he had been identified.

Therefore, what luck it had been when he decided that they come to this house instead of the one in Dale City!

Immediately after he thought out what to do, he instructed the man on the phone to stay where he was and then "Call again in an hour. Come to this house but not until you talk to me or someone else here to see if it's safe."

After he hung up, he signaled the two other men on their feet in the bedroom and led them into a study room at the other end of the hall. On their way, by the top of the stair, Omar called downstairs at Kashim Najoub, Hassan Bahaji and one other man—Marwan Razzak, a team leader from New York, to join them.

After everyone heard about the FBI raid in Dale City and how it possibly came about, he said the first thing they needed to do was get all the cars out of the driveway, park them at strategic spots on the road approaches to the house in both directions and post a man in each car. Just in case they'd also located this house.

And what if they had? They could be coming even at this very minute. Each man searched every other face in the room looking for an answer.

"The rear of the house opens to the thick wooded area in the back," Abu Kamal said. "I've taken walks out there many times. I know the way to get back to the cars on the road. As soon as we get the call from one of the men in the car, we'll make a break through there before they get close. We'll have time."

"Let's hope we won't have to go through that," said Omar Husain. Everyone nodded in agreement.

Hassan Bahaji then got up quickly to tell the men downstairs what had been decided and to do it immediately. Three men who had been guarding the house were given exact instructions what to do and then pulled to sit in the car they parked separately on the side of the road at least a hundred yards from the house.

After that, Omar Husain gathered the men close, assuming a somber appearance they rarely saw on the man.

"Gentlemen, today I believe I have come near the remaining days of my stay in America," he started out in a measured voice. "The missions which the Organization had entrusted upon me are nearly completed. Thanks to every one of you and all the young brothers downstairs and out there throughout the city, throughout this enemy country. To those who had fallen into the hands of the enemy, and especially those who had made the ultimate sacrifice and gone to Allah.

"But as you know, there is work left to be done before us. We have only a few days before we launch the operation. I think at this point, we've made good time in our preparation for this last mission." He turned to the three team leaders—Kashim Najoub, Hassan Bahaji and Marwan Razzak, with an inquiring look. The men responded with a nod of assurance.

"Good," said Omar with absolute confidence. "Because of this recent development, however, for which I take sole responsibility—"

Several of the men gestured with a hand to speak. It was Kashim Najoub Omar Husain turned to first.

"Commander, if I may," said Kashim, a man eleven years Omar's senior and who had dedicated the last thirty years of his life fighting Christians and Jews. "We're all in this together. We pull together as one, always, especially where one may have suffered a setback."

The other men echoed their agreement:

Yes, yes, at all times.

Most definitely, Commander.

We work together against our enemy.

We all take responsibility for everything as a group.

Omar had to wave them down so he could speak again.

"Gentlemen, thank you very much. *Shukran gazillan*," he said appreciatively. "Next to our faith in the almighty Allah, nothing is greater than our faith in each other. We need to look after each other, and this is exactly the reason why I must now tell you this—our enemies are closing in on us fast. We must therefore have the ability first to elude them, save ourselves from them, or destroy them. Destroy them before they destroy us. Each of us then must have the resources to save himself, or to fight the enemy."

He turned to Khalil Majid and spoke to the men of what great act Khalil had done for all of them, and for the Organization. Khalil then brought out the luggage bag containing the millions he literally hand-carried from the bank in Detroit.

"I want each one of you to have the personal resources that would allow you to function individually," Omar explained carefully. "Whatever situation you find yourself in, at least for a given time."

He then instructed Khalil to distribute funds to the men in the room. Sixty thousand dollars each. The nine other men in the house, downstairs, and the three posted in the cars on the road who together so far made up the three teams that would carry out Operation Capitol West in six days, were given forty thousand each. Khalil took the stacks of bills out of the luggage bag and gave them to the team leaders.

Abu Kamal, with help from some of the men downstairs, took the task of calling all the other houses throughout the area. None of the brothers residing in each one of them should be in danger, except the ones in Baltimore where Samir Osmani lived, and no one was there at the moment according to Samir. He had a roommate who was supposed to be at school. Those who were at home were given the message to be on heightened alert for government agents. Clear up any evidence in the house, they were told, that could point to any connection to the Organization and its activities. In any event, be prepared to abandon the residence at any time. Get in touch with the team leaders as soon as possible should this happen.

In the meantime, two phone calls came in for Abu Kamal. The first was from the brother in Dale City. The man was told to come in at this time. The second came within three minutes of the other. It was from Samir Osmani's roommate in Baltimore who, much like the man in Dale City, had come close to home and saw the FBI raiding the house, as Omar Husain had counted on. He too was told to come in and report everything that happened.

The men agreed at this point to go downstairs and gather everyone in the house back into the large family room. The planning of Operation Capitol West which had been proceeding for the past few days was resumed. Now that they had renewed financial resources, some changes were introduced to the initial plan. The money had allowed them more mobility and to expand their area of operation; cut down on the time they had allotted to accomplish some activities involving travel and transportation and staking out positions at different stages of the operation, gathering intelligence, watching out for the enemy and looking after each other.

It took them well into the afternoon but the plan was at last finalized. Everyone understood his part in the operation from beginning to end, every step of the way in between.

Then they dispersed. Most of them went back to the residences they were assigned to live in for the time being. One of the men who was staying in the Dale City house went with another. Those who had taken rooms in the other houses temporarily checked into inexpensive motels where they could move about inconspicuously. One instruction given each man before he left was to alter his appearance by shaving his facial hair, putting on clothes to look more local American residents; attract as little attention or curiosity as possible.

Khalil Majid went back upstairs to check up on the wounded man in bed while Abu Kamal stayed with Omar Husain downstairs. Four men remained with them. Two of the men who had been guarding the house and the other two sitting in separate cars on the road a hundred yards from each side of the house.

Both of them, Abu Kamal and Omar Husain, had much on their minds, much more than just the upcoming operation. The situation they now faced was unfamiliar. Abu Kamal Ramshallah, more than Omar Husain, felt he was literally on the run. And rightly so because he was now a known fugitive from the U.S. government. Finally going underground after years of living a comfortable, normal life in America was totally unsettling. He was doing his best to adjust and it wasn't easy. He looked forward to the day after the mission when he hoped to leave America and return to the life he left in Syria a lifetime ago.

For years, Omar Husain himself had been living an underground life in many ways not just in America but everywhere he went in the world. In that respect, he was used to this situation except this time there was this added complication involving his identity—one big reason why he wouldn't rest till he had Julie Santorelli.

But now, could it be she was telling him the truth? That they now knew who he was and what he looked like?

The two men sat facing each other for a while without saying a thing, in their silence knowing what each was thinking, what burden they carried inside. Abu Kamal had made contact with the leaders of the Organization in the homelands, once to report on what happened to the company in Dearborn, Michigan, and the company officials, including him. A second time to report on the planning of Operation Capitol West which the Organization was counting on them to pull through successfully even more than their previous missions in America.

Omar Husain knew, as he told the men earlier, his days in America at this time were numbered. Like Abu Kamal, he longed for the successful passing of the next seven days, after which he planned to return to his native Lebanon for some rest and contemplation.

But at the moment, he was a man much more burdened than Abu Kamal, and more now than at any time since he returned to live in America a year ago. It wasn't the fear and worry of the enemy, not even the fear of dying, this burden. It was something else he knew was in him, taking time and space in his consciousness, in his heart and mind.

Something from the past that began on that day, a whole lifetime ago. That fateful day she brought him the Book. Never in his life before then had he imagined ever laying a hand on the Christian Holy Book. But, lost in the fire of young love, nothing came between them—him, an inquiring young Islamic intellectual at twenty and seventeen-year old Kamilah (perfect), a Lebanese beauty raised in America by a Christian mother and a Muslim father.

When she asked him to share her knowledge of her mother's faith, he opened his mind willingly to it, not knowing that the day he turned the cover of the Holy Bible, he would from then on suffer this burden of the spirit. It had been like an overseer that never slept, lurking in his subconscious and coming forth everytime there was a flare of anger and hatred in his mind or whenever he turned east to say a prayer.

He had been trying to ignore it for many days now, since the weeks of the past Ramadan. But it just kept coming back, each time becoming more and more persistent. It had become a voice coming behind everything he did, every decision he made. And there was a person behind it, a woman, from a distant time and place; her words soft and fragile and yet overpowering him with its pleading and loving kindness.

He remembered when it encumbered him most strongly, one day several weeks ago during his morning prayer, and again that same day during the evening prayer. He prayed for peace among all peoples of all beliefs, as it was taught and learned in the Quran by all the faithful, and immediately the voice came leaping in his mind, triggered by the prayer, seeding his mind with unfamiliar thoughts. Thoughts of conflict and inconsistency between the motivation behind his actions in life and his prayers and especially the *hadiths* that spoke of the many good things written in the Quran which he had recited for many years since youth and tried to live by, at times successfully and at others not quite so or not at all.

It was these, these conflicts within him, in his heart and soul, that now burdened him more than anything else did. It felt as if the flame of hatred and anger he had harbored for most of his life since the deaths of all his loved ones at the hands of the enemy had started melting away. And within him, he had been struggling to keep the flame alive and burning.

He resolved time and again that he must never forget what had been taken away from him, and those who took them away must pay. There can never be room in his heart to forgive and forget.

But then in his *salat* during any of the five times in the day, the voice would come in his mind and speak of the opposite. And then he would pray for it. Pray for peace and reconciliation, for the Almighty to fill everyone's heart and mind with kindness and humility. Again and again, the voice in his mind would speak: *For in kindness, there is no greater wisdom. In humility, no greater peace.*

It tore him apart inside. And he would shut his mind and turn a cold heart. And he did, until the next prayer of the day.

Sitting at the end of the table with eyebrows knotted, deep in thought, he suddenly shot to his feet involuntarily, pushing the chair inches away behind him, almost toppling it. Abu Kamal, sitting two arm lengths away at one side of the table, gave a start.

"You must rest," he said to Omar Husain. "There is much left to do before this is all over. But it will soon be over."

"I will, don't worry, Abu," Omar replied. "I will just see to downstairs, then I will join you for lunch."

CHAPTER 31

▼

The basement floor at the back of the house where the bedrooms were was seven feet below grade. The only window was a fixed-glass opening looking out to an areaway, a small trench outside to allow some natural light in. The ground sloped fast from the rear to the front and side of the property so that out in the basement living room, the door opened out to a patio on one side. But in the bedroom where Julie was kept, all around was solid masonry wall but for the small areaway opening.

The walls were thick and well insulated so that the silence was pervasive. In this silence, Julie had no trouble organizing her thoughts, keeping herself calm and rational. She had almost totally convinced herself that these people were not in the drug business. Not mobsters but—terrorists.

Their business is not making money, she thought. What they do is driven by ideology, world politics and, no doubt, culture and religion. Money is not the object of their operations. They must already have money. It's the disruption of social order, society, and the killing of their perceived enemies, through the menace of terrorism. That has to be their objective, driven not by material gain but sheer hatred of America, her allies, and what she stands for.

This gave her an idea how to communicate to them, this Omar Husain, for a start. Apparently a well respected leader, and firmly in command, from what she saw up there. She wondered what they're up to at present—another air hijacking, suicide bombing, or another all out armed assault like the Pentagon II? She also wondered for a dozen times now what they planned to do with her, and when?

There was an entertainment cabinet which covered a length of the bedroom wall at the foot of the bed. A small stereo and a 20-inch TV sat on top of it. She had turned the tube on earlier in an attempt to relax. It had been more than an hour since she was locked in the room. But nothing on TV interested her. Not the news or the daytime talk shows.

Now she started to feel the isolation and confinement. And she was thirsty, and getting hungry. So she decided to rap on the door and demand some attention, an audience. What else was there to do?

Masoud Faisal, her guard, was sitting at the far end of the living room near the door to the patio soaking in some sunlight. He raised his head from the newspaper he was reading and got up when he heard the banging on the bedroom door and Julie's muffled voice behind it. At that same moment, Omar Husain came down the stairs and followed him to the door.

As soon as Masoud unlocked the door, it swung in wide open and he was quick to stand in the middle of the doorway to block it. "What do you want?" he asked, looking down at Julie standing three feet in the room holding the doorknob.

"A number of things," she said pointedly. "I want something to drink, something to eat, and I demand to talk to somebody."

Omar Husain, standing behind the guard, said something to him in Arabic and Masoud stepped aside.

"Yes, of course," Omar said politely. "We are just getting something ready for lunch. That's what I came down to talk to you about. Please." He motioned her to follow him to the side of the living room which led to the area of the dining room and the kitchen.

She followed him to a breakfast table in the kitchen where he offered her a seat but she remained standing. Masoud hovered close behind her. When he turned and spoke to her, she looked closely at him to ascertain once again, that he was indeed the same man as the picture that emerged in the FBI's laptop computer. And he was, without a doubt, when he turned to pour her the glass of water she asked for from a decanter he took out of the refrigerator, and handed it to her.

She observed him closely every moment, listened to his tone of voice, the way he said things, the way he moved and looked at her. Gradually, she formed an idea how to talk to him, what kind of language to use.

He didn't look like the killer type although now she wondered if he would not have shot her at the park if he had caught up with her. Being a leader and obviously one who had the high regard of his followers, he let the others do what needed to be done as she saw in the park. But that didn't change her perception of him as being no different than the man who pulled the trigger, or her belief that he would have done it himself if he had had to.

There were several things she wanted to ask him at once and she knew he knew this. Thus, when he sent the guard back out to the living room and asked her again to sit down, she complied. Then she geared up to start asking her questions. But he opened up first before she could speak.

"I am ready to listen to your questions but I won't promise I will give you an answer to every one of them," he said, sitting down across the table from her.

"The first one is—what are you going to do to me?"

"We will hold you for as long as necessary, and then we will decide what next."

"And how long is necessary?"

"A few days from now. A week."

"Why? Why not tomorrow, or day after tomorrow. Or two weeks from today? A month?"

"That I can not tell you."

"Who are you people?" she asked next, expecting to get no straight answer or any answer at all.

He knew that was coming next. Contrary to her expectation, he wanted to give her an answer. Not a direct one, but something to tell her what they represented, what brought people like them about into the world, particularly here in America, and why they did what they did. Including the killing of Robert Grundell.

They locked eyes for a few moments. She—waiting to hear any kind of an answer he might give her, not at all counting on anything meaningful or substantial. He—sizing her up, the knowledge and interest she might possess of the cultural and ideological issues that by sheer luck or perhaps the will of the Providence brought the two of them together at this kitchen table today.

Sitting five feet away from her wasn't the same as watching her come out of her car in a parking lot from a greater distance. Now, knowing the words to say to her—even as he had decided long before that nothing about her as a person, especially as a woman, should get in the way of what he must do, wasn't as easy as he thought it would be. As he felt in the parking lot, again he couldn't see her as a threat. And now, he found it even harder to imagine destroying her, doing her harm in any way.

He stood up and turned his back to her, unable to sustain her gaze. She felt triumphant. Clearly, she now thought, this was not the kind of man capable of a total disregard of human life. This was a man with certain sensitivities, a good amount of intelligence and some measure of personal values he would uphold to a great extent.

"Who are we," he said more to himself, looking through the window across the room. Turning slowly to her, he continued: "I can only give you an answer to tell you what we are. We are a people at war. A people just like you, Americans, who would fight to the death defending their way of life, their belief, their culture, and their land."

She sat looking up at him, now more convinced of the kind of people she was dealing with.

"You're terrorists," she declared in a calculated tone of voice.

That changed the calm expression on his face quickly to a look of anger, much to her surprise.

"I could shoot you right here now and end your life for saying that," he said, his eyes suddenly drilling fear into her entire being. "But then you would never realize how wrong you were to think that of us and not of your government and its allies, in Israel, Europe and the whole Christian world."

Scared as she had never been before hearing a threat to her life as real as the presence of the man who said it, she summoned enough strength to sit still and keep herself from falling to pieces. She kept her eyes at him in a daring expression, even defiant. Behind this, she now shuffled new thoughts with old ones. About him, about their operation, and about her chance of coming out of this alive.

Indeed, he may be a man of certain values and sensitivities, but those very same things, when defied or threatened, could very well be what turned him into a cold-blooded killer in the blink of an eye. After what he said, she no longer doubted who they were and what they were about.

She was right from the first about their business. She must now make an adjustment to how she communicated with him and the rest, first by making sure she didn't give any of them enough reason to kill her.

The moment of anger had passed and a look of calm had returned on Omar Husain's face.

"I'm a school teacher," she said, stating a fact. "I teach mathematics. I only see things as they are, based on what I learn about them. I see people as they are. Christians, Muslims, Jews and anyone else in between."

"There's more to what people are called," he argued.

"I agree. People become known by what they do, how they behave, not by what they're called."

"But not here in America," he countered. "When a Muslim blows up a bus in Jerusalem, crashes a jet plane on a building, it's called terrorism, not war. And he's branded a terrorist, not a warrior or a soldier. When America and her allies invade a weaker, defenseless country and kill innocent people, women and children by the hundreds, thousands, it's called a liberation, a fight for freedom and democracy. And Americans are viewed as heroes, saviors, from the eyes of those who benefit from their killing. Not terrorists, not murderers, not evildoers as they are viewed by those they oppress, those whose culture and way of life they destroy and replace with theirs. The world never hears of these oppressed people who are rendered voiceless, because they're either denied the freedom to be heard, or they're dead."

There were so many ways she thought she could respond to that but she chose not to, now knowing how she should feel her way around him first, avoiding the sore spots. She sat quietly, keeping her expressionless eyes at him and waited to hear more.

He paused and drew a long breath. It felt good to have been able to let that out on somebody, an American, particularly this type. Educated, middle-class at least, and apparently of above average intelligence.

There were a great many other things it would feel good to let out of him, things he had bottled up inside for as long as he could remember. What he would do to have the freedom and the opportunity to voice them all out, to be heard by all these infidels throughout the western world, starting with this country. What he would do if only he had the power to make them understand, not with violence and bloodshed but with trust and understanding, with words of reason.

Once again, he was filled with regret more than anger that his enemies had always left him with no choice but the path of war and violence. They simply would not listen. How he longed that wisdom and compassion would prevail upon them one day to make them listen so that the bloodshed, the horrors and the heartaches may soon end.

He was lost in thought for a long time when suddenly he heard one of the men from upstairs standing in the living room addressing him.

"Commander?" It was one of the guards.

"Yes. What is it?" he asked.

The man from Dale City had arrived and was very anxious to report to their leader. Also, food was being ordered from a carry-out and they needed to know what people wanted to eat. They gave the man their order then Omar Husain called Masoud in the living room and prepared to leave.

"Wait for just a minute, please," Julie said, getting up quickly and standing in his way. They came within three feet of each other. Being that close to her gave him a sense of vulnerability. He wasn't sure how much he bared the effect she had on him. He looked at her as coldly as he could, a man with no thoughts or feelings that concerned her whatsoever, wishing this were so.

"I'm sorry for what I said." Her voice was subdued and true, and this went a long way into him. He struggled to maintain his cold appearance and he did, not easily. "It was good that you sounded out how I had upset you. I had no idea. But we must talk more. I have other questions."

"I know you do, but not now," he said hurriedly. "It'll have to be later."

He motioned Masoud as he turned to go and the guard escorted Julie back to the bedroom.

*   *   *   *

Chris Phillips had called in sick for two days now since the gruesome night in his place. He kept thinking how lucky he was that he wasn't one of the two who got shot. He still had a hard time believing it all happened right there in his living room. A dead terrorist and a police detective with a near-fatal bullet wound, not to mention him doing battle with another terrorist, chasing the man and shooting him.

And it's not over yet. Everytime he turned around, he was hung up with the idea that it was just the beginning. Now, with the disappearance of Julie, everything that had happened so far had been for nothing. Everyone was in a quandary. The police, the FBI and most of all the Santorelli family. Not to mention himself.

He'd had very little sleep the past two nights. Jim, his brother, came over the following day while he was working hard scrubbing the bloodstains in the living room and Jim too couldn't believe what had taken place the night before. He said he wished he had been with Chris when it happened. But thank goodness Chris came out of it all right.

Between the local police and the FBI, he had hardly found time for himself. The cops invited him to the station and got all the information they could out of him. So did the FBI. Today was more of the same. The Feds, two agents, came and took him with them to see Julie's parents in Chevy Chase. That wasn't something he had looked forward to after he learned the horrible news from FBI agent Bartley yesterday afternoon that Julie had been taken. Actually, it was he who had asked to go with them and be kept abreast of what was going on.

Richard Bartley came with agent Doug Jones, the partner of Hector Gomez who was on duty at the time and saw Julie at school get into the car, willingly, with a man. She had been missing since then. What happened was anybody's guess and Chris suspected that nobody outside of Gomez himself would ever know. And who knows what story Gomez, who incidentally wasn't on assignment today, could come up with?

Joe Santorelli, Julie's father, had to help his wife absorb the shock when they were first told. It took him awhile to come out to the living room and listen to what the agents had to say further.

It was a repeat of what Chris had already heard when they came to pick him up. It all felt and sounded so helpless. Nobody had any idea where Julie had been taken. Anything could have happened to her by now.

The house in Dale City where, they had been almost certain, she was taken turned up only a couple of college students who were now in custody on suspicion of being connected with terrorist activities. How they connected the house to Julie's abduction was one thing, the only thing, that the lawmen had hoped would come to anything—either Julie's whereabouts ultimately or at least someone who would lead them to her. The car that was supposedly used by the abductors had appeared on the surveillance videos taken at Julie's apartment for several days. The vehicle's garage residence address was at the house. The car, a Pontiac Grand Am sedan, and the car owner weren't in when they raided the house, and neither were Julie and her abductors.

At this point, no one had any doubt who one of the abductors was. In the video from the night before, he was seen with another man, identified as the owner of the Grand Am, going through every room in Julie's apartment.

They now had a positive ID of Saladin in live video for the first time ever. A nationwide all points bulletin was issued immediately for the Grand Am following the raid of the house in Dale City. The same was done for the Ford Mustang Cobra that was seen in the surveillance video the night of the break-in at Chris Phillips' place.

The Bureau, however, continued to keep Saladin's picture and identity a secret. This was what Joe Santorelli, not knowing who Saladin was, got into a heated argument with the FBI agents about, after he had been listening to them for a few minutes. Chris stood right beside Julie's father on that.

Joe Santorelli insisted that the government release all the information they had on the man immediately, telling the FBI agents that it could very well be what could free his daughter from her captors. The reason they took her was to prevent her from identifying them for the murder. With their identity known, there wouldn't be as much reason for them to keep her.

He knew her daughter, he said. She would reason with them that way and try to talk them into letting her go.

Richard Bartley argued that he was following orders from headquarters. It was policy decision, he said but which he himself now thought had grown thin in the last couple of days. Joe Santorelli got upset and raised his voice at the agents. "The hell with office policies!" he argued. "It's my daughter's life that's at stake here!"

Chris got into this and made a slip, saying to the agents: "They must do it now. Release the identity of Saladin to the media immediately. Every minute he thinks he remains unknown to the government, he feels Julie is a risk to him and his operation."

Joe Santorelli turned to Chris first, then to Richard Bartley and asked: "Who is Saladin?"

The three men in front of him exchanged glances like there was something icky they passed around between them which no one wanted to end up with. It was Richard Bartley who wound up with it, finally taking on the unsavory task of telling Joe Santorelli who Saladin was: the man the Bureau had been after for at least two decades now but was unable to positively identify; the man who the government believed had been responsible for a number of terrorist attacks in America and other parts of the world; the same man who the government had positively identified as having plotted, engineered, and executed the suicide bombing of the Veteran's Day ceremony at the Punchbowl Memorial in Hawaii.

And—it followed in Joe Santorelli's mind—the man, the sonofabitch who killed my brother. And now, now he had my dear sweet Julie too. God Almighty, he thought in anguish. Why us? Why my family?

He looked, glared at the men in front of him one after the other, including Chris. But with him, he softened the angry look on his face a little when he finally noticed the bandage that held the thick lump of gauze covering the stitches on Chris' forehead.

Chris simply lowered his head apologetically and waited to be scorned by the man. He was relieved when Julie's father, instead, raised a hand and gave him a pat on the shoulder.

Bartley continued: "Sir, I agree with you and Chris. It is time to release the man's identity. The reason to keep it secret has absolutely nothing to do with the killing your daughter witnessed at the park. It is a matter of national security. We want this man caught so bad the government would do anything not to jeopardize any chance we might have of finding out who he is, where he is, what he is doing or planning to do and who he works with. But now that we have positively identified him, I believe it would actually be more advantageous for the world to know what he looks like, who he is and what he has been doing."

He went on to say that he would do everything he could today, the next hour, to convince the office to uncover Saladin to the media immediately. He looked at the time. It was a few minutes before eleven in the morning. With some luck, he said, it would be in the 'breaking news' of all the network and cable newcasts before six o'clock tonight.

Then his phone rang. It was agent John Jacobs. He had assigned JayJay and Hector to continue searching for any leads they could dig up in the Dale City house. Jacobs had thought of something, real simple he said and real dumb of them for not having thought of it earlier in all the excitement during the raid.

He and Hector had gone back to the house which was now in the state of government quarantine, to check up the telephone units in the house one more time. There were two. One upstairs in one of the bedrooms. That one had a caller-id where they found over a dozen numbers they'd already investigated and turned up nothing. Lots of junk calls, telemarketers. The other one was a cordless in the living room. It had several features in it. A built-in caller-id, a phone-number directory and a memory that stored the last ten numbers that had been dialed on the unit for re-dialing. The numbers displayed in an LCD window screen on the phone along with the time and date they were used.

The calling numbers were the same as the ones captured in the unit upstairs. They found one of them several times. The same number of times it showed in the re-dial memory. This turned out to be a significant lead. It was the telephone in a house in North Arlington on Military Road, owned by an Egyptian family.

The big tip-off came from the telephone company which reported records of calls between the house and numbers listed under MidEast Continental Ltd. of Dearborn, Michigan, and other numbers in other Detroit suburban areas.

The same two SWAT teams that were used in the Dale City raid were re-assembled immediately and were now preparing to raid the house. Target strike time was 1600 hour. Bartley told Jacobs he and Jones were on the way and would be right over. Good work, JayJay, he told his partner. He hung up and turned to the men around him to tell them what was happening.

On their way out of the house, Bartley stopped a moment to take the hand Joe Santorelli offered gratefully while saying: "I didn't mean to be rude to you. I'm sorry."

"Not at all, sir. And thank you for your courage, Mr. Santorelli. Don't worry too much. We're doing everything we can to find this man. And we'll get your daughter back safely. Please tell your wife too."

They drove to Arlington first to drop off Chris Phillips before proceeding to Washington. Along the way, agent Richard Bartley spent no less than twenty minutes on the phone talking to his Section Chief and the case analysts, trying to convince them as he told Joe Santorelli he would, to reveal Saladin to the public. It was a battle as usual between the field and the headquarters.

Most ordinary field agents usually didn't stand much of a chance with head-quarters especially on something like this, a high-visibility case, national security, involving an international figure. But as one of the senior agents in the Bureau who had built himself a good service reputation, Richard Bartley commanded an audience at headquarters. People inside listened to this one field agent. They had, many times. And the times they did, they never regretted it afterwards.

When they finally agreed with him after Bartley described the agony the Santorelli family was going through at the moment, discussed at length the rationale behind not keeping Saladin a secret anymore, they hoped this would be another one of those times they wouldn't regret.

They told him they'd have the Bureau's Communications and PR working on it right away. Listen to the news within the next three to four hours.

CHAPTER 32

▼

Listening to Muhammad Shah, the man from the house in Dale City, report what happened, Omar Husain imagined the government's fishnet now cast over a wider area and closing in on everyone fast. It had been a costly mistake on his part. Hopefully, the losses would not go beyond the houses in Dale City and the one in Baltimore.

He had the Grand Am and the Mustang Cobra removed from the house and hidden in the garages of other houses. Then he posted Muhammad Shah who came in the Toyota Land Cruiser SUV in place of one of the lookout men on the road. He would recognize a government raid better if one came, having seen it himself. The uniforms, the vehicles, the approach and the deployment.

Ahman Farooq, the man from the Baltimore house who had had the same experience as Muhammad Shah, replaced the other roadside lookout man on the other side of the house. He too came in an SUV, a Ford Explorer.

Omar Husain then posted one of the two former lookouts just off the front of the house in a car, a Buick LeSabre. He was given orders to take off in an emergency, drive a couple hundred yards down the road to help, along with the lookout SUV, pick up people from the house coming out of the backwoods. The other one he posted in the house with the other guards.

He had been feeling edgy about remaining in the house since yesterday and had spoken to Abu Kamal Ramshallah and the men about relocating to another safehouse. Either the one in Bethesda or Reston.

Everyone in the house had been constantly on alert after hearing about the raids. Some suggested moving out to some inexpensive motels like many of the other people from yesterday had done.

It was half past two in the afternoon. He had meant to go down the basement twenty minutes earlier to talk to Julie as he had promised her the day before but he had been tied up on the phone most of the day. In the meantime, Julie had turned on the TV in the bedroom to catch up on the news. At exactly two o'clock, a 'breaking news' came on CNN from the Press Room of the FBI. It was about the continuing investigation of the Punchbowl suicide bombing. The lead was the identity of the man the FBI finally revealed as the mastermind of the attack. He had also been linked to a number of other terrorist attacks over the years in the U.S. and abroad.

Julie nearly dropped the bottle of spring water she had been drinking when the picture of Omar Husain appeared on the screen. One of the FBI's most wanted men in the world, the news reporter announced, finally identified. Because he had been unsparingly using many aliases with his disguises, the government not knowing his true identity had pursued him over the years in secret. Until now, said the reporter.

However, no one is still sure, the news report continued, what his real name is. Records from the Bureau's worldwide investigations listed such names as Sulaiman Zatari, Yussuf Zadran, John Tyler, Sultan Salahudin, Rahim Akbar, Muhammed Moussa, among many others. For years now, he had only been known by a code name chosen by the FBI—Saladin.

Omar Husain was on his way to the basement after he finally got done with the phone calls when he heard Khalil Majid, up in the second floor, calling him to come up quick. He rushed up the stairs and walked into the bedroom where he found Khalil Majid and Samir Osmani, now sitting up in a chair, watching the same news Julie was watching in the basement bedroom.

He froze for a lot longer time, it seemed, than the five minutes he watched. The fishnet was closing in faster than he thought. He felt pressured, personally threatened as he had never felt before. He was right and so was everyone else, he now thought, to be constantly on alert and to keep all the lookouts on the road and in front of the house. He told the two men in the room to keep watch through the window from here on.

He was ambivalent about the code name they had given him. At first, he felt flattered that he would be likened to the man considered to be one of the greatest leaders of the Muslim world, a wise and benevolent warrior, the curse of the Crusaders, conqueror of Jerusalem. On second thought, he felt how irreverent it was of them to use the great leader's name in a way, perhaps, to show contempt and disrespect for the Muslims.

Only five days now remained to Operation Capitol West. He couldn't let anything happen to throw it off after all the planning and preparations these past few weeks. It would be a big disappointment to the Organization. Their primary interest was to see it happen. Nothing came before it, not even the loss of their leaders, even Commander Omar himself.

With this in mind, he hurried downstairs to work out a contingency plan with Abu Kamal Ramshallah to cover the succession of command among the team leaders should Omar Husain be unable to function as their commander. They would gather the men back later or the next day to explain their decision and include it in the ops plan. Next, Omar Husain finally made his way down to the basement to talk to Julie. He was very curious to know, remembering what she said about the authorities knowing his identity, if she had seen the news about it. Even more than that, he wanted to know if she had anything to do with it.

When the guard, Masoud Faisal, let her out of her confinement in the bedroom, she looked different from the day before. She didn't appear to have any fight left in her. She looked subdued but underneath, Omar Husain could see the upset, the anger at the hopelessness she felt. He could tell she had a lot on her mind. He was curious to hear what it was and waited for her to open up. And she did.

"You sonofabitch!" she snarled at him, surprising the two men standing no more than four feet away from her, Masoud on her left, Omar on her right. Before either one saw it, her left knuckles were on each side of Masoud's nose-bridge so fast he didn't even know it as he went floundering a few steps back from the impact. Then it was her right-foot snapping on Omar's face, again so fast it caught him on the chin as he was turning back to her from looking at what happened to Masoud. He stumbled a few steps back facing the ceiling, feeling his brain bouncing around like a ball loose inside his skull.

She kept after Omar as he was recovering from the front-snap kick. He took another hit from her, a roundhouse kick to the ribs before Masoud jumped her from behind and subdued her by looping his arms around her and immobilizing her with his sheer size and strength.

"You murderer! All of you!" she screamed at Omar, struggling in Masoud's massive arms.

"Commander?" Masoud said, his eyes querying his leader for a quick answer. From the expression on his face, it sounded and looked as if he awaited an extreme order: whether or not to kill her now simply by breaking her neck or strangling her.

"No!" Omar replied firmly, waving him down with one hand and feeling his chin with the other. "I came to talk to her and I will, for now."

"Yes, talk to me," Julie said in a voice shaking with anger. "Talk to me about how you killed my uncle, how you murdered him and all those hundreds of other innocent people in Hawaii who couldn't care less about what you're fighting for, what you believe in!"

Omar stood still for a long moment, studying her. The anger burning in her eyes, the hurt mirrored on her face and the tears now smeared all over her face like that of a child as she continued to struggle helplessly against Masoud's hold.

There was no point talking to her at present. She was engulfed in a storm of emotions stronger than he had anticipated. He waited till it had peaked, her energy spent and she started to calm down. One of the house guards came running down the stairs to see what the commotion was about. Omar turned to him briefly to tell him there was no problem and told him to go back to his post.

He took time turning back to her while a number of things went through his mind at the same time. They had both seen the news about Saladin but only within the past few moments, that had given way to what he just learned from her. Seeing her now slumped in Masoud's arms, exhausted, resigned, jarred him more than he expected. To his surprise, all the apathy, indifference and vengefulness that had withstood the thoughts and images of death and destruction of past operations did not hold up against the sight of her—lifeless, spent and uncaring about her fate at his hands.

But he could not let this happen. Not now. Not ever. He must remain strong, apathetic, stoical. Soon he will be out of this country, back to his homeland, and all these would have come to pass like an illusion.

He said something to Masoud in Arabic and the big man hauled Julie back into the bedroom. He dropped her in bed face down and went out to the living room, leaving Omar standing just inside the doorway.

She didn't move a limb. It looked like she was out but she was just numb. Tears kept fogging her eyes, now wetting the bedcovers. She cried quietly from grief and sadness now that she had used up her anger and fighting bravado, reason and practicality setting back in.

For several long minutes, Omar found himself unable to say or do anything while he did battle with the demons within. What's happening to him now, after all these years? Why can't he just destroy her and anyone else that may get in their way and move on with the plans? Simply obey the orders from the homeland without regard to the consequences especially to the enemy.

They're fighting a war. Wars are meant to be deadly, violent and destructive. They must be victorious or be subjugated, dominated if not altogether destroyed by the enemy. Their way of life mocked, despised and a different one forced upon them. But when he thought of Julie outside a moment ago struggling in anger and grief, and now crying helplessly in bed, resigned to her fate—whatever that might be—at his hands, he backtracked from all that, the voice again speaking in his mind, telling him differently:

'What good is a victory if it turns you into your enemy?'

He argued with the voice, recalling the day in June 1982 when he had come home only a few days ago from the madrassas he was attending in Pakistan, just finishing up a rigid two-year study in Islamic fundamentalism. The Israeli invasion had began early that day and reached their location in southern Lebanon by midday.

The IDF rained mortars mercilessly on their village, one of them demolishing their home. As the dust and smoke cleared, images came to view: his parents bathed in blood, torn to pieces; his twelve-year old sister, Hibah (gift), herself bathed in blood but still alive, crawling out of a pile of rubble, one arm reaching out to their dead parents. And him, then only twenty years old, miraculously alive though critically wounded, rushing to claim her in his arms and take her away from the ruins of the house still coming down on them.

She struggled against his hold, desperately trying to free herself to go to their mother and father, hauntingly similar to the sight of Julie a moment ago struggling helplessly to free herself. He ran away cradling her in his arms as fast as he could, for the mortars kept coming. Half a kilometer later, he took cover at the ruins of an ancient stone building that had been hit earlier, behind a thick wall where he found a wooden cot covered by a rug. There, he rested the bleeding Hibah, his beautiful sister and only sibling.

For a few moments, he watched her lie there motionless, exhausted, her face covered with tears, again much like Julie now lying in bed. He spoke words of comfort to her to make her feel safe. But she did not respond. She was dead.

That same week, in a refugee camp near Sidon, he learned that everything he held dear was lost. He went to visit Kamilah with whom he had made wedding plans only weeks before. But he never saw her. He learned from her relatives that she too was dead.

He continued to wrestle with the voice in his mind.

I do not regret what I have done, all these years, he argued, and what I have yet to do.

I am obligated to do them, for my people, my homeland, and Allah.

I am not the same as my enemy.

He started to leave but in the last moment lifted his head to look at Julie in bed. Instead, he saw Hibah lying there in the cot, covered in blood. Tears came to his eyes and blurred his vision. The same tears he shed more than two decades ago for his loved ones. He tried to prevent them but simply couldn't. He hurried to dry them with a tissue he quickly fished out of his pocket. And when his vision was again clear, he saw Julie sitting at the edge of the bed looking at him.

Suddenly, he heard himself say to her, his voice in agony: "I'm sorry. Please...I'm sorry—"

She herself had wiped away her tears before she sat up in bed and saw him with his head low between his shoulders. What she saw was a man troubled by inner burdens, his voice unable to conceal the anguish, the pain inside.

They held each other's eyes for a few moments, both caught in the confusion of anger and sadness in each one, for each one. Julie hated it that she should even glimpse a trace of humanity in him. She just wanted to curse him but wasn't able to. Omar loathed his inability to feel nothing for her especially at the expense of the memory of his family. He hated the voice in his mind. He just wanted to focus on the mission ahead and beyond when he would be back in the homeland, free from this confusion.

He withdrew his eyes from her and cast them down at his feet again as he walked out. Julie watched him until the guard came and shut the door. After what she just saw of him, she remained convinced he was not a cold-blooded killer. He was a man she could reason with. He was a leader, a thinker, and he had sensitivities that made him act and think the way he did. She wondered what those were. Something in the past. Something lost but not forgotten. She would find out. And she would, sooner than she thought.

*   *   *   *

The caravan of Bureau vehicles headed by the Chevrolet Malibu sedan with agent Richard Bartley at the wheel slowed down not long after it made the right turn to Military Road from Lorcom Lane. With him was agent Doug Jones in the passenger seat. Two dark armor personnel transport vans loaded with the SWAT teams followed. Behind these were two other sedans. The first one carrying agents John Jacobs at the wheel and Hector Gomez in the passenger seat. The last car had agent Eddie Green at the wheel and three other men newly assigned to the operation as reinforcements.

Bartley drove past a number of cars parked on the side of the road, seeing the Toyota Land Cruiser but not paying particular attention to it enough to notice Muhammad Shah sitting low in the driver's seat. He came to within fifty yards of the house on the same side of the road and stopped. The rest of the raid party stayed close behind within a car length of each other.

Muhammad Shah was on the phone as soon as he saw the caravan go by and was frantically punching the number he was given to call in the house. This looked exactly like a repeat of the scene he saw yesterday at the Dale City house. It was Commander Omar, he recognized right away, who got on the line. He spoke only a few words rapidly in Arabic to his leader. Get out now. Hurry. FBI raid.

Omar Husain was talking to Abu Kamal and Khalil Majid in the second floor study room when the call came. The first thing he did upon hanging up was tell Abu Kamal to give the emergency order to the LeSabre outside and order everybody downstairs to evacuate the house immediately as planned. He had Khalil Majid help the wounded man in the bedroom, Samir Osmani, get out of the house. Next he quickly gathered the personal belongings he had brought to the house the past few days before hurrying down the basement.

Four of the people in the house had exited through the backdoor, gone down the steps to the backyard and disappeared into the backwoods inside of three minutes. When the guard, Masoud Faisal, burst through the door of Julie's bedroom and ordered her to come with him, she resisted, wanting to know what was going on. It took another man—Kamran Salama, a sleeper from Baltimore and one of the house guards upstairs, to persuade her to come along. On their way out to the basement exit to the backyard, Omar Husain came down the stairs carrying a duffel bag and a woman's winter coat.

"You could at least have the decency to tell me where you're taking me!" Julie demanded, catching the coat he tossed at her.

Omar appeared to be a different man from the one she saw only a short while ago. He glared viciously at her and barked, "I don't have to tell you anything. Just do as you're told!"

One of the two guards remaining upstairs came halfway down the stairs holding a phone to his ear and called out to Omar: "Commander, they're coming!"

Omar ordered the men to head out the exit door to the backyard but the two men didn't make much progress with Julie resisting, delaying them further.

"They're here!" They heard the other guard upstairs call out. The first of the SWAT Team members had appeared on both sides of the road some thirty yards away from the property.

"There's no time," the guard at the stair said. "Commander, what do we do?"

Omar gave him an order in a firm and high-spirited voice, in Arabic, and the guard saluted him.

"*Inshallah.* Allah be with you." Omar said, returning the salute.

"*Inshallah.*" said the guard and went back upstairs to join the other. Their order was to do battle with the raiders, open fire now and hold their position in the house as long as possible, to the end.

Julie was bound and gagged after she put the coat on. Once she was adequately controlled, Omar stepped out to the backyard, waited a moment until the burst of gunfire from the house commenced and led their way quickly into the backwoods.

The first burst from the house felled three of the SWAT Team members, two of them killed instantly. This prompted an all out assault on the house. Both uniformed and plainclothes forces deployed rapidly as close to the front and the near side of the house as possible. They poured hundreds of rounds through every window visible from their positions. A hand grenade landed at the entrance and demolished the canopy above, the door and part of the exterior wall they were attached to.

After two minutes of the non-stop salvo, Richard Bartley gave the SWAT Team leaders the signal to cease firing. As quickly as the battle had erupted, an eerie silence—along with the snow that had started falling, as predicted for the day, now descended upon the surrounding. Everyone stayed low in his position in the ditch across the road, behind a tree or a ground cover. Bartley and the team leaders waited a full minute before they gave the signal for the troops to close in.

Two men rose from their separate positions and advanced a few yards, one scurrying behind a two-foot high tree stump on the house side of the road, the other one behind a power pole right across the road from the house. The next two followed, one of them zigzagging from behind a tree to another ten yards closer to the house. The other did the same but was cut down by a burst of 40mm automatic rounds that suddenly ripped through the silence before he reached the tree.

Bartley cursed himself as he watched the team member hit the ground face down with a bullet in his head, roll onto his back and lay there lifeless. Damn! He could see his career of nearly two-decades with the Bureau getting cut down too after this. Minutes into it, the operation had surpassed the number of casualties of Columbia Plaza.

For a while, everything was at a standstill. Nobody moved anything but his eyeballs. It was up to the SWAT Team leaders to make the next move. One of them, the one behind a clump of trees across the road with a direct view of the house, spoke to one of his men nearby who was carrying an M203 grenade launcher with his M16A2 rifle. The man, crouched below in the shallow ditch at the edge of the road, quickly got a shot ready and waited for the order to fire. The team leader then signaled the rest of his team to let out another salvo before he gave the order to fire the grenade.

The explosion blew out nearly a quarter of the house on its right side. It was followed by a succession of tear gas shots from two other gunners. In a matter of seconds, it looked like the whole house was on fire as it filled with smoke at both levels.

Inside, only one of the two house guards remained alive, barely. He bled profusely from head and body wounds but was determined to fight to the end as he had sworn to his commander. He held an AK-47 on one side of him through the kitchen window sill and a .45 caliber automatic handgun in the other hand. The other man lay on the living room floor in a pool of blood, dead from multiple shrapnel wounds.

The man in the kitchen knew he only had minutes, seconds, if that, before he's finished. The smoke tore at his eyelids and was suffocating him fast, so he opened up with both firearms in his hands, spraying rounds wherever he had heard shots coming. The SWAT teams responded with another salvo, another grenade, and in another few seconds, everything fell silent again.

Through a narrow footpath in the woods, Omar Husain along with the two men who held Julie captive had traveled over a hundred fifty yards when the Ford Explorer and the LeSabre in front of it came to view on the side of the road. The sound of the battle they left behind gave Omar a great sense of assurance that their escape plan was working. It was a clean getaway so far. A four-inch snowfall was forecast in the area. It looked like it could be an accurate prediction as it got heavier, the white stuff starting to stick and accumulate on the ground and the treetops. Julie felt glad for the winter coat but she fought any feeling of gratitude to Omar Husain.

She had decided minutes ago that there was no point resisting her captivity for the moment. Once she realized that a battle had begun and that she was caught in the middle of their plan of escape, she simply let her captors drag her along. There was nothing to gain struggling but the risk of getting shot dead for holding them up further.

All four of them got into the LeSabre, Julie and her two escorts in the back seat. She felt glad when her gag was taken off and was too exhausted to offer any resistance when she was blindfolded. Before getting in the front seat, Omar took a moment to look back down the road and listen. Everything had quieted down from the deafening ruckus of a minute ago.

He thought of the men they left behind in the house and said a brief prayer for them. "May Allah be merciful," he said in his mind. Then he got into the car quickly and told the driver their destination. He looked back and saw the Ford Explorer, now half covered with snow, get on the road behind them.

CHAPTER 33

▼

The snow came steadily for the next forty-five minutes. Turning south from North Glebe Road in north Arlington to the GW Parkway, they got in the middle of the rush-hour traffic and crawled for miles. People in the area were so paranoid about snow. Give them an inch or two and the whole region freezes. Schools closed or were delayed two hours and there were all kinds of cancellations.

Omar Husain didn't mind at all as the Buick LeSabre plodded along the parkway through the whole of Arlington and Alexandria, past the Pentagon, Reagan National Airport and downtown Old Town. In fact, he even felt glad. What better way to elude your pursuers, not that he thought they had any, than lose yourself in a crowd on a snowy day?

Past the Beltway and into Fairfax County, they picked up speed, the Ford Explorer keeping close behind. Ten minutes later, they made the switch from the parkway to Fort Hunt Road still going south towards the house where he had taken up residence the week before. A right turn to Old Stage Road and another, past a middle school, to Stockade Drive brought them to a one-story brick split-level with a full basement, the fourth house on the right. Three bedrooms with two baths on the ground level, one in the basement with a half-bath. Julie was deposited and locked in the basement bedroom.

The four inches of snow predicted did come, looking more like five or six by the time it slowed down. By six o'clock in the evening, the suburban roads were hardly navigable. Then the temperature dropped to the twenties.

Julie found out soon enough that the room did not have enough heat. Later in the evening, she was about to bang on the door to ask for a blanket when one of her guards came with fried chicken, french fries and a glass of soda for her dinner. He left, came back a few minutes later and tossed her the blanket.

Other than the bed and the nightstand next to it, the furnishings consisted of a dresser, a chair, a small bookshelf with a 14-inch TV on top. She wrapped herself with the blanket while still wearing the winter coat, sat in the chair and ate the chicken in front of the TV.

She was tired, and hungry, but she no longer agonized over her captivity. After seeing how determined these people were—none of them gave much thought to engaging the government forces in the gunbattle and sacrificing however many lives they lost in it—she decided the best thing for her to do was try to be as tough as they were and be equally determined to face whatever lay ahead. Letting herself be sad or angry anymore would only cloud her judgment and lower her defenses for her survival.

At eight o'clock at night, news of the 'FBI raid on a suspected terrorist hideout, a house in north Arlington, Virginia' finally hit the airwaves. Network and local stations picked it up at the same time and for the next whole hour, everything else in the news media got shoved aside to cover the item from every angle and anybody's point of view, even those who weren't there and barely had anything to say about it. The local police, the neighborhood residents three blocks away, some cab drivers.

Julie watched intently every minute of it for a half hour, surfing the channels, waiting to hear one authentic account of what did happen, what it was really all about—a government operation to rescue a murder-witness hostage abducted by one of the murder suspects who happened to be Saladin, newly identified by the FBI as one of its most wanted terrorist figures in the world. But there was none of that in any of the coverage, local or national. She learned that three SWAT Team members were killed, several others wounded, and two suspected terrorists armed with automatic assault rifles and high-power handguns were also killed in the encounter. Everything that was reported came from government people who took over the scene after the participants in the event had left, and from local 'eyewitnesses' who didn't witness but only heard what happened.

For the next three days, Julie was to see no one except the two guards who stayed in the basement rec room outside, when they brought her food. She alternated passing her time between the TV and the paperbacks she found in the bookshelf. She didn't sleep in the bed after she inspected it the first night. She saw yellowed maps on the mattress and the sheets so she took the bedspread instead, folded it in half on the floor at the foot of the bed and slept on it bundled in the winter coat with the blanket over it.

For three nights, she didn't sleep till after one in the morning. She got in the habit of worrying about how worried everyone was about her—her family, the school, and Chris. She wished somehow there'd be a way to get in touch with him, or any of her family. When she turned the light out to lie down, she heard footsteps upstairs. She tried to listen to their voices too, including those outside her bedroom, but they spoke mostly in Arabic.

Then she would slowly drift into a light sleep, curled up in a fetal position on the floor, in the same clothes and with the same personal possessions she had in the tote bag which she kept near her under the bed. For two nights in a row, she fell half-asleep and then there were sounds that woke her up. They sounded like the same ones she tried to listen to when she was fully awake, intensified in the deep silence of the night.

But there were other sounds from a different source, she couldn't be sure where—from some distance outside the house or maybe inside the house but from another room in the basement, or maybe even in her room coming from the closet, the bathroom or under the bed. It wasn't a voice. It was more like an electronic sound. Very faint, somewhat like a tune that played in a cell phone but slower.

The weather remained much the same the next few days. Temperature rose to the thirties and went down again to the twenties. Snow came again two days later, less than two inches, and it got even colder. Julie thought she wasn't going to last much longer before she froze to death in that room. Then late in the afternoon of the third day, Omar Husain suddenly paid her a visit.

"I have to get out of this room or you might as well just shoot me dead," she told him, breathing fog, wrapped in the blanket she kept on all day.

He was clearly taken aback by the sight of her. He wanted to show some sympathy but would not afford her this. Instead, he spoke to her in a gruff voice, saying: "I'll see what I can do," and left. A couple of hours later, he came back to move her into one of the rooms upstairs. It was one of the two bedrooms he occupied, the one he used as a work room next to the one he slept in, and where he said his prayers five times a day.

On one side, it had a double bed which looked much cleaner and appeared it hadn't been slept in. The door to the bathroom was at the foot of the bed. At the opposite wall was an office-size desk with two chairs and at the wall where the door was, a mirrored dresser and a 20-inch TV set stood next to each other. Across the room from this was a double-hung window looking out to the woods behind the house. It had been nailed to its side frames and sill to make it permanently shut and inoperable as she found out later in the night when she tried it before she finally decided to go to bed.

Julie sighed with relief when Omar led her through the door and she felt the warm air in the room. Much as he avoided thinking about it, he couldn't help feeling bad that he had let her suffer in the cold room downstairs. Like she said, he could've just as well put her out of her misery in captivity by shooting her. But at this point, after the visions of 1982 in the other house, it was no longer a question that he was incapable of doing that.

For the past three days, he cursed how they had happened to cross paths in life. The Punchbowl bombing and her uncle, the killing of Bobby at the park. At the same time, he fought the feelings he had growing for her. That's why he avoided seeing her since they arrived in the house.

And then there was that voice that came and intruded during his prayers through the day. It seemed there was no foreseeable end at present to the struggles with his inner burdens. One thing he knew would help unload them was being able to voice some of them out to those whose lives had been touched by his actions, by his sworn duties and commitment to his Faith, his country and his people. He must justify himself to them, especially to Julie.

One of the men staying in the house followed them into the room carrying a tray of hot water, packets of tea, instant coffee and the works, as Omar had ordered. He placed it on top of the dresser, gave Omar an obedient bow and left.

"Please," Omar Husain said, holding out an open hand to Julie. She had unwrapped the blanket and was now taking off the winter coat too which she dropped on the bed along with the tote bag.

Omar closed the door partially, leaving an inch gap while Julie helped herself to the hot drink. They could sense the need to talk to one another. Julie spoke first with her back to him after taking a long sip of tea while she stood looking out the window.

"Please let me go," she said to him, not demanding or pleading but making a simple, rational statement.

"I can't do that," he answered plainly.

"What does it matter now that I saw what I saw at the park?" she said, still with her back to him. "What does it matter that I saw you there? That's just another crime you're involved in. They want you more for the killing of hundreds of other people, God knows how many others, including innocent victims."

"Collateral damage. That's what they call them in this country. Innocent victims. The term given by your government, specifically their killers both in the military and civilian armed services," Omar explained matter-of-factly. "When they plan an operation, they project a number of casualties on both sides, including a percentage of collateral damage. Innocent victims who are none other than the local people of the land, the country they're attacking or invading. What we've been doing is no different than what your country has been doing everywhere in the world. The only difference is nobody hears as much about it or not at all when you do it."

Julie finally turned around and regarded the man standing a few yards from her as if this was the first time she'd seen him.

"This country has never done and will never do anything like the Punchbowl bombing," she countered. "No one in the government, the media or the American people will ever allow or condone any such act as strapping explosives on a living human body or hijacking an airplane and killing innocent people with it. Thousands of innocent people, many of them were not even Americans or people you have nothing against.

"That's not our way. We will never attack any person or place that does not mean us harm. But if we do, it will be as an act of self-defense. That is our way."

"That's what you believe," Omar replied, a half-smile forming at a corner of his mouth. "Or are made to believe. From all that you are allowed to know. Of course you never see it done by your people. It's because either you're never told about it or they have it done by somebody else. They pay their allies and armies of hired killers to do it. The almighty American dollar does it all. In a way, I don't blame you and many other Americans for seeing things only from the American or the Judeo-Christian side. You are as much a victim of all your government's lies as we are."

"We have laws that govern everyone's action in this country without exception, especially those in government, including the president."

"Don't talk to me about your president and your laws!" Omar said, screaming out the first few words and then lowering his voice toward the end. "Your American laws! They're nothing but a convenient way to justify and hide your aggression and interference in other people's way of life. Listen," He paused, holding out a hand and lowering his head for a moment to gather his thoughts before continuing: "You want to know what it is that has been preventing our people and your people from seeing eye to eye? Or why they don't—see eye to eye, just like you and me right now? It's because Americans only see things from their own point of view. You are completely ignorant of how things look from somebody else's point of view. It's all about point of view."

Julie took a sip of the tea, pulled one of the desk chairs to her side of the room and sat down. She was just going to sit and listen for a while. Might as well get comfortable for she can see that Omar Husain, or Saladin as he was now known to the world, had much more to say and she wanted to impress upon him without saying it that she's willing to listen to his point of view. If that's what the problem is between them and between his people and her people.

He can let it all out on her, she thought, especially if that's what it might take to win her freedom. She'd have to hold herself back, though, and not contradict what he was saying no matter how strongly she felt against it.

She tried—not very successfully.

But Omar was desperate to be heard even by this one American that he made room for her arguments even as she got somewhat impudent. The urge to justify his actions as well as those of the Soldiers of Islam he commanded, had gotten too strong to hold back.

We are not murderers! We are not terrorists! We are soldiers, the same as your armored Christian crusaders who took our land and ravaged our people for two centuries. The same as your soldiers now deployed in many Muslim countries, and many other countries, imposing American power upon other people in their own land! The difference is, we are fighting to defend our way of life, our freedom to worship the way we want, to preserve our belief, our culture and tradition. We simply want to exist the way we want for ourselves. We do not force our way upon others, like you do.

Julie almost leaped up from her seat on this with:

We are not in those countries by force; we are asked and welcomed to be there; and we're not there plotting to kill and destroy like you do.

But she sat tight through it and listened some more.

Now, as if he read her mind:

This country does more evil than its victims think. When it forces its way upon other people, sometimes it does it with bullets and bombs. In reality, it's better that way because you can fight it fair and square even if it has more firepower than you. But other times, it uses lies, propaganda and brainwashing. That's when America works its evil ways the most—when it forces its values upon innocent people. Planting seeds of discontent and contempt, in their hearts and minds, contempt for their own way of life, and making them believe and adapt the American way. The American way of thinking, the American way of behaving at home, at school, everywhere. The American way of worshipping God, and the American way of living one's life altogether. This is so wrong, so uncalled for. This is a most vicious form of aggression.

That she was not able to take in silence. She had to say something just to get it off her chest.

"Someone knocks on your door," she said, "you don't have to answer it. And if he comes again, you open the door and tell him to go away."

"You open your door and your hungry children see the food he carries with him," Omar said disdainfully. "You see the devil with all the temptations he possesses, then you're finished. That's how America does what she does so well."

"Then you must make yourself stronger. Don't blame it on the devil. Blame it on yourself for not being strong enough to resist the temptation. You have a choice."

"You have no right to exploit our lacking! You prey on the weak, the hungry, the underprivileged people everywhere. You evangelize to them, capture their minds and turn them against their own culture and heritage. You poison their minds with your depravity, you defile them and rob them of their dignity!"

"They have a choice. You have a choice!" She repeated, raising her voice, for a moment abandoning her discretion. "All we do is show you—possibilities! Possibilities to better your life, to help yourself out of your lacking. What's so wrong about that? We mean no harm! Can you understand that?"

Their exchange accelerated in the next few minutes. It was no longer just Omar Husain trying to justify his actions, past and present, and arguing the values and traditions his people were trying to preserve against the corrupt and immoral western culture. It was Julie as well, trying to do the same for the actions of her country, her government, defending the merits of a democratic society, the preservation of human dignity, the respect for each individual human life and, yes, the pursuit of happiness, material comfort, pleasure and all that which Omar only saw as unrestrained debauchery. As they dueled, Omar appeared to have proven himself right about one thing—that each one, more often than not, did not care to see things from the other's point of view. Because either they come to a point where one refuses to do so for fear of being cornered to submission or for being so stubbornly ignorant of the other, being so self-righteous, fanatical or held down by some xenophobic prejudice.

Omar: We will not tolerate America's disrespect for our values and traditions. Our way of life! We will not be ignored! We will fight your meddling, your secret interference, your incursions into our society. We will make you pay a high price for what you're doing if we have to come here and disrupt your society, the same as what you're doing to ours.

We will defend our country, our people and natural resources from your economic and ideological exploitation. We will show no respect for your values, your belief and anything you hold dear in your life, the same as what you have been doing to us. We will make your mothers and children weep. We will bring them the same sorrow and grief you have caused us, until you see the evil in your ways and you leave us in peace in our land.

Julie: America has nothing against anyone's values and traditions. If it does, it can not survive. It might not even exist. You know why? Because it is a country founded upon the good in those very same values and traditions from different peoples and cultures of the world, including yours.

America is nobody's country and at the same time it is everybody's country. People here are now descended from every human race in the whole world. This is God's country if there ever was any that came close to being one on this planet! This is every people's country, people who believe in human rights and all the freedoms necessary to make something out of their lives. Freedom to think and believe as they choose, freedom to dissent, freedom to change and better themselves.

Omar: That is a lie! America is not my country. This country is a Judeo-Christian country. It is dominated by Anglo-Western-European cultures and traditions that despise and defile the Muslim people all over the world. It supplies three billion dollars worth of economic and military aid to its outpost in the heart of the Muslim world—that American puppet country, Israel—to kill our people and continue its exploitation of the region. It poisons the minds of our innocent people and turns them against their own country.

It's no different than an outright colonization of our land and people. That's what America is doing and we will continue our struggle to stop it no matter what it takes and how long it takes. And take your so-called American way some place else. Don't keep shoving it down our throats. Not everybody wants to look like you, behave like you, think like you and live like you.

Julie: Why don't you ask the millions of Muslim and Arab Americans who live in this country?

Omar: They're no longer our people! They're the sad victims of your vicious exploitations, lies and deceptions. They're lost people. People without a country, without values, without self-respect.

A couple of more minutes of that brought Julie to believe they could carry on another couple of hours or even the whole day and not get anywhere. Like spinning their wheels in the mud. The time they had just spent talking, from each one's point of view, might as well be the hundreds of years that the conflict between the two sides had been going on. As far back as the start of the Crusades in the eleventh century, the entry of King Richard the Lion Hearted into the fray, and the emergence of the real Saladin himself.

It was obvious how they both needed to uncork so that after a while, they felt relieved, cooled off mentally and emotionally. They started to see each other again as single individuals, not as representatives of a people or a culture.

But now, Julie saw something even more about Omar than she did before. He was undoubtedly a man of high intellect. A loyal follower, one who would die—or kill—fighting for what he believed in. He was also an effective leader, likeable and for that reason easily admired by his followers and commanded their great respect as she had seen the past few days.

Much as she detested it in herself, like Omar she wondered what it would have been like between them had they met under a different circumstance or, at least, had they not come from such conflicting backgrounds. And again, like Omar, she thought how impossible it was that now she would even care to look into his character, be curious what manner of a man he was and—for the most impossible part of it all—feel any kind of sympathy, sadness, for him and have a sense of loss in the way their paths in life had crossed.

What's happening? Here she was in captivity by one of the FBI's most wanted men in the world, a sworn enemy of her Church and country, a man she feared and despised for the killing of her dear uncle, and she allowed such thoughts and feelings in her about him.

It was all so difficult to comprehend. She grappled with herself internally late into the night but it did not get any easier. Not until she remembered something he said earlier—why they don't see eye to eye; it's all about point of view.

She allowed for a moment that he was right about her in that regard, and put herself in his shoes, so to speak. Then, as if lost in a dark night and now finally seeing light in the way ahead, she began to understand those thoughts and feelings she had for him. A man of such intellect and integrity is of great value to whoever, whatever, he supports. And so it is a sad thing to see such character in a person become an instrument of discord. But more than that is the loss of opportunity for the person himself to live a peaceful and happy life. And to share such life with loved ones. This was what the sadness she felt for him was about.

Sitting at the desk trying to get into the first few pages of a paperback she found on the nightstand beside the bed, she remembered vividly the look on his face hours earlier when they talked. She had noticed, not for the first time, that he always had that far away look in his eyes. Like a yearning to belong, or an expression of some irrecoverable loss. He was always quick to hide it with a frown or an induced expression of anger. But the times it showed on his face, she caught it and took note of it. She remembered thinking that this man carries a lot of burden although he appears to have the strength of mind and body to bear them. For he is a thinking and patient man. True to his purpose in life and whatever motivates him.

Presently, she let go of the paperback and laid her hand on top of another book with a black leather cover. At the same time, her eyes fell on a couple of pictures on a built-in shelf in the wall above the desk. The one on the right looked like a family picture: a young mother with a six- or seven-year old daughter sitting on her lap; close to their left the father standing behind the son, fourteen or fifteen years old. It was black and white and had partly faded around the edges over the years. A date printed near the lower right-hand corner showed Jan/1977.

The picture on the left was of a young girl, perhaps fifteen or sixteen years old with a shy look in her eyes in a half-smile. Dark long hair gathered over her left shoulder. Centered at the bottom, a handwriting read: Kamilah, 1979.

She can only guess how Omar Husain must value that family picture, for him to be taking it with him wherever he went in the kind of life he had been living. She wondered where they were now, what had happened to them since it was taken. She would not venture to guess who Kamilah was. She was definitely not the little girl in the family picture.

She took it off the shelf for a closer look. What a lovely young girl. She had no doubt what a beautiful woman Kamilah must have grown to be. She turned it around to look at the back of the frame as she was putting it back on the shelf but held it momentarily. A handwriting similar to the one on the front read: d. June 1982.

She put it back on the shelf and looked at the back of the family picture next. That too had the handwriting: d. June 1982.

She sat still for a couple of minutes. It was almost ten o'clock. In the silence of the night, she could almost hear her thought as she weighed what she learned about him, that which must be a very significant part of Omar Husain's life, and what appeared to have happened to it. How and why, she found it hard to imagine.

And so did Omar Husain, even after more than twenty years, since he wrote that date on the back of the pictures. A great part of him died with them on that day, with Kamilah as well. There was nothing left to his life in the world, nothing but to make the enemy pay for what they had done.

Julie pulled herself back from her thoughts and found herself looking at the black book which she now held in front of her. For some strange reason, she felt fixated to it.

She turned the cover and saw that it was the Holy Bible. Now she felt even more drawn to it as if it exerted an irresistible power upon her. An odd sense of familiarity swept through her. It was comforting and for one swift moment brought her the memory of her aunt, Sister Caterina, who had passed away a few years ago in Rome shortly after retiring from her career mission in the Philippines. She held the Bible closer, puzzled by how it affected her, and then she was back to her thoughts of Omar Husain.

She frowned upon this discovery. A Muslim who is a devout believer and a formidable defender of Islam, reading the Christian Holy Scriptures?

Even some of the Jews she had come in contact with over the years and had known personally wouldn't come near enough to turn its cover. The Jews do believe in the Messiah and his coming but according to them, it is yet to happen. They would not accept that it already did with the coming of Jesus as the Lord, the one and only Son of God. But for a Muslim, especially such a leader as Omar Husain, to be found with a copy of the Holy Book instead of the Quran was even more surprising to her.

It could be that the copy did not belong to him. Maybe it was just there like anything else in the room. The TV set, the furniture, the other books. Perhaps the owner of the house from whom they may be renting it owned the book.

All that speculation went out when she turned the book at a place marked by something which turned out to be another picture of Kamilah, a larger one—four by six black and white, dated 1981. It showed her, two years older, noticeably grown into a beautiful young woman. Pressed against it in the book was a yellowed two-page letter folded in half. Julie hesitated only for a moment before she unfolded it. She'd take every opportunity that might help her understand her captor better and deal with him more effectively.

Dearest Omar,

I really appreciate that you have expressed an honest interest in wanting to read the Bible and learning about my mother's religion. I think it's wonderful that we accept each other as we are.

I wish my father had been more like you in this respect. Open-minded and intelligent enough to give himself a chance to see things from someone else's point of view. I'm glad that my mother has the strength to stand up to him and does not just submit to his demands. I think they have finally come to a common ground where they agree to respect each other's belief.

Although I feel glad that this now brings peace in our family, it puts me in an uncertain place, not only in our home but outside of it as well, espe-

cially that between us. You are a Muslim and what am I—half-Christian and half-Muslim.

I knew this is what would happen even while I was growing up in America, before my father brought us back here to Lebanon five years ago. It had been difficult for me since then, but thank God you've come into my life.

Both my mother and father like you very much. I hope by knowing about Christianity, you will also learn the other half of me, and know me better as a whole person.

With much Love,

Kamilah

Julie sat for two minutes relishing the sweetness of every thought she just read of a young woman in love, imagining Omar when he first unfolded the letter as a young man, feeling the love and truthfulness in every word Kamilah wrote. There was so much feeling it raised in Julie that tears came to her eyes.

Curious about the place in the Bible where she found the picture, she looked at the page and saw that it was in The First Book of the Kings of the Old Testament—1 Kings 3. Before she knew it, she was reading about King Solomon's reign in Israel when he went to Gibeon where he made sacrifices at the altar there.

She read about the Lord appearing to him in a dream in which he asked God to give him wisdom, *'an understanding heart to judge the people that I may discern between good and bad…',* instead of a long life and riches for himself.

She read about the king arising from his dream, going to Jerusalem and there facing two women who stood before him, each claiming to be the mother of a child.

'Bring me a sword,' the king said in the book. *'Divide the living child in two, and give half to the one, and half to the other.'*

And the true mother, whose *'bowels yearned upon her son'* spoke to beg the king to *'give the other woman the living child, and in no wise slay it.'*

But the other said *'Let it be neither mine nor thine, but divide it.'*

And the king answered: *'Give her (the true mother) the living child, and in no wise slay it. She is the mother thereof.'*

Julie sat for a minute admiring the human drama she just read, its simplicity and effectiveness, even if she had read it many times before. Then she returned the letter and the picture of Kamilah where she found them and closed the book.

There was plenty of hot water left in the thermos Omar brought in. She made herself a cup of tea, sat up under the covers in bed and turned the TV on. She was still feeling the relief being in this room now, thinking about the cold she had endured for three nights in the basement. She had been in captivity for five days. After today's exchange with Omar Husain and the revelations that came out of it, she felt less fearful for her life at his hands than with his followers. In fact, she now saw him in two ways—as her captor and her protector.

But now, knowing who he was since the escape from the other house, she had gradually resigned to the idea that he won't let her go. She started thinking that her role itself in this personal crisis had changed from a murder witness to a hostage.

The most she was hoping for now was that whatever it was they had coming up shortly—a few days, a week, when Omar said they would hold her as long as necessary—would happen soon. Anything to see any kind of resolution or change from her present situation. Of course the best thing she could hope for was another operation to rescue her, and a successful one. But what were the chances now of anyone looking for Saladin finding him?

What could she do to help? With her locked up and guarded twenty-four hours a day in the room, she simply dismissed the thought of this altogether. Any possibility of escape was non-existent at all. And communicating with outside? The only possibility was breaking out of the room quietly in the middle of the night and getting to a phone in the house. But if she could break out of the room, why not just break out of the house and run like hell to a neighboring house or anywhere—a gas station, a fast food store, any public place, for help?

She flipped through several cable news networks, thinking maybe there'd be something on Saladin, or even her. Nearly all of them were simultaneously covering another major event in the Middle East between the Palestinians and the Israelis. The never-ending crisis. Another Israeli army task force of a dozen or so tanks with support helicopter gunships rumbled into a Palestinian section of the city of Hebron in the West Bank. Several buildings suspected of being a training site for suicide bombers and snipers for Intifada activists and Hamas Islamic fundamentalists were leveled. This was in retaliation for a suicide bombing of a commuter bus that killed ten people a few days ago in West Jerusalem.

This must be the longest on-going conflict between peoples in the entire history of civilization, she mused, feeling distressed just thinking about it. And how much longer would it go on, she wondered, how many more peace talks and broken agreements would there be? How many more people killed, homes destroyed;

how much more anger and hatred and human suffering before it all came to an end, if ever?

One land, two peoples. Two beliefs, two religions, but all descended from one patriarch, worshipping one God, one supreme being.

Julie glanced at the Bible on the desk across the room. She couldn't help imagining the similarity of the whole thing to what she had just read in The Old Testament. A king endowed with wisdom from God made a judgment and upheld the truth. If only a similar judgment could be made to settle the age-old conflict over the land one people calls Palestine, another calls Israel. But...no. It is as if King Solomon sleeps and is yet to arise. Oh, if only he would. Soon.

Suddenly feeling tired physically as well as mentally, her eyelids getting heavy, Julie started to fall asleep. As she drifted away, her mind continued to work with the last thing she had in it. As if the words had a life of their own, half-consciously she recited a few times—arise, King Solomon, arise.

A few minutes later, just before she was completely lost in sleep, a sound came to her ears. It persisted in the silence of the room many times. The same kind of sound she heard the night before. Faint, electronic. A series of two short and three long pulses, repeating in regular sequence. She started drifting back out of sleep and listened to it half awake, eyes partly open, trying to figure out where it was coming from. It lasted another fifteen, twenty seconds perhaps for a duration of about one minute and then it stopped. She closed her eyes again, sank deeper under the covers and fell asleep.

*   *   *   *

Brigit Santorelli had decided to stay with her mother in Vienna from the day her cousin Julie disappeared. For the past three days now, since she remembered the proto-type copy of the ESCard V2 she gave Julie to test, she had been making the call to it, hoping against hope for three things: that it worked and, second, if it did, it would not jeopardize Julie's position wherever she might be at the time and, third, that she would have it where she could hear the call signals. She was counting that if Julie had the smart card with her, she would also have the manual with it, in case she needed it.

It was twenty past ten at night. She was pretty sure the call she just made to the V2 went through, for she heard it ringing. Question was—could Julie hear it too? She let it ring for a whole minute before she hung up. She had been making the call late at night the past three days, thinking that would be the time Julie would most likely be by herself. Maybe she should also try calling another time.

The wake-up time instead of just the bedtime. In fact, she might have better luck with that when Julie would be fresh, rested, and she could hear the signals better.

She was positive the card worked. There was only one thing she thought might be a problem—the solar-powered battery might be dead and needed to be recharged. Again, if Julie had the manual, she would know that all she needed to do was put the card under a light for twenty, twenty-five minutes—any ordinary table lamp would do—to load up the photo-voltaic cells of the strip battery with enough voltage to power all the circuits in the card. But first she must remember that she had the card, *if* she had it with her.

CHAPTER 34

▼

It was a pleasant ride, thought Kashim Najoub of the trip they took to Pittsburgh the day before on the Capitol West train from the Union Station in D.C. A bit long—over eight hours. There were six men who started out. Two teams of three. One led by Kashim Najoub and the other by Marwan Razzak, the man from New York, a graying mild-mannered man one would think did not keep with the company he did.

Kashim's team members got off at Martinsburg, West Virginia, Marwan's the next stop an hour and a half later at the Cumberland, Maryland station. The two team leaders then continued on to Pittsburgh and spent the night there. They drove back today in a rented Chevrolet Monte Carlo and had just now arrived at the house in Fort Hunt, Alexandria, to report to Omar Husain in the final hours of preparations before the launch of Operation Capitol West tomorrow.

Everything appeared to be as they had expected from all the information they had been gathering over the past two weeks. The layout of each car of the superliner train: the couch and the sleeper cars, the dining and the lounge cars. The actual departure-arrival time between stations which averaged within three to five minutes of schedule. The crew which consisted of two conductors, one engineer and twelve service personnel, and the approximate number of passengers the train carried—under two hundred.

There were a few who got off before Pittsburgh and a few who got on after the train left Union Station. They were hoping this would be the case. The plan called for the men now in Martinsburg and Cumberland to catch another Capitol West train that would be leaving Union Station in D.C. at 9:40 A.M. tomorrow, and it would be good if there were other passengers boarding with them so they wouldn't be the sole focus of attention if anyone was watching. The same with Omar Husain and the two men with him who would board at the Rockville, Maryland station, the first stop from Union Station.

Everyone agreed it was a good plan, thanks to Bobby Grundell's drop. From it, they learned that Union Station would be closely watched. The place would be crawling with the Feds and the D.C. police. Only four men would board at the station. Two together and the other two separately. They would scope the situation at boarding and in the train, from one end of it to the other as soon as it got on the way, and relay the information to the rest in the next three stations.

On their way back in the Monte Carlo, the two team leaders made a detour stop in Martinsburg and Cumberland to meet with the men there and see how the details of the plan checked out. Everything does, the men reported of the two train stations. Nothing to worry about security in boarding the train. Both stations were unstaffed. People boarding the train were supposed to have purchased tickets already someplace else and all they had to do was be at the station on time and hop in.

The two men Omar Husain had sent out to Rockville earlier reported the same setup at the station when they returned. Nothing at all to cause any change in the plan.

There were seven men already in the living room of the house when the two men arrived from Pittsburgh in mid-afternoon. They were immediately served refreshments, given time to relax from the long drive. Then Omar Husain and Abu Kamal Ramshallah gathered everybody around for the final rehash of the plan of operation for the next day.

They went over every single detail they'd gone over several times, days before, making sure everybody involved understood his part in it. Each man was made aware that his responsibilities throughout the operation, whether or not he lived to see the end of it, were solely his. He was not to expect anyone else to take over if he was rendered unable to handle them. He had his orders in the name of the Jihad and he must carry them out to the ultimate sacrifice of his life if needed.

The meeting went through the rest of the day and into the early evening when Abu Kamal reminded everyone of the fourth *salat* of the day. The group then wrapped it up and everyone knelt on the floor facing the direction of the *Makkah* to begin their end-of-day prayers.

Later at night, after dinner was served and some of the men had left, Omar brought Julie tea. He found her holding the picture of Kamilah in her hand, admiring it.

"She's very beautiful," she said after pouring herself a cup.

"Thank you. I was going to marry her, twenty-two years ago," Omar said, surprising Julie with such casual openness, and himself as well. "But she died suddenly. Another innocent victim of this insane conflict between two peoples."

Julie, standing near the desk holding the cup of tea with the other hand, lowered her head through a few moments of silence. "I'm sorry to hear that," she muttered, meaning it well. "It's such a tragic waste."

"Yes it was," Omar replied, stepping up to reach for the family picture across the table on the wall shelf. "And so were they," he said, looking at his long gone family. "I was twenty years old. Hibah, my little sister, was twelve, when it all ended for us. The Israelis rained artillery on our village for several hours that day. One thing I could never forgive myself for, even more than what the Israelis did to us, was having survived that day. I would have done anything if there had been a way to trade my life for theirs. But, no. I am the one who must live. The one who must live and suffer this anger and hatred all these years, and be a part of this unending war. Turn a cold heart to all the killings, the death and destruction of—yes, even innocent people."

Julie was caught off-guard by this outpouring more than surprised. For the past two nights since she first saw the pictures, she looked at them while having dinner, reading a book or watching TV. She had a pretty good idea what happened to everyone in the pictures based on the handwriting she found on them. She would look at one and then the other. The family picture, a well-balanced unit: husband-wife-children; mother-father-son-daughter. Just like her own family.

Then she would focus on the young man and move her eyes to the picture of Kamilah. She didn't have to guess who they were to each other, what they meant to each other. She imagined them together, alone, and with the family. The happy days. Life was young and in bloom. Then one day it all came to a swift end.

Now, twenty-two years later, it didn't surprise her at all to hear him spill it out perhaps for the thousandth time. Exactly the way she felt when her uncle Steve was taken away from the family. When she first saw the news and talked to her cousins and their bereaved mother, at the funeral, and lately at the Thanksgiving dinner table.

Before she dwelt on this another moment, she snapped out of it, refusing to relate her experience of life's tragedy with his, denying him any sympathy and understanding. But with the picture of Kamilah still in her hand, she struggled to turn a cold heart at him, at what he had been going through, at the kind of life he had to live.

This was not happening! This can not happen!

She can not let herself feel anything for this man after what he had done, not only to her family but to a lot of other people. She reached over the desk to replace the picture on the wall shelf, making a conscious effort to obliterate the image of Kamilah from her mind.

It was more than she could bear thinking of her uncle while facing the man who took him away from them. She turned her back to Omar, afraid she'd bare one shred of sympathy she was trying to smother inside her.

She wished she hadn't learned anything at all about him. She'd much rather have him here now as someone similar to one of his men even if she constantly feared him for her life. She hated finding herself now fighting against any kind of feeling about him. She just wanted to continue to despise him, spend every moment thinking of how to escape and get away from him, defeat him and make him pay for what he had done.

But now, behind all that, a new kind of awareness had come into play, rising from years of Catholic upbringing at home and school from an early age. She couldn't turn around and tell him she hated him any more than she could say one more word to comfort him more than she already had.

She wanted him to just go away without saying another word. Time felt at a standstill as she waited. But she didn't hear him step out of the room. Instead, she heard him say: "I'm deeply sorry about your uncle. Please accept my apology."

Instantly, a wave of anger rose to her head. But as quickly as it had come, it gave way to a calmer feeling the moment she had turned around and was facing him, looking at a man weary of his grief and burden in life. A needful and helpless man. A very lonely man.

Now she had lost herself and felt as helpless as he appeared. They were two people in conflict with each other and with each one's self. Omar regretting the life he lived and yet knowing only that what he had done and was yet to do tomorrow was all he lived for. Julie not knowing which part of her now to put forth—the hurt and angry one or the sympathetic and forgiving.

Suddenly, she heard herself say to him, not with malice but resignation and a touch of pity in her voice: "And I am sorry for you. I am sorry for the life you lost, and what's left of it. But I hardly think one's grief is worth those of so many other people. What you and your people have done is selfish and cruel and can never be justified in any way. I don't care what faith or religion, what ideology you're coming from."

It was hard for him to stand there and listen to that. It mattered to him what faith one had, especially his, for this is what he and his people lived and died for.

But now, there was a part of him that stood up before this, a voice in his mind questioning his faith and raised by what Julie said.

He wished he had not lived to see this day, to be standing in this room before this Christian woman and find himself wavering in his belief, tempted to make something out of what's left of his life from the tragedy of long ago.

"Whatever you think of me," he said in a low voice, almost a whisper, "or whoever you think I am, I accept freely. I only hope that you don't hate me."

"I don't hate you," she responded. "As I said, I feel sorry for you. But it isn't too late. It is never too late to start living again."

"I have nothing to live for but what has kept me going all these years. That is all I know and care about."

"You know that's not true. I know you don't believe that. But you must keep up the anger and the hatred of the Jews and of us Christians and anyone you perceive to dishonor your faith and reject your way of life. So you'd rather spend your whole life trying to get even rather than to find peace with your enemy, and with yourself. You know that never works and never will. That's why this war you're fighting never ends. You get back at someone for something he did to you and do the same thing to him, you're no different than he is."

If Omar knew a way to silence her, he would have done so before she got to the end of that. But now he couldn't even stop the voice in his mind:

What good is a victory if it turns you into your enemy?

He took a step backwards, toward the door, as if afraid to be nearer her than where he was standing. In truth, he was trying to get away from himself, that part of him that was just now seeing how much he had been in denial. But the other part of him would not give in. Rather, he would not let it give in.

"I am not like my enemy!" he argued to Julie, inching farther away from her. "My country is not the same as America or Israel. We are not the same as you Americans or the Jews in Israel. We are not the oppressor. We are the oppressed!"

Julie watched him closely as he spoke while backing away to the door. This was what she saw of him. A man in retreat—from the life he had fallen into—but who would not admit it to himself.

Now she wished he would not leave. She wanted to speak to him more, help him overcome his self-denial. And by doing so, she thought, perhaps prevent further bloodshed and violence in the future, save lives and spare the world the same grief that had come upon her family.

She now saw a totally different man from the one she saw a few days ago. He gave her one last look before turning to leave. It was a long look, pleading, helpless and full of self-pity. She put her head down for a moment and breathed deeply before she stepped forward to go after him. But when she looked up, he was gone.

*   *   *   *

She opened her eyes with the impression of coming from a long sleep. And the first thing she tried to comprehend, or remember, was how she got into this place. A prison cell. She was looking through a full-height wall of cell bars so fat she couldn't even wrap her hand fully around each one of them. There was no door on it. Only a glass-paned window which was odd being in a cell wall. It was exactly the same window that had been nailed shut in her bedroom so she couldn't escape.

What's even more odd was that she was looking directly at a vast expanse of land starting right outside the cell. It was green and flat. Above was a clear silver sky. At first, it was all quiet. Then a moment later, she heard a distant hum coming from the sky. It got louder as it approached rapidly. Next, she saw a crowd of people appear from the left side of the green field. They were running as fast as they could diagonally to the right. Her impression was that they were trying to get away from the increasing thunder of noise in the sky.

Then a monster of a fighter plane appeared above, sweeping low and cutting down many of the people under it with a long burst of devastating gunfire. She watched in horror as bodies, torn to pieces, were scattered throughout the green field. Those who survived continued running and disappeared from her view. But more appeared where they had come from. Julie recognized some people as they got nearer. One of them was her uncle. Another was Kamilah. They were running near each other, almost touching, as the sky rumbled with another approaching fighter plane.

All of a sudden, Omar Husain came to view from the right side. He was hurrying to get to the two before the plane started shooting. But it was coming too fast and there was nothing he could do to save them.

Julie had the impression that she was watching a war movie as she kept her eyes on the approaching aircraft. It was so vivid, coming fast, closer and closer until she could actually see and recognize the pilot when he turned the guns on his helpless victims below.

The same moment she heard the deafening gunfire, she saw the face of the pilot. It was Omar Husain.

She bolted up from the bed, staring catatonically through the window. She let out a long sigh from a deep breath and shook her head. She was half awake, her eyes heavy with sleep. The curtains were partially drawn and for a moment she looked hard to see what's out there. It was pitch black outside. She pushed the light button on her digital wristwatch which showed 5:15 AM.

She slid down under the covers and went back to sleep.

Two hours later, she stirred and slowly became conscious to the now familiar sound she'd heard before for several nights now. Except this time, it's early morning.

She pushed herself up in bed so she could raise her head slightly and listen to it more carefully. As before, it was a series of two short and three long pulses, repeating in regular sequence. Somehow, perhaps because she was fresh from sleep and her senses were sharp when they initially get to work, it sounded a little louder and she was able to home in on its source easily.

It was coming from under the bed. When she looked under, she had no doubt it was coming from inside her tote bag which she had stored near the edge of the bed where she could easily reach it.

She hurried to look in the bag and realized the signals were coming from inside her purse. Prying it open, the first thing that drew her attention was a speck of light blinking on a corner of a card in one of the rib compartments of the purse. The instant she realized what it was, she got so excited that she had to suppress the squeal that nearly escaped her throat.

Brigit, her cousin, was calling her—and she had been for days now—on the ESCard! Why didn't she think of it sooner, the first time she heard the signals days ago? She took the smart card out as quickly as she could before the signal stopped and pressed the tiny answer button with the tip of an index fingernail.

"Hello! Hello, Brigit! Can you hear me? Hello!" she said under the bed as loud as possible, hoping no one could hear her outside.

She held the card close to her ear and listened. At first she thought the tiny voice she heard from it was a play of her imagination. So she held it closer and closer until she was pressing it to her ear. The transmission was fragmented as it came out of the tiny speakers embedded in the smart card.

Julie heard: *Ju......you......erre? Can y.....er......me? ....lie...wh.... a...you? ...ell me wh......are!*

"Brigit! Speak louder! I can't hear you!"

Brigit had been out of bed for fifteen minutes when she made the call as she had planned the night before. She went downstairs first to make herself a quick cup of instant coffee, came back up to her bedroom and made the call with the cordless home phone.

She knew Julie finally answered her call this time because the ringing stopped long before she had intended to hang up. They stayed connected for nearly two minutes before the line cut off and her dial tone came back.

Although she didn't hear anything back, she believed Julie heard her. The card had a special long-life rechargeable standby power cell that lasted weeks and allowed it to receive transmissions anytime. But the main battery might be quite low in which case there would not be enough power to transmit. Seconds before the line cut off then, she hurried to give Julie instructions which she managed to repeat twice.

I can not hear you, Julie! You need to recharge the card battery. It's solar. Just put the back close under a table light. Twenty to twenty-five minutes. Got that? Then call me right away.

Just before the line cut off, Julie got busy putting together pieces of words coming from Brigit. The third time she heard them, she was able to put the message together clearly.

She was reeling with excitement as she crawled back out from under the bed and bumped her head on it. There was a table lamp on the desk which she found had a 65-watt bulb in it. She didn't waste a second to follow Brigit's instruction.

Her hand got hot under the light after a minute so she put her gloves on. Then she switched hands under the lamp every few minutes.

Ten minutes later, there was knocking on the bedroom door. She put the card back in the purse and turned the light out.

"Just a minute," she called out as she headed to the bathroom.

The knocks came again after a few seconds. Then she heard the door being unlocked and Masoud Faisal came through the door.

"Coming in," he said, carrying a breakfast tray. He put it on the desk as he had done before but this time he didn't leave until she came out of the bathroom. When she did, he told her: "Get ready to leave in half an hour."

"I don't imagine you're anxious to tell me where we're going," she said.

"Half an hour," he repeated and stepped out of the room. Instead of closing the door, he swung it wide open and sat in a chair outside to keep an eye on her.

She wondered what's happening so early in the morning. Whatever it is, she thought, it's perfect timing for them to decide to keep her closely guarded, just as she was about to get a break and bring her ordeal to an end by calling for a rescue. On the other hand, as she had thought before, she welcomed the possibility that the day had come for a change in the condition of her captivity. Any change at all would be better than being dragged through day after day of this confinement.

She sat down at the desk and had the breakfast—tea, buttered toast and scrambled eggs. The time on her wristwatch read 7:35 AM. While she ate, she listened carefully for every sound she could hear both in the house and outside. Earlier, she remembered hearing somebody, could have been two people, leave the house. A few moments later, she heard a car start and leave the driveway.

With the door wide open, she could hear voices coming from the outside. The far end of the living room or back in the dining room. They spoke rapidly as if they were in a hurry. And they were not speaking in English. She could tell people had been up much earlier than she was which gave her the impression that everyone was now getting ready to leave. Something was definitely afoot. She must get through to Brigit, or anyone outside—Chris, her father, the police, the FBI, anybody.

Damn! She came so close to springing a surprise on Saladin and his men and bringing this whole crisis to an end. She needed fifteen minutes more for the card to recharge. Maybe not even that long. Ten or five. Maybe she could make the call even now. But now she had to have the opportunity to do it and make sure she didn't get caught.

One opportunity she realized she had right now, sitting within a short arm's reach of the desk lamp, was to continue to recharge the card. A ten-inch high file-holder box on the desk hid the lamp partially from the view of the guard at the door. She could hold the card under the lamp for another ten minutes at least. Perhaps that would be enough. Only thing was, she hoped the guard wouldn't notice when she turned the light on.

No problem. She dropped the fork with the scrambled egg on it for a moment to pick up some papers from the file-holder box and, very casually, turned the light on. Masoud Faisal turned his head slightly into the bedroom. He briefly glanced at Julie reading the papers while eating, the fork back in her hand, and looked away again.

Now Julie let go of the fork again from her right hand and took the smart card out of her purse on the desk. She held it up as close as possible to the light behind the ten-inch high box and pretended to chew on her breakfast while reading the papers in her left hand.

She had been looking at it for two minutes before she finally focused on what was written on the paper. She had wondered what was going on so early in the day since the guard came and there it was, the answer, right in her hand—Operation Capitol West, the title handwritten in upper-case block letters, underlined and dated today by someone who she surmised was Saladin. Below the title was a list of activities, like a schedule, tagged by the time for each item.

6:30 am—Kamal and Ghulan leave for Cumberland
7:30 am—Kashim and Hassan leave for Union Station
8:00 am—Leave for Rockville Station
9:40 am—Capitol West departs Union Station, D.C.

Not knowing where she was, now she guessed that she must still be in the metro D.C. area, going by the time in the list.

Her first thought was they're going on a train trip. To where she couldn't come up with the wildest guess. For what—this she could, but she was reluctant to imagine what it might be.

Ten minutes had passed since she started recharging the card. It had to be enough to power a call, she thought, and got up to go to the bathroom. The guard simply turned his head at her and didn't mind her at all. As soon as she shut the door, she wore the data-entry ring around her index finger and called Chris. She decided to call him instead of Brigit because he was closer and could act more quickly. She could explain everything to her cousin later, counting on herself being reunited with her family soon.

The call went through. She heard the other end ring three times before it was picked up. There was a little static at first when she heard Chris' voice from his cell phone. It cleared up the next time he spoke.

She imagined him shooting up from his cozy chair in his government office in disbelief at suddenly hearing from her by phone. And he did, filling with excitement and apprehension at the same time.

"Where are you?" was his first question, pressing the telephone receiver hard on his ear. Her voice was tiny in it, sounded like coming from a remote location.

"I don't know," she said, feeling at a total loss on suddenly realizing she didn't know what to tell him. "I was blindfolded when I was brought here. I'm in a one-story house somewhere, probably within the metro area. Listen—find out about Capitol West."

"What is it? Julie, tell me first—where do you think you are? Do you see anything to indicate where you might be? Look everywhere around you."

"It's a train leaving Union Station in D.C. at 9:40 this morning. We will be in it." She was doing at least three things while she talked—looking around in the bathroom to do as he said, thinking fast for the most important thing to say next, fearing the guard might have heard her and burst through the door at any moment, and making the noise with what one normally did in the bathroom such as running the sink water.

She moved closer to the small bathroom window thinking the smart card would work better nearer the outdoors so she wouldn't have to raise her voice.

Over the property fence a few yards outside, she saw the top of a brick building some forty yards across a playground. On the four-foot deep fascia running the full length of the wall, a sign read: SANDBURG MIDDLE SCHOOL. She was looking straight at it.

As soon as she told him, he said: "You're in Fort Hunt, Alexandria. Near Mount Vernon. I know that school. I have cousins who went to that school. You know what street the house is on?"

"No. But it's behind the school."

"That's good enough," he said in a hurry. Knowing the school fronted Fort Hunt Road, the house had to be one on the street parallel to Fort Hunt, perhaps directly behind the school.

"I only have a few minutes," she said quickly. "If no one's here, go to Union Station in D.C. Check the Capitol West train schedule. Hurry! And, honey, please tell my family, and Brigit too."

"Yes. I'll get with the local police and the FBI right away. Be careful, sweetheart. Hang in there. We'll get you back. Call again any time you get a chance."

She hung up and pocketed the card as soon as she heard footsteps approaching outside the bathroom door. Then a loud knock came.

"Come out now," commanded a voice. "Time to go!"

Omar Husain had seen five men leave since shortly after he got up at six o'clock. The first three were Abu Kamal Ramshallah, Marwan Razzak and the driver, Ghulan Wahid. Their mission for the day was to cover the 150 miles to Cumberland in the Toyota Land Cruiser SUV two hours before Capitol West arrived there. Marwan Razzak was to rejoin his team at the station. This after working out some details of the operation with Kamal and Ghulan, their role in it, which was to serve as the pick-up and rescue support team during or after.

The next two were the team leaders Kashim Najoub and Hassan Bahaji, two of the four men who were to board at Union Station in D.C. They were the ones Julie heard leave shortly after she got up. The other two were Hassan Bahaji's team, Jabir Yasin and Mullah Ahmadullah, a pair of New York sleepers, traveling separately from the other safe houses to the station and were to be there earlier as the advance scout along with the two team leaders. The three parties—the two who 'didn't know each other' and the two traveling together—were to be total strangers to each other at the station and in the train. There were to be twelve of them in the train by the time it leaves the Cumberland station in the early afternoon. Those who weren't traveling together weren't to make any kind of contact unless it was absolutely necessary. Not until it was…time.

The next to leave, in fifteen minutes, would be the people remaining in the house: Omar Husain, Julie, Khalil Majid the money-man from Detroit who would be at the driver's seat, and the two who now formed Omar's team as well as his personal security—Masoud Faisal and the young GWU sleeper, Haji Madari.

Julie was blindfolded, her hands cuffed behind her, and led into the backseat of the Buick LeSabre between Omar on her left and Masoud Faisal. It was five minutes before eight when she glanced at her wristwatch a moment before she was blindfolded and led out of the house. A few minutes later she could tell they got on a high-speed road, probably the Beltway, as they traveled non-stop and faster. Perhaps another twenty-five minutes later, they again slowed down for some distance, came to a stop briefly and traveled another two minutes at a surface-road speed. Finally, they turned from the road into what sounded like a gravel top and then a paved surface, and came to a stop.

When she removed the blindfold herself after Masoud took her cuff off, she saw Omar outside the car door on her left offering a hand for her to come out. She grabbed the tote bag at her feet, took his hand and got out of the car. But Omar didn't let go. He turned and walked some distance away from the car, pulling her along toward a large sycamore tree.

They were in an empty parking lot. Beyond was a small playground and farther beyond that, the ground dipped to where the white steeple of a small church could be seen from where they now stood under the tan hardwood tree.

Julie waited to hear anything from Omar after he let her hand go. She could see that they were out of sight of the road they came from, whatever that road was. The only sound to be heard other than the faint hum of traffic from some distance, was from nature—the birds, the breeze in the treetops, the insects.

She didn't fear for her life, though. Her main concern of the moment was her whereabouts, next to what Omar Husain planned to do now.

"You're free to go," Omar said plainly without looking at her. His eyes went past between her and the tree, gazing far away in the sky.

"Where are we?"

"We're in Virginia, near the Potomac river." Now he turned his eyes on her, in them a look of so many unspoken words that only he would ever know or hear from the voice in his mind.

But Julie knew. And she didn't have to hear them. She saw them with that sad, distant look she had seen before on his face. That grudging look underneath his eyebrows that mirrored the pain, the loneliness he endured for so long now; the burden of extreme commitments he carried in the life he lived, the burden of anger and hatred in his heart and what must be an unyielding desire to find peace and a way to somehow free himself of those burdens. But there were more Julie saw in his eyes as he now turned away to leave her. A reluctance. A pleading she could almost hear him say to her. And behind all that, a sense of helplessness at the distance that must now separate him from her.

"Omar," she called after him before he was two steps away. It felt odd addressing him by name for the first time. "Please—"

He stopped and turned around slowly. Seeing her with a hand reaching out to him as if she didn't want him to leave made her appear a different person. Not one who had been his prisoner but someone with whom he shared something. Something they cared about equally.

"Please, whatever it is you plan to do," she continued in a voice equally pleading as the look on his face. "I'm asking you not to do it. I know you're obligated to do it but it's also hard for you to do it, because you know in your heart it's not really the right thing to do. Listen to your heart, Omar."

"I have to leave now. There's a church over there where you can get help."

He turned away again but before he could take one step, Julie stopped him, saying: "No amount of killing and violence is ever going to bring Kamilah and any of your family back into your life. The only thing it will do is bring more grief into other people's lives. The same as you had been feeling all these years. Does that really help you bear your sorrow any easier, help ease your pain and anger?"

"How dare you speak to me of my sorrow and grief! You know nothing of how I feel, how I suffer!" As it got louder, his voice quivered with latent emotions that had been buried deep inside for a long time.

"Oh, yes, I do!" Her voice now went up a notch higher than his. "I know exactly how you feel, what you feel. I feel it right here in my guts. I feel the same anger and hatred you do, the same hurt. Maybe not as long as you have been feeling them but I will feel them for a long long time."

Omar froze where he stood. Once again, he was caught between the conflicts within: his longing to be free of the life he lived, to be free of Saladin, the reluctance to let go of the anger and now the regret, the gnawing guilt that no way in hell he could ever undo, the guilt for the grief he had caused Julie Santorelli and her family.

He wished he had just kept going, run as fast as he could back to the car and taken off without looking back to hear one word she said. But he had to stop, turn around to look at her one last time. He wanted to hear what last words she had to say to him, or he would forever be wanting to bring back this moment, wondering what those words might have been no matter how bad they made him feel about himself, how hurt she may sound for what he had done to her and her family, and how sad it felt that he must leave her.

"I feel what you feel, Omar," she continued, every word of it tearing at him mercilessly and all he could do, wanted to do, was simply stand there and take the beating. "So does my uncle's wife, their children and the rest of my family. And so do all the people who lost their loved ones at the Punchbowl in Hawaii, at the Pentagon, the World Trade Center in New York and every place else that this anger, this hatred we now feel touches. And that's why I'm not going to live my life nurturing it like you do. I'm going to try very hard to forget it, to stop it from becoming a part of my life so that I can find peace and also, somehow...learn to forgive."

Now he really wished he had kept on going the moment he turned his back on her. But, no. He had to hear her minister her Christianity to him, challenge his faith. As if he needed it to deal with these last few hours before Operation Capitol West. As if he badly needed to be reminded of another instance in his life, a significant one, when Kamilah became part of his life, and with her—Christianity.

"Please, Omar. Don't do it," Julie pleaded again. "Please...for Kamilah."

Hearing that name from her again, Omar felt the ground shake under his feet, his whole body tremble. Immediately, his eyes began to moisten. And before she could see a sparkle of tears in them, he backed away a step at a time.

"No!" he cried out to Julie, blinking his tears away.

"Please, listen to your heart, Omar!" Julie pleaded once again, her own voice shaking.

"No!" he cried out one more time, louder, then turned away and hurried to the car.

CHAPTER 35

▼

After Chris heard from Julie, first he tried Bartley on the agent's cell phone. He got the machine and left a voicemail message. He called his office next. Same thing. He called his cell phone a second time and left another message. He tried another agent, Eddie Green, one of Bartley's partners. Same thing. He left a voicemail message.

By that time, he had taken it upon himself to take the rest of the day off, hurry down to his car in the garage and drive out to Fort Hunt, Alexandria. He got in the thick of the eight o'clock rush-hour in the District and started feeling desperate sitting at red lights, inching along just to cross the Potomac to Virginia. Then he thought of Harold Duke and dialed his number. It took him one call to get through to the Alexandria Police detective.

As soon as he learned everything from Chris, the detective briefed his supervisor in a hurry. They decided something like this, they would need some help from big neighbor Fairfax County, the State Police and of course the FBI.

Duke had told Chris they, the police, would take care of notifying the FBI immediately and everything else. He also told him not to go near the house or do anything on his own. But he couldn't dissuade Chris from heading out to Fort Hunt and so agreed to meet him there at the corner of Old Stage and Stockade Drive. In a matter of minutes, law enforcement forces consisting of the Alexandria City, Fairfax County and Virginia State police began to gather at their separate locations in Northern Virginia: a Special Operations Team and a hostage negotiator from the city Police Department, a heavily-armed Specialty Team from the VSP's Bureau of Field Operations, and an assault team from the Fairfax County Police Department's Special Operations.

Duke couldn't get FBI agent Richard Bartley either. Nobody could. The agent's phone only took messages. Instead, he got through to agent Henry Tucker, the man he became acquainted with during the Robert Grundell missing-person investigation. Henry Tucker knew a way to get a call through to Richard Bartley, which he did.

When asked by the detective what's with the unavailability of agent Bartley, the lead man in the investigation, at such a time, Tucker simply answered: "That's classified top-secret, highly-sensitive information at this time."

Gotcha, whatever, thought Duke who knew better than to question it, hearing something like that from a Fed. He told Tucker his people, the Fairfax County and the VSP troops were on their way to the house. Tucker said to expect him there at about the same time, give or take.

Like a swarm of iron particles being pulled from all directions towards a powerful magnet, everybody got on the road at the same time from Fairfax, Alexandria and the District, converging towards Fort Hunt. Chris got there first, followed by Harold Duke and the city and county police forces at the same time. The state police showed up next.

It was a quiet neighborhood of mostly upper-level federal government workers who left home early to beat the rush-hour to the District so that the deployment attracted little attention. Both ends of Stockade Drive, a one-block street, was sealed. From Julie's description to Chris, they had narrowed the address to either the third or the fourth house from Old Stage Road. Some men were positioned as close as one house away across the street on both sides of it. At the rear, others hid behind the trees and bushes inside the school grounds a short distance from the house fence.

Both suspect houses were completely surrounded. The siege was in place. Then Chris' cell phone rang.

"It's me, honey," Julie said excitedly over the phone. "I'm free! I'm okay. Omar...Saladin let me go!"

"Julie! Where are you?"

She was on Georgetown Pike, very near the exit from the Beltway. On Balls Hill Road, north of the Pike. There's a small chapel nearby, she said. Chris repeated everything to Harold Duke as soon as he got it from Julie.

The house is empty. Everybody's gone.

Saladin, real name Omar Husain, and his men are on their way to the train stations.

They will board the Capitol West train leaving Union Station at 9:40.

They have a plan to do something. I don't know what.

Tell the police and the FBI right away.

Henry Tucker and a team of agents, meanwhile, came and was briefed quickly by Harold Duke. As soon as he was caught up, Tucker asked Chris to keep Julie on the phone while he called Richard Bartley. He talked to Bartley for two minutes, speaking rapidly, listening closely to what he was being told, bobbing his head in agreement. When he hung up, he turned quickly to Chris and asked to talk to Julie.

Apparently, she was now safe and out of danger. But the FBI must get to her without delay, he told her. They needed her help to identify Saladin—now also known by his real name, Omar Husain—and his men at the train station.

After listening to everything Bartley told him, Tucker had quickly mapped out in his head the order of priorities minute by minute, starting with the next, say, twenty minutes—the time he was given by the Virginia State Police it would take to get to Julie from where they were in Alexandria.

With the help of two VSP cars, Henry Tucker, along with Chris Phillips in the backseat and one of his team members, agent Doug Jones, got in the bureau car they came in and thundered up Fort Hunt Road to the inner loop of the Capital Beltway. Chris Phillips thought if the three cars had wings, they would have taken off the road at the speed they were traveling. He kept an eye on the speedometer for a few seconds at one time and saw it rise and fall between 105 and 110 MPH.

It was 8:30 when they got off the Beltway on the Georgetown Pike exit, seventeen minutes from the time they got on the road. They turned north on Balls Hill Road, the first intersection, drove up a short distance through a parking lot and saw Julie standing in front of the chapel.

One skill Henry Tucker or any other agent didn't train for at Quantico was talking to three people at the same time and not all of them in person. That while pressed for time. As soon as they were sure Julie was unharmed and well, he had to talk real fast to her and Chris while he was on the phone with agent Richard Bartley at the same time. This lasted about ten minutes which was all that could be spared before they all got back in the car and sped to Union Station in Washington, D.C.

At first, Tucker tried to discourage Chris from getting involved more than he already had been, taking note of the wide Band-Aid covering the cut on his forehead from the night incursion at his home only a week ago. But Chris would not be dissuaded. If Julie goes, he said, no way he's going to see her face any more risks than she had already gone through, without him. In the end, Tucker and

Bartley agreed, thinking it would actually be a better arrangement. They could travel as a couple, help cover each other. They would be a natural.

While they barreled down the G. W. Parkway alongside the Potomac between the two VSP cars, agent Tucker with approval from the ops lead agent Richard Bartley carefully unraveled what he would not even hint at to his local law enforcement colleague back in Fort Hunt—Operation Big Thunder.

With the data uncovered in the OCDL floppies from the bust of the Treasury office, the Bureau analysts were unanimous, along with Richard Bartley and Nancy Schneider, on the decision to plan the operation immediately. No one doubted that the enemy had targeted the Big Thunder event. The nuclear plants in Norfolk, Virginia and in Raleigh, North Carolina, were too protected. Near impossible to penetrate and sabotage.

The presidential (POTUS) inauguration was a distant event. The only one happening was the inauguration of the Big Thunder infrastructure projects in the west. Saturday morning, two days from now, to be attended by the chairman of the Senate Committee on Energy and Natural Resources, and most of the members of its Subcommittee on Water and power.

For the past two weeks, every anti-terrorist brain in the Bureau had gathered day after day to explore every possible scenario for one or more attacks: against the senators on the train between Washington and North Dakota, in North Dakota against them and other dignitaries at the project site, and against the finished project itself.

The logistics and security plan for the event—presumably leaked to the enemy—were kept as was shown in the floppies and as the attackers would expect, except it was beefed up with twice as much the resources of the original design. Union Station as of this minute was teeming with Federal agents and local police undercovers. Agent Richard Bartley and his team, directing the operation, were among them.

At the Big Thunder projects in North Dakota and Montana, security, likewise, was doubled. And again, the security plans and schedule of events for the inauguration were not changed from what was described in the floppies.

The intent was to lure the attackers, Henry Tucker explained to Julie and Chris in the car, into what they expected to take place based on what they must have paid good money for to some traitor or traitors working in the U.S. government. A handful of people in Robert Grundell's office at Treasury's Office of Civil Defense Logistics had been arrested, without bond, on suspicion of treason, Tucker said. The latest on that was, the government had a very solid case against every one of them. None of them stood a chance of walking.

The trap was all laid out and ready to spring on the attackers at both ends of the Capitol West train route. But up until Julie's release, no one knew for sure how imminent a terrorist attack was. And even if it was certain that it was going to happen, the Bureau was severely lacking in intelligence on the identity of the attackers, the logistics and plan of their attack.

Everything was a guessing game involving the high risks not only in the Bureau's assets but potentially in some collateral damage which included primarily the U.S senators. A big headache for the planners of Operation Big Thunder at headquarters. There was no question that the thing to do then was to put highly trained members of the Bureau's HRT (Hostage Rescue Team) into expensive Capitol Hill suits, touch them up some and substitute them for the senators.

They had to create the appearance that they knew nothing of the (presumed) impending attack or they could very well have a no-show on their hands. The pressure was on to bag Saladin this time and at the same time foil a repeat of the Punchbowl bombing, even at such high risks.

But now, thanks to Julie, they had something concrete to work with. She could identify some of Saladin's men, and Saladin himself better than anyone else in the force. And quite possibly—after having been in contact with him for several days, listened to his voice, observed his gestures and mannerisms—even if he disguised himself. *Possibly.*

It was absolutely vital to the operation that the enemy did not get a hint they were expected at the times and places they planned to be; that nothing led them to suspect they were walking into a trap. Not in one's action or speech and most of all in one's appearance.

Hurtling down the parkway past the morning rush-hour, they had covered most of the distance to the Potomac river crossing at the Roosevelt bridge when Richard Bartley rang Henry Tucker's cell phone. He asked to talk to Julie, wanting to know her apparel sizes. Everyone in the car caught on to what Bartley was up to after a few moments.

Did she wear glasses? And did she ever wear a hat?

What size was her winter coat?

Afterwards, Bartley gave them instructions where to approach the Union Station and where to meet them inside. It was now 8:45. There was less than an hour for them to get to the station, for Bartley to shop for Julie's—and Chris'— cover, and for everyone to take up their positions.

Omar Husain slowed down a few moments getting back into the car after leaving Julie. There was a side of him he could not let any of his men know even existed. One he was not able to hide from Julie. He had to steady himself, take a few long deep breaths and reconstitute his mental and emotional state to that of Saladin before he got back in the car and faced Masoud Faisal next to him in the backseat, Haji Madari in the passenger seat and Khalil Majid in the driver's seat of the LeSabre.

They got back on the Beltway and in less than three minutes crossed the Potomac to Maryland. While they had waited for the Commander to come back to the car, Masoud had moved the bag from the trunk into the backseat. Now, after a quick glance at the time on his wristwatch, Omar Husain dug into the bag and began what was now a routine process of transforming his appearance into one of his many disguises.

First a shade of golden brown to cover the olive eastern Mediterranean complexion on the face and neck. Next, some streaks of gray on the eyebrows and the sideburns to match the dark brown of the hairpiece. No mustache, this time. Clean-shaven, this look. Then the stainless steel-framed eyeglasses.

Lastly, the one thing he was reluctant to do but, since the release of his picture in the media, he knew he must—removing the crescent-moon-and-star earring, the symbol of Islam, given to him by a teacher he was close to years ago in the madrassa he attended in Pakistan. He took it off and offered it to Haji Madari who hesitated a moment and then glowed with enthusiasm when Omar himself hung it on his left ear.

"This is a great honor, Commander Omar," said the younger man. "I will wear it with pride and respect."

Why does it always have to turn out like this? Bartley thought to himself as he looked at the time You get a last-minute break—Julie Santorelli, and Chris Phillips. Great. Now perhaps they can ID Saladin and his men and corral them before they can get going with whatever they had planned for today. But why did it have to happen this close? The train leaves in twenty minutes. Why couldn't last-minute be more like an hour or two instead of literally the last few minutes?

He marveled at how agent Henry Tucker, even with the help of the Virginia State Troopers and the city police, got them to the train station from the other side of the river in the few minutes since he talked to him through the morning rush-hour in the District. Together with agent John Jacobs, Bartley met them at a side entrance and hustled them into the station's security office.

There was no time to see if the outerwear they bought at the station shops for Julie and Chris fit. The first thing that had to be done was wire them and while they're doing it talk to them about Operation Big Thunder, where it's at now and what their part in it would be.

Bartley reassured that agents wouldn't be more than a few steps away from either of them at all times. But remember one thing, he told them—all you need to do is identify Saladin and his men. Don't do anything else on your own. Leave the rest to us.

He and partner John Jacobs went out first, separately, going through the sprawl of shops and eating places, past the long ticket counters and into the waiting areas outside the row of arrival and boarding gates. Jacobs with a small duffel bag, Bartley a briefcase. Two passengers apparently already with tickets. One went straight to one of the waiting areas, the other (Bartley), strolled up to an arrival/departure monitor out in the wide hallway to check the schedule.

The station, with its early 20th century Beaux Arts architecture, giant arched ceiling and dozens of Roman statuary looking down at over a hundred specialty shops, a food court and several restaurants, looked more like a fashion galleria or a mall than a train station. Millions of people passed through its marble floor every year either to shop, eat or catch an Amtrak, a VRE, a MARC or a Metro subway train to somewhere. Most everyone always in a hurry, it seemed.

Agent Richard Bartley didn't appear to be in a hurry. And he wasn't.

He placed himself amid the traffic of early morning commuters, travelers and shoppers where he had the best view of the waiting areas and the gate where the stage was set for the arrival of the 'senators' and a brief pre-boarding ceremony. With a slight head and eye movement, he could also see all the activities around him. At the hallways from the shops, the ticket counters and the eateries, including those of the other undercover agents already in place and working—either sipping a cup of coffee at a fastfood, browsing at a souvenir store or reading the paper on a bench.

One of them was agent Eddie Green looking like one irritated waiting passenger while reading the schedule at another monitor screen. Bartley tapped him on the radio, turned his head slightly down and muttered: "'Sup?".

"Nothing, so far," Green mumbled through his nose.

"Patience. They're here. Coming out now," Bartley said, referring to Julie and Chris.

Eddie Green tipped his head a little to the side and saw a couple coming into the main concourse from the shopping section on the right where he saw Bartley and Jacobs come from. The woman wearing a gray basque beret, a wing-collared fleece coat, light-tinted winter glasses and a thin-strapped leather purse. The man in a suede car coat, a pair of darker-tinted glasses that covered part of a large Band-Aid on his forehead and carrying a gym bag. He didn't recognize either of them right away. Not until they got nearer and went by him towards one of the waiting areas, gradually discerning their faces from that day he saw them in Vienna.

"I see them," Eddie Green muttered to his tiny microphone.

Ten yards behind them, he also saw agents Henry Tucker and Doug Jones, engaged in an animated conversation, heading in the same direction. Henry Tucker glanced sideways at him as they went by.

"Stay sharp now," Bartley said over the radio, glancing at his watch. "Get ready to move. Twelve minutes and counting."

"Roger," replied Green.

Bartley tapped the rest of them scattered in the area and told them the same.

Julie and Chris stood near a bench under a monitor just outside the waiting area of Gate E. After spending a few moments reading the schedules, they sat down on the bench talking. Julie had actually been busy from the moment they walked out of the security office observing the people around them. Where they were now, she discreetly scanned the main concourse and all the areas as far as she could see of the large station, the same as Bartley and the others had been doing. But she had an advantage in that she knew who to look for.

In another minute, a crowd gathered around the waiting area at Gate G where passengers would go through to board the Capitol West train. Several of the 'senators' had appeared and were now preparing to go through the gate. The media was there with video cameras trained on the scene along with the expected plain-clothes security, deliberately made quite visible and identifiable at Bartley's direction. Sunglasses and fresh pressed suits, radio wire behind their ears, heads moving like submarine periscopes. He wanted Saladin and his men to see, and think, that the security plans for the event was as what they learned in the floppies.

One of two things he and everybody else in the force worried about—the substitute senators. None of the real senators was a high-profile personality on Capitol Hill and therefore not a recognizable national figure, except perhaps the Committee Chairman. They were counting that none of the enemies knew any of them at all by appearance. The other thing which concerned everybody, including the FBI Director, more than anything was the risk itself involved in the operation. The enemy's plan could simply be to launch an attack right here at the station. Blow the senators and everybody else around them to smithereens, with a suicide bomber.

The Bureau analysts debated it for two weeks, in the end making the decision to go ahead with the operation. They just couldn't pass up a good chance to catch Saladin although until Julie's release less than an hour ago, the possibility remained that the operation might be called off. The HRT didn't flinch at being the target of the attack but still the Bureau wasn't comfortable at deliberately throwing them or anybody in for a live bait.

But after Julie told them what she learned in that room they kept her in, they were able to relax a bit with the decision to go through with the operation. It was clearly not the enemy's plan to attack at the station. They would hit in the train. It was a relief, for now. Again, another last-minute break but one Bartley couldn't complain about.

Bartley had most of his men now move closer to the center of activity. Agent Henry Tucker, Doug Jones, John Jacobs and several others who had been working the area earlier were also alerted. Bartley got on the radio to Julie.

"Anything?"

"No," Julie said, looking hard all around as fast as she could, moving her eyes more than her head. She focused on adult men of average weight and height, not paying attention at all to how they were dressed. She and Chris were now standing side by side carefully eyeballing the entire place. "Still looking."

Two men coming from behind them brushed past Chris. They were clean-shaven, early middle-age, dressed for white-collar work it appeared—coat and tie under their winter coats. Chris overheard a few words they spoke as they went past. Sounded mainstream Americans.

And they did. That's because Kashim Najoub and Hassan Bahaji had been practicing to sound that way for months now just for such an occasion as today. Omar Husain himself had spent hours with them, coaching them not only on how to sound but how to move and look and appear like American men. They headed directly towards the gathering outside Gate G. Neither Julie or Chris paid any special attention to them.

The two men stood a few feet from the swell of the crowd around the waiting area of the gate to watch the scene. Over in the next waiting area beyond the crowd, Hassan saw Mullah Ahmadullah, one of his team members, rise from a bench and look at the scene too. They had a brief eye contact. Over by a coffee vendor across the concourse from the waiting area, he noticed Jabir Yassin, his other team member, holding a steaming cup and also watching the activity around Gate G.

They had no need to communicate no matter what they saw or found out at the station. Whatever information they needed to share with each other they will do so in the train. Between here and Cumberland before the train leaves there.

At the moment, everything they observed had been common knowledge to them since they arrived over an hour ago: the suits who had been hanging around from one end of the concourse to the other, the uniformed federal protection security, in addition to the uniformed private security roaming the lower level, the street level and the mezzanine of the huge station complex. Everything appeared to be exactly as they had expected according to the data contained in the floppies bought—they were told by their leaders—from some disgruntled American government worker.

The media cameras now focused on one of the senators as he delivered a short speech before they went through the gate to begin their journey to North

Dakota. The first leg would take them to Chicago via Pittsburgh and Cleveland. A nineteen-hour trip. The second to Fargo via St. Paul-Minneapolis. Thirteen hours. The last a 190-mile bus ride to Bismarck near the Big Thunder project site. The journey was a symbolic gesture depicting the westward push of the industrial revolution in the late 19th and early 20th century in America.

More people had converged around the waiting area mostly with small shoulder-bags and hand-carried luggages on wheels, passengers hurrying to catch the train the last few minutes. The setting was similar to being at an airport boarding gate except for the awareness that you're not flying. In another three minutes, applause broke out and cameras flashed as the brief ceremony concluded. The scheduled departure of Capitol West must be met to the minute.

The senators shook hands with the people at arm's reach, raised an arm to wave at the crowd before turning around to go through the gate. Once they disappeared inside, the rest of the passengers followed. So did Kashim Najoub, Hassan Bahaji and his team.

Agent Richard Bartley had most of his men mix in evenly with the crowd, some of them actually coming in contact with a couple of the men they were hunting. Julie and Chris joined the line to the gate near the end. Agent Doug Jones two ahead of them, Bartley two back of them. Several more passengers came after him before the gate security, a couple of uniformed federal police, raised the yellow cords and hooked them to their stanchions to close the gate.

Chris didn't feel comfortable having Julie take the upper-level aisle seat in the coach 1 car of the Superliner train. Had this been one of their vacation trips like the one they took to Europe last year, he wouldn't have minded the arrangement. He always enjoyed sitting by the window on land or in the air. But this wasn't a pleasure trip. This wasn't any other kind of trip the two of them had ever taken.

Shortly before the train started moving, he had so many thoughts run through his head about how in the world the two of them ended up where they were now. They didn't need to be in this scene after what Julie just went through, not to mention what he went through last week with the bloodletting in his house. He shouldn't have let her talk him into it. And she shouldn't have let the FBI talk her into it in the first place.

But after they came to pick her up where Saladin had left her by that little chapel and they started telling her how much they needed her to help, how important it was that she did not just to the whole country but the whole world, she was simply overwhelmed. So was he. For her, in addition to that, it meant also the possibility of bringing those responsible for the killing of her uncle to justice.

When Julie insisted on sitting by the aisle, he didn't give her a lot of argument. After all, she was right. She needed to be where she could have a wider view of their surroundings for a better chance of seeing the people she was brought here to identify. The only thing he worried about was her being too exposed, more than he was, in case things started to happen. That's when she told him a little bit more about her captivity, and about Omar Husain. Saladin.

He felt relieved to learn that after all the discomfort she went through for lack of sleep at one time, the cold she endured in that basement room for three days and all the inconveniences from being forced to live outside of her normal life, she didn't sustain any physical or psychological damage, and she was not violated. On the contrary, he admired how she so courageously fended for herself, stood up against them and even gained insight into the making of Saladin.

"He is angry," she told Chris. "He had so much hatred for the Jews and us Americans that for years, that's all he lived for, he told me himself. But now, he's desperate to be heard. He wants so much to voice out his anger, so he did—to me."

Chris listened intently while she spoke.

"He's tired of living the life he had been living for more than twenty years now," Julie continued, recalling the man she first feared, then hated, and later on pitied. "He's tired of hating and fighting and doing what he had been doing. He continues to grieve the loss of his family and the girl he was going to marry. But he wants it all to end now. The killing, the violence. When I found this out about him, I stopped fearing for my life. I knew he couldn't possibly do me harm, personally. There are two sides of him in conflict with each other."

"And it appears the one who wants to keep doing what he had been doing is in command right now," Chris said. "He's not letting the other side of him call this thing off which is why we're on this train right now. I wouldn't exactly count on him sparing anyone for any reason from becoming another victim of his violence. Anyone."

Julie laid a hand on his arm to listen to Richard Bartley who had just signaled her on the radio. "Everything alright?" agent Bartley asked.

He was sitting in an upper-level sleeper car seat that converted into a deluxe bedroom at night. Up ahead were four of the senators in the same deluxe accommodations, two on his side of the aisle and two directly across the others. The other two senators were down on the lower level of the car. Across the aisle one row back were agents Henry Tucker and Doug Jones in a deluxe bedroom accommodation for two.

Julie lowered her chin slightly and with her lips hardly moving spoke: "Fine."

"How does it look?"

"I didn't see him, or anyone close." She used as few words as she could to say what she had to.

"And the others?"

"None of them either."

The traditional 'all aboard' announcement came on the p.a. and the train started moving.

"I'm coming over now," Bartley said. The plan was for Julie and Chris to follow him on a quick tour of the train, starting at the upper level of the coach 1 car where they were seated.

"He's on the way," Julie told Chris after she got off the radio.

In a couple of minutes, they followed Bartley through the upper level of coach cars 1 and 2 toward the rear of the train, keeping distance from him to avoid even an accidental eye contact. They moved purposefully and in no hurry. When they approached a row of seats from its back, Julie eyeballed the passenger by turning her head slightly around to catch a glimpse of the occupants through her peripheral.

Coming back on the lower level past the coach 1 car, they entered the snack lounge. Not too many people in it. No one they might be interested in giving a second or a third take. Just the server behind the coffee bar pouring a fresh brew in the cups of an older couple and several other people who looked like a family eating donuts and pastries at a couple of tables.

They walked through the whole length of the car into the next which was the dining car. There, they climbed back up to the upper level, Chris and Julie staying a discreet distance of some twelve feet behind Bartley. It was Bartley's idea to go through each car of the train open to the passengers in the direction of the front of the seats on each level. The sleeper and coach cars, the lounge and dining cars, including the sightseer lounge in the upper level of the dining car.

There was a little traffic going through the cars, other people looking the Superliner train over like they appeared to be doing. In the sightseer lounge above the dining car, there were people sitting on both sides of the aisle taking in the early morning sun as the train picked up speed. Walking down the aisle, Julie couldn't get a good look at the ones she was interested in because the seats were all facing the window. So she slowed down and stopped briefly, as did Bartley when he noticed what she was doing, to take in the passing scenery outside.

Behind her sunglasses, she focused more on some of the men sitting nearby than on the scenery. Chris stood next to her and appeared to be absorbed by the view of the city they were leaving behind—the Capitol Hill, the Mall and its surrounding area.

One of the men Julie noticed through the corner of her eye for a couple of seconds was Mullah Ahmadullah. He was reading a magazine behind a pair of sunglasses. Early thirties, neatly dressed. Sports jacket over a tan sweater.

Two seats away on the other side of the aisle was Hassan Bahaji, an older man. Some gray hair, respectable-looking in a beige jacket and blue tie, enjoying the scenery. Julie only gave him a passing glance and moved her eyes to the other people nearby before continuing down the aisle, following Bartley by a small bar with a few tables near the end.

The bar was nearly empty being so early in the day but for the bartender who was busy restocking the shelves and the service staff tidying up the tables, getting things ready for the long-distance journey. They went past to the end of the car where Bartley took the stair back down and proceeded into the first of the two sleeper cars, the one before that where he and the senators were staying.

Immediately, they were facing dozens of people either just getting situated in their bedroom seats, tucking luggages in the overhead storage, peering into hand-carried bags and luggages, or sitting comfortably with their traveling companions and starting to enjoy the train ride. Walking along the aisle, again one got the sense of being in an airplane but for the passing scene outside the windows.

With people coming the opposite direction or out of their seats, Bartley got held up so that Julie and Chris caught up with him and ended up walking slowly right behind him. Julie and Chris spoke a few words to each other but not to Bartley. They were companions. They didn't know Bartley at all. A total stranger who happened to be walking ahead of them.

And that's how Kashim Najoub saw the three of them from his aisle seat. While Julie got busy surveying both sides of the aisle the way she was instructed by Bartley—small head movement if you can't help it, but mostly eye movement only—she glimpsed the veteran Soldier of Islam once directly. She had eye contact with him as she inched behind Bartley and even gave him a half-smile when she looked down at him. He gave her a friendly nod in return as she moved on. Chris, following close behind her, watched through his peripheral vision.

They continued through the length of the car and into the next where two of the senators were staying. The two HRT undercover in their kevlar bulletproof vests posing as the lawmakers looked up from their cups of coffee and papers when Bartley paused briefly to give them a tiny nod as he went by. Julie kept busy surveying the passengers on both sides of the aisle, Chris tagging along a step behind. At the end of the car, Bartley led them upstairs where he and the four other senators were staying. Here, Bartley made eye contact with the four HRT undercover, went past them and returned to his seat.

Julie and Chris continued down the aisle of the sleeper car and the next, now going back to where they came from downstairs. They stayed in the upper level of the train to return to their seats in the coach 1 car. There, Julie went straight to the restroom so she could talk freely to Bartley on the radio.

"Anything?" Bartley asked.

"I don't think Saladin is here. Not yet," she said, thinking. Thinking about the paper she found in the bedroom in the house in Fort Hunt.

In her excitement then over her discovery of the ESCard in her purse, she hardly retained what was written in the paper which later on she realized she should have taken with her. But she was able to piece parts of the texts together enough for the FBI to figure out what it was all about. What stood out in her mind right now was *Capitol West, Cumberland,* and...*Rockville.* Yes. *Rockville Station.* And what was the word before *Rockville?*

She concentrated hard for a moment. Then she recalled.

Leave for Rockville Station.

Now she remembered there were names associated with the other stations. But not with Rockville. And who could be leaving for Rockville? Who else but Saladin?

"I know some of them are in this train," Richard Bartley said on the radio, his voice sounding gravely serious. "I can feel it."

"I believe it," she replied. "I can feel it too. I felt I was looking at some of them without knowing it. How long to Rockville Station?"

"Twenty minutes," Bartley replied, looking at his wristwatch. "A little less now."

"I think that's where Saladin is boarding."

At 9:20, the LeSabre pulled into the short-term parking of the train station at Hungerford Drive in Rockville. Haji Madari and Masoud Faisal got out of the car with their hand-carried luggages and walked to the station concourse. Two men, both caucasian with what looked like permanent tans, clean-shaven. One was about a foot taller and eighty pounds heavier than the other who was younger

and leaner. They both looked very athletic and could easily be taken for a college athlete and a coach. Omar Husain and the driver, Khalil Majid remained in the car.

Another car arrived at the parking lot a minute later. The driver hurried to let out a graying middle-aged couple from the backseat while a ten-year old girl helped herself out of the front passenger seat. All four of them headed to the station, the two men carrying the luggages they hauled from the trunk. A couple of minutes later, the driver got back in the car and drove off.

Omar Husain watched the comings and goings from the passenger seat of the LeSabre, next to Khalil Majid at the wheel.

Ten minutes later, another car arrived at the parking lot. Three people, a young couple and an elderly woman, came out of the car. The driver popped the trunk open with the remote lever on the floor and remained in his seat The man outside went to the trunk and came back to the women with two pieces of luggage. Then all three of them said what looked like a quick thank you and goodbye to the driver who waved at them and drove out of the parking lot.

From the car, Omar Husain watched them walk to the station. Just as they reached the concourse, he saw Haji Madari stand there, raise a hand at waist level and discreetly wave at him, a signal that everything was clear.

Omar nodded to acknowledge it. He looked at his watch then turned to the driver. "Allah be with you, brother Khalil," he said to his friend from Detroit, an associate from many other missions over the years.

"Allah be with you, Commander Omar," Khalil Majid returned, remembering similar occasions in the past when they said the same parting words to each other. "You know, we don't have to sound so glum every time we say goodbye to each other."

Omar gave a small laugh. "I didn't know we did," he said.

"Yes," Khalil replied, laughing the same way. "I think it's because we get so caught up with the...the logistics of what we do. How things will turn out, even when we know we can't control what may happen."

Omar nodded, gazing long at the other man.

"We should be cheerful instead," Khalil continued. "Because what really matters, as far as the Jihad is concerned, is that we live to see this day come. Another opportunity to make sacrifices for The Faith and to serve Allah. Another opportunity perhaps to be united with Him, and those who have gone before us."

"You are absolutely right, brother Khalil," Omar agreed. "It is very easy to be so self-preoccupied with one's work and worldly concerns, and so easy to forget what we do them for. Thank you, brother, for helping keep us in the right path. I will keep you in my prayers."

"And you in mine, Commander."

"Please say the same to the other brothers in Cumberland when you get there," Omar said, referring to Abu Kamal Ramshallah and the three other men in Cumberland where Khalil Majid would now proceed to join them.

"I will, Commander. And we'll see you later."

"Yes, definitely. Sala'am aleikum," Omar said, putting out a hand.

"Sala'am Aleikum," Khalil replied, taking the hand and shaking it warmly.

Omar got out of the car with a duffel bag he took from the backseat and watched the LeSabre drive out of the parking lot before he turned toward the station. At the concourse, he saw Haji Madari and Masoud Faisal talking at the other end. The plan was—he wasn't with them. He was traveling alone.

He took a few steps to a long bench against a wall of the station shed where the couple and the little girl were sitting. He gave every one of them a nice smile and a hello and immediately got into a friendly conversation with them.

As he thought, the couple was not the parents but the grandparents. Their son who dropped them off at the station was the father, divorced from the mother who lived in Cleveland, as did the grandparents. The father had recently moved to the Washington, D.C. area a few months ago due to a job transfer and his parents came to visit together with his little girl.

"And how did you like Washington, Kate?" Omar asked the girl ten minutes into their conversation.

"It's just like I've seen in pictures and books," Kate replied with sparkling eyes. "I like it a lot. It's a pretty place. Do you live here?"

"Yes. In Virginia."

"I like Virginia too. We were there last weekend. Are you going to Cleveland too?"

Omar took a moment to come up with the answer. "No," he replied. "I'm only going to Pittsburgh."

"My grandma is from Pittsburgh," Kate said interestedly. "Aren't you, grandma?"

The woman, early sixties, some gray hair but holding on to vestiges of her youth twenty years ago, inched closer to the girl, smiling coyly. "Yes, I am," she said to Omar. "Born and raised there, as a matter of fact."

"And grandpa was a school perfessor there and that's how they met," the girl said to Omar. "Isn't that right, grandpa?"

"Yes, honey, that's right," said grandpa, nodding fondly at his granddaughter. "But I was born and raised in Cleveland. Just like you and your mom and dad."

A handsome American couple, thought Omar. Seemed like a long-time successful marriage, not very common nowadays with their children's generation. Goes without saying with this western egocentric culture. Shallow, materialistic and rife with infidelity.

By the time the train arrived a few minutes later, Omar had managed to get so acquainted with them that anyone seeing them the first time would think the four was one group traveling together. That was how Julie and several of the FBI agents watching from the train saw them when they boarded the train: Omar, a bespectacled middle-aged man, traveling with an older couple, probably his parents, and his little girl.

They were the first to get on board, Omar dutifully helping with the luggage. They got very little attention from those watching inside. Julie, next to Bartley behind the curtain of a window at the lower level of the coach 1 car, didn't recognize Omar Husain at all.

She was about to turn away from the window as the last of the passengers, fourteen of them, were stepping up when she saw, first, Haji Madari—the young man who lured her from the school and helped Omar Husain in her abduction— coming up behind one of the black women. Next she saw her guard at the house in Arlington and Fort Hunt, Masoud Faisal, third from the end of the line.

"I see two of them," Julie said to Bartley in a hurry, identifying which ones. Bartley got on the radio immediately to agent John Jacobs and Henry Tucker on the other side of the door to identify the two to them.

Tucker followed them at a safe distance to the upper level of coach 2 car, the last passenger car of the train. He saw them take the two front seats on the right.

At Bartley's direction, Tucker posted a team of two agents led by Eddie Green. Green took an aisle seat halfway back of the car across the aisle. He put his partner, agent Art Guerrero, a Desert Storm veteran from the Army's 2nd Armored Division, now a five-year undercover, one back of him across the aisle for cover. Their instruction was from here on, let them out of your sight only when you blink. Anything they do—look at somebody for more than two seconds, make any kind of move that could mean a signal to somebody, check it out, follow up on the contact and don't let up no matter who it is, what the person looks like. Young or old, man or woman.

Anybody they contact, mark them.

Moments after the train left the station, everyone sensed tension building up. For the first time, the FBI had a positive ID of some of the people they were looking for. Whatever doubt they had about the enemies' plan was replaced by the now real and growing uncertainty of what that plan was, what they had set out to do and when.

Bartley thought about perhaps calling for a full-blown assault reinforcement now to interdict the train at the next station, Harper's Ferry or if there weren't enough time, the one after that, Martinsburg. But there wasn't enough time! Harper's Ferry was just under an hour. From there, Martinsburg was only a half hour away.

His mind raced to make a decision. If the enemy planned an operation for this day which he was now almost sure of, they would launch an attack when they could do the most damage. Meaning—as he rehashed many times over with the analysts at the Bureau—get as many of the senators as they can in one quick strike. And the time to pick was when the senators would be gathered in one place such as?—the lunch caucus they were scheduled to hold in the dining car at 1:30; dinnertime at 7:00 or bedtime anytime between 10:00 o'clock and midnight. From the data in the floppies, the enemy knew the senators' schedule of activities in their journey from Washington, D.C. to Bismarck, North Dakota, and throughout the Big Thunder inauguration event there. They knew what car of the train the senators were in, what accommodations. In reality, they could strike anytime they chose to between the beginning and the end of the whole event..

They might have a plan already worked out, days, weeks ahead, and then decide to change it, depending on how they see things going. What we're dealing with here now, Bartley summarized, was a cat-and-mouse game. You don't know what hole to plug, where to set a trap, when to spring it.

On the other hand, and this was what he hoped might happen, they might decide for whatever reason to call everything off. And why would they do this? What might perhaps force them to do this?

Simple. Let them know they're found. First, capture the two men Julie had already identified, then bring in the reinforcements, lay siege to the train and search everybody. And if they had plans at the other end, in North Dakota, force them to call everything off there too by postponing the event to another time and place.

The only problem with that was the capture of Saladin, the main reason the Bureau decided to go ahead with Operation Big Thunder even at such a high risk of collateral damage as they faced possibly anytime now. Also—he blows this operation, it's his job. Most likely the end of his career with the Bureau.

No, Bartley decided. Go ahead with the operation, he thought to himself. You still need the job, dammit. Not ready to retire yet and he hated to think of himself taking on a PI or an armed security job out there in the private industry. Just hope nothing happens between now and Bismarck, or at least not before Julie identified more of the enemy, including Saladin himself.

Twenty minutes before Harper's Ferry, Kate persuaded grandma to let her go to the snack lounge for a soda and chocolate bar. With Omar volunteering to accompany her, Grandma gave her permission.

Omar walked her to one of the soda machines and asked: "What would you like?"

"I want a root beer," she said, searching for it on the vertical row of buttons.

"It's over on this one," said Haji Madari standing in front of the other machine next to them. He dropped the last of the three quarters in the coin slot and pressed the Coke button. A can came hurtling down the chute instantly.

"Thank you, mister," Kate said after the man picked up his purchase and stepped out of their way. Omar looked at him and thanked him too.

"You're welcome," Haji replied to both, hardly glancing at his Commander.

At the far end of the lounge, agent Art Guerrero, enjoying a cup of coffee with the morning paper, sat at a window table facing their way. He too gave Omar a short glance. And he would a number of more times as Omar helped Kate at the soda machine and at the candy machine next. At the same time, he kept track of every move Haji Madari made, every gesture and any further interaction he might have with the other people in the room.

The agent saw no other contact his quarry made with anybody else as Haji walked to a table and sat down, drank the Coke and ate a bag of peanuts. The man and the little girl moved next to a candy machine and got a chocolate bar. They walked by him on their way out, the girl saying 'bye, the bespectacled man, obviously the father, returning his friendly smile with a nod.

Nothing to worry about with those two, Guerrero thought. But he'd keep an eye on this fellow. It could be he's expecting somebody to show up here. He studied the young man from the distance of nearly the full length of the car. If he hadn't been identified as one of the enemies, Guerrero wouldn't have thought anything of him. He looked like any twenty-something mainstream American; sounded, moved and dressed like one.

A minute went by as he studied Haji some more through his peripheral vision, thinking maybe he'd get a closer look by going to one of the food dispensers near the man. Then someone came into the lounge at Guerrero's end of the car, standing at the entry way a couple of yards away from him for a few moments. He was an older man, middle-aged, showing some gray on both sides of his head but with the build of a younger man. Trim, broad shouldered, powerful-looking arms and legs.

As soon as he spotted Haji Madari at the table near the other end of the car, Kashim Najoub started towards the coffee bar halfway through the car on the left side, cautiously eyeing the people in the lounge. He had to wait for his turn with the server who was busy with a customer ahead of him. While he did, he continued to survey the surroundings carefully.

Some people sat with company, others by themselves. For one moment, his eyes fell on the man near the far end of the car at a window table reading the paper. He remembered brushing past him during boarding at Union Station and getting a suspicious feeling about who, what, he might be.

Did he look like someone traveling to his relatives in Pittsburgh? Chicago? Someone on a leisure travel? Or someone on the job, a government agent looking for America's enemies? An undercover agent, in addition to the senators' plain-clothes security everybody already knew about, in their neatly pressed suits and sun goggles?

Why the additional security? Could it be they knew something was coming down? Could they possibly know about Operation Capitol West? And did this man already know who they were? If this were so, then there must be others on the train. Many others. Commander Omar must be told. And he must give the order to execute the alternate plan—launch the attack sooner than Cumberland.

His team was yet to board at Martinsburg, two stations and forty-five minutes away. That would bring their strength to nine men, up from seven now. With the possible increase in the enemy force, that would make a difference.

Forty-five minutes.

If he was right about this, they're trapped. They must make use of that time to allow the Commander to make a decision. But a decision based on what? Right now, just a suspicion that this man sitting by himself reading the paper by the window was a government agent?

There's only one way to find out, thought Kashim Najoub as he now paid the server for the coffee and stepped over to a shelf on the wall for the cream and sugar. And what if he was wrong about the man who might happen to be just an ordinary passenger? He could simply apologize for the inconvenience and say he was only doing his job as an employee of the U.S. government.

He turned from the bar and walked directly toward Haji Madari across the car, his eyes moving between the coffee he was careful not to spill in his hand and partly in the direction of agent Guerrero. He sat across the table from Haji facing Guerrero at the far end of the lounge after Haji made a welcoming hand gesture for him to sit down.

If he was indeed a government agent, Kashim was now thinking, then he must be after Haji, spying on him. It follows that they must at least know of an existing threat if not about Operation Capitol West specifically. And now that he'd seen the two of them together, he must be feeling really productive about his sleuthing job. Another subject identified.

At the other end of the car, Guerrero lowered the paper a fraction of an inch, allowing himself a narrow view of the two over the edge. He didn't really have to have them in sight because he had his listening earpiece turned up and honed in on them. But it helped authenticate what he was hearing to catch a glimpse of them talking to each other.

"It's a nice day for a train ride," said the older man.

"Yes," replied the younger one. "A very nice winter day."

"How is everything with you and the others?"

"Very well. We're all doing very well. Thank you. And you?"

"The same. But, listen," said the older man, lowering his voice. "I'm beginning to think we have company, besides the ones we know about."

Agent Guerrero tuned in harder on hearing that. He took a quick glance at Kashim over the edge of the newspaper then moved his mouth down closer to the tiny microphone under his collar. He tapped agent Bartley on the radio and reported what he had going on.

"I'm sending agent Jones over right now," Bartley said after listening to Guerrero. "You stick with the young one."

"There's no time," Guerrero said as he watched Kashim Najoub now get up and start to leave after taking a couple of longs sips of the coffee. "The older guy's getting ready to go. We're going to lose him."

"Alright, you tail him instead. I'll get Jones to take over the young one for now. But we won't worry about him. We know where to find him."

Guerrero followed Kashim with his eyes for a few seconds, watching him go upstairs to the entertainment bar lounge. As soon as he was out of sight, Guerrero followed. In the upper lounge, the same man restocking the shelves behind the bar at the sightseer lounge was now doing the same here. He was all work, hardly noticing Guerrero coming up the stair into the lounge. Guerrero saw no one else in the room.

He walked up to the bar and greeted the man with a cheerful hello. The man glanced up at a clock above him on the wall and turned to Guerrero briefly, saying: "Too early. Come back at eleven."

"Thanks," Guerrero said, looking amused. "Nice place you got up here."

"Sure is. There's big-screen movie playing later on, video games, music you care to listen to. A piano over there you can play, if you know how."

"I wish. I'll just look around, if you don't mind."

"Help yourself."

He stepped away to the middle of the car and scoped the entire layout. Looked just like a small neighborhood bar lounge. Neat cozy little tables for two and four, a couple of alcove seating against each side of the car, an upright babygrand at a corner, a couple of video game boards on the other side, an audio entertainment center at the opposite end on one side of the doorway to the lounge just outside the restroom. He waited a moment before moving toward the restroom, standing outside the closed door near enough to hear any sound inside.

Nothing.

Then, suddenly, the door swung wide open, a hand came out right behind it and grabbed him by the lapel of his jacket. And that was all agent Guerrero was aware of before Kashim Najoub delivered the succession of blows to the back of his head and neck with the grip end of his Glock 20 pistol.

After closing the door and locking it, Kashim hurried to wet a handful of paper towels and wipe the blood off his hand and gun. He noticed some smudges on his coat too and worked on them quickly. When he heard Guerrero outside the door, he knew it was him although a small doubt lingered in his mind about his identity. It could be that the man was some kind of a weirdo or gay who had taken a fancy on him—a thought he found revolting. For that reason, he felt relieved though only for a moment to find that he wasn't wrong about him in the first place when he looked inside the man's wallet and saw the shiny government badge and ID cards.

FBI field agent Art Guerrero…33 years old. Well, what do you know. Just as he had suspected. He's getting good at picking these guys out.

Next he tore the man's shirtfront open and saw what he expected.

Just look at that teeny-weeny microphone and mini-speaker wired from under his clothes. And what is this other thing inside his ear. A high-tech listening device of some kind.

This guy is wired to the bones, he thought. He knew Guerrero wasn't just reading the newspaper aloud to himself when he noticed his lips moving. He was talking on the radio to somebody while listening to his conversation with Haji, making an instant report to the others about what he saw and heard.

The agents must know they're on the train and are hot on their trail, now he realized with alarm. The question is, do they know who they're after? Any of the brothers? Which ones? Haji Madari, apparently. And him, Kashim Najoub? Commander Omar? Hassan? How would that be possible unless somebody had ratted on them, pointed a finger at any of them. He hurried to take out the cell phone and dialed his Commander.

Omar Husain was about to leave Kate and her grandparents to go back to his seat four rows back of them in the coach 1 car when his cell phone vibrated. He listened for two minutes to Kashim's report without interrupting, until Kashim was saying: "We must do it as soon as possible. After Harper's Ferry. Or, at the latest, after my team gets on at Martinsburg."

"You said you joined Haji at his table?" Omar said, backtracking on what Kashim had told him. He had moved out of the seating area to the open space at the end of the coach car leading to the next to avoid being heard by anybody.

"Yes. But I wasn't with him more than two minutes before I decided to leave and see what this man would do."

"It didn't matter if you'd stayed with Haji or not. That's all he wanted to see. That you made contact with Haji." If ever he had to think real hard and fast to make a decision, Omar realized this was the time. Consider the possibilities from what Kashim reported. Somehow Haji picked up a tail. Being a traveling companion, so must have Masoud. But where did they pick up the tail, and since when? Never mind that. Deal with what's at hand.

No one else must make contact with the two between now and after Cumberland. Everyone must now be on high alert, especially Haji and Masoud. And since they're now known to the enemy, he thought, this could in effect work to our advantage. Use them as decoys to identify any more undercover agents. Hopefully, the enemy wouldn't decide to capture them now.

He looked at the time. Cumberland was two hours away. The train was now only a few minutes to Harper's Ferry station. At the moment, he had to give Kashim an answer whether to strike sooner or wait till it was time according to plan.

"Continue according to plan," he ordered, looking out the window at the end of the coach, the low hills of the West Virginia countryside rushing past. "Wait for a new order after Martinsburg. Meantime, notify the other team leaders."

"Yes, Commander," replied Kashim dutifully.

He trusted Omar Husain's judgment now as he always had, the same as all the other team leaders and their men did. But at the moment he had the strongest urge to ask their leader how seriously he considered, if at all, the very real possibility that the government knew about Operation Capitol West and that many other undercover agents were deployed throughout the train in addition to the regular suits escorting the senators to North Dakota. He found out and caught one, so far. How are we to identify the others? He couldn't hold this back to himself and asked Omar to excuse him for bringing it up.

As in the past, Commander Omar had an answer to fill the perceived gap in the others' thinking. "We don't know them, but they don't know us either. At least, from what we now suspect, not all of us. From now on, we avoid contact with the brothers we're not traveling with. You made contact with Haji and I did not. That was very fortunate of me. But you did well with that agent Guerrero, brother Kashim."

He went on to instruct Kashim to put everyone on high alert immediately and explain how they may identify more of the enemy by using Haji and Masoud as decoys from here on. He would call one of them as soon as they hung up.

Following up on that, a similar idea came to Kashim. He looked at the bleeding and unconscious FBI undercover agent sprawled face up on the floor of the men's room, the radio equipment and wiring hidden under his clothing. He suggested the idea to Omar. Something about how Guerrero may be of some use to them as well.

"Brilliant," praised Omar. "Let's move quickly, but carefully."

CHAPTER 37

▼

Shortly after he had sent agent Doug Jones out to the snack lounge car, the announcement came through the p.a. The train will not stop at the Harper's Ferry station and will continue on to Martinsburg to arrive there at the scheduled time. One less worry, thought agent Richard Bartley. The less people coming on board the better.

He was still feeling the boost from agent Guerrero's radio call about the contact his quarry had made. That got him thinking about Saladin. Could he have slipped in at Union Station? Or got past Julie at Rockville? It's not at all too remote a possibility that the contact may be Saladin. But how do we know it's him?

Julie.

Not right away, though. Tag him first, see where he sits, then get her to have a look at him. He hoped there would be more of them, contacts to be made by the two men Julie had identified. And perhaps before anything happens, they could round them all up, including Saladin.

Then Guerrero's second call came. It wasn't anything he expected at all the way the agent sounded. In addition, Bartley wasn't sure it sounded like Guerrero at all. He couldn't tell because after identifying himself on the radio, Guerrero spoke only a few harried words.

Need backups fast...I'm hit! Bad!

Where are you?

Restroom...bar lounge...hurry!

He pulled four men out of their posts quickly. Agent Henry Tucker, Tom Hayden, a young 28-year old undercover—six years Navy, three years out of

Quantico, assigned to the two senators in the lower-level sleeper seats; and two of the suits escorting the four other senators in the upper-level.

They figured the thing to do was plug both ends of the lounge car as well as the stairs to the snack lounge in the lower level. He posted Tucker below, at the foot of the stairs. Doug Jones had come and gone, tracking his quarry, Haji Madari, when Tucker took his position in the snack lounge. Bartley posted himself at the doorway between the sightseer lounge and the bar lounge near the restroom with Hayden close behind him as his backup.

He had the two suits enter the lounge from the other end. One of them, fellow named Buck Hudson, an ex secret service and still looked it in his gray suit and red tie, took a position a few feet inside to cover the doorway at that end of the car; also, to back up the other suit, Darrel Ford, ex Marine sergeant and another Desert Storm vet like Guerrero. He was Bartley's pick to get in there first and find out what happened in the restroom.

Minutes before the agents deployed, Omar Husain made sure his men were in position to see them arrive at both ends of the bar lounge car and downstairs at the snack lounge. Hassan Bahaji took a cup of coffee and a donut to a table in the snack lounge. A minute later, a man with a noticeably wary look on his face pulled out a magazine from a rack on the wall and took a seat near the stairs. Even from across the car, Hassan could tell the man was not reading. He was listening, watching the place.

Kashim Najoub appeared to be enjoying the scenery in the sightseer lounge in the upper level, seated near the doorway to the next car which was the bar lounge where, minutes before, he had pretended to be Guerrero when he contacted Bartley on Guerrero's radio to ask for backups.

Capitol West was now coming out of the Shenandoah valley, leaving the scenic juncture of the Potomac and the Shenandoah river at Harper's Ferry and chugging northwest towards western Maryland through the easternmost part of West Virginia. Kashim would have liked to pay more attention to the scenery. But not long after he was seated, a man sat across the aisle from him facing the other side of the train. He was visibly preoccupied and kept his attention more on the doorway to the bar lounge than on the scenery outside.

Shortly before that, at the other end of the lounge, Omar Husain came up the stairs of the coach 1 car where he was seated. He turned towards the doorway to the bar lounge from the coach just in time to see the suits moving inside. First Darrel Ford walking stealthily towards the restroom at the other end, one hand tucked under his coat ready to pull out something in an instant. Stepping across the aisle to a view window of the coach car, Omar saw Buck Hudson, the backup suit, through the door standing alert near the audio equipments of the bar with one hand also concealed under his coat.

Seeing the suits didn't make any difference since they already knew who they were. They would be the first to get hit, with the senators, when things got going after Cumberland. He was expecting to see some undercovers show up too, rushing to the bar lounge perhaps, but none did. Omar hoped Kashim and Hassan had better luck at the other end. He would learn later that they did. Three they saw, they would tell him and identify to him later during a quick tour of the train Kashim led shortly before the train reached Martinsburg.

Inside the bar lounge, when Darrel Ford reached the restroom door, he finally drew his 40 caliber Glock. The door was open about four inches towards him and a man's foot, toes up on its heel on the floor, was visible. He flung the door and swept the Glock in front of him in both hands from one corner of the restroom to the other. Seeing his sudden movement, Buck Hudson pulled out his pistol too and rushed right behind him. Ford hurried down the floor on one knee and pressed two fingers on the side of agent Art Guerrero's neck.

No pulse.

He noticed how Guerrero's head just lay loosely on its side on the floor as if it wasn't connected to his body. He turned it slightly sideways then looked up at Hudson behind him. "He's dead," he declared. "Somebody broke his neck. Let's get Bartley in here quick."

Hudson took the few steps out to the middle of the car and came directly to view of Bartley in the sightseer lounge outside. He gave Bartley an urgent head signal to come in and from his facial and body expression, Bartley knew to hurry the hell into the lounge. Behind him in the sightseer lounge, agent Tom Hayden moved just as quickly as if he was tethered to him when he saw Bartley go through the doorway.

Hayden didn't go in but only stood near where Bartley was seated to cover the doorway. All this happened in plain view of Kashim Najoub sitting a few feet away among a number of other passengers enjoying the scenery. The few minutes that Bartley sat across the aisle from him, he made sure he got a good look at the undercover agent and could identify him the next time he saw him. Now, here's another one of them. Tall, young and strong. In addition, he would learn later that Hassan Bahaji downstairs had one other undercover agent identified.

The idea certainly worked as well as he and Commander Omar had expected. At least, now they knew some more of the enemy. The odds had evened out some.

As soon as they were told, the train conductors moved immediately to seal the lounge bar. A sign was posted at both ends of the car declaring it 'Closed Temporarily'. The snack lounge below stayed open except for the stairs which were blocked with a chain.

Bartley spread the word of what happened, to the 'senators' and to the rest of the force in the train. He put everyone on high alert, this time in anticipation of the enemy striking at anytime. Then he reported immediately to the command and control analysts at headquarters in D.C.

He was ordered to stay the course till after Cumberland—the priority still to identify and capture Saladin. But given the increased risks they now recognized after agent Guerrero's fatal encounter with the enemy, he was given the option to—in their own words—'call the shots' as he deemed necessary to give themselves a fighting chance and protect the innocent, or reduce collateral damage, that is.

He thought about going for a number of options now but none of them sounded solid enough an alternative to the order he was given. There's calling in an assault reinforcement now as he had thought earlier, using the local law enforcement and any military available in the area within the next hour, then frisking everybody as they emptied the train at the next station. He balked at the idea even more now as he imagined someone at headquarters saying: "Sure. Like Saladin—if he was now in the train—or his men who are now in the train, would simply identify themselves and lay down their arms at the station concourse. And even if they did, if it turns out Saladin is not one of them, we'd have been better off calling off Operation Big Thunder in the first place. Forget the possibility that they might take everyone hostage, commandeer the train and…where does it all end?"

Then there's profiling all the passengers and emptying the train of the highly-probable-no-threats a little at a time at the next two or three stations. Martinsburg, now only twenty minutes away; Cumberland, an hour and a half after that and Connellsville in Pennsylvania, two and a half hours from there. Headquarters: "Sure. And how would it look to the enemy when no one else is left in the train but male passengers between the ages of seventeen and sixty?"

Here, Bartley thought to himself: "Dammit, then we should not have launched Operation Big Thunder at all. It just doesn't seem right no matter how you look at it to deliberately risk so many lives to capture Saladin. He's still one man against many innocent people."

The worst-case scenario which may be the safest but possibly most disgraceful for the Bureau was, in a way, calling off the operation by revealing to the enemy that the senators were not in the train. Headquarters: "And then what? Simply ask them to come forward and give themselves up? What if they just started shooting anyway? What if..."

The what-ifs were simply too destabilizing that Bartley opted to just follow the order: stay the course. If Saladin was not in the train yet, Julie may not be entirely wrong about Rockville. He could've changed plans and decided to board at Martinsburg or Cumberland.

He decided he'd bite the bullet, tough it out at least for the next two hours, hoping nothing would happen in that time other than Saladin coming on board and Julie making a positive ID of him. He realized he didn't have much choice other than be so optimistic, so why not? But after Cumberland, he must steel his nerves and make some really hard decisions.

Two minutes before Martinsburg, Omar was back in his aisle seat in the lower level of coach 1 car. The idea of going from one end to the other at both levels of the sleeper 1 car had seemed at first a long precarious journey when Kashim led him and Hassan through it. Four of the senators were in the upper level, the other two down below. He knew security in the car was the tightest and even more so now that they found out there were undercovers as well.

But they went through both levels unnoticed and saw the faces of agents Henry Tucker and Richard Bartley along with the suits in the upper level several seats back of the senators; agent Tom Hayden in the lower level sitting across the aisle from a suit a few seats back of the other two lawmakers. Now, sitting quietly in his coach seat and looking at a travel magazine, his mind didn't see the alluring pictures of Ireland and England he appeared to be concentrating on. An older African-American man in the window seat next to him couldn't have guessed that he was, instead, busy weighing how much difference the undercovers really made to Operation Capitol West.

Considering the end-game of the whole operation, he decided—not a whole lot.

It's good to know now they were here versus being surprised the last minute. And it certainly helped that they identified some of them. Hopefully, there weren't many more.

"Thinking about going there?" he heard the man next to him say suddenly, looking over at the magazine.

He shook his head slightly to snap out of his mental activity and turned to the man, smiling. "I'd like to. Maybe one of these days."

"I heard it's real nice. I have a son, he's an air force pilot. He was stationed there for a while, couple years back. He said it was beautiful there."

"I believe it, looking at these pictures. Where is he now? Your son."

"Ever heard of a place called Qatar?"

"Yes. A small country in the Persian Gulf."

"That's where he's stationed right now, flying patrol missions around Kuwait, southern Iraq and Saudi Arabia. Keeping an eye on those crazy ay-rabs and Muslims over there. Making sure they don't step out o' line."

"Sounds like a big job."

"Oh, yes. And he likes it," the old man said. And beaming proudly, added: "He's a good boy. He always says he hopes whatever he does in life makes a lasting difference to the world. I think that's exactly what he's doing."

"I believe you're right," replied Omar Husain, taking in the measure of pride the man radiated. He wondered how many other Americans think the way this old man did, believed the same way he did about 'those ay-rabs and Muslims'. God Almighty, he thought, when is all this going to end?

The train slowed down as it approached Martinsburg station, gradually coming to a full stop a few seconds later. He closed the magazine and sat back. He thought about the two men, Kashim Najoub's team, who were to board the train at the station. He worried a little, now knowing about the undercover agents. Kashim was to call him to report when they're safely on board.

He turned to look out the window past the old man and saw only a couple of passengers on the concourse moving toward the other cars up front. There was a line ahead of them beyond his view. He turned the other way to avoid possibly having another small talk with the old man. That's when he saw her, coming down the aisle. Behind her, seven or eight feet back was one of the undercovers. They were definitely *not* with each other. Just happened to be passing through in the same direction.

He kept his eyes on her as she got closer. At first he was almost certain it was her especially when she looked down momentarily and her eyes fell on him. The walk, the height and the shape under the fleece coat. He couldn't be a hundred percent sure, though. The hair looked different from how he saw it three hours ago. If only the woman didn't wear that hat and those sunglasses.

He turned back to the window as she went by, followed by agent Richard Bartley. If he had only turned back after they went past him, he could have recognized Chris Phillips, following not more than five feet behind Bartley, on their way to see if Julie might recognize any of the passengers coming on board.

Twelve passengers boarded the train. Eight were men between the ages of twenty and the late fifties, the way they looked to Julie and Bartley and a couple of other agents watching through the view window at the rear of the boarding car. None of them looked anywhere near Saladin's build even as Julie imagined him disguised as one of them. The rest were women casually dressed in jeans, cold-weather jackets and winter waistcoats pulling their light luggage on rollers. Some of the men politely helped them lift their load up the steps to the car from the concourse.

It was a quick call at the station. Within a few short minutes, the two conductors at both ends of the train blew their whistle and the train got on the way again.

The next one and a half hours would prove to be the most tenuous for agent Richard Bartley in the train ride so far. No one had come up with a suspect for Saladin. His last hope as far as Julie was concerned, was Cumberland. They had one fatality, so far. Eddie Green was left alone in coach 2 car watching the two men Julie had identified. Bartley took care of that immediately by having Doug Jones take Guerrero's post, putting him in a vacant seat away from Eddie Green across the aisle and back a few from their quarry in front.

Since the encounter at the snack lounge, it would only be reasonable to count on the enemy thinking—knowing—that their presence in the train had been discovered by the agents. They must now be operating on the belief that two of their men, traveling companions, had both been identified after one of them turned out to be under surveillance by Guerrero. Realizing this, Bartley cautioned Green and Jones to keep a distance between the two of them since they weren't traveling companions, the reason Jones took the seat where he was now. The enemy, after having found Guerrero and killed him, could very well be trying to lure more of the undercovers into exposing their identities, similar to what the agents had been trying to do with the enemy since Julie identified Haji Madari and Masoud Faisal.

Both sides were using the two men and each side knew it. Sounded rather silly when Bartley thought about it, but deadly silly. They're playing cat and mouse using the same bait. So far, he's one man down. One too many.

His mind suddenly paused for a moment from the tangle of everything that had and had not yet happened. Focusing on one luring the other to the open, he went back to thinking about the second call Guerrero made to ask for backups. Thinking about how he was found by agent Darrel Ford on the floor in the restroom. His shirt torn wide open, his wires exposed. Now Bartley recalled how 'he' sounded on that radio call. Oh, damn!

Damn! Damn! How could he have been so careless?

That wasn't Guerrero. Guerrero was out, or already dead, when the call was made. Somebody else made that call, and the purpose was to lure more of them into the bar lounge and blow their cover.

Sonofabitch! That means which UC had been ID'ed by the enemy? Himself, Bartley. The young Tom Hayden, Henry Tucker, and possibly Doug Jones.

This changes everything in the operation from here on, Bartley thought, his mind racing, groping for something to hold on to steady his sensibility. First thing to do is calm down. Stay rational and then go a step at a time.

Perhaps it's a good thing he's now compelled to come to a major decision, not like a couple of minutes ago, when he didn't know exactly what to do, how and when. He called headquarters and after giving them a summary and status of the operation told them: "I'm using my option to call the shots I now deem necessary."

Their position, he told them further, was now at a level of vulnerability that required immediate preemptive action. No one argued with him. The only question was the timing. All the analysts agreed to begin profiling the passengers now, according to Bartley's plan, using the train conductors and service attendants along with the UCs whose covers were still intact. It was agreed too that Bartley will call the shots on the timing which would depend on when they get done with securing the probable-no-threats which should reduce collateral damage by a large percentage or, hopefully, eliminate it altogether. Headquarters felt much better with this prospect.

Bartley spent the next couple of minutes after talking to headquarters conditioning himself, mind and body, to what he knew lay ahead in the next two hours, quite possibly much less. Cumberland was now less than seventy five minutes away.

He considered skipping the station. It was a bigger town than the last two stops and he was reluctant for the train to pick up more passengers, more risks. But he could never live it down if it turned out Saladin was there waiting to board the train so Julie could ID him and they could just grab him.

Profiling the passengers visually would be a most delicate thing to accomplish. In the bar lounge which was now off-limits to the passengers, he quickly but stealthily gathered four people. One of the conductors and a service attendant, agent John Jacobs from his coach 1 car seat behind Julie and Chris, and another agent in the same car across the aisle from Jacobs but traveling separately—Ty Ellis, a 35-year old African-American, seven years UC with the Bureau with a good reputation for being reliable and a team player.

The UCs were fitted in the train uniforms the conductor got from the maintenance closet in the service car. Then the four of them were given instructions on what they needed to do, and how. Very carefully, they were made to understand above all.

Carrying a copy of the passenger manifest on a clipboard, each went out to his assigned passenger car and looked into each passenger in it. Going by seat number instead of name, they asked the passenger one thing—the destination. And they did so with a smile, in a very pleasant and friendly way.

They would start with "Hello, how is everything?" and then, "Destination, please?"

Every now and then, someone would ask and they would simply say: "Routine regulation."

To the left of the passenger list, they marked the probable-no-threats with an 'x', looked at the passenger one last time with a smile and moved on to the next. When they were done, they would return to the bar lounge and pick up the 3 x 4 notes, folded in half, they were to hand to the x'ed passengers in the car somebody else profiled. The message in the note simply said

> *You are required to go to the service car*
> *at the end of the train.*
> *Do not let anyone else see this note.*
> *Please move NOW.*
>
> *—Security.*

They would deliver the notes randomly on each side of the aisle in each car over several passes. This so as not to create the appearance of a mass evacuation. The fact that the seat backs in the coach cars were high enough that the passengers could not be seen from behind helped. The whole car could be empty and any passenger remaining either front or back of the car would have to get up and look to find out. The sleeper cars were even better in that respect because the seats which converted to bunkbeds were partly enclosed for privacy.

"A message for you, sir (ma'am)," they would say in a soft voice, again with that friendly smile especially in the presence of one who's not getting the note.

Kashim Najoub's team, Muhammad Shah and Yussuf Al Mukhtar, traveling separately, settled in their sleeper 1 car lower-level seats near the rear of the car without attracting anyone's curiosity, particularly those of Julie and the FBI, neither of whom had ever seen them before. A minute later, their team leader, Kashim Najoub who sat in the next car, sleeper 2 at the same level, came by from the front end. He gave them an accidental take, an ever subtle nod, and kept going down the aisle back to his seat in the other car.

"They're on," Kashim reported to Omar Husain on the phone right away.

"Good," replied Omar, adding to reaffirm to both of them: "They know what to do."

"Yes, of course. They're ready. Brother Muhammad will be in the dining car in...fifteen minutes, waiting for you."

While the profiling was in progress in the passenger cars, part of that time Muhammad Shah, one of Omar's GWU student sleepers, went into the dining car carrying what looked like a laptop case. There were six people in the car including the two service attendants behind a counter preparing lunch when he walked in and took the table one away from the stairs that led to the sightseer lounge in the upper level. The other four were two teenage girls sitting at a table near the far end of the car from the stair. Across the aisle from them were Julie and Chris.

After Martinsburg, things started to happen one after the other. First, the conductors closed the bar lounge. Next, Julie got a call from Bartley telling them to be prepared to move to the service car at the end of the train after Cumberland or, possibly, even before. He didn't—wouldn't—say why.

"I have no idea," Julie replied when Chris asked. "Your guess or mine."

"Something must have happened or is about to happen," Chris said. "I think we deserve to know, after what they'd been putting us through. Especially if it has something to do with our safety. What's your guess?"

Two more people came in, an older couple. They took a table across from them, next to the two girls. Julie was getting hungry and she had opted to just go to the snack lounge in the next car. But it was too crowded there so they came in here and decided they might as well get lunch. After all, it was almost noon, except service in the dining car was running a little late, they were told by one of the attendants.

"They've been tracking the two I identified at Rockville," Julie answered, taking off her sunglasses temporarily to read the menu. "My guess is they've picked up some intelligence from them. Maybe the two have made contact with the others already on board and Bartley and his men heard them talking."

"So now he's making his move, getting ready for something to happen."

"We'll see what happens when we get to Cumberland."

"Or before," Chris said. "Like any minute now, from what he said."

Over near the other end of the car two rows from the stair, Muhammad Shah, a Soldier of Islam with intensive training in incendiary and controlled explosives was delighted to find out that he didn't need the duct tape he had with him in the case when he positioned the 36-ounce bomb on the wall of the train car up against the underside of the dining table. The flat side of the bomb which he had fashioned with a highly magnetic thin steel plate attached itself to the stainless steel interior finish of the train wall with a snap once he held it within an inch of the metal surface. But for assurance, he double secured it anyway with a length of the two-inch wide duct tape. Then he activated the bomb, which had the power to demolish the whole car upward and sideways, by simply turning the detonator toggle switch on.

In his coat pocket was a multiple-channel RF remote control that had an effective range of four hundred feet through solid objects of any kind. He could be anywhere in the train or outside of it within that distance and set the bomb off. He took it out and made sure the safety switch was off before he accidentally pressed the transmit button and prematurely blow up the dining car with everybody in it including him.

Two cars away in the sleeper 1 car, Yussuf Al Mukhtar, another one of Omar Husain's GWU sleepers, newly activated for Operation Capitol West, had left his seat in the lower level of the car and gone into the restroom of the upper level. He was now getting up from crouching on the floor after taping the 24-ounce bomb on the floor against the back wall of the sanitary supply cabinet.

Back in the dining car, lunch was ready to be served. The servers had finally shown up and begun taking orders. More people had come in. One of them was Omar Husain. He came down the stair from the sightseer lounge above and was looking straight at Muhammad Shah when he stepped on the floor. They had a brief eye contact before Omar turned towards the restroom on the other side of the car. Muhammad waited a minute, looked around stealthily before following. He stood at the door and knocked twice, did it again after a short pause. The door opened and Omar came out, taking the remote control from Muhammad as the latter stepped out of his way and entered the restroom.

Omar pocketed the remote with a three-channel FM transmitter now programmed to signal the receivers (bombs), the two now in place and a third one Muhammad would plant next in the snack lounge, and headed towards the other end of the car. Two tables before the doorway, he looked ahead and nearly held himself in the middle of the aisle when he saw the same woman he saw earlier. Except this time, she didn't have her sunglasses on and he found himself looking at the face of Julie Santorelli at the table with Chris Phillips. She glanced up at him for a moment as he came nearer and turned back to Chris without showing any reaction.

He looked away as soon as he recognized her and kept going. Past the doorway into the snack lounge in the next car, he found a vacant seat with a direct view of the couple at the table in the dining car. He took his time looking at the paper he pulled off a wall rack and eating a sandwich he got from the food dispenser. A while later, he saw them get up and come his way.

He followed them through the snack lounge car into the upper level of coach 1 car. Once he saw where they were seated, he turned and went back down to his seat in the lower level of the car.

That's how they identified brothers Haji and Masoud, he thought as he sat down next to the African-American man in the window seat. At Rockville. But she hadn't recognized him, he felt sure because she had seen him at least three times now.

The man next to him was about to start a conversation when agent Ty Ellis, looking natural in the uniform of a train service attendant, excused himself to the two of them and handed the older man a piece of paper.

"A message for you, sir," said Ellis in a low voice, friendly smile on his face. He regarded Omar Husain with the same smile, gave him a nod and moved on.

Shortly after he got Julie's radio call at fifteen minutes to Cumberland, Bartley finally made the decision to capture Haji Madari and Masoud Faisal. With the help of the two suits, Darrel Ford and Buck Hudson, he gave the order to Eddie Green and Doug Jones. The four of them quietly shadowed the two in their coach 2 seats without incident and escorted them into the bar lounge which now served as the agents' base of operation.

Since Rockville, Julie remained convinced Saladin was either already in the train or would be boarding at either of the next three stations. Then coming back to her upper level seat in coach 1 with Chris from the dining car, they passed Haji Madari along the aisle. He was coming from his upper level seat in coach 2, apparently heading for lunch, when she saw him and was immediately transfixed by what she saw—the crescent-moon-and-star earring on his left ear. She secretly looked long and hard at him behind her sunglasses, thinking for a moment that she might be looking at Saladin. She knew she was not, but at that instant, she became certain that Saladin was already in the train, boarded either at Union Station or Rockville. He must have put on a disguise, without the earring. She then radio'ed Bartley as soon as she got back to her seat.

After Julie's call, Bartley assessed the situation: the profiling was progressing smoothly; the enemy apparently hadn't become aware of anything else since learning of the presence of the undercovers; having had their cover blown, several of the UCs including him now faced a real danger, considering what happened to Guerrero; playing cat-and-mouse with the enemy using the two identified men as bait could take too long to do the FBI any good now that the profiling is on the way, after which the main thrust of the alternate plan of Operation Big Thunder would commence; might as well secure the two men, get them out of the way and eliminate some risk sooner.

At this time, the service car at the end of the train contained nearly a hundred people, about two-thirds of the paying passengers of Capitol West, mostly women of all ages, children, teenagers under sixteen and men visibly sixty and older. The agents realized, as did headquarters, that there's some risk involved in the process, grave risk, so that once a passenger was in the end-car, he or she was searched and interrogated immediately. Several men who turned out to be in their fifties were grilled more thoroughly and held separately in the car, under guard. Some of the passengers demanded to know what's going on. The agents had to come up quickly with something like health and sanitation or environmental protection measures. Sorry for the temporary inconvenience, folks. This won't take long.

Up to the last minute before Cumberland, Bartley debated whether it had been the right decision not to skip the station. But two things nagged at him— the one last chance Saladin might board there, in spite of Julie's feeling about it, and the undercover reinforcements headquarters had requested from the local police.

CHAPTER 38

▼

Capitol West pulled into the Cumberland station on schedule at twelve minutes before one o'clock in the afternoon. Julie and Bartley were promptly at the view window of the boarding car at one side of the door, with Bartley this time staying out of plain view. Agents John Jacobs and Ray Burke, another young twenty-something UC, three years out of Quantico, whom Bartley teamed up with Tom Hayden but had to pull out quickly when Hayden's cover was blown, watched from a distance at the other side of the door.

Ten passengers boarded the train. Two women traveling together, a middle-aged couple and their two pre-teen children, and four men traveling separately. Julie hardly blinked all the time she kept her eyes on the four, switching from one to the other, back and forth like a scanner, recording, analyzing, as they moved up the line. She profiled only two of them as probable threats and neither one came near to looking like Omar Husain: late twenties, early thirties, neatly dressed in their cold-weather outerwear, one carrying a duffel bag, the other a gym bag in one hand and a book in the other.

The other two—one was a gray-haired bearded man wearing dark clothes and a hat, unmistakably Amish, the other a handsome bespectacled late middle-aged man with a small hand-carried luggage, also with some gray hair and with very refined manners. Along with the two women and the family of four, they would be handed the note by a conductor to move to the end car even before the train left the station.

Moments before the whistle blew to warn of the train's departure, agent Jacobs, with a slight hand motion through the rear side window, signaled the four undercover reinforcements waiting behind a wall at the end of the concourse to come on board. The men hurried stealthily one after the other without being seen to the end of the train. They hopped over the steps onto the deck of the service car amidst the dozens of passengers whose growing impatience was now becoming a real concern to the agents and the suits Bartley had pulled from the passenger cars to handle the situation here.

One of the UCs was agent Tom Hayden, the other was Henry Tucker, the two whose cover was blown. Hayden was now teamed with a suit in the lower level of the end car, Tucker with another in the upper level where they were watching over the other passengers, at the same time keeping several men, possible threats, under guard.

One man they should have kept closely guarded but didn't was Marwan Razzak, the newly boarded mild-mannered middle-aged man who was profiled and sent to the end car with the Amish and the other new passengers.

The four reinforcements, undercover detectives from the local surrounding law enforcement jurisdictions, went straight up the FBI base of operation in the upper level bar lounge, three cars up from the end car. There they were briefed quickly in less than three minutes and deployed to take part in the next step of Operation Big Thunder.

Everyone in the passenger cars was seated by the time the train left the station. Shortly before then, Richard Bartley was back in the bar lounge with agents John Jacobs and Doug Jones. Together, they made a last-minute attempt at getting something out of Haji Madari and Masoud Faisal, now cuffed, fully restrained and held apart beyond earshot of each other. They worked on them separately.

Who are you with?

Where are they seated?

How many are aboard?

What is the plan?

Bartley tried bargaining with them. He made them offers, telling them they hadn't actually done anything and if they cooperated, the more likely the government would see fit to let them go. He even brought in Julie briefly to surprise them, hoping either of the men might soften up their stance through her and cough up some information.

While this was going on, the process to ignite the powder keg that was waiting to wreak havoc upon Capitol West began happening. It started with the first whistle before the train started moving.

The team leader of the HRTs, the 'senators' who had been keeping still all this time playing their role, raised Bartley on the radio. It's time, the man said.

They're ready for the next step of the operation which was to round up the remaining passengers and herd them into the bar lounge.

The whistle blew again. As if prompted by this, Bartley gave his go-ahead in two words: "Do it."

Starting from where they were seated, both levels of the sleeper 1 car which was the first of the passenger cars from the front of the train, a dozen FBI agents in suits—the six 'senators' and the six suits guarding them—rose from their seats and began extracting the remaining passengers from their accommodations out to the aisle.

Three minutes earlier in the next car, sleeper 2, Ahman Farooq and Kamran Salama, Marwan Razzak's team who boarded the train and were now seated separately in the upper level, were puzzling over what they saw on their way to their seats.

Where are most of the passengers?

Could Wednesday be a really slow day for the rail business?

It didn't look this way when they took the ride only yesterday.

Thus, Farooq called his team leader, Marwan Razzak, whom he expected to be sitting a few seats nearby in the same car.

In the service car back of the train, Marwan Razzak at that moment had removed himself from the crowd to a corner at the end of the car. He was about to alert Omar Husain to what was going on when Farooq's call came in his cell phone.

He quickly explained what was puzzling Farooq by telling him where he was and what he now realized was happening. He gave instructions for him and Kamran Salama, the other team member, to proceed immediately as planned—move to coach 1 car, their ops base, where Commander Omar as well as leader Hassan Bahaji and his team were seated. Then he called their Commander.

Omar Husain was still trying to get over the surprise at seeing Julie in the train. She's in the same car, he thought somewhat incredulously, in a seat in the upper level right above him.

He was sitting alone. The old man next to him hadn't come back so that he was free from any distraction as he now started preparing himself mentally for what was to occur in the next few minutes. It's time for everyone to gather into the car, he thought, holding the compact RF remote control in one hand. The cell phone in his pocket vibrated.

He listened to Marwan Razzak for a minute without interrupting—a minute too long. A moment after he hung up, the last departure whistle blew. And then he heard a succession of gunshots coming from the snack lounge in the next car.

Through the open doorway, first he saw Kashim Najoub running towards him, turn and shoot at his pursuers. Two men in suits ducked and held their positions back at the far end of the snack lounge behind some furniture. Next, he heard more gunshots this time coming from a greater distance like two cars farther away. But they got nearer, intermittently, every shot.

Kashim Najoub crawled his way through the doorway into the coach car and when he got near enough, he called out to Omar: "Now! Now!"

Sitting across the aisle from Omar, Hassan Bahaji and his team, Jabir Yasin and Mullah Ahmadullah, meantime had risen from their seats and at gunpoint herded the three passengers remaining in the car besides them, into the front-row seats. They were all male in their thirties and forties and had no clue at all what was going on as they obeyed the order of the men holding guns to their heads.

Kashim had been hit. Seeing him bleeding on the floor, Hassan and his men started returning fire at his pursuers. Omar Husain got out of his seat to pull Kashim away from the line of fire and take him to the rear of the car.

A minute before, Muhammad Shah and Yussuf Al Mukhtar, Kashim Najoub's team sitting across the aisle from each other in the lower level of sleeper 1, were about to move to coach 1 through three cars—sleeper 2, dining and snack lounge—according to plan before the train started moving. Then two suits appeared before them and ordered them to put their hands up and get up. They looked up and immediately recognized the two 'senators' they'd been keeping an eye on since they got on board at Martinsburg.

"They knew," thought Yussuf Al Mukhtar, a sudden chill creeping up his spine to the back of his neck. "They faked us. The senators aren't in the train. It's a trap!"

"Mind telling me who you are and what this is all about?" Yussuf Al Mukhtar asked the suit, a skinny blonde thirty-something agent—didn't really look like a senator at all, standing by the front of his seat waiting for him to come out.

The suit was terse and would not be delayed by words: "Federal agents," he said, flashing the badge. "Please do as you're told, now!"

As they were about to get up, the gunbattle in the next car, sleeper 2, involving their team leader, Kashim Najoub, broke out. Kashim had noticed what was happening up front with the few male passengers in the car. When he realized it was his turn and saw the suits approaching along the aisle, he pulled out his gun and bolted. They ordered him to stop. He took a shot at them instead as he kept running through the dining car and into the snack lounge car and felled one of them. The others, two of them—agents Buck Hudson and Darrel Ford, broke their chase in the dining car and took cover behind the seats where they returned fire.

In sleeper 1, everyone got distracted when the shooting in the other cars started. Muhammad Shah saw the opportunity and moved quickly to take advantage of it. He got up fast and rushed the suit—an older man who he thought did look like a senator—standing at his side of the aisle, ramming his head against his solar plexus and knocking the wind out of him. The man fell on top of the other who was also caught off-guard.

The train started moving.

By the time Muhammad turned around and got a start, he saw Yussuf already near the doorway to the next car, running as fast as he could. Muhammad jumped to his feet and followed, sprinting to separate himself from the suits quickly without looking back. He heard one of them, the young one, bark an order for them to stop. He kept going. Then the agent fired a warning shot, shattering a window on the right side of the car. Muhammad tripped as he was crossing the doorway to the next car and fell. Agitated by the shot, he pulled out his gun and turned over on the floor. He raised his upper body partially, aimed and fired twice. The agent fell back.

He got back up and continued running through the sleeper 2 car until he heard a succession of shots and suddenly felt a jolt like somebody punched him hard on the back of his right shoulder. He fell again and realized he had been hit. Yussuf, a good twelve yards ahead of him, turned and saw him on the floor. Yussuf took cover, gun in hand, dropping low behind a seat and began shooting back into the other car.

The exchange of fire continued and intensified with the arrival of agent Ray Burke to reinforce the two agents, now reduced to one after the other—the younger one—chasing Muhammad Shah and Yussuf Al Mukhtar was fatally wounded. Farther back of the train, through the next two cars—the dining and snack lounge—Yussuf heard and actually saw the other gunbattle going on. That between agents Buck Hudson and Darrel Ford who had taken positions just past the doorway between the dining car and the snack lounge, and the men in coach 1 car.

Muhammad and Yussuf had them bottled up but they themselves were in the same situation with the men behind them. There was only one thing to do—hold their position and shoot in opposite directions: Muhammad, bleeding from a shoulder wound but not disabled by it, holding off Ray Burke and the suit, Yussuf helping Hassan Bahaji and his team in coach 1 take out Hudson and Ford from his end in the sleeper 2 car.

As soon as Hudson and Ford became aware somebody else was shooting at them from behind, they did the same, Ford turning around and returning Yussuf's fire.

Bullets flew non-stop for several seconds throughout the train at the lower level. The few remaining passengers scattered throughout hugged the floor in terror, deafened by the noise of the gunfights. But all that was suddenly muted by a horrendous explosion when Omar Husain, in coach 1, set off the bomb in the upper-level restroom of the sleeper 1 car. The shock wave traveled in both directions of the train, spiraling like a horizontal tornado through every car.

The roof and upper-level sidewalls of sleeper 1 flew out in shards, pieces of furniture hurtling in every direction along with numerous body parts of both the government agents and the remaining passengers they were rounding up. The floor bent and gaped open from the restroom to half the length of the car as if a hundred tons of rock dropped on it and fell through.

Trapped at the end of the snack lounge, outgunned by the enemy and lacking cover on both sides, Hudson and Ford took advantage of the shooting break due to the blast and clambered up the stairs to the bar lounge. Yussuf went in pursuit, squeezing a couple of rounds up at the stairs but thought better. He turned and called out to Muhammad to follow him into the coach 1 car.

Muhammad, slowed by the bullet in his shoulder, waved at Yussuf to go ahead, he'd follow momentarily. He let out a quick volley at Ray Burke and the suit with the 9 mm MAC M11 submachinegun, backing up a step at a time, then turned to hurry after Yussuf. He didn't take three steps before another round from the agents struck him in the upper torso, and then another and another. He was dead before he hit the floor.

Back in the service car at the end of the train, after he talked to Omar Husain on the phone, Marwan Razzak immediately worked his way to get back in the coach 2 passenger car. But he ran into agent Tom Hayden and the suit.

"I need to get back to my seat and get my belongings," he told them.

"We'll take care of it for you shortly, sir," Hayden replied, holding out a hand and blocking the doorway to the other car.

At this moment, the departure whistle blew.

Suddenly, the mild manners and the refined man disappeared as Marwan Razzak pulled out a powerful .40 caliber Smith and Wesson pistol and shot Hayden point-blank. He aimed next at the suit who raised his hands up quickly and backed off helplessly with the crowd of horrified passengers behind him.

Marwan Razzak moved through the doorway by backing up to it. Then the train started moving—that part of the train behind him which was the coach 2 car, but not the service car where they were. He turned and saw that the end car had been loosened from the next, the gap widening between the two. Stepping over to the edge of the end car while keeping the gun pointed at the suit inside, he leaped head first diagonally to the coach car before it got too far.

He landed just inside the door, crashing on his right knee on the floor, left foot hanging out over the edge. He pulled himself up and in, pain radiating from his knee up and down his right leg. But a moment later, a sharper pain suddenly erupted on his lower backside and he fell back on the floor. The suit in the stationary end car had started shooting several rounds before the train got outside thirty yards of it. One of them found its mark just below Marwan Razzak's left rib-cage, the .40 caliber bullet tearing through his flesh but missing the bones and exiting straight out to his front as he now felt with his right hand.

He crawled on his belly away from the back door, leaving a trail of blood behind him on the floor. A few more bullets ricocheted over his head through the doorway until the train turned northwest and got farther away.

In the upper level of the coach 1 car, before the train left the station, Julie returned to her seat from Bartley's interrogation of the two captives in the bar lounge. All they got out of the two men were surprised looks at seeing Julie again. They were men totally committed to their cause. Bartley admired their commitment. He wished it had been for a better cause.

Julie found Chris getting impatient at not being informed about what the hell was going on. He asked her if she knew when they should move to the end car, and why.

"He didn't tell me why," she answered. "But he said stay put for now. We didn't have time to talk much. They were real busy in there. Bartley's constantly on the radio with different people, the phone with the bosses at headquarters in D.C. And then six men, more agents I imagine, came in and reported for duty. They had a quick briefing with the other agents already in there and they went out again."

Chris looked at Julie directly and asked: "Tell me, do you really think he's aboard?"

"Yes," she replied a bit abruptly. "I know he's here. Bartley thinks so too."

The six men Julie talked about consisted of the two African-American agents Ty Ellis and Eddie Green, and the four-men reinforcement Jacobs had brought in. Ty teamed up with two of them, locals named Perkins and Grayson, and Eddie with the other two—Holden and Peebles. An air of discomfort became apparent among them at first, everyone suddenly realizing the oddity in each team: a pair of homegrown white law enforcers, in what may be a race-sensitive small town, being led by a black man. But the moment they were deployed out in the passenger cars to round up everybody into the bar lounge, face a common enemy and look after each other, they were a team, men to whom nothing mattered but their common mission and getting the job done.

They moved quickly, starting with the last passenger car, the coach 2 car, one team at each level. Eddie's team worked the lower level. They were halfway through, frisking two young men on each side of the aisle when the last departure whistle blew. They could see the end car with some of the people in it staying put as the train started moving moments later.

Then they heard a shot. A man in the end car collapsed. Another man leaped over from the end car through the doorway of the departing train at the back of the coach 2 car and landed face first. Bullets flew into the coach car from the unmoving end car. Everybody hit the deck.

The shooting stopped as the train picked up speed and got farther away form the end car. Marwan Razzak crawled farther into the coach 2 car, bleeding on his side. As he began to pick himself up, he raised his head and found himself staring at the gun barrel of Eddie Green.

Ty Ellis and his team had gone through the upper level fast and rounded up three men without any problem. They were now moving into the coach 1 car, coming in from the rear.

Julie and Chris saw them frisk a couple of men two seats back of them. Before this, they had been listening to what they thought at first as firecrackers coming from a distance in the lower level. Chris wasn't entirely sure but it sounded to him like firearms discharging. And if they were, there must be one hell of a gunfight going on downstairs, he thought.

In the next instant, they become oblivious of that when the bomb exploded.

They felt the train rattle along the track and thought it would derail. With that came an overwhelming turbulence that swept upon them through several cars, turning the train into a moving wind-tunnel. Their first reaction was to abandon their seats and secure themselves in the lower level of the car. Pulling Julie behind him by a hand, Chris led the way to the stair.

The moment he set foot on the lower floor, he looked up and saw three men gather around, all pointing their guns at him. Hassan Bahaji, one of the three, immediately ordered them to the seats behind the three other passengers they were holding captive in the front row.

Three more of their men had arrived in the car and they couldn't have come any sooner: Yussuf Al Mukhtar, from the gunbattles with the agents in the sleeper cars and Marwan Razzak's team of Ahman Farooq and Kamran Salama, from sleeper 2 upper level. Marwan Razzak himself, their team leader, appeared at this time to have been lost.

A minute earlier, Omar Husain together with the other leaders, Kashim Najoub and Hassan Bahaji, had quickly agreed on a change of plan to Operation Capitol West. After they killed the senators with the bomb and overpowered their security, they were going to remain where they were and have a couple of men take over the locomotive car to commandeer the train to the planned rendezvous with Abu Kamal for their getaway. But because of the presence of the undercovers which they didn't count on during their weeks of planning and who were now closing in on them on both ends of the coach 1 car, they were now going to move to the front end of the train.

Given the situation of the moment, they had less of the enemy to overcome going in that direction after the blast and the damage Yussuf, Muhammad and Kashim had inflicted upon the agents at that end. But they had no idea of the strength of the enemy force that was yet awaiting them from both levels and at either end of the train.

No matter, they had to move now, and fast. This they realized even more so in the next moment when, to their surprise, they heard Marwan Razzak—wounded and held captive by the agents in the next car—shout a warning to them in Arabic, urging them to move up the train. And they did.

The shooting that followed was twice as fierce and loud as before. Three men—Yussuf Al Mukhtar leading Ahman Farooq and Kamran Salama, headed the move up front through the snack lounge and the dining car, spraying rounds from their MAC11 subs along the way. Some passengers caught in the gunbattle earlier remained cowering under the tables and seats of the lounge. Hassan Bahaji's team brought up the rear, stepping back as they returned the fire that had started coming from agent Eddie Green's team in the coach 2 car.

Hassan took a hit on the left arm as he hopped the doorway from the coach 1 car to the snack lounge. Omar and the wounded Kashim Najoub were pinned down on the floor behind a row of seats next to Julie and Chris. More fire was now coming at them as Ty Ellis' team came down from upstairs and joined Eddie Green's. The agents had yet to cross the doorway to coach 1. They tried but were met with a barrage from the group, taking some hits. Omar now realized that when that happened, they better be out of there and as far as they could be in the dining car or beyond. He moved a hand to feel the RF remote control in his shirt pocket to make sure he still had it.

They must make it out of the coach car, past the dining and into the sleeper 2. But first, they had to get through the obstacle of the doorway as Hassan did, before the agents made it through their own obstacle at the other end.

With more of the enemy shooting at them now, there was only one way to do it. The moment he touched on the idea, he told everyone in rapid Arabic. It was to be a concerted effort which they did not a moment sooner. Agent Bartley and several others upstairs had started to descend the stair but was repelled by a burst of gunfire and had to pull back up. Omar then gave the signal to open up non-stop, rise and grab a hostage for a shield and back up through the doorway into the snack lounge car.

With powerful guns blazing inches away from their faces, the hostages were petrified and simply let their captors drag them backwards into the next car. It worked. Bartley's group didn't dare fire a shot, the same with Ty Ellis and Eddie Green's forces at the other end.

Hassan's team, Jabir Yasin and Mullah Ahmadullah, held the position at the doorway to hold back the agents while the rest went through the next two cars, dragging the hostages along. Every one of them believed it was just a matter of time—minutes, seconds—before their captors turned their guns on them and finished them up. They waited in horror, except Julie.

Earlier, when she first heard Omar speak, she recognized his voice immediately. And moments ago when he grabbed her for his hostage, wrapping his arm around her neck and dragging her backwards, she knew he had recognized her and Chris. She was more afraid of being shot by the agents than of Omar hurting her.

She waited for a good time to speak to him. This came while they were halfway through the snack lounge car. Most of his men and the other hostages had moved farther away in the car than they had. She felt as if Omar deliberately wanted to separate himself from them for the moment.

"Omar, please stop these killings now," she pleaded to him. "It's absolutely senseless. None of the senators are even here. You must see how meaningless all of it is."

"Nothing makes any sense any more," he said without feeling. He had known from Yussuf earlier about the fake senators. "Life is meaningless. For me it is."

"No life is meaningless," she said. The words came out of her as if they were just there, cached in her mind waiting to be spoken at the right moment. "Look at me, Omar." She twisted away from his arm's hold around her and locked her eyes with his. "It's never too late to redeem one's self. To save one's self. Please listen to what's really inside you. I know it's there, within you."

They stood little more than a foot from each other with his arm over her shoulder, hand clutching her back. He had never been this close to her for as long with their eyes locked on each other and him touching her.

As in the house in Arlington and in Fort Hunt, he felt so vulnerable to her. There was no escaping her knowing his thoughts, the guilt that ate in him for the grief he had caused her and many others through the years, the anguish he now suffered for what he had allowed himself to become, for living the life he lived.

He felt they were back in their moment of parting at the parking lot by the chapel a few hours ago with her pleading to him and him backing off, hiding his tears from her while the two sides of him continued to do battle: one with that voice in his mind pleading to him, like Julie; the other with all that anger and hatred that would not relent. But seeing her so close, touching her and looking into her eyes, into her soul, the voice in his mind prevailed, all that hatred and anger in one side of him abated.

He did not look away this time even as his eyes began to moisten.

Even as Julie continued to hold that imploring look in her eyes and in a quiet voice, pleaded to him one more time: "Please?"

There was a loud explosion of what sounded like a grenade, just outside the doorway in the coach 1 car, shattering what remained of the glass walls and windows in the car. One of the men defending the entry, Jabir Yasin, face covered with blood tossed in the air and fell dead on his back. The agents had now entered the coach 1 car and were coming up, zigzagging from one side of the aisle to the other behind each row of seats.

It came only in a flash of a second but Julie saw it clearly on Omar's face. That yearning to be free of his burdens, the weariness, and the most telling of all that sad look in his eyes followed by an ever subtle but quite distinguishable nod he gave her in answer to her pleading.

He put his arm back around her neck and continued to drag her backwards as a shield against the advancing government forces. She understood what he was now doing, what he would do, to free himself of his burden, of Saladin, and relieve the anguish that tortured his soul.

With this understanding, all her apprehensions vanished, even her anger. If he must be brought to justice, she thought, and atone for everything he had done, this was the time for it. Not to judge and punish but to allow the opportunity to make up for past wrongdoings by preventing future ones. And not just the killings and destruction but the clashes of belief, the disrespect of one another, the resulting hatred and alienation.

For this, she would be willing to be a part of it if it meant risking her life more than she ever had before this day. But first, he must survive. He must continue to live.

He caught up with Hassan Bahaji and Kashim Najoub who had now joined forces with Yussuf Al Mukhtar and the other two to dislodge the enemy blocking their way to the front end of the train—the locomotive car. Agent Ray Burke and the one suit with him, both severely wounded, had pulled back to the far end of the sleeper 2 car. With the increased firepower coming at them, they decided they didn't stand a chance and hurried up the stairs to escape to the upper level.

Yussuf and his men then simply walked to the next car, the baggage car, blasting their way through into the locomotive car, and took control of the train from the two terrified engineers.

The three leaders, Kashim Najoub, Hassan Bahaji and their commander, Omar Husain, had now reached the sleeper2 car with the half dozen hostages in their hands. Everything was now turning out almost exactly as they had planned—take control of the train, maintain a distance between them and their pursuers in the train, keep going to the rendezvous point with the pickup team a mile and a half up state Highway 40 from Cumberland.

A couple of things remained to be seen. Did the FBI call for support? I would, thought Omar, if I were their leader. With all the government resources at their disposal, either ground or air support. The other leaders agreed. If they had, then how long before it gets here? And if they hadn't yet, then prevent them from doing so before they did.

The agents had now advanced to the near end of the coach 1 car. They had pushed the two men, Mullah Ahmadullah and Ahman Farooq who had joined him from the engine car, past the snack lounge and into the dining car.

The leaders in the sleeper 2 next to the dining car listened to the gunbattle as it got closer. The hostages sat on the floor near the end of the car curled up against a seat or the wall. One of the leaders, Kashim Najoub, turned to Commander Omar.

"Commander, there's little time left," he said urgently.

As if they heard, the men now controlling the locomotive car powered up the engine. The train picked up speed rapidly. Omar Husain didn't react at once and for a moment, Kashim Najoub saw him hesitate, deep in thought.

Another explosion occurred in the snack lounge, near the doorway to the dining car, pushing the men farther back into the sleeper 2.

"Commander," Kashim called again amid the heightened noise of the speeding train and the gunbattle coming closer. The agents had now entered the snack lounge.

Realizing this, Omar suddenly turned to Kashim and handed over the remote control. Then he and Hassan Bahaji herded the hostages into the next car, the sleeper 1.

A moment later, seeing the agents move closer in the snack lounge car and one of the men, Ahman Farooq, take a fatal hit, Kashim pressed the button that set off the bomb in the car. The whole train seemed to have lifted off the track for an instant. It felt as if the whole world exploded as again the shock wave traveled horizontally through the cars in both directions and everything flew out of the exploded car's sides—pieces of furniture, food dispensers, people, kitchen equipment.

The cars wobbled and whined on the tracks for a while and everyone thought the train was going to derail this time. But it didn't and kept going at the same speed. The blast appeared to have deadened everything. There was an eerie calm that descended on the train in the absence of the gunfire that a minute ago filled the air, that sense of death and destruction in the battlefield when the fighting was over.

But it wasn't. When they were pushed back in the upper level earlier, agent Richard Bartley with his group, coming from the bar lounge above the snack lounge, decided to approach the enemy from above and surprise them by coming down from different cars. One thing they didn't count on, however, was another bomb hit.

Two men, Ray Burke and the suit with him who were halfway down the stairs, along with most of the people in the snack lounge below: the team of Ty Ellis, Perkins and Grayson, one of Eddie Green's team members—Peebles, and several passengers trapped in the car, perished in the explosion. Eddie Green and Red Holden, his other team member, who had not yet entered the snack lounge, survived.

There were three men left in the upper-level bar lounge when the explosion occurred downstairs—a suit, Darrel Ford, who was left to guard the captives, Masoud Faisal who was chained to a four-inch round steel post by the bar and Haji Madari, chained separately to the newel below the handrail at the stairs at the other end of the car near where the bomb was in the snack bar below. Darrel Ford was standing right at the top of the stairs watching Ray Burke and the other suit get halfway down the stairs when the bomb blew up.

He had the luck of having been assigned to stay upstairs and not descending the stairs with the others to their deaths. But he was knocked down by the impact of the blast, hit his head on the edge of a table and dropped out cold on the floor a short distance from Haji Madari.

Haji Madari had resigned himself to seeing his part through the duration of Operation Capitol West chained to the post. But now, he came to life as he watched the FBI agent knocked out, bleeding on the floor. He could see the Glock .40-caliber semi-automatic partly showing under Ford's suit coat. His hands, restrained by the cuffs around the post, were no use so he extended a foot to reach the man on the floor. The thing to do was hook the tip of his shoe under the belt and pull. The agent was slightly beyond reach at the waist. But it might be possible. He'd have to try doing it with either foot, see which has a better reach, and stretch hard. Stretch really hard...and then pull...

In the sightseer lounge in the next car, Bartley, moving carefully to the front of the train together with the remaining agents, worried about another bomb. He had finally decided to call for the choppers minutes earlier and now couldn't wait to see them appear in the sky.

With the bombs, the whole operation had taken a completely different direction and was turning into one of the deadliest he had ever been a part of. So far, the casualties on their side, not counting collateral damage, had gone far beyond he and anyone at headquarters had imagined. One thing he could almost certainly count on right now—the end of his career with the Bureau, whether or not he came out of this in one piece.

He could have called the whole thing off, insisted on it. He could've argued more than he did. Saladin and his backers would have pulled out as well had the FBI revealed that the government knew about their planned attack, that the senators weren't going to be in the train. Never mind that his bosses and the analysts at headquarters had overridden his argument and given the order to proceed as planned.

So, maybe headquarters might take the brunt of the responsibility for going ahead with Operation Big Thunder even at such high risks in both assets and collateral damage as he told them repeatedly. But he's as much a part of the operation as anybody else. Never mind that he took measures to minimize those risks and that a major part of it paid off—saving most of the passengers in the end car of the train and filtering out the potential suspects. Never mind that they had now identified the enemy and known who to shoot at. It wasn't enough.

Nearly a dozen agents, UCs, HRTs and the locals, wiped out in an operation they weren't even sure at first was going to happen, where they deployed nearly blindfolded and used live decoys as sitting targets. On top of these, the main objective of the operation—Saladin—hadn't materialized. Not to mention that Julie, this time with Chris Phillips and other passengers, was again taken hostage. He continued to have the gut feeling, though, that Saladin was aboard, that he was one of the men they had been doing battle with.

He now believed they had all underestimated the man. His skills and intelligence. Clearly, this was a man who had made a lifetime commitment to destroy his enemies and their allies. Even those who might only be his perceived enemies perhaps because they did not share his belief and ideology. What they're dealing with here was either one of the following or any combination of—a religious zealot, a cultural and social extremist, an individual bearing deep personal grudges against America and the West, the Christians and the Jews, or simply a highly paid, cruel, cold-hearted and calculating mass killer

Agent Richard Bartley couldn't have been more right about the man he was in pursuit of in every way he thought of him now, but not since the last time Julie spoke to Omar Husain only minutes ago.

Coming back into sleeper 1 from talking to Yussuf Al Mukhtar in the engine car, Omar Husain spoke briefly to Hassan Bahaji in rapid Arabic. Some of the hostages, including Julie and Chris, on whom Hassan kept his submachinegun trained menacingly as if ready to finish them off any moment picked up on what was said when they noticed Hassan point his weapon away from them, nod dutifully to his commander and back off. Omar stepped through the doorway into the sleeper 2 car and spoke next to Kashim Najoub and Mullah Ahmadullah. The men, guns at the ready for anything that moved as the smoke of the devastation from the bomb explosion cleared, likewise responded agreeably to what they were told by their commander. A moment later, Omar received a call on his cell phone.

"Commander," said Khalil Majid, sitting in the LeSabre at a high ground a short distance from Highway 40 overlooking the railroad track. He could now see the train approaching about three quarters of a mile and told Omar. A few yards from him beside a shade tree was the Toyota Land Cruiser SUV with Abu Kamal Ramshallah in the front passenger seat and Ghulan Wahid at the wheel.

"Everything is going well according to plan. Stand by," Omar said on the phone. He talked fast. Everything happening at the moment happened fast. In seconds, half seconds, such as when they heard shots in the sightseer lounge above the dining car, followed by loud voices, footsteps rushing, and more shots.

In the upper-level bar lounge, a few moments ago, Haji Madari had finally taken possession of Darrel Ford's pistol just as the agent was coming to. They had a brief struggle which ended with the agent taking a bullet in the head. Haji Madari discovered a second pistol in the agent's coat, a semi-automatic .357SIG Sauer, which he gave to Masoud Faisal after freeing him from the steel post. The shot alerted agents Doug Jones and Buck Hudson in the sightseer lounge in the next car. They turned back and engaged in a gunbattle with the two enemies in the bar lounge.

Directly below them, another gunbattle started when agent Eddie Green and local lawman Red Holden who had now crawled out of the devastated snack lounge into the dining car, surprised their enemies in the sleeper 2 car by opening up with their handguns. Mullah Ahmadullah who was positioned nearest the doorway between the cars took a hit but managed to fall back halfway through the car and take cover behind the seats. He and Kashim Najoub with Omar Husain across the aisle near the end of the car then returned fire, pouring rounds through the doorway from their submachineguns.

At this time, the train had reached the rendezvous point with the pick-ups waiting some fifty yards up on the side of the road, and came to a quick stop. Omar Husain was stepping back to go into the sleeper 1 car when he heard Hassan Bahaji's call to duck. But it was a little late. An agent had started to descend the stair from the upper level of sleeper 2 and opened up as soon as he saw Omar Husain. The agent jumped back up when Hassan opened up at him through the doorway from sleeper 1. Omar Husain stumbled through the doorway after taking a .40-caliber round in his right shoulder.

"Hurry!" he called to Hassan, getting back up on his feet. "Let's get them all out now!"

They opened the door and at gunpoint told the hostages to disembark quickly. In the process, an agent, followed by another, again appeared at the top of the stairs spraying rounds into the sleeper cars randomly. Seeing them, Hassan grabbed one of the hostages, Chris, and used him as a shield as they were disembarking. Omar Husain did the same with Julie, snatching her on his way out through the door. They fell diagonally feet first and rolled on the ground away from the train into a grass area. The train then started moving again and picked up speed quickly.

After setting the speed at 80-mph, the two men operating the train, Yussuf Al Mukhtar and Kamran Salama, left the locomotive car and joined the battle with the agents.

In the sleeper 2 car, Kashim Najoub now turned his attention on the agents coming down the stairs while Mullah Ahmadullah kept busy holding off the enemies in the dining car, agent Eddie Green and Red Holden, who had now been joined by two other agents from upstairs. In the bar lounge, Haji Madari and Masoud Faisal couldn't get past agents Jones and Hudson. They decided they would go downstairs and see about working their way through the lower level to get to the front of the train.

Coming down the ruins of the snack lounge, they immediately came under fire when they walked near the doorway to the dining car. Masoud Faisal took two rounds in the upper body from agent Eddie Green and a suit. Knowing at that instant his life was coming to an end, he gathered all the strength he had left and hopped into the dining car, pumping rounds to his last breath at everyone he saw in the car. He took another four rounds before he dropped. Haji Madari was right behind him and did the same, killing Red Holden in the process before being gunned down by the suits.

At that same moment, Kashim Najoub—bleeding with multiple wounds and no longer able to return fire at the agents who had now made their way down into the sleeper cars from upstairs, pressed the third button of the remote control in his left hand and set off the bomb under the table in the dining car.

Once again, the cars wobbled on the tracks, the wheels screaming as the shock from the explosion forced them in different directions, causing the train to twist and wriggle like a wounded serpent. The entire dining car blew up. The blast which appeared twice as powerful as the ones before tore up the sides clean and split the structure of the upper level wide. Parts of everything in the car and most of what held it together flew in all directions. No one in it was spared this time. Even some of the agents in the adjoining car, the sleeper 2, suffered injuries from the flying debris.

Agents Richard Bartley, John Jacobs and a number of suits, some of them still coming down from upstairs, were just steadying themselves on their feet when a submachinegun barrage came at them through the doorway from the sleeper 1 car. Two suits went down, fatally wounded. Bartley took a round on the right leg but was able to take cover behind a row of seats next to Jacobs.

In a suicide charge, Yussuf Al Mukhtar and Kamran Salama plunged into the sleeper 2 car spraying rounds everywhere. One of the suits halfway down the stairs managed to keep his calm and with full concentration took them out quickly one at a time, one sure round each to the head from his Glock 20 pistol.

Moments later, everyone rose to their feet, gun trained at every direction they turned. But now, outside of the sound of metal against metal the train made on the tracks, there was only silence throughout.

Agent Richard Bartley noticed a shiny object near the doorway to the dining car as he inched up from behind a row of seats. Limping from the bleeding gunshot wound on his right leg, he went to pick it up.

After looking at it a few seconds, a tiny smile formed at a corner of his mouth, on his face an expression of great satisfaction. Agent John Jacobs saw him and came over.

"What is it?" he asked curiously.

Bartley laid the object flat on the palm of his hand and showed Jacobs the crescent-moon-and-star earring he remembered seeing worn by Saladin.

They watched Capitol West get farther away, curve slightly northward in the direction of its next stop at Connellsville, Pennsylvania. The hostages stayed low on the ground either crouching on hands and knees or flat on their stomach, afraid to move with Hassan Bahaji keeping his submachinegun on them while waiting for Omar Husain to make the next move.

Up on the side of the road at a distance, Khalil Majid, Abu Kamal and Ghulan Wahid waved at them urgently.

"Commander!" Hassan Bahaji, looking much weakened now from the wound in his left arm, called to Omar.

Omar raised a hand to him and said something in Arabic. He took Julie by the arm to help her get up and the two of them stood close for a few moments, unable to take their eyes off the train. The sound of the explosion still rang in their ears.

"I'm sorry about that," Omar said in a contrite voice, now turning to Julie. "There was nothing I could do."

"I know," Julie said. "I understand."

Their eyes were fixed on each other for a long time, speaking words neither one had to say to each other. There was a sense of loss mirrored on both their faces and this too they both knew. They both understood so well. Their grief for what had been, how their paths in life had crossed and how irrevocable everything else was between them.

"You made me want to live," Omar finally said, unable to contain the urge. "You saved my life."

"I'm glad I did," replied Julie. She regarded him kindly before she suddenly turned her eyes away from him to listen to a distant sound in the sky.

Omar Husain looked far to the south over Julie's head and saw the helicopters approaching fast. The wound on his right shoulder throbbed.

"Thank you," he said, touching her face lightly with his left hand before stepping away. "You won't regret it. I promise."

EPILOG

▼

Since Herod Hardin and several of his Branch staff were hauled out of the office in handcuffs, their offices and workstations were sealed, a yellow 'Off Limits' sticker set on the doors. No one knew exactly what had happened outside of the rumor that a serious breach in data security had occurred in the office.

Suddenly, everybody in all the Branches throughout the Division got worried. In their daily activities, most people working in any IT environment, especially in government, usually concerned themselves only with hackers, viruses and worms, or abuse of use. But not a security breach bad enough for somebody to be hand-cuffed and summarily thrown in jail.

Then came the news of Robert Grundell's disappearance and, later, murder. That brought on a grim atmosphere in the office nobody ever imagined.

A series of investigations followed. Everybody was on edge. Anybody could be a suspect for no reason at all, and without even knowing about it. The FBI had set up a case field office next to that of the head of the Treasury Office of Civil Defense Logistics in the tenth floor. Everyone employed in OCDL was called in for an investigative interview.

Agents Nancy Schneider and Frank DiPaolo were placed in charge of the investigations. They were supported by a panel of three analysts from headquarters and a couple of IT specialist contractor staff.

The people in Milton Pheasant's Interstate Logistics Division were the first to be interviewed, including him, the Division head. An hour before on the day he was called in, Pheasant asked Max Poysen, one of his most senior and experienced IT staff in the Division, to come into his office.

"I need somebody in the Plans and Security Database Branch. To take Herod Hardin's place, for the time being," the Division Chief told Max Poysen. "You're the best I could think of in the Division."

Max was real slow responding.

Over the weekend, he had a quick talk again—for the second or third time—with his wife of twenty-seven years about retirement. It came up when he was telling her about what was happening in the office but he initially meant to bring it up by itself.

Since he became eligible for regular retirement when he made the 55/30 rule two and a half months ago, he had been itching to make the decision. One itty-bitty good reason to go, he thought in the back of his mind, he'd do it.

"I'll think about it," he told his wife whom he loved very much, the last time they talked about it.

Now, both he and his wife were convinced the investigation provided more than enough reason for him to do it.

Money was no longer a problem. He had a good nest egg built with his mutual funds, IRAs, Thrift Savings Plan—the federal government's equivalent of the 401K in the private industry, where he had tons of money, credit union savings and CDs, to top off his thirty-year federal civil service pension for life.

And if he got bored and got the itch to go back to work like a lot of retirees were doing instead of just hanging around waiting to drop, it wouldn't take him more than a phone call to a couple of contractor project managers he had kept busy working over the years even during lean times to get something lined up in a week or two. All he had to do, like some people in the Division had done, was wait six months before coming back as a double-dipper contractor staff.

When he told this to his wife, she said matter-of-factly: "You'd be getting two paychecks."

"Easily," he said. "For doing the same things I do now."

"Go for it," she said. "If you want to keep working, you'd be losing money by staying. What for? You could either make more money—if that's what we want—or enjoy life now, go see the world. Just don't forget to take me with you."

The following Monday, he started gathering papers—personnel records and retirement forms and started filling them out. He went down to personnel and talked to a retirement counselor for an hour. Two days later, this morning, he was ready to go back and submit the completed forms. Then Milton Pheasant called him in.

He gave Pheasant a discerning look as if he was thinking hard about what he just heard. Actually, he was trying to find a way to say something like 'Take that job and shove it up your...' or similar to 'You got the place into this mess, it's your problem. Don't look at me. I'm getting out of here.' And you should've gone to jail with the rest of them, he thought in addition.

He had other things in the back of his mind, most of which concerned Robert Grundell and how he was tied up to all that had happened, possibly including the terrorist attack on the Capitol West train just the past week. No one else in the world had the slightest idea of what he knew. Unless perhaps some of these FBI IT people conducting the investigation now were thorough enough to...

He switched positions in his chair in front of Pheasant's expensive shiny desk, suddenly remembering one thing he just now realized he should have done right away after people in the office were rounded up by the FBI. They could be looking at it right now.

Shit!

"By the way, I also plan to make the announcement," he heard Pheasant say next, "that a decision to abolish the position held by Leon Justice had been made by the Undersecretary of the Treasury for OCDL, and myself."

Pheasant also informed him that all the Classified Clearance categories—Critical, Critical Sensitive, Secret and Top Secret—had been suspended throughout the Division.

Everything the man said to him now sounded meaningless. News of the success of the protest against Leon Justice's position gave him some lift but even that meant nothing now. Nothing could top seeing Leon Justice and the bunch of them in jail.

"As the acting Branch chief, of course you'd be compensated with the salary of that position and grade which must be higher than your current salary."

Max didn't give a shit, thinking you could offer me even your job and I'd be equally tempted to tell you what you can do with it.

He decided he'd jerk the guy around a bit for a few days, not telling him of his decision to retire the end of the next pay period.

"Gee, Milton, this is totally unexpected," he started out. "You caught me totally off-guard with this."

"As I said, you're the best I got."

"I appreciate your confidence."

"I'm up for the interview upstairs in a few minutes. Let's talk about it some more later if you want more time."

"Yes. I'll think about it."

As soon as he got back to his workstation, Max brought up the source program of the system monitor software that logged accesses to any file, especially classified ones. The software itself documented any change made to its source program the first time it executed after the source was updated, creating a log record showing the date and time of the update and the userid that did the update.

He scrolled down through the source program until he got to the routine Robert Grundell had asked him to insert in the program:

> *If &&userid = OCDLRAG and &&termid = ILD41 and &&time = 1000 thru 1200*
> *userid = OCDLLTJ, termid = ILD70   endif*
> *If &&userid = OCDLRAG and &&time = 1500 thru 1700*
> *userid = &&enter   endif*

He deleted all four lines and replaced it with what's known in programming jargon as the universal truth, a dummy code,

> *If 1 = 1 endif*

and saved to update the source program quickly. Then he sat back and breathed a sigh of relief for a minute before getting up again to go down to personnel to submit the retirement forms.

The following day, coming back from lunch, he looked at the Washington Post and saw the pictures of Herod Hardin and Leon Justice at the bottom half of the front page.

The article heading read: '*U.S. Tightens Access to Government Data*'.

And the sub-heading: '*Intense Investigation Underway on Treasury Espionage Case*'.

At two o'clock in the afternoon, still carrying the front section of the paper, he sat in the FBI case field office in the tenth floor across the table from Jerome Bolden, Ray Huai-lo and Nancy Schneider. They grilled him for nearly an hour. Each had a copy of his resume, actually the old federal government standard application form SF-171, now obsolete, he submitted when he applied for the job eighteen years ago.

After they got past the academic background and employment history including present job, forty minutes into the investigative interview, they started digging into his present duties and responsibilities. The three of them took turns. They were very thorough, especially the Chinese guy, who was apparently a more experienced system software engineer than he was. He asked detailed technical questions that zeroed in on what he worried about the day before.

"You have update access to the system software in your Branch, is that correct?" he asked.

"Yes. Actually, I have access Division-wide. System software are used by all the Branches throughout the Division."

"Operating System, Job Control, Text Editors, Data Audit, Journaling and Monitoring software, to name a few. Is that correct?"

"Yes, sir."

"I see here—" Ray Huai-lo said, running a finger down the middle of a printout page he had in front of him on the table. Max's heart skipped a beat when he recognized it as a copy of the source program of the Journal Monitor system software, the one he updated yesterday. "I see that you have recently made a change to the Monitor source program. You are OCDLMHP. I mean, that is your userid, I believe?"

"Yes, that's my userid. And, yes, I did an update of that source program yesterday."

"I see it here with your userid, the time and date," said Ray Huai-lo. And then the real edgy question: "Mind telling us what you did?"

But Max was ready. "I *added* one line," he answered nodding at the place on the printout where Ray Huai-lo had his finger pointing.. "It's a dummy line that does nothing."

"And for what purpose, if I may ask?"

"It's a standard practice we do here. Periodically we test these software packages by inserting new routines. That dummy line indicates to whoever does the test where the routine should be inserted when it's time to run the test."

"And what kind of test routines, may I ask?"

"Mostly error handling routines. We force errors to occur in the system and see how the routines handle them. Then we do the upgrade based on the result."

"One last thing, Mr. Poysen," Ray Huai-lo said, looking Max straight in the eye. "What was there before—which you changed to this one dummy line?"

Max caught on even before the man finished the question. It was a trick question, very subtle. The guy had a good head on his shoulders. But Max was right there with him.

"I did not make a *change* update. I made an *add* update, as I said," he lied. "There was nothing there before."

Ray Huai-lo turned to Jerome Bolden on his left, then to Nancy Schneider on his right. They spoke something to each other with their eyes that was totally impossible for Max Poysen to decipher.

He imagined the horror of Ray Huai-lo or any of the others suddenly coming up with another printout, one printed before he made the *change* yesterday. God help me, he thought. That would exonerate Herod Hardin, Leon Justice and the rest of them now being held in federal detention in Alexandria, and bring out the discovery of Robert Grundell's guilt. But Robert was dead. He, Max Poysen, was the only one who had any idea what Robert may have done and what he himself did to help Robert. He may not fry for he had actually done nothing as far as compromising data security was concerned. He didn't know for sure what Robert might have been doing outside of switching userid's in the access log. But still, it's his word against—no one else's.

One thing he's sure of, though—the fate of Herod Hardin and Leon Justice and their buddies now in jail, he held in his hands.

No one made a move to produce any other printout. Instead, Jerome Bolden who was the one to speak next, said: "Thank you, Mr. Poysen. Thank you for your time and cooperation." And Max let out his breath slowly.

"For your information," added agent Nancy Schneider, pushing a card across the table to Max, "we have not ruled out the possibility of a frame-up here against your accused co-workers. So, please, if there is anything else you happen to think of which you believe might help us in any way, give us a call. Anytime."

"Yes, I will. I'll think about it," Max replied, picking up the card.

On his way back to his workstation, he glanced at the pictures of Herod Hardin and Leon Justice in the paper he carried. Then he thought about the last thing he said in there: I'll think about it.

It seemed he had gotten into the habit of dropping the line of late. That's what he said to his wife the last time he talked to her about his retirement. Then, yesterday, he said it again, to Milton Pheasant. And then again, today, to the FBI.

Two things he was sure of right now, he thought, which he didn't have to think about at all—his retirement and the answer Milton Pheasant would get from him today or tomorrow, sometime before the end of the week. He looked again at the picture of the two men in the paper and recalled their presence in the office, months, years before. How they used their position, their friendship and cronyism to their advantage, taking credit for other people's good work, holding them back and keeping quiet about it. Fucking assholes.

Then he imagined them now in jail, confined twenty-four hours a day, their rights and freedom taken away. He could almost flip off the floor and click his heels in mid-air a-la Fred Astaire at the thought that it's up to him whether they stayed in jail or not. Or how long. It's all up to him.

Somewhere in the Holy Bible, it said 'Be kind to your enemy...' Or was it somebody else said or wrote it someplace else? Well, maybe that's the right thing to do. But not right now. He's feeling too good to be so kind. When? He didn't know.

"I'll think about it," he said, to himself, one more time.

978-0-595-34715-5
0-595-34715-0